PRAISE FOR *THE LIVING DEAD*

"The best collection of zombie fiction stories ever collected. Fans of zombie fiction shouldn't just read this anthology—they should own it."

—Paul Goat Allen, *BarnesAndNoble.com*

"Believe the hype. *The Living Dead* is absolutely the best zombie anthology I've ever read (and I've read many)... If you have even a vague interest in zombie fiction, you MUST buy this book."

—*HorrorScope*

"The best selection of zombie fiction I've ever encountered. A satisfyingly thick volume with excellent variety."

—*Book Spot Central*

"YOU NEED THIS BOOK! As terrific a short story collection as I've ever encountered, *The Living Dead* gathers together 34 of the cleverest, creepiest and most brain-freezing zombie tales. These are not your grandpa's *Late Late Show* walking dead, either, but direct descendants of the modern post-Romero gut-ripping, intestine-crunching undead hordes. A collection to die for—or with."

—Joe Dante, award-winning director of *Gremlins*, *The Howling*, and *Homecoming*

"*The Living Dead* contains stories of heartbreak, drama, and man's eternal struggle against himself. The focus doesn't fall squarely on violence and horror, which earns it a place among the best of zombie fiction. *The Living Dead* is not a book to be ignored; it demands a read through—maybe a couple."

—Robert Kirkman, writer of *The Walking Dead* and *Marvel Zombies*

"A superb reprint anthology that runs the gamut of zombie stories. Great storytelling for zombie fans as well as newcomers."

—*Publishers Weekly* (Starred Review); named one of *PW*'s best books of 2008

THE LIVING DEAD 2

Other Books edited by John Joseph Adams

Wastelands
Seeds of Change
The Living Dead
By Blood We Live
Federations
The Improbable Adventures of Sherlock Holmes

Forthcoming Anthologies

The Way of the Wizard
The Mad Scientist's Guide to World Domination
Brave New Worlds
The Book of Cthulhu

THE LIVING DEAD 2

Edited by John Joseph Adams

NIGHT SHADE BOOKS
SAN FRANCISCO

Cover art by David Palumbo
Cover design by Michael Ellis
Interior layout and design by Ross E. Lockhart

An extension of this copyright page can be found on pages 495-496.

First Edition

ISBN 978-1-59780-190-4

Printed in Canada

Night Shade Books
Please visit us on the web at
http://www.nightshadebooks.com

CONTENTS

INTRODUCTION

By John Joseph Adams

Turns out, zombies *really* don't want to die.

When Night Shade Books and I put the first *The Living Dead* anthology together a couple years ago (which I will refer to hereafter as *Volume One*), we had the sense that zombies would be big, but I don't think any of us realized just *how big* they would become.

When the book actually came out in September of 2008, it seemed like the timing was perfect, that we would be hitting right at the crest of the zombie's popularity. But now it looks like they've only become *more* popular in the intervening period, spreading throughout an unsuspecting population like zombiism itself.

In the last couple years there have been a slew of new zombie entertainments released, across all media. There have been new movies (*Quarantine*, *REC²*, *Deadgirl*, *Diary of the Dead*, *Survival of the Dead*, *Dead Snow*, *Zombie Strippers*, *Zombieland*); video games (*Plants vs. Zombies*, *Dead Rising 2*, *Dead Space*, *Left 4 Dead*, *Left 4 Dead 2*); and a veritable *horde* of books (*Pride and Prejudice and Zombies* and its sequel, books from several of the contributors to this anthology, and even a *Star Wars* zombie novel called *Death Troopers*). *Plus*, a film adaptation is in the works for Max Brooks's *World War Z*, and Robert Kirkman's *The Walking Dead* is being made into a television series.

And all of that's just off the top of my head—if I wanted to make an extensive list, I'm sure it could be ten times longer. If you were inclined to have zombies in all of your entertainment, I expect you'd have very little trouble finding things to watch, play, or read, all of them chock-full of zombie mayhem.

But since zombies have continued to dominate the popular consciousness—and *Volume One* was so popular with readers and critics—it was an easy decision to do a second volume of zombie stories; after all, even at 230,000 words, I couldn't fit everything I wanted to into the first book!

And while it's obvious that the public can't get enough of zombies, well, I guess it's just as obvious neither can I.

Let's talk a bit about this anthology in particular, and how it is similar to and different from *Volume One*.

Volume One was comprised entirely of reprints (except for one original story, by John Langan), but this volume is mostly original with a mix of selected reprints. Twenty-five of the forty-four stories appear for the first time in this anthology.

With the popularity of zombies infecting the pop culture like it has, more writers than ever have been itching to try their hand at a zombie story, so it was not difficult to find writers eager to participate in the book. I asked some of the top names in zombie fiction—Max Brooks (*World War Z*), Robert Kirkman (*The Walking Dead*), David Wellington (*Monster Island*), Brian Keene (*The Rising*), and others—along with some bestsellers and rising stars of the science fiction, fantasy, and horror fields—to write me original stories. And boy did they deliver.

For *Volume One*, I chose stories that I felt represented the best of the best and together showcased the range of what zombie fiction was capable of. This time around, because my intent was to include the best *new* stories, I focused on finding the best material that had never previously appeared in a zombie anthology before. So while nineteen of the stories are reprints, there's a good chance that—even if you're a hardcore zombie fan—they'll be entirely new to you.

To bring this introduction to a close, let's bring it back to where it started: Why *are* zombies so appealing?

Since *Volume One* came out, that's one of my most frequently asked questions. (It's kind of a curious question, as if there's some reason zombies *shouldn't* be popular. Do people ask NFL football players why football is so popular?)

I can't claim to know exactly why it is that people love zombies so much, but there are a number of common theories about their popularity.

Zombies are:

- an enemy that used to be us, that we can become at any time;
- a canvas writers can use to comment on almost anything;
- a morality-free way to fulfill a world-destruction fantasy;
- a monster that remains scary and cannot be easily romanticized.

I'm sure that's all part of it, and we could continue to speculate *ad nauseam*—I'm sure there are dissertations being written on the subject as we speak. But one thing is clear: Zombies aren't going to be dying off any time soon, and we'd better learn how to live with them.

ALONE, TOGETHER

By Robert Kirkman

Robert Kirkman is best-known for his work in the comics field as the writer and creator of the critically acclaimed, bestselling zombie comic *The Walking Dead*—which is considered by many (myself included) to be one of the greatest comics series of all-time. Other comics he's written for include *Invincible, Haunt*, and *The Astounding Wolf-Man*. He has also worked on many Marvel titles, such as *Marvel Zombies, Captain America, Ultimate X-Men, The Irredeemable Ant-Man*, and *Fantastic Four*. Despite all of these writing credentials, this is his first piece of published prose fiction.

In *The Walking Dead*, Robert Kirkman set out to tell a different sort of zombie tale. Most such stories focus on a brief period of intense danger—a single night, as in the original *Night of the Living Dead*—or perhaps a few days or weeks, and concern the characters eluding predators and obtaining the immediate exigencies of survival—food, shelter, weapons.

The Walking Dead follows the characters for month after month after month in their grueling quest to stay alive and, more importantly, to stay sane. The stories present searing portraits of disaster psychology—survivor's guilt, depression, and hopelessness, as well as the grim humor and small acts of kindness that allow people to carry on. The zombies in this world are an ever-present threat, but for long stretches of the story they fade into the background and the emotional landscapes of the characters take center stage as they feud, break down, fall in love, lose heart, and ultimately endure...or not—for this a gritty, realistic world where no one is safe. The characters learn the hard way that other survivors can be more dangerous than zombies, and that the most dangerous foe of all is your own heart.

Our first story shares this focus on human psychology. This is a zombie story and a love story, the story of an ordinary man in a terrible situation, and of the woman who just might be his only hope to make it out alive.

She was dressed like a private detective from a low-budget TV show—a pair of slacks, modest high heels, and the most ridiculous trench coat I'd ever seen, one of the shorter ones, that hung just above the knees. I couldn't help but laugh, and it was obvious my reaction annoyed her, but she did her best to hide her feelings as she pressed a finger to my lips, quieting me, and gently nudged me back inside my apartment.

We'd been dating for nearly three months. The next day was our anniversary, and we were supposed to do something together. I can't remember what now, but she had some sort of last minute work obligation crop up. She called to tell me she wanted to see me that night. I had hung up the phone maybe five minutes before she arrived. She must have called me on the way. She had nothing in her hands. No present. I was suspicious.

As she closed the door she flashed a naughty grin and opened the trench coat. It's not an overstatement to say that that moment changed my life. Her slacks stopped shortly above where the coat ended. She'd cut the legs off of a pair of her pants and attached them to a garter belt.

She wore nothing else under the coat.

To say this looked slightly ridiculous wouldn't be a lie but in that moment I couldn't care less about how silly she looked. She was gorgeous, full-figured in all the right ways, dark hair, bright eyes. I instantly fell in love with her, head over heels, hopelessly smitten, and all that. I already knew she was smart, funny, kind, and all that other good stuff, but to see this work of genius— these pant legs, concocted to better sell the old naked-under-the-trench-coat gag, knowing how much thought and preparation went into something so completely and utterly silly—I instantly knew that this was the woman for me.

I proposed to her in that very moment. She thought I was joking, of course, but when I did it again two weeks later, properly and with a ring, she accepted. We were married six months later.

We were married four wonderful years before the world around us fell apart. The world as we knew it quickly disappeared, leaving us and everyone else lost without any hope of regaining the lives we'd grown accustomed to. Diane died two weeks after we abandoned our home.

My name is Timothy Stinnot, and if it's Christmas I'm twenty-eight. Yes, it's as horrible as you would imagine, growing up with a birthday on Christmas. An entire childhood of receiving exactly one more present on Christmas day than my little brother, only to watch him celebrate essentially a second Christmas a few months later. It's not easy for a kid to overcome that kind of jealousy. Justin is probably dead by now; I have no way of knowing for sure. Some days, I'm jealous of him for that, too.

My father—who I must also assume is now dead—had this saying when we were growing up: "If not today, when?" It was usually just to get me to clean my room or some other chore I'd been avoiding. He didn't really give me much advice that didn't have a direct correlation to something he wanted me to do at the time. It's really just another way to say: "Don't put off until tomorrow what you can do today." But his way was a little catchier. Of course, these days I've altered the saying to better reflect the times. Now it's, "If not right now, when?"

These days, tomorrow is much less of a guarantee.

I should be sleeping. Instead, I'm sitting next to the window looking down at the grocery store across the street, listening to Alicia breathe as she sleeps on the floor next to me. I saw the store on our way in earlier tonight. Dad's motto be damned, it was much too dark to try anything then so I didn't even mention it to Alicia. Maybe I wanted to surprise her; maybe I just didn't want to let her down. But I can't stop fantasizing about what we might find in that worn-down, abandoned building.

Tomorrow.

So, I should be sleeping, but instead I sit here, in this empty apartment, surrounded by trash and belongings that weren't quite worth taking when the owners left. I alternate between staring at the store, and watching the quiet rise and fall of Alicia's chest as she sleeps.

She's not the most beautiful woman in the world, or at least she wouldn't have been—*before*. Now she very well might be. Blonde and bone-skinny with a boyish figure, she's pretty much the exact opposite of Diane and not at all the type of girl I would have dated in my previous life.

Have you ever heard of Smurfette Syndrome? Smurfette was the lone female Smurf on the children's cartoon of the same name. The syndrome dictates that when a group of men have only one female, the men in that group will grow to find her attractive, no matter how much they may otherwise not be attracted to her if there where other females present. The male desire to procreate takes over your brain and forces you to suddenly consider the only female available to be extremely desirable.

I desire Alicia extremely.

When Diane was still alive I used to think that I could never be with someone else if something ever happened to her. I know it's something people do all the time but I just couldn't imagine doing it myself. It seemed like such a betrayal. That was, of course, before Diane died. I never considered what complete and utter loneliness felt like—how tormenting it was, and just how much that torment could make you desire to connect with someone.

We started out as a group of six—five guys plus Alicia. I met up with them about six months ago, almost a month after I'd lost Diane. Alicia and I have been alone for two. Guess what happened to everyone else.

There was David Never-Got-His-Last-Name. He lasted all of ten days: rounded a corner as we were leaving town when the walkers got him. He distracted them long enough for the rest of us to get away.

I never really walked out front much after that. I do more now that it's just Alicia and I, but even still, not very often. One of the things I love about her is how strong she is, and brave. Things I'd never even *say* I was, she *is*. Sometimes I feel like I'm the one protecting her, but really we're protecting each other. I sometimes wonder what she'd say on the matter.

The Carson twins lasted a little longer than David. We were at a used car lot, trying to siphon enough gas out of the cars and trucks to fill the tank of a passenger van we'd commandeered. There were just four of us by that point and we really should have tried to get something with better gas mileage, but I think we wanted a vehicle we could all sleep in.

Carson One—that's what I called him when I had to call him by a name—got his leg mangled up by a walker that had been hiding under an old Ford Taurus. I don't know if it had done that on purpose or if it had ended up there by chance. Either way, Carson One's leg got mangled all to hell and we knew right away that he was done for, soon to be one of them—we all know what the bite does.

Carson Two—I *think* it was Two…. Come to think of it, I could have them reversed in this story. (That happened a lot.) Anyway, Carson Two saw his brother mangled up, bleeding all over the asphalt, crying and carrying on—and he just *loses it*. Maybe it was a twin thing, where he was feeling the pain of his brother, but he wailed on that thing like a man possessed, which isn't something you should ever do—cutting your fists up and rubbing open wounds on one of them is about the same as getting bit. Alicia, James, and I all yelled for him to stop, trying to get him to see what was coming for him. All his screaming and carrying on had drawn a lot of attention—the kind that gets you killed.

The three of us ran away as Carson Two got torn to bits. James and Alicia hadn't seen as much of that kind of thing as I had. They didn't talk very much for the next few days.

James was Alicia's fiancé. They were both very young, about the same age Diane and I were when we got married. Before the whole damn world went to shit, they were in love.

I'm getting upset just thinking about it—the three of us, alone…them hugging and holding each other all the time. The way they slept in a tangled mess, stealing each other's breath throughout the night. Me off to the side, the worst third-wheel situation in the history of the world. I was still in agony over the loss of my wife and now here I was, trapped with two honest-to-god lovebirds. I wouldn't have thought that this hell on Earth could be made any worse, but seeing those two so in love with each other somehow did.

The day he died, James and I had been looking for medicine for Alicia. She had been sick for almost a week. We'd been out all day, and it was starting to get dark when we headed home. I was lost in thought, agonizing over all the time I was likely to spend over the next few weeks watching James and Alicia together. Seeing him watching over her, tending to her every need, reminding me of how alone I was, how much I missed Diane.

In a split second it was over. When the walkers moved in and swarmed around him, I watched, unable to save him as they tore him apart. Just like that, he was gone.

I might've said that my prayers had been answered but then I'd have to stop and consider who it was that had answered them.

"They got him," was all I could say to her when I returned to camp. She recovered from her illness in a few days, even without the medicine; she didn't stop crying until much later.

Over time, the spells between tears got longer and longer and we began to talk about the things we had each lived through. I couldn't talk about what happened to James without crying, something about being so close to it. I saw Diane slaughtered in front of me, all the others, and now James. It was all too much. Both our hearts had been broken. We were two people, alone, sharing in each other's agony over what we'd lost. All we had now was each other.

After James was gone, I started to notice things about Alicia that I hadn't noticed before: the point of her nose and how it was slightly off center; the dent in the middle of her bottom lip; the way her voice would crack ever so slightly when she got excited about something. There was no TV, and no movies, so my main—no, my *only*—pastime had become obsessing over Alicia.

Alone together, we talked. For hours, day in, day out, about nothing in particular. I told her all about Diane and all that she had meant to me. She talked about meeting James on their college campus. I told her about my mother's horrible childhood, relaying the stories I'd hear as a child when complaining about absolutely anything at all. She told me about her sister's heart condition, about the long trips to the hospital, how she occupied herself in the waiting room. No story too mundane, no detail too personal. We had nothing but time and so we talked.

As I look at her now, sleeping on the floor beside me, I realize I've never known anyone so intimately. Even Diane had her secrets. But when the world is falling apart around you, secrets become just another luxury that you have to give up...or risk dying for them.

It is a strange thing for me, to feel like I am falling in love all over again. My grief over the loss of Diane has transformed into what feels like real affection for Alicia. But is it real? Do I really love her as much as I loved Diane? Or do I just feel the need for companionship so badly that I would find a way to love anyone?

Is this, in fact, just Smurfette Syndrome?

If it is, I don't care. My every waking thought for the last two months has been of Alicia. *Is she okay? Is she happy? Is she scared? Is she tired?*

As I sit here watching her chest rise and fall as she breathes, every so often letting out the faintest hint of a snore, I find my thoughts of the grocery store below shifting away from *What will I find for myself?* to *What might I find for Alicia? What she might like to eat? What things left behind by other survivors might she find some value in?*

If there is anything left in that grocery store at all, of course.

But I can't dwell on that. I have to stay positive. I have to sleep. Tomorrow we'll go to the store and find out what is left.

When we arrived here, it had been getting dark, and we had only had enough time to make sure this apartment was secure. In the hustle of preparing for nightfall she didn't even notice that the window overlooks the grocery store. She's unaware of the possibilities tomorrow could hold—which is why she fell asleep right away, and I'm still up, obsessing over what we might find.

Maybe they'll have saltine crackers. I know she loves them, and they'd still be relatively edible, if a little stale—those things last forever. Tomorrow we'll know.

Tomorrow.

"Did you see it?"

The question wakes me. Alicia is standing near the window, looking down. I should have closed the curtains. Maybe her opening them would have woken me up and given me enough time to see the surprised pleasure in her smile. Too late now; the news has been broken. Still, the look on her face is full of hope and anticipation. I love how excited she gets about little things, even surrounded by all this death and misery.

"I was going to surprise you," I tell her.

"Oh, that's so sweet."

The look on her face fades instantly as she begins to rush me out of our makeshift bed. Somehow I find even her impatience adorable.

"Now get ready, I'm dying to see what's inside," she says as she pulls the tattered blanket out from under me.

Clothing is not something that is hard to find—clothes that fit perfectly, sure, but there's a wealth of clothes a little too loose or a little too tight. We can't really wash them, so we change clothes every other day or so, rotating through found clothes, trying to stay as clean as we can.

Alicia brushes her hair constantly, not so much for appearance but to keep it from turning into a tangled mess. We have a small bottle of shampoo, but only use it once a week. I made that rule because she blew through the last one so quickly.

I can't fault her for wanting to stay clean. She still uses way too much toothpaste, though. The tube is already almost empty and we've only had it for a month. I cover maybe a quarter the length of my toothbrush with toothpaste when I brush. She uses the full-length, as if you could go down to the corner and buy a new tube when you run out. I'll need to make a point to look for toothpaste once we get into the grocery store. And soap. And definitely shampoo.

I tighten my belt to hold up my two-sizes-too-big jeans, which I have to admit, I have been wearing for almost three weeks. They still look remarkably close to clean for as much walking as we've been doing. The only other pants I've found are a bit tight. I wore them for a day and it was miserable. I'm searching this apartment for pants before we go. T-shirts I have plenty of. I usually discard a few before ever wearing them in favor of newly discovered ones. I favor the ugliest ones I can find because they always get a smile out of Alicia. I have a hot pink "Don't Worry Be Happy" t-shirt that I just can't get rid of, no matter how many times I've worn it.

"Just let me tie my shoes and I'll be ready," I tell her.

She impatiently hovers over me and feigns annoyance. Alicia always sleeps in her shoes, just in case we ever have to leave in a hurry. It's a practice she has often tried to talk me into, but I just can't sleep with shoes on my feet. She watches me roll my eyes and then offers me a fruit bar.

"Have you eaten anything?" she asks as I tie my other shoe.

"I kind of wanted to wait until we checked the place out before I ate anything. Wouldn't want to spoil my appetite."

Alicia shakes her head at me. "You know that's never a good idea."

She's right. I'm sure many people have rushed into such places looking for something to eat, only to get eaten themselves. We could find anything down there, including a large group of walkers. It's never a good idea to do anything dangerous on an empty stomach.

I eat a blueberry fruit bar. It's stale and hard to chew, but it's the best we've got. After I choke it down, we make our way to the grocery store.

We very rarely find doors.

I don't know why, but for whatever reason there aren't a lot of doors left that haven't been torn off their hinges. Nearly every door I've seen since all of this started has had at least one busted hinge. Especially places like gas stations and grocery stores.

A fair bit of looting took place early on, before people really started thinning out. Sometimes I feel like you've almost got better luck finding a large supply of food in an abandoned residence than you do in a grocery store. They've all been...ransacked? I think that's the word I'm looking for. Most places known for having food have already been ransacked. I suppose during that period a shitload of doors got torn off their hinges.

So as a result, the insides of most places are dangerous as all hell. The walkers can just come and go as they please. Seems like a lot of them like to be inside. They seem to be drawn indoors, perhaps because that's where they mostly stayed before. I don't really know why, and I don't much care; all I do know is that when looking around in a grocery store like the one Alicia and I are about to enter, you need to be careful.

The Carson twins had carried guns. I don't know if they had them before or just found them along the way. Whatever kind of guns they were, I never noticed. Didn't matter anyway—when the twins died, they took those guns with them.

I've never fired a gun. I never really felt qualified to handle one. I think if I had a gun, I'd probably just shoot myself in the foot, or worse. It's not like a toy; the triggers actually require quite a bit of pressure, or so I've heard.

The mechanics of the whole thing seem beyond me. Point, stay steady, shoot... It seems so simple; maybe I'm overthinking it. But don't you have to cock most guns? And aren't they supposed to be cleaned regularly or else they jam up? I've watched movies where people take guns apart to clean them and there's all kinds of little springs and shit inside. That baffles me. I'm supposed to somehow figure out how to take a gun apart and put it back together? No fucking way.

Then there's the sound, which is the number one thing that will draw walkers to you. Firing a gun is like ringing the dinner bell. You may think to yourself: *Well, how do you attack them, then?* You don't. Or *I* don't, anyway. I run. Anyone who's smart runs. You see one, you go the other way. If it hasn't seen you, just keep walking—even at a leisurely pace—and you'll be just fine. Shoot it and the next thing you know you're surrounded, and then you'll be dead.

Guns just aren't practical.

So if you find yourself in the middle of a large group of walkers—gun or no gun—you're dead. That's all there is to it. Only reason you'd want a gun in that situation is so you can turn it on yourself before they tear into you.

That's another reason I don't carry one: I know I might be tempted to do just that, and I was always told growing up that suicide was a one-way ticket straight to hell. Not that I necessarily buy into all that, but I'm hedging my bets, or rather, I had been. I don't know if that should be a concern of mine anymore.

So I carry a knife. You'd be surprised how easy it is to push a knife into one of their faces. If they get too close, or you don't see them until they're practically right on top of you, which has happened to me exactly once, you stab them in the face. Didn't kill it right away the time I did it. More like made a handle on the thing's head for me to push it away with. They're not very strong. I knocked it over and wiggled the blade around until it messed its brain up enough that it stopped moving.

Alicia is what you would call petite, so you wouldn't think a bat would be much use to her, but that's her weapon of choice. Thing is, you don't really have to bash a walker's brains in. The idea is to knock them off balance, and Alicia's a pro at that. She knocks them in the head with that bat, next thing you know they're down on their side trying to figure out which way is up, and by then we're long gone.

Alicia is walking out front. She turns to me just before stepping into the store, shushing me, as if I don't already know to be quiet. The windows in this place have all been smashed out and there's broken glass all over the ground, so being quiet is going to be pretty much impossible. If there's something in there, we're going to know it right away. And vice versa.

The grocery store is dimly lit from the daylight outside. The front area of the store is in clear view, but anything past that fades into black quickly, especially with our eyes adjusting from the brightness of the midday sun. I've never understood why these types of places don't have windows anywhere but in the front.

The store is small, not a big-time grocery. It's old, dated, like it's from the late seventies—the kind of place that just never updated its look. I would have hated shopping here before. It would have reminded me of my childhood, depressed me. This is the kind of place Diane liked. Nostalgic, she would have called it.

"Get your flashlight out," Alicia whispers.

Looks like I'll be going into the back. That's fine, I certainly don't want Alicia taking the big risks. I can run faster than her. That's the one thing I'm sure I'm better at.

In places like this, turning the flashlight on causes me no end of anxiety. I'm standing next to a wall of blackness, fiddling around in my backpack for the flashlight. When I finally get it out, there are those few seconds that tick by between turning it on and pointing it at what you're going to see.

I dread those seconds.

There's no telling what the flashlight is going to show. There could be a dozen walkers, standing there, patiently waiting to inform me that there will be no treasures to be found here and that I will soon be dead.

Empty shelves, for the most part.

That's what I see. It's at once a relief and a huge disappointment. This place has been picked clean.

Alicia is calling me over; she's found some beef jerky. Usually that's one of the first things people grab, but this box fell behind one of the check-out counters. I find a can of opened Pringles near a pile of other cans that have been stepped on. I'd eat them, stale and all, but there are bound to be bugs—or worse yet, *mice*—inside.

In the back of the store I struggle to spend the proper amount of time examining the shelves. The meat section is in the back. As you go down the aisles, the putrid smell intensifies. With each step I think, *This is as bad as it's going to get*...until I take another.

Nobody ever took the meat at any of the places we'd been to. The lack of refrigeration makes storing processed meats pretty much impossible. I doubt anyone ever took so much as one package. They just sit in the dark and rot. Even the animals know better than to eat it after a while; they just tear the packages to shit, treating us to the smell.

It stinks in here almost worse than the walkers. You'd think after a while you would become accustomed to all the smells of today's world. No running water, the stench of death hanging in the air at every turn. Really, though, they aren't the kind of smells you get used to. You spend so much time in the open air that you have no chance to build up a tolerance. The good part about that is that half the time you smell the walkers before you ever see them.

Of course, if you're standing near a months-old meat cooler in the back of a dark grocery store, one of them could practically be standing right beside you and you wouldn't even know it.

And I don't.

It lumbers forward, reaching for me with that blind grab they all do. I step back, quickly, but careful not to back myself into a corner—I'd done that far too many times to let it happen again.

The walker comes at me, turning the corner, coming at me from the end of the cereal aisle, and all I can think of is Alicia.

"You okay up there?" I yell to her.

"Oh, my God, Timothy!"

She's rushing down one of the aisles behind the thing, coming toward us. I can't see her, but I can hear her footsteps as she rushes to my rescue.

"I'm okay! Stay where you are! Don't—"

Her scream keeps me from finishing my sentence. Another walker has gotten to her.

I continue to struggle with the walker, keeping its gnashing teeth at bay, then manage to jam the knife into its neck. I'd been aiming for its face but there was no time to try for a kill shot now. Pushing it aside I make a break toward the sound of Alicia's voice. I'm still not quite sure exactly where she is. I blaze across the aisles looking for her, but she's farther away than I had thought.

I round the corner and see only a mass of dark movement. Is Alicia beneath? On top? Is she even here at all?

I only hear the grunts of a struggle. I can't immediately tell that they're hers, but then...yes, it's her. As I near the struggling mass, I tuck my head down, knowing what I'm going to do. With my arms stretched out at either side, I tackle the beast.

I knock it free from Alicia and the thing and I roll off of her in an instant. I swear I hear the sound of bone breaking from the impact, as if I'm demolishing the thing. I fear that's only my imagination. As I roll on top of it Alicia's safety is still my only concern, and I never once consider that I'm wrestling a walker, with no clue as to where its mouth is or how in danger of being bit I might be.

I can feel its fingers clawing at my thigh, and my only instinct is to get away, but by then it's got me—its fingers locked in a death grip around my thigh and my arm. I'm hitting it, kicking at it with my free arm and leg with all my might and I don't even know what I'm hitting. Suddenly I realize I have my eyes tightly shut, and so I open them—just in time to see Alicia, bathed in light, bringing the baseball bat down on the walker's head.

She bashes its skull in with a single blow. My arm and thigh now released—Alicia has saved me. She stands over me with the bat, watching the walker—dead for real now—collapse into a heap.

Alicia collapses shortly after.

"Alicia!"

She offers no response. I can barely stand.

"Were you bitten?" I crawl over to her. She's concealed in darkness; I can't see any blood. I don't know if she's hurt or if her malnourished body couldn't take the strain of all this exertion. Whatever the case, I have to get her out where I can see her, to the road where it's safe and well-lit. I begin dragging her frantically toward the light; no time to lift her up—there could be more of them.

I get halfway to the exit before I remember the broken glass in the front of the store. So I drop to my knees and gather her onto my lap, nearly toppling a nearby shelf as I use it to support me as I force myself to stand. I think I hear rustling as I lumber out of the store; a figment of my imagination and not more of them, I hope.

Out in the street I gently lower her down to the pavement. I examine her face. No blood. Her shirt. No blood. Her pants, the same—but there are rips and tears in her clothing, and it's possible she received a scratch or a minor bite not yielding much blood. The shoes pop off with little effort, having not been untied and retied in more than a day's time. Getting her pants over her hips is another matter. She's always insisted on wearing snug-fitting jeans, or at least as snug-fitting as she could find. She claims she doesn't want to risk having her clothing get caught on something during an escape, but I think that fashion is the last part of civilization she's willing to let go of. As I start to pull her shirt off she wakes up, helping me the rest of the way.

There's not a scrape on her; must have been exhaustion from the struggle. She smiles up at me, and the emotion of the moment shifts. We're starting to feel safe now.

"How do I look?" she asks.

It sounds cheesy, but I say the first thing that comes to mind: "Perfect."

Nearly naked, completely vulnerable, in the middle of the road, directly in front of the grocery store, out in the midday sun, she sits up and pushes me onto my backside.

Checking me for wounds is just a formality. I've heard of at least two different cases where the adrenaline rush and the shock of the attack kept a person from realizing they had been bitten for several hours. Never witnessed this first hand but I never like to risk anything. Laughing to herself as she struggles to pull off my shoes, she begins to undress me. The urgency in the moment is gone; she takes her time. By the time Alicia begins unbuttoning my pants, I have my own shirt off. I smile at her.

"Nothing to see here," I tell her.

And so we survived. Again. Our third such close-call together.

We seem to be good luck to each other.

I look into her eyes and she smiles back at me in relief. There's no feeling more exhilarating than the feeling of being in *no* danger, immediately after escaping *mortal* danger.

I try to stand up, wanting to get dressed and go back inside and find my knife, but Alicia pulls me to her and kisses me, and whatever danger I just put myself in for her, this is worth it. If I had a large gash on my ankle in the shape of a bloody bite mark that meant I only had a matter of hours to keep living, this would still be worth it. She's kissing me, I'm kissing her, and despite my instincts screaming for me to stop, we continue on, kissing faster and more passionately.

I can't help but question her actions.

"Right here?" I ask.

She tells me to shut up.

Funny, that's what I wanted to say to myself.

There are any number of things that could come up this road in one way or another. Once we were watching a gas station surrounded by walkers trying to figure out the safest way to get inside when a band of marauders arrived in a large truck. I remember a mean-looking woman with a sword who nearly single-handedly staved off the walkers while other members of her group broke in to clean out the place. I hate to think about what could have happened had they found us inside. They certainly didn't look like the kind of people we'd want to get to know. That's how things are now, running into another group of survivors is just as dangerous as finding a group of walkers. You never know how people are going to act. At least the walkers are predictable.

I don't want to think about what would happen if anyone were to come walking up the street right now, so I don't. Alicia and I lose ourselves in each other. I don't know what brought this on—maybe it was her waking up to me stripping her down, seeing me labor and stress over her well-being, or the general excitement of the whole ordeal, but whatever it is, I don't care.

It is only the second time we've made love.

Diane, please forgive me.

You may find yourself thinking about how uncomfortable it would be to have sex in the middle of an open road, next to a ransacked grocery store littered with shards of broken glass. Don't dwell on it. This rural road already has large patches of weeds growing up through the cracked asphalt, soft little patches of lawn in the middle of harsh pavement. Between that and our discarded clothing, we do just fine.

When it's over my mind is racing. The one thing we've never talked about is how she really feels about me. We spend every waking moment together, but we do that because we have to. If there was anyone else to talk to, maybe she would favor them instead. Maybe I would, too, but I doubt it.

No, this is real. The look in her eyes when she looks at me: that's *love*. I may not know much, but I know what that looks like. She may not feel it for me as strongly as I do for her… but it's there.

I can tell.

Alicia loves me.

She loves me! I think to myself, at first excited, and then burdened with the guilt of officially having a new relationship after losing Diane less than a year ago. My mind races as I return to the grocery store to retrieve my knife. That's not something I can just leave behind.

I'd reconciled myself to never loving again after I lost Diane. I've learned to live with it. I remember her, and it makes me sad. That was my burden, the pain I carry inside me. Alicia, I thought, liked me and was with me because I was all that was available. She found comfort in my arms. I was fine with leaving it at that.

This is something else entirely. This makes the relationship real. She's getting over James, I'm getting over Diane, and we have mutual feelings for each other. This isn't something I can take lightly. This is something I have to treat with respect. That's what Alicia deserves.

She deserves to know the truth.

There were a few houses in the area and a lot of daylight left. We decided to explore them, and see if we could find more supplies. Over the course of the day we found clothes, another bottle of shampoo, some soap, toothpaste, and a whole mess of food: canned soup, crackers, and various things that were either completely unspoiled or edible, but only if you were *really* hungry.

There were a few walkers milling about, in or around the houses but we saw them early and easily avoided them. This was a small miracle, as distracted as I was. I couldn't stop thinking about what I had to tell Alicia, what I was going to say to her tonight. By the time we returned to the apartment across the street from the grocery store, darkness had already come.

The thing that kept running through my head all day—the thing I had to tell Alicia—was how James really died.

The day James died, it had just been the three of us—James, Alicia, and I—for weeks. I missed Diane so much. My grief over losing her was still fresh in my mind. I like to think I wasn't myself. I just wanted things to go back to the way they were before, and knowing that that would never be possible made me more angry than

I'd ever been in my life.

They say people are capable of doing things when they're grieving that they would never consider otherwise.

Seeing Diane die right in front of me scarred me. Watching those things tear into her, unable to do anything about it. Seeing the terror in her eyes as she screamed for help, only to see her life fade away moments later. There are things that we're now forced to deal with on a daily basis that I don't think we should have ever had to deal with.

I loved Diane. Alicia loved James. I didn't want to see her go through that much pain. I didn't want to kill James.

But I thought about it.

He and I were alone that day, all day. I knew that if he were to die, maybe I wouldn't get Diane back, but at the very least, I wouldn't have to see the two of them together anymore. I wouldn't have to see, in them, exactly what I wanted for myself.

I had opportunities. My knife in hand, his back to me. I wouldn't have even had to see his face. In the end, I couldn't do it. It was too much, I could never go that far. I couldn't kill him myself.

Luckily, it was a dangerous world we were living in.

The day was nearly over. We were talking, deciding whether or not to search one last house for medicine before starting our journey back.

I saw them coming.

He didn't.

There was a moment, just after he saw them—too late!—that he looked at me, screaming for help. In that moment I could have stepped in and helped him fight them off. Instead, I stepped back. Everything I'd been thinking about that day affected that split-second decision.

Immediately, I realized what I'd done, and I suddenly wanted to help him but by then it was too late, there were too many of them.

James was dead.

It was only a second—a brief moment where the pain of seeing them together had reached a crescendo within me and made me do that awful thing.

People were dying every second of every day. Most everyone I'd ever known was probably dead. *What's one more?* I thought. What's one more if it means I'll be happier?

What's one more if she never has to know what I've done?

But now Alicia loves me, and I can't keep this from her any longer.

Maybe we were meant to be together. Maybe Diane and James were meant to die. Maybe that was necessary to bring Alicia and me together to ensure our survival.

Standing in the apartment, moonlight filling the room from the open window, I embrace Alicia and tell her I love her. She responds in kind, like I knew she would. I take one final look at her, and take a mental snapshot of the Alicia who is unaware of the evil I have done.

Then I tell her everything.

I tell her because I love her. I tell her because I respect her. I tell her because I hope she'll forgive me.

When I'm done, the look on her face surprises me. She looks at me not with anger, but with sorrow. She looks at me as if I told her I'd killed myself, and maybe that's what I just did. The man she'd fallen in love with was a lie. She starts crying, and before long is sobbing heavily.

I didn't expect the screaming.

"I'm sorry," I say.

She begins pounding on my chest with her fists, hitting me repeatedly, but it's all I can say: "*I'm sorry*. I'm sorry. I'm sorry."

I weather the storm; it's what I deserve. Before long her anger fades and she collapses. I embrace her and we cry together for a while.

All we have to lean on is each other. *Neither of us can get through this alone.*

She has forgiven me, I think, as we lie together in the darkness. I'm all she has. She can't stay mad at me forever. The fact that I told her has to count for something, doesn't it? She has to know this is something I regret, that it will haunt me for as long as I live.

I think it will be a long time before things will be back to normal between us. But we'll get there and when we do our bond will be that much stronger now that there are no secrets between us.

We're going to have to make the best of this world around us if we're going to survive. Everything is going to be okay. That's what I think as I drift off to sleep, Alicia sobbing in my arms.

The sun of a new morning shines through the open window, waking me. The bedding beside me is colder than it should be. I reach for Alicia but she's not there. My eyes open, I look around.

Gone.

She's gone. And she's taken all our food, all our supplies, and all of our weapons.

Whether she's meant to or not, she has killed me.

I won't last more than five days alone.

Truth be told—without her, I don't want to.

DANGER WORD

By Steven Barnes & Tananarive Due

Steven Barnes and Tananarive Due are frequent collaborators; in fiction, they've produced film scripts, this story, and three Tennyson Hardwick detective novels, the latest of which is *From Cape Town with Love* (written with actor Blair Underwood). In life, they're married.

Barnes is the bestselling author of many novels, such as *Lion's Blood*, *Zulu Heart*, *Great Sky Woman*, and *Shadow Valley*. He's also worked on television shows such as *The Twilight Zone*, *The Outer Limits*, *Andromeda*, and *Stargate*. Due is a two-time finalist for the Bram Stoker Award, and her novels include the My Soul to Keep series, *The Between*, *The Good House*, and *Joplin's Ghost*.

Barnes's short work has appeared in *Analog* and *Asimov's Science Fiction*, while Due's has been published in *The Magazine of Fantasy & Science Fiction*, *Dark Delicacies II*, and *Voices from the Other Side*. Stories by both have been included in the anthologies *Dark Dreams* (where this story first appeared), *Dark Matter*, and *Mojo: Conjure Stories*.

It's a universal human urge to leave the world a better place than you found it, and to pass on to your children a world where they can have a happier, more prosperous life than you had. This has mostly been the case throughout human history, as ever-expanding infrastructure and knowledge have generally made life more secure and comfortable generation after generation, through innovations such as fertilizers, vaccines, antibiotics, indoor plumbing, and electronics. But now adults are facing the despairing sense that today's youth will experience significantly more hardship than the previous generation, as today's young people confront a world of economic ruin and environmental catastrophe that they had no hand in creating.

Recent works have grappled with this generational guilt in different ways. One of the best-known examples is Cormac McCarthy's novel *The Road*, a post-apocalyptic story in which a father attempts to guide his young son through a devastated landscape, all the while knowing that their situation is hopeless. The notion of enduring anything to protect your children is a primal one, and one of the worst things that most people can imagine is being helpless to aid their children. Our next story deals with this theme in a powerful way.

For a generation facing the prospect of bequeathing to their children a shattered world, one fear stands out even more than being helpless to protect your child: that you yourself might be the architect of your child's undoing.

When Kendrick opened his eyes, Grandpa Joe was standing over his bed, a tall dark bulk dividing the morning light. Grandpa Joe's beard covered his dark chin like a coat of snow. Mom used to say that guardian angels watched over you while you slept, and Grandpa Joe looked like he might have been guarding him all night with his shotgun. Kendrick didn't believe in guardian angels anymore, but he was glad he could believe in Grandpa Joe.

Most mornings, Kendrick opened his eyes to only strangeness: dark, heavy curtains, wooden planks for walls, a brownish-gray stuffed owl mounted near the window, with glassy black eyes that twitched as the sun set—or seemed to. A rough pine bed. And that *smell* everywhere, like the smell in Mom and Dad's closet. Cedar, Grandpa Joe told him. Grandpa Joe's big, hard hands had made the whole cabin of it, one board and beam at a time.

For the last six months, this had been his room, but it still wasn't, really. His Spider-Man bed sheets weren't here. His G.I. Joes, Tonka trucks, and Matchbox racetracks weren't here. His posters of Blade and Shaq weren't on the walls. This was his bed, but it wasn't his room.

"Up and at 'em, Little Soldier," Grandpa Joe said, using the nickname Mom had never liked. Grandpa was dressed in his hickory shirt and blue jeans, the same clothes he wore every day. He leaned on his rifle like a cane, so his left knee must be hurting him like it always did in the mornings. He'd hurt it long ago, in Vietnam.

"I'm going trading down to Mike's. You can come if you want, or I can leave you with the Dog-Girl. Up to you." Grandpa's voice was morning-rough. "Either way, it's time to get out of bed, sleepyhead."

Dog-Girl, the woman who lived in a house on a hill by herself fifteen minutes' walk west, was their closest neighbor. Once upon a time she'd had six pit bulls that paraded up and down her fence. In the last month that number had dropped to three. Grandpa Joe said meat was getting scarce. Hard to keep six dogs fed, even if you needed them. The dogs wagged their tails when Kendrick came up to the fence, because Dog-Girl had introduced him to them, but Grandpa Joe said those dogs could tear a man's arms off.

"Don't you ever stick your hand in there," Grandpa Joe always said. "Just because a dog looks friendly don't mean he is. Especially when he's hungry."

"Can I have a Coke?" Kendrick said, surprised to hear his own voice again, so much smaller than Grandpa Joe's, almost a little girl's. Kendrick hadn't planned to say anything today, but he wanted the Coke so bad he could almost taste the fizz; it would taste like a treat from Willy Wonka's Chocolate Factory.

"If Mike's got one, you'll get one. For *damn* sure." Grandpa Joe's grin widened until Kendrick could see the hole where his tooth used to be: his straw-hole,

Grandpa Joe called it. He mussed Kendrick's hair with his big palm. "Good boy, Kendrick. You keep it up. I knew your tongue was in there somewhere. You better start using it, or you'll forget how. Hear me? You start talking again, and I'll whip you up a lumberjack breakfast, like before."

It *would* be good to eat one of Grandpa Joe's famous lumberjack breakfasts again, piled nearly to the ceiling: a bowl of fluffy eggs, a stack of pancakes, a plate full of bacon and sausage, and homemade biscuits to boot. Grandpa Joe had learned to cook in the Army.

But whenever Kendrick thought about talking, his stomach filled up like a balloon and he thought he would puke. Some things couldn't be said out loud, and some things *shouldn't.* There was more to talking than most people thought. A whole lot more.

Kendrick's eye went to the bandage on Grandpa Joe's left arm, just below his elbow, where the tip peeked out at the edge of his shirtsleeve. Grandpa Joe had said he'd hurt himself chopping wood yesterday, and Kendrick's skin had hardened when he'd seen a spot of blood on the bandage. He hadn't seen blood in a long time. He couldn't see any blood now, but Kendrick still felt worried. Mom said Grandpa Joe didn't heal as fast as other people, because of his diabetes. What if something happened to him? He was old. Something could.

"That six-point we brought down will bring a good haul at Mike's. We'll trade jerky for gas. Don't like to be low on gas," Grandpa said. His foot slid a little on the braided rug as he turned to leave the room, and Kendrick thought he heard him hiss with pain under his breath. "And we'll get that Coke for you. Whaddya say, Little Soldier?"

Kendrick couldn't make any words come out of this mouth this time, but at least he was smiling, and smiling felt good. They had something to smile about, for once.

Three days ago a buck had come to drink from the creek.

Through the kitchen window, Kendrick had seen something move—antlers, it turned out—and Grandpa Joe grabbed his rifle when Kendrick motioned. Before the shot exploded, Kendrick had seen the buck look up, and Kendrick thought, *It knows.* The buck's black eyes reminded him of Dad's eyes when he had listened to the news on the radio in the basement, hunched over his desk with a headset. Kendrick had guessed it was bad news from the trapped look in his father's eyes.

Dad would be surprised at how good Kendrick was with a rifle now. He could blow away an empty Chef Boyardee ravioli can from twenty yards. He'd learned how to aim on *Max Payne* and *Medal of Honor,* but Grandpa Joe had taught him how to shoot for real, a little every day. Grandpa Joe had a roomful of guns and ammunition—the back shed, which he kept locked—so they never ran low on bullets.

Kendrick supposed he would have to shoot a deer one day soon. Or an elk. Or something else. The time would come, Grandpa Joe said, when he would have to make a kill whether he wanted to or not. "You may have to kill to survive, Kendrick," he said. "I know you're only nine, but you need to be sure you can do it."

Before everything changed, Grandpa Joe used to ask Mom and Dad if he could teach Kendrick how to hunt during summer vacation, and they'd said no. Dad didn't like Grandpa much, maybe because Grandpa Joe always said what he thought, and he was Mom's father, not Dad's. And Mom didn't go much easier on him, always telling Grandpa Joe no, no matter what he asked. *No,* you can't keep him longer than a couple weeks in the summer. *No,* you can't teach him shooting. *No,* you can't take him hunting.

Now there was no one to say *no.* No one except Grandpa Joe, unless Mom and Dad came back. Grandpa Joe had said they might, and they knew where to find him. They might.

Kendrick put on the red down jacket he'd been wearing the day Grandpa Joe found him. He'd sat in this for never-ending hours in the safe room at home, the storage space under the stairs with a reinforced door, a chemical toilet, and enough food and water for a month. Mom had sobbed, "Bolt the door tight. Stay here, Kendrick, and don't open the door until you hear Grandpa's danger word—NO MATTER WHAT."

She made him swear to Jesus, and she'd never made him swear to Jesus before. He'd been afraid to move or breathe. He'd heard other footsteps in the house, the awful sound of crashing and breaking. A single terrible scream. It could have been his mother, or father, or neither—he just didn't know.

Followed by silence, for one hour, two, three. Then the hardest part. The worst part.

"Show me your math homework, Kendrick."

The danger word was the special word he and Grandpa Joe had picked because Grandpa Joe had insisted on it. Grandpa Joe had made a special trip in his truck to tell them something bad could happen to them, and he had a list of reasons how and why. Dad didn't like Grandpa Joe's yelling much, but he'd listened. So Kendrick and Grandpa Joe had made up a danger word nobody else in the world knew, not even Mom and Dad.

And he had to wait to hear the danger word, Mom said.

No matter what.

By the time Kendrick dressed, Grandpa was already outside loading the truck, a beat-up navy blue Chevy. Kendrick heard a thud as he dropped a large sack of wrapped jerky in the bed.

Grandpa Joe had taught him how to mix up the secret jerky recipe he hadn't even given Mom: soy sauce and Worcestershire sauce, fresh garlic cloves, dried pepper, onion powder. He'd made sure Kendrick was paying attention while strips of deer meat soaked in that tangy mess for two days and then spent twelve hours in the slow-cook oven. Grandpa Joe had also made him watch as he cut the deer open and its guts flopped to the ground, all gray and glistening. "Watch, boy. Don't turn away. Don't be scared to look at something for what it is."

Grandpa Joe's deer jerky was almost as good as the lumberjack breakfast, and Kendrick's mouth used to water for it. Not anymore.

His jerky loaded, Grandpa Joe leaned against the truck, lighting a brown cigarette.

Kendrick thought he shouldn't be smoking.

"Ready?"

Kendrick nodded. His hands shook a little every time he got in the truck, so he hid his hands in his jacket pockets. Some wadded-up toilet paper from the safe room in Longview was still in there, a souvenir. Kendrick clung to the wad, squeezing his hand into a fist.

"We do this right, we'll be back in less than an hour," Grandpa Joe said. He spit, as if the cigarette had come apart in his mouth. "Forty-five minutes."

Forty-five minutes. That wasn't bad. Forty-five minutes, then they'd be back.

Kendrick stared at the cabin in the rearview mirror until the trees hid it from his sight.

The road was empty, as usual. Grandpa Joe's rutted dirt road spilled onto the highway after a half-mile, and they jounced past darkened, abandoned houses. Kendrick saw three stray dogs trot out of the open door of a pink two-story house on the corner. He'd never seen that door open before, and he wondered whose dogs they were. He wondered what they'd been eating.

Suddenly, Kendrick wished he'd stayed back at Dog-Girl's. She was from England and he couldn't always understand her, but he liked being behind her fence. He liked Popeye and Ranger and Lady Di, her dogs. He tried not to think about the ones that were gone now. Maybe she'd given them away.

They passed tree farms, with all the trees growing the same size, identical, and Kendrick enjoyed watching their trunks pass in a blur. He was glad to be away from the empty houses.

"Get me a station," Grandpa Joe said.

The radio was Kendrick's job. Unlike Dad, Grandpa Joe never kept the radio a secret.

The radio hissed and squealed up and down the FM dial, so Kendrick tried AM next. Grandpa Joe's truck radio wasn't good for anything. The shortwave at the cabin was better.

A man's voice came right away, a shout so loud it was like screaming.

"...and in those days shall men seek death and shall not find it...and shall desire to die and death shall flee from them..."

"Turn that bullshit off," Grandpa Joe snapped. Kendrick hurried to turn the knob, and the voice was gone. "Don't you believe a word of that, you hear me? That's B-U-double-L *bullshit.* Things are bad now, but they'll get better once we get a fix on this thing. Anything can be beat, believe you me. I ain't givin' up, and neither should you. That's givin'-up talk."

The next voices were a man and a woman who sounded so peaceful that Kendrick wondered where they were. What calm places were left? "...mobilization at the Vancouver Armory. That's from the commander of the Washington National Guard. So you see," the man said, "there *are* orchestrated efforts. There *has* been progress in the effort to reclaim Portland, and even more in points north. The Armory is secure, and running survivors to the islands twice a week. Look at Rainier. Look at Devil's Wake. As long as you stay away from the large urban centers, there are dozens of pockets where people are safe and life is going on."

"Oh, yes," the woman said. "Of course there are."

"There's a learning curve. That's what people don't understand."

"Absolutely." The woman sounded absurdly cheerful.

"Everybody keeps harping on Longview..." The man said "Longview" as if it were a normal, everyday place. Kendrick's stomach tightened when he heard it. "...but that's become another encouraging story. Contrary to rumors, there *is* a National Guard presence. There *are* limited food supplies. There's a gated community in the hills housing over four hundred. Remember, safety in numbers. Any man, woman, or teenager who's willing to enlist is guaranteed safe lodging. Fences are going up, roads barricaded. We're getting this under control. That's a far cry from what we were hearing even five, six weeks ago."

"Night and day," the cheerful woman said. Her voice trembled with happiness.

Grandpa Joe reached over to rub Kendrick's head. "See there?" he said.

Kendrick nodded, but he wasn't happy to imagine that a stranger might be in his bed. Maybe it was another family with a little boy. Or twins.

But probably not. Dog-Girl said the National Guard was long gone and nobody knew where to find them. "Bunch of useless bloody shit-heads," she'd said—the first time he'd heard the little round woman cuss. Her accent made cussing sound exotic. If she was right, dogs might be roaming through his house, too, looking for something to eat.

"...There's talk that a Bay Area power plant is up again. It's still an unconfirmed rumor, and I'm not trying to wave some magic wand here, but I'm just making the point—and I've tried to make it before—that life probably felt a lot like this in Hiroshima."

"Yes," the woman said. From her voice, Hiroshima was somewhere very important.

"Call it apples and oranges, but put yourself in the place of a villager in Rwanda. Or an Auschwitz survivor. There had to be some days that felt *exactly* the way we feel when we hear these stories from Seattle and Portland, and when we've talked to the survivors..."

Just ahead, along the middle of the road, a man was walking.

Kendrick sat straight up when he saw him, balling up the tissue wad in his pocket so tightly that he felt his fingernails bite into his skin. The walking man was tall and broad-shouldered, wearing a brick-red backpack. He lurched along unsteadily. From the way he bent forward, as if bracing into a gale, Kendrick guessed the backpack was heavy.

He hadn't ever seen anyone walking on this road.

"Don't you worry," Grandpa Joe said. Kendrick's neck snapped back as Grandpa Joe speeded up his truck. "We ain't stoppin'."

The man let out a mournful cry as they passed, waving a cardboard sign. He had a long, bushy beard, and as they passed, his eyes looked wide and wild. Kendrick craned his head to read the sign, which the man held high in the air: STILL

HERE, the sign read.

"He'll be all right," Grandpa Joe said, but Kendrick didn't think so. No one was supposed to go on the roads alone, especially without a car. Maybe the man had a gun, and maybe they would need another man with a gun. Maybe the man had been trying to warn them something bad was waiting for them ahead.

But the way he walked...

"No matter what," Mom had said.

Kendrick kept watching while the man retreated behind them. He had to stop watching when he felt nausea pitch in his stomach. He'd been holding his breath without knowing it. His face was cold and sweating, both at once.

"Was that one?" Kendrick whispered.

He hadn't known he was going to say that either, just like when he'd asked for a Coke. Instead, he'd been thinking about the man's sign. STILL HERE.

"Don't know," Grandpa Joe said. "It's hard to tell. That's why you never stop."

They listened to the radio, neither of them speaking again for the rest of the ride.

Time was, Joseph Earl Davis III never would have driven past anyone on the road without giving them a chance to hop into the bed and ride out a few miles closer to wherever they were going. Hell, he'd picked up a group of six college-age kids and driven them to the Centralia compound back in April.

But Joe hadn't liked the look of that hitcher. Something about his walk. Or, maybe times were just different. If Kendrick hadn't been in the car, Jesus as his witness, Joe might have run that poor wanderer down where he walked. An ounce of prevention. That was what it had come to in Joe Davis's mind. Drastic measures. You just never knew; that was the thing.

EREH LLITS, the man's sign said in the mirror, receding into a tiny, unreadable blur.

Yeah, I'm still here, too, Joe thought. And not picking up hitchhikers was one way he intended to *stay* here, thanks a bunch for asking.

Freaks clustered in the cities, but there were plenty of them wandering through the countryside nowadays, actual packs. Thousands, maybe. Joe had seen his first six months ago, coming into Longview to rescue his grandson. His first, his fifth, and his tenth. He'd done what he had to do to save the boy, then shut the memories away where they couldn't sneak into his dreams. Then drank enough to make the dreams blurry.

A week later, he'd seen one closer to home, not three miles beyond the gated road, *not five miles from the cabin.* Its face was bloated blue-gray, and flies buzzed around the open sores clotted with that dark red scabby shit that grew under their skin. The thing could barely walk, but it had smelled him, swiveling in his direction like a scarecrow on a pivot.

Joe still dreamed about that one every night. That one had *chosen* him.

Joe left the freaks alone unless one came at him—that was safest if you were by yourself. He'd seen a poor guy shoot one down in a field, and then a swarm came from over a hill. Some of those fuckers could walk pretty fast, could *run*, and they weren't stupid, by God.

But Joe had killed that one, the pivoting one that had chosen him. He'd kill it a dozen times again if he had the chance; it was a favor to both of them. That shambling mess had been somebody's son, somebody's husband, somebody's father. People said freaks weren't really dead—they didn't climb out of graves like movie monsters—but they were as close to walking dead as Joe ever wanted to see. Something was eating them from the inside out, and if they bit you, the freak shit would start eating you, too. You fell asleep, and you woke up different.

The movies had that part right, anyway.

As for the rest, nobody knew much. People who met freaks up close and personal didn't live long enough to write reports about them. Whatever they were, freaks weren't just a city problem anymore. They were everybody's problem.

"Can you hold on, Dad? My neighbor's knocking on the window."

That's what Cass had said the last time they'd spoken, then he hadn't heard any more from his daughter for ten agonizing minutes. The next time he'd heard her voice, he'd barely recognized it, so calm it could be nothing but a mask over mortal terror. "DADDY? Don't talk—just listen. I'm so sorry. For everything. No time to say it all. They're here. You need to come and get Kendrick. Use the danger word. Do you hear me, Daddy? And...bring guns. Shoot anyone suspicious. I mean *anyone*, Daddy."

"Daddy," she'd called him. She hadn't called him that in years.

That day he'd woken up with alarm twisting his gut for no particular reason. That was why he'd raised Cassidy on the shortwave two hours earlier than he usually did, and she'd sounded irritated that he'd called before she was up. "My neighbor's knocking on the window."

Joe had prayed he wouldn't find what he knew would be waiting in Longview. He'd known what might happen to Cass, Devon, and Kendrick the moment he'd found them letting neighbors use the shortwave and drink their water like they'd been elected the Rescue Committee. They couldn't even *name* one of the women in their house. That was Cass and Devon for you. Acting like naive fools, and he'd told them as much.

Still, even though he'd tried to make himself expect the worst, he couldn't, really. If he ever dwelled on that day, he might lose his mind...and then what would happen to Kendrick?

Anytime Joe brought up that day, the kid's eyes whiffed out like a dead pilot light. It had taken Kendrick hours to finally open that reinforced door and let him in, even though Joe had used the danger word again and again. And Kendrick had spoken hardly a word since.

Little Soldier was doing all right today. Good. He'd need to be tougher, fast. The kid had regressed from nine to five or six, just when Joe needed him to be as old as he could get.

As Joe drove beyond the old tree farms, the countryside opened up on either side; fields on his left, a range of hills on his right. There'd been a cattle farm out here once, but the cattle were gone. Wasn't much else out here, and there never had been.

Except for Mike's. Nowadays, Mike's was the only thing left anyone recognized.

Mike's was a gas station off exit 46 with porta-potties out back and a few shelves inside crammed with things people wanted: flour, canned foods, cereal, powdered milk, lanterns, flashlights, batteries, first aid supplies, and bottled water. And gas, of course. How he kept getting this shit, Joe had no idea. "If I told you that, I'd be out of business, bro," Mike had told him when Joe asked, barking a laugh at him.

Last time he'd driven out here, Joe had asked Mike why he'd stayed behind when so many others were gone. Why not move somewhere less isolated? Even then, almost a full month ago, folks had been clumping up in Longview, barricading the school, jail, and hospital. Had to be safer, if you could buy your way in. Being white helped, too. They said it didn't, but Joe Davis knew it did. Always had, always would. Things like that just went underground for a time, that's all. Times like these the ugly stuff festered and exploded back topside.

Mike wasn't quite as old as Joe—sixty-three to Joe's more cumbersome seventy-one—but Joe thought he was foolhardy to keep the place open. Sure, all the stockpiling and bartering had made Mike a rich man, but was gasoline and Rice-A-Roni worth the risk? "I don't run, Joe. Guess I'm hardheaded." That was all he'd said.

Joe had known Mike since he first built his cedar cabin in 1989, after retiring from his berth as supply sergeant at Fort McArthur. Mike had just moved down from Alberta, and they'd talked movies, then jazz. They'd discovered a mutual love of Duke Ellington and old sitcoms. Mike had always been one of his few friends around here. Now he was the only one.

Joe didn't know whether to hope his friend would still be there or to pray he was gone. Better for him to be gone, Joe thought. One day he and the kid would have to move on, too, plain and simple. That day was coming soon. That day had probably come and gone twice over.

Joe saw a glint of the aluminum fencing posted around Mike's as he came around the bend, the end of the S in the road. Although it looked more like a prison camp, Mike's was an oasis, a tiny squat store and a row of gas pumps surrounded by a wire fence a man and a half tall. The fence was electrified at night: Joe had seen at least one barbecued body to prove it, and everyone had walked around the corpse as if it weren't there. With gas getting scarcer, Mike tended to trust the razor wire more, using the generator less these days.

Mike's three boys, who'd never proved to be much good at anything else, had come in handy for keeping order. They'd had two or three gunfights there, Mike had said, because strangers with guns thought they could go anywhere they pleased and take anything they wanted.

Today, the gate was hanging open. He'd never come to Mike's when there wasn't someone standing at the gate. All three of Mike's boys were usually there, with their greasy hair and their pale fleshy bellies bulging through their too-tight T-shirts.

No one today.

Something was wrong.

"Shit," Joe said aloud before he remembered he didn't want to scare the kid. He pinched Kendrick's chin between his forefinger and thumb, and his grandson peered up at him, resigned, the expression he always wore these days. "Let's just sit here a minute, okay?"

Little Soldier nodded. He was a good kid.

Joe coasted the truck to a stop outside the gate. While it idled, he tried to see what he could. The pumps stood silent and still on their concrete islands, like two men with their hands in their pockets. There was a light on inside, a super-white fluorescent glow through the picture windows painted with the words GAS, FOOD in red. He could make out a few shelves from where he was parked, but he didn't see anyone inside. The air pulsed with the steady burr of Mike's generator, still working.

At least it didn't look like anyone had rammed or cut the gate. The chain looked intact, so it had been unlocked. If there'd been trouble here, it had come with an invitation. Nothing would have made those boys open that gate otherwise. Maybe Mike and his boys had believed all that happy-talk on the radio, ditched their place, and moved to Longview. The idea made Joe feel so relieved that he forgot the ache in his knee.

And leave the generator on? Bullshit.

Tire tracks drew patterns in hardened mud. Mike's was a busy place. Damn greedy fool.

Beside him, Joe felt the kid fidgeting in his seat, and Joe didn't blame him. He had more than half a mind to turn around and start driving back toward home. The jerky would keep. He had enough gas to last him. He'd come back when things looked right again.

But he'd promised the kid a Coke. That was the only thing. And it would help erase a slew of memories if he could bring a grin to the kid's face today. Little Soldier's grins were a miracle. His little chipmunk cheeks were the spitting image of Cass's at his age.

"Daddy," she'd called him on the radio. "Daddy."

Don't think about that don't think don't—

Joe leaned on his horn. He let it blow five seconds before he laid off.

After a few seconds, the door to the store opened, and Mike stood there leaning against the doorjamb, a big, ruddy white-haired Canuck with linebacker shoulders and a pigskin-sized bulge above his belt. He was wearing an apron like he always did, as if he ran a butcher shop instead of a gas station. Mike peered out at them and waved. "Come on in!" he called out.

Joe leaned out of the window. "Where the boys at?" he called back.

"They're fine!" Mike said. Over the years, Joe had tried a dozen times to convince Mike he couldn't hear worth shit. No sense asking after the boys again until he got closer.

The wind skittered a few leaves along the ground between the truck and the door, and Joe watched their silent dance for a few seconds, considering. "I'm gonna go do this real quick, Kendrick," Joe finally said. "Stay in the truck."

The kid didn't say anything, but Joe saw the terror freeze his face. The kid's eyes went dead just like they did when he asked what had happened at the house in Longview.

Joe cracked open his door. "I'll only be a minute," he said, trying to sound casual.

"D-don't leave me. Please, Grandpa Joe? Let me c-come."

Well, I'll be damned, Joe thought. This kid was talking up a storm today.

Joe sighed, mulling it over. Pros and cons either way, he supposed. He reached under the seat and pulled out his Glock 9mm. He'd never liked automatics until maybe the mid-80s, when somebody figured out how to keep them from jamming so damned often. He had a Mossberg shotgun in a rack behind the seat, but that might seem a little too hostile. He'd give Kendrick the Remington 28-gauge. It had some kick, but the Little Soldier was used to it. He could trust Little Soldier not to fire into the ceiling. Or his back. Joe had seen to that.

"How many shots?" Joe asked him, handing over the little birder. Kendrick held up four stubby fingers, like a toddler. So much for talking.

"If you're coming with me, I damn well better know you can talk if there's a reason to." Joe sounded angrier than he'd intended. "Now…how many shots?"

"*Four!*" That time, he'd nearly shouted it.

"Come on in," Mike called from the doorway. "I've got hot dogs today!"

That was a first. Joe hadn't seen a hot dog in nearly a year and his mouth watered. Joe started to ask him again what the boys were up to, but Mike turned around and went inside.

"Stick close to me," Joe told Kendrick. "You're my other pair of eyes. *Anything* looks funny, you point and speak up loud and clear. Anybody makes a move in your direction you don't like, *shoot.* Hear?"

Kendrick nodded.

"That means *anybody. I* don't care if it's Mike or his boys or Santa Claus or anybody else. You understand me?"

Kendrick nodded again, although he lowered his eyes sadly. "Like Mom said."

"Damn right. Exactly like your mom said," Joe told Kendrick, squeezing the kid's shoulder. For an instant, his chest burned so hot with grief that he knew a heart attack couldn't feel any worse. The kid might have *watched* what happened to Cass. Cass might have turned into one of them before his eyes.

Joe thought of the pivoting, bloated freak he'd killed, the one that had smelled him, and his stomach clamped tight. "Let's go. Remember what I told you," Joe said.

"Yes, sir."

He'd leave the jerky alone, for now. He'd go inside and look around for himself first.

Joe's knee flared as his boot sank into soft mud just inside the gate. Shit. He was a useless fucking old man, and he had a bouncing Betty fifty klicks south of the

DMZ to blame for it. In those happy days of Vietnam, none of them had known that the *real* war was still forty years off—but coming fast—and he was going to need both knees for the real war, you dig? And he could use a real soldier at his side for this war, not just a little one.

"Closer," Joe said, and Kendrick pulled up behind him, his shadow.

When Joe pushed the glass door open, the salmon-shaped door chimes jangled merrily, like old times. Mike had vanished quick, because he wasn't behind the counter. A small television set on the counter erupted with laughter—old, canned laughter from people who were either dead or no longer saw much to laugh about. "EEEEEEEdith," Archie Bunker's voice crowed. On the screen, old Archie was so mad he was nearly jumping up and down. It was the episode with Sammy Davis Jr., where Sammy gives Archie a wet one on the cheek. Joe remembered watching that episode with Cass once upon a time. Mike was playing his VCR.

"Mike? Where'd you go?" Joe's finger massaged his shotgun trigger as he peered behind the counter.

Suddenly, there was a loud laugh from the back of the store, matching a new fit of laughter from the TV. He'd know that laugh blindfolded.

Mike was behind a broom, one of those school custodian brooms with a wide brush, sweeping up and back, and Joe heard large shards of glass clinking as he swept. Mike was laughing so hard, his face and crown had turned pink.

Joe saw what he was sweeping: The glass had been broken out of one of the refrigerated cases in back, which were now dark and empty. The others were still intact, plastered with Budweiser and Red Bull stickers, but the last door had broken clean off except for a few jagged pieces still standing upright, like a mountain range, close to the floor.

"Ya'll had some trouble?" Joe asked.

"Nope," Mike said, still laughing. He sounded congested, but otherwise all right. Mike kept a cold six months out of the year.

"Who broke your glass?"

"Tom broke it. The boys are fine." Suddenly, Mike laughed loudly again. "That Archie Bunker!" he said, and shook his head.

Kendrick, too, was staring at the television set, mesmerized. From the look on his face, he could be witnessing the parting of the Red Sea. The kid must miss TV, all right.

"Got any Cokes, Mike?" Joe said.

Mike could hardly swallow back his laughter long enough to answer. He squatted down, sweeping the glass onto an orange dustpan. "We've got hot dogs! They're—" Suddenly, Mike's face changed. He dropped his broom, and it clattered to the floor as he cradled one of his hands close to his chest. *"Ow! SHIT ON A STICK!"*

"Careful there, old-timer," Joe said. "Cut yourself?"

"Goddamn shit on a stick, shit on a stick, goddamn shit on a stick."

Sounded like it might be bad, Joe realized. He hoped this fool hadn't messed around and cut himself somewhere he shouldn't have. Mike sank from a squat to a sitting position, still cradling his hand. Joe couldn't see any blood yet, but he hurried toward him. "Well, don't sit there whining over it."

"*Shit* on a *stick, goddamn shit on a stick.*"

When Mike's wife, Kimmy, died a decade ago, Mike had gone down hard and come up a Christian. Joe hadn't heard a blasphemy pass his old friend's lips in years.

As Joe began to kneel down, Mike's shoulder heaved upward into Joe's midsection, stanching his breath and lifting him to his toes. For a moment Joe was too startled to react—the what-the-hell reaction, stronger than reflex, which had nearly cost him his life more than once. He was frozen by the sheer surprise of it, the impossibility that he'd been *talking* to Mike one second and—

Joe snatched clumsily at the Glock in his belt and fired at Mike's throat. Missed. *Shit.*

The second shot hit Mike in the shoulder, but not before Joe had lost what was left of his balance and gone crashing backward into the broken refrigerator door. Three things happened at once: His arm snapped against the case doorway as he fell backward, knocking the gun out of his hand before he could feel it fall. A knife of broken glass carved him from below as he fell, slicing into the back of his thigh with such a sudden wave of pain that he screamed. And Mike had hiked up Joe's pant leg and taken hold of his calf in his teeth, gnawing at him like a dog with a beef rib.

"Fucking *son of a bitch.*"

Joe kicked away at Mike's head with the only leg that was still responding to his body's commands. Still Mike hung on. Somehow, even inside the fog of pain from his lower-body injury, Joe felt a chunk of his calf tearing, more hot pain.

He was bitten, that was certain. *He was bitten.* Every alarm in his head and heart rang.

Oh, God, holy horseshit, he was bitten. He'd walked right up to him. They could make sounds—everybody said that—but this one had been *talking,* putting words together, acting like...acting like...

With a cry of agony, Joe pulled himself forward to leverage more of his weight, and kicked at Mike's head again. This time, he felt Mike's teeth withdraw. Another kick, and Joe's hiking boot sank squarely into Mike's face. Mike fell backward into the shelf of flashlights behind him.

"*Kendrick!*" Joe screamed.

The shelves blocked his sight of the spot where his grandson had been standing.

Pain from the torn calf muscle rippled through Joe, clouding thought. The pain from his calf shot up to his neck, liquid fire. Did the bastards have venom? Was that it?

Mike didn't lurch like the one on the road. Mike scrambled up again, untroubled by the blood spattering from his broken nose and teeth. "I have hot dogs," Mike said, whining it almost.

Joe reached back for the Glock, his injured thigh flaming, while Mike's face came at him, mouth gaping, teeth glittering crimson. Joe's fingers brushed the automatic, but it skittered away from him, and now Mike would bite, and bite, and then go after the Little Soldier—

Mike's nose and mouth exploded in a mist of pink tissue. The sound registered a moment later, deafening in the confined space, an explosion that sent Mike's useless body toppling to the floor. Then Joe saw Kendrick just behind him, his little birding gun smoking, face pinched, hands shaking.

Holy Jesus, Kendrick had done it. The kid had hit his mark.

Sucking wind, Grandpa Joe took the opportunity to dig among the old soapboxes for his Glock, and when he had a firm grip on it, he tried to pull himself up. Dizziness rocked him, and he tumbled back down.

"Grandpa Joe!" Kendrick said, and rushed to him. The boy's grip was surprisingly strong, and Joe hugged him for support, straining to peer down at his leg. He could be wrong about the bite. He could be wrong.

"Let me look at this," Joe said, trying to keep his voice calm. He peeled back his pant leg, grimacing at the blood hugging the fabric to flesh.

There it was, facing him in a semicircle of oozing slits: a bite, and a deep one. He was bleeding badly. Maybe Mike had hit an artery, and whatever shit they had was shooting all through him. Damn, damn, damn.

Night seemed to come early, because for an instant Joe Davis's fear blotted the room's light. He was bitten. And where were Mike's three boys? Wouldn't they all come running now, like the swarm over the hill he'd seen in the field?

"We've gotta get out of here, Little Soldier," Joe said, and levered himself up to standing. Pain coiled and writhed inside him. "I mean now. Let's go."

His leg was leaking. The pain was terrible, a throb with every heartbeat. He found himself wishing he'd faint, and his terror at the thought snapped him to more alertness than he'd felt before.

He had to get Little Soldier to the truck. He had to keep Little Soldier safe.

Joe cried out with each step on his left leg, where the back of his thigh felt ravaged. He was leaning so hard on Little Soldier, the kid could hardly manage the door. Joe heard the tinkling above him, and then, impossibly, they were back outside. Joe saw the truck waiting just beyond the gate.

His eyes swept the perimeter. No movement. No one. Where were those boys?

"Let's go," Joe panted. He patted his pocket, and the keys were there. "Faster."

Joe nearly fell three times, but each time he found the kid's weight beneath him, keeping him on his feet. Joe's heartbeat was in his ears, an ocean's roar.

"Jump in. Hurry," Joe said after the driver's door was open, and Little Soldier scooted into the car like a monkey. The hard leather made Joe whimper as his thigh slid across the seat, but suddenly, it all felt easy. Slam and lock the door. Get his hand to stop shaking enough to get the key in the ignition. Fire her up.

Joe lurched the truck in reverse for thirty yards before he finally turned around. His right leg was numb up to his knee—*from that bite, oh, sweet Jesus*—but he was still flooring the pedal somehow, keeping the truck on the road instead of in a ditch.

Joe looked in his rearview mirror. At first he couldn't see for the dust, but there they were: Mike's boys had come running in a ragged line, all of them straining as if they were in a race. Fast. They were too far back to catch up, but their fervor sent a bottomless fear through Joe's stomach.

Mike's boys looked like starving animals hunting for a meal.

Kendrick couldn't breathe. The air in the truck felt the way it might in outer space, if you were floating in the universe, a speck too far in the sky to see.

"Grandpa Joe?" Kendrick whispered. Grandpa Joe's black face shone with sweat, and he was chewing at his lip hard enough to draw blood.

Grandpa Joe's fingers gripped at the wheel, and the corners of his mouth turned upward in an imitation of a smile. It's gonna be all right," he said, but it seemed to Kendrick that he was talking to himself more than to him. "It'll be fine."

Kendrick stared at him, assessing: He seemed all right. He was sweating and bleeding, but he must be all right if he was driving the truck. You couldn't drive if you were one of them, could you? Grandpa Joe was fine. He said he was.

Mom and Dad hadn't been fine after a while, but they had warned him. They had told him they were getting sleepy, and they all knew getting sleepy right away meant you might not wake up. Or if you did, you'd be changed. They'd made him promise not to open the door to the safe room, even for them.

No matter what. Not until you hear the danger word.

Kendrick felt warm liquid on the seat beneath him, and he gasped, thinking Grandpa Joe might be bleeding all over the seat. Instead, when he looked down, Kendrick saw a clear puddle between his legs. His jeans were dark and wet, almost black. It wasn't blood. He'd peed on himself, like a baby.

"Are you sleepy?" Kendrick said.

Grandpa Joe shook his head, but Kendrick thought he'd hesitated first, just a little. Grandpa Joe's eyes were on the road half the time, on the rearview mirror the rest. "How long before your mom and dad got sleepy?"

Kendrick remembered Dad's voice outside of the door, announcing the time: "It's nine o'clock, Cass." Worried it was getting late. Worried they should get far away from Kendrick and send for Grandpa Joe to come get him. Kendrick heard them talking outside the door plain as day; for once, they hadn't tried to keep him from hearing.

"A few minutes," Kendrick said softly. "Five. Or ten."

Grandpa Joe went back to chewing his lip. "What happened?"

Kendrick didn't know what happened. He'd been in bed when he heard Mom say their neighbor Mrs. Shane was knocking at the window. All he knew was that Dad came into his room, shouting and cradling his arm. Blood oozed from between Dad's fingers. Dad pulled him out of bed, yanking Kendrick's arm so hard that it popped, pulling him to his feet. In the living room, he'd seen Mom crouching far away, by the fireplace, sobbing with a red face. Mom's shirt was bloody, too.

At first, Kendrick had thought Dad had hurt Mom, and now Dad was mad at him, too. Dad was punishing him by putting him in the safe room.

"They're in the house, Kendrick. We're bitten, both of us."

After the door to the safe room was closed, for the first time Kendrick had heard somebody else's footsteps. Then, that scream.

"They stayed for ten minutes, maybe. Not long. Then they said they had to leave. They were getting sleepy, and they were scared to come near me. Then they went away for a long time. For hours," Kendrick told Grandpa Joe. "All of a sudden I heard Mom again. She was knocking on the door. She asked me where my math homework was. She said, 'You were supposed to do your math homework.'"

Kendrick had never said the words before. Tears hurt his eyes.

"That was how you knew?" Grandpa Joe said.

Kendrick nodded. Snot dripped from his nose to the front of his jacket, but he didn't move to wipe it away. Mom had said not to open the door until Grandpa Joe came and said the danger word. No matter what.

"*Good* boy, Kendrick," Grandpa Joe said, his voice wavering. "Good boy."

All this time, Joe had thought it was his imagination.

A gaggle of the freaks had been there in Cass's front yard waiting for him, so he'd plowed most of them down with the truck so he could get to the door. That was the easy part. As soon as he got out, the ones still standing had surged. There'd been ten of them at least; an old man, a couple of teenage boys, the rest of them women, moving quick. He'd been squeezing off rounds at anything that moved.

"Daddy?"

Had he heard her voice before he'd fired? In the time since, he'd decided the voice was his imagination, because how *could* she have talked to him, said his name? He'd decided God had created her voice in his mind, a last chance to hear it to make up for the horror of the hole his Glock had just put in her forehead. "Daddy?"

It had been Cass, but it *hadn't* been. Her blouse and mouth had been a bloody, dripping mess, and he'd seen stringy bits of flesh caught in her teeth, just like the other freaks. It hadn't been Cass. Hadn't been.

People said freaks could *make noises.* They walked and looked like us. The newer ones didn't have the red shit showing beneath their skin, and they didn't start to lose their motor skills for a couple of days—so they could run fast, the new ones. He'd known that. Everybody knew that.

But if freaks could talk, could recognize you...

Then we can't win.

The thought was quiet in Joe's mind, from a place that was already accepting it.

Ten minutes, Little Soldier had said. Maybe five.

Joe tried to bear down harder on the gas, and his leg felt like a wooden stump. Still, the speedometer climbed before it began shaking at ninety. He had to get Little Soldier as far as he could from Mike's boys. Those boys might run all day and all night, from the way they'd looked. He had to get Little Soldier away...

Joe's mouth was so dry it ached.

"We're in trouble, Little Soldier," Joe said.

Joe couldn't bring himself to look at Kendrick, even though he wanted to so much he was nearly blinded by tears. "You know we're in trouble, don't you?" Joe said.

"Yes," the boy said.

"We have to come up with a plan. Just like we did at your house that time."

"A danger word?" Kendrick said.

Joe sighed. "A danger word won't work this time."

Again, Kendrick was silent.

"Don't go back to the cabin," Joe said, deciding that part. "It's not safe."

"But Mom and Dad might..."

This time Joe did gaze over at Kendrick. Unless it was imagination, the boy was already sitting as far from him as he could, against the door.

"That was a story I told you," Joe said, cursing himself for the lie. "You know they're not coming, Kendrick. You said yourself she wasn't right. You could hear it. That means they got your father, too. She was out in the front yard, before I got inside. I had to shoot her, Little Soldier. I shot her in the head."

Kendrick gazed at him wide-eyed, rage knotting his little face.

That's it, Little Soldier. Get mad.

"I couldn't tell you before. But I'm telling you now for a reason..."

Just that quick, the road ahead of Joe fogged, doubled. He snapped his head up, aware that he had just lost a moment of time, that his consciousness had flagged.

But he was still himself. Still himself, and that made the difference, right? He was still himself, and just maybe he would stay himself, and beat this damned thing.

If you could stay awake...

Then you might stay alive for another—what? Ten days? He'd heard about someone staying awake that long, maybe longer. Right now he didn't know if he'd last the ten minutes. His eyes fought to close so hard that they trembled. *There'll be rest enough in the grave.* Wasn't that what Benjamin Franklin had said?

"Don't you close your eyes, Daddy." Cass's voice. He snapped his head around, wondering where the voice had come from. He was seeing things: Cassie sat beside him with her pink lips and ringlets of tight brown hair. For a moment he couldn't see Little Soldier, so solid she seemed. "You always talked tough this and tough that. Da Nang and Hanoi and a dozen places I couldn't pronounce. And now the one damned time in your life that it matters, you're going to sleep?" The accusation in her voice was crippling. "We trusted you, and you walked right into that store and got bitten because you were laughing at Archie Bunker? I trusted you, Daddy."

Silence. Then: "I still trust you, Daddy."

Suddenly, Joe felt wide awake again for the last time in his life.

"Listen to me. I can't give you the truck," Joe said. "I know we practiced driving, but you might make a mistake and hurt yourself. You're better off on foot."

Rage melted from Kendrick's face, replaced by bewilderment and the terror of an infant left naked in a snowdrift. Kendrick's lips quivered violently.

"No, Grandpa Joe. You can stay awake," he whispered.

"Grab that backpack behind your seat—it's got a compass, bottled water, jerky, and a flashlight. It's heavy, but you'll need it. And take your Remington. There's more ammo for it under your seat. Put the ammo in the backpack. Do it now."

Kendrick sobbed, reaching out to squeeze Joe's arm. "P-please, Grandpa Joe..."

"*Stop that goddamned crying!*" Joe roared, and the shock of his voice silenced the boy. Kendrick yanked his hand away, sliding back toward his door again. The poor kid must think he'd crossed over.

Joe took a deep breath. Another wave of dizziness came, and his chin rocked downward. The car swerved slightly before he could pull his head back up. Joe's pain was easing, and he felt stoned, as if he were on acid. He hadn't driven far enough yet. They were still too close to Mike's boys. So much to say...

Joe kept his voice as even as he could. "There were only two people who could put up a better fight than me, and that was your mom and dad. They couldn't do it, not even for you. That tells me I can't, either. Understand?"

His tears miraculously stanched, Kendrick nodded.

READ REVELATIONS, a billboard fifty yards ahead advised in red letters. Beside the billboard, the road forked into another highway. Thank Jesus.

The words flew from his mouth, nearly breathless. "I'll pull off when we get to that sign, at the crossroads. When the truck stops, *run.* Hear me? Fast as you can. No matter what you hear...don't turn around. Don't stop. It's twenty miles to Centralia, straight south. There's National Guard there, and caravans. Tell them you want to go to Devil's Wake. That's where I'd go. When you're running, stay near the roads, but keep out of sight. If anyone comes before you get to Centralia, hide. If they see you, tell 'em you'll shoot, and then do it. And don't go to sleep, Kendrick. Don't let anybody surprise you."

"Yes, sir," Kendrick said in a sad voice, yet still eager to be commanded.

The truck took control of itself, no longer confined to its lane or the road, and it bumped wildly as it drove down the embankment. Joe's leg was too numb to keep pressing the accelerator, so the truck gradually lost speed, rocking to a stop, nose down, its headlights lost in weeds. Feeling in his arms was nearly gone now, too.

"I love you, Grandpa Joe," he heard his grandson say. Or thought he did.

"Love you, too, Little Soldier."

Still here. Still here.

"Now, go. *Go.*"

Joe heard Kendrick's car door open and slam before he could finish.

He turned his head to watch Kendrick, to make sure he was doing as he'd been told. Kendrick had the backpack and his gun as he stumbled away from the truck, running down in the embankment that ran beside the road. The boy glanced back over his shoulder, saw Joe wave him on, and then disappeared into the roadside brush.

With trembling fingers, Joe opened the glove compartment, digging out his snub-nose .38, his favorite gun. He rested the cold metal between his lips, past his teeth. He was breathing hard, sucking at the air, and he didn't know if it was the toxin or his nerves working him. He looked for Kendrick again, but he couldn't see him at this angle.

Now. Do it now.

It seemed that he heard his own voice whispering in his ear.

I can win. I can win. I saved my whole fucking squad. I can beat this thing...

Joe sat in the truck feeling alternating waves of heat and cold washing through him. As long as he could stay awake...

He heard the voice of old Mrs. Reed, his sixth-grade English teacher; saw the faces of Little Bob and Eddie Kevner, who'd been standing beside him when the bouncing Betty blew. Then he saw Cassie in her wedding dress, giving him a secret gaze, as if to ask if it was all right before she pledged her final vows at the altar.

Then in the midst of the images, some he didn't recognize.

Something red, drifting through a trackless cosmos. Alive, yet not alive. Intelligent but unaware. He'd been with them all along, those drifting spore-strands gravitating toward a blue-green planet with water and soil...filtering through the atmosphere...rest...home...grow...

A crow's mournful caw awakened Joe, but not as much of him as had slipped into sleep. His vision was tinged red. His world, his heart, was tinged red. What remained of Joe knew that *it* was in him, awakening, using his own mind against him, dazzling him with its visions while it took control of his motor nerves.

He wanted to tear, to rend. Not killing. Not eating. Not yet. There was something more urgent, a new voice he had never heard before. *Must bite.*

Panicked, he gave his hand an urgent command: *Pull the trigger.*

But he couldn't. He'd come this close and couldn't. Too many parts of him no longer wanted to die. The new parts of him only wanted to live. To grow. To spread.

Still Joe struggled against himself, even as he knew struggle was doomed. Little Soldier. Must protect Little Soldier. Must...

Must...

Must find boy.

Kendrick had been running for nearly ten minutes, never far from stumbling, before pure instinct left him and his mind woke up again. Suddenly, his stomach hurt from a deep sob. He had to slow down because he couldn't see for his tears.

Grandpa Joe had been hunched over the steering wheel, eyes open so wide that the effort had changed the way his face looked. Kendrick thought he'd never seen such a hopeless, helpless look on anyone's face. If he had been able to see Mom and Dad from the safe room, that was how they would have looked, too.

He'd been stupid to think Grandpa Joe could keep him safe. He was an old man who lived in the woods.

Kendrick ran, his legs burning and throat scalding. He could see the road above him, but he ran in the embankment like Grandpa Joe had told him, out of sight.

For an endless hour Kendrick ran, despite burning legs and scalded throat, struggling to stay true to the directions Grandpa Joe had given him. South. Stay south.

Centralia. National Guard. Devil's Wake. Safe.

By the time exhaustion claimed Kendrick, rain clouds had darkened the sky, and he was so tired he had lost any certainty of placing his feet without disaster. The trees, once an explosion of green, had been bleached gray and black. They were a place of trackless, unknowable danger. Every sound and shadow seemed to call to him.

Trembling so badly he could hardly move, Kendrick crawled past a wall of ferns into a culvert, clutching the little Remington to his chest.

Once he sat, his sadness felt worse, like a blanket over him. He sobbed so hard he could no longer sit up straight, curling himself in a ball on the soft soil. Small leaves and debris pasted themselves to the tears and mucous that covered his face. One sob sounded more like a wail, so loud it startled him.

Grandpa Joe had lied. Mom had been dead all along. He'd shot her in the head. He'd said it like it hardly mattered to him.

Kendrick heard snapping twigs, and the back of his neck turned ice-cold.

Footsteps. Running fast.

Kendrick's sobs vanished, as if they'd never been. He sat straight up, propping his shotgun across his bent knee, aiming, finger ready on the trigger. He saw a small black spider crawling on his trigger wrist—one with a bloated egg sack, about to give birth to a hundred babies like in *Charlotte's Web*—but he made no move to bat the spider away. Kendrick sat primed, trying to silence his clotted nose by breathing through his mouth. Waiting.

Maybe it was that hitchhiker with the sign, he thought.

But it didn't matter who it was. *Hide.* That was what Grandpa Joe said.

The footsteps slowed, although they were so close that Kendrick guessed the intruder couldn't be more than a few feet away. He was no longer running, as if he knew where Kendrick was. As if he'd been close behind him all along, and now that he'd found him, he wasn't in a hurry anymore.

"I have a gun! I'll shoot!" Kendrick called out, and this voice was very different from the one he'd used to ask Grandpa Joe for a Coke. Not a little girl's voice this time, or even a boy's. It was a voice that meant what it said.

Silence. The movement had stopped.

That was when Grandpa Joe said the danger word.

Kendrick's finger loosened against the trigger. His limbs gave way, and his body began to shake. The woods melted away, and he remembered wearing this same jacket in the safe room, waiting. Waiting for Grandpa Joe.

There had never been a gunshot from Grandpa Joe's truck. Kendrick had expected to hear the gunshot as soon as he ran off, dreading it. Grandpa Joe always did what needed to be done. Kendrick should have heard a gunshot.

"Go back!" Kendrick said. Although his voice was not so sure this time, he cocked the Remington's hammer, just as he'd been taught.

Kendrick waited. He tried not to hope—and then hoped fervently—that his scare had worked. The instant Kendrick's hope reached its peak, a shadow moved against the ferns above him, closer.

"Breakfast," Grandpa Joe's watery voice said again.

ZOMBIEVILLE

By Paula R. Stiles

Paula R. Stiles is the author of more than two dozen stories. Her work has appeared in *Nature*, *Albedo One*, the zombie anthology *History Is Dead*, *Shine*, *Writers of the Future XXIV*, *Jim Baen's Universe*, *Space and Time*, and in many other venues, such as the South African magazine *Something Wicked*, where this story first appeared. She is also the editor of *Innsmouth Free Press*. From 1991 to 1994, Stiles served as an Aquaculture Extension Agent with the Peace Corps in Cameroon, West Africa.

Resident Evil, a 1996 video game set in a haunted mansion, combined polygonal characters with pre-rendered backgrounds, and was one of the first games in the "survival horror" genre, following the model of *Alone in the Dark*. The game has spun off numerous sequels, as well as three feature films starring Milla Jovovich and written by Paul W. S. Anderson, most recently the *Mad Max*-inspired *Resident Evil: Extinction*. The most recent video game in the franchise, *Resident Evil 5*, is set in Africa, which has provoked some criticism of the game's handling of racial imagery.

The author of our next tale says, "I kept hearing they wanted to do a *Resident Evil* movie set in Africa, and I groaned a little, thinking about how many boring clichés they'd come up with for that. Then I thought, 'Well, self, why not do your own take on an African Zombocalypse?'"

Stiles made the protagonists of the story Peace Corps volunteers because she used to be one. "AIDS was already at epidemic proportions in Cameroon by the time I left in '94, and that's a pretty scary atmosphere to be in for two years," she says. "So when I was hearing people talk about the zombocalypse as if it would be this catastrophic event, I kinda laughed and thought, 'You know, I should just write a zombocalypse tale that's a metaphor for AIDS in Africa.' It's not actually the first AIDS-in-Africa metaphor tale I've written. Probably won't be my last, either."

The *gendarme* had wandered out into the middle of the road. His already well-fleshed form had swelled to bursting, and his skin, once the color of the stash of dark chocolate we'd traded for in Yaoundé, looked almost as green as his stained army uniform. He looked like he'd been from the Bulu, a tribe down in the South Region near the port of Douala, down the railroad line from Yaoundé. He stood there, waving his arms in a parody of his old *contrôle*-point routine of stopping bush-taxis and other traffic to check their papers, hunt up the odd bribe.

Our taxi, a gray Peugeot, stuffed with ten live passengers and driver, cleared the hill and slammed down on all four wheels into a nasty pothole. We hit the *gendarme* about dead center five meters later to the tune of ABBA's "Dancing Queen," which the Hausa Muslim driver had been blasting on the Peugeot's tape deck. The *gendarme* flew up over the roof, landing hard—and in pieces—on the paved road behind the car. The driver didn't so much as ease off the gas. Just as well. We'd all sooner stop for a cobra than a zombie.

"That was pretty spectacular," Josie said. She was a reasonably good-looking blonde and my housemate, crammed half onto my lap and half up onto the armrest of the right rear door. That might sound like a good thing, but only if you've never been stuck in a Peugeot with ten other people for three hours on a tropical afternoon. Our only break was the half-hour we'd spent on the side of the road to allow the six Muslims in the car to pray and the rest of us to pee.

"Yeah, pretty spectacular…if you like blood and guts splattering all over the road," I said. "Bet he'd have stopped if the guy had been Muslim."

"Since he was obviously a *gendarme*, he couldn't have been Muslim, so I'm sure the driver thought it was perfectly reasonable to run him down," Josie said.

Cameroon's president just before everything had gone to zombie hell had been from the South. His predecessor had been a Fulani Muslim from the Extreme North. There'd been bad blood between the Muslims and the Government ever since. Considering this was a country where a Muslim friend had once told me that his Christian neighbors were "cannibals" because they ate cats and a good host always popped the top off your beer in front of you to prove he or she hadn't poisoned it, it was a wonder the driver hadn't turned around and run over the *gendarme* twice.

Josie and I were the only *nassaras* (foreign whites) in the car. Technically, I was Chinese-American, not white, but Cameroonians didn't make those distinctions with Americans—except when they expected me to do kung fu like Bruce Lee. Didn't help that my name really was Bruce, or that I'd clear six feet easily in my bare feet. They got a lot of martial arts flicks over here—used to, anyway. Before.

Running over the *gendarme* may not have been such a hot idea. His guts had gotten snarled on the roof of the car and now dangled through the driver's-side window like a sausage brand of fuzzy dice and bumped against the driver's shoulder. They smelled—literally—like shit. The driver ignored them. He'd probably smelled worse.

We rolled across the bridge over a river of sand and into Maroua, provincial capital of the Extreme North Region of Cameroon. If you had to get stranded someplace during a zombie epidemic, you could have done worse than Maroua. The place looked like a city out of *Arabian Nights*. The local Hausa and Fulani Muslims were friendly, rich and regionally well-organized. They lived in large, walled compounds along tree-lined streets, the walls whitewashed or cement-*crépissagé* mud-brick, with wells inside and fruit trees. Some of those civic features had helped save most of the city's population, that and the usually dry climate—mixed savannah and desert. During the initial outbreak, we'd all just shut ourselves up and waited. We'd only gone out, heavily armed, for food and other necessary supplies. Many nights I'd lain in bed, listening to the zombies claw and bang on the *tolle* gates. In the morning, we'd venture out to club and burn any walking dead in sight. Nobody took them on at night, even now.

The taxi bumped past the main taxi park, an open, flat place of beaten red dirt near one of the round hills that just popped up out of the landscape this far north. The taxi park was surrounded by dusty green trees with low-spreading limbs. We were only a day's journey south of Lake Chad, not all that far from the Sahara.

As we passed the park, I spotted two men torching a zombie dog. They had it staked down with a spear and were burning it in sections, from the tail up. I could see its dry ribs shining in the afternoon sun all the way from the taxi. The dog snapped at its tormentors as they danced around it. I loved animals, and I pitied what that dog had been, but there was no way I would have tried to save it now.

The driver dropped us off at our compound in the "safe" part of town. Josie and I peeled ourselves out of the taxi along with the rest of the passengers. After stretching the kinks out of our backs, we snagged our equipment from the overstuffed-and-strapped-down trunk. The passengers stood by looking over their shoulders as the driver handed out the machetes, matches, and canned goods we'd looted during our "shopping" trip down south. Even with the curiosity that anything we *nassaras* did generated, our equipment post-outbreak was too ordinary to mark.

Josie banged on the gate. No one answered, but that wasn't uncommon. She got the tin gate open while I hauled out our bags. The driver took off as soon as he'd cinched things back up with strips of black rubber inner tube called *caoutchouc*. Josie and I liked to joke that the entire country was held together with it. Keeping an eye out, we tossed the bags in through the gate quickly and slammed the door behind us.

The virus had raged during the rainy season the previous year and had gotten into the water supply. The traditional clearing of the savannah brush by fire in December at the beginning of the Dry Season had helped considerably with suppressing the initial epidemic. Christmas had passed fairly uneventfully. With the end of January and the reheating of the weather, though, some isolated outbreaks were starting up again. Josie and I had come back from Yaoundé, the country capital not far north of Douala, just in time.

The compound's dogs, Cujo I and II, came bounding up to us for a head-rub as soon as we came in. Like most Cameroonian dogs, they barely came up to Josie's knees. They reminded me with a twinge of the zombified dog I'd seen in the taxi park. A tawny cat from our small colony lazed on a chair on the porch. We'd had some feline mortality initially, but they'd learned fast to avoid zombie rats and the like. They mostly stayed inside the compound now. The day guard, Adamou, woke up in his chair near the cat and came down off the porch, scratching his head and yawning.

"*Bonsoir*, Adamou," I said. He nodded and waved distractedly, then went back to his nap. He wasn't big on helping out with heavy lifting.

"We're here!" Josie shouted toward the house. It was a cement, ranch-style structure with a *tolle* roof, barred windows and an open front porch. Nothing you'd ever see in *Out of Africa*. Buckets and panniers were lined up under all the eaves from the last rainy season. We had a well, and running water still ran in the pipes sporadically, but less and less often since the beginning of the outbreak. We kept the water in big containers and we always boiled it before we drank it or bathed in it. That cut a bit into our supply of propane tanks, and the rate of indirect infection from the virus, in strict epidemiological terms, was pretty low, but nobody wanted to end up like that *gendarme* from brushing their teeth in the morning.

Two of our group came out onto the porch. There were still nine non-missionary foreigners that we knew of in the region—five volunteers from the Peace Corps (three of us here in town), two Italian aid workers and a couple of young tourists who'd just been passing through when everything had gone to a hot place in a hand conveyance back home. Cyndi and Roger had decided to stay in their village up near Waza National Park. The rest of us had wanted everybody to stick together. We'd heard rumors that poachers had spread the virus to some of the animals in Waza. Facing off with a zombie elephant? No thanks. But Roger and Cyndi felt differently.

Personally, I thought Roger was just being his usual antisocial asshole self and that Cyndi stuck with him out of loyalty. She was still dating him, after all. But it wasn't my decision, or anybody else's but Cyndi's and Roger's. With everything we'd lost, we weren't about to curtail each other's freedom on top of it.

"How was Zombieville?" Alicia, one of the Italians, asked. She meant Yaoundé, after Brazzaville in the Congo. But it could have applied to any large city, even Maroua, just eight months ago. She was a tall, thin brunette who smoked a lot, more now than before the outbreak.

Josie and I looked at each other. We didn't much want to talk about our trip, especially considering we'd barely made the last train to Ngaounderé that was liable to leave Yaoundé for a while. But our buddies needed a report.

"Messy, as usual," I replied. "Whole sections of the city are overrun at this point. Everybody who's still got a pulse has gone back *en brousse*, as far as we could tell, though the Muslims are still running a closed *marché* and the like. The Peace Corps Admin office is picked pretty clean, but we found some meds—Chloroquine and Mefloquine—and some antibiotics that we don't think are too spoiled."

"How's the situation back home?" That was Silas, our third volunteer. He was a big black guy in his forties who looked like he'd been born in the Marines. He'd have gone with us if he hadn't broken his leg in a motorcycle accident a few months back. He'd left family back in the States—hadn't we all—but he'd probably been the least homesick of us until the outbreak. Now, he spent a lot of his time working a two-way short-wave radio he'd found in the *marché* while laid up, burning through car battery after car battery, hoping to get an answer. Sometimes he did from the oddest places, like Siberia or Bosnia or Cape Cod, but most of the time he just got static. Nobody told him to give it up. We were all hoping along with him.

I hadn't heard from either my mom or my sister in San Francisco since before the outbreak. Didn't expect to, either, but you know, you like to hope.

Josie shook her head to Silas' question. "It's total radio silence. The last anybody heard, things were getting pretty ugly, nothing your contact on the Cape hasn't already told you about zombies hating salt water. That was before the Rainy Season began…end of February or March, maybe. Who knows what it's like now?"

"Now" was January. If we hadn't heard from anybody else in the U.S. by now, that meant we probably never would; the country was gone. And Italy. And the rest of Europe and the Americas. And Asia. And Australia. All gone, at least as far as civilization was concerned. Drowned in an apocalyptic flood of mostly dead carrion beasts with the shelf-life of rotting hamburger.

And here we were in Cameroon, West Africa, cut loose like the rest of the expats, scrambling to make a living, to make a permanent life and put down roots in a country where we'd expected only to have a passing adventure for two or three years. Needless to say, it had been a shock all round that we were stuck here for the duration. Not even a year had helped us get used to it.

Cameroon is a radically different culture from any in the West. You think you'll be fine and then you get here and…well, you're not always fine. Psychovacs hadn't been all that uncommon among volunteers before the outbreak. They were no longer an option.

The rest of the world had succumbed so fast. But not Africa. Africa, cradle of humanity and civilization, had simply shrugged and collectively said to this latest pandemic, "You want a piece of *Homo sapiens*? Get in line." And someday—maybe not so soon, but someday—we'd spread out once again and repopulate the world, pushing aside another hominid species, this time *Homo mortuus*. It was only a matter of time.

But now it was January, and the yellow Harmattan wind was rolling in off the Sahara, pushing the rains south and drying everything out, including the zombies. A good time for a little zombicide.

Alicia said, "We have some bad news of our own."

Josie looked down and started scuffing the red dirt, probably not too keen to face whatever Alicia had to say. I decided to face it straight on; maybe it would hurt less. I looked back and forth between Alicia and Silas. "What?"

Silas took the plunge. "We haven't heard from Roger and Cyndi since before you guys left."

"I'm sorry, Bruce," Alicia said. "I know you three have been worrying about them."

"Uh, that was over two weeks ago," I said, feeling my stomach clench up into some serious heartburn. I felt a sudden need for a shot of Gordon's gin. They didn't answer, just looked grim.

"No bush-taxi notes?" Josie asked, finally looking up. "Nothing?"

"I wanted to go out and pick them up," Silas said, shaking his head, "but the others argued that we'd better wait for you guys, what with my bum leg. You're the ones with the connections and experience and we only really started to worry a few days ago."

"Shit," I said. Josie didn't say anything. She didn't need to. We'd had a little business going for a couple of months now, cleaning out centers of zombie infection. It kept the money coming in, so nobody complained. Silas was right. We were the logical ones to go find out what had happened to Roger and Cyndi, just like we'd been the logical ones to go down to Zombieville and reconnoiter.

"Well, we can't go right now," Josie said with her usual practicality. "It's only two hours to sunset and way too hot. We'll go tomorrow at sunrise."

Sunrise wasn't until six a.m., but she was right. You couldn't get much done in the Cameroon heat after nine in the morning, especially in the north, and evenings weren't a good time to be outside. The bandits who had infested the roads of the region for many years had been some of the first to get zombified. Like that *gendarme* on the road, their rotten minds kept them at their old habits. Sure, being half-dead slowed them down, but Cameroonian nights were dark. In a noisy taxi, we'd get no warning of an attack.

Josie and I only got some sleep that night because we were so tired. We tried a little fooling around, but dropped off in the middle of it. Right before dawn, in *Le Grande Matin*, we set off in a bush-taxi, not long after the first call to prayer for the day wailed out to the Muslims from mosques all over town. Bush-taxis looked like milk trucks with holes cut out for windows, but they were sturdier than car taxis when it came to zombie attacks. Along the way, we saw a zombie giraffe come out of the trees and stagger along the roadside in a parody of a live giraffe's stately walk, trying to outpace us, no doubt. Most of its mottled hide had worn off in patches or was hanging in strips around its long legs. Its tendons looked so brittle it was a wonder it could keep its feet. Even so, a pride of very-much-alive lions on the other side of the road just lounged on large tree branches, wistfully observing it from a distance. They knew better than to try that kind of meat. I wondered if the virus might even end up saving the wildlife. They sure were venturing out of Waza with increasing boldness. All the more reason to persuade Roger and Cyndi to come back with us, even if it turned out they were fine.

We got hit up for a job as soon as we rolled into town around eight. The *sousprefet* himself met us at the little taxi park. *Sousprefets* were federal government officials in charge of the *arrondisement* around a township. A big city like Maroua had a *prefet*, instead, in addition to at least one local mayor and a *chef* for each tribe.

This guy was an Anglophone from the Northwest Region above Yaoundé, which meant he was probably even more industrious than the Muslims. The super-efficient inhabitants of the two Anglophone regions and the neighboring Francophone West Region had a mutual hostility with the other seven Francophone regions, which sometimes got Anglophone officials lynched in the south during times of unrest (like national elections). It wasn't so bad up here, where the Anglophones and the Muslims shared a work ethic and a common cause against our now-defunct federal government. Probably why the locals hadn't replaced this guy with a Muslim. A long-running joke was that the country would never elect an Anglophone because he'd make everybody work, and nobody wanted that.

The *sousprefet* seemed happy to see a couple of Western *nassaras* and chatted for a little while with us in English. Then he told us he needed our services even before we mentioned our own mission.

The job would pay our rent for the next couple of months—40,000 CFA or its equivalent in supplies to burn out a house of zombies. You'd think people wouldn't use paper money or coins anymore. But you can't carry that much in supplies everywhere you go and there was no way in hell anybody would take credit the payer probably wouldn't honor. So, money still got passed around, increasingly tattered and with different countries on it, but still useful. A bit like the bottles people still brought to bars in exchange for beer and soda because some enterprising souls were still making both. The *sousprefet* and his *gendarmes* could have done the job themselves, but this was in the compound of a local traditional *chef*. *Nassaras* were good for the more delicate zombicide jobs. Being from a foreign tribe, we weren't supposed to have a stake in the local politics, so we had a rep for being impartial.

Josie and I discussed it. We wanted to get over to see Roger and Cyndi right away, but we already knew from experience that whatever condition they were in, they'd probably been in it for two weeks already. Besides, we could really use the money and the *sousprefet*'s goodwill if things had gone sideways with them. We agreed to do it.

We stocked up on kerosene in the *marché*, buying it in old, plastic palm-oil bottles. There was red sediment at the bottom of each one. Any petroleum product was strained through a cloth to get out the dust, but that wasn't 100 percent successful. That would matter for a car, but not for our purposes. Zombies would burn just as well with dirty kerosene.

They'd shut up all the infected, living and dead, inside a large hut in a compound. Nobody had been out for seven days. That made the job a simple one of torching and watching it burn, slicing and incinerating the zombies who tried to escape. The only glitch came when a woman burst out of the burning hut, clutching a baby. We nearly hacked her before she screamed and the baby started howling.

Zombies don't talk. They can make a weird sort of grunt, with air coming out through the vocal cords, but they can't talk. Or scream.

We doused both woman and child with gin (my own way of dealing with the outbreak, so I always had some on me) to disinfect them as best we could. Then we pronounced mother and child "clean." This practice didn't usually thrill the local Muslims, but they were fine with the logic of cleaning off zombie virus as long as the booze didn't make the person drunk. Judged living again by the *nassara* zombie-hunters, both survivors were taken away gently to be fed and given a real bath.

And that was the job. We'd insisted on the 40,000 CFA up front. That would have been not quite a hundred bucks American if the U.S. still existed. Normally, we'd have pocketed it and gone back to Maroua in high spirits.

But we weren't here on business, or fun. We were here to check up on two of our own.

The *sousprefet* grabbed two *gendarmes* and led us there himself. He seemed to know what we were in for, but, our friends being *nassaras*, he'd probably been hesitant to go in.

"If you find anything, we'll pay the usual rate," he said. This seemed awfully generous until he took off down the road with the two *gendarmes* without paying us first. Figured we wouldn't get any backup, though I could see the hold-off on payment. Roger and Cyndi might be okay. And if they weren't, he might want the house after we burned it out. The cement walls wouldn't be damaged, nor the *tolle* roof.

The compound was ominously silent as we let ourselves in through the gate with a little machete-prying. We went in machetes-first. Once we established that the coast was apparently clear, we brought in our bottles of kerosene. We laid them out along a line on the dirt path up to the cement porch, dropping small matchboxes as we went. We'd long since learned how to play zombie-hunting like a video game. You wanted to lay down ammunition coming in along the routes where you'd be most likely to come hell-for-leather back out, screaming and scrambling to avoid those clutching hands and snapping teeth. Zombies weren't too fast and they weren't too bright. They didn't last all that long, either, maybe six months. But once they got fixated on you, they'd keep coming and they'd run you down if you didn't burn them, pin them or find sanctuary.

The house was probably bigger than would be comfortable, or safe, for a single volunteer or even two. Peace Corps Admin had made some weird decisions in the past about security on that score, not that it mattered now. I'd learned fast during training to take care of my own safety as much as possible; in fact, Josie and I had bonded then over our cynicism about some Peace Corps policies. We'd been in Community Development before the outbreak, if you can believe it.

We busted into the house fast, machetes and matches out. We thought we were ready for what we'd find.

We weren't.

The house had an open plan to allow for the February heat in the middle of the dry season. It had three bedrooms coming off a huge, airy living room that shaded off into a back porch with big clay pots, round and red.

In the middle of the living room, near a wooden couch that had been turned over and smashed, lay a zombie. It had been staked down with a metal spike through the ribs. Impressive. Whoever had done it must have used a sledgehammer. The zombie kept trying to get itself free, but couldn't do so without ripping itself in half. Even so, it was still trying, scrabbling feebly at the cement floor.

It took me at least a minute to recognize Roger. His face had bloated up and slid sideways in the heat. His guts had burst out onto the floor. He had to have been dead for most of the past two weeks. The soiled t-shirt gave him away. We'd been in training together and he was still wearing the shirt our group had designed, along with the usual Peace Corps uniform of jeans and hiking boots that we were wearing for the job. A lot of volunteers eventually went native in their clothing styles, switching to cooler tailored cotton pajamas and flip-flops. Not Roger.

"Sweet Mary Mother of God," Josie said, recognizing him at the same moment. She looked ready to puke. I wasn't surprised. She and Roger had dated for about a week in training before she found out he was an asshole. Training relationships usually burned fast and furious, then guttered out just as fast.

"That's one way to put it." I could see her having a few issues walking in on a zombified person she'd once fooled around with.

As our voices echoed, I realized that the house seemed awfully quiet, as if someone was hiding further in, holding his or her breath. If Cyndi had been zombified, why would she be hiding from us? Why not attack? Where the hell was she?

I sidled up to Josie. Sound really carried off gloss-painted walls and polished floors. I leaned close and whispered, "I think Cyndi's still in here."

She nodded and whispered back, "You think we should check before we clear the house and start burning?" Cyndi had never liked Josie, being a tad jealous about the training fling, but Josie was a pro. She wasn't going to let that stop her from finishing the job.

"Well...*yeah*." At the very least, we'd need to make sure we'd located every zombie in the place or we might not get paid. Somebody had staked Roger to the living room floor, somebody who seriously didn't want to die or get zombified. It was probably Cyndi, but that didn't mean she was still human.

We catfooted down the hallway toward the bedrooms, covering each other. Machetes can be pretty effective, especially considering how much practice we'd gotten in with them. But they were close-up weapons, which meant we could get infected by body fluids or a bite if we didn't watch it. No way in hell did I want to get infected and end up like Roger. Or that *gendarme* on the road from Ngaoundéré.

Josie came behind me, watching my back. One of the fun parts of being a guy was getting to be on point. As I snuck down the hallway, I thought I heard a noise. I stopped dead, Josie ramming into my back.

"What the hell is that?" I whispered. Josie was practically clinging to my shoulders. Then I heard it again. It was a whimper. It came from down the hall.

We edged into the room. The noise was coming from the closet. Somebody was hiding in there.

We eased up to either side, machetes raised high. Then, at a signal from Josie, I yanked open the door.

Good thing we didn't stand right in front of it. Whoever it was came right out of the closet, flailing around with a big spear. We almost hacked her to pieces right there, even as I recognized Cyndi. But then she started screaming at us. Actual words, mostly curses.

"Hey!" I yelled, backing up fast from the spear. "Hey, Cyndi! Calm down! It's Bruce and Josie!"

Cyndi didn't seem to notice. Josie and I had to dodge and hop around the room until I managed to hack the spear in half with my machete. Josie clomped Cyndi over the head with the butt of hers. That dazed Cyndi long enough that we were able to get her down and tie her up. I guess she finally realized then that we weren't zombies—they don't tie you up, just eat you raw. She started to cry, so we stopped trying to tie her up. We chivvied her out of there, checking the backyard to make sure it was clear and burning everything flammable as we went. We managed to save a photo album and some letters, though we weren't sure if they belonged to Cyndi or Roger.

Last, we torched Roger. Or I did, that is. On the front porch, Josie sat on top of Cyndi to squash her ongoing hysterics and to keep her from watching while I went back into the living room to take care of the thing that used to be her boyfriend.

"Sorry about this, Roger," I said. Just because he'd been an asshole when he was alive didn't mean he deserved this. Nobody did. I doused him with kerosene, coughing at the smoke oozing through the house while he grunted and snapped at my hands. Then I lit a match. It took five or six, but he went up. The grunting didn't get any more intense as the flames took him. If anything, it died down. He moved aimlessly around while he burned. Finally, something popped or broiled or I-don't-know-what inside what was left of his brain and he settled down on the floor to smolder, mostly in silence, aside from the odd pop and crackle. And that was the end of Roger. The second end. The final one, I hoped. I backed away with a shudder and went out onto the porch, leaving the doors open to get better circulation for the fire. That sure as hell wasn't how I wanted to close out *my* Peace Corps service.

We took Cyndi back to the taxi park after an alcohol bath, got our money from the *sousprefet* and caught a car taxi back with no other passengers. It cost a little extra to get the whole car, but it was worth it. We were covered with dried sweat already, the heat of late morning wringing out more, and Cyndi was acting pretty claustrophobic. About halfway home, Cyndi started to get semi-coherent and more than thankful. That was actually worse because then she had to tell us all about how Roger had been bitten by a zombie rat out of nowhere and turned a few days later. How she'd survived the past two weeks being chased around the house by her zombie boyfriend, afraid to go out in case she was attacked by more zombies. Damn. That was almost as bad as ending up like Roger.

On the way back, the driver took a detour to pick something up from his house, so we ended up coming in on the same road we'd taken the day before from the train station in Ngaoundéré. The remains of the dead *gendarme* our taxi had hit lay all over the road. The limbs still moved feebly.

Suddenly, I needed a really stiff drink, but we'd used up all my gin for disinfectant purposes. I'd have to go dry until we got back to the house.

"*Arrêtez!*" I shouted to the driver. "Stop! Stop the car!"

The driver thought I was nuts, but he pulled over. We hadn't paid him the full fare yet. He wouldn't leave.

"What're you doing?" Josie said, getting out with me. Cyndi just huddled in the back seat of taxi.

"I'm not leaving that poor bastard in the road." I started getting the kerosene and matches out.

"Ahhh," she said, following my line of sight to the twitching arms and legs.

We didn't even bother to gather the body parts together, too much risk of infection. We just went up and down the road in the noon heat, pouring kerosene on the pieces and setting them on fire. I hoped that somehow it gave that *gendarme* some peace. I hoped I'd never have to do the same thing to Josie. And I hoped that if I got unlucky, too, someone would give me the same mercy.

THE ANTEROOM

By Adam-Troy Castro

Adam-Troy Castro's work has been nominated for several awards, including the Hugo, Nebula, and Stoker. His novels include *Emissaries from the Dead* and *The Third Claw of God*, and two collaborations with artist Johnny Atomic: *Z Is for Zombie*, and *V Is for Vampire*, which comes out in October. Castro's short fiction has appeared in such magazines as *The Magazine of Fantasy & Science Fiction*, *Science Fiction Age*, *Analog*, *Cemetery Dance*, and in a number of anthologies. I previously included his work in *The Living Dead* and in *Lightspeed Magazine*. His story collections include *A Desperate, Decaying Darkness* and *Tangled Strings*.

People throughout history have had many different conceptions of what an afterlife might look like. The Greeks imagined the sunny fields of Elysium and the unending drudgery of Hades. The Vikings imagined that great warriors would go to an endless kegger in Valhalla. Dante imagined Hell as a massive multi-tiered pit. (The image of the underworld as a place of fire may have been inspired by the volcanic island of Crete, and the word Gehenna, associated with Hell, is named after a fiery garbage pit outside Jerusalem.) But what sort of an afterlife might await those who have been transformed into zombies?

"The most bone-chilling horror of the zombie sub-genre has always been that the plague turns us into things we don't want to be, things capable of committing depraved acts that would have appalled the people we used to be," Castro says. "We laugh when the hero of a zombie story blows away the shambling rotter in his path...but we tend to forget that the rotter used to be a person, and might have even been a human paragon. Stephen King wrote about his rabid St. Bernard Cujo, from the novel of the same name. You can't hate the dog. The dog always tried to be a good dog. But something got into him, something that eliminated free will from the equation. How would Cujo feel if somebody returned to him the capacity to understand what he'd done? How would a human being?"

Your mercy killer, who knew you well in life and weeps for you even as he does what he must, presses the rifle barrel against your forehead with a gentleness that renders the gesture more a goodbye kiss than a murder. He even apologizes to you, calling you by name and telling you how sorry he is. You do not understand the apology or recognize your name or even appreciate that you are being put out of your misery. You only know that you have been prevented from shuffling forward, the atavistic impulses that drive your rotting limbs still urging you toward the very man who is about to end you. You don't attempt to evade the bullet, because that kind of problem-solving is beyond you. You simply moan in protest. And then he pulls the trigger and the world fills with fire and your head comes apart in an explosion of bone and blood and brains. The wall behind you drips with everything good you were in life and everything obscene you became in death.

Your best friend will tell himself that you're in a better place now. And here we leave him, wishing him well, whether he manages to survive or at least dies without becoming infected. Because his story is unremarkable. There have been many thousands just like it, in the world plagued by the living dead.

But your own story is not yet done.

In fact, your story might never be done. And this is why.

You wake an infinite distance away, blinking on your back beneath a sky that is neither dark nor light, but rather a shade of gray that reminds you of sheets that have gone unwashed. You are naked, to the kind of air that raises goose bumps on your skin and assures you that you're once again alive. You are hungry, but it is not the hunger that you have been feeling in the days since the contagion turned you into a thing neither alive nor dead; it is the hunger a human being feels, the hunger of skipped meals, the hunger of a body beginning to tremble from need but not yet forced to desperation. It is not pleasant, but it is better than what you felt as a corpse: a gnawing, painful emptiness powerful enough to drive ambulatory meat.

It's cold. The air has the kind of chill only possible in caves. The dirt against your back feels dry, and so solid that it might as well be concrete, but there is no warmth in it, no sense that it has ever known sun or sprouted so much as a weed.

But that's not the force that makes your face contort in pain. A flood of unwanted memories has reminded you of the man you were, in the world before everything turned to shit, and taken you through every shambling step of the journey you began when you rose as one of the living dead. You recall facing people you'd once known, and seeing only meat; hearing the screams of somebody who had been wounded and left behind, and feeling only hunger; digging with your bare hands through the steaming belly wound of a victim who begged you to finish her off, and knowing only the compulsion to shovel more of her sweetmeats into your idiot maw. You remember exactly the long minutes she lasted, and you remember failing to see her as a living thing, even when she called you Daddy. You remember losing interest in her after her heart stopped, staying near her only out of indecision, walking away after she sat up a thing hollowed out both body and soul, noticing but not caring that she tried to follow you but fell behind with every step.

As a mindless walking corpse, preying on the warm, you were spared these memories. As whatever you are now, something capable of knowing what they mean, you will never be able to escape them. You will never be able to forget what it had been like, before, to watch that bulge in your wife's belly grow until it became a great big promise of imminent life; to hold the squirming little miracle in your hands, unprepared for the sheer intensity of the love that seized you as you looked into the baby's indignant face; to feel that wonderment again the first time she smiled at you; to live for the moments when she laughed; to watch her run around you in circles, her laughter like music; to hold her in your arms as the world turned to shit and the skies filled with soot and everything you saw became an atrocity, clutching for you both. You will never be able to forget the way she'd fallen into a lasting silence well into the plague after your wife died from a simple fever, one that killed without forcing her to rise. You will never be able to forget watching your daughter's exhausted sleep while foul things moaned on the other side of a flimsy wall. You will never be able to forget telling her, without waking her, that you would never let the bad things get her, that you would never become one of them, that you would never let her become one of them either. You will never be able to forget the long weeks of bitter struggle that followed. You will never be able to forget the moment when your own chances ran out, or the way she regained her powers of speech and called you Daddy just before you put an end to her.

You weep until you have to stop from sheer emotional exhaustion.

Only when you fall silent, for a moment, do you register the many other wails in the wind.

Standing hurts. The ground is covered with a thin layer of concentrated grit that irritates your skin where it adheres to the soles of your feet. You wipe the particles away with a brush of your hand, but more accrues with your next step, which makes a nasty crunch as you sink a millimeter or so into the surface. Your body's going to have a hard time generating enough warmth to replace what the dirt leeches from your flesh; and while you should be better off standing than you were lying flat on your back, the air is no real improvement. It's thin, frigid, and tasteless. Your lungs derive no nourishment from it.

The surrounding landscape is just as barren. The gray plain extends to a gray horizon that feels farther away than any you would have found in any desert on Earth; there seems no obvious dividing line between dirt and sky, no border drawn that mitigates this emptiness by establishing any kind of limit. There are no distant hills, no sense that any one direction is preferable than any other. If you had to guess you would say that there might, might, be a dull glow somewhere off to what you arbitrarily decide to be east. But that might be imaginary, too. It might just be your eyes, imposing detail on a landscape that otherwise offers none.

This is not the same thing as calling this flat purgatory uninhabited. Because it happens to imprison many thousands of other people, crouching or sitting or lying down, as far as your eyes can see. Wherever they come from—and you can only assume that it must be the same place you have come from—they have been plopped down at equal distances, hundreds of paces apart, and they all remain alone, unwilling to expend the energy it would cost to get up and form groups. There are many weeping and many screaming, but most are just stewing in their own silence, finding enough torment within the confines of their own skulls.

Another memory comes to you: a man who had been shot in the knee. The round had turned his leg to a broken twig, trailing along at a sickening angle as he used a rifle butt to lever himself across a city street strewn with corpses and garbage and broken glass. For some reason you had been the only one of your kind still ambulatory, and this promised great things for you as you shambled toward him, announcing your approach and your intent with a low moan that made the doomed figure try to crawl faster. By the time you were within twenty paces of catching up with him, he was looking back over his shoulder once for every yard he managed to crawl. By the time you'd halved that distance he was shouting empty obscenities, calling you a stinking bastard. When you halved the distance again he was swinging his ruined rifle like a club, offering a threat that deterred you not at all. Once you came within reach of him he clubbed you in the belly, knocking you on your back; and he cried out with the savage glee of a Neanderthal who had just managed to spear the attacking tiger.

He spent the time it took you to get up dragging himself another five yards, but then collapsed, gasping. Another sweep from that rifle put you down a second time, but this time he only managed to retreat half the distance before you were on him again. Too late he decided to do what he should have done the first time, which was club you in the skull and hope he could do enough damage to your brain to smash the terrible miracle that kept you moving. But by now his strength was fading. He only succeeded in flattening your nose, adding your own clotted blood to the gore already painting your lips. You fell down again and got up again. This time he had only crawled a foot. He swung the rifle again and this time did not knock you down, but only drove you back a step or two, which was not far enough at all.

No longer able to summon voice, he whispered one last defiant "Fuck You," before giving up on the rifle he could no longer lift and trying to fend you off with his bare hands.

That slowed you down for longer than you can now believe: maybe an hour, as the magnificent doomed bastard continued to refuse to submit. The best you can say about him is that there was a little less left of you by the time he was done. The worst is that it didn't help him, and that he really should have saved a bullet for himself.

Afterward, you took your time, starting with his face while he made the few sounds he still could.

Reliving that now, just one returning horror out of many—and wishing for something solid in your stomach, so you could vomit something other than air—you finally understand why none of the other people you see would stir themselves to approach any of the others. All of these people are haunted by the people they killed, the flesh that they ate, and the loved ones who lived to see them become something reeking of the grave that wanted to drag them into the same bottomless darkness.

Who would want to see another human face, with that on their conscience?

Like them, you want to just sit alone and stew in your misery.

But then something drives you forward anyway. You select one of your closest fellow prisoners, a pale fat mound sitting on the ground about a hundred paces away. She looks up long enough to see you coming, but then turns her attention back to the dirt and doesn't move at all as you cross the gulf between you. As you draw near, you see that her skin is just as colorless as the sky, except for the places where particles of grit now cling, like parasites. She's not obese, not really, but she has enough excess flesh to form a donut around her waist. There is a tattoo on her arm, but it's an old one and has become a faded purple smudge that no longer conveys whatever it had once been meant to signify.

When you stop before her, she glances at you, her weariness heavy enough to fill up a world. "What do you want?"

"What is this place?"

She barks a bitter laugh. "Did you just arrive?"

"Is it Hell?"

She shifts her weight just enough to set the excess flesh jiggling, a sad little dance that gives the impression of life for all of two seconds before inertia reasserts herself and the rolls of flesh once again take on the character of stacked corpses. For long minutes you imagine her intent on waiting you out, but there's little point in that, not here in this place where every direction is exactly like every other. And then she murmurs, "I was a nurse."

"What?"

"I was a ward nurse at an old age home, the floor where they kept all the patients with dementia. It was the last stop. They'd already been through the forgetful stage, the confused stage, even the dangerous stage most people don't know about, when their frustration with a world they no longer understood turned them unreasonable and violent. They didn't come to me until they'd forgotten who they were, and what they'd lost. Most of them were bedridden, and some were so weak with age that they didn't have enough energy to move much...but always, always, there were some who'd gotten it in their sixties, or fifties, when they were still ambulatory, with energy to burn. I even had some in their forties, from time to time: one a college professor with a beautiful little wife twenty years younger than him, an ex-student who had to watch as her robust middle-aged husband suddenly started turning into an old man only two years into their marriage. He could run a marathon every day, that one. And we let him walk up the hallway and back, up the hallway and back, up the hallway and back, nodding a kind hello to us on every pass, never remembering that he'd ever seen us before. Understand: we knew that he was in a terrible situation. We knew that he didn't deserve what had happened to him. But, for a long time, it was almost pleasant, getting that smile from him every few minutes. He wasn't unhappy, not at all. He didn't know it was a care facility. He just thought it was a hotel, and figured that he'd be able to return to his life if he could just...if he could just find his room. He just needed to find his room. I always thought, if I ever come down with it, let me be like him. It wouldn't be too bad, if all I cared about was...finding my room."

You don't understand why she's telling you this. It seems random, not the answer to your question at all. As she winds down, you come within a breath of interrupting. But then she continues.

"After a while, he got worse. The smile went away. He forgot everything else but the shuffling walk up and down the corridor, and the skin of his face went slack, like a blanket draped on a chair. He was no longer looking for anything. There was nothing behind his eyes but the next step, and the step after that. He was transferred to another facility, so I never found out what happened to him. But when the dead rose…when they started coming after us…the look on their faces was nothing new to me. They looked like everybody in my ward. Some of the people I ended up with called them names like '*those things*,' and '*those sons of bitches*,' but I always remembered the old people on the ward, the ones who'd also forgotten everything, and had also never asked to become what they were. I never forgot that it *wasn't their fault*, that they were just looking for something they couldn't have anymore." Her tired gaze, long fixed on the dirt, manages to move upward, long enough to meet yours. "Some of us may have been evil bastards before. But what we did after the infection took us was just the infection. It wasn't our fault. Unless God's a total maniac…it wouldn't condemn us to Hell. And it hasn't. I believed in Hell. I still believe in Hell. It may have taken me a long time to figure out, but this place isn't even remotely terrible enough to be Hell."

"Then…I'm sorry. I don't get it."

She stabs the dirt with her thumb, and draws an angry circle, one that fails to connect back to itself as the curve comes around to its starting point. She rubs it out and draws it again, once again breaking the curve at the point where it should become perfect. You get the impression that she has spent much of her time here, however long that's been, trying and failing to make this one simple shape. And then she says, "After what we've done…why would anybody already in Heaven want us there?"

The size of it almost knocks you over. You spin in place, taking in hundreds, thousands of immobile figures with all that horror behind them and nothing that offers comfort in front of them. There must be millions, all told, maybe hundreds of millions or even billions: the poor, abused world getting pretty damn unpopulated by attrition by the time your own life was ripped out. You might be looking at much of the Earth's population, but for those lucky few fortunate enough to suffer so much damage when they died that the terrible phenomenon was unable to affect them: the lucky few who had not been tainted.

You say, "But that's so fucking unfair."

She nods without sympathy before returning to her hopeless drawing. "The whole thing's unfair. Isn't it?"

You stumble away, so blinded by despair and horror that you don't even thank her for the information. You are still stumbling as you pass the next hopeless figure, and the next figure after that; the ones who look up at you and the ones who don't, the ones who seem half-mad and the ones who act that way because it's the only rational response to an irrational eternity. You want to scream at them, raise an army of them, and march together toward that light in the east, the one you now know to be the Eden that will never let you in. You know that you will never get another to stand with you, let alone walk with you. They all know they carry the taint. They all know that while they're not quite damned they're as close to damned as human beings can be without actual consignment to the pit.

And then the rage rises out of nowhere and you throw your head back and you howl at the empty sky. You know exactly who you're yelling at, but you don't care. You only know that what happened wasn't anybody's fault. Or even if it was somebody's, if the plague was some exotic bug escaped from a government lab or something, nobody who caught it had ever been given a choice. You were no more responsible than loving family dogs gone rabid, or sane men turned violent by tumors in their brains. You don't deserve this emptiness, this punishment that amounts to no more than the stubborn refusal to judge you.

You scream until you run out of breath and stand there panting as you wait for an answer. But nobody answers. Nobody answers. You scream again and this time you face the gray sky and try to bring forth a pattern in the miniscule differences in shade between one patch of emptiness and another: the face of a kind and benevolent, or even stern and maniacal creator, looking down on you, taking note of what you say, and either changing his mind or smiting you for your temerity in daring to criticize him. But again, though you scream for a timeless time, maybe longer than you existed as one of the living dead, maybe longer than you existed as one of the warm, no face emerges. You are alone.

And again you wind down and sink to your knees and face the prospect of doing what all these other lost people have done, which is sit your ass on some forsaken patch of dirt and let the years, the centuries, the millennia accrue like dust.

You want to. That's the terrible thing. You want to.

But the Bastard has left you with one thing worth doing.

And so you lurch back to your feet and begin to trudge forward, stopping in front of every immobile before moving on to the next, aware that there may be millions or even billions left to go, but not caring at all, because you have nothing but time.

She was just a little girl. *Your* little girl.

It may take about as much time as it takes some mountain ranges to crumble to dust...but sooner or later, you'll find her.

WHEN THE ZOMBIES WIN

By Karina Sumner-Smith

Karina Sumner-Smith is the author of several stories, including "An End to All Things," which was a finalist for the Nebula Award. Her work has appeared in the magazines *Lady Churchill's Rosebud Wristlet, Flytrap, Challenging Destiny, Fantasy Magazine*, and *Strange Horizons*. Anthology appearances include *Children of Magic, Mythspring, Jabberwocky 3, Summoned to Destiny, Ages of Wonder*, and *Why I Hate Aliens*. Sumner-Smith is a graduate of the Clarion Writers Workshop and works part-time as a bookseller at Bakka-Phoenix Books, Toronto's science fiction and fantasy bookstore. She says she is currently battling a novel.

The ending of George Romero's *Night of the Living Dead* is pessimistic about human nature but seems optimistic about the chances of human survival in the face of a zombie pandemic. After all, come morning, we see squads of militiamen rounding up zombies and consigning them to bonfires. However, in the sequel, *Dawn of the Dead*, we are presented with the reality that the zombie plague cannot be contained and will continue to expand exponentially and irreversibly, and by the time *Day of the Dead* rolls around the world is completely dominated by zombies and only a few clusters of survivors remain.

The final outcome seems inevitable. Sumner-Smith writes, "In a discussion about the apocalypse, I joked that someone should write a story set after everyone has been eaten or turned into zombies. What would the zombies eat? What would they do when there's no one left to infect? Once I'd considered the consequences, a total zombie apocalypse seemed not horrific, nor comedic, but tragic. It's not just that everyone has died, but that we have died and yet continue to stumble through the ruins of our world with no way to understand or acknowledge what's happened, or mourn the loss of everything we once were."

When the zombies win, they will be slow to realize their success. Word travels slowly on shambling feet.

It will take years to be sure that there aren't still humans hiding in high mountain camps or deep within labyrinthine caverns; that the desert bunkers are empty, the forest retreats fallen; that the ships still afloat bear no breathing passengers.

And then: victory. Yet the zombies will not call out to each other, or cry in relief, or raise their rotting hands in triumph. They will walk unseeing beneath telephone wires and over cell phones, computers, radios. They will pass smoldering rubble without thinking of smoke signals, trip on tattered bed sheets and not consider making flags.

They are zombies; they will only walk and walk and walk, the word spreading step by step across continents and oceans and islands, year by year. And the word, to them, will feel like hunger.

When the zombies win, their quest to eat and infect human flesh will continue unabated. They will have known only gorging, only feasting; they will not understand the world as anything other than a screaming buffet on the run.

Yet there will be only silence and vacant rooms where once there was food, and the zombies, in their slow and stumbling way, will be surprised. Stomachs once perpetually distended will feel empty and curve inward towards their spines, the strength of even animated corpses beginning to fail without fuel. They will look about, cloudy eyes staring, and they will groan, unbreathing lungs wheezing as they try to push out enough air to ask slowly, hungrily, "*Brains?*"

But there will be no one left to find. Only each other.

Zombies, they will learn, do not taste good.

When the zombies win, they will become restless. There is little to do when one is dead.

Their old pastimes—their favorite pastimes—will hold no satisfaction. They will shamble down streets, arms outstretched as they groan and wail, yet inspire no fear. Together they will pound on doors, beat on windows with decaying hands until the glass shatters, hide in rivers and lakes, stumble after cars on the highway. But the cars will all be stopped, forever in park; the breaking glass will elicit no screams; and no swimmer's hands or feet will break the water's surface to be grabbed. When the doors burst open there will be no one cowering behind.

There will be no people to stalk, no food to eat, no homes to build, no deaths to die. Lost and aimless they will turn as if seeking a leader's guidance, and find none. With zombies, the only leader is the one who happens to be walking first.

So they will walk alone, all of them alone, with no destinations, only the need to keep putting one unsteady foot in front of the other, over and over without end. The world is a big place to wander, even when inhabited only by the dead.

When the zombies win, they will not think of the future. There will be no next generation of zombies, no newborn zombie children held in rotting arms. The zombies will not find comfort in each other, will not rediscover concepts like friendship or companionship, will not remember sympathy or empathy or kindness. They will not learn or dream, or even know that they cannot.

They will build no buildings, fix no cars, write no histories, sing no songs. They will not fall in love. For zombies, there is only an endless today—this moment, this place, this step, this need, this hunger, this hunger unrelenting.

And the streets will begin to crumble, and windows break, and buildings fall.

Cities will burn and flood, towns will be reclaimed by grassland and forest, desert and ocean.

The human world will go to pieces, decaying to nothing as empty eyes stare.

When the zombies win, they will not fear. They will not laugh or rejoice, they will not regret, they will not mourn. And the world will turn and turn, seasons burning and freezing across the landscape, the sun flashing through the sky, and they will continue.

When they zombies win, they will not stop. They will still moan and cry and whisper, on and on until the lips rot from their faces, their vocal cords slide away. They will never truly think again, never know the meaning of the words they try to utter, only flutter endlessly on the edge of remembering. Still they will try to speak, bone scraping on bone as their ruined jaws move, and they will not know why.

One by one they will fall. In the streets they will fall, legs no longer working, arms too broken to drag them forward. Inside buildings they will fall, tumbling down stairs and collapsing in hallways, slipping behind beds and in closets, curling into the gap between toilet and wall, not knowing, not seeing, not understanding these trappings of the places they once called home. They will sink to the bottoms of rivers and oceans, and lie down in fields, and tumble from mountainsides, and fall apart on the gravel edges of highways.

One by one they will stop moving, flesh and bone and brain too broken to do anything more. And in that silence and stillness they will struggle—trapped and ruined, they will still yearn, still hunger, always reaching for that which was taken from them. That which they granted to so many of us, in such great numbers.

To stop. To sleep. To rest, just rest, and let the darkness come.

MOUJA

By Matt London

Matt London is an author and filmmaker who lives in New York City. He is a graduate of the Clarion Writers Workshop, and a columnist for Tor.com. This story is his first piece of published fiction. He has no less than three escape plans should the zombies take Manhattan.

The samurai were a warrior caste in feudal Japan who wore distinctive armor and often fought with a sword in either hand, one long (a katana or tachi) and one short (a wakizashi or tantō). Though they were feared because they had the authority to execute any commoner who displeased them, they were bound by a strict code of honor—Bushido—which demanded they commit seppuku—ritual suicide—should they dishonor themselves.

Samurai have had a massive impact on popular culture, everything from westerns (*The Magnificent Seven* and *A Fistful of Dollars* are remakes of Akira Kurosawa samurai movies) to *Star Wars* (the film is heavily influenced by the Kurosawa film *Hidden Fortress*, and Darth Vader's helmet is modeled after a samurai helmet).

Our next story explores what happens when these highly trained soldiers face off against their first horde of zombies. The author says, "Lore would have us believe that samurai were almost superhuman in their devotion, but of course people are people. I wanted to create a character who is a slave to what he is, much as the zombies are slaves to what they are. I studied film at NYU, where I had a passionate interest in Kurosawa and horror cinema. *Seven Samurai* essentially has the same plot as most zombie movies: protagonists improve the defenses of a location, deal with social problems among the survivors, and then fight off the horde."

London's primary resource in writing the story was the *Hagakure* by Tsunetomo Yamamoto, a samurai how-to pamphlet written in the eighteenth century. Its opening line is: "I have found the essence of Bushido: to die! In other words, when you have a choice between life and death, then always choose death." Which somehow seems appropriate as a lead-in to a zombie story.

From the window of his guard hut, Takashi Shimada watched the trees. Three of the mouja lurked at the edge of the forest on the far side of the rice paddies. Takashi could just make out their shapes through the thick misty rain that made the flooded paddies seem to boil. Two of the figures at the edge of the forest were men in muddy tunics, caked with blood; the third was a woman, her kimono shamelessly open. Takashi watched, waiting, as the shadowy figures shambled toward the village. It did not matter if they traveled one mile per day or a hundred. The dead were coming, and they carried with them a hunger for human flesh.

A loud twang pierced the silence, like the string of a shamisen harshly plucked; an arrow whizzed through the air, cutting through raindrops as they fell to the earth. It struck one of the men in the forehead, splitting his rotting skull like a ripe kabocha. Undeterred, the other mouja lumbered forward as the man's body fell to the ground in a heap.

In the next hut over, Seiji stood motionless, unwavering since letting the arrow fly, his falcon eyes peering into the distance. Takashi wondered if Seiji was admiring his precise shot, or if his mind was elsewhere, asking himself why he had come to this inconsequential farming village to fight these monsters. All of the samurai had doubted their mission since arriving at the village, though none of them shared their concern with the others—such behavior was unbefitting of a samurai. Seiji finally lowered his bow, then knelt on the ground. After a moment of silent meditation, he drew an arrow from his rabbit-hide quiver, nocked it, and rose to his feet once more.

When the mouja first arrived, it was discovered they only fell when struck directly in the head by an arrow, sword, or spear. Takashi recalled the samurai's confusion as they watched the creatures approach the village looking like blowfish, their bodies riddled with arrows. Seiji's technique was so precise he never wasted an arrow. When only a few wandering mouja appeared at a time, the other samurai left it to him to eliminate the threat.

Watching the fluid elegance of Seiji's ritual put Takashi at peace. Seiji raised the bow so that the horizontal shaft of the arrow was level with his eyes. He extended his hands, his movement loose and calm. His knuckles were curved, as if he held two tiny teacups in his fingers.

Had Takashi been the one holding Seiji's bow, he would have found it difficult to fire at a woman. He might have needed Seiji to place a nimble hand on his shoulder and remind him that it was not a woman anymore.

Seiji's drawing hand opened like the wing of a bird, and with remarkable grace he let the arrow fly.

It was a perfect shot. The arrowhead pierced the woman's eye, erupted out the back of her skull, and passed through the remaining man's eye socket as well. The arrow continued on, finally coming to rest in the soggy bark of a lilac tree.

Takashi looked away, feeling the vomit crawl up his throat. He wondered whose grandmother, dead and buried years before, that had been. He wondered whose father, too slow to escape the mouja, had just been defiled.

In this new world, Bushido was just a specter lurking in the dark caves of samurai minds. Takashi knew a curse had fallen over the five islands, that none could die without rising as a perverse rotting thing, mindless and hungry for flesh. To obey the honor laws was to set a place for Death at one's own table.

Edo, Kyoto—for all Takashi knew all of the major cities had already fallen. This little village would have been defenseless. But the farmers had known that the mouja were on their way, so they had sought out a champion.

They had found Takashi at a trading post and begged him to take up their cause. It was a hopeless task. They needed an army to stand a chance. But hell was coming, and honor dictated it is better to go down fighting, protecting those who could not protect themselves. Bushido or no, doing anything was better than sitting around and drinking sake, awaiting the inevitable. So Takashi had agreed, and recruited a few other ronin to join him in protecting the town.

"Look alive," Seiji called from his window. The words were a suggestion as much as a greeting. "I am going to retrieve my arrows. You never know when we may need more than we have. Shout if you see anything that needs killing."

Seiji bounded from the hut and splashed across the rice paddies, the rain beating down on his gray cloak. When he reached the three mouja corpses, Seiji checked to make sure they were truly dead by prodding them with his katana. Takashi marveled. He had not even seen Seiji draw his sword. Other samurai had been recruited to defend the village, but Takashi would have traded any two of them for another Seiji. He was more dangerous with a fish knife than the others were with swords.

Days earlier, Isao, the youngest among the samurai protecting the village, had been watching Seiji's unmatched accuracy at work. "Your aim is perfect every time," he had said. "What is the trick?"

"The trick," Seiji had said, "is not caring if you hit the target."

The rain stopped. As the sound of roaring water faded, Takashi came out of his reverie. On the edge of the forest, Seiji was examining his arrows. One shaft had broken two inches below the fletching, so Seiji snapped off the arrowhead and kept it. The other arrow—the one that had killed two mouja with one shot—was fine once the gore was stripped off.

After sliding the arrow into his quiver, Seiji started back across the paddy field, but then suddenly froze. His ears pricked up, and he looked like a thirsty buck at a stream. From his expression the cause of his concern was clear: he was being hunted.

With the slightest motion of his head, Seiji turned. Takashi followed his gaze. Through the trees he could see a chubby, bearded man wearing a leather armor breastplate and deerskin chaps, with a brown bandana around his head. His face was ashen, his eyes the color of bird droppings. The man's left arm and his teeth were missing, and a ropy line of blood and saliva dribbled from his mouth.

If not for the beloved hatchet slung across the man's back, Takashi never would have believed it was Minoru. Poor Minoru, the first of the samurai to fall, had now vacated the funeral mound where the others had buried him. He stood leaning against a tree, staring at Seiji with a hungry mouth and those swirling eyes. All of his good humor was gone. Only the hunger remained.

Seiji raised his sword into a medium stance and looked at Takashi as if to ask "Should I?" Takashi had to tell himself that this creature was no more Minoru than a palace raided by bandits was still a king's home. Minoru's mind had new tenants. Takashi nodded to Seiji, then looked away. He shut his eyes as he heard the heavy thud of Minoru's severed head hitting the ground.

As Seiji returned to Takashi's hut, the young samurai Isao came running up to the rear window. "Masters! Masters! Come quickly!" he shouted. "The villagers—there was something they didn't tell us about the outlying homesteads. We just found out, there's a hunting lodge about an hour's walk from the center of town. Long walls, strong wooden building. Apparently, an old woodsman used to live there, but he died a few years ago. Master Takashi, Master Seiji, the farmers say there are rifles hidden in the lodge. Master Toshiro wants to go get the rifles. Do you think the rifles will fend off the mouja?"

Takashi and Seiji ordered two farmers to take their posts and followed Isao to the town square. On the way, they passed the fields where old men and women not fit for sentry duty were up to their elbows in murky water. They harvested the rice impassively. These farmers were a simple people, simple and simple-minded. They had no music, no art, no higher purpose. All they cared for was the harvest, and they would defend the harvest at any cost. Their only drive was to feed their families.

Daisuke, Toshiro, and the mayor were waiting for the other samurai by the old well in the center of town. The situation was as Isao had described. Toshiro was shouting at the mayor, furious that he had not told the samurai about the rifles.

But of course the farmers had kept it secret. In tough times, samurai could be just as greedy as the mouja, consume just as much. Ronin were known to burn villages, rape daughters, steal property, and even kill men for no reason.

Daisuke was in favor of retrieving the rifles, but not so close to dark. Toshiro and Isao wanted to fetch them right away—Toshiro for the adventure, Isao out of fear. The young one did not think they would last the night without stronger arms.

Takashi agreed with Daisuke. At least three samurai would have to go to the hunter's lodge, and leaving the village's defenses so thin at night would be suicide.

Toshiro slapped the ground with both hands. "Don't you see? You fool! With those rifles, we could fight them from a safe distance. We lost Minoru because he was forced to get close to the mouja and draw his sword. Rifles can be fired from a safer distance than bows. We must retrieve these weapons now. The boy is right. The sun sinks quickly; the darkness calls those foul things like a hungry dog to supper. We need the guns."

In the hope that Seiji could sort out this mess, Takashi turned to receive the skilled warrior's advice, but when he looked, the samurai was gone. This argument was not his concern. Slaying the foul creatures and protecting the villagers were all that mattered to him. So Takashi was the deciding vote. He was the leader, after all. They would wait until morning, and at dawn's first light, he, Daisuke, and Isao would set out for the hunter's lodge to retrieve the guns.

Day turned to dusk, and the sun splattered the western ridge with fire. Takashi squinted at the horizon. The silhouettes of the monsters looked like scarecrows, jutting up from the crest of the hill overlooking the village.

"Master Takashi! Master Takashi!" Isao again. He ran up to Takashi, breathless. "It is Toshiro, master. He told me he was going off to the hunter's lodge alone. He is going for the guns."

Takashi felt his stomach tighten into a thick knot. They could not spare a man. Without assistance, Toshiro would be lost, and with him the village. Takashi ordered Isao to take his bow and join Daisuke at the barricade. He posted most of the townspeople at the river, where the water would slow the creatures enough for the farmers to pierce them with their spears.

Takashi then ran to Seiji's post to tell him what had happened, and together, their swords glinting in the light of the setting sun, they made for the hunter's lodge.

Regret crept into Takashi's mind. To leave the village when so many mouja were on the move, when so few villagers were primed to defend...the desertion shamed him. His fear, unbecoming of a samurai, fogged his mind all the way through the woods.

On occasion, Seiji halted their progress and drew his sword just long enough to finish off the mouja that lay tangled in ferns along the path. "It is fortunate we have encountered so few on this journey," Seiji said as he wiped his blade clean. "If our luck holds up, Toshiro may still be alive when we find him."

As they walked, Takashi noticed groves of flowers lined the hillsides. The trees had white, pink, and yellow blossoms, each dripping gemstones of rain. The samurai's thoughts wandered back to the village. Hopefully the farmers had picked up the patrols Seiji and he were missing. The farmers' vigilance would be integral to their survival. If they kept the watch, they might just make it through the night. Apprehension coiled around Takashi's throat like a serpent. He should have left Seiji in charge of the village's defense, and taken Daisuke with him to the lodge.

But the truth was Takashi feared what hid in the ever-darkening woodland. His concern for his own life and the knowledge that Seiji was at his side kept him feeling safe, so he chanced to leave the village with weakened defenses and tried to stay optimistic. Perhaps they would retrieve Toshiro and the rifles, return safely, and defend the village with great success. His gamble still might pay off.

They stepped through a small grove of trees and saw the hunter's lodge in the distance. The building was the same width as the farmers' cottages, but three times as long, about the size of a small barn. Seiji stepped cautiously toward the building.

"I smell blood," Takashi said, but Seiji ignored the warning and entered the lodge. Takashi sniffed the air, scanning the trees.

Inside, the floor was sprinkled with dry hay. Tanned animal skins hung from the walls. A dusty bedroll took up one corner of the room. A hunched figure, bathed in shadow, crept around the far side of the lodge. A large clay pot smashed to the floor as the figure tore open a storage crate. He pulled out a long stiff bundle wrapped in blankets and began to unravel it.

"Toshiro?" Takashi called out.

The rugged samurai turned to face them. The barrels of three muskets were visible in his arms. He grinned, his teeth flashing in the darkness, and laughed a monkey's laugh. "You see this?" He spat on the floor. "With these we can take out those filthy mouja for sure. And you were going to let them just sit here and collect dust. Ha!"

Takashi was about to reprimand the stubborn fool when Seiji said, "We must go at once." He made for the door.

The instant Seiji opened the door he slammed it shut again. He took a pitchfork from a rack of tools on the wall and slid it through the door handles, barring the entrance. "They are upon us," Seiji said. "At least twenty. Load those muskets. We must fight!"

A cacophony sounded outside the lodge. Rotting fists banged on the walls, the windows, the door, even the ceiling. Takashi could hear unbearable suffering in their groans. The creatures were starving.

The samurai each grabbed a rifle. Seiji swiped Toshiro's weapon away from him. "We do not have the time or ammunition to teach you how to aim." Carrying a gun in each hand, Seiji ran to the window and fired the first rifle, then took the other and slew a second mouja.

Takashi aimed out the window on the opposite side of the lodge and fired into the crowd assembled there. The lead ball struck one of the mouja in the throat. The creature gurgled and kept moving forward. Takashi gritted his teeth and stabbed the wounded mouja in the head, using the barrel of the musket as a spear. It collapsed outside the window, dropping from view.

Seiji tossed the two muskets to Toshiro. "Reload," he demanded, drawing his sword. A flash of glinting steel left three of the dead in pieces outside Seiji's window.

Takashi released his second round, incapacitating another mouja so only an infinite number remained. Behind him, he heard Toshiro fumble with the ramrod, trying to pack the gunpowder into place. As soon as he finished, Seiji snatched the muskets, then aimed them out the window and fired off two quick shots.

"I would also like to fight. I am not your student!" Toshiro barked as Takashi hurried to the center of the room to load another round.

Seiji grabbed Takashi's rifle and threw it to the ground. He kicked the muskets from Toshiro's hands, sending them skittering across the floor. "Forget it," Seiji said. "It is no use. Takashi, Toshiro, draw your swords for the last time. Better we go down fighting with steel in our hands."

But the despair of Seiji's words only seemed to energize their blades. Takashi rushed to the window and began to jab and thrust, piercing the brains of any mouja close enough to strike. Toshiro and Seiji matched Takashi's tactic. They struck down dozens in this way, and the bodies piled up in front of the windows, obstructing the approach of the others.

"Ha ha!" Toshiro whooped. "We're making our own barricade of flesh. Perverse, but effective!"

Time moved fast in the thick of battle. Bodies accumulated in three mounds outside the windows of the lodge. Before long, the windows were covered completely.

With the windows blocked, the chamber darkened and the foul noises dampened, but the smell...the smell penetrated them. It saturated their clothes and skin, even their topknots. The samurai retched at the overwhelming reek of death. Even Seiji was not immune.

Takashi covered his nose. "Perhaps the smell will fool them into moving on. If we wait, they might pass by, leaving us behind, so we may escape."

Toshiro appeared hopeful, but Seiji gave them a skeptical look. "I am sorry, my friends. But the only way we are leaving here is mindless and hungry."

A noise broke the silence, louder than before, but it was something different, not the groaning of the creatures. Takashi looked up and wiped his blade. It was coming from the ceiling. The wooden-slatted roof creaked and shifted under the weight of something.

"Is that the wind?" Toshiro asked.

"No," Seiji said. "Them."

The roof collapsed in a hail of splinters and bodies. The samurai screamed, squinting against the flurry, and flailed their weapons. They hacked at the waterfall of ghouls that rained down on them from above. Black blood spattered the walls—the hunting lodge became a butcher shop.

As the bodies continued to fall to the floor, quick strikes from the samurai's blades destroyed them. Takashi leaped into the air, attacking the mouja before they could drop down into the lodge. He stabbed the head of one of them, and the body brought his weapon to the floor as it dropped. As he struggled to remove his sword from the skull of one of the fallen, he chanced a look up, and saw a mouja dangling above him, about to fall. Seiji cried out Takashi's name and pushed his comrade out of the way. He grappled with the mouja as it fell upon him.

Toshiro hurried to the rescue. He stood over them, following the mouja's head with the tip of his blade. The thing was a young man, no older than nineteen. Toshiro pushed his blade straight through the young man's ear...but it wasn't really a young man anymore. It was a dead thing.

Seiji sat up, clutching his bloody hands. The creature had bitten off the third and fourth fingers of his left hand. He glanced at Takashi expectantly. Toshiro backed away, waiting for Takashi to make a move.

Takashi had always viewed Seiji with a certain invincibility, and seeing him in that state, unable to shoot, barely able to wield a katana, it set Takashi's heart on the edge of a blade.

Seiji howled. His body snapped rigid and flailed about on the floor. His muscles hardened, his skin turned to the color of the ocean depths, and his eyes clouded like dirty cubes of ice. He emitted one last sound, a sound like steel against a rough stone. Beneath the grating noise, Takashi discerned a single word—kaishakunin.

Seiji retained none of his masterful dexterity in the afterlife. His stiff legs fought to propel him forward, limping and forcing every jerky step. His arms dangled. His fingers could not flex. His sword forgotten, Seiji's mouth and shredded fingers dripped dark blood as they reached for Takashi.

Was Seiji's final word a request? Kaishakunin. When a samurai committed seppuku, the kaishakunin served as the principal's second; once the samurai had disemboweled himself, the kaishakunin decapitated the principal to alleviate the immense pain. It was a difficult job, physically and emotionally. Was this what Seiji asked of Takashi? It sickened him to think of destroying a great warrior such as this. To kill a friend.

Seiji lunged at Takashi with a growl. Takashi's blade flashed.

For all of Seiji's proficiencies, his neck was no thicker than any other man's. His head rolled into a dark corner of the room.

The silence that followed unnerved the remaining samurai. Takashi opened the door and inspected the area surrounding the lodge. There were bodies all around, but the rest of the mouja appeared to have vanished.

Toshiro wrapped the muskets in the belt and blanket the way he had found them and strapped the parcel over his shoulder. "They may still be useful," Toshiro said as he joined Takashi outside the lodge, "from a distance."

Takashi was too stunned to lead the way, so Toshiro guided him back to the village. The forest was dark. Without a torch, Takashi had no idea where they were going. He was amazed that Toshiro was able to find the right direction, weaving between trees, dodging exposed roots, and not once did they come across what they both feared—more of the mouja. Takashi's thoughts were of Seiji, the elegant work of art that he had been forced to destroy. No. That he had chosen to destroy. There must have been a way Takashi could have saved Seiji, or at least preserved him in his undead state long enough to find a cure for this illness. The wound was superficial. With skill such as his, a few short digits would not have slowed Seiji for long.

A pain twisted in Takashi's stomach again, a dull rotting pain, tying his guts into knots. It was tragic, really, what happened to Seiji. "Is there no honor left in this world?" Takashi shouted over the noise. There was a grumbling roar in the distance, growing louder. "A man such as Seiji deserved better. I should not have cut him down, Toshiro. I have dishonored myself. I must face consequences for that."

But no, Takashi thought. Seppuku was not the way. He had a mission. He had sworn an oath. It was his duty to protect these helpless farmers.

Toshiro was not listening. They had reached the ridge overlooking the town. Down in the pit, the town served one final purpose. It would act as a signal fire to warn neighboring villages that the swarm was on its way. The houses were all aflame, the air was polluted with acrid black smoke, and countless mouja prowled the streets. Takashi couldn't see any people. They must have been in the streets, among the mouja, driven only to feed on their families. Isao and Daisuke were nowhere to be found.

Looking down at the village, Takashi's heart sank. He fell to his knees and drew his tantō. Slowly and carefully, Takashi untied the sash of his kimono and pulled it open. He tucked the sleeves beneath his knees. He wanted to be sure to fall forward. "I swore to protect these people, Toshiro, and I have failed. This is my fault."

"This is no one's fault," Toshiro said.

"It was my decision to leave the village, and this is the result. Toshiro, you will have to be my kaishakunin. Once I make the cut, be very quick and careful. I do not want to return as one of those things. When I am gone, hurry to the next village. You are fast in the dark. Perhaps you can warn them before those creatures arrive."

Toshiro sneered. He grabbed Takashi by the collar. "No. I will not allow you to do this. Better we go down fighting with steel in our hands. Besides, two samurai with katanas are more powerful than the tallest tsunami. We will take many of them with us. We may even find survivors.

Takashi's eyes met Toshiro's intense gaze. Where Seiji had skill, Toshiro had spirit. Takashi held out his hand; Toshiro grasped his arm and pulled him to his feet. They drew their swords, walking with deliberate steps down the ridge. Their eyes glowed with fire. They navigated around the fallen bodies, cutting down mouja whenever one came near. Takashi whispered, "These poor farmers. They never stood a chance."

Toshiro spat. "It is their lot to suffer."

At the center of town, a crowd of mouja had congregated. Their shadows danced on the sandy ground like demons in the firelight. One thousand cloudy eyes found the samurai at once. The mouja charged. Takashi and Toshiro swung hard.

Blood and fire glinted on their blades.

CATEGORY FIVE

By Marc Paoletti

Marc Paoletti is the coauthor (with Patricia Rosemoor) of the novels *The Last Vampire* and *The Vampire Agent.* He is also the author of *Scorch*, a thriller that draws upon his experiences as a Hollywood pyrotechnician. His short fiction has appeared in anthologies such as *Young Blood, Book of Voices, Horror Library Vol. 2, The Best Underground Fiction, The Blackest Death Vol. 2, Cold Flesh*, and *Thou Shalt Not.* Earlier this year, he had a story published in *First Thrills*, edited by Lee Child.

Hurricane Katrina in 2005 was the worst natural disaster in U.S. history. Almost 2,000 people died, both in the storm itself and in the severe flooding that followed. And bad as the storm was, the real horror was the human element—the engineers' failure to maintain the levees, the incompetence of the federal response, and the disorder that ensued. People attempting to flee the storm-ravaged city of New Orleans were turned back at gunpoint by locals who feared looters. FEMA director Michael Brown, a political appointee whose most relevant prior experience had been managing horse shows, became a laughingstock after the president absurdly praised him for doing a "heck of a job."

Most of us never imagined we'd see corpses lying unattended on the streets of an American city. The author of our next story writes, "I watched Hurricane Katrina decimate New Orleans live on CNN. Talk about horror. I was shocked by the devastation, and appalled that the most disadvantaged people were bearing the brunt of the disaster. I finished the first draft of this story in one sitting. Funny what happens when you're fueled by outrage. Also my childhood home in Sacramento was almost flooded a few years back. I was in Los Angeles at the time. Believe me, it's grim to get a call from your folks in the middle of the night and hear the fear in their voices as they tell you the levee—which is less than a mile away from them—is about to break."

Remy listened to the wind beat the walls, listened to the rain whip the windows. Since the power was out and it was after sundown, he'd lit candles in the bedroom and rest of the house. He might have considered the thrashing beat a hip tempo if not for what he'd heard over the battery-powered radio crackling on the dresser.

Category five.

This hurricane was supposed to be the worst in a generation, like nothing they'd seen, yet the mayor had done little to get folks like him and Marta out. They were late seventies. Too poor to afford a car. Too old to venture far on their own. They were black. They didn't matter.

Their home was ramshackle, single story, built long ago in a crumbling ward that sat below sea level and lacked the comfort of close neighbors. On the radio, he'd heard that the 17th Street Canal levee was under assault by storm surge from Lake Pontchartrain. If the levee failed, the ward didn't stand a chance. Their home didn't stand a chance.

He sat next to Marta who lay under thick covers, eyes closed, breathing fitfully. He placed a wrinkled palm on the wrinkled forehead of his love, her sweaty skin the color of coffee and sooty with age, but still beautiful to him after fifty years of marriage.

Remy touched her as he listened to the radio's thick crackles, to the broken bits of news, to the random chatter. Other wards had been flooded, he'd made out that much. The water had carried away cars and trucks, had swept houses from their foundations, and had caved in crypts and mortuaries freeing the bodies within.

That's where things got strange.

He thought he'd heard reports that said disinterred bodies were coming back to life. Witnesses on the radio had sworn it was true. Supposedly, dead bodies had writhed and flailed as floodwaters swept them along and when they'd washed against higher ground, they'd clambered to their feet and walked. *Walked.* He shook his head. Here people were spinning foolish tales about the walking dead when Marta couldn't walk at all.

"We'll get through this, you 'n' me," Remy whispered, taking his wife's hand. "Like we got through so much else."

She moaned softly. Marta had been sick for a long, long time. So long, in fact, that he'd nearly forgotten what their life had been like before the disease. Ovarian cancer. It didn't make sense to him since she was far past childbearing age—not that they'd had children—but her ovaries had become polluted just the same, and the cancer had spread to her stomach and then her spine.

"We'll get through this, hon," he repeated, but didn't know how to make good on the promise if the levee broke. How could he when most of the city had run off? When the police and fire fighters had run off as well?

Lightning flashed, casting the room bright white, and then thunder growled as fiercely as the apocalypse.

Taking the radio, Remy shuffled down a dark hallway into a kitchen lit by candles. He fetched more matches from a cupboard, and then counted cans. They had enough food for a week, which would have been fine if the morphine he'd dripped so carefully onto Marta's tongue with a baby's eyedropper hadn't run out that very morning. He couldn't call the hospital for more, either, because the landline was dead and he'd never been able to afford a cell phone. Of course that was assuming the hospital staff hadn't left town, which they probably had.

Without morphine, Marta had nowhere to hide from the pain; already it was becoming too much for her. One moment she'd be lying there peacefully, and the next she'd be mewling and balling her fists and crushing her eyes closed with such force that he'd feel her agony like it was his own.

Mewling… that was the only sound she could make now.

Remy looked into the living room at his trumpet, which hung on the wall in a glass case above the fireplace. He'd put it away over a year ago when Marta got so sick she couldn't sing along with him any more.

At times he'd fooled himself into believing that folks had come to the Bourbon Street clubs they booked to hear his sharp-noted riffs, but deep down, he'd always known they'd come for her. Achingly hourglass in form-fitting blue, Marta would take the stage as quietly as an afterthought, press her full lips to the mic, and then float her voice sweetly, robustly, through a room's smoky air in time with his trumpet's plaintive moan. Jazz, blues, gospel, rock—she could sing them all. *Transform* them all. Her soulful, smooth-rasping lullabies never failed to transfix, to shake free what was hidden, to soothe like promises of hope the damaged spirits of those who listened. None more than his. None more.

No more.

Marta's voice had been siphoned by the cancer. What he would do to give Marta her voice back. To stop her constant suffering.

The radio crackled. Remy placed it on the kitchen counter and fussed with the dial.

"…broken…" he heard the broadcaster say. "…17th Street Canal levee…mercy on our souls…"

Remy went cold with fear. So it had happened. He had to get Marta outside and up onto the roof, but how could he when he lacked the strength to move her fast enough to beat the coming floodwater?

Suddenly, an idea occurred to him. He dashed to the utility closet, whipped out his raingear: an opaque-plastic poncho to cover his tweed jacket, shabby white shirt, and gray slacks, and galoshes to cover his cracked Oxfords. And then, as he grabbed a shovel, he heard it.

A deep and distant roar that swelled like the charging thrum of a thousand battle tanks—a sound he'd last heard as a young man in the killing fields of Korea—until it shook the floor, the walls, the house. The glass case surrounding his trumpet shuddered then cracked down the middle as plaster dust fell in streaks from the ceiling. The roar—nature's own terrible riff—grew so thick that he thought he might feel it slide against his fingers, and then came a cracking, trembling *boom* followed by a mad-static hiss.

The house groaned and held. But for how long?

Lightning flashed, giving him a glimpse of the flood through the living room window. A dark wave tumbled past, followed by another and another. Grimy water flowed underneath the front door, soaking fast across the carpet, as the flood level surged against the sill.

And then he saw something else.

At first he thought it was debris held in place by opposing currents, but then he realized it was the naked corpse of a man—one washed from a cemetery and long dead, judging by the decay. The flesh was shriveled and fish-belly white, the eyes were worm-eaten, and the jaw, a skinless mandible, opened and closed like the corpse was trying to describe the destruction it had witnessed. Open and closed. Open and closed. The jaw opened and closed so much it made him think for a moment that stories of the dead coming back to life might be true.

Remy chided himself for entertaining the silly idea when the corpse lashed out and grabbed the window frame. He could only stare in disbelief as the thing pulled itself toward him through the roaring deluge, and then slammed its rotted face into the glass. The window shattered and let in a thick rush of black, foul-smelling floodwater.

Remy threw up his arms to protect his face from the glass as the thing clutched both sides of the window frame and stepped a twisted, rotted foot onto the flooding carpet.

He continued to stare in shock, not wanting to believe what he saw but unable to deny the truth before him. *Alive! Alive! The radio was right!*

When the thing brought its other leg through the window and then reached for him, Remy snapped out of his fugue and swung the shovel. The flat of the blade struck the thing's chest with a wet-sack slap, pushing it back. But then it kept coming, growl bubbling in its throat, like it hadn't felt any pain at all.

He swung again, striking the thing's face this time, and the rotted skull imploded in a gush of pink. The headless body took a final step before it collapsed splashing into the water, which was high enough now to soak Remy's pants above the galoshes.

Still clutching the shovel, Remy bolted from the flooding living room. It wouldn't be long before the water flowed down the hall and reached the bedroom.

That thing was alive!

Mind still reeling, he slammed the bedroom door closed and then wedged clothes underneath it. That would hold back the floodwater for only a minute or two, but it was something, at least.

Holding the shovel under one arm, he dragged the dresser to the middle of the floor then clambered on top of it and stood as straight as he could without hitting the low ceiling.

"I'll be right back, hon," Remy said, trying to keep the panic from his voice. "Just wait there as best you can." Marta mewled, gripped the blankets. The morphine was wearing off, and he felt her growing agony in his chest, in his heart.

Age had taken a toll on him, but he knew it had taken more of a toll on the cracked, off-grade ceiling. He jabbed the shovel up again and again, shattering thin plaster, rending pink insulation, splintering worm-eaten beams. Finally, he broke through brittle shingles and saw the night sky. Raindrops pelted his face as he wormed up through the ragged hole and then stood on the roof near a small brick chimney, wind whipping his poncho.

By light of the moon, he saw that the water had taken the entire neighborhood, uprooting trees, rolling cars, flooding houses, creating a trash-strewn sea in every direction. He and Marta could expect to be stranded for a long time. Too long.

And then he noticed flailing silhouettes flowing among the houses when lightning revealed what the moon hadn't—dozens of animated dead, like the one that had broken through his window, caught in the rushing floodwater. Rotted bodies, broken bodies, bodies with limbs missing, bodies stripped of flesh. Some floated and thrashed while others strode through the chest-deep water, straining to escape the vicious current. Over the din of rushing water came a flat, plaintive sound. Moaning, he realized. A wailing chorus from the dead that rose up with a life of its own.

Remy closed his eyes and considered his only choice.

God willing, he'd have the strength to hoist Marta through the hole and onto the roof, and then he'd do his best to cover her with his poncho to keep her dry and hide her from the dead things that surrounded them. But they'd still be stranded. And Marta would still be without her morphine.

Below, Marta cried out in agony. Desperation shot through him. What else could he do?

He scrambled around the roof, looking for a safe way off, but the water was everywhere, rushing past in black, white-capped fury. He scanned the surface for debris, for a bobbing chunk big enough to use as a raft, but again there was only black water. Black water and the thrashing, floating bodies of the animated dead.

Marta cried out again, voice tinged with such pain, such agony, that Remy moaned in frustration and blind emptiness as rage blossomed along with his fear. He beat the chimney until his knuckles were bloody, crying out himself, his own anguish mingling with Marta's cries and the moans rising up from the dark water around him.

And then he felt a sudden calm come over him. There was another way out of this. Another way. For a moment he felt a flicker of doubt, but another cry from Marta decided the issue.

The animated dead moved with ease and felt no pain. That much had been clear from the thing in his living room. As unbelievable as it seemed, he could not doubt what he had witnessed or question the opportunity that had been placed before him.

He wondered about Marta's voice as he lowered himself back through the hole in the roof and onto the dresser. Would it return when her pain disappeared? He listened to the moans coming through the wall as clear as a back-up chorus. Maybe the dead could do more than moan. Was that so hard to believe in the face of all this? Maybe the dead outside *chose* to moan their woe, *chose* to moan in eulogy for the living who no longer grieved for them.

But such would not be the case with Marta and him. They would choose to do otherwise. They had each other. They'd always have each other.

Remy clambered down from the dresser, rushed to Marta's side, and leaned over to kiss her forehead. She opened her pain-stricken eyes.

"Do you trust me?" he whispered.

She blinked her eyes once slowly in reply. *Always.*

Nodding, he turned and opened the bedroom door.

The floodwater rushed in to soak the tops of his galoshes, then chilled his calves, then his knees. The cold water kept rising as he sloshed back to the bed, sat by Marta's side, and stroked her forehead.

It had to be something in the water that brought the dead back. It had to be.

"Close your eyes, hon," he said.

But she didn't close her eyes. He knew she could sense his doubt. His fear. In fifty years, he could never keep a secret from her.

She might have known what was about to happen, too, because she reached out, gently pulled his face to hers, pressed her lips to his ear. And began to sing. For the first time in so, so long.

Her raspy, pain-etched voice scraped only the bottom of the notes she used to reach, but it soothed his spirit just the same, long enough and completely enough until the floodwater delivered them into their new beginning.

LIVING WITH THE DEAD

By Molly Brown

British Science Fiction Award-winner Molly Brown is the author of the novels *Invitation to a Funeral* and *Virus*. Her short fiction has appeared many times in *Interzone*, and in the *Mammoth Book* anthologies: *Jules Verne Adventures*, *New Comic Fantasy*, and *Future Cops*. Other anthology appearances include *Steampunk*, *Time Machines*, *Celebration*, *Villains!* and *The Year's Best Fantasy and Horror*. Many of these stories have been gathered in her collection *Bad Timing and Other Stories*. In addition to writing prose fiction, Brown has written and appeared in a several short zombie films, and some of her stories have been optioned for film and/or television.

One of the challenges of assembling an anthology of zombie fiction is deciding exactly what constitutes a "zombie" story. The term originated in the Caribbean and originally referred to recently deceased individuals who had been brought back to life through magic to serve as slave workers. After the word zombie was used in connection with the marketing of George Romero's 1978 film *Dawn of the Dead*, the term has mostly been associated with masses of mindless, hungry undead who kill and convert the living. In recent years, the film *28 Days Later* and the video game *Left 4 Dead* have depicted zombies as belligerent infected who aren't actually undead. However, they are otherwise so similar to Romero zombies that everyone calls them that, and they can really be classified no other way.

But where do you draw the line? In this anthology series we've chosen to take an inclusive view and expose readers to the broadest possible spectrum of zombie fiction. Which brings us to our next story. One thing that's been interesting to watch is how the term "zombie" has fallen into colloquial usage—i.e., we often refer to people as zombies when they're performing mindless tasks, or planted in front of the television, or in a state of emotional detachment, even if they're not trying to kill anyone. On this view, the defining feature of zombies is that they're animate but not present. Our next story is a quiet tale of suburban life that explores this side of zombiehood.

I went to the park today, and for the first time in five years, Alice looked at me as if she knew me.

Alice used to be my best friend. We were in the same class at school. We used to do each other's hair and borrow each other's clothes until one night when we were both sixteen, and everything changed.

The details don't matter now. All you need to know is we were at a party in a basement, and we both snorted something that we thought was cocaine, but it wasn't.

The next thing I remember is waking up in the hospital with everyone telling me it was a miracle I was alive because the other girl was dead.

There'd been a story in the local paper a couple of months earlier about a guy who'd collapsed in the park. He was declared dead on arrival at the hospital and was taken to the hospital mortuary. A few hours later, he woke up.

No one thought much about it at the time, everyone just assumed he'd been mistakenly declared dead when he was actually in a coma. These things happen. Not often—and never before in the kind of place where nobody dies without the whole town knowing about it—but they happen.

The man hadn't spoken once since waking; they said he just stared into space.

I remember they interviewed some expert on the news who used a lot of big words just to say sometimes it's like that when you wake up from a coma.

Alice had been dead a little over twenty-four hours when she opened her eyes. Like the guy before her, she never spoke or reacted to anyone or anything; she just seemed to stare into the distance as if she was looking at something no one else could see.

A few weeks later they sent her home, saying there was nothing they could do.

I wasn't that well myself—as everyone kept reminding me, I was lucky to be alive—but I went to visit Alice every day. We would sit in her room with me talking and her staring straight ahead as if I wasn't there. And every day as I left, her mother would beg me to come back again tomorrow: "You're her best friend. Keep talking to her; maybe you can bring her back."

When a forty-nine-year-old man named Sam Jenkins woke up the morning after he'd died of a heart attack, people finally began to suspect that something strange was going on. This man was definitely dead, the doctors insisted. They were being especially careful about who they declared dead these days; Sam Jenkins had been repeatedly checked—and double-checked—for any signs of life, and his body had been cold when they finally allowed it to be taken to the mortuary.

Like the previous two people to wake in the hospital mortuary, Sam Jenkins never spoke. Unlike the other two, Sam Jenkins had risen naked from his mortuary slab, walked home without being noticed (it was four a.m. and the streets were empty), and got into bed beside his wife.

By the time Rosemary Harold died of cancer, they'd decided the problem must be something to do with the mortuary, so they kept her body upstairs. This didn't make any difference; Rosemary was awake the next day.

Then everyone thought maybe it was something to do with dying in the hospital, so—as much as possible—people started dying at home. Once again, no difference. They all opened their eyes within twenty-four hours.

People eventually came to the conclusion that the problem was the town—as far as anyone knew, this wasn't happening anywhere else—so the next time someone died, the body was immediately shipped to another state. But the guy still woke up. The other state wouldn't allow him to stay—they said it was not their taxpayers' responsibility to support another state's walking dead—so he was brought back here.

Soon the dead fell into a routine of spending their afternoons in the park. You'd see them there from one o'clock every day, sometimes sitting on benches with their faces tilted up to the sun, other times just standing in a kind of loose formation. And every day at dusk they would go their separate ways, returning to the homes they'd known in life.

Some, like Alice, were obviously cared for by the living. Alice's mother always made sure that her clothes were clean and her hair was combed.

But others were not so comfortable with their dead. On finding her husband in bed with her, Sam Jenkins' widow had at first moved into the spare room, but having a dead man in the house soon became too much for her and she changed the locks, with the result that her dead husband spent his nights standing on the front lawn. It was around this time that I first heard the word "zombie" being used.

The first thing that happens when the dead start waking is not that they go on a rampage like you see in the movies, it's that you find out all your insurance policies are worthless. Sam Jenkins had a life insurance policy with his wife as the beneficiary, but the insurance company refused to pay out because they said Sam didn't meet their definition of dead.

Then Alice's mother got a huge bill from the hospital because her daughter—being officially deceased—was no longer covered by her health insurance.

The second thing that happens is property values plummet. Sam Jenkins' widow, unable to pay the mortgage, tried putting the house up for sale. But nobody wants to buy a house with a dead man standing on the lawn. Even if—like Sam's widow—you try to make the dead man a selling point by explaining he deters burglars.

The third thing that happens is church attendances rise. The fourth thing is they fall again as everyone comes to the conclusion there's no point in worrying about the afterlife if you're only going to spend it hanging around the park.

The fifth thing is all the jobs go, as businesses tend to prefer locations where the dead stay dead.

The next thing that happens is the town itself begins to die as everyone who can get away gets as far away as possible, until the only people left are the dead and those few who refuse to abandon them.

Sometimes I go to the park and watch the dead together. Despite being all different ages and backgrounds, they seem at ease in each other's company.

The silence of the dead when faced with the living can seem awkward, but when the dead are together, their silence is a comfortable one, their blank faces not so much vacant as serene.

And though their faces are far from expressive, I was there one day as a newly deceased came to join them for the first time, and I am sure I saw recognition in their eyes.

Five years ago, there were more than three thousand people in this town. Now there are less than three hundred. As the town's living population continues to move away, more of the dead are being left to fend for themselves.

With no one to dress them or comb their hair, some of them were getting into quite a state until a woman named Hilary Frentzen stepped in. The first thing Hilary did was to get a shelter built so the dead would have somewhere to get out of the rain. Then she set up a charitable foundation to collect donations of food and clothing, which she distributes in the park.

The dead *do* eat, just not a lot. Every day Hilary hands out slices of day-old bread donated by supermarkets, and watches as the dead take one or two bites and then scatter the rest on the ground for the pigeons. Of course the pigeons—being dead themselves since the town council poisoned them all a couple of years ago—are no more interested in the bread than they are. Not even the insects are that interested since the park was sprayed, so every day before she leaves, Hilary picks up the leftovers.

She's tried giving them vegetables, but the dead won't touch them. If you ask her, she'll tell you that no matter how hard she tries, she cannot get the dead to eat broccoli.

Once, as an experiment, Hilary bought a dozen chocolate cakes and took them to the park. The dead didn't leave a single crumb behind. She told me she can't afford to do that every day, but now once every month or so, she'll buy them some chocolate cakes as a special treat. (Even dead wasps perk up at the smell of chocolate, which is another reason she doesn't bring it too often.)

Hilary used to get very annoyed when tourists turned up with portable sound systems playing *Thriller* at full blast, or shouting: "They don't want bread, they want brainzzz!" but that kind of thing has been happening less and less since the state barricaded the highway and put up all of those "Quarantine" signs.

And there's hardly been a single crime since the day a guy who was stripping the lead off a dead person's roof slipped and fell, breaking his neck. He's been in the park ever since, walking sideways with his head twisted over one shoulder.

I don't think the dead feel any pain. When I used to visit Alice in her room, I'd always ask her: "Do you feel any pain? Do you feel anything?"

But she'd never answer.

Then one day as we sat with me talking and her staring into space, I picked up a pin and jabbed it, hard, into her arm.

She moved her head slightly, just enough to look down at the pin.

"You felt that, didn't you?" I said. "Does it hurt?"

She went back to staring into space.

When she stood up to leave for the park, the pin was still protruding from her arm.

I reached up and pulled it out; she didn't notice.

The dead don't seem to age, either. Eating only a few bites of bread a day—plus one piece of chocolate cake a month—they've all lost a bit of weight, but otherwise they haven't changed.

I'd kind of expected their hair to keep growing, but that doesn't seem to be the case. Which is probably just as well because the dead's hair is invariably a mess. Someone living always has to comb it for them because for some reason they will not do it themselves.

The one exception to this is Rosemary Harold, who died without a single hair on her body—not even an eyelash—because she'd been in the middle of chemotherapy.

Alice is one of the few dead people in the park who hasn't been reduced to wearing hand-me-downs thanks to her mother, who still buys her new clothes when she needs them.

The first couple of years, she used to take her to the mall, which wasn't easy since the sales people didn't like serving the dead and wouldn't let her try anything on, and there was one guard who'd obviously seen *Dawn of the Dead* on television and would always follow them around, scowling, from the minute they arrived. But Alice's mother persevered because she said it was the one time Alice actually seemed to know where she was and why she was there. She even claimed Alice would invariably head straight for the most expensive thing in the shop, just like she did when she was alive.

Not that it matters now the mall is shut.

At one time this town had five churches, four cafes, six bars, two auto dealerships, three banks, two primary schools, a high school, a motel, a funeral parlour, and a meat-packing plant (which closed the day after a calf's head on a shelf in the freezer room was seen blinking). All of them are boarded up now. So are most of the houses.

The streets are full of abandoned dogs and cats. It's the live ones you've got to watch out for, because they're nervous.

My next door neighbour adopted a dead dog. When I asked her why, she said, "Why not? He's no trouble and he doesn't bark."

Five years ago, they said it was a miracle I was still alive. Three weeks ago they told me the miracle was coming to an end; my organs were shutting down one by one. All because of one stupid thing I did one night when I was sixteen.

People told me my only hope was to get out of this town before I died. They told me it only happens here; if I die somewhere else, I won't wake up. I won't end up with those zombies in the park.

I'm sure all those people were right, but I knew something they didn't know.

I've been going to the same doctor since I was a kid—he's the only doctor in town these days—and the last time I saw him, he said he was going to tell me a secret.

Remember I told you about when it all first started, and how they shipped a man's body to another state to see if he would wake up, and he did?

It turns out my doctor was sent along to accompany the body. He was there when the man woke up, and he'd asked him: "What was it like being dead? Do you remember any of it?"

And to his amazement, the man had answered him.

"He spoke?" I said.

My doctor nodded. "Only that one time, and never again. Considering what he said, I thought it was best to keep quiet about it."

"Why? What did he say?"

"All you need to know is: there are a lot worse places a person could end up," my doctor said as I left his office that last time, "than in the park."

I went to the park today and saw a dead man sitting on a bench with Hilary Frentzen combing his hair.

What is it about the dead that they refuse to comb their own hair? For five years I had been telling myself that I would be the exception. I would be the one who speaks, who dresses herself, who eats vegetables, who continues to do simple things like comb her own hair... but with every moment that passed, these things seemed less and less important.

The next thing I knew, I was standing face to face with Alice. And for the first time in five years, she looked at me as if she knew me.

TWENTY-THREE SNAPSHOTS OF SAN FRANCISCO

By Seth Lindberg

Seth Lindberg's short fiction has appeared in the anthologies *Phantom, Denying Death, The Darker Side, Brainbox, Brainbox II, Haunting the Dead, Jack Haringa Must Die!, Jigsaw Nation*, and in the magazines *Not One of Us, Twilight Showcase, Gothic.net*, and *Chiaroscuro*. He is also a former editor of *Gothic.net* and currently works as a sysadmin in San Francisco, where, as the title implies, this story takes place.

In nineteenth-century photographs, nobody is smiling. The subjects sit rigid and stare out at you with cold, serious expressions. You might think humor hadn't been invented yet, but actually cameras in those days had such long exposure times that no one wanted to hold a smile for that long. People, at least, can be instructed not to move; photographing animals proved more challenging. One early photographer decided that the only way to get a pair of stray dogs to sit still long enough for him to take their picture was to shoot them with bullets, stuff them, and position their stiff, lifeless bodies in front of his camera. In the resulting photographs, of course, the dogs appear to be alive.

This brings us to our next story, which also features photos of things that seem to be alive but aren't. Photographs connect us to the past, fading only a little over time, especially compared with our memories, which quickly become vague and distorted. Since the dawn of photography people have obsessively compiled photo albums, keeping important memories locked safely in place. With the advent of digital cameras, it's not unusual for a person's personal collection to run to hundreds or even thousands of images. But what if all of that disappeared? What if a handful of photos were all that remained to remind you of an entire world, now lost?

Our next story is about just such a collection, and, as in nineteenth-century photographs, in most of these photos, nobody is smiling.

My ex-girlfriend May used to accuse me of starting every story or joke straight in the middle. Like she had to ask a thousand questions just to figure out what the hell I was talking about. I'd just babble on and she'd have to route me back to all the concrete facts about the case at hand. I can't help it! I'm bad with beginnings: I'm suspicious of them as they are. Life doesn't begin, not really.

Well, life begins in the physical sense, but as far as your memories go, it's not like that. It's not like one day you remember things, the day before you didn't. These memories kind of fade out back, little moments, like a vision of your dad's face, the way the back porch smelled. The rest you got to fill in, you suppose all together. A lot like pictures, really. People all frozen in these expressions they never really have because you caught them in mid-motion or something, you have to fill in who it is and what they're about based on that one moment.

So I was talking about them the other night, but here they are for real. Twenty-three snapshots of San Francisco; the last roll of shots I ever took, the last roll I ever got developed. The end of my brilliant amateur photography career.

I guess the roll had twenty-four exposures, so I'm not sure why I only got twenty-three. Maybe it got underexposed or overexposed, maybe there was some kind of error when it got developed. I'll never know. I lost the negatives, so these prints are all I have.

#1

Freeze frame of me, awkwardly leaning into a picture with May and her Japanese pen pal, Kyoko. May's got an expression from the tail end of a laugh, Kyoko has this half smile while flashing a peace sign at the camera for some reason. I'm standing there, looking like an idiot. Forgot to brush my hair, my hands are shoved tightly in my pockets. I made the mistake of putting my arm around May while Kyoko was around before all this, and May got all weird on me. So I'm just standing there.

If you look hard enough, you can sort of see Alcatraz in the distance, sitting in the waters of the San Francisco Bay. Behind that, faded by haze, is the Marin Headlands.

Yes, this was before everything happened. Maybe you think so because we were smiling in that picture. But I think people smile for pictures out of habit, really.

#2

Picture of the famous "Painted Ladies": Victorian houses in old San Francisco, in a park in the middle of the Western Addition. You can see a few people sunbathing in the grass just before it to the left. I've never lived in houses like that, but I bet it's nice. Admittedly, they look better in the post cards, but they're still quite pretty.

Behind the Painted Ladies lies the whole San Francisco skyline, including the Transamerica Pyramid. To the right you can see a pillar of smoke rising from the southern part of the city.

#3

Just May and Kyoko, hugging each other and grinning. Close up zoom on their faces, so close you can see Kyoko's acne scars. That old gray 7 Seconds tee shirt that May's wearing, that's mine.

In the background people walk past and stuff. I think this one was taken in the Japantown Peace Plaza, but I don't remember.

#4

Picture of my neighbor, Mr. Sumpter. He's standing in the hallway, wearing an old polyester button-up shirt, leaning to one side and putting his weight on one foot. He has his head tilted and eyes open, mouth closed. One fist is clenched.

Mr. Sumpter's eyes didn't glow red when I took the picture, it just looks that way now. I think it was the flash from the camera. I didn't know then what I know now.

The hallway frames Mr. Sumpter. You can't see where he's looking at, but he's looking at a blank wall. I was walking down the hallway and saw him like that. I called out to him but he didn't say anything, so I took a picture.

#5

Face of my roommate, Bradley. He's grinning and the color of the photograph is bleached out by the flash. His eyes are red, too. You can see that blond stubble of a goatee that he has, and the blur in the corner is his hand holding a bottle of Miller Genuine Draft. This is important because it was the only alcohol he ever drank. He wouldn't even drink Miller Lite or Miller High Life. Just MGD.

Bradley was always a little bit weird. I took this picture at a party we had in our apartment. It got shut down a little after this because of noise complaints from my neighbors.

#6

Picture of May, caught in a half-laugh. May hated this picture the most, though I personally think she looks really cute. That thing in her hand is a bottle of beer, I think, but I don't remember what brand she drank. Behind are the windows of the apartment Bradley and I shared. You can't really see the view of the west side of the city that we got, though.

Yeah, the smudges and rip on one side is from my fingers handling the sides once or twice too many.

#7

Group shot. I don't remember a lot of these faces anymore. The couple to one side, those were May's friends. The two guys in faded computer tee shirts, those were my coworkers. Of course, May, Kyoko, and Bradley are easy to spot. I'm not in the picture because I was behind the camera. You can't tell where this was taken, but I'm pretty sure it was in my apartment at the party.

#8

Blurred picture of Kyoko. She's standing in the living room with one hand raised with half of her coat off. She has her head tilted and her mouth is open, but you can't quite see that. She just got stuck that way putting on her coat. Kind of an odd time for it to hit. The blurry black cloud-looking thing is the couch that Bradley and I bought with our tax returns. It doesn't look like a lot in the picture but it was really comfortable.

I think the picture got blurred because May was moving past me and bumped my shoulder. This was just before we took Kyoko to the hospital.

#9

Those big brick buildings are San Francisco General Hospital. You can see all the cars in the parking lot and the crowd to one side. I took this from across the street, on Potrero Avenue.

#10

Picture of inside the emergency room waiting area. You can see it was really packed. In the corner, the guy dressed in blue, that's a security guard who got angry at me soon after this. May you can see over by the side standing over something that doesn't look like Kyoko but is her sleeping, I think maybe just her shoulder and maybe a leg is all that's in the picture, but she fell right asleep in the middle of the waiting area.

Over at the corner you can see a television set, note the four people watching it and one of them is just staring off into space. You can tell his head is angled just a bit differently than the others, but you have to hold the photograph up close to your face.

I think that was the last time I saw Kyoko. Nice girl. Odd sense of humor. I can't describe how. I guess some people who learn English but don't speak it natively, they get caught up with one word or two that just sounds interesting to them. With Kyoko it was words like "susurrus." She'd fit it into any conversation she could. I don't think she even half-understood what it meant. She was just fooling around.

#11

This is Bradley and May at the Jack in the Box which was down by Bernal Heights, which is pretty far south in the city without being South San Francisco. There are a lot of warehouses and stuff there. You can't see what May's looking out the window at but it's just the road, I think. There might have been a McDonald's or something across the street, I'm not sure. But it was a pretty busy road.

Behind Bradley you can sort of see a figure that looks like someone standing in that awkward position again. But I don't remember anyone like that when we were there so the picture probably just caught someone mid-stride.

#12

Picture of the four-car pileup outside our apartment building. I'd seen a few car crashes before, but nothing like this one. Usually you'd see a car crash and it'd be two cars, one dented, and a bunch of people arguing. Not here, though, obviously. The building to the left is ours, the shattered window is the coffee house where I used to always get double mocha lattes with extra whipped cream in them. Those mochas ended up somehow tasting like some perfect mix of hot chocolate and coffee. It's one of the things I miss the most these days.

You can only see three of the four cars, because the smoke from the first two is obscuring the last one. That's Bradley standing to one side with a stupid grin on his face, near him are two cops. If you look closely you can see one of them has a gun in his hand; something I never noticed or even vaguely remember from the real event. But there it is, pictures don't lie.

The big car that's spun out and on the other side from the two other cars you can see, by the shattered window, that's a Pontiac Bonneville of a make and model that's nearly exactly like the old Bonneville I used to drive around when I lived back in the Midwest.

#13

Picture of our neighbor's door. Note the scratch marks: I think the doors were made of metal so whoever put their shoulder into this one had to have messed himself up.

Although there are Christmas decorations on the door, it says less about the time of the year that all those awful events happened and more about just how odd my neighbors were. I never knew their names. I saw them once or twice. Seemed like nice people. But the fact that they put up the Christmas decorations in December and then never bothered to take them down… well, it seemed a bit curious.

#14

Picture of Bradley and Mr. Sumpter. Thankfully, most of the blood here is Mr. Sumpter's, but the bastard nearly took both of us down. He was hiding in the trash bin and leapt out, clawing at my face. We'd been alerted by this awful odor and were all keyed up what with all the blackouts and weird events in the city the two days before. Or we were just damned lucky.

Anyways, Bradley has poor Mr. Sumpter propped up here and is crouching next to him. He looks a lot more exuberant than we were, the camera sort of caught him in this smile so he looks more wide-eyed and mad than he was. Even in death, Mr. Sumpter's muscles have a certain rigidity, like they all do. Just look at his neck. It's crazy.

#15

Some National Guardsmen, smoking cigarettes on the Fillmore bridge over Geary Street Across the street and over the bridge you can see some buildings and some graffiti up there, and that little blues club. I think the Guardsmen were there to keep us from looting too much, which, now that I think of it, would have been a pretty good idea. None of us thought of it, though.

You can just barely read the headline on the newspaper in the rack, it reads

"CHAOS!" Depending on what you read or which radio station you hear, the cause is all sorts of things. You know, a virus or some kind of biological warfare gone wrong, or God's vengeance or a comet or…I don't know. Everything. They've got all sorts of excuses for this mess.

May was with me. We were heading down the street to find a good corner store and to see if the ATMs were working again: sometimes we had service, other times we didn't. We would have gone to the supermarket just a block back but the Guard had camped out in the parking lot. There was another one a few blocks away on Eddy Street but I'd never been there, and besides, I heard that the projects had gotten hit really hard and figured it'd be better to stick to routes I knew.

#16

Bradley and me with our makeshift weapons. At that point I spent a lot of time wishing I was a gun nut like my cousin back in Ohio. Of course, ten to one he got turned into one of those monsters and is using his prize semiautomatic AR-15 "that the Government will never take away" as a sturdy club.

Bradley's weapon you can see is brightly colored—I think he had this weird idea that they were attracted to bright colors, like bulls or something. The whole idea being since they're essentially ex-humans, creatures who have abandoned their intelligence for some razor sense of cunning, that they'd be somehow animalistic. In practice it never worked too well. Confused the hell out of one for a moment, though, which was just enough time for me to bash its head in.

Mine was my Louisville Slugger. You see, when I came to San Francisco, I had this idea I'd meet all these young, active people and every Saturday we'd hit the park and toss around a few balls or something and enjoy being in the California sun. It never happened. Too foggy, and everyone was always too damned stressed out about work.

Guess I found a use for the bat after all.

#17

Kind of hard to tell what's going on here. I took this picture while running. To one side, those bright yellow blobs right there? I think that's the flash from guns. The blur on the left side is someone else running away as well.

The Guard dragged us out of our homes and there was a ton of us milling about in the middle of the street. That's when a bunch of the creatures attacked—and quickly, too. Like cheetahs jumping into a herd of gazelle. I saw two of them literally rip a woman in half before the Guard started opening up on them.

The Guardsmen were firing into the crowd. They didn't even care.

#18

This one's blurry. The picture is tan, there's some sort of large dark object in the center.

I don't know how this one ended up here. I think I took the picture by accident. But I keep it anyways.

#19

Group shot of refugees in a truck. That's May there, frowning and looking directly at the camera. May was pissed that I wasn't going with her, but there wasn't a lot of room on the truck anyways. She'd stolen my favorite tee shirt of my collection and was wearing it on the truck. I'm not sure if it was extortion to try to get me to go, or if she wore it out of spite, knowing I'd probably want to stay.

Word was, that the Presidio camps were only temporary. The Government already set up bigger, more permanent facilities in the old internment camps they put all the Japanese-Americans in during the Second World War. I heard about the slaughters in those camps, but every once in a while I can imagine her up by Mt. Shasta or someplace like that, working in a field. Maybe doing laundry, I dunno.

#20

Shot of Bradley. Like the first shot of him, the flash has sort of bleached out a lot of the color here. Look at the beginnings of a beard he has. Sometimes I look at this picture and picture #5 right next to each other. It's hard to think that only a few weeks have passed between the two shots, because he looks so much older in this one. It's set in his face, a kind of constant panic.

And, yeah, his neck muscles are taut here. And his emotionless grin, too: I'm pretty sure that's the muscles in his face constricting. When I woke up, he was stuck that way.

I slashed his throat a few minutes after taking this picture. It seemed to take forever. I cut into his neck, and nothing happened at first, and this dark blood began to flow, and I remember flinching back, like this was the first time or something. Then...then he started screaming like he woke up and the panic hit me like a flurry of fists. I shut my eyes and stabbed over and over again until the screaming stopped.

I'd killed before, mostly with Bradley, but we had to. When they come for you, faster than anything, eyes so desperate, you learn to think on that level. You get in their mindset, and it's okay. Before I killed Bradley, I'd killed or helped kill four of those beasts, but when I did it I was a beast myself. Bradley was the first one I had to murder as a person.

No one should have to do that.

#21

Shot of my "family" I ran with for a few months down south by the Castro. After Bradley died, I thought I was dead. No way I could hope to stand off against one of those things face-to-face, not even with my bat. It was pure luck that got me in with some looters over by the Haight, then I wandered down into the Castro after half of those guys died in an ambush.

The old guy with the rifle, that's Jamal. Peter and his boyfriend Graham are in the center. Terence is the one saluting, his wife Alicia's the one laughing and raising up the bottle of champagne. They used to be both into computers or something before this whole mess. The small one is Karen. Always had a soft spot for her, really.

#22

Picture of San Francisco from the hills in South S.F. You probably recognize the Transamerica building. There are other buildings here, but I can't name them. The center bit of rubble there used to have a bunch of those buildings. Some people say the military bombed that area but I'm pretty sure it was just a gas explosion of some kind.

Up on the hills to the left of the city you can see the lovely Sutro Tower as the fog rolls in like a white blanket to cover the city. We were on our way out, hearing about some army forming up on the Peninsula. It seemed like a good idea to me. After Karen died, I just…I knew I had to leave. I'd had enough.

They say there's less of them out in the country, but they're more dangerous. One's likely to stalk you for miles without you knowing, I hear. It'll follow you like it has nothing better to do in the world, dog you down until you're tired and afraid and used up any ammo or reserves you might have. But I didn't care. I was willing to take that risk.

Recently, I've started to think about May again, to tell you the truth. It's like every once in a while I remember her, just something little, like the way her hair smelled or how confused she got by sitcoms. Never the important things. Just, you know, dumb stuff.

I wonder what it would have been like if I had gotten on that truck. I don't know why I didn't go. I think I was still in the pre-disaster mindset. Things weren't working really well there, towards the end. It was a lot of little things, you know? The day those attacks started happening, the day our civilization was brought to its knees, all the rules changed with it. All that petty bullshit, it was nothing, but we had no perspective to see that. Until the end, but out of habit, I pushed her away anyways.

I guess I still have pictures of her, though.

#23

No, it's not one of the beasts attacking me. But it sure looks like one, doesn't it? This is actually a picture of the guy who developed my film for me. I traded him my camera because I can't find film for it anyways. He and I sort of set up this shot because we thought it'd be funny. He could mimic one of the monsters really well, just sort of huff up and get all tense and bug-eyed.

Smart guy, too. Haven't found anyone that knew how to develop pictures until him. He even had the chemicals. Some of them came out sort of weird, but what can you do? No matter what happens now, even if I twitch out and become one of them, I have my pictures, I have my memories.

Even if they are fragments, I don't care. I can't make a story out of my life, it's never worked out that way. I just remember things as a collection of moments, you have to fill in the rest. That's maybe why I got so upset the other night. The way people tell stories, it's dishonest. They stretch those moments together, they put a framework that's not there.

These pictures are my life, at least at that time. Like memories, only fragments. Impressions, really.

Like memories, incomplete. Twenty-three snapshots from a roll of twenty-four. Like the rest of my life, those pictures came out odd.

Some nights, when I feel the cold breezes come off the Pacific, I stare up at the sky and the thousands of stars I never knew existed, wondering how I'll document these memories of mine: the sunsets over the sea, the valleys of redwoods that feel like sacred groves. The trees that are starting to grow through suburban homes. The people I've met, both good and bad. The scars on their faces, the calluses on their hands. Is it right to live life knowing every detail will die?

I've never been good at endings either, to tell you the truth. I mess them up all over the place. May could tell you that. She used to tell me that my stories were all jokes without punch lines. I never did figure out what she meant by that. I bet Kyoko'd say I was bad at endings, too. And Bradley, and Karen in her own way. So you might have to help me:

Breathe in, keep breathing. Shut your eyes, then open them again. Take a good look around you, then back at me. Try to remember every little detail, no matter how unimportant. Freeze this split second in time.

It's important, this moment. Every stupid detail about it. It's you and me, unwilling to forget we're alive.

THE MEXICAN BUS

By Walter Greatshell

Walter Greatshell is the author of the novels *Xombies: Apocalypse Blues* and *Xombies: Apocalypticon*. A non-zombie novel, *Mad Skillz*, is forthcoming. On his website, waltergreatshell.com, Greatshell says that the last real job he had was as a graveyard-shift nuclear-submarine technician, and before that he was the general manager of the Avon Cinema, a Providence, Rhode Island, landmark. In addition to writing, he currently dabbles in freelance illustration, numerous examples of which are available on his website.

In 1957 Jack Kerouac published *On the Road*, a lightly fictionalized memoir of his road trips crisscrossing the U.S. and Mexico. The novel was written single-spaced and without paragraph breaks on a 120-foot long roll of tracing paper that Kerouac called "the scroll." (It originally used the real names of Kerouac's friends and acquaintances, including the free-spirited ex-con Neal Cassady and the poet Allen Ginsberg, but their names were changed in the published manuscript, at the publisher's insistence, to Dean Moriarty and Carlo Marx.) The book has been massively popular, influencing artists from Bob Dylan to Jim Morrison to Hunter S. Thompson, most obviously in the latter's 1972 road novel *Fear and Loathing in Las Vegas.*

On the Road also seems to have exerted an influence on our next author, who writes, "This story is an offshoot of my Xombies storyline. It's about a young guy, a college dropout, who is bumming around Mexico and has the extreme misfortune of being caught in the middle of a zombie-type epidemic—what I call the Sadie Hawkins Day Massacre. Almost every woman in the world simultaneously turns blue and goes berserk." He adds, "I actually was a college dropout, because once I discovered hitchhiking I was done with school. I have all these notebooks of stuff I wrote while on the road, hundreds of pages of obsessive beatnik musings that I hoped might come in handy someday. Who knew it would be for a zombie story?"

T*res Estrellas de Oro*. Three gold stars on a green medallion, possibly signifying the Holy Trinity—or perhaps nothing at all. It didn't matter; what was important was that his two years of high school Spanish were not completely wasted. He was not just a college dropout with little money, no prospects, and all his remaining possessions stuffed into a rain-soaked dufflebag, but a romantic figure: a bohemian man of the world. What did he need with Aristotle and Copernicus?

Tres Estrellas de Oro—beautiful.

This wasn't the bus he had started out on. That one had been red and white, with the words *Norte de Sonora* on the side. But heavy rains had washed out the road, and the bus had been forced to turn back. All that headway south, hours of travel, just to return to the border and start over! But it was okay; he had nothing but time, and no place he would rather spend New Year's Eve than on a Mexican bus going anywhere. He had learned what was possible if you had a map...and time...and a little money. Just follow the dotted line.

It was near midnight when the second bus stopped.

The young man awoke from his doze and realized he had been drooling. His neck hurt and his face was sore from being pressed against the vibrating window, but he didn't dare move lest he disturb the beautiful Canadian girl who was using his left shoulder as a pillow. An elderly man across the aisle winked at him. There was nothing to see outside but flat black—the windows might as well have been painted over. Inside the bus it was dim and cozy, with cigarette smoke drifting across the overhead reading lights. Muted Spanish conversation simmered in the cabin, and it wasn't necessary to understand the words to know what they were saying: *What now?*

Gears clanked and the bus moved forward, weaving around a line of cars. Another highway accident, that's all—they had passed enough of those. The passengers relaxed as the bus swerved clear and gathered speed. Things were looking good, but a moment later it abruptly stopped again with a hiss.

They waited. Perhaps there was still a chance this was only a short delay. The sense of collective yearning was palpable, forty people hanging on the edge of their seats. Then the driver turned off the engine and all hope collapsed. Without a word, he opened the door and got out.

Abandoned, the passengers gave in to resignation. Actually there was a certain sense of relief, as if everyone could now relax and be themselves. No one was particularly angry or upset. This was why he loved Mexico.

The Canadian girl came half awake, taking her fragrant head off his shoulder. "What's going on?" she groaned.

"Nothing. We've just stopped. It's probably a car accident or something."

"Where are we?"

"I don't know. Nowhere."

The Mexicans were making a party of it. Cigarettes were lit, snacks brought out, and the volume of conversation increased. A radio was turned on, playing a live New Year's Eve countdown from Mexico City. Some folks got up to stretch their legs, and the young man decided to do the same. He would scope out the situation and bring the girl a full report—show her he had everything under control. As if a sixteen-year-old girl traveling alone through the backlands of Mexico needed reassurance from him.

Outside it was quite a scene. The bus was part of a long line of stopped traffic in the middle of the desert—a festive-looking chain of lights spanning the void.

Many people had gotten out of their vehicles and some were wandering down the road trying to find out what was going on. There was a lit Pemex sign ahead, but the gas station itself was hidden by a dip in the fathomless landscape.

The young man wanted to walk down there and see, but he was reluctant to venture too far from the bus. What if the traffic started moving, or the bus turned around and went back? Last thing he needed was to be stranded out here. But he figured he was all right as long he kept the driver in sight, so when that officious old character and some other men started down the hill, he tagged along behind.

It was nice to be outside in the fresh air. He had been a prisoner for hours, afraid to budge. And it was so stupid: as if he had any chance with this incredible girl. Confidence with the opposite sex was not his strong suit; his record with women was a catalogue of rejection—it was a rejection, in fact, that led to his dropping out of college and impulsively heading for Mexico. He tended to rush things, that was his problem. Unrequited love was a bitch.

But…he couldn't help feeling that this situation was different. For one thing, this was *Mexico*—a whole different universe. For another, he and the gorgeous Canadian were the only gringos on the bus. Initially they had been in separate seats, but jolly Mexican ladies had insisted they sit together, playing matchmaker for the clueless *estudiantes*. Embarrassed, he had been all too ready to decline—*no, no, gracias*—but to his amazement the girl came over and sat by him. And from that moment on, he was in love.

Yet…he didn't want everything to depend on a girl. Not again. Not here. As he walked, he tried to fully immerse himself in the moment, in the extraordinary fact that he was alive, here, now, on this beautiful Godforsaken highway somewhere in Mexico. The gravel crunching under his feet, the rolling horizon like a black cardboard cutout under dimly luminous clouds, the tiny flecks of rain in the breeze—it was all marvelous.

Below the highway embankment he could see an army of tall, pale figures with arms upraised—saguaro cacti. For a second he had a wild impulse to run down there: a hike out into the desert would put things in their true perspective. But he knew he wouldn't really do it.

The Pemex station came into view, an island of sickly fluorescent light. It looked as desolate as a base on the Moon. Now he could see the trouble: there was another bus down there, a sleek white charter bus, straddling both lanes of the road. It didn't look damaged, but there must have been an accident of some kind because a lot of people were laying on the ground, with a bunch of nurses giving them CPR. Not nurses—*nuns*. A busload of nuns. Other people were running around frantically yelling for help.

Was he crazy or were some of the nuns *chasing* them?

The bus driver and his party ran to offer assistance, other men joining them along the way until the group snowballed to twenty or thirty people. They passed at least as many running in the opposite direction, who frantically tried to warn them off, shouting *¡Monjas locas! ¡Locas!* but they kept going. Meanwhile, police and military vehicles began arriving from the south, pouring on their sirens as they sped along the shoulder of the road.

Having fallen behind the driver, the young man was about halfway down the hill when he realized he was walking into something very wrong—and he stopped.

An olive-drab truck full of soldiers pulled into the gas station first. Before it could even begin unloading, a group of people—including several nuns—rushed the truck's bed and leaped in among the surprised troops. The canvas cover bounced cartoonishly from the violence within. A police Bronco stormed onto the scene and four smartly uniformed federal officers charged out, shouting orders. Nuns rushed them and they disappeared from view. Was it the fluorescent light, or did those nuns' faces look weirdly blue?

At the same time, the bus driver's posse was nearing the outer realm of glare from the gas station. The men's elongated black shadows stretched behind them as though reluctant to get any closer, but the determined hombres did not waver. From their vantage it was likely they could not properly see what was happening to the police and soldiers. Weirdly manic female silhouettes rushed to meet them, and in a second the two groups collided.

It was a massacre: the thirty volunteers suddenly found themselves senselessly, viciously assaulted. Tackled in flying leaps, half of them were pinned to the ground before they knew what hit them, their faces crushed under the searching mouths of their attackers. Stranger still, some of these attackers were the "accident victims" who had themselves been receiving CPR only moments ago. And more were jumping to life every second.

Frozen in place, the young man watched all this with increasing disbelief, unsure of how to react, but at the sound of gunfire he realized he was in over his head. The bus driver obviously had the same thought: As the rest of his party got caught up in the fighting, he had an abrupt change of heart and ran for his life. It was a close thing. He was a heavy smoker, and not young either, but he could move when he had to.

"Come on, man, come on!" shouted the American. It had occurred to him that he wasn't going anywhere without that bus driver.

The driver was faltering, wheezing badly. He had already run quite a distance, and now the running was all uphill. In desperation, the young man sprinted down to him and took the driver's leathery arm around his neck, half-carrying him up the road. The older man smelled of sweat and Old Spice—it reminded him of his grandfather.

As they retreated alongside the line of traffic, they passed the bizarre spectacle of what appeared to be people making out in some of the cars: mismatched couples locked in furious sexual combat...though the men were clearly not the aggressors. In fact the women seemed to be sucking the very life from their reluctant male prey. *Like spiders,* the American thought wildly. *Black widow spiders.*

A man's flailing leg kicked through a windshield, spraying them with glass as they hurried by. A car pulled out of line and drove down the steep embankment, plowing into the ditch at the bottom. Truck horns brayed, and they could hear small children screaming. Over it all was a shrill, rising din—the hyena laughter of the insane.

Now the young man was tiring. Almost there...almost there. They had crested the hill, and he could see the bus—*Tres Estrellas de Oro*—but all around them things were getting sketchier by the second. People were bursting from cars and fleeing in all directions with blue-faced monstrosities hot on their heels. Any second one of those things would notice them and it would all be over. The number of scary maniacs was doubling as the victims revived and joined their ranks—very soon there wouldn't be anyone sane left. From the direction of the gas station, they could hear a demonic host approaching. It was hopeless.

But nothing noticed them—or perhaps they were beneath notice, this shambling, silent pair, so ploddingly steadfast amid the general panic—because suddenly they were there, miraculously at the bus, *on* the bus, clambering up the steps and slamming the door behind them.

It was empty.

"*¡Lupe! ¡Lupita!*" the driver called, searching frantically, but the bus was completely deserted. It was also a ransacked mess, the aisle littered with women's shoes and spilled luggage, as well as teeth and tufts of ripped hair. And blood—blood everywhere—flung in drabs and spatters and hectic smears, as by the hand of a mad impressionist. It was just as well that the two men couldn't see much of this in the dark. The only sound was a high-pitched whine coming from the radio.

Bad things had happened here, as everywhere else, but for now the bus was empty; it was dark; it was safe. It was life. For a brief moment, the terror outside was muffled and remote. The two exhausted men fell into seats, crying and gasping for breath. "*Se viene abajo...se viene abajo*," the driver sobbed.

"What the fuck is this, man?" the younger man babbled. "What the fuck is going on out there? What's happening to everyone?"

"*La ley ya no está en vigor...*"

"It must be some kind of chemical weapon! A gas attack or some kind of mind control thing...but then why don't we have it? It doesn't make any sense!"

"*Sea lo que sea, no lo puedo creer.*"

They continued like this for a few minutes, purging the raw adrenaline from their systems. Catching his breath a bit, the driver reached into the overhead rack and turned off the radio. He then pulled down two plastic bottles of milky liquid. Handing one to the American, he said, "*Pulque*," and took a deep drink.

"Don't you understand? I'm fucking losing it, man! I'm losing it!"

"*A otro perro con ese hueso.*"

"I don't understand a word you're saying! I don't understand anything! *No entiendo*—you get it?"

Shaking his head, the younger man swigged from the bottle and nearly choked at the soapy, medicinal taste—he had been expecting lemonade. But the alcohol in it helped his shakes and he forced down another gulp.

Reaching a decision of some kind, the driver sighed and got up. "*Me he hartado de esto*," he said gravely.

Alarmed, the American caught his arm. "No, what are you doing? Sit down, man, they'll see us."

The driver patted his shoulder, saying gently, "*Hombre de muchos oficios, pobre seguro.*" He walked forward and climbed behind the wheel, belting himself in. Then he smoothed his hair back and started the engine.

"Dude, what do you think you're *doing?* We can't go anywhere—we're blocked in, bumper to bumper! We should just wait here for help to come!"

"*No siempre es fácil salir de un apuro.*"

"I don't speak Spanish!"

"Seet down and shut up."

At the sound of the diesel, things started happening again. The naked, blurred creatures outside suddenly froze into sharp focus, gaping mouths and black eyes all trained on the bus. There were hundreds of them now: men, women, and children. They came fast. Bodies slammed against the sides, leaping for handholds, while others swarmed the door and front windshield. Hard objects starred the glass, quickly knocking out holes through which blue arms lunged like snakes. The young man couldn't stand to look, but worse than the sight was the *sound* of them: "*¡No hay cuidaaado!*" they screamed. "*¡No hay cuidaaado!*"

The bus lurched forward, smashing a dozen creatures against the rear of a trailer truck and shaking off the rest like fleas. The impact destroyed what was left of the windshield, but succeeded at ramming the truck a few feet ahead so that it rear-ended another vehicle. Then the driver shifted gears, jumping the bus into reverse and slamming into the traffic immediately behind, plowing a wide space in which to maneuver. At once the American realized what he was trying to do: a U-turn! It made a certain amount of sense because the northbound lane of traffic was clear, but the narrow highway didn't look nearly wide enough to swing this huge bus around—certainly not before those maniacs out there got inside. With the windshield gone the bus was open to all comers. But surely the driver himself must know better than anyone what was or wasn't possible; he was a professional. Flinching at each crash, the American hung on tight and surrendered to hope.

A loud drumming of feet could be heard on the roof. Hideous blue faces were gibbering upside-down through crazed windows. It was now or never: the bus driver cranked the wheel to its limit and backed over the near edge of the roadway, his rear tires settling deep into the soft bank. Then he rolled the steering wheel hard to the left and gunned forward into the massing loonies. With a lurch, the vehicle came back onto the pavement, turning in as tight a radius as was physically possible...and it was *almost* tight enough. But no—now the front of the bus was dangling over the opposite shoulder! One more correction was necessary, one more reverse...

Too late. As soon as the bus stopped again, those blue horrors were inside. They came like locusts, heedless of injury as they leaped and scrambled over the sill. The driver produced an old machete from under his seat, hacking furiously, but it didn't slow them down one bit: multitudes of hands pinned him down while a terrifying madwoman straddled him and crushed his resisting mouth under hers. Was it worse because he recognized her? Would it have been better if it was a stranger?

For the inhuman beast stealing the breath from Don Diego's lungs was someone he dearly loved, who often kept him company on these long road trips since his wife had passed away: his virtuous eldest daughter, Lupe. They were inseparable. As her mouth turned inside-out, filling him like a sack of live eels, he convulsed as though electrocuted...then went limp.

Watching the others come, the American suddenly realized that they were familiar to him as well, if only of brief acquaintance—they were his fellow bus passengers! Women, for the most part, though such a word hardly seemed to describe them now. Hags. Furies. Banshees. Blue-skinned ghouls, storming the bus as though it belonged to them, and why not?—they had paid the fare. They came piling in like grubs, brazenly naked or wearing only scraps of clothing, their black eyes fixed on him with implacable, cold lust. Old or young, male or female, they *craved* him.

Backing down the aisle he felt like an object; a piece of meat. It was a new sensation, being wanted, and not as pleasant as he might formerly have imagined. Leading the pack was the Canadian girl, her pale, perfect beauty now transformed into something washed up on the beach: all jaws and cartilage and kelp-like red hair. That hair obscured her eyes, but it seemed to him that they were messed up—empty holes crying black tears.

She came fast and there was no place left to go but the restroom. Ugh. No time to think about it—he fell inside and turned the latch. As violent blows started falling on the flimsy door, he pressed his back against it, bracing his legs against the opposite wall.

They didn't give up. They weren't going to give up. Ever. Looking at himself in the mirror, he thought, *This is it, man: now you're stuck like this.* Trapped for eternity in a Mexican toilet, with women clamoring for his body—it had to be a joke. The thought wrung a ragged, involuntary laugh out of him, or was it a scream? He clamped his hands over his mouth to silence it. Please God let it be a joke.

The pounding became more frenzied, jarring his spine. The whole bus shook with it. As the door deformed in its frame, blue fingers wormed in at the weak spots, clamping tight and pulling with inhuman strength—any second they were going to rip the thing right off its hinges. The man closed his eyes, whimpering through gritted teeth...when all at once the hammering stopped.

As if by magic, the monsters disappeared.

Then he realized why. The bus was moving.

The cause was simple: the driver hadn't set the brake, they were on an incline, so the bus was rolling backwards. It glanced off another vehicle, then tipped sickeningly over the edge of the roadway and down the high bank. Veering sharply right from the angle of its tires, it toppled over onto its side, hitting the desert floor like a great carcass.

The young man emerged. He climbed out of the vehicle and dropped to the sand, vomiting his guts out. He was dyed blue from head to foot, soaked with raw sewage and the disinfectant liquid from the exploded toilet. Defenseless, half-blind, he expected to be attacked any second. When no maniacs came for him, he realized their fevered attention was being drawn elsewhere—to a caravan of new arrivals. He could hear the screams. It was a hellish fly trap up there, with more flies arriving by the minute. Down here, in the dark, he was already forgotten.

Hugging his aching ribs, he dragged himself as far from the road as he could, a mile or more, huddling under a bush amid stands of tall cacti. At one time he would have been worried about snakes or scorpions, but now he didn't care about much of anything. He would wait here until morning—wait for help to come. Then, as if a switch was thrown, he was out.

White. He came to in a world of muffled whiteness, with surreal ranks of cacti looming above him like sentinels. It was fog—dense morning fog. His body hurt all over, and he was cold, curled up in a ball with his jacket collar around his ears. It took him a second to remember where he was and why—much longer to believe it. How long had it been? Five or six hours at least. Everything was dead quiet. Maybe it was over.

Stiffly climbing to his feet, he hobbled back in the general direction of the highway. Just to see. He was a little disoriented, but it didn't matter if he went back the exact same way he had come, as long as he found the road. And a drink. Definitely a drink.

It was a long hike, much longer than he remembered. The terrain became very rocky. He didn't dare consider that he might be lost. *When the fog clears, I'll see exactly where I am*, he thought, but when the fog cleared there was nothing—just more rocks and a barren vista of brown hills. Topping each rise, he kept praying to see something hopeful, preferably a *mercado* with a cooler full of ice-cold sodas…and was forever disappointed, falling deeper and deeper into despair until by the time he finally did sight the road he had practically given up. But there it was.

"Oh thank God," he croaked.

It was the highway all right, however a different, more level stretch than the one he had left behind. There was no traffic-jam here, no Pemex station—the lanes were clear in both directions. Hiking down to it, he fell on the pavement with the gratitude of a shipwreck survivor. But was he north or south of the pile-up? Rather than heading into trouble, he decided to stay where he was and wait for help to come to him. Which was just as well—he couldn't move another inch. His blisters had blisters. But the thirst was getting out of control; if someone didn't come along soon…well, someone had to come along.

He got as comfortable as possible and waited. As he sat there, a couple of large black birds landed nearby. It took him a minute to realize they must be vultures. That was interesting, sitting under the hot white sky and watching turkey vultures waddle along the opposite side of the road like fat little undertakers—it was the corniest thing ever. Real vultures! Back and forth, back and forth, exactly as if they were pacing. Which they were, of course. It was too stupid.

An hour passed. Then two. Dozing under the makeshift cowl of his jacket, he heard the truck before he saw it. It was a big one—some kind of heavy construction vehicle. It came rumbling around the bend of a hill, and at the sight of it the American let out a hoarse cheer: it was a huge red dump-truck bristling with armed men. His body had stiffened from sitting so long; it took a painful effort to get to his feet. By that time the truck was much closer, coming on fast. Its wheels were taller than he was, and there was a railed walkway around the high cab on which several men were standing. They were pointing at him and calling to the driver.

Tears streaking his face, the American waved his arms and shouted as best he could, "*¡Por favor! ¡Por favor!*"

The truck slowed, its passengers shading their eyes to see him better against the late-day sun. He could see them well enough: a harsh-faced bunch in dirty coveralls, bearing picks and shovels—a prison road crew escaped from their keepers. He didn't care; to him they looked like angels of mercy. But at the last minute the truck swerved wide and throttled up.

Crying, "No, no!" the young man ran to intercept it, to block the road if he had to. "I'm not crazy!" he shouted. "*¡No estoy loco!*"

The truck grew bigger and bigger; the truck took over the landscape, expanding like the Big Bang until its right wheel alone was bigger than the entire world—the whole universe. A black rubber sky studded with shiny pebbles, turning over on him.

The last thing he saw was stars.

THE OTHER SIDE

By Jamie Lackey

Jamie Lackey's short fiction has appeared in *Atomjack Magazine*, *Bards and Sages Quarterly*, *Drabblecast*, and in the anthology *It Was a Dark and Stormy Halloween*. She is also a slush reader for *Clarkesworld Magazine* and an assistant editor for the *Triangulation* annual anthology series. She hails from Pittsburgh, where George Romero filmed *Night of the Living Dead*.

For most of history, human beings have been throwing up walls. Walls seem to offer protection from a hostile world, and give us a sense of control, of keeping people where we think they ought to be. But walls definitely have a spotty history when it comes to their actual usefulness. The magnificent Great Wall of China never really did keep the barbarians out, nor did the walls of the Roman Emperor Hadrian. The Berlin Wall ultimately failed to keep Germany divided, and the strenuous efforts by the Israelis to put up walls between them and the Palestinians haven't really proven effective.

Can we have much confidence that walls would do any better against zombies? And of course with any wall there's the question not just of what are you keeping out, but also what are you holding in. Our next story is about fences, about boundaries, and being on the wrong side of them, and, of course, about zombies. The author says, "This story is about high school students almost twenty years after a zombie apocalypse. And unrequited love. I started thinking how the world would be different if there were zombies, but they'd been driven back decades ago. The zombies might still be a threat, biding their time, waiting to strike again, or they could have all rotted away without anyone noticing. The emotions in the story are what make it personal to me—the need to fit in, the fear, and in the end, the sorrow and regret."

No one has seen a zombie in my lifetime. The twelve-foot-high electrified chain-link fence that protects us from the dead land passes behind my house, and I used to stare into the woods for hours on end, looking for zombies. I saw a raccoon once, peeking out through a broken window in a half-burned townhouse. It might have been undead. But it might not have been.

There used to be regular armed patrols on the dirt road inside the fence, back when I was little, but eventually the manpower was diverted to other projects. Federal troops still come around once a year in a tanker truck and burn back the vegetation in the buffer zone with napalm.

We have about fifty feet of scorched earth so that if they do come out of the woods, we can see them before they get to the fence. It keeps them from using trees to climb out, too. But like I said, no one has seen a zombie for well over a decade. Some of the kids in my school want to take the fence down and see what's beyond it, see if there are any people up in Canada anymore. But anybody who was alive during the apocalypse is set against ever taking the fence down. *Just in case*, they always say. *Just in case. Let them keep the dead land.*

There was a group of guys in my high school who wanted the fence down. They were idiots, but they were cool, and I wanted desperately for them to like me. They threw Katie over the fence because they could, and because they wanted to prove that the zombies were gone.

Katie and I were best friends. Best friends outside of school, anyway. She'd always been kind of a dork, and she didn't even drink or party anymore, not since the previous Fourth of July. Something had happened while I was away at a family picnic, and no one would tell me about it. Anyway, Katie wasn't someone to hang out with in public, since I wanted to be cool.

I was an asshole to her. But she put up with it. I didn't figure out why till too late. She had thick glasses and curly hair and average everything else. But none of this would have happened if she hadn't been so smart.

But she was brilliant and didn't bother to hide it from anyone, so they picked her to hurl over the fence. They were jerks, but they weren't murderers, so I didn't think they'd do it till her body actually hit the ground on the other side.

They used the volunteer fire truck. They put up that ladder meant to save people and stranded kittens and tossed my best friend into the dead land. She landed in the fresh ashes, and for a second everyone was silent.

Then I started screaming at them, which pretty much killed my hopes of high school popularity. They laughed and opened some beers and settled in to see if the zombies would show up. I cried and screamed for them to get her out until they punched me, then I got my cell phone and called the police.

They left in a hurry after that.

All through it, Katie sat on the ground and stared at the fence. She didn't look toward the woods once. She didn't look at me either.

The police were no help. They wouldn't get her out. She was outside the fence. She counted as infected. It didn't matter that I'd been watching the whole time and that she didn't have a mark on her. They couldn't let her in. She might be a zombie.

They dragged me home and took my statement and I didn't see the guys again who tossed Katie over. I heard that they were taken away in the night and executed.

She was still there the next day, sitting and staring.

"Katie?" I called through the fence. "Are you okay?"

She looked at me, and her eyes filled with tears. "I'm not going to get out of here, am I?"

"I'll figure something out."

Katie just shook her head and went back to staring. Her tears made trails through the ash that had settled on her skin. I'd never touched the fence before. I knew some people who had, but I never did, till that day. I was watching Katie's tears, and I reached out and grabbed onto the fence.

When I woke up, my head felt like it had exploded and I couldn't move my arms.

Katie was standing on the other side of the fence, one finger reaching through the chain links. "Are you okay?"

When I woke up again, she was still there. "Thing really packs a punch," I said.

"It was made to put a zombie down long enough for a clean headshot."

At least she wasn't crying anymore. But it was getting dark. I got up slowly, flexing my fingers to make sure they still worked. "I have to go home."

"I know," she whispered.

I touched her fingertip, staying carefully away from the fence. Her skin was cold and dry. I wanted to hug her. "I'll get you out."

I tossed her a bottle of water and my peanut butter and jelly sandwich. That night, I called every government agency I could find a number for, but they all repeated the same thing. She's outside the fence, she could be infected. No one wanted to risk another outbreak. I called the volunteer fire chief, and he said the same thing.

So did Katie's parents.

I heard it enough times I started to half believe it. After all, I hadn't been watching her the whole time. She could have been bitten. I wouldn't know.

I skipped school and went straight out to see her. "Are you infected?" I asked. She looked the same as always. But sometimes, they looked the same. Sometimes, they could even still talk.

"Of course I'm not," she said.

I wanted to believe them so I could give up on her and mourn. "You'd say that if you were."

That pissed her off. "You think I'm bitten? You think I'd be horrible enough to want out of here if I was? Do you think I want to be the cause of another outbreak?" She pulled off her shirt, then her pants, and unhooked her bra, all faster than I could think of a response. "See? No bites."

She kept her underwear on. She'd whipped off her bra, but left those on. "What about on your hips?" I said.

Her face turned red, as if she suddenly realized that she was standing in front of me almost naked. "How could a zombie bite me through my underwear and not leave any marks on them?"

"Maybe it happened when you were going to the bathroom or something," I said. I stared at her, searching for signs of the change.

"I didn't get bit there." She sounded close to tears.

"Prove it!"

She didn't move.

I took a step back. She was lost. Dead. No, *worse* than dead—a monster. I started to walk away.

"Wait!" she shouted. "I swear, I didn't get bitten."

"Then prove it."

"I was drunk." Her voice shook. "I didn't know what I was doing, and I've been saving up to get it removed."

"What are you talking about?"

She took off her panties very slowly, then turned for my inspection.

There was no bite, but she had a tattoo that I hadn't known about, just below the crest of her pelvis.

My name.

She was crying. Sobs this time, with painful gasping breaths between them. "I'm not infected." Her voice was different when she was crying. I'd never heard it like that before. "I'm not!"

I didn't know what to say to her. How could I? She was in love with me, and some tattoo artist somewhere knew it—half the school probably knew it—and I hadn't? She was my best friend.

"Is this what happened on the Fourth of July?"

She nodded and wiped her eyes, but she refused to look at me.

"You should have told me," I finally managed.

"What good would it have done?"

I couldn't answer her. I just didn't feel the same way about her and we both knew it. "I'm still looking for a way to get you out of there."

"I love you," she said. Her voice still sounded different.

I wanted to cry. I ran home.

The next day, she wasn't there.

There was a dark spot in the shadows of the woods. It might have been blood. But it might not have been.

WHERE THE HEART WAS

By David J. Schow

David J. Schow's most recent novels are *Gun Work* and *Internecine*. He is also the author of the novels *The Kill Riff*, *The Shaft*, *Bullets of Rain*, and *Rock Breaks Scissors Cut*. One of the early innovators of zombie fiction, he is the author of the notorious story "Jerry's Kids Meet Wormboy," which, along with several other zombie tales, appears in the collection *Zombie Jam*. Schow has done a lot of work in television and film, including co-writing (with John Shirley) the screenplay for *The Crow* and writing teleplays for Showtime's *Masters of Horror*. Schow is also generally considered to be the originator of the term "splatterpunk."

Our lives are full of things that we wish would just go away: worries, fears, doubts. Also bills, advertisements, and enemies. And also, of course, rotting corpses. Them most of all. Alas, in the case of zombies, these things we never wanted to see again have returned, and while they may run amuck in our streets, cause our civilization to collapse, and bite and convert our neighbors and friends, at least we can be consoled by the knowledge that they can be stopped by a bullet through the brain, and that this time—dammit—they're staying down.

It's troubling when something you're trying to get rid of comes back once when all the laws of reason and common sense say it can't, but how much worse is it when that same unwanted thing keeps coming back over and over again? As children, many of us were given nightmares by a Warner Bros. cartoon in which a family goes to ever more elaborate lengths to abandon its incredibly annoying dog, only to have the dog show up at the front door again and again and again. If the cartoonists thought this sort of thing was amusing, they were wrong—it's terrifying, a fact Stephen King well understood when he wrote his story "The Monkey," about a cursed toy that simply cannot be disposed of. Our next story combines these two ideas. It's bad enough when a rotting corpse comes crawling home. But what if it turns into a habit?

Victor Jacks ambled through the back door to ruin their lives on Thursday. Which was a pain, since Victor had been pronounced dead the previous Saturday.

"Stubborn sumbitch." Renny reached under the bed for the ballbat. He was on hands and knees, forced to paw around until it finally came out with dustballs and hair kitties chasing it. Renny, who was allergic to animal dander, sneezed ear-poppingly. This trebled his rage.

Renny's life was one that Victor's back-from-the-dead encore was designed to ruin. Barb's was the other. Just now she was backed into a corner, shrieking like an ingenue in a fifty-year-old horror film. Unlike those World War II heroines, she was naked. Renny still had his socks on. Apart from his Timex, he was garbless, but for the baseball bat. This, he refused to yield in the name of mere modesty.

Victor looked a bit shaggy, having been deceased for the better part of the work week. His shoulder blades, butt and legs down to the heels were blue-black with dependent lividity. His eyes were so crusty that one was welded shut. His hair was lank and wild, the most alive thing about him; his skin tone hung somewhere between catgut and bottled pig's knuckle.

He crackled as he moved. That would be rigor.

He had obviously been walking for some time. At each of his joints the dry flesh had split into gummy wounds with chafed and elevated flaps. The distance from the morgue to Barb's bedroom was about twelve pedestrian miles.

Provided, that is, Victor had come here directly, after sitting up on his slab and deciding to ruin their lives, Renny thought. And that pissed him off even more.

Renny's next explosive sneeze spoiled his aim. He wiped his nose with his forearm. Barb kept screaming, totally out of character for her, and Renny wished in a mean flash that she would either faint or die.

Enough.

At the crack point it was the batting that mattered, not the invective. The bulb end of the bat smashed Victor's dead left ear deep into the dead left hemisphere of his dead brain. Victor wobbled and missed his zombie grab for Renny. He didn't have a chance.

Renny was foaming and lunatic, swinging and connecting, swinging and connecting, making pulp. It was what he had ached to do to Victor all along. What he had fantasized about doing to Victor just last week, when Victor was still alive. His yelling finally drowned out Barb, who was still shrunken fetally into her corner, her eyes seeking the deep retreat of trauma.

Renny's eyes were pink with rage. Flecks of froth dotted the corners of his mouth. He kept bashing away with the bat, pausing only to sneeze and wipe. Victor put up as good a fight as a dead person could, which is to say, not much.

While the Renny on the outside was cussing and bludgeoning, the Renny on the inside was smirking about several things. Number one—zombie movies. In the movies, reanimated corpses boogied back from the dead with all kinds of *strength* and *powers*. What a bagload. Cadavers had all the tensile strength of twice-cooked pasta. Even in the movies, you could put them down with a headshot. What threat, where?

Deeper down, Renny was *enjoying* himself. He thought Barb watched too much cable. When he had first proposed murdering Victor—just as a hoot, mind you, nothing serious—she burdened him with *probable cause* and *airtight alibis* and *where-were-you-on-the-night-of*. Ridiculous, in a world where people simply dropped off the planet on a daily basis, never again a peep. You break his neck, you dump him in the first available manhole, the sewer is a disposal system, end of story.

Barb had wanted to play faithful and loving right up to the climax of the drama. Loving, hah. Faithful, not since she'd met Renny.

In the end it hadn't come down to murder, but right now Barb sure was reaping some drama.

Things were so lively right now that Renny had busted a workout sweat and Barb's vocal cords were rawing. He finally turned around and told her to shut up while what was left of Victor Jacks twitched in a pile on the floor. The business end of the bat was a real mess.

"Is he dead?" said Barb, cowering.

"I don't think he's gonna move no more right now." Renny would have wiped his be-gored hands on his pants; his pants had been off since just after dinnertime. He let his hands hang in the air as he looked around, uselessly. He said *sheeeit,* slow and weary. It didn't help.

"How? How did he? He…we…I don't…it just." Barb was still having a bit of trouble being coherent.

"Victor was always a stubborn sumbitch, you *know* that one, babe."

Barb stood up and risked moving a little closer to what was left of Victor. "Maybe he, you know, didn't really die. Went into a coma or something."

"Barb, Victor was dead. He was dead last week and he was *still* dead when he walked in on us. He is the deadest thing I ever saw."

"You knocked his head off," she said, dully.

"Stopped him, didn't it?"

"What're we gonna *do,* Renny? He's all…ehh."

"Shush. What we're gonna do is call the morgue and tell them some pervert snatched the body and mutilated it, and dumped it here as a joke. Some old boyfriend of yours. You can make up a description. Nobody'll bug us."

"What makes you so smart?"

Renny had to stop a moment to ponder a good answer to that one.

"I mean, you think they'll buy it?" There she went again. Barb was one of those people who strolled through life obliviously, thinking a call to the police would sling her free of any sort of trouble. Now she was just as convinced that the Authorities—capital A—would swoop down at any moment to *point j'accuse.*

"Babe, just dream up a good description. Say he was a Mexican in a green windbreaker."

"But Renny, I'd never go out with no Mexican, and how come I have to say he's my old boyfriend? I mean—"

Renny sighed, held her by the shoulders, met her eyes. "We'll *deal.* Trust me. Please." He forced a smile for her. It was like jamming a finger down his throat to chuck up an emotion. He needed to divert her, to say something that would get her mind off police procedure, so he said, "Uh—got any towels?"

Renny mopped off. Barb brought a big Hefty bag. Renny stuck the bat back under the bed. Touching it again made him re-experience the sheer satisfaction of pounding ole Victor right back into death, and this gifted him with a healthy and urgent erection.

Barb glimpsed what was coming up, and managed to finish him off before the police came knocking. Once again she told Renny that she'd never done *that* with Victor, and Renny smiled and stroked her head, keeping to himself the private notion that Barb could probably suck the stitches off a hardball through a flexi-straw. Victor Jacks would never have hung with a china doll. Renny would never have been tempted by one, either.

Then the Authorities arrived, and Renny and Barb set about making up stories.

Funerals never were much of a hoot. Neither Barb nor Renny had RSVPed many in their combined forty-odd years, but this time they dutifully duded up in basic black, and held hands, and dabbed at crocodile tears as the rearranged remains of Victor Jacks were boxed up and delivered six feet closer to Hell.

Half an hour after the services, both of them were naked and neither of them was very depressed.

Most annoying of Barb's bed-play habits was her wont of lighting off to the toilet as soon as...well, right after. Renny had once joked about it: "I make all that effort to give you something, babe, and you just go piss it away." Barb had made a face. Crude, her face told him. Not funny. Then hi-de-ho, off to the can again.

Fine. Renny grunted manfully and rolled to his right side, his favored side for dozing. Swell.

In the bathroom, Barb watched herself in the mirror for a long time, not quite sure what her surveillance was in quest of. Victor had hit her in this bathroom. He'd also done it to her, same day, in the tub, which was too small for love. Victor's tendency to boil over all at once was frightening, a pit bull on a very iffy leash, thought Barb. Whether it got hostile, life-threatening, might depend on a dozen factors. When it last ate. Whether it was pissed off. Whether it liked you. Whether it liked your smell. Victor Jacks had been like that.

But when Victor got to the part where he put his big hands all over her, large, powerful, warm hands, unbuttoning and unzipping her, making her naked and telling her she was wanted, touching her in places only *she* touched—curve of ass, inside of thigh, underside of breast, smooth-shaven armpit—oh, my. He made her moist, filled her up; she would practically *hallucinate* and she had always slept gorgeously afterward. The sex was never violent between them; only the occasional backhand was.

Barb knew she would never get around to enjoying the way men apologized, every time, *after* they smacked her.

When she had met Victor Jacks, she was a waitress-newly-turned-exotic-dancer. Petite-chested, with good hips and sturdy, if not long, legs, she figured it was virtually the same aggravation for better tips and weirder hours; she fancied she needed more weird in her life. She got Victor. All he lacked was a puff of smoke to appear in.

When Victor had met Barb, he was comfortably into pharmaceutical dexedrine pops and on the cusp of crystal meth. He made do with the odd frame-weld for RUBs—Rich Urban Bikers—and bashed big-blocks for muscle-car meatheads with too much leisure cash. He paid Barb to table-dance and made her sit, just sit, while he looked at her. Management did not approve. Victor did not make a scene. He merely smiled and showed Barb's bosses more money. To Barb, whose concept of foreplay was someone bigger than her saying *shut up and lay down*, this was romance with a big R indeed. After a week of this bizarre courtship, she went out with him...and he stayed in with her.

When Renny Boone had met Barb, he was so chemical-free you could almost see his halo. To Barb, by this time shell shocked by two years of biker-speed tantrums and eight-ball insomnia, Renny's well-cut bod and addictionless turn smelled like that myth come true, the Better Life.

"You look like you could use a rest," Renny had told her, and so telling her, he took her straight away to bed.

Five days later the two of them were still trying to dope out some rationalization that might convince, say, a jury that she, Barb, and he, Renny, were Meant To Be. But Barb lacked the heart to dump someone as spontaneous and romantic as Victor Jacks.

Truth was, Renny preferred Barb as a rental. And that Victor wasn't such a bad dude. He'd even nailed the chronic carburetor wheeze suffered by Butch, Renny's black '66 Impala.

Truth was, Barb preferred Victor's flash-fire spats to shaking her ass for the beery swine who bellied up to the runway at Nasty Tramps.

So Truth held sway, and Victor stayed ignorant, dangerous and sexy. Barb had Renny for the topics she could never broach to Victor. And Renny had Barb, the way cowboys have spittoons. And they all lived happily ever after for about two more weeks, until Victor came back to the house, unannounced, to fetch his set of Allen wrenches, and...

...well, you can imagine.

The "tool excuse" had been Victor's cover story. That afternoon, unbeknownst to Renny and Barb, Victor had fallen in love again—this time, with a smokable amphetamine called ice. He was pretty saturated, on top of his morning fistful of vitamins, and when he walked through his front door and caught Renny and Barb doing the bone dance on his sofa bed, the speed made his anger instantaneous; his reaction time, zero.

Victor had snarled. Literally snarled, lip curling. He came for his betrayers, his face bright crimson, the sclera of his eyes pinking. Two steps closer he stopped, stiffened, pawed at his left arm, and fell stone dead of the most concussive goddamned heart attack his mesomorphic build could contain. Victor's fulsome, romantic-if-crazy heart shut down like a phone sex line with no callers, and all that remained was for the coroner to scribble *death by chemical misadventure* into the appropriate box...while Victor himself was trucked away to fill up another appropriate box.

Which brings us back to Barb, in the bathroom.

She flushed the toilet. Flushed, then blushed, in a match-head flare of anger as she remembered Renny's idiotic joke about her having to urinate after sex. She would never forget it. Crude, Renny could be so crude. Maybe dumb, too—dumb enough never to have heard of Honeymooner's Cystitis, an inflammation of the bladder that was easy to get when you had too much foreign juice rammed up your tubes. And perhaps uncaring, as well—maybe Renny didn't give a big manly damn what havoc forty-five minutes of the missionary position could wreak on even a healthy girl's poor need to pee.

In her mirror, by nightlight, she spotted a hickey on her neck. Crude.

But she loved the way Renny liked to chew on her, just nibble and bite and suck all the right places, as though he was desperately hungry for her, physically starving. She always orgasmed first, even when she tried to outlast him, and once she was coitally zoned, she really *did* want him to leave marks. Little ones she'd see in the morning, when she felt the delicious residual ache of their workout.

She liked to tease Renny about all the women he must have learned his bag of tricks from. If she had a headache or a rotten mood, Renny could bang it right out of her. Victor would never even touch her at her time of the month; Renny did not have that particular cultural problem. He made her feel more desirable on her doggiest days, and feeling desirable made Barb feel womanly indeed. Renny even understood about her having to go back to work at Nasty Tramps, now that Victor was no longer winning the bread. In fact, Renny had *suggested* Barb rejoin the working world. What a guy.

Crude, dumb, uncaring, and boy-howdy opportunistic. Yeah, Renny was a prize, for sure. Prize catch of the day.

Except that *this* day, somehow, Victor had found time out from his busy schedule to come back from the dead. This did not shock or befuddle Barb overtly. Maybe she'd seen too many monster movies, and lacked the emotional capacity for astonishment. She stared down her reflection eye-to-eye and reminded herself that Victor had done a *lot* of uppers in his thirty-odd years on the planet. Hell, he was probably spinning in his new grave right now—at 78 rpm.

The bathroom light was harsh. It made her feel lonely. She was fortunate to know that it was a loneliness she could drive away. She wanted Renny on her, inside of her, the fastest way she knew not to feel lonely anymore.

She found him semiconscious and semi-erect. Renny functioned best with a five-minute nap between rounds. Barb woke him up with her mouth. She didn't say a word, but he awoke anyway. They made a great deal of noise over the next half-hour. Renny always lasted longer once he'd "primed his pump"; his words.

They were both on their backs, kicking away sheets to let their own sweat cool them off, when Barb said, "Did you hear that?"

"Hear what?"

"Little scritchy noise. Like a mouse."

"Probably that stupid cat of yours."

"No, he doesn't make noises like that."

"Then it probably *is* a mouse. This house is—"

"No, listen."

Renny listened. If the thing making the noise was a mouse, it was dragging off a dog for a bit of fun.

Barb pounded his shoulder. "It's under the bed!"

"Jesus Christ." Renny stayed calm and leaned overboard for a look-see.

From beneath the dust ruffle, the baseball bat shot out like a piston, hitting Renny foursquare in the chin and making him see night sky. It still had clots of Victor drying on it. Then something whip-snaked tight coils around Renny's throat and dragged him down to tussle.

Renny made a gargling noise in the dark as he was reeled in. Discombobulated, he thought he was being engulfed by a giant wiggle-worm with a whole lot of little worms attached. He dug his heels into the rug and fought to breathe. Barb was already making those screamy gasps that truly *bugged* him, deep down.

It was a hand on his throat. He peeled it off. As he did, another appendage trapped his hand.

Renny pulled back and dragged his rubber-limbed assailant out from under the bed—the preferred place of concealment for seasoned, traditional boogeymen.

It was Victor again.

Moreover, it was Victor as he had been buried that afternoon. Bones all smashed. No head.

Renny was instantly mummified in a barbwire-tangle of leathery muscles and nonliving rubber flesh; it was like trying to wrassle a waterbed. What *used* to be Victor's arms and legs—now freed from bones and framework—coiled and constricted into tentacles that were much quicker than Renny's fist. They slithered snug around his windpipe, his chest, his stomach, and Renny could feel it coming—the big squeeze that would make the life jump right out of him.

Now Renny was making those screamy noises.

He was clawing at his own face when Barb, no longer wailing, charged back from the kitchen, brandishing the biggest meat cleaver Renny had ever seen.

Victor had threatened her with the cleaver once; that was how she'd known where to find it.

And Barb had, in fact, seen too many monster movies. Especially the ones about psychos and kitchen implements; you could get every-damned-thing on cable nowadays. She hacked and chopped and slashed and hollered and only nailed Renny by accident once.

The grabby Victor-thing began falling to pieces faster than a clay vase run through on the wheel with a cutoff needle. Tearing a suffocating creeper of skin free from his mouth, Renny flailed to a sitting position and sucked air.

"Barb—you cut me *open*, goddammit!"

"*I missed*, honey, I'm *sorry*, okay? That thing was all over the place!"

She helped him stand. He was wobbly, unused to needing help, to being nearly beaten. Their feet buried in the desiccated meat on the floor, she felt him shake. He hugged her tight and genuinely.

"I know. I know, babe...but that thing is ole you-know-who again."

"Can't be. No way." She pressed her face into his neck, not looking. He lifted a scrap of now-inanimate flesh and turned it to the faint light, so Barb could see the tattoo. A cherubic, comic book devil-child looked back at her from a corona of flame.

"Aww, *shit—it's* Hot Stuff, Renny!"

"Yep." Jesus, wasn't there *anyone* whose life hadn't been touched by Harvey Comics?

Victor Jacks had gotten his ink at a Sunset Boulevard parlor called Skin Illos, at the behest of Nikki, who had been his girlfriend of record prior to Barb. Barb had heard you could bleach tattoos by using a laser. She hadn't been able to work up the spit to suggest this to Victor prior to his very timely demise.

"Renny...hon...I don't want to make you *mad* or nothin, but—"

"But?"

"What if Victor...you know, keeps coming back every time we, you and I...you know."

"Victor ain't coming back again."

"What're we gonna do?"

"What I wanted to do originally. Dump him in the sewer. What's left of him. Let the rats chow down."

"Guess we're gonna need another Hefty bag, huh?"

Barb grimaced at the sliced-and-diced assemblage of tissue on the floor. It relaxed and settled, shifting softly. Renny stared at it, too, panting, with shiny eyes, the sweat leaving his chin in droplets.

"But first, babe—hand me that meat cleaver."

The manhole cover weighed ninety-five pounds, give or take. Renny had the advantages of a pry bar and good upper torso strength. Thus were the headless, autopsied, dismembered, broken-boned earthly remnants of Victor Jacks consigned to LA County waste disposal network.

Hacking Victor into itty-bitty bite-sized morsels had given Renny a peculiar thrill—the same excitement that had granted him a full-on chubby while bludgeoning Vic-baby the *first* time.

Sucker just wouldn't give it up. Renny had to admire that, begrudgingly.

And if Vic-baby somehow managed to make a third curtain call, why, that'd be the tits, too. Because Renny was starting to enjoy the new, fun things he could do with his hands.

Like what he might do if Barb lost her marbles and started that gawdawful shrieking again...

Nahh. Just a vagrant thought. No problem, there.

Renny yanked his fingers clean and the lid seated with an iron clank. An old pal of his had once broken three fingers by not letting go soon enough, after chasing a frisbee into the sewer. That made Renny think again of Barb. Maybe it was getting time to let *her* go. True, she'd come to his rescue and handled herself well enough tonight, but what if Victor was some kind of *curse* or something, specific to her?

You don't pull back your hand in time, you lose. And it wasn't his fingers that Renny had been parking inside of Barb, most of the recent past.

Just now, in fact, he was up for another bout. His body urged him to hurry home to her. She would be fresh out of her bath, tasty and scented, and Renny wanted to ride her until she screamed for real.

"Do you hear something? A noise, or—"

"Oh for *Christ* sake, Barb!"

"I'm serious. Stop it."

Feeling like a wiener, Renny backed out and listened to the double-time of his own heart, backdraft from his urgent need to climax, soon-sorta-like-immediately. Barb listened intently—she resembled a grade-schooler trying too hard to concentrate—not for sounds from the heart, but telltales of nearing monsters. She was still head down, ass up after coyly asking Renny to do her *that way,* and she clung to the mattress as though it could render her some psychic truth.

"I don't hear anything, babe, except maybe your own paranoia bouncing back at us from the walls." Fed up, he grabbed his smokes off the nightstand. Pretty glib, he thought, for a guy who was strangling on a rope of living dead ligaments about an hour ago.

"I thought I heard the seat fall down in the bathroom."

"My fault. I left it up." When Renny strove to impress, he could be the most courteous, thoughtful man on earth. Then, as he procured what he wanted, he let the courtesies slide. Like tonight: He'd left the seat up on purpose, a territorial assertion he knew she'd notice, yet tolerate. The brilliant trick of Renny's life was that he made sure people always noticed him when he was being a swell guy, so there was less risk of him being singled out when he was being a turd of ethics. Voila—he was known far and wide for being fair, wise and trusty. No way he'd ever sleep with another man's partner, or murder someone, or even *think* of doing the deed.

Even to someone already dead.

Renny could take blame artfully, too—whamming it back the way a tennis pro returns a smartass serve. Like the toilet seat thing.

"I admit I left the seat up, babe. Your house, your rules. But that fuzzy cover on the tank makes it fall down again, and—"

"Shh!"

He smoked in silence, having scored his point. Barb took the cigarette from between his lips, stole two quick puffs, and replaced it as though afraid of being caught tampering with the evidence at a murder scene.

Renny gave up and went to use the bathroom. He left the seat up.

"Barb, there's water all over the bathroom floor. I think maybe your pipes are backing up. Roots, maybe."

"Oh, no! Is it all—you know, messy?"

"Just water. Like a big splash, all over."

"Renny!"

That brought him back quick enough. What a man.

As he skidded in barefoot, he caught Barb shrinking and pointing. Something had just moved near the juncture of wall and ceiling above her cosmetic table. Renny squinted. The something was low-slung, slid along lizard-fashion, and was now watching them both coldly from seven feet up.

"What the hell is it?" said Renny. "A rat?"

"You ever see a white rat with no hair, with eyes that big? Jeeezus, Renny!" Barb could see pretty well in the dark after all. "Where's the bat?"

Renny almost chuckled. "I'll get the damned thing. Whatever it is."

She stopped him, open palm to naked chest. "No you won't, either, Renny. Now, I've been doin some thinking, and you're a nice guy and a good man and a good male protector and all that, and I haven't been holding up my end on this deal, and like you said, this *is* my house…so let me do this. It's my turn."

When Barb let loose with stuff like that it stopped Renny deaf and dumb; how could he even consider dumping a woman this good?

She watched his cigarette glow near the bathroom door. "You just stay right there and hit the overhead lights when I tell you, okay?"

"Yes'm."

"Go!"

The hundred-watter Barb kept in the ceiling fixture blinded them. The thing on the wall recoiled and dropped behind the mirror. Renny and Barb heard it hit the floor and scrabble into the shadows.

"See it?"

"I see it," Barb lied. She shielded her eyes and groped around until she found the bat.

"I don't see it."

Renny could see the tail of Barb's cat, poking from beneath the dresser. It was a miserable calico Renny felt was responsible for every one of his sneezes since he and Barb had linked up. When it wasn't skulking around the kitchen trying to eat everything in sight, it was shedding pounds of hair and clawing the furniture to ribbons. It had some kind of inane cat name Renny could not retain. It didn't listen when Barb told it no. It never had.

It had probably knocked the toilet seat over, numb little fart.

The tail twitched in that spastic way that announced the cat was revving up for the old chase-and-disembowel routine. Barb told the cat *no,* loudly. It didn't listen.

She tried to block it with her foot, but the cat executed a tight dodge and zipped under the dresser, way ahead of her. There followed an unseen, brief and violent encounter that *sounded* pretty awful, though neither Barb nor Renny could see any of it.

The cat's tail whapped Barb in the chest. The cat was no longer connected to it. Tufts of calico fur followed, held together mostly by blood.

Barb began making cave-person noises and wedged herself into the combat zone, dealing short, blind strokes with the bat. The bureau began to scoot with each hit, bunching the area rug.

The intruder darted out from the far side. It looked like a hand.

"Barb, it's a *hand.*"

"What!" Barb backed off, frantic and hollow-eyed. "What! What! A hand? I don't *care!* It hurt my cat!"

"Barb, it ran under the bed." Renny stepped back from the edge, just in case Barb started swinging again.

Hot for combat, Barb spun. "It hurt Rumplecatskin!" The kill light was in her eyes.

She swept aside the dust ruffle. Two eyes returned her gaze from about a foot in. Then it charged, before she could bring the bat into play, and got a tight grip on her throat.

It was Victor's hand, all right. He'd grabbed her throat enough times for her to make a lightning ID. Whatever else had befallen Victor's mortal parts, his right hand was still strong and mean as ever. Barb's wind was cut and in seconds she'd see the purple spots. Victor knew *exactly* how to throttle her.

She collapsed into a heavy, spread-legged sit-down as Renny dived across the bed, not as fast as he could have been. He didn't really want to touch it. The severed wrist terminated in a reddish-white bag of muscle, like the fat, nontapered tail of a Gila monster. Renny grabbed that end and tried to yank it off.

Goddamn it, but this was getting to be much more trouble than *anything* was worth.

Barb's face had shaded to mauve. Renny crawled in tighter, bent back the clutching index finger, and heard it *pop* as he broke it at the base joint.

Shouldn't he just let it polish Barb off? Would this all be over then?

Nope, he thought as he levered the middle finger out of the flesh of her neck. No way he was going to be beaten and humiliated by disorganized body parts. He cocked the finger away savagely and smiled when he heard it snap.

There were eyeballs on the back of the hand, and they swivelled a full one-eighty to glare at Renny. The pupils dilated. Barb was sucking wind in big horsey gasps, her face flushing crimson.

Renny remembered the first time he had ever shaken this hand. Howyadoo. Victor Jacks was the sort of guy whose very existence dared you to be better than him, and promised to humiliate you if you tried.

The thumb and ring finger could not hang on alone; apparently Barb had smashed the pinky, a lucky hit with the bat; it jutted crookedly, alienated from the choking operation. Renny pried the hand free and chucked it across the room as Barb fell down. The hand bounced from the wall to the floor, leaving red impact smears. Clumsily, it tried to locomote.

Barb stumbled over and started stomping on it. She got gook all over her heel, slipped and nearly fell again. This enraged her enough to bash the hand with the bat until it didn't move anymore.

Both of them squatted down at a safe distance and got their first really clear look at it.

Apart from the killer hand and about four inches of forearm, there were Victor's eyes. Eyes that had always been the color of pastel blue enamel, opaque eyes that did not deal in emotional shades, with the hair-trigger flecks of silver buried deep like vague rumors of madness. The eyes were seated across the first three knuckles on the back of the hand, and looked roped down by strings of muscle and threads of optic nerve. One eyeball had just been imploded by Barb's death-dance. At last, Renny could recognize the bulbous bag that hung off the far end of the wrist.

"That's his heart."

The whole assemblage reminded Renny of something that Victor might jerry-rig on his auto workbench. He was known to be miraculous when it came to solving your vehicular woes with a bent coat hanger, spit and a soldering iron.

"His *heart.*" This was not the sort of news Barb was eager to hear. "His *heart,* oh godddd...how could it be his *heart,* they took it *out,* you beat him to *pieces,* didn't you break his hand? *Last* time?"

Renny honestly could not recall.

"I mean...he didn't have no *head,* Renny! What'd the eyeballs do, *roll* here by themselves—?"

As they watched, the heart-end caved in, voiding blood in a final death-spurt. It made a large, wet, wide stain on the finished wood of the now-exposed floor.

It appeared to Renny as though it had farted. It was kind of funny. "Wow. You *really* broke his heart."

She began slapping him. The blows were openhanded and basically harmless. "Renny, goddammit, that's not funny! That's his fucking *hand!* It's been around my throat plenty of times, and for a minute there I could actually *see* him, like he'd come back whole to beat me up again, and *it's not funny!*"

Barb was a pace and a half from an asylum. Her tirade petered out and left her sobbing. Renny did the right thing and tried to hold her. She let him. If he had given her a Kleenex, she would have dislocated his jaw.

"Okay, okay. Sorry I'm such a jerk."

Pangs of selfishness could occasionally make Renny feel guilt, or something like guilt. More important right this minute was the abrupt deduction he'd made while keeping an untrusting eye on the no-longer-moving hand thing.

Victor had been slabbed and gutted...and had come walking back. He'd had all his bones busted and he'd come *blobbing* back. And Renny had dumped Victor in the sewer and Victor had come back again, from the sewer. Up through the toilet, just like those urban legends about scuba-diving rats, and snakes, and crocodiles, all of which the eyeball-hand resembled.

"Look, babe—I know what this thing needs. I'll make sure there ain't nothin left this time."

"And how do you plan on doing that?" Barb had regained enough of her equilibrium to peek at herself in the bureau mirror to ensure she didn't look *too* messed up.

Renny lifted the interloper by its broken pinky. He could feel himself piling up jungle smarts by the minute.

"You got any charcoal starter out back?"

It stank. Truly. It sizzled when it burned, a roundly unappetizing spectacle that Barb forced herself to witness. They both watched it cook down and Renny periodically batted the chunks apart with barbecue tongs until it was reduced to black goo and bone ash.

Barb plodded back inside to take her third shower in twenty-four hours. There was just no washing Victor off her life.

Renny watched the goo smolder and bubble on the coals. Kind of like pork, the smell.

He rubbed the smoke from his reddened eyes and finished up, not really wanting to enter the house again. He no longer wanted to play bed games with Barb. He just wanted to get some sleep.

By the time Barb towelled off, she discovered Renny deep in slumberland. *Igg*, she'd have to change the sheets despite her shower. A job for tomorrow. She sat on what was, de facto, "her" side of her own bed, successfully not waking her partner in crime.

Renny was different, she knew. Their relationship had turned. Flowers decay. Banquets spoil. Water evaporates. And their sneaky victory had soured. At first it had been a delicious, shared secret; now it had become a horrid quickmire that bonded them like a pair of panicked dogs struggling to uncouple.

She felt, well, *dead* inside, to hammer a phrase. Blown out, wasted, spent, scorching at the edges. She did not want to feel anything so much as she wanted to feel nothing.

Renny was sleeping with his mouth unhinged, as usual, just beginning to snore. That snore would tell her that she was far, far away from his thoughts. She gently grabbed his nose and tilted his head so he no longer faced her. The incipient snore died with a gurgle.

She felt unusually sensitized, to the point where the dust on the sheets and comforter bothered her. Grit was in her eyes and she fancied more dust layered upon her soul, like wet snow. The thought that it might be the powder of dead bones made her start crying, and she never stopped.

Caught up in her own grief, she missed seeing the tenacious little gob of charred protoplasm as it wormed past Renny's slack lips, to slide easily down his esophageal tract. Soon it would renew its work deep inside of him, where the heart was.

GOOD PEOPLE

By David Wellington

David Wellington is the author of the zombie novels *Monster Island*, *Monster Nation*, and *Monster Planet*, and the vampire novels *13 Bullets*, *99 Coffins*, *Vampire Zero*, and *23 Hours*. A werewolf novel, *Frostbite*, came out last October. Another zombie novel, *Plague Zone*, was serialized on his website, davidwellington.net, but is not yet in print. Wellington's short fiction has appeared in the zombie anthologies *The Undead*, *The Undead 2: Skin and Bones*, and *The New Dead*, and he also has a story in my vampire anthology *By Blood We Live*. He recently made his comic book writing debut with *Marvel Zombies Return*.

George Romero's 1968 film *Night of the Living Dead* established our modern image of zombies—mindless corpses with pale flesh, wild hair, and dark-ringed eyes who stumble clumsily about, hungering after the flesh of the living. Since then we've seen a vast proliferation of zombie stories and a corresponding increase in their variety. We've seen zombies who aren't technically dead (*28 Days Later*), zombies who sprint after their victims (Zack Snyder's *Dawn of the Dead*), zombie dogs (*Resident Evil*), zombie Nazis (*Dead Snow*), zombie superheroes (*Marvel Zombies*), even zombie strippers (*Zombie Strippers*). We've also seen zombie comedy (*Shaun of the Dead, Zombieland*), zombie romance (Amelia Beamer's *The Loving Dead*), and even zombies invading classic nineteenth-century literature (*Pride and Prejudice and Zombies*). And of course we've seen David Wellington's gonzo *Monster* trilogy, which features smart zombies, superpowers, mummies, and an epic battle for the future of humanity.

But sometimes all you're in the mood for are some good old-fashioned moaning, shambling zombies, which our next story delivers—in spades. Here David Wellington takes the zombie story back to its roots—a bunch of regular folks just trying to survive, figuring out what they're willing to do to make it, and the horrible things they have to do after the end of the world. After all the variations, parodies, and mashups, the classic Romero-style zombie is still alive and well (so to speak) and still, after all these years, coming to get you.

The sun was coming down over the desert, painting the red rocks a hundred different shades of purple, silver, and ocher and making spiky silhouettes out of the few creosote bushes that eked a living out of the barren land. I watched the hot pink clouds scud by overhead for a while before turning my attention back to the fence.

Then my heart stopped beating.

The dead man was only a couple feet away from Candy when I saw him. He was on the wrong side of the chain-link fence but he was leaning on it, hard, and it was starting to sway. His clothes were bleached white by the sun and his skin was gray. His lips had rotted away, like most of his face, and his teeth were huge and yellow and broken until they looked very sharp.

Candy was three years old. She didn't even look up. There'd never been a time in her life when the dead people weren't around, weren't reaching for her, gnashing their teeth at her. There'd never been a time when Mommy wasn't right there to save her.

I wasn't going to let her learn different. Not until she was old enough to hold a weapon.

So I didn't shout at her, didn't scream for the dead guy to back off. I brought up my bow and nocked an arrow. Drew back, nice and steady, and took my time to aim. My bow string twanged but my arrow didn't make a sound as it went right through the chain link, and right through his skull. The point came out the other side.

He fell down in a heap. Silently.

Thank you, Girl Scouts of America, I thought.

I went over to Candy then, to get her away from the corpse. They don't smell so bad anymore—the sun down here dries them out—but you can still get sick just by being near them. And sometimes they aren't as dead as they look.

Candy was squatting down on the ground by the pump house that used to fill up the swimming pool. She had a bunch of credit cards and she had laid them out on the yellow grass, sorting them by color. The plastic had gone white around the edges over time and the silver ink had rubbed off the numbers, but the holograms still flashed back and forth in the sun as I reached down to pick her up.

"Look at the bird," Candy said, pointing at one of them. "It flies if you close one eye, then the other."

"Sure does, pumpkin," I said, and kissed the side of her head.

It's been a year and a half since I saw a bird. I don't know when she ever had, but she knew, birds fly. Birds fly away. People have to stay on the ground, right where they are.

Bruce and Finster came out of the shade of the motel complex wearing gloves and bandanas across their faces. I covered them with my bow while they dragged the corpse into the empty pool and set it on fire. The bottom of the pool used to be painted blue but the paint had chipped away months ago and now the bare concrete showed through. There were black scorch marks like flat craters all over the concrete.

The guys couldn't just drag the body out into the desert to rot away. That would just draw more of the dead—they don't eat their own kind, but once you destroy the brain, all bets are off. Anything that could hurt us, anything that would draw attention to us, was dragged down into the pool and burned until there was nothing left but ashes and bones.

I didn't stick around to watch. I took Candy back to our room instead, to let her play inside where the air might be stuffy but she couldn't just wander away. Then I went into the dark bathroom and stared at myself in the mirror for a while.

I did that every time I killed somebody. I was looking for any sign of fear, or weakness. If I found my lips were shaking I made them stop. If my eyes looked too wide I forced myself to squint. If I had gone white as a sheet I held my breath until my color came back.

I could have been an actress. You know, Before. I was a dancer in Vegas—yes, that kind of dancer—but I was saving my money to go to LA. Then it got overrun and everybody there died. Guess it was a good thing I never got my big break.

This time, when I stared in the mirror, I didn't see anything looking back. My face was there, my cheekbones more hollow than they used to be, lines around my eyes a little deeper. Blond hair bleached by the sun. I looked even skinnier than I used to when I was dancing. But there was nothing there in my face, no expression at all.

I wondered if that was a bad thing. If that was worse than finding signs of weakness there.

Then I decided that was a stupid thing to worry about. Times like these, you learned pretty fast what was important and what was bullshit, and you let the bullshit go.

The rules were that when you even see a dead guy, you had to tell Vance. I headed out, leaving Candy alone where I knew she was safe, and walked down the row of motel rooms toward the reception office, the place he was most likely to be. As I stepped in through the glass doors I found about half of the survivors there. It was the stuffiest part of the motel, and there were no curtains on the windows so the desert light came glaring in, but ever since the dead came back people tend to want to congregate in central places where they can see each other, so reception is always crowded. There were old folks logging in cans of food from the last foraging expedition, and young guys bristling with weapons, just standing guard. Good people, all of them. I've known plenty of the other kind, but we left all of them behind.

Of course Simon was there, tinkering. Just like always. Simon was the only one of us who couldn't walk, because he'd lost both his legs. Whether that happened Before or After, nobody knew, because he didn't like to talk about it, and if you pushed Simon on something he didn't like to talk about he usually started screaming.

He claimed he had Asperger syndrome. When we first met him most of us just thought he was crazy. A lot of us still thought he was a drain on our resources, which is one thing we don't normally forgive. But Vance had refused to leave him behind when we headed south from Scottsdale. Said he would come in useful, eventually.

Lucky guesses like that were what made Vance our leader. Simon, it turned out, had a way with machines. He could take them apart in his head and figure out why they didn't work, and how to fix them. He'd put a truck back together from spare parts back at Scottsdale and that was the only way we got out of that hell alive. The truck had brought us all the way here before it ran out of gas and we couldn't find anymore. When Vance found the motel, with the little creek running behind it, it was Simon who figured out how we could pump water up from the creek and survive in the desert.

Just looking at Simon, you would never believe it. He was maybe fifteen years old. He had a mop of black hair that hung down over his eyes. He was overweight, even after a year and a half of eating no more than I had. His fingers were pudgy and short and the nails were always cut down so far his fingertips bled.

With a couple dozen yards of PVC pipe, though, and some parts from the empty swimming pool's pumps, he gave us running water. He gave us water for cooking, and washing, and even cleaning our clothes. He gave us water to drink in a place where you could die in four hours without it.

When I walked into reception he was fiddling with an old clock radio from one of the rooms, picking at a circuit board with those non-existent nails of his. "I wanna build a radio transponder," he said. "So's the Army can find us. I wanna build a computer so we can get back onna innernet." In many ways Simon still lived in the Before—or maybe he just took the extremely long view, and assumed that this wasn't the end of the world, just a momentary pause in civilization. "I wanna check my website, check my traffic. Traffic—traffic, we can get the traffic lights back on."

Vance stepped out from the back office and nearly tousled the kid's hair. He stopped himself before he actually touched him—Simon does not like to be touched. "Don't worry," Vance said. "You and me, buddy, we're going to rebuild the entire world together."

Simon looked up with an idiotic smile on his face. "I like to build things."

Vance smiled back. "Darcy," he said, turning to look at me. "You have something to report?"

He probably already knew what had happened out at the fence. Bruce and Finster had probably already let him know. But he wanted to hear it again, from me. Vance is not a big guy but you can see in his eyes that he's always thinking. He's always two steps ahead, which is how he keeps us alive. Nobody ever voted for him to be leader, and he didn't have to fight anybody for the right. He led us because he was always on top of things when the rest of us were just trying to survive. "One dead guy, out by the southwest fence. I got him with an arrow."

Vance nodded. "And did you retrieve the arrow?"

"Yeah," I said.

He nodded and reached over to touch my arm. Most guys I've known, they would have grabbed me around the waist, or maybe patted me on the shoulder if they were trying to be PC. Vance squeezed my bicep. "I hear he was going for Candy."

I shrugged. "Not anymore."

He gave me another squeeze, on the strongest part of me. Like he knew. Just somehow he knew what was inside of me, and he approved.

A guy like Vance, back in Before? I wouldn't have bothered giving him a second look. Now I'd move into his room if he just asked.

"Three this month," Simon said, his face curling up. He looked like he might start screaming. "Three: one, two, three."

Vance frowned. "That's right," he said. "More than we're used to."

I shrugged. "Some months we don't see any. Sometimes we get a few. We can handle it."

Vance nodded, but his brow was furrowed and I knew he was thinking of something. He went over to the drinking fountain that Simon had rigged up to be our main water supply. An inch-wide pipe stuck up out of the top of the box, and there was a crank on the side that pulled the water up from the creek. Vance started turning the crank but you could see on his face he was still thinking. "Simon," he said, "is there any way to make that fence stronger?"

The boy started bouncing up and down in his chair. "Yeah, lots of ways! I wanna sink the posts in concrete, and double up on the chain link, and uh, and uh, we could 'lectrify it if we had some solar panels, and there's barbed wire—"

He stopped suddenly, which wasn't strange for Simon. Sometimes he just stopped talking and that was it. He would be silent for the rest of the day. Sometimes it was just a pause while he worked something out in his head.

This time he started screaming.

Vance was still winding the crank. You had to pull hard to get water out of the little trickle of the creek, and sometimes pebbles got in the pipe and you had to crank even harder. This time Vance was really working it, his arm flashing around and around. He'd been too preoccupied to notice why he had to work so hard. Something was in the pipe, something bigger than a pebble.

When he heard Simon scream, he stopped cranking—and then everybody saw what set Simon off. A human finger was sticking out of the top of the pipe, gray and mottled and topped with a broken yellow nail.

"Don't throw up. Don't do it," I said, rubbing Finster's back. When your entire food supply is comprised of tin cans you scavenge out of abandoned dollar stores, you can't afford to waste a meal. Finster was looking green and starting to double over. Slowly he straightened up and started breathing deeply.

"Thanks. I just—ulp." He closed his eyes and turned away.

Simon kept screaming. Sometimes when he got that way he wouldn't stop for hours. This was a kid who used to freak out when his father couldn't find the right brand of chicken tenders for his dinner. The new world was full of triggers, and not a lot of comfort.

Vance grabbed the finger out of the pipe and shoved it in his pocket so nobody would have to see it. "Mike, Joe, I want this system taken apart and all the parts boiled until it's sterile," he said. The two men he'd named rushed over to the water fountain to start disassembling it. They were good people and they didn't wait until things had calmed down to get to work.

"You okay now?" I asked Finster. He'd gotten some of his color back.

"Yeah. But—"

"What?" I asked.

"That thing. That—finger. It means—"

Bruce shook his head. "It doesn't necessarily mean anything. The creek out back flows all the way from Tucson," he insisted. "Some dead guy just lost his finger off the side of a bridge, that's all."

"—or it could mean there's a horde of them downstream, splashing around in our water supply," Finster said.

Everyone looked at Vance. Even Simon stopped screaming long enough to hear what our intrepid leader would say.

He glanced around the room, making eye contact with each of us. Then he shrugged. "We can't afford not to know for sure. So we check it out."

One of Vance's rules was that nobody ever went outside alone. When he decided to form a search party to go check out the stream, he took almost everybody with him. There were miles of canyons and gullies to check out, washes that could hide hundreds of the dead from view that had to be explored. In the end he left only a handful of us behind. Finster and myself, to stand watch and to coordinate the search via radio. Simon, whose wheelchair couldn't make the trip. And, of course, Candy. Candy never left my side.

The morning they left he had me do a radio check for him. Simon had rigged up a solar charger for a set of walkie-talkies we found in an overrun police station, and the radios had gotten us out of some pretty tight spots. We depended on them, but we didn't trust them—you couldn't really trust any technology from Before that relied on electricity. So Vance went up to the top of a hill about a quarter-mile from the hotel, while I went behind the motel's detached laundry building and waited for him to call.

"Are you getting this?" he asked, and I confirmed. "How about now? Good. So we should be back in three days. If it takes longer, I'll let you know."

"I'll be listening," I told him.

"I don't think we're going to find anything. If that's the case, it's still a good excuse to do some foraging, turn up some more cans of food. You sound worried."

"Do I?" I asked. I was surprised. I'd been keeping my voice very carefully casual. "I guess I'm always going to be concerned, when we split up like this." That was one of the first things I'd learned, when this all began: Stay together. Let other people watch your back—you're going to be busy enough watching your front. People who could work together, good people who cared about each other, stayed alive. People who couldn't get along or who wanted to go it alone got weeded out pretty fast.

"Don't be. We'll take the guns, and there'll be enough of us to take care of just about anything. You know I wouldn't put any of us at risk unnecessarily."

"I know."

"I have to say I'm glad you'll be back here, safe. Though, listen—Finster has said some things, when you weren't around. Well, a lot of the guys have. But when you're alone with him, he might try to take advantage of that fact."

"I'm not following," I said.

"I know you can take care of yourself, but… he might… offer his services, if you catch my drift."

I laughed out loud. I couldn't remember the last time I'd laughed. "Well," I said, "in the absence of a better offer, maybe I'll take him up on that."

Vance laughed then, too. "Okay. Just make sure one of you is always watching the fence."

The conversation ended there because we didn't want to drain the radio batteries.

An hour later, the search party left, heading out through the big gate in the fence while Finster and I waved from the roof of the reception building, both of us covering their exit. Vance and his group took all of our guns, but I had my bow. I watched them go for hours, winding in single file down the road that ran alongside the creek, Vance marching along tirelessly at their fore.

"When are they coming back, Mommy?" Candy asked. I had her in a makeshift papoose on my back.

"Real soon."

"We caught a couple of them today, working their way up the creek," Vance said over the radio. "They were eating weeds and cactus, anything they could find." He sounded tired. He'd been gone for only a day but already he'd covered ten square miles. He was pushing himself and his people hard, which made me nervous. "Honestly, Darcy, I didn't expect to see even one out here. But I'm worried these might just be stragglers from a larger group."

"How so?" I asked. I spooned cold baked beans onto a plate for Candy, the walkie-talkie cradled between my ear and my shoulder.

"One of them was wearing a business suit. One sleeve was torn off but his tie was still knotted around his neck. He didn't look like a rancher or a tourist. He looked like somebody who belonged in a big city. I'm worried that we're seeing people from Tucson."

I stopped what I was doing and put down the spoon, careful not to spill any food. "That—would be bad," I said.

When it happened, when the dead came back to life, most people in this part of the country lived in the big cities. There were millions of them packed into small geographical areas. That just meant that when the end of the world came, there was more food for the dead. They rarely ventured out into the desert, which is why we had made our home there. But we had always considered the possibility that the city dead would eventually exhaust their food supply and start wandering out into the country looking for more. The dead are always hungry, and they don't sleep.

"It's too soon to start panicking," Vance told me. "How are things back on the home front?"

"Fine," I said, steeling myself. He was right, there was no need to get worried—yet.

"Finster's been a perfect gentleman. Simon took apart the cash register and now it's in pieces all over your office. He says he wants to build an electric water heater so we can have hot showers."

"It would be nice," he sighed. "All right. I'll check in eight hours from now."

"I'll be listening."

Candy picked up a finger full of beans and put it in her mouth. I watched her face, curled up in concentration. She was still learning such basic things—like how to feed herself. I smiled and she smiled back, then ate some more.

I stood the next watch, during which nothing happened. Candy played quietly while I walked back and forth on the roof of the motel, making long circuits from the rooms back to the reception building to the poolhouse, keeping my eyes open, keeping moving so I didn't fall asleep. The red rocks beyond the fence never changed, and nothing moved. A breeze picked up for a while, which was kind of nice.

When my watch ended, I sank down in a folding chair and sucked some water out of a bottle. Finster climbed up behind me and just stood there for a while, not saying anything, just looking out at the horizon. I wondered if he was looking for Vance, the way I had been for hours.

Then he put his hands on my shoulders and started to rub. "You're tense," he said. "Worried about them?"

"Yeah." I reached up to push his hands away. Then I stopped myself. If something happened, if Finster made a pass, would that be so bad? It would help pass the time. And it had been a very long time since anyone touched me like that. There had been a time when I'd gotten too much male attention, when it had been a drag. But that was Before.

It wasn't like Vance was responding to my veiled hints, after all.

I started leaning my head back, eyes closed, letting things happen. The tension of eighteen months started draining out of me.

Which, as we all know by now, is exactly when the bad things happen. This time, it was the radio squawking. I sat up straight and grabbed for the walkie-talkie.

"We're coming back fast," Vance said. There was a lot of static and he was barely whispering, but my heart raced as I made out his words. "Get everything you can into the backpacks. We're going to have to bug out."

"What did you find?" I asked, whispering myself. Behind me Finster crouched down to try to hear better.

"About fifty of them, all coming up the same canyon. They're spread out pretty loose, and I think I haven't seen them all. There's probably more. Probably a lot more. This is Tucson. Go, now. Get things ready—we won't have time to pack when I get back."

"Understood," I said, and signed off. I turned to face Finster. His face was as white as—well, as white as a dead guy's. "Let's move," I told him.

We cracked open one of the motel rooms we used as cold storage and found the back packs waiting for us on an unmade bed. Ten of them, still half-full of stuff we never bothered to unpack. Bottles of purified water, bags of beef jerky and boxes of hard crackers. Canned food is heavy and if you're carrying your supply on your back it slows you down. Into each pack we put survival gear, camp stoves, thermal blankets, first aid kits. Knives, lots of knives and other basic weapons. As much water as we could shove into the packs. If we were going to walk across the desert until we found another safe place we would need a gallon per day per person. There was no way we could carry enough, but the supply we had would just have to do.

Finster and I didn't talk while we worked. Candy was slung on my back, fast asleep. She learned how to do that very early on. When Mommy's busy, you just go to sleep—that's a survival strategy. Good girl.

I didn't feel bad about having to abandon the motel. It had been a good place, a shelter in a dangerous world, and I had no idea where we would find anything like it again. But the rules of this world are very clear: When you have to move on, you go and you don't look back.

The search party had taken all our guns, which wasn't saying much—they had two revolvers and a .22 pistol between them, and enough ammo to reload once. I had my bow and my quiver and Finster had a slingshot, a high-tech geek toy that could put a ball bearing through a dead guy's skull at twenty yards. We geared ourselves up and hauled the packs out to the motel's courtyard so the search party could just grab and go.

It was only when all that was done that I realized neither of us had been watching Simon. Nobody would expect the boy genius to help us get ready, so I guess we just ignored him until it was time to get him prepared for the move. Vance and Joe, the two strongest men in our group, had a kind of stretcher they had built so they could carry Simon around. It even had a little canopy to keep the sun off of him. Simon hated the thing, though, and we never brought it out until it was absolutely necessary. Just seeing it would be enough to trigger one of Simon's screaming fits.

"He's probably in reception playing with the cable box, wondering why he can't tune in *The Brady Bunch* or something," Finster said, when I asked where Simon was.

"You check there. I'll look in his room," I told him.

But he wasn't in his room. Finster shouted to say he wasn't in the office, either. I jogged back and forth across the parking lot, calling him, but got no response. He didn't seem to be anywhere inside the fence.

Then I spotted him, and I nearly yelped in horror.

He was outside the fence.

Lord knows how he made it all that way, crawling around on his arms. He had the gate open and had crossed both lanes of the highway beyond. There was a stoplight out there that hadn't worked since Before, with a big electrical junction box at the base of its pole. Simon had the box open and was pulling wires out, making neat piles around him sorted by color. I called his name but he didn't even look up.

"Damn it," I said, exasperated. This wasn't the first time Simon had put us in danger, and I doubted it would be the last. I ran over to him, my heart pounding the second I was outside the fence, even though there was no sign of the dead in either direction. I tried to grab his arm and lift him up but Simon just went limp and his arm slithered through my hands. "Simon, come on, we have to go."

"Busy. Busy building," Simon said. "Vance says I can build. Vance says you have to leave me alone while I'm building."

"Sure," I tried, "but right now we need you to build something inside the fence."

"I'll do that later," Simon said.

There was nothing for it. I just didn't have the upper body strength to pick him up and carry him, not when he was going to fight me. I needed to get Finster to help. So I hurried back toward the gate, shouting for Finster to come help.

I don't know if he heard me or not. He was pretty busy just then.

Tucson had come for us.

Hundreds of them. Maybe a thousand.

I hadn't seen anything like it since the last days of Vegas.

Their clothes hung on them in tatters, and their flesh had shriveled on their bones. They must have run out of food in Tucson a while back and desperate hunger had driven them this far. Their eyes were cloudy with sun damage and their skin was covered in sores. Many of them were missing limbs, or at least fingers, but they all had their legs intact. When I saw them I understood what had happened. The fifty Vance had found in the canyons were the slow ones, the ones that didn't keep up.

This was the crowd that could still move at a good clip. The ones that were still mostly healthy, who had gotten ahead of the rest.

You always expect them to be an unruly mob, shoving at each other and snarling at the ones who would rob them of their food. It wasn't like that, though. They were barely aware of each other, but all of them wanted the same thing. They knew Finster and I were inside that fence. They moved in concert, pushing forward all at once. Never making the slightest sound. It was easy for the dead to take us by surprise, because they were as silent as the grave.

They hit the fence like a human tsunami. That side of the fence had been the strongest part—we had reinforced an existing fence there that had been made to keep out coyotes. The dead had no trouble with it at all. It came jangling down and they climbed over what was left.

Finster was working overtime with his slingshot, firing his giant-sized BBs one after the other, grabbing them out of a sack on his belt. He was a crack shot with that thing and he didn't hesitate, but he didn't waste shots either, making sure every round he fired was a clean head shot that took down his target.

I could have run up and joined him, and fired every single one of my arrows into that crowd in the time we had. Even healthy dead people move slow. I could see right away it was pointless, though. Neither of us had anything like enough ammunition. "Finster," I shouted, "stop—you can't get them all!"

"You have a better idea?" he asked me. His eyes looked crazed and I thought he might be hyperventilating.

"Yes! Come on, this way." I grabbed at his arm and he followed.

"Come on. The reception office has the thickest walls, and we can get a couple of doors between us and them," I told him, dashing around the side of the pool's pump house. The dead were hot on our heels but we had no problem outrunning them. I rushed out onto the pool deck with my bow in my hand, an arrow already half-nocked. Good thing, too, because a dead woman in a pantsuit was already there waiting for me. She came stumbling toward me with her arms out, like she wanted to give me a big hug. I put my arrow right through her eye and jumped over her as she collapsed.

"But what then?" Finster demanded. "We just wait for them to go away?"

"No! We wait for Vance and the others to come rescue us," I told him. Why couldn't he see what we needed to do? I saw a dead man wearing a police uniform come stumbling through the weak part of the fence and shot an arrow through his forehead. "Just stick with me, Finster. We'll be okay if—"

Finster screamed. The dead woman I'd put down was still moving. She had grabbed at the leg of his pants as he stepped over her.

He kicked at her furiously, even as her teeth came closer and closer to his flesh. One bite and it was all over—nobody ever survived a bite. I nocked another arrow, but couldn't be sure of hitting her the way Finster was jumping around.

"It's okay, I'm okay," he shouted, as he stumbled away from her. "She didn't get me." She was still crawling toward him so I put another arrow in her ear. That stopped her. "I made it," he said, gasping for breath. "I—"

He wasn't looking where he was going. So happy that he'd escaped a fate worse than death, he didn't watch his step, and he fell into the pool.

I rushed over to the edge of the pool and looked down. He'd fallen into the deep end and he was crying in pain. One of his legs was bent the wrong way.

"Finster, come on, get up!" I shouted at him, and he waved one hand at me to indicate he just needed a minute, that he would get up any time now.

We didn't have a minute. The dead were streaming around the sides of the pump house, coming straight for us. I felt Candy stir against my back as she woke up. Why couldn't she just have slept through this?

I should have left Finster there, of course. That's how it was supposed to work. If you couldn't walk, you couldn't survive. But then, Simon couldn't walk, either. Vance had changed some of the rules. He'd changed who we were. He'd made us into good people again. Given us something to live for.

"Take my hand," I shouted at Finster, thrusting my arm down into the pool. "Take my goddamned hand!"

He blinked away his tears and struggled to get up. When he tried moving his broken leg he screamed in agony.

I looked away to check on the dead. They were very close now. Before I could look back at Finster, he reached up and snagged my arm. I hauled him upwards, pulling so hard I thought my arm might come out of its socket. He got his free hand over the lip of the pool, though, and helped me pull him up.

"Stand up. Lean on me. We have to run, now," I said, once he was out of the pool. "Think of it like a three-legged race, okay?"

He didn't say anything. His face was a mask of pain. But he hopped on his good foot, his arm clutched tight around my shoulders. We were still faster than the dead.

Inside the reception lobby it was dark and cool once I closed all the window shutters. The dead hammered on the steel core door from the outside, their fists banging away at the wood veneer. It was holding, for the moment. I locked it, though I doubted any of them were smart enough to try to turn the knob. Then I headed into the back office, where I'd left Finster and Candy.

I barricaded the door of the reception office as best I could, shoving furniture up against it in a way that might slow the dead down for a minute or two. Candy had fully woken up by that point and wanted to know what was going on.

"Nothing, honey, we're safe," I told her. And she believed me. It's amazing how trusting a three-year-old can be.

I had Finster laid out on the desk, his leg propped up on a pile of old file folders. There was blood on his jeans. That could mean one of two things. Either when he'd fallen his leg had suffered a compound fracture—which was very bad—or that he'd lied when he said the dead woman hadn't bitten him.

Which would be a lot worse.

The only way to find out was to take his pants off, which I didn't have the time or the steady nerves to do just then. I shoved my back up against the wall farthest from the door and sank down to sit on the floor. I just needed to calm down. I just needed to breathe carefully. This didn't have to be the end for us. We could survive this.

I wanted to cry. I wanted to scream and bang on the walls with my fists, and shout for the dead to go away, and tear my hair out, and curl up in a ball, and throw up in horror. I didn't do any of those things, because Candy was watching me very closely.

I could have been a good actress. I could have won an Oscar.

"Darcy," Finster said, his breath coming in ragged spurts, "I want you to know something. I want you to know how I feel, since I may not get another chance, and—"

"Save it," I told him. Which was maybe a little cruel. But I couldn't afford to hear what he was going to say.

I pulled the walkie-talkie off my belt and checked the battery. Still about twenty minutes of talk time left. "Vance," I said. "Vance, if you can hear me, come in." There was no response, so I waited a minute and tried again. After that I waited five minutes before I tried a third time.

Meanwhile I could hear the dead in the lobby. They'd gotten through the door somehow. They didn't make any noise but I could hear it when they knocked over furniture or crashed into the walls. How long did we have?

Not very long.

"Vance, come in, please," I said.

"Darcy? What's going on?"

I closed my eyes and thought about how much I loved that man. This was the man who was going to save Candy. And me. And Finster. "Vance, we have a couple hundred of them here. We're locked in the reception office and can't get out. You have to come save us."

"I can see them," Vance said. "I'm about a mile away."

"Oh, thank God," I said. "Oh, thank you Jesus."

"Stay with me, Darcy," Vance told me. "Is everyone okay?"

"Candy and I are fine. Finster broke his leg, and it's bleeding." I didn't want to say what I suspected, that he might already be dying of a bite wound.

"Understood. How's Simon holding up?"

"Simon?" I asked. As if I didn't know who he was talking about.

"If he's screaming too much, just let him play with his electronics." Vance was quiet for a second. "Why don't I hear him screaming?"

"He's not in here with us," I admitted. "The last time I saw him, he was outside of the fence. Opposite the gate."

Vance didn't respond for a while.

"Vance, come in," I shouted.

"I'm still here, Darcy. Just trying to save my breath. We're moving fast. You say Simon is outside of the fence. Okay. That's good."

"It is?"

Vance sounded determined. Steadfast. "All of the dead are inside the fence. Maybe they didn't see him there. Maybe they just think you're the better meal, since there's three of you." He took his mouth away from the microphone, but I could hear him giving orders. "Joe, Bruce, Phil, get down there and get that gate closed—that'll give us a second or two. Arnold, do you see Simon down there? Take Mary and just pick him up. Don't stop if he fights you, just hold him still and pick him up. Yes, damn it. That's exactly what I'm saying. No, we are not leaving him behind. We need him if we're going to rebuild anything. If we're going to have a future."

"Vance," I called. "Vance, what should we do? I don't think we can get out of here without help. Tell me your plan."

"Hold on, Darcy," he said, and went back to issuing orders.

Outside, the dead started pounding on the office door. The furniture barricade jumped every time they struck. It was loud, very loud in the tiny office, and the air in there started to feel very stale.

"Vance, please. Tell me how you're going to get us out of here," I said.

The radio was silent.

"Vance. Please. Vance, you son of a—"

"We're not, Darcy."

I opened my eyes. Finster was staring down at me. The barricade started to fall apart.

"We can't. We don't have the numbers. If I tried, I would just get all of us killed. I'm sorry. We got Simon to safety, if it's any consolation. He's going to be a big help. He's going to teach us how to build things."

"That's—no consolation at all! Listen, you stupid motherfucker, my baby is in here! My little baby. She's scared, and alone, and—"

"Darcy, it has to be this way. We're going to run away, and hope the dead don't follow us. I think they'll be too busy trying to get at you to notice. Thank you for that. Your sacrifice is going to let other people live."

"My baby, Vance. My baby is in here."

"Call me names. Tell me what an asshole I am. If it helps," Vance told me. "I promise, I won't turn my radio off until I know it's over. But I'm sorry. That's all I can do for you."

"What is he saying?" Finster demanded. "I can't hear him!"

"Mommy?" Candy asked. Three-year-old trust only goes so far, I guess.

I swore and screamed at Vance, then, used every nasty, obscene insult I could think of. Called him a prick. Called him impotent. Called him a traitor and a baby-killer. Thought up some new names just for him.

But I knew. Even as the barricade collapsed and the dead poured into the room—even then, I knew, he wasn't a bad man.

He was good people.

But these are evil times.

LOST CANYON OF THE DEAD

By Brian Keene

Two-time Stoker Award-winner Brian Keene is the author of more than a dozen novels, including zombie novels *The Rising*, *City of the Dead*, and *Dead Sea*, the latter of which shares the same milieu as this story. Other novels include *The Conqueror Worms*, *Castaways*, *Ghost Walk*, *Ghoul*, *Terminal*, *Dark Hollow*, *Urban Gothic*, and his latest, *Darkness on the Edge of Town* and *A Gathering of Crows*. Other recent work includes his new, ongoing comic book series *The Last Zombie* from Antarctic Press. Keene's short fiction—which has been collected in *Unhappy Endings* and *Fear of Gravity*—has appeared in a variety of magazines and anthologies, including the zombie anthologies *The New Dead* and *The Dead That Walk*.

All that remains today of the dinosaurs are their fossilized bones, towering assemblages of which adorn museums around the world. As children, many of us gazed up at these skeletal monsters and imagined what it would be like if all these spines and ribs and skulls and teeth suddenly came to life and tried to devour us.

Brian Keene was likely one of those children. He says, "This story is about cowboys, dinosaurs, and zombies—the three things all little boys love. I wrote this story after finishing a long, serious novel. I usually write something pulpy and fun after finishing something serious—sort of like a palate cleanser."

Science has learned a lot about dinosaurs, who were once thought to be slow, lumbering reptiles unable to cope with a changing climate. We now know that dinosaurs were warm-blooded and agile, that they were nearly wiped out by a devastating meteor strike, and that the survivors evolved into modern-day birds (a fact attested to by beautiful transitional fossils such as Archaeopteryx).

One mystery that remains largely unsolved is what color dinosaurs were. Scientists had long assumed that dinosaurs were green like lizards, or maybe gray like elephants. But in recent years scientists have speculated that dinosaurs may have had more varied, colorful patterns, like certain kinds of snakes. Recent analysis of fossil melanosomes may provide some insight.

The dinosaur skin in our next story, however, could probably best be described as green...and mottled...and rotting.

The desert smelled like dead folks.

The sun hung over our heads, fat and swollen like that Polish whore back in Red Creek. It made me sweat, just like she had. It felt like we were breathing soup. The heat made the stench worse. Our dirty handkerchiefs, crusted with sand and blood, were useless. They stank almost as bad as the desert. Course, it wasn't the desert that stank. It was the things chasing us.

We'd been fleeing through the desert for days. None of us had a clue where we were. Leppo knew the terrain and had acted as our guide, but he died of heatstroke on the second day, and we shot him in the head before he got back up again. We weren't sure if the disease affected folks who'd died of natural causes, but we figured it was better to be safe than sorry. Since then, we'd been following the sun, searching the horizons for something other than sand or dead things. Our canteens were empty. So were our bellies. We baked during daylight and froze at night.

All things considered, I'd have rather been in Santa Fe. I knew folks there. Had friends. A girl. From what we'd heard, the disease hadn't made it that far yet.

Riding behind me and Deke, Jorge muttered something in Spanish. I've never been able to get the hang of that language, so I'm not sure what he said. Sounded like "There's goats in the pool" but it probably wasn't.

I slumped forward in the saddle while my horse plodded along. My tongue felt like sandpaper. My lips were cracked and swollen. I kept trying to lick them, but couldn't work up any spit.

"They still back there?" I was too tired to turn around and check for myself.

"Still there, Hogan," Deke grunted. "Reckon they don't need to rest. Don't need water. Slower we go, the closer they get."

I wiped sweat from my eyes. "We push these horses any harder and they're gonna drop right out from under us. Then we'll be fucked."

Behind us, Janelle gasped at my language. I didn't care. According to the Reverend, it was the end of the world. I figured rough language was the least of her worries.

"The good Lord will deliver us," the Reverend said. "Even you, Mr. Hogan."

"Appreciate that, Reverend. Give Him my thanks the next time you two talk."

Deke rolled his eyes. I grinned, even though it hurt my lips.

We were an odd bunch, to be sure. Deke and I had come to Red Creek just a month ago. We'd bought ourselves a stand of timber there, and were intent on clearing it. Jorge had worked at the livery. The Reverend was just that—had himself a tent on the edge of town and gave services every Sunday. Terry was just a kid. Couldn't have been a day over fourteen. No hair on his chin yet. But he shot like a man, and I was pretty sure that he was sweet on Janelle. It was easy to see why. Women like her were hard to find in the west. Janelle was from Philadelphia. Come to Red Creek after marrying a dandy twice her age. Don't know if she really loved him or not, but she'd certainly carried on when those corpses tore the old boy apart in front of the apothecary like a pack of starved coyotes.

Red Creek wasn't a big town, but it was large enough that none of us had known each other until we fled together. Except for me and Deke, we were strangers, thrown together by circumstance. That made for an uneasy ride.

The first any of us heard of the disease was when a man stumbled into town one night, feverish and moaning. There was a nasty bite on his arm, and a chunk of flesh missing from his thigh. The doc took care of him as best he could, but the poor bastard died just the same. Before he did, he told the doc and his helpers about Hamelin's Revenge. That's what folks back east were calling it, on account of some story about a piper and some rats. The disease started with rats. They overran an Indian reservation back east, which wasn't a surprise, as far as I was concerned. I'd seen the conditions on those reservations, and figured those people would be better off sleeping at the bottom of an outhouse. It was a terrible way to live. The thing is, these weren't no ordinary rats. They were dead. Guts hanging out. Maggots clinging to their bodies. But they still moved. And bit. And whatever they bit got sick and died. Mostly, they bit the Indians. The Indians took ill and died off, and the government didn't seem to care—until the Indians came back and started eating white folks. By then, it was too late.

The man told the doc about this, and then died. Doc got some of the town bigwigs together, and while they were having a meeting about it, the dead fella got back up and ate the doc's helpers. Then they came back and started eating folks, too.

Hamelin's Revenge spread fast, hopping from person to person. Other species, too. Before we hightailed it out of Red Creek, I saw dead horses, dogs, and coyotes attacking townspeople in the streets. And lots of dead people, of course. By then, there were more corpses stumbling around than there were live folks. Lucky for us, the dead moved slowly. Otherwise, we'd have never escaped. Even then, it wasn't easy. They swarmed, trapping us inside the saloon. We had to fight our way out. Burned most of Red Creek down in the process.

How do you kill something that's already dead? Shooting them in the head seems to work. So does smacking them in the head with a hammer or a pick-axe or a length of kindling. You can fire six shots into their chest and they'll keep on coming. You can chop off their arms and legs and they'll keep wriggling like a worm on a hook. But get them in the head, and they drop like a sack of grain.

I glanced up at the sky, squinting. The sun hadn't moved. It felt like we hadn't, either. Our horses shuffled through the sand, wobbling unsteadily. Janelle coughed. I turned around to see if she was okay. She fanned her hand in front of her nose. When she saw me looking at her, she frowned.

"They're getting closer, Mr. Hogan, judging by the stench."

"I know."

"What do you intend to do about it?"

I looked past her, studying the horizon. There were hundreds of black dots—dead things. The population of Red Creek, and then some. Every infected animal had joined in the pursuit, too. I'll give the dead one thing—they're determined sons of bitches.

"I intend to keep moving," I told her. "Stay ahead of them. We don't have enough bullets to kill them all, and even if we did, I reckon they're out of range. Ain't none of us gunslingers. Even if we were, nobody's that good of a shot—not even your boyfriend there."

I nodded in Terry's direction. The boy blushed.

Scowling, Janelle stuck her nose into the air. I turned around again, trying to hide my grin. Deke chuckled beside me.

"She's taken a shine to you," he whispered.

I shrugged. It took a lot of effort to do so. I was trying to work up enough energy to respond, when something ahead of us caught my eye. The flat landscape was broken by a smattering of low hills. It looked like God had just dropped them right there in the middle of the desert. Jorge must have seen it too, because he jabbered and pointed.

"Look there." Deke patted his horse's flank. "We could hole up atop one of them hills. Make a stand. Shoot them as they climb up."

"Until we run out of bullets," I reminded him. "Then we'd be surrounded."

"We could drop boulders on them."

"Don't know about that, but I reckon we'll make for those hills, anyway. Maybe if those things lose sight of us, they'll give up. Or maybe there's something on the other side."

"Water?" Terry's tone was hopeful.

Before I could answer him, the sky got dark. We glanced upward. Janelle screamed. Jorge made a kind of choking sound. Deke and Terry gasped. The Reverend muttered a prayer. I just stared in shock.

The sky was full of dead birds. They moved like they were still alive, circling and careening as one, but slow. Parts of them kept falling off. They stank. The flock headed right for us, dropping down like hail.

"Ride!" I dug my heels into my horse's sides, hoping she had more energy than I did. Apparently she had some reserves, because she took off like lightning, stirring up clouds of dust beneath her hooves. Deke's mare did the same, keeping pace with us. The others rumbled along behind us. I looked around for some cover, but there wasn't any.

"Head for them hills," I shouted. "Might be some trees or a cave."

I glanced over my shoulder to make sure that Jorge understood the plan, and what I saw stopped me cold. Janelle sat motionless, face upturned, gaping at the flock of dead birds. Her horse danced nervously beneath her. Terry held onto her horse's reins and kept his own mount in check. He was urging Janelle to flee, but if she heard him, she gave no sign.

As I rode up to them, Terry fumbled with his shotgun. His hands were shaking and he was having one hell of a time freeing it. I grabbed his arm. He looked up at me and I saw the fear in his eyes. It echoed my own.

"Don't bother," I said. "All you'll do is waste ammunition. Skin on out of here."

He glanced at Janelle. "But Miss Perkins—"

"I've got her. You go on and ride."

He stared at me, clearly reluctant to leave Janelle's side. I reckon he had visions of coming to her rescue and then she'd repay him by sharing his bedroll if we ever found a safe place to make camp, but I went ahead and crushed those dreams. We didn't have time for nonsense.

"Go on, now." I slapped his horse on its rear. "Get!"

It took off after the others, and I turned to Janelle. I seized her horse's bridle and gave it a tug. The mare whinnied, baring her teeth. Janelle did the same thing. I hollered at them both as the birds drew closer. I don't reckon Janelle heard me over the terrible racket the birds were making.

Frustrated, I turned my horse around and kept a grip on Janelle's mount, too. My other hand clutched my Colt. I knew it was pointless as a defense against the birds, but having it in my hand made me feel better. I squeezed my mount with my legs and prodded her on, hoping Janelle's mare would keep up with us.

She did—for about the first two hundred yards. Then fatigue, heat, and thirst took their toll. She stumbled, snorted, and then sagged to the ground. She didn't fall. If she had, that might have been it for Janelle and me both. Instead, the horse sort of eased down. I snatched Janelle from the saddle and plopped her down behind me. She slapped my shoulders, pulled my hair, and insisted we go back for her horse. I ignored her. Gritting my teeth, I spurred my mount on even harder.

I only looked back once. What I saw made me glad and sad at the same time. Screeching and squawking, the birds fed on Janelle's horse, covering it from head to toe, pecking at its eyes and flesh. But they weren't chasing us anymore, now that they had easier pickings.

Deke and the others waited for us. I shouted at them to go on. Wasn't any sense in wasting our momentary advantage. The birds would strip that carcass soon enough. Then they—and whatever was left of Janelle's horse—would be back after us again, along with all those other dead things loping along behind us.

We caught up with them and I found myself in the lead again. Deke and Jorge flanked me. Terry and the Reverend rode along behind. I kept my eyes on the foothills and said nothing, but I noticed the wounded, hurt look that Terry gave Janelle and me.

The day grew hotter. I wished it would rain.

We lost Jorge's horse before we reached the hills. The rest of our mounts were stumbling badly, the last of their strength spent. Jorge wept as he took a hatchet to the poor animal. I wondered how he managed the tears. I was so dry, I couldn't spit, let alone cry. We all dismounted, leading our horses the rest of the way. I didn't much cotton to the idea, but it was either that or let them keep dropping out from underneath us. Janelle complained about having to walk, but none of us paid her any mind, except for Terry, who offered to carry her. He blushed, withering under her scornful glare while the rest of us chuckled at the image of Janelle riding piggyback on his shoulders across the desert.

The terrain changed, becoming rockier. Soon enough, we reached the foothills. Deke stopped us, shading his eyes with his hands.

"Y'all see what I see?"

We looked where he was pointing, and I whistled.

"I'll be damned."

There was a narrow canyon entrance wedged between two of the hills. The landscape seemed to arch over it, and for a moment, it almost looked like a door. Then I wiped the sweat from my eyes and looked again. Nope. No door. Just sloping canyon walls, shadowed and probably a lot cooler than where we were standing.

"Let's make for that," I said. "At the very least, it'll get us out of the sun for a spell, and give us a place to hide. Might even be a stream or a pool."

The others seemed to brighten at this. They picked up their pace. Even the horses seemed to sense that our luck was changing. They trudged forward with renewed strength. I looked back the way we'd come. There were a few birds circling in the haze. From that distance, I couldn't tell if they were dead or not, but they weren't heading in our direction. There were, however, three small objects limping across the desert. Judging by their size and movements, I figured them for dead dogs or coyotes. They were too far away to be any real danger, but I figured we should put some distance between them and us.

We made our way into the canyon mouth, and again, I was reminded of a door. We went single file—Deke and me in the lead, and Jorge and Terry bringing up the rear. A cool breeze dried the sweat on my forehead. I smiled. Despite everything we'd been through, I suddenly felt better than I had in days. Underneath those sloping cliff walls, the sun couldn't touch us. With luck, the dead wouldn't either.

The passage narrowed. There was a slight but noticeable downward descent. It went on like that for a while. Then the walls pressed closer. I was just starting to doubt that we'd be able to squeeze the horses through it when the canyon rounded a corner and opened wide.

I stood there gaping, half-convinced that what I was seeing was a mirage, until Deke cleared his throat behind me.

"Get a move on, Hogan. What's the hold up?"

"See for yourself."

I moved my mount aside so that they could come through. One by one, they walked out of the narrow fissure and stopped, sharing my reaction.

"This sure ain't on no map I've seen," Deke whispered.

"No," I agreed. "I don't reckon it is."

Spread out before us, from one horizon to the other, was the biggest damned valley I've ever seen. It was filled with all kinds of trees and plants—things that had no business growing in the desert. The lush, green foliage was quite a shock after the barren wasteland we'd just crossed. A broad, clear stream ran through the center of the valley—not quite a river, but too big to be a creek. The air in the valley was different. It smelled just like the aftermath of a thunderstorm, and it was more humid, but not as hot as the desert had been. Although we couldn't see any, the trees and bushes echoed with the sounds of wildlife—deep-throated rumblings and shrill bird-calls like nothing I'd ever heard before. Understand, this wasn't just some desert oasis. This was an entire hidden valley, nestled between the surrounding canyon hills. The terrain was unlike the rest of the desert. I couldn't figure out how such a thing could be.

The Reverend must have been thinking the same thing, because he said, "If I didn't know better, I'd think I was back home."

"Why's that?" Terry asked.

"Because it reminds me of the forests back in Virginia."

"It's an oasis," Deke said.

"Too big for that," I told him. "It's a whole valley."

Janelle stared at the treetops, swaying in the breeze. "How is this possible? Wouldn't someone in Red Creek have known about this?"

"Does it matter?" Deke shrugged. "Whether they knew about it or not, we're here now. I reckon the Reverend ought to thank God for us, cause as far as I'm concerned, our prayers have been answered. We've got shelter, shade, food, and water. These trees will hide us from those dead birds."

We led the horses down to the stream. The thick undergrowth slapped our legs and brushed against our faces. Clouds of mosquitoes and gnats buzzed around our eyes and ears, but we didn't pay them any mind. Unlike the dead, the bugs only ate a little bit.

The horses drank eagerly. We did the same, laughing and splashing. The water was cold and clear, which struck me as odd. There'd been no snow atop the hills. Running in from the desert, the stream shouldn't have been so frigid. Drinking it made my teeth hurt, but I didn't care. I gulped it down until my stomach cramped. Then I threw up and drank some more, splashing water across my face.

Whooping, Deke plunged into the stream and waded out until the water was up to his waist. Terry, Jorge, and I stripped off our gear and followed him. I turned back to Janelle and the Reverend, who were watching us from the bank.

"Come on in," I said through chattering teeth. "The water's fine."

"I doubt that." Janelle smiled. "Your skin is turning blue."

"Hell," Deke laughed. "My damn balls are shriveling up."

We all chuckled at that, even Janelle. Terry and Jorge splashed each other. Deke ducked below the surface and came up sputtering. I motioned to Janelle and the Reverend.

"Seriously, y'all should come in."

"I'm fine here," Janelle said. "It wouldn't be ladylike."

The Reverend shook his head. "I'm afraid that I can't swim, Mr. Hogan."

"It ain't that deep," Deke told him.

Before the Reverend could respond, Jorge interrupted.

"What's he saying?" Deke asked.

Jorge put one finger to his lips and cupped his ear with his other hand.

"I don't hear nothing," Terry said.

The bushes along the stream bank rustled. The horses whinnied and glanced around, stomping their feet. I reached for my pistol, realizing too late that I'd left it on the shore with the rest of my gear. Then the undergrowth parted and Janelle and the Reverend both screamed.

I was expecting another dead thing—maybe a horse or a person—but what charged out of the bushes was no corpse. It was the biggest damn lizard I'd ever seen. It stood on its hind legs, towering over the horses, about fifteen feet long from head to tail and probably weighing a ton. Despite its size, the thing moved fast. Arms outstretched, it ran on two legs towards Janelle and the Reverend. Each hand had three fingers. The middle fingers were equipped with claws the size and shape of a grain sickle. It had a big head and an even bigger mouth full of arrowhead-sized teeth. Its tongue flicked the air as it made a hissing, throaty sort of roar.

Shrieking, Janelle dove into the stream. The Reverend ran after her. I noticed that he'd pissed his pants. He paused, glancing back and forth from the water to the lizard, as if trying to decide which one he feared the most.

The creature slashed the throat of Terry's mount. The poor beast took two faltering steps and then fell over. The other horses scattered. As they did, three more giant lizards emerged from the bushes and attacked them. The cries the horses made as they were slaughtered was one of the worst sounds I've ever heard.

We hurried to the far side of the stream while the lizards busied themselves with their kills, tearing and ripping, sticking their snouts into the horses' abdomens and rooting around. I glanced back and noticed that the Reverend had waded into the water up to his knees. He stood there trembling, watching in horror as the lizards feasted.

"Come on," I shouted. "While they're distracted!"

He shook his head.

"Somebody has to help him," Janelle said. "One of you get back over there."

"The hell with that," Deke said, wading onto the shore. "I ain't even going back for my gear. You think I'd go back for him?"

Janelle gasped. "He is a man of *God*."

"Then I reckon God will keep him safe," Deke replied. "Either that, or he'll meet God real soon."

"I'll get him." Terry splashed into the stream.

Cursing, I jumped in after him.

"Hogan," Deke yelled. "Where the hell are you going? Get back here!"

"Our guns are over there," I told him. "We're going to need them."

That was my excuse, anyway. Deep down inside, I wondered if I was doing it for Janelle, instead. I waded after Terry. We made it about halfway across the stream before pausing. The lizards were still eating. So far, they'd ignored the Reverend. He stood there, glancing back and forth between them and us. His chin quivered and his legs shook.

"Come on, Reverend." I waved at him, trying to keep my voice low. The movement attracted the attention of one of the lizards. It raised its bloody snout and snorted, cocking its head sideways and studying Terry and me. I'd been charged by a bull once, while crossing a pasture. The lizard had the same look in its eyes as the bull right before it charged.

"Terry," I whispered, "don't move. Just stay still."

He nodded. The color drained from his face.

"Reverend," I said, keeping my voice calm and steady. "You need to get in this creek right now. It don't matter if you can't swim. Terry and I will carry you. But get your ass over here."

Nodding, he inched forward. The water rippled around his knees. His lips moved in silent prayer. His eyes were closed.

"That's it," I whispered. "Easy now. Nice and slow."

I glanced at the lizards. All four of them watched us now. They stood stiff and tense, ready to spring. One of them was missing an eye. The left side of its face was a mass of scar tissue left over from some long-ago fight.

"Giants in the Earth," the Reverend muttered. "Leviathan."

It was hard to hear him over the churning water. "What?"

"It's a Bible verse, Mr. Hogan. There were giants in the Earth in those days."

"Only verse I know is 'Jesus saves'. Reckon I'll take your word for it."

He stopped, gasping as the water reached his crotch. One of the lizards crept towards the stream.

"C-cold," the Reverend stammered. "It's so cold."

"That's okay. We've got you. Terry, give him a hand."

"Hogan," Deke called.

"Little busy right now," I said.

The lizard on the bank lowered its head and sniffed the spot where the Reverend had been standing. The other three turned away from us and stared into the forest. I followed their gaze and saw why. The three dead coyotes I'd noticed earlier had followed us into the canyon. Now they stood under the tree line, watching us with blank, lifeless eyes. One of them was missing an ear. Another's broken ribs were sticking through its fur. They didn't pant. Didn't growl. They just stared. Flies hovered around them in clouds.

"Oh hell," Terry said.

The Reverend's eyes grew wider. "What is it? What's wrong?"

He started to turn around, but I stopped him.

"Never you mind. Just give Terry your hand. Let's get out of here before they decide to have us for dessert."

As Terry reached for the Reverend's trembling hand, the lizard on the bank leaped into the stream, splashing water over our heads. At the same time, the dead coyotes lumbered into the clearing. The other three lizards went for them. The one with the missing eye seized a coyote in its massive jaws and shook the corpse back and forth.

The Reverend and Terry both slipped, sinking below the surface. They came up sputtering and flailing. The Reverend clung to Terry's shoulders, almost dragging him back down again. The lizard surged forward, squealing. I splashed water at it in an attempt to scare it off, but all I did was make it swim faster.

"Let go," Terry choked. "Can't breathe..."

Sobbing, the Reverend clutched him tighter. They both went down again, and then the lizard was on them, close enough that I could feel its breath on my face. It smelled like rotten meat. Its jaws closed around Terry's head and lifted him out of the water. His legs and arms jittered, and I could hear him screaming inside its mouth. The creature gutted him from groin to neck with one of those sickle-shaped claws, while holding the Reverend beneath the surface with its hind legs.

On the far shore, Janelle, Deke, and Jorge screamed. I backpedaled, unable to take my eyes off the slaughter. The lizard was busy with Terry and the Reverend, and paid me no mind. Neither did the other three. They feasted on the horses and coyotes.

I stumbled out of the stream and shouted at the others to run. Without looking back, we plunged into the forest, panicked and terrified. Soon, the greenery swallowed us.

We made camp inside a hollowed out tree. I'd never seen anything like it before, though I'd heard tell of some big trees out in California, and reckoned this might be like them. It was large enough for the four of us to sit inside comfortably. The top had snapped off at some point, but the trunk was still standing. We were able to fashion a crude roof using leaves and branches. There were bugs inside—beetles and ants and such—bigger than any I'd ever seen, but harmless. Janelle was afraid of them, but she was more afraid of what might be outside.

All we had was what had been in our pockets—a bit of paper and a pencil, Deke's compass, a pouch of chewing tobacco, Janelle's frilly lace handkerchief, some money, and other odds and ends.

It got cold after the sun went down. We had no matches or flint. We huddled together for warmth. Janelle fell asleep with her cheek resting on my shoulder. When she breathed, her breasts rubbed against my arm, soft and warm. That made everything we'd been through almost worth it.

A few lizards passed by, close enough for us to see them. None of them were like the ones from the creek. One was the size of a cow, with a long neck and even longer tail. It sniffed around the base of the tree, but was more interested in eating leaves than it was in us. Another one, a baby judging by its size, had a bill like a duck. One of the creatures shook the ground as it lumbered by. Trees snapped, crashing to the earth. We saw its legs and hind end, but not the rest of it. Some of the lizards had feathers. Most didn't. Right before sundown, the forest got real dark as something flew overhead. I poked my head out and looked up. Through the branches, I caught a glimpse of a flying creature with a fifteen-foot wingspan. It reminded me more of a bat than a bird.

We stayed there all night. We didn't talk much. When we did, it was in short, hushed whispers so we wouldn't attract attention. Janelle and Deke slept. Jorge shut his eyes, but opened them every time there was a noise from the forest. Deke cried in his sleep, but I didn't mention it to him. After all, I cried, too. Only difference was my eyes were open.

"What are they?" Janelle asked the next morning.

"Big damn lizards," Deke told her.

"I know that. But where did they come from?"

"I've got an idea," I said. "Y'all know about these big bones in the rocks that folks dig up out of the ground, right?"

"Sure," Deke replied. "There's rich people who collect them."

Janelle nodded. "They're called fossils—all that remains of the dinosaurs."

"Yeah," I said. "That's the word. I reckon these lizards are living versions of those fossils. They're dinosaurs."

"The Reverend might have disagreed with you on that," Deke said. "He seemed to think they were something out of the Bible. I don't remember any dinosaurs in the good book."

"Well, the Reverend's dead. I don't reckon he'll be any more help."

Janelle frowned. "You should be more respectful of the dead, Mr. Hogan."

"I usually am. But our recent experiences with the dead have soured me a bit. It's hard to be respectful of something when it's trying to eat you."

"But the Reverend wasn't like *those* dead."

"No, he wasn't. I reckon he was one of the lucky ones."

"You're forgetting one thing," Deke said. "I thought dinosaurs were supposed to be extinct."

"Somebody forgot to tell them that."

Jorge glanced at each of us as we talked, clearly trying to follow the conversation. His expression was desperate. I smiled at him. He smiled back and then pointed outside.

"I'm with him," Deke said. "Let's get out of here."

"We need to find our way back to the desert," I agreed.

"But the dead are still out there," Janelle said.

"They're here in the valley, too," I reminded her. "But there aren't any dinosaurs in the desert. Given a choice, I'd rather take my chances with just the dead, rather than worrying about them both."

Deke rubbed the whiskers on his chin. "You remember how to get back to the canyon entrance?"

"No." I shook my head. "I got all turned around when we ran. I was hoping one of you knew the way."

Neither Deke nor Janelle remembered, and when we tried asking Jorge, he just stared at us in confusion and pointed outside again.

"Try your compass," I told Deke. "Let's get a bearing on where we are, and which direction we'll need to go."

He pulled it out, wiped condensation from the lens, and then stared at it.

"What's wrong?" Janelle asked.

"Damned thing ain't working," Deke muttered. "It's just spinning round and round, like it can't find north."

"Let me see." I tried it for myself. Sure enough, the needle just kept spinning in a circle. I handed it back to him. "How much did you pay for that?"

"Five cents."

"That was five cents too much."

"It worked in the desert."

"Well, it ain't working now."

Jorge pointed outside again.

"We can't just go stumbling around through this valley," Deke said. "We'll get eaten."

"That might be so," I agreed, "but we can't stay here, either."

"Then what do you propose, Hogan?"

"I say we head for high ground. The valley is ringed by those hills. I say we get to the top of one of them, and then work our way back down to the desert. Should be easy without the horses."

"That's another problem," Deke said. "With no mounts, how do we stay ahead of the dead once we make it out of here?"

I shrugged. "They're slow. And judging by the shape those coyotes were in yesterday, I'd say the desert has been harder on them than it was on us. Long as we keep moving, we should be able to outpace them. With any luck, they'll fall apart before too much longer."

"And if you're wrong?" Janelle asked.

I didn't have an answer for her. None of us did.

Soon as it was light, we crept outside and held our breath. When nothing charged out of the undergrowth, we relaxed. I shimmied up a tree and got a fix on our location. The hills were there on the horizon, ringing the valley. Pale clouds floated above them, almost touching their tips. I saw a few dinosaurs—long-necked, soft-eyed things with square, blunt teeth, chewing on the treetops. They reminded me of cows. I shuddered, watching them warily. Big as they were, they could have reached me in no time. Luckily, they paid me no attention.

We set off on our trek through the valley. I took the lead, followed by Deke and Janelle. Jorge brought up the rear. We went slowly, communicating with each other through hand gestures. The forest was full of animal noises, but they weren't sounds that I recognized. There were croaking, raspy grunts and long hisses and chirps that sounded almost, but not quite, like birdsongs.

The first sound we recognized was a tree snapping—a loud crack, like a schoolmarm's paddle smacking someone's behind. We couldn't tell which direction it was coming from. Then we heard it crash to the ground. The forest floor vibrated with the impact. Another tree snapped. We caught a glimpse of the thing—a tail as long as a stagecoach and hind legs taller than a barn. It was walking away from us. We hurried straight ahead, not wanting to attract its attention. We moved so fast that we didn't see the dead dinosaur until it lurched out of the undergrowth.

Janelle's shriek echoed through the valley. Deke and I dove to the side. Jorge stood there gaping as it towered over him, staring down at him with one good eye. I recognized the lizard right away. It was the same one we'd encountered the day before. The missing eye and the scars on its face were unmistakable. When we'd last seen it, the dinosaur was still alive. Apparently, the dead coyote it had eaten hadn't agreed with it, because now it was dead—infected with Hamelin's Revenge. It already stank. A swarm of flies hovered around it. Its movements were sluggish, but it was still quick enough to catch Jorge. He tried to run, but it swiped at his back, plunging its talons into his skin and lifting him off the ground. Jorge jerked and jittered like a drunk at a square dance. He opened his mouth to scream and vomited blood instead. The lizard's claws burst through his chest. Then the dinosaur ripped him in half.

I grabbed Janelle's hand and forced her to run with me. Deke was at my side, breathing heavily. His cheeks were flushed. I wanted to ask him if he was all right, but couldn't spare the breath. We plunged through the greenery, heedless of where we were going or what was around us. One-Eye lumbered after us. We couldn't see him, but his steady, thudding footfalls kept pace.

The ground started to slope upward. The trees tilted forward, then thinned out. Janelle stumbled and fell, but I scooped her up in my arms and continued on. Deke's face turned beet red. He was drenched with sweat.

"Not much farther," I panted. "Just keep climbing."

They nodded. Janelle tapped my shoulder, indicating that she wanted down. She was wobbly when she first tried to stand, but soon regained her footing. We scrabbled upward. The vegetation thinned to scrub, and the soil turned rocky. Huge boulders thrust from the earth. I glanced back down into the forest and saw treetops swaying back and forth as One-Eye passed beneath them. Then he lurched into sight. Without pausing, he started up the hill.

"It's no use," Deke sobbed, mopping his brow with his shirttail. "That thing's dead. It won't tire. It'll just keep coming until we tucker out, and then get us."

"I ain't gonna let that happen," I said.

"Well, how do you reckon you can stop it?" Deke glanced back down at the dinosaur, creeping closer but still a long way off. "We ain't got any weapons."

"Sure we do." I smiled, patting the boulder next to me.

"Hogan, you've lost your damned mind." Deke stumbled to his feet. "What are you gonna do? Spit at it?"

"No. When it gets closer, I'm gonna drop this rock on its head. That was your idea yesterday, remember?"

"Will that work?" Janelle asked.

I shrugged. "Depends on whether I hit him or not."

We waited for it to get closer. Janelle got nervous, but I calmed her down, assuring her that my plan would work. And it did. When the dinosaur was right below us, close enough that we could smell it again and hear the insects buzzing around its corpse, Deke and I rolled the boulder out over the ledge and dropped it right on the lizard's head. There was a loud crack, like the sounds the snapping tree trunks had made. One-Eye sank to the ground. The boulder tumbled down the hillside. After a moment, the twice-dead dinosaur did the same.

Cheering, Janelle and Deke both hugged me. Then, before I even realized what was happening, Janelle kissed me. Her lips were blistered and cracked from the sun, but I didn't mind. I pulled her to me and kissed her back. We didn't stop until Deke cleared his throat.

"We ought to get going," he said. "I reckon there will be more like him coming along shortly."

"You're probably right," I agreed. "Let's go. I'll race you both to the top."

We scrabbled to the summit, laughing and talking about our good fortune. It occurred to me that we should feel bad about Jorge and the others, and I did, of course. But at that moment, I was just happy to be alive, and even happier about that kiss. I felt something I hadn't felt in a long time.

Hope.

That sensation crumbled when we reached the summit. We stood there, unable to speak. Janelle began to cry. Instead of desert, spread out before us was more forest—an endless sea of green treetops swaying as things passed beneath them.

"No," Deke whispered. "This can't be right. This ain't on any of the maps."

I put my arm around Janelle. "I don't think we're on the maps anymore, Deke."

Deep in the valley below, something roared. I glanced over my shoulder. Another dinosaur emerged from the forest. Its head was as big as a full-grown buffalo and its teeth were the size of tent pegs. It was obviously dead. It might have escaped extinction, but it couldn't escape Hamelin's Revenge. Death is funny that way. In the end, it gets us all.

As we ran, I wondered if, one day, folks would dig our bones out of the ground like they had the dinosaurs, and if so, which kind of dead we'd be.

PIRATES VS. ZOMBIES

By Amelia Beamer

Amelia Beamer works as an editor and reviewer for *Locus Magazine*. She has won several literary awards and has published fiction and poetry in *Lady Churchill's Rosebud Wristlet, Interfictions 2, Red Cedar Review*, and other venues. As an independent scholar, she has published papers in *Foundation* and *The Journal of the Fantastic in the Arts*. She has a B.A. in English Literature from Michigan State University, and attended the Clarion Writers Workshop in 2004. Her first novel—a zombie tale called *The Loving Dead,* which she describes as "a darkly humorous story of sex, relationships, and zombies"—was published this summer. Our next story is set in the same milieu.

Many people dream of owning a yacht. Who wouldn't revel in the freedom to sail the seas while enjoying all the amenities? Problem is, yachts are kind of expensive—the world's largest yacht, the 525-foot Project Platinum, owned by the Crown Prince of Dubai, is estimated to cost upwards of $300 million. In 2004, a former child actor named Skylar Deleon (who once starred on *Mighty Morphin Power Rangers*) took a yacht out for a test drive, then tied the yacht's owners to the anchor and threw them overboard. That's one way to get a yacht—at least until you get arrested and sentenced to death.

If people are willing to do stuff like that to get their hands on a yacht now, just imagine what they'll be doing when boats become the only way to put some distance between you and the zombie-infested mainland. This strategy may not always work out, of course—just take a look at the ending of Zack Snyder's 2004 remake of *Dawn of the Dead*, in which the survivors forsake the safety of a shopping mall for the freedom of the open seas, with unfortunate results.

As the title implies, our next story is a tale of piracy (and zombies) on the high seas, a warning about how, in a disaster, empathy is often the first casualty, and a reminder that though a plague of zombies may sweep away the world you knew, the person you are and the problems you face often stay depressingly the same.

The noise a zombie makes when it's eating someone is a lot like the sound of drunk people having sloppy sex—grunting and moaning and wet smacking.

Kelly was in a rowboat below, eating people. You couldn't help but hear it, over the sound of water against the ship.

We hadn't known there was a rowboat down there. We hadn't known he'd turn into a zombie. What were we supposed to do? When your friend turns into a zombie, you have to do something. We'd grabbed him by his hands and feet and swung him like you swing a little kid. And then we flung him into the water. Only he didn't splash. He thudded. We looked down over the side of the ship and swore. The person he'd landed on was smashed so badly, we couldn't tell if it had been a man or a woman. The other person in the rowboat had fainted.

"Sorry!" we'd called.

Both of the people in the rowboat woke up before they died. They screamed. *We* screamed. And then we vomited off the side of the ship, until our stomachs heaved dry and our noses ran and our eyes watered.

"Did you bring water?" we asked one another. "Where is the water? Who has Kleenex?"

"When was I supposed to get water?" we asked. "Before or after the customers started rioting? When we were running to the car, or running to the pier?"

We took stock of the ship. Ten paces from front to back. No cabin, no facilities, no supplies. No water. It was the only ship left. A replica of the *Niña*, Columbus's ship. The sign had said so, when we'd stolen it.

Our phones didn't have service. No one knew we were out here. We wiped our faces on our sleeves and spat. One of us had a box cutter. We supposed we could use it to open our wrists, if we had to. We sat down to wait for help. The sun was setting, and it was going to be a cold night.

It takes a while to eat a person. This would be the last thing that Kelly taught us. At Trader Joe's, he'd trained us, and introduced us around, and let us know who was friendly and who wasn't. He'd brought us to the bay, too, after people had started turning into zombies in the coffee aisle. Maybe zombies could swim, he'd said, but it would be a lot easier to defend your territory on a boat.

Now there were three zombies in the rowboat. They were quiet but for a soft moan now and again, like the sounds we all made when hung over. The whole bay was foggy with screaming. Boats of all sizes littered the water, motoring or drifting. There were screams from the Emeryville shore, and the Berkeley shore, and from Oakland further south and inland, and we thought we could hear them from the Bay Bridge, and Treasure Island, and across the water from San Francisco. The world was over, and it wasn't even 2012 yet.

We were thirsty. We looked over the side, at the rowboat. It was starting to drift away. There were gallons of water in it. Safe, plastic gallons. Plus backpacks that surely had clothes and first aid gear and food. Bedrolls. Oars. Those people were far better prepared than we were, and see what it got them. We looked at one another, but the decision had already been made. Help wasn't coming. If we were going to survive, we had to lower our standards.

We lowered a length of rope, cooing and beckoning to the zombies. Kelly grabbed onto it, and started climbing up. He'd lost his glasses, but maybe zombies weren't nearsighted. We swung the rope away from the boat and let it go, dropping him into the water.

Turns out zombies can't swim. So we did the same thing to the other zombies. They sank. That was the one thing the ship had: rope. We took turns climbing down a rope and taking the water and gear from the little boat, like the Grinch stealing Christmas. And it felt like Christmas, after; we had enough supplies to last a few days. Plus we didn't drop each other.

We cleaned up, and then we did something secret. We gave ourselves pirate names. Juicy Liu, Highwater Mark, and Justin Case. It seemed fitting. We'd stolen a boat. We'd killed Kelly. (Twice.) That made us pirates.

We were no longer the kind of people we thought we were, so we had to give up something.

Juicy volunteered to take the first watch. She wouldn't be able to sleep anyway, she said. But then she kept me and Highwater up, singing, "*A three-hour tour*" over and over. She didn't know any of the other words, so she kept singing those. When she got bored of that, she sang, "Row, Row, Row Your Boat." Voices from neighboring boats joined in. For the first few minutes, it made me believe that humanity could survive.

I dozed but came awake when she nudged me with her foot. The singing was over. Juicy snuggled into my bedroll. I paced the deck, understanding why someone would sing. It's like making noise when hiking, to warn the rattlesnakes. If you were singing, you were too crazy to be bothered.

So I started singing. Christmas carols, because I couldn't remember any other songs. Then James Taylor, the Beatles, Dylan. I found that I knew all of the lyrics to "In da Club" by 50 Cent, so I shouted those a few times. I thought I heard Kelly rapping with me. That was impossible, but I looked for him anyway. The water was calm and unbroken.

I woke Highwater as the sky started turning a friendly blue. I hadn't seen dawn in ten years or more, not since early morning marching band practice in high school. I watched the sky warm while I lay in Highwater's bedroll, and I remembered how everyone, even cute girls, looked lumpy in band uniforms. Girls with their hair up in the uniform hats, like librarians. Librarians with chin straps. Marching in formation with books in their mouths instead of clarinets.

"No way Columbus sailed the ocean blue on this thing," Juicy said. "I don't even *know* anyone who can sail a square sail. It's *got* to have an outboard motor."

I squinted against the light. Juicy was beautiful. It's funny, I had no recollection of her previous name, and no desire to remember. Whatever it was had never suited her.

"But where are we going to go?" Highwater was sunburned and he smelled like the kitchen of a Long John Silver's at the end of the night.

I could still see the empty dock, far off the port bow. Unless it was the starboard bow. I wondered which way it worked. If it was like stage directions.

"Avast!" a voice called. Down below, in the water, there was a little man in a little motorboat. He pointed a little handgun at us.

We put our hands up, trained by cop dramas.

"Put your hands down. D'ya think I'd have bothered you if I thought you had weapons?" he said. He had a smile like a fighting dog. "Just toss your supplies over, water and food, blankets, first aid, whatever you got. Sunscreen, especially." He wore sunglasses, the bastard, but his bald head was a deep, painful pink. "I mean it," he said. "I don't want to waste my ammo."

"Okay, okay, give us a minute," Highwater said. Always the fast thinker. "What do we *do?*" he whispered.

I found that I was very thirsty. "We're pirates," I said.

"So…what?" Juicy whispered. "We *parlay?*"

I squirmed out of the bedroll, came to the edge of the boat. "Let's join forces, man," I called. "We're resourceful folks, the kind you want on your side. We stole all of this stuff ourselves, and dispatched three of… You know. Those things!" Nobody had said the Z word yet, and I didn't want to be the first.

The little man shot his little gun. The three of us on the *Niña* hit the deck—was that where the phrase came from?—and waited. My ears rang.

"I mean it," the little man shouted.

"Okay, you win," I called.

So we lost our supplies, and the little man motored off.

"This can't be a full-size ship," Juicy said. It's maybe ten-twelve paces from bow to stern."

"Maybe it's a scale model," I guessed.

We were going to die of thirst. Unless one of us turned into a zombie out of nowhere, the way Kelly had, and then we'd die of being zombies. Maybe dying of thirst wasn't the worst way to go. The *worst* way to go, I thought, was being lashed head-to-head with a decomposing skeleton, and left to starve. Some king did that to his enemies, back in the day when people could do things like that and not get put on trial for being a terrorist. Although probably you'd still just die of thirst.

We searched the place, now that we had daylight. We didn't find any water, but we found a whip, lashed to the wall below deck. (Whether it was a full-sized whip, or just to scale, I don't know.) It was big. I went to show off and hit myself in the ear. It didn't even snap.

Back when phones and the Internet still worked, people on Twitter had said that you could use whips to control the zombies. That, and how zombieism was an STD, incubating before it turned its victims. Those people had to be zombies by now, due to their total lack of bullshit detectors. But we were thirsty enough to try anything. Juicy took the whip from me. She switched it without hitting herself. It popped like when Indiana Jones does it. She called for Kelly.

A few minutes later, Kelly bobbed up out of the water. So maybe zombies *could* swim. Maybe they were just lazy. They needed external motivation. Juicy talked to him, using the whip for punctuation. She said his name. He still responded to it, which didn't bother any of us, though maybe it should have. He knew *our* names at one point. Someone did.

Kelly climbed up the rope we dangled down for him. He stood, dripping onto the deck, eyeing us as if we were a hundred dewy virgins. He looked that way at all of us, which probably upset Juicy. He didn't seem to remember that they'd been together. But it was nice to have him back. I told him so, but he didn't say much.

"We need you to attack them," Juicy said, pointing. She'd picked out a nice little motorboat, the kind that has a cabin with refrigerators and beds and a big-ass water tank. Kelly made a noise like the Incredible Hulk, and wiggled his hips like Elvis. I think he still loved Juicy.

She told him to go wait in the water, and act like he was drowning. With luck, he wouldn't look dead that way. He smiled at Juicy, and he went.

It was like bioterrorism, what we were doing. It was like giving smallpox-infected blankets to the Native Americans. It was like taking someone else's towel off the hook on the locker room wall when they're in the shower because yours got wet—it was just plain mean.

We waved to the motorboat. We pointed to Kelly. We pointed at the rigging. Or the spar. Or the mizzenmast. Whatever the sail was attached to. There was no wind.

The elderly couple understood, and they motored over to where Kelly bobbed and waved. They seemed like such nice people, helping out a stranger like that. We reminded ourselves that it was us or them.

The couple threw out a rope. They pulled Kelly out of the black water, and by the time they dropped the rope and backed away, he was wiggling onto their deck. And then it was like an L. L. Bean catalog gone terribly wrong: flannel tearing and sensible shoes flying.

While Kelly ate, we argued about whether we should have done something differently.

We called our new home the *SuperBall*. It'd had a different name before, but the paint got messed up when Juicy pulled the boat up next to the *Niña*. She's never been good at parallel parking. But you should have seen her, boldly swimming over to get the boat, with the whip in her teeth, her clothes all wet and clingy. It was all Highwater and me could do not to jump on her, once we got aboard the boat. I saw the way he looked at her, and he saw the way I looked at her. We were both ashamed of ourselves, going after Kelly's girl. Although it wasn't like he was taking care of her anymore. And he'd always been flirting with other girls. Rumor had it he'd been screwing around.

We let the old couple stay. They obeyed the whip, like Kelly, and it was their boat, after all. We started calling them Homer and Marge, which are terribly old-fashioned names when you think about it. Their hair was thin and fine and pale, and both of them were balding. They wandered around on the deck, moaning. They were always together. Groping each other, even. Kelly followed them around, but they ignored him.

Us pirates stayed inside the cabin. That way, all of the other boats that went past would think that we were already a ghost ship. We would be safe.

Back on shore, it would be like every zombie movie you've ever seen. Here it was peaceful. We played with the Ouija board we found, but we couldn't contact any ghosts. You'd think with this many dead people around we could find a ghost willing to talk. We checked the radio, but no one would talk to us on that either. Or maybe the batteries were dead. I taught Juicy some hymnals that I remembered from *O Brother, Where Art Thou?* Also the chorus of a screamer by this band Lordi called "The Night of the Loving Dead." I couldn't remember any of the words except for the title, but I sang it and she smiled.

Even then I knew. She'd already chosen Highwater. They hadn't even kissed yet, not in front of me, but I knew. It shouldn't have bothered me, but it did.

Juicy asked me to go outside. The look she gave me when she closed the door told me she knew how I felt. Her eyes were wet with desire. Or maybe grief. Or need. She couldn't stop herself; she was trying to tell me.

I paced, waiting for her to open the door. I wanted to call out her name—her *real* name—but the only one I could remember was Kelly's. I opened my mouth to say it, just in case. Then I heard grunting and moaning and wet smacking.

THE CROCODILES

By Steven Popkes

Steven Popkes is the author of two novels: *Caliban Landing* and *Slow Lightning.* His short fiction has appeared in *Asimov's Science Fiction, The Magazine of Fantasy & Science Fiction, Twilight Zone Magazine, Science Fiction Age, Realms of Fantasy, SCI FICTION*, and in the annuals the *Year's Best Science Fiction, The Mammoth Book of Best New Science Fiction*, and *Year's Best Fantasy*. His story "The Color Winter" was a finalist for the Nebula Award. He is currently working on a novel about flying witches.

When it comes to horror, Nazis and zombies are like peanut butter and chocolate—very *evil* peanut butter and chocolate, that is. Dr. Mengele's gruesome experiments on living subjects, German technological prowess—as demonstrated by the V2 rockets—and Hitler's obsession with supermen and the occult make it all too easy to imagine fiendish Nazi experiments reanimating dead soldiers. A well-known example is the video game *Wolfenstein*, in which you play a lone American agent who must penetrate secret Nazi labs crawling will all manner of grotesque monstrosities. The recent horror movie *Dead Snow*—which features a memorable scene in which one of the heroes chainsaws off his own arm after it is bitten by a zombie—is about a group of tourists who inadvertently awaken a colony of frozen Nazi zombies left over from World War II. It must be said that these examples, and several others we could name, are pretty campy, with Nazis used as a convenient shorthand for faceless evil.

Our next tale is a completely different sort of story. This is a tale told from the point of view of a World War II-era German scientist, a man who loves his wife and child, which makes his inhuman detachment about his work all the more chilling. This is Nazi zombies as high art, a tale so full of plausible-sounding scientific and historical detail that you'll start to wonder if maybe these sorts of experiments were real after all.

I could not make a silk purse from a sow's ear. But I went over the data again to see if I could find a tiny tatter of bright thread in the otherwise disappointing results. There had to be a better use of a well-educated chemical engineer than cannon fodder. Willem, my wife's uncle, called me.

"Max," he said, a happy disembodied voice over the phone. "Very sorry about your work and all that. How was it going?"

It didn't surprise me he already knew. "We didn't get the results we'd hoped for," I said. "But there are other areas in the war effort where fuel filtration research would be entirely applicable. Aircraft engines, for instance—"

"No doubt," he said, chuckling. "However, by an astonishing coincidence I was planning to call you anyway. I have a good use for your skills."

"Oh, really?" I said with a sinking feeling. I had no desire to work for the Gestapo. Uncomfortable work at the very least.

"Yes. There's a Doctor Otto Weber doing some very interesting biological work in Buchenwald. He can use your help."

"What sort of work?"

"I'm sure I'd be the wrong person to discuss it with you, not being a scientist or an engineer. I'll work out the details of the transfer and send round the papers and tickets."

"I really ought to find out how I can be of service—"

"There's always the regular army. I'm sure a man of your caliber—"

"I'll be looking for your messenger."

"Fine. Oh, and Max?"

"Yes?"

"Weekly reports. On everything and everybody. All right?"

"Of course," I said.

You don't argue with the Gestapo. Even my Elsa's uncle.

Otto Weber was a thin, elderly gentleman. Once he had been quite tall. He was now stooped with age. His eyes were washed out and watery, like blue glass underwater. But his hands were steady as he first lit my cigarette, then his own.

Weber called them *tote Männer.* Once he showed me their decomposing condition and single-minded hunger, I thought the term apt.

Weber was brought the first host in 1938 and had to keep the disease alive with new hosts from the Gestapo—which they were always willing to supply, though in small lots so he never had more than a few laboratory subjects at a time. He was never told where that first host came from but he surmised South America. Later, in 1940 when the laboratory was at Buchenwald, the Gestapo supplied him with a slow but steady trickle of Gypsies.

What he had discovered when I joined the project in 1941 was that infection was only successful by fluid transport from the infected host, infection was in two phases, and there were at least two components to the disease.

In one experiment, Weber took fluid from a *toter Mann* and filtered three samples, one through a 100 micron filter, one through a 50 micron filter, and one through a Chamberland filter. The 100 micron wash caused full infection. The 50 micron also caused a partial infection involving quick and sudden pain, followed by an inevitably fatal stroke. He called this partial infection type I-A. The Chamberland wash caused a particularly quick and virulent form of rabies—Weber referred to that as type I-B. Hence, Weber's hypothesis of two components for a full infection, one large and the other the rabies virus. He had isolated a worm as the possible large component in that, when collected and washed of any contaminants, it seemed to cause an I-A infection similar to the infection caused by the 50 micron wash. When the Chamberland wash was recombined with the worm, full infection ensued.

Weber had even characterized the partial infections and the stages of the full infection. I found it interesting that the partial infections were both dismal, painful affairs, while the full infection showed up first as euphoria, followed by sleepiness and coma. The subject awoke in a few days as a *toter Mann.*

Even so, I was surprised that there hadn't been more discovered in four years. After all, Weber had the *tote Männer* themselves and their inherent ability to infect others. The Gestapo was willing to provide a constant, if limited, supply of hosts. But Weber's horror of contagion was so strong that every step had to be examined minutely until he had determined to his satisfaction that he could properly protect himself and his staff. Dissection was a long and tedious process; vivisection was almost impossible. I suppose I could not blame him. Even a partial infection would be fatal and full infection always resulted in another *toter Mann.* No one wanted to risk that.

Thus, my first task was the design and construction of a dissection and histology laboratory where Weber could disassemble the subjects in safety. It was not a difficult task. I came to Buchenwald in July. By the end of the month I had the design and began construction. Weber dissected his first wriggling subject by the first of September.

My fuel work had been much more interesting. It was exacting, exciting work with great applications. Here, I was barely more than a foreman. The war in Russia seemed to be going well and I wondered if I should have protested more to Willem.

But Elsa and our son Helmut loved Weimar. The city was pretty in a storybook way. It didn't hurt that the bombers left Weimar largely undisturbed, instead striking in Germany proper. It lent the city a relative calm. Several young couples had taken over the empty housing. This was early in the war and food and petrol, though rationed, were still plentiful.

I didn't work weekends and the three of us spent many summer days in the Park on the Ilm. It occurred to me, during those pleasant hours watching Helmut playing in front of Goethe's House, that this was, perhaps, a better use of my time than the factory or the lab.

Within a week of opening the new facilities, Weber made some astonishing discoveries. Histological examination of the brain tissue of the *tote Männer* showed how the worms nested deep in the higher functioning brain—clearly explaining why there were only *tote Männer* and not *tote* rats and *tote* cats. He speculated that there could be *tote* gorillas and *tote* chimpanzees and went so far as to request animals from the Berlin Zoo. The Zoo was not cooperative. Weber reconsidered his New World origin of the disease and attributed it to Africa or Indonesia where the great apes lived. It stood to reason that a complex disease found suddenly in humans would require a similar host in which to evolve prior to human infection.

However, the worms were only one half of the disease. The virus followed the nervous system through the body, enabling worm entry into the brain but also enabling the growth of strong cords throughout the body. This was further proof of the two-component infection model Weber had developed. In the case of partial infections of the worm or the virus, the process only went so far. Forced by the absence of the virus to remain within the body's major cavities, the worm caused fevers and paralysis, blocking blood vessels mechanically, causing a heart attack or stroke. The virus enabled the worm to penetrate directly into the brain, leaving the heart and circulatory system intact—at least for a while. Without the worm, the virus merely crippled the nervous system, causing fevers, seizures, and great pain. The cords only appeared when both were present. Weber was convinced by the pathology of the disease that the *tote Männer* virus was a variant of rabies, but the biological history of the virus, the worm, and the virus-worm combination was mysteriously speculative.

I dutifully reported this to Willem, along with descriptions of Weber, his assistant, Brung, and his mistress, Josephine, whom we had met at dinner in Weimar earlier in the summer. Unsure whether Willem's desire for detail extended to the subjects, I included the names of the last couple of Gypsy hosts left from the Buchenwald experiments and the newer Jews we had appropriated from the main population of the camp. Weber was curiously reluctant to use the handicapped and mentally deficient and he hated using Poles. Perhaps this stemmed from some event in his past of which I was unaware.

Willem paid his niece a Christmas visit, visiting our laboratory only coincidentally. He was impressed with our progress. "With the *tote Männer* we will crush Russia," he said over drinks that evening.

Weber paled. "There will be problems using the *tote Männer* in winter," he said obliquely.

"Eh?" Willem looked at me. "Speak plainly."

"The *tote Männer* cannot thermoregulate. This doesn't show up in laboratory conditions but below ten degrees Celsius the worms do not function properly. By freezing they die and the host dies with them."

Willem considered that. "We can clothe them."

Weber grew excited. "They do not generate enough heat. Humans maintain temperature. Cats maintain temperature. Crocodiles do not. They do not eat—the hunger for brains is no more than the desire of the disease to perpetuate the infection—the way horsehair worms cause crickets to drown themselves. They do not consume what they put in their mouths. Metabolism keeps the body temperature above ambient somewhat like large lizards. Clothing lizards would have no more effect than clothing *tote Männer*."

"I see," Willem said. He patted down his vest until he located his cigarettes and lighter. "I'm going out on the porch for a smoke. Max, will you join me?"

Weber looked as if he'd swallowed a lemon. He rose as if to join us but Willem waved him back. "Don't bother. This gives Max and me a chance to exchange a little gossip."

Outside, we lit our cigarettes and watched the snow fall.

"It's true what Weber said? We can't use them as soldiers?"

I thought for a moment before answering. "Comparing them to crocodiles is apt. You can't make a soldier out of an animal. And it's too cold for them in the east."

"Then what good are they? Is this all for nothing?"

"I did not say they could not be a weapon."

"Tell me."

"The crocodile simile is better than you know. They are very fast and very strong. There is so little to their metabolism that they are hard to kill. And they are terrifying—you've seen them. You know. We must be able to make some use of them." I shook my head. "I don't know enough yet. I need to perform some experiments. Weber has discovered the basic science. Now it is time to apply some German engineering."

Willem nodded. "I'll do what I can." He grimaced. "Two weeks ago the Japanese attacked the Americans. The Americans declared war on Japan. We declared war on each other. They allied themselves with the British, which brings them into the war in Europe."

"The Americans are too far away. They don't have the strength of mind to make much difference."

"So we thought in the last war. The point is I may not have much time to give."

The goal was to deploy *tote Männer* to a suitable front and have them wreak havoc on the enemy while leaving our own troops alone. The *tote Männer* would terrify and demoralize the enemy. Our troops would march in behind them, clearing the area of enemy soldiers and *tote Männer* alike. Simple.

Only, we did not have a means by which we could create a large number of *tote Männer* simultaneously or a means by which we could be sure they would discriminate between our soldiers and the enemy.

Weber attacked the discrimination problem while I considered issues of scale.

Buchenwald was too small and low volume to be useful to us. Auschwitz was more appropriate to our needs. However, Auschwitz was already overwhelmed with the volume of its operation.

In October, the Birkenau expansion of Auschwitz had begun. It was scheduled to be complete in the spring. Willem had shown me copies of the plans. It was clear that only minor modifications to the Birkenau plans would accommodate our needs much more easily than building an addition to Buchenwald or moving to Auschwitz proper.

In January of 1942 I kissed Elsa and Helmut goodbye and boarded the train to Krakow. From there, I took a car west. It was beautiful country, full of gently rising mountains over flat valleys. Curiously unspoiled either by industry or by the war.

Auschwitz was a complex, not a single camp like Buchenwald. There were several smaller camps near the headquarters. Birkenau was further west. Here, construction was going on apace in spite of the winter weather.

The foundations for gas chambers and crematoria had already been laid. But that didn't matter as far as I was concerned. The addition of some larger chambers and holding areas was an insignificant change to a well-managed engineering project. I went over the modifications in detail with the chief engineer, a man named Tilly. Willem had sent me with a certificate of authority. That gave me the full support of Tilly and the chief of the camps, Rudolf Hoess, even though they did not know the reason for the modifications. I finished working out the details in two weeks.

I spent a few days in Krakow. I planned to move Elsa and Helmut into an apartment in Krakow and then travel to work by automobile. It was not far and the roads were good. If that proved impractical in a hard winter—something difficult for me to predict as the weather was now mild—I could just stay in the camp for a few days or come home on weekends.

When I returned, I found I had been gone just long enough for both Elsa and Helmut to miss me terribly. It made for a sweet homecoming.

Weber was reluctant to plan the move but saw my logic. He was preoccupied with the discrimination problem. Since the *tote Männer* were attracted to normal humans as hosts, he had reasoned that it was easier to *attract* them to a particular prey rather than *repel* them from a particular prey. He had performed several experiments with different hosts to see if there was any preference for differing types, such as racial subtype, diet, or other variables he could control.

I looked over the data and noticed that there was a marked difference in attack percentages not according to his typing but to the time the subjects arrived at the camp. Those subjects that were at the camp the longest were the most attractive to the *tote Männer.* I showed my figures to Weber. He instantly grasped the significance in ways I could not. The older inmates at Buchenwald were considerably thinner than the newer inmates since the rations were short. Fat utilization caused excretory products to be exuded by the skin and from the lungs. Weber reasoned these were what attracted the *tote Männer.*

Immediately, he called Willem for a mass spectrometer and a technician to run it.

We were all very tired but elated at this new direction. We decided to take a few days off. Elsa, Helmut, and I went for a trip into the mountains.

Birkenau opened in March of 1942. Weber and I stopped work on the subjects, except to keep an incubating strain alive, and took the month to pack up the laboratory for the move. In May, we moved the equipment, materials, and *tote Männer* to Birkenau. Once the planning for the move was complete, Weber supervised the staff and aides Willem had supplied. Elsa and Helmut traveled down to Krakow by train and took up residence in the apartment I had leased for them. As for myself, I left Buchenwald and returned to Berlin for meetings with representatives of Daimler-Benz and I. G. Farben. The delivery mechanism for the *tote Männer* still had to be devised.

The mood in Berlin that spring was jubilant. The army was driving towards Rostov and trying for Stalingrad. Sevastopol was about to fall to Germany. The use of the *tote Männer* could only be necessary as a last resort. A doomsday scenario. The Reich would never need it.

Personally, I felt the same. Still, I had no wish to help in cancelling the project unless I could find better work. So I met with the Daimler-Benz mechanical engineers and utilized the I. G. Farben labs. I had brought with me a pair of *tote Männer* for testing purposes.

Not being a mechanical engineer, the problem of deployment was more difficult than I had initially imagined. *Tote Männer* were a curious mixture of toughness and fragility. You could shoot a *toter Mann* until he was merely chopped meat and he might continue to advance. Blowing apart his brain would kill the worms and stop him. But the *tote Männer* were so resilient and resistant to anoxia that they could still advance with their hearts shattered and their sluggish black blood pooled beneath their feet.

However, their flesh was soft enough and loosely enough attached to their bones that heavy acceleration, such as dropping them with parachutes, would cause them to come apart. Clearly, they had to be preserved long enough to reach their target.

The Daimler-Benz engineers were the best. On a chalk board, they drew up several ways of conveying them to enemy lines. The simplest idea was a cushioned cage dropped with a parachute. An impact charge would blow the doors off the cage and the *tote Männer* would be free. The engineers didn't like the idea. They said it lacked elegance and style.

I pointed out the *tote Männer* could tolerate significant time without ambient oxygen, operating as they did largely on a lactic acid metabolism. They tossed the cage idea with abandon and attacked the problem again, coming up with a sphere containing carefully restrained *tote Männer*. A compressed-air charge would open the doors and break loose the restraints. This had the advantage of being quiet.

I only donated a little knowledge here and there as needed, letting their minds fly unfettered. It is a grand thing to watch engineers create works of imagination with only the germ of a requirement, a bit of chalk, and some board to write on. When they found I had brought a couple of *tote Männer* for experiments, they were overjoyed. I tried to explain the danger but they did not listen until one of their own number, Hans Braun, was bitten. He and his friends laughed but stilled when I came over. Wearing surgical gloves and a mask I carefully examined the wound but I already knew what I would find.

"You are an idiot," I said as I sat back.

"It is a small bite—"

"It is a fatal wound." I gave him a pack of cigarettes. "You have been killed by that thing out there."

"But—"

"Shut up." I couldn't look at him: tall, healthy, brown hair and a face in the habit of smiling. "You have been infected. By tomorrow, you will feel wonderful. You will want to kiss and fondle your friends out of love for them. Then, after a few days, you will—still enormously happy—feel an overpowering urge to sleep. Sleep will turn to coma. Then, after three days, you will be one of those things out there."

His hands trembled. "I didn't realize—"

"No."

Hans steadied himself. "There is no hope?"

"None."

He nodded and for a moment he stood straighter. Stronger. I was proud of him.

"Do you have a gun?"

"I do. Is there a furnace where we can dispose of the body?"

He nodded, shakily. "Will you accompany me?"

"I would be honored." And I was.

After the funeral, realizing the power and speed of the *tote Männer* and the infection they harbored, the Daimler-Benz engineers were more careful.

In a couple of weeks, my part was done and I took the train to Krakow to have a long weekend reunion with my Elsa and Helmut. The following Monday, I drove to Birkenau to address the problem of *tote Männer* production.

Elsa had mixed feelings about the rental. While she liked the apartment itself and the proximity of Park Jordana, she found the leftover debris and detritus disturbing. These were obviously Jewish artifacts and Elsa's excitement might have come from a mixture of womanly wariness of another female's territory combined with an aversion to having anything Jewish in the house. I assured her that the original owners would not be returning and she relaxed somewhat.

Helmut had no reservations about his new environment. Finding small objects of indeterminate origin covered with unfamiliar characters fastened in unexpected places gave mystery to the place. No doubt he observed I was more inclined to answer questions about this or that artifact than I was about the American bombers or air raid drills or what Father did at work. I protected my family as best I could from such things.

For the next several months we were collecting the breath and sweat of subjects into vials, injecting the vial contents into the mass spectrometer, and determining what was there. Then we concentrated the effluvia and tried it on the *tote Männer* themselves. Immediately, we found that the *tote Männer* were not attracted to merely any object smeared with the test substances, only when those attractants were applied to a possible host. Weber thought this quite exciting. It suggested that the *tote Männer* had a means of detecting a host other than smell.

In October of 1942, we hit on a combination of aldehydes and ketones the *tote Männer* found especially attractive. I synthesized it in the growing chemistry laboratory we had been using and applied it to a collection of test subjects. Control subjects who had no application of the test attractant were also present in the experiment and were ignored until the test subjects had been thoroughly mauled. At that point, the controls were attacked. We made careful note of this as it would strongly influence how troops would recover an infected area after the enemy succumbed.

We had proved our attractant in the laboratory by the end of October of 1942. But the war appeared to us to be going so well, our little military experiment would never be needed. We would win the Battle of Stalingrad in a month and concentrate on the western front.

That changed in November.

The Battle of Stalingrad evolved into what I had feared: a siege over a Russian winter. The Red Army began their counter-offensive along with the winter. Like Napoleon, the German army was stuck.

The Germans lost ground in other places. Willem suggested if I could hurry up the program, I should.

We were in part saved by problems encountered by the Daimler-Benz engineering team. Developing a deployment methodology had been proved harder than the engineers had foreseen. They had broken the problem into three parts. The first, and most easily solved, was how to restrain and cushion the *tote Männer* until they could be released. The remaining two issues revolved around deploying on an advance and deploying on a retreat. In both cases, they resolved into two kinds of scenarios: how to deploy the *first* time and how to deploy *after* the first time. If secrecy was kept (and Willem assured us the enemy did not know what we were working on), then the first deployment would be relatively easy. Deploying on a retreat could be as simple as leaving sealed containers transported by trucks to the target zone to be opened pyrotechnically by remote control. Similar containers, with additional cushioning, could be released by parachute.

But once the secret was out and the Allies were looking for *tote Männer* delivery devices, we would need a means to overcome their resistance. This had stalled the Daimler-Benz engineers. I saw presentations of stealth night drops, blitzkrieg raids with tanks carrying large transport carts—one enterprising young man demonstrated a quarter-scale model trebuchet that could catapult a scale model container holding six *tote Männer* as much as three kilometers behind enemy lines. Not to be outdone, his work partner showed how bracing a *toter Mann* could enable it to be fired from a cannon like a circus performer.

These issues so dwarfed our own minor problems that we were given, for the moment, no close scrutiny and I had the opportunity to address shortcomings in our own production.

In February 1943, Russia won the Battle of Stalingrad. Willem warned us that we would have to expect to send *tote Männer* against Russian troops before long. I argued against it. It would be foolish to waste surprise in an attack that could not work. At least, it would not work until summer.

I went home and spent a week with Elsa and Helmut. Each morning I sat down and drew up production schedules, scrapped them, smoked cigarettes, and tried again. In the afternoon, I played with my son. It was cold in Krakow and with the war not going very well, heating fuel was hard to come by. I was able to requisition what we needed due to my position but even I couldn't get coal for the theater or the restaurants. Often, we spent intimate evenings together with just ourselves for company. I didn't mind. Elsa and Helmut were company enough.

All that spring Willem told us of defeat after defeat—I don't think we were supposed to know what he told us. I think we served as people in whom he could confide as his world crumbled. Germany retreated in Africa. The Warsaw Uprising. The Russian advance.

I buried myself in my work. I resolved that if there were to be a failure in the program, it would not be where I had control. Production was, in my opinion, our weak point. Weber's approach to creating *tote Männer* was haphazard and labor intensive. I wanted something more robust and reliable. Something more *industrial.*

I came to the conclusion that our production schedule had to revolve around the progression of the disease. For three days there was a strong euphoria. Often, the new hosts tried to kiss anyone who came near them, presaging the biting activity of the fully infected *toter Mann.* Sometime on the third day, the host fell into a sleep that progressed rapidly into coma. Breathing decreased to almost nothing. The heartbeat reduced to a slow fraction of the uninfected. Body temperature dropped to nearly ambient though the infected were able to keep some warmth above room temperature.

The coma period lasted as long as five days, though we saw it end as soon as three. Arousal was sudden, so often precipitated by a nearby possible victim that I came to the conclusion that after three days, the *toter Mann* was ready to strike and merely waiting for the opportunity.

After that, a *toter Mann* was mobile for as much as ten weeks, though during the last weeks of infection the *toter Mann* showed significant deterioration.

Therefore, we required an incubation period of six days, minimum. Effectiveness could not be counted upon after eight weeks. This gave us a target window. If we wanted, for example, to deploy on June first we had to have infected our *tote Männer* no later than May twenty-fifth. This was the time domain of our military supply chain.

The first order of business was to synchronize the incubation period. I performed a series of experiments that showed that, as I suspected, once the coma period had been entered the *toter Mann* was ready to be used. However, there was unacceptable variation in the time between exposure and coma. We couldn't reliably produce *tote Männer* in six days.

The new Chief Medical Officer, Mengele, delivered the necessary insight. Zyklon B was the answer. Though the standard Zyklon B dose would kill the subject quickly, a reduced dose weakened the subject sufficiently to allow infection almost instantly. Commander Hoess was able to supply me with enough experimental data that I could proceed with my own tests. We introduced the gas, waited for ten minutes, then sprayed the subjects with an infecting agent. The remaining three days were sufficient for subjects to recover from the gas just in time to provide healthy hosts for the organisms. This method had the added bonus that the same production chambers could serve two purposes.

By November, when the march up Italy by the Allies had begun and Germany seemed to be losing on all fronts, we could incubate as many as a thousand at a time, six days after exposure. The trains supplying the rest of the camp came in full and left empty so by using the empty trains for transport, we could send *tote Männer* anywhere in Germany or Poland. Delivery to the deployment launch point would have to be by truck. We were ready. Now, it was up to the Daimler-Benz engineers to deliver our *tote Männer* the last kilometer to the enemy.

Christmas 1943 was uneventful. Weber and I worked on various refinements to an already prepared system without damaging it too badly. My teachers back in Berlin had taught me the idea of *schlimmbesserung:* an improvement that makes things worse. At that point, the natural tendency of idle minds and hands to improve a working system into uselessness was our only real enemy.

Given that, we resolutely turned our attention away from the weapons system we had devised to a different problem we had discussed a year before: Why deliver *tote Männer* at all? The worm and virus were perfectly able to create *tote Männer* for us. Why did we have to supply the raw material?

Delivering a disease substance was perilously close to delivering a poison gas—something forbidden us from the previous war. However, we had already made some excursions into the territory with the production and delivery of *tote Männer* attractant—a colloid I had developed that would evaporate into the proper aldehyde and ketone mix the *tote Männer* found so irresistible. We had also attempted to deliver an infecting gas along with the Zyklon B but the attempt had failed. The worm succumbed to the Zyklon B before the subjects.

Creating an inhalant that carried both the worm and virus proved to be an interesting problem. The virus was stable when dry and the worm could be induced to encyst itself. However, it took time for the worm to de-cyst and by the time it did, the subject was fully infected with an undirected virus. Rabid humans made a poor host.

We went back to the colloid I devised for the attractant. Colloids are neither liquid nor solid but partake of the traits of both. Gelatin is a colloid. By adding nutrients to the colloid so that the worm could stay alive and not encyst, the virus could be delivered along with the worm when both were at their most infective stage. It was interesting work for a couple of months. Weber was quite elated with it. He called it the *Todesluft.*

In May of 1944, Willem paid us another visit. This time, he took both Weber and myself aside and spoke to us privately.

"It is clear the Allies are preparing a counter-invasion. The likely location is somewhere across from England on the coast of France." He held the cigarette to his lips thoughtfully.

"We're ready," I said boldly. "We've been ready for months. What do the Daimler-Benz engineers say?"

Willem breathed out smoke. "They have made several methods available to us. Since this is to be the first deployment, we have chosen the retreat scenario. We will place the *tote Männer* in a bunker in the path of the Allies and detonate it when they come."

"Are we expecting to be overrun?"

Willem shook his head. "Of course not. The *tote Männer* are a backup plan only. We will deploy them behind our own lines and only release them if we are forced past them. If the front line holds, we will not release them at all."

I nodded. "How many?"

"We estimate six thousand."

I thought quickly. "It takes six days for each group. Six thousand will take us thirty-six days."

Willem smiled at me. "Did you know of the expansions of Birkenau commissioned early last year?"

"Of course," said Weber. "They were a dreadful nuisance."

"They are about to pay for themselves," retorted Willem. "I developed Max's original plans for Birkenau beyond his conception. The new facilities can serve as incubator."

"How many?"

"At least forty thousand at once. Six thousand should not be a problem." He pulled from his briefcase a set of plans.

I looked them over. I was impressed with the innovations I saw. "This is better than I had hoped."

"I'm glad you are pleased. When can the first squad be ready?"

I looked over the plans again and did some figuring on a piece of paper. "May 12, if Daimler-Benz can provide the bunkers and the transportation."

"I've been assured this will not be a problem."

"Then we will be ready to deploy."

Willem pulled a map from his briefcase. "Our sources say we will be struck here." He pointed to the map. "Pas-de-Calais. That is where our defenses are located and just three kilometers behind them, our *tote Männer.* The Allies will not know what hit them."

This was by far the largest group of *tote Männer* we had ever attempted to create. Weber took a fatherly approach to them. When the hosts entered the euphoric stage and called to him with affection, he responded, calling them his "children" and other endearments. I found this unnerving. When the *tote Männer* were finally ready and installed into their transportation containers I was glad to see them go. Weber watched them leave with a tear in his eye. I went home to my wife and son.

But, of course, the Allies did not strike at Pas-de-Calais but at Normandy, over three hundred kilometers to the southwest. The *tote Männer* were in their bunkers. The Daimler-Benz engineers had packed them like munitions. There was no way to extract them without releasing them.

It was terrible timing. All of the available *tote Männer* were in Calais and the next squad would not be ready for deployment until June 9: three days!

Willem conferred with his staff and said that if we could drop enough bunkers in the Cerisy Forest and fill them with *tote Männer*, we would let the Allies overrun the forest and open the bunker.

At this point the new squad was just entering the coma stage. We'd found the *tote Männer* were vulnerable to jostling during this period and had always transported them towards the end of the coma. But desperate times require desperate measures. Willem and I led the crew that took the newly comatose *tote Männer*, eight thousand strong, and trucked them to the forest. Meanwhile, three large prefabricated bunkers were erected on the sites. I barely had time to phone Elsa to say I would not be home that night. Weber, affectionate to the *tote Männer* as before, elected to stay and incubate the next squad. I was just as glad not to have him along.

The bunkers were not particularly explosive-proof but would stop bullets. They looked more like officers' quarters than anything else. We locked them and moved away to nearby Trevieres. This was June 8th. By the afternoon of June 9th, the *tote Männer* would be alert. When fired, the bunker would first explode a smoke bomb containing the colloid and attractant we had devised to mask the area. A few minutes later, small explosives would release the *tote Männer* and break the outside walls. The *tote Männer* would have to do the rest. We hoped the smell of nearby prey would waken them to fury as we had observed in the lab.

The time passed slowly, punctuated with small arms fire and a few large weapons. The wind moved back and forth, sometimes bringing us the firecracker smell of the battlefield and then replacing it with the pine smell of the forests.

The afternoon came. An odd aircraft I'd never seen before, called a *Storch*, was made available to us. The pilot, Willem, and I boarded the airplane along with the radio equipment. The heavily laden craft took off in an impressively short distance and in a few moments we were high enough to see the bunkers and, worse, the advancing Allies. Willem pressed the button.

Smoke poured out of the three buildings. I could not hear the reports as the internal explosives ignited but there was motion—furious motion—through the smoke. Seconds later the advancing Allies were running down the hill away from the smoke. Directly behind them were the *tote Männer*.

The *tote Männer* were much faster than the humans they pursued and more clever than ever I would have guessed. One *toter Mann* leapt from human to human, biting and clawing, not even pausing to enjoy the "meal." Eight thousand *tote Männer* poured over the Allies. Guns didn't stop them. They were in and among the soldiers so quickly none of the supporting artillery or machine guns could fire. The smoke switched over them and we could no longer observe.

"Fly over them," Willem ordered, "so we can look down."

"Sir, we will be shot."

"Fly over them, I say," Willem shouted and brought out his pistol. "Or I will shoot you myself."

We flew over the churning mass of *tote Männer* and humans. They took no notice of us. All of their attention was focused on the horrifying apparitions among them.

"Good," said Willem grimly. "Return."

It was a safe bet that each of the *tote Männer* had likely managed to bite at least three soldiers. Assuming an overlap of twenty percent, that meant better than thirteen thousand Allied *tote Männer* would be awakening in a week. This was a conservative estimate, assuming the infected soldiers would not infect others during the euphoric period.

We landed, and General Marcks himself joined us. Willem told him of the adventure and the anti-*tote Männer* equipment—mostly flame throwers and protective jackets—waiting in trucks not ten kilometers distant. The Allied invasion would not succeed.

And it did not.

The Allies, so demoralized by the Reich's new weapon, were unable to advance. German bombers were able to sink support craft in the channel. The war stalled in western France all that summer.

When I returned to Krakow in July to see my wife I still smelled of burning diesel and gunpowder. She made me bathe before I could kiss her.

The Daimler-Benz flying barges were deployed. These, I had not known about. They were gliders filled with forty or fifty *tote Männer*, towed overnight by bombers and released near the front to land where they would. The crashes released most of the *tote Männer* but mechanical relays released the remainder. Willem informed us that there were now highly localized *tote Männer* infections in Britain, where wounded men had been returned before they had turned completely and before the Allies had realized what they were dealing with.

But the Russians continued to advance. They were no less ruthless than the *tote Männer* and had devised a simple but effective defense. Any group of *tote Männer* they found they slaughtered without regard to coincident casualties. We estimated they were killing as much as 10 percent of their own men with this technique. But it was effective. It was only a matter of time before they reached Germany.

The Allied advance had not been routed as we'd hoped but only stalled as they tried to cope with their own problems. Had Germany remained the fighting force it had been at the beginning of the war, this would have been enough. However, now the Allies had a foothold in France and would not give it up. Antiaircraft batteries were brought over the channel and the bombers could no longer eliminate the shipping. Soon, the Allies would figure out a method of containing the infection just as the Russians had done. A stalemate in this war would inevitably lead to an Allied victory.

Willem created the *todeskommandos.* These were the last paratroopers still left in the Luftwaffe. They were infected without their knowing and dropped far behind enemy lines. Their mission was to spy on the enemy and return in two weeks' time. Of course, they transformed in less than half that time and infected the Russians.

I refused to participate in this activity. I would not be a party to infecting unwitting German soldiers. Willem did not press me at that point though I knew a day of reckoning was coming. Knowing this, I persuaded Willem to loan me one of the Daimler-Benz engineers—preferably Joseph Bremer, a friend of Hans Braun and the engineer who had later proposed the trebuchet. I liked the way his mind worked. Willem sent him to me with the warning that something needed to be done about the Russians.

Bremer, being a mechanical rather than a chemical engineer, immediately saw solutions to the issues we had not solved. We had to maintain the environment of the worm and virus for the duration of delivery and then spray it out into the surrounding area without shredding either. Weber and I had already determined that *inhaling* the inoculum would not infect the host unless some portion was swallowed. The worm needed to actually enter the digestive tract to enter the blood stream. The only result from a purely pulmonary inoculation would be a sterile partial infection.

It was Bremer who devised an irritant to be added to the mixture. The irritant would not be poisonous in any way but would cause a mucous flow from the nose. The subjects would be forced to swallow. It worked in Birkenau experiments with great success.

By this time, Hitler had been sending V1's against Britain for a few weeks. My purpose was to be able to replace the explosive in the V1 with a Todesluft canister and infect the Allies in their home territories.

Once we had the Todesluft device perfected, we approached Willem with it. Willem at once saw the possibilities but denied us the chance to try it out in a V1. Instead, he told us of a new rocket, vastly more powerful and accurate. It was to be called the V2.

The bombers over Berlin never stopped during that summer. Up until we released the *tote Männer*, Auschwitz, Buchenwald, and the other camps had been spared for some reason. By July, we had a version of the Todesluft device ready for the V2 and after the first few reached their targets, the Allies, realizing where our production facilities must be located, started bombing the camps. I had to drag Weber from our burning laboratories. He wanted to save his "children." I triggered the containment-failure devices and incinerated the last remaining *tote Männer* squads but saved inoculum samples and the Todesluft devices to operate elsewhere. It was curious: the incubation pens and the holding areas were completely destroyed but the gas chambers survived the bombing.

I had thought to travel immediately to Krakow to be with Elsa. But before I could, Elsa showed up at the camp. Weber, Elsa, Helmut, and I were able to find safety in the basement of the headquarters building. I managed to locate an intact phone and called Willem to tell him where we were.

The bombing ceased in a day or so. The inmates were taken care of and we had food and water. Power was restored the following day.

Weber liked to be near us. Something profound had come undone in him. He mourned the death of his squad over and over. On the third day he accosted me out in the street as I cleaned up the front of the building.

"Could it have been the Jews?"

"What are you talking about?"

"The failure of our *tote Männer*."

I sighed. "The *tote Männer* did not fail."

"How can you say that? Germany is *still* losing the war!"

I considered responding to this. How could any single weapon ever win a war on its own? It was *our* failure, not any failure of the *tote Männer*. But that would only have encouraged him. "We haven't lost yet."

He ignored that. "We made *tote Männer* out of the Jews. Perhaps there was a *judengeist* that impaired them."

"What would you have done instead? Made them out of Germans as Willem did?"

"I should not have been so reluctant to use Poles," Weber said and sat on the bench, sunk in apathy.

I continued shoveling broken concrete and shards of wood out of the street.

Willem showed up that night. He was half-drunk and I was surprised he'd managed to drive all the way from Berlin. Morose and untalkative, he refused to speak until after dinner when Elsa had taken Helmut and herself to bed.

"The Americans are smarter than we are."

"Beg pardon?" I said, ready to defend German intelligence.

"It had to be the Americans. The British would not have considered it."

"Considered *what?*"

Willem stared at me. "Of course. How could you know? They have been raining *tote Männer* on Berlin. All over Germany."

"That's impossible. Did they drop them out of the bombers? Did they think we would be intimidated by smashed body parts?"

Willem shook his head. "Nothing so complex. All they did was harness them to a big parachute and then tie them together with a bow knot so they would not escape during transport. Then they shoved them out the back of a bomber on a strip line. It undid the bow knot and released the parachute. Some of them were killed, of course. But so what? Between ours and the ones generated from their own ranks, they have enough."

"How were they released from the parachutes?"

"We found a wind-up spring clip. When the spring wound down, the clip opened and they were released. Diabolical simplicity."

I drank some wine. "There are *tote Männer* in Berlin." I tried to frame it as a logical proposition. I could imagine them lurching through the city.

"There are *tote Männer* all over Germany. There are *tote Männer* in London from the V2 Todesluft attack. Von Braun even managed to extend the range of the V2 with a V1 attachment. There are *tote Männer* in Moscow. Tell me, Weber. How many *tote Männer* must there be to become self-sustaining?"

Weber peered at him owlishly. "They cannot be self-sustaining. Eventually all of the raw material would be used up."

"You are so comforting," Willem said dryly.

I stared at the wine bottle. "When will they reach here?"

"They were behind me when I crossed the border. One day? Two days? They move slowly but steadily and they will be brought here by our scent."

We had all underestimated them. They were in the camp by morning.

They had broken through the barbed wire holding the inmates easily. The inmates were bitten and mauled by the hundreds. The guards died when they insisted on firing on the *tote Männer* and the *tote Männer*, of course, did not fall.

The scent of the inmates was so strong that it overpowered our own smells. The *tote Männer* did not know we were there. We took care to remain hidden in the headquarters building. With so many possible hosts around, the *tote Männer* ignored the buildings. Each time a few seemed to take interest, there was another inmate to attack.

Elsa refused to let Helmut near the windows. During a lull in the fighting she sat next to me as I watched through the window.

"What are those things?" Elsa said quietly. Her face was milk white but her voice was calm. "Max? Uncle? What are those things?"

"We call them *tote Männer*," I said.

"Is that what you were building in the camps? Is that your weapon?"

"Yes."

She shook her head. "Did they escape from another camp?"

"No." Willem laughed dryly. "The Allies were kind enough to return these to us."

"Helmut must not see them."

"Yes," I said. "More importantly, they must not see us."

She nodded.

Eventually, the inmates were all infected. We had discovered in experiments that infected hosts were ignored by *tote Männer*. But there were still so many of them our own scent remained undiscovered. The *tote Männer* wandered off in small groups, heading east toward Krakow.

The remaining freed inmates, now euphorically infected hosts, were not so ignorant as the *tote Männer*. They tried to enter the headquarters building. Willem and I defended the place as best we could. Hoess and Mengele tried to gain entrance by sweet reasonableness and grumbled when we shot at them. They wandered off arm in arm.

By the end of the third day after the attack, we saw hosts finding small places to sleep. That evening the camp was entirely still.

"We have to leave," Willem insisted. This was Monday morning. By Wednesday night we would be fighting for our lives.

"I'm ready," Elsa said. "Those *things* will not hurt Helmut. I will kill him first."

I nodded. It pleased me that Elsa understood the situation. "Where shall we go? Our *tote Männer* are to the west and south. *Their tote Männer* are to the north and east. We have no petrol—the depot was blown up in the bombing."

"What shall we do, then?" demanded Willem.

"They are not very intelligent—as I said a long time ago, think of them as crocodiles. They can use their eyes but largely they depend upon scent. Therefore, we can block ourselves up in one of the gas chambers. They are air tight."

"We will smother," said Elsa.

"No." I shook my head. "We have three days. I can devise air circulation. It will be slow and diffuse up through the chimneys. But I do not think it will be sufficient to cause the *tote Männer* to attack the chamber. We can hold out for help."

It took most of those three days to set ourselves up. We had to change the locks on the doors so we could get ourselves out and convert the exhaust fans to give us a little air. We stockpiled as much food and water as we could carry. I even built a periscope through which I could observe the courtyard in front of the chamber and the areas around.

We were carrying one of the last loads into the chamber when a *toter Mann* leapt on Willem from the roof. Willem grabbed his pistol as he hurled the *toter Mann* to one side. Weber cried out and wrestled with Willem. The *toter Mann* attacked both of them. Finally, Willem threw down Weber and emptied the clip of his pistol into the *toter Mann*'s head. He turned to club Weber but Weber climbed the wall and was gone. Willem turned his attention back to the *toter Mann,* which had ceased moving as its head had ceased to have any shape. The worms wriggled out like thin spaghetti.

Willem looked at me and held up his arm. His fingers and wrist were bitten. "Do I have any chance at all?"

I shook my head.

"Well, then." He replaced the clip in the pistol. "Perhaps I have time enough to kill Weber for this."

"Don't wait too long," I advised. "Once you start to feel the euphoria you won't want to kill him at all."

"I won't."

He nodded at me and I saluted him. Then I went inside the chamber and sealed the door.

Which brings me to the present.

It has been ten weeks since we sealed the door of the chamber. No one has come to help us. Sure enough, the *tote Männer* have not detected us though they often walk around the building sensing something. Our scent is diffuse enough not to trigger an attack.

But they do not wander off as the previous *tote Männer* did. They have remained. Worse, instead of degrading in ten weeks as our experiments suggested, they remain whole. I am now forced to admit that the deterioration we observed in our experiments was more likely the result of captivity than any natural process.

I watch them. Sometimes a group of them will disappear into the surrounding forest and then return with a deer or the corpse of a man or child. Then they eat. We never took an opportunity to observe their lifecycle. It seems that once the initial infection period is over, they can, after their own fashion, hunt and eat.

We ran out of water two days ago. We ran out of food nearly a week before that. Helmut cries continuously. The sounds do not appear to penetrate the walls of the chamber—at least, the *tote Männer* do not respond.

I had planned to hold out longer—perhaps attempt an escape or brave the *tote Männer* and try to bring back supplies. It is now September. Surely, the impending winter would stop them. Then, when they were dormant, we could leave. But in these last days I have witnessed disturbing changes in their behavior. I saw one *toter Mann* walking around the camp wrapped in a rug found in one of the camp buildings. A small group of five or six gathered around a trash barrel in which smoldered a low fire. At first, I thought the disease might have managed to retrieve the host memories or that the hosts were recovering—both indicated disaster for us. We would be discovered.

But this is different. The *tote Männer* stand near the fires until they smolder and only then move away. They drape blankets and clothes completely over their heads but leave their feet unshod. Whatever is motivating them, it is not some surfacing human being but the dark wisdom of the disease itself.

They are still *tote Männer* and will infect us if they can. There is no hope of escape or holding out.

Always the engineer, I prepared for this. I kept back a bottle of water. In it, I dissolved some Demerol powder. Elsa and Helmut were so thirsty they did not notice the odd taste. They fell asleep in minutes.

I am a coward in some ways. The idea of me, my wife and my child living on only as a host for worms and microbes horrifies me. Death is preferable. Nor do I trust drugs. The faint possibility they might come upon us in our sleep fills me with dread. I have my pistol and enough bullets for Elsa and Helmut and myself. If they find us we will be of no use to them.

I believe that you, Germany, will triumph over these creatures, though that victory will no doubt be a hard one. The Third Reich will not live forever as we had hoped but will, no doubt, fall to the *tote Männer*. But good German strength must eventually prevail.

For my own part, I regret my inability to foresee my own inadequacies and I regret that I must die here, without being able to help. I regret that Elsa and Helmut will never again see the sun and that they will die by my hand.

But you, who read this, take heart. We did not yield. We did not surrender here but only died when there was no other way to deny ourselves to the enemy. You will defeat and destroy them and raise your hand over a grateful Earth.

It is there waiting for you.

THE SKULL-FACED CITY

By David Barr Kirtley

David Barr Kirtley has been described as "one of the newest and freshest voices in sf." His work frequently appears in *Realms of Fantasy*, and he has also sold fiction to the magazines *Weird Tales* and *Intergalactic Medicine Show*, the podcasts *Escape Pod* and *Pseudopod*, and the anthologies *New Voices in Science Fiction*, *The Dragon Done It*, and *Fantasy: The Best of the Year*. I've previously published him in the first *The Living Dead* anthology and in my online science fiction magazine *Lightspeed*. He also has a story forthcoming in my anthology *The Way of the Wizard* that's due out in November. Kirtley is also the co-host (with me) of the *Geek's Guide to the Galaxy* podcast.

This story is a sequel to one that appeared in the first *The Living Dead* anthology. In "The Skull-Faced Boy," Dustin and Jack, two recent college grads, die in a car accident and rise as intelligent zombies. Dustin—called "the skull-faced boy" due to his injuries—organizes hordes of mindless zombies into an army and declares war against the living, while Jack becomes his reluctant accomplice. Their rivalry over a girl named Ashley eventually leads Dustin to carve off her face as well.

When "The Skull-Faced Boy" appeared on the *Pseudopod* horror podcast, it was very well received, and several listeners requested more material set in the same universe. So it was in the back of Kirtley's mind for a while to possibly expand the story into something longer. When I told him I was editing *The Living Dead 2*, I encouraged him to submit a sequel story.

"This is the first sequel I've written, and it's hard," Kirtley says. "For a long time I was stuck, since by the end of 'The Skull-Faced Boy' the conflicts and agendas of the characters are all pretty much on the table. My big break came when I considered creating a new main character, Park. And so as not to repeat myself, I made him completely different from my original protagonist, Jack. Jack is an ordinary young man, sensitive, kind of a doormat type, whereas Park is a very, very dangerous soldier."

Park watched from his car as a pickup screeched to a halt in front of the supermarket. He'd known they would come. The armies of the living were on the march, and the living needed food.

The pickup's doors flew open and two figures leapt out—a black man and a blond woman. The man, who was older, maybe forty, carried a shotgun. He sprinted toward the store and the woman ran close behind him, her hands wrapped tight around a large silver pistol. The man threw open the entrance doors and vanished into the darkness while the woman waited outside, keeping watch. Smart. But it would not save them.

Park slipped from his car, his scoped rifle clutched to his chest. He crept forward, using abandoned cars as cover. Finally he lay down on the asphalt and leveled his rifle at the pickup.

A dead man in a green apron wandered around the side of the building. He spotted the woman, groaned exultantly, and stumbled toward her, his arms outstretched. The woman took aim at his forehead.

Park pulled the trigger at the same moment she did. The report of her pistol drowned out the soft pinging that his round made as it drilled a neat hole through her pickup's gas tank. The dead man's skull smacked against the pavement, and the woman lowered her gun. She didn't notice the gas pooling beneath her truck.

Park sneaked back to his car and got in. He waited, watching as the woman took down several more of the moaning dead who strayed too close. Later her companion emerged, pushing a loaded shopping cart. The woman hurriedly tossed its contents into the bed of her truck while the man dashed to the store again. This was repeated several times. The commotion attracted an ever-growing audience of moaners, which the woman eyed nervously.

Finally the man and woman leapt into their vehicle and peeled out. The pickup careened across the parking lot, and the dead men who staggered into its path were hurled aside or crushed beneath its tires.

Park donned his black ski mask, pulled his goggles down over his eyes, and started his car. He tailed the pickup along the highway, keeping his distance. When the truck rolled to a stop, he pulled over too and got out.

The man and woman fled from their vehicle and into a nearby field, which was crawling with the dead. Park followed them through the grass and into the woods. He watched through his scope as the pair expended the last of their ammo and tossed away their guns, and then they stood back to back and drew machetes against the clusters of moaners who continued to stumble from the trees all around.

Park approached, using his rifle to pick off the nearby dead men. One shot to each head, cleanly destroying each brain—what was left of them.

He pointed his rifle at the living man and shouted, "Drop it."

The man shouted back, "Who are you? What do you want?"

Park shifted his aim to the woman and said, "Now. I only need one of you alive."

"Wait!" the man said. "Damn it." He tossed his machete into the brush. "There. Okay?"

"And you," Park told the woman. She hesitated, then flung her weapon away as well.

Park said, "Turn around. Kneel. Hands on your heads."

They complied. Park strode forward and handcuffed them both. "Up," he said. "Move."

The pair stood, and marched. The woman glanced back at Park.

"Eyes front," he ordered.

She gasped. "Oh my god." To the man she hissed frantically, "He's one of them! The ones that can talk."

The man turned to stare too, his face full of terror.

"Eyes front!" Park shouted.

The man and woman looked away. After a minute, the woman said quietly, "Are you going to eat us?"

"I don't intend to," Park said.

"So why do you want us?" she asked.

"It's not me that wants you," Park answered.

"Who does then?" the man demanded.

For a long moment Park said nothing. Then he removed his goggles, exposing dark sockets and two huge eyeballs threaded with veins. He yanked off his ski mask, revealing a gaping nose cavity, bone-white forehead and cheeks—a horrific skull-visage.

"You'll see," he said.

As dusk fell Park drove down a long straight road that passed between rows of corn. In the fields, dead men with skull faces wielded scythes against the stalks.

"Crops," said the man in the back seat. "Those are crops."

Beside him the woman said, "What do the dead need with food?"

"To feed the living," Park answered.

For the first time her voice held a trace of hope. "So we'll be kept alive?"

"Some are, it would seem," Park said.

And Mei? he wondered. He just didn't know.

In front of his car loomed the necropolis, its walls clumsy constructions of stone, twenty feet high. Crews of skull-faced men listlessly piled on more rocks.

The woman watched this, her jaw slack. She murmured, "What happened to your faces?"

Park glanced at her in the rearview mirror. The car bounced over a pothole, and the mirror trembled as he answered, "Faces are vanity. The dead are beyond such things."

He pulled to a stop before a gap in the stone wall. The dirty yellow side of a school bus blocked his way. He rolled down his window.

From the shadows emerged one of the dead, a guard. This one did have a face—nose and cheeks and forehead—though the flesh was green and mottled. A rifle hung from his shoulder. He shined a flashlight at Park, then at the captives.

"For the Commander," Park said.

The guard waved at someone in the bus, the vehicle rumbled forward out of the way, and Park drove on through.

The woman said, "That one had a face."

"That one is weak," Park snapped. "Still enamored with the trappings of life. And so here he is, far from the Commander's favor."

Park drove down a narrow causeway bordered on both sides by chain-link fences. Every few minutes he passed a tall steel pole upon which was mounted a loudspeaker. Beyond the fences, scores of moaners wandered aimlessly in the light of the setting sun. The man and woman lapsed again into silence. Plainly they could see that this army of corpses presented a formidable obstacle to either escape or rescue.

Park remembered the first time he'd come here, almost three months ago, pursuing a trail of clues. Upon beholding the necropolis his first thought had been: The city that never sleeps.

He passed through another gate and into a large courtyard. "End of the line," he said as he opened the door and got out.

A group of uniformed dead men with rifles and skull-faces ambled toward him. Their sergeant said, "You again. Park, isn't it? What've you got?"

"Two," Park replied. "Man and woman."

The sergeant nodded to his soldiers, who yanked open the car doors and seized the prisoners. As the pair was led away, the sergeant said to Park, "All right. Come on."

Park was escorted across the yard. From a loudspeaker mounted on a nearby pole came the recorded voice of the Commander:

"Once you were lost," said the voice, "but now you've found peace. Once you were afflicted by the ills of the flesh. The hot sun made you sweat, and the icy wind made you shiver. You sickened and fell and were buried in muck. You were slaves to the most vile lusts, and you gorged yourselves on sugar and grease. But now, now you are strong, and the only hunger you feel is the hunger for victory, the hunger to destroy our enemies, to bend them to the true path by the power of your righteous hands and teeth. Once you were vain, preoccupied by the shape of your nose, the shape of your cheeks. You gazed into the mirror and felt shame. Shame is for the living. Let them keep their shame. We are beyond them, above them. Your face is a symbol of bondage to a fallen world, a reminder of all that you once were and now rightfully despise. Take up your knife now and carve away your face. Embrace the future. Embrace death."

Park was taken to a nearby building and led to a room piled high with ammo clips and small arms—the currency of the dead. He filled a duffel. As he made his way back to his car, another skull-faced man came hurrying over and called out, "Hey. Hey you."

Park looked up.

The man gestured for him to follow and announced, "The Commander wants to meet you."

This is what Park had been waiting for. He dumped the duffel in the trunk of his car, then followed the man to an armored truck. They drove together toward the palace. The building had been a prison once, but now hordes of dead laborers had transformed it into a crude and sinister fortress.

The truck arrived at the palace, then stopped in a dim alley. Park got out and was led inside. He surrendered his handcuffs to an armed guard, walked through a metal detector, then retrieved them.

He was shown to a large chamber. Against the far wall stood two throne-like wooden chairs, in one of which sat a slender skull-faced young man who held an automatic rifle across his lap. Beside him sat a skull-faced girl with long auburn hair. She wore an elegant white gown, and Park imagined that she must have been very beautiful once. The man in the chair wore a military uniform, as did the row of a dozen skull-faced men who stood flanking him.

Park stepped into the center of the room.

"Welcome," said the man in the chair. "I am the Commander. This is my wife." He gestured to the girl beside him. "And my generals." He waved at the assembled dead. "And you are Park."

"Sir," Park said.

"You're quickly becoming our favorite supplier."

Park was silent.

The Commander leaned forward and regarded him. "Tell me, Park. How did you die?"

Park hesitated a moment, then said, "Friendly fire. When my base was overrun."

And he'd been damn lucky in that. Those who died after being bitten by the dead always came back as moaners, as the rest of his company had.

The Commander said, "You were a soldier?"

"Scout sniper, sir."

The Commander nodded. "Good." He added wryly, "I like the look of you, Park. You remind me of myself."

"Thank you, sir."

"But tell me," the Commander went on. "Why do you keep bringing us the living? I'm grateful, but you can't still need the reward. You must have plenty of guns by now."

"I want to do more," Park said. "Help you. Convert the living. End the war."

The Commander settled back in his chair. "Yes," he said thoughtfully. "Perhaps you can help us. We'll discuss it after dinner."

Dinner. The word filled Park with dread. Fortunately he had no face to give him away.

She reminded him of his grandmother. A woman in her seventies, naked, gagged, and tied to a steel platter. When she was placed on the table, and saw a dozen skull-faces with all their eyeballs staring down at her, she began to bray into her gag and thrash against her bonds.

The Commander, who now wore his rifle strapped to his shoulder, said to Park, "Guests first."

Park leaned over the woman, who whimpered and tried to squirm away. He wanted to tell her: I'm sorry. I have no choice.

He bit into her arm, tore. The woman screamed. Park straightened and began to chew. No flavor at all. The dead couldn't taste, though he did feel a diminishment of the perpetual hunger that the dead bore for the living.

The Commander turned to the skull-faced girl and said, "Now you, my dear." She began to feed. Soon the others joined in.

When it was over, Park looked up and noticed that the living man and woman he'd just brought in were now present. They stood in the corner, naked and trembling, held up by dead men who clutched them by the arms.

What now? Park wondered.

The old woman was moving again, moaning. The Commander ordered her released. He murmured, "We eat of this flesh, and proclaim death." To the woman he added, "Rise now in glory. Go."

There wasn't much left of her, really. A crimson skeleton festooned with gobbets. The thing that had once been a woman dragged itself off the table and lurched as best it could toward the exit.

"Now," the Commander said. "We have a bit of after-dinner entertainment. Some fresh material." He waved at Park. "Thanks to our friend here."

Park followed as the captives were dragged out the door, down a long corridor, and into another chamber. This room was smaller, with chairs lined up along one wall, all of them facing a king-sized bed. The man and woman were brought to the bed and dumped upon it, where they sat dazed. The seats filled with spectators. The skull-faced girl sat beside the Commander, who assumed the centermost chair.

The Commander pointed at the living man and said, "You. Take her. Now." The generals watched, silent but rapt.

The man stood, made a fist. "Fuck you, freak." Behind him the woman sat pale and stricken.

The Commander shrugged. "Maybe you're not in the mood. We have something for that." He turned to the door and called, "The aphrodisiac, please."

For almost a minute nothing happened. Then from the corridor came a terrible groaning. The sound grew louder, closer. The woman on the bed wrinkled her nose and whispered, "No." A dark form appeared in the doorway.

It was one of the ones who had been buried in the ground before coming back. They always returned as moaners too, and had always rotted terribly.

The man and woman scrambled away, onto the floor.

Around its neck the moaner wore a steel collar, which was attached to a chain held by a skull-faced guard. The moaner shrieked, and slavered, and swiped at the air with clawlike fingers. It lunged at the living, and its handler, just barely able to keep it under control, was half-dragged along behind it. With each charge, the creature came closer to the man and woman, who cowered on the floor in the corner, the man kicking feebly in the direction of the monster.

When the thing was just a few feet away the man shrieked, "All right! All right! Get it off me!"

The Commander lifted a hand, and the moaner was hauled back.

The man and woman trooped grimly to the bed. The woman was young, maybe twenty. Mei's age, Park thought. Had Mei gone through this? No. Don't think about it.

The woman lay down on the bed and the man climbed awkwardly on top of her. The Commander stared. He reached over, took the hand of the skull-faced girl, and held it. For a long time the living man nuzzled the woman, pawed her, rubbed against her, but he was too frightened, and couldn't become aroused.

Finally the Commander called out, "Enough!"

The figures on the bed froze.

The Commander stood. "This grows tedious. Another night, perhaps?" The pair on the bed pulled away from each other and watched anxiously. The Commander said to them, "Don't worry. There'll be other chances. Next time will be better." To the generals he instructed, "Take them away. Put them with the rest."

The rest? Park thought.

"Park," said the Commander. "Walk with me."

Park followed him through several doorways, then up a few flights of stairs. They emerged onto what must have once been simply a rooftop, but which had been augmented through the exertions of the dead with a sort of parapet.

The Commander said, "So how did you enjoy that?"

"I… it was… "

The Commander said sharply, "Don't dissemble. I don't like that." All of a sudden there was real anger in his voice, and Park was afraid, but just as suddenly the man's eerie calm returned. He went on, "You were uneasy."

Park thought fast. "I just… you always say lust of the flesh is—"

"For the masses," the Commander cut in. "Black and white. Right and wrong. But men like you and I must take a more nuanced view. Besides, it's for a greater purpose. You'll see."

"I'm sorry. I didn't mean—"

"And don't apologize," the Commander said. "Now… there's something you want to discuss?"

"Yes." Park collected his thoughts. Then: "In what way does one become an officer in your army?"

"I am the way," the Commander said. "Tell me why you want to join."

"I hate the living," Park said. "Always have. Even when I was one of them. Especially then. But I never saw any alternative. Until now."

"I understand," the Commander told him. "You seem a useful sort, Park, and I'm always damned short of good men. I think I'm going to be glad I met you."

The Commander turned away and gazed out over the battlements to admire his city, his domain. There in the darkness, with the man's back turned and no one else around, Park allowed himself one fleeting instant to glare at the Commander with pure hatred.

No, Park thought. You won't be glad. Not at all.

So Park was designated a "lieutenant," and given a room in a far corner of the palace, and often he was called on to perform routine tasks, mostly drilling the other officers in marksmanship. The Commander's voice was a constant presence, as the loudspeakers blared forth an endless mix of propaganda and instructions for the maintenance of the city. Sometimes pairs of living prisoners were brought out to perform for the Commander and his wife, but Mei was never among them.

Most information was still restricted from Park, and most areas of the palace were still off-limits. A few times he heard men refer to the top floor of the east wing as the "petting zoo." Was that where the living were kept? The palace was severely undermanned, but even so trying to slip in where he wasn't wanted would be chancy at best. Patience, he told himself. Wait, and watch. This is who you are. This is what you do. And when you strike, you strike hard, and they never see it coming.

One day Park returned to his room to find someone waiting in the hall. It was Greavey, a heavyset man with a scattering of red hairs whose jowls hung slack below his skeletal face.

Park nodded to him. "General."

"Park," said Greavey. "Can I ask you a favor? A private lesson?"

"Of course," Park said.

He retrieved a pair of rifles from his car, then took Greavey to a muddy yard nearby, where Park lined up empty cans upon a wooden table. The two of them positioned themselves at the far end of the field.

Greavey took aim and fired. His shot went wide. He growled, and said, "I was a soldier too, in life. Like you. Never was a terrific shot though."

Park fired and knocked over the first can. "It's easier now. Your body is more still."

Greavey raised his rifle again. As he sighted, he said casually, "You may have fooled him, but you don't fool me." He fired. A can went flying.

Park didn't answer. He took another shot, took down another can.

Greavey's voice was gruff. "You don't buy all his bullshit. His little cult. And neither do I." He fired again. Missed. "Damn."

Park had been expecting something like this. He took aim again. "And what if I don't?" He fired. Another hit.

"Listen," Greavey told him. "You're new around here. You don't know what he's like. We're losing this war, losing bad, because of him. We don't have enough officers, and every time one of us shows a little promise... well, he doesn't like rivals much. So watch yourself. It's only a matter of time before he turns on you too."

"So what's the alternative?" Park said. "The moaners are loyal to him. They've been listening to his voice every day and night now for how long? What's going to happen if he's gone? You think they'll obey you? You think you can control them?"

"Man, they'll listen to anyone—" Greavey waved at a loudspeaker— "who gets on that PA."

Park raised his rifle to his shoulder and sighted downrange. "It's too much of a risk."

"That's not what you'll be saying when the living storm in here and blow our brains out."

Park fired. Another can. "Who then? If not him?"

Greavey said, "You know he never did shit before all this? He likes to play soldier—all of them do—but he's just some college kid. Now, he's smart, I'll give him that, but not as smart as he thinks he is. We need someone in charge who knows this army and who's got real military training."

"You then?" Park said.

Greavey shrugged. "Seems sensible."

"I've got training," Park said. Another shot. Another can.

"Look," Greavey said. "You shoot real good, but come on. You just got here. Back me and I promise I'll—"

"No."

Greavey was silent a while. He raised his rifle, hesitated, lowered it. Finally: "What do you want?"

"Half," Park said.

"Half what?"

"Half everything. The guns, trucks, troops—"

"No way."

Park raised his rifle again. "Maybe I should see what *he* thinks about all this."

Greavey stared as Park took down another can, then said, "Fine. If that's the way it's got to be. You and me. Full partners. All right?"

"All right." Park glanced toward the palace. "Except... no one but him's allowed to bring weapons in there. He's always armed, obviously he never sleeps—"

"He comes out sometimes," Greavey said. "To supervise things personally, or lead his army in the field. And like I said, you shoot real good."

At this, Park nodded slowly. "I see," he said, as he took down the final can.

Later, as Park strode through the palace, he thought: A good try. Convincing. Much of it likely true. Greavey plotting assassination? A lie. But the Commander too reliant on his legion of moaners? Eliminating clever officers who might become rivals? Probably yes. Also true: The Commander not as smart as he thinks he is.

Park turned a corner toward the Commander's private suite. Two skull-faced men stood guard.

"I have to see the Commander," Park said.

The men eyed him. One of them said, "Wait here," and disappeared around a corner. A short time later he returned and said, "All right. Come on."

They walked down the hall to an office, where the Commander sat behind a desk, his rifle leaning against a nearby wall. He held a combat knife, which he fiddled with absently as he said, "Talk."

Park said, "Sir, Greavey is plotting against you."

The Commander leaned back in his chair. "Give me details. Everything."

So Park relayed the conversation, leaving out nothing.

Afterward, the Commander stood and began to pace. "This is good to know."

Park said, "Sir, let me handle Greavey. I'll—"

"Greavey's fine."

"Sir?"

The Commander pointed his knife at Park and said, "Listen to me carefully. Nothing happens in this city without my knowledge, without my order. Do you understand?"

Park feigned bafflement. "You mean it was... a test?"

"An exercise," the Commander said. "I apologize, but it's necessary. I've been betrayed before. I have to make sure."

A few weeks later, just after dawn, Park heard a rumble from outside, as of distant thunder. He hurried to the window of his chamber and looked out. A giant plume of black smoke was rising from the southern end of the city.

A short time later the Commander's recorded speech cut out abruptly. Then the Commander came on and announced, "The city is under attack. The south wall has been breached. Muster at the south wall. I repeat, the south wall." The message continued in this vein, until the moaners got the idea and began to march to the city's defense.

Park lay low, hoping to be missed in the confusion. He waited until he saw a column of trucks go speeding away to the south. Eight trucks—enough to carry most of the officers who lurked about the palace. Park knew he might never get a better chance to scout out the "petting zoo."

He raced through the halls, but saw no one. The east wing seemed deserted. If anyone caught him—

No. They would not catch him. He'd make sure of that.

One time he heard footfalls approaching. He slipped into a shadowed alcove, and a guard passed by, heedless. Another time, as Park climbed a staircase, he imagined he heard wailing, but when he stopped to listen there was nothing.

He reached the top floor and moved quickly down a long hallway lined with windows. To his right was a door, open just a crack. He crept up to it and peeked inside.

On a nearby couch sat a woman with auburn hair, who was bent over something in her lap. She was murmuring, "Hey. Hey, it's okay. Mommy's here."

Park shifted slightly and scanned the room. The walls were painted yellow. He saw cribs, toys...

Children.

Living children, six of them, none more than a year old.

The petting zoo. It was a goddamn... nursery. But... why?

No, he told himself. Ponder later. Get out now. Mei's not here.

The woman on the couch raised her head, and Park caught just a glimpse of her skeletal profile as he eased away from the door.

He heard voices then, back the way he'd come. He hurried in the other direction. He slipped through a door and onto a balcony. At its far end was another door.

The wall to his left was crenellated, and as he hurried along he could see down into the yard below, where a few dead men wandered, moaning, "The south wall..." Apparently they were attempting to join the battle but were too witless to find their way there.

A voice at his side said, "Oh. Hey."

Park leapt back, almost stumbling.

A decapitated human head was impaled on an iron spike between two battlements. The head was that of a young man, blond, who even in this grisly state retained a look of gentle innocence. "Sorry," said the head. "Didn't mean to startle you."

"It's all right," Park said, turning away.

"Wait," the head called. "Who are you? I've never seen you before. I'm Jack."

Damn it. Park said, "Look, I really have to—"

The head narrowed its eyes. "You're not supposed to be here, are you?"

Shit. Park eyed the head. It could report him to the others. Should he destroy it?

"Don't," the head warned, anticipating him. "He'll know something's up. Listen, you can trust me. I'm not on his side. I mean, he's the one who put me here."

Park was at a loss.

"I can help you," the head added. "I know things. What are you doing here?"

Park hesitated. Did he dare trust it? But what choice did he have? He said, "I'm looking for my sister. She was captured. I don't—"

"How old is she?" said the head.

"Twenty."

"Good." The head gave him an encouraging look. "Then she was probably kept alive to breed. The prisoners are in the south wing, down in the basement. But you'll need keys to the cells. Dustin's got a set, and Greavey's got the other."

"Dustin?" said Park.

"The Commander," the head explained. It added, "I knew him before all this. We were friends."

Park whispered, "Why did he do this to you?"

The head gave a sad, wry smile. "I tried to free the prisoners," it said.

Park slipped from the east wing without being noticed. Hours later one of the trucks returned. Park lurked in the corridor and watched as the Commander and Greavey strode back into the palace. The two men conferred, then the Commander headed off in the direction of his suite. Park tailed Greavey down a hallway.

After a minute, Greavey turned. "Oh, it's you."

Park sidled up. "What's the situation?"

Greavey was grim. "The living are inside the walls. They'll be here by nightfall. Tough bastards. Militia types, called the Sons of Perdition."

Park knew of them. They had a ghastly reputation.

Greavey said, "The Commander's gone to issue new orders. Where the hell have you been?"

Park nodded at some metal piping that ran up the wall from floor to ceiling, and said, "Over there." Greavey turned to look.

Park grabbed the man and ran him into the pipes. Greavey's skull-face rebounded with a crack, and he went down. Park straddled him, seized the man's left wrist and cuffed it, then slipped the cuffs around the pipes and bound Greavey's right wrist too.

Park dug through the man's pockets. A keyring. Park hoped the head on the wall—Jack—had been telling the truth.

As Park made his way to the south wing, the Commander's voice came over the loudspeakers: "Fall back to the palace. Defend the palace at all costs. I repeat, defend the palace."

Park spent maddening minutes navigating the unfamiliar corridors. Finally he clambered down a set of metal steps and emerged into a dim, grimy hallway lined with cells. He donned his mask and goggles, then moved from door to door. "Mei?" he called out. "Mei? Are you here?" Vague figures huddled in the darkness.

Then, from a cell he'd just passed, a weak voice: "Hello?"

She was there, her tiny fingers wrapped around the bars. He ran to her. "I'm getting you out," he said, as he tried a key in the lock. It didn't fit.

"Park?" she said, unbelieving. "I thought—"

She stiffened then, as she watched him. In a near-whisper she said, "Take off your mask."

He tried another key.

"Park," she said, insistent.

He stopped. For a moment he just stood there. Then he carefully removed his mask and goggles, revealing his terrible skull-face for all to see.

Mei recoiled. "But… you're one of them, one of his—"

"It was the only way," Park said. He tried another key.

Beside her in the cell, a skinny white man with curly black hair said, "I know you. You're the one who captured me, who brought me here."

Mei said, "Is that… true?"

"Yes," Park said. He couldn't meet her gaze. He tried another key, which turned with a click, and he slid the door open.

The skinny man tried to rush out, but Park stiff-armed him back and said, "Only her."

"No," Mei said. "We can't—"

"Mei, come here," he told her.

She shook her head, withdrawing. Park looked down and saw that she was pregnant. She asked, "What's happened to you? You're—"

"I'm what I have to be!" he shouted. "To save you. Now come on!"

For a moment he thought he had her. She took a tentative step forward.

Then he heard clanging footsteps on the stairs behind him, and knew it was over.

The Commander strode into the hall, his rifle raised. Behind him came the skull-faced girl and Greavey. The handcuffs dangled from Greavey's right wrist, and half his left hand was gone—he'd chewed it off to get free.

The Commander stared at Park with baleful eyes. There was a long silence. Then the Commander barked, "Get away from there!"

Park took a few steps back.

"Keep going! Move!" The Commander advanced. When he was even with the cell, he glanced at its occupants. "You brought us so many," he said slowly, to himself. "Why a change of heart?"

Park glared back, said nothing.

"No," the Commander declared then, with sudden triumph. "You're not the compassionate sort. You only care about… one." He swung his rifle around so that it menaced the skinny man in the cell, and demanded, "Who's he here for?"

The man shrank back, holding up his hands defensively. "Her! The girl! Please."

Park inched forward, but instantly the gun was back on him. The Commander said to Greavey, "Get her."

Greavey strode into the cell and with his good hand snatched Mei by her long dark hair and dragged her stumbling into the corridor. He stood her there in the middle of the hall, then stepped aside. She trembled.

Behind the Commander, the skull-faced girl said softly, "Dustin, she's pregnant."

"Not for long." He leveled his rifle at Mei's belly.

Park stared at Mei, his sister, as she stood there right in front of him after so long, and he knew there was nothing he could do to save her.

Then the skull-faced girl shoved the Commander as hard as she could.

His rifle discharged, spraying rounds into the cement as he sprawled. The gun flew from his grasp and skittered across the floor, coming to rest at Mei's feet. She spun and kicked it to Park, but not hard enough. The rifle slid to a stop near Greavey, who fell to his knees, grasping for it.

Park leapt forward and tackled him, and they went down together, grappling. Park wrapped both arms around Greavey's meaty right bicep, pinning it. The man's mutilated left hand brushed over the rifle's stock, but couldn't get a grip on it. The Commander scrambled to his feet.

Park pushed against the floor with his heels, pivoting him and Greavey. Park kept hold of Greavey's bicep with one arm while with the other he reached out and snatched the rifle. He shoved the muzzle up under Greavey's chin and held down the trigger. Chunks of the man's fleshy jowls spattered across the floor, and his body went limp.

Park rolled off him and came up in a crouch with the rifle aimed at the Commander, who slid to a halt just a few feet away. "Back!" Park said, and the Commander slowly retreated, holding up his hands.

Park said, "Mei! Come here."

She staggered toward him. "Park… we can't—"

He held out the keys to her and said, "Get these goddamn cells open. Now."

The skull-faced girl approached him. The prisoners watched her with a mix of unease and wonder. She said quietly, "And the children. Please."

Park considered this. "All right," he told her. "And the children."

An hour later Park returned to the cell block with a duffel slung over his shoulder. The prisoners were free now, around twenty of them, and were armed with weapons from the trunk of his car. The skull-faced girl had fetched the children, each of whom was being carried by an adult. The guards had fled, and Park had taken care of the Commander.

Park said to the crowd, "You know the city's under attack by an army of the living. They're called the Sons of Perdition. You all know who they are?"

The crowd was somber.

"Anyone want to join them?" Park said. "Now's your chance."

No one moved.

"All right," he said. "Then let's get the hell out of here."

They formed a convoy of vehicles and set out north, away from the fighting. Park drove his car, and the others followed. On the seat beside him rested the duffel, and in the back seat sat Mei and the skull-faced girl, each of them holding a child. At first Park was forced to barrel through clusters of moaners, but once he got away from the palace the streets were mostly deserted.

The skull-faced girl stared out the window. One time she spoke faintly, "I said I wanted children. I was just… I didn't think… He wanted to—when they got older—make them like us. He—"

"It's okay," Park said. "It's over."

The girl fell silent.

"What's your name?" Mei asked her.

"Ashley," she said.

The convoy passed through the north gate without encountering any of the invaders. Park was faintly hopeful about slipping away unnoticed, but as he followed a two-lane road toward a cluster of wooded hills, a small fleet of pickups came racing out of the west, throwing up great clouds of dust.

"Shit," Park said. He hoped he could at least make it to the treeline before being overtaken.

He did. Barely.

"Get out," he told Mei and Ashley then. "Move to another vehicle." He passed the duffel to Ashley and said, "Take this. It's Jack. Look after him."

"I will," she promised.

Mei lingered. "How will we meet up after—?"

"Go, Mei," he said.

She insisted, "I don't want—"

"I said go!" he screamed.

She gave him one last worried look, then fled.

Park backed up his car so that it blocked the road, then he got out, fetched his scoped rifle, put on his mask and goggles, and crouched in the shadow of his car. Behind him, the rest of the convoy sped away.

The pursuers drew near, seven trucks. Park lay his rifle across the hood of his car, then put a round through the windshield of the lead vehicle. The truck slid to a halt, and the others pulled up alongside it. Men with rifles poured out, taking cover behind the doors of their vehicles. Thirty guns, maybe more.

The driver of the lead vehicle, a giant man with a blond beard who was dressed all in black leather, shouted, "You shot my truck."

Park didn't respond.

The man yelled, "You have any idea who you're fucking with?"

Again, Park said nothing.

"Listen," the man called. "This is real simple. We saw you all coming out. We know you've got women. We need them, your guns, and your vehicles. And you're all drafted."

They didn't seem to realize that Park was one of the dead. Good. He shouted back, "We don't want anything to do with your army."

"Drafted means you got no choice," said the man.

Park crept into the underbrush and took up a position behind a tree.

"Hey," the man called. "What's your plan, huh? Just how do you think this is going to end?"

For you? Park thought. Like this.

He fired. The man's body toppled against the truck, then slumped to the pavement.

Park crawled away as the other men started shooting, their bullets shredding the foliage all around him.

By dusk Park was down to his last bullet. It didn't matter. He'd won. Thirty men had come charging up the hill after him, and he'd kept ahead of them, taking them out one by one. He'd dropped nine already, and there were moaners in these woods too who'd surprised and overwhelmed maybe two or three more. Mei and Ashley and the others were well away.

Park had been hit twice in the chest, and many more times in the arms and legs, but those scarcely troubled him. By now his pursuers must know that he was one of the dead, and they would be going only for headshots.

One of the men emerged from behind a boulder and crept closer, scanning the bushes. Make the last shot count, Park thought, as he eased his rifle into place and peered through the scope.

He was shocked. My face, he thought. My old face.

No, he decided then, studying the man. But close. We could be brothers.

Park's finger twitched, tapping the trigger. He could easily put a bullet through that face, but he hesitated. It had been such a long time since he'd looked in a mirror. Since he'd recognized himself.

Any moment now he'd be spotted. Take the shot, his mind urged. Do it. But what difference did it make? Mei was safe. Park continued to stare. He didn't want to see that face destroyed.

No. Not *that* face.

He imagined the eyes of all the people he'd delivered into the horrors of the necropolis. He imagined the old woman screaming as his teeth tore into her. He heard Mei's voice crying, "What's happened to you?" and his own replying, "I'm what I have to be. To save you."

Slowly he reached up and grasped a handful of fabric.

There. The man had seen him, was taking aim. For an instant the two of them stared at each other through their scopes.

Park removed his mask.

Dustin watched from the wall of his palace as an army of the living battled through the city toward him, but he was powerless to do anything.

In the yard below, one of his followers came into view.

"Hey!" Dustin shouted. "You! Up here!"

The man stopped and looked at him.

"Listen to me very carefully," Dustin said. "This is your Commander speaking. You are to walk around this palace to the main entrance. Once inside, turn right and keep going until you reach the stairs. Take them to the top floor and continue on the way you were. You'll come to a door leading out onto this balcony. Then remove me from this fucking spike! Do you understand?"

The man stared back with vacant eyes. "Walk around the palace..." it moaned.

"Yes," Dustin said. "And the rest of it. Turn right—"

"Walk around the palace... " The creature took a step toward him, then away. "Walk around the palace... " it repeated, as it wandered, back and forth.

OBEDIENCE

By Brenna Yovanoff

Brenna Yovanoff's first novel, a contemporary young adult fantasy called *The Replacement*, should be out from Razorbill around the same time as this anthology. Her short fiction has appeared in *Chiaroscuro* and *Strange Horizons*. On her LiveJournal (*brennayovanoff.livejournal.com*), she claims to be good at soccer, violent video games, and making very flaky pie pastry, but bad at dancing, making decisions, and inspiring confidence as an authority figure.

One of the most wrenching aspects of a zombie plague that makes it completely different from, say, an invasion of alien arachnids is the knowledge that these hordes of enemies were once our friends and neighbors, were once decent, loving people. As we perforate their faces with a .50 caliber machinegun, or hack at their clutching hands with a machete, axe, or chainsaw, it's impossible not to wonder whether these moaning ghouls retain any trace of their former personality. Are the people they once were still trapped in there somewhere, aware of what's happening around them? Might they ever be cured, the way a mentally ill patient can be, with the right treatment?

Books and films are filled with incidents in which survivors try to show mercy to zombies—as with the barn full of zombies in Robert Kirkman's *The Walking Dead*—or will even fight to protect them, as with the zombified newborn in the 2004 remake of *Dawn of the Dead*. Michael Crichton's novel *Jurassic Park* suggests that it's impossible to safely keep dinosaurs in captivity, and much the same thing seems to be true of zombies. The temptation is always there, though—what if it were just one zombie? Just one little girl, surely we could handle that?

But if zombie stories have taught us anything, it's that keeping zombies around, whether out of mercy or as research subjects, seems to have a way of ending up badly for everyone involved—and by "badly" we mean with teeth, blood, and screams.

When the first drinking glass hit the floor and broke, Private Grace pressed her back against the wall and steadied the sidearm with both hands. The window above her was single-paned, the weather-stripping rotten. To her left, a free-standing radiator was rusting gently. The house was a summer cabin, cramped, and redolent with the smell of mice. They'd spent the better part of an hour nailing the windows shut, then gathering glassware—pitchers, vases, dinner plates, a souvenir ashtray with a cartoon walrus painted in the bottom—and arranging the dishes in rows along the sills.

Now, they hunkered down, waiting. There had been food at least, canned, coated in dust. They ate quickly, passing the open cans back and forth as evening fell. The sound the glass made when it landed was explosive, a mortar going off.

"What do we show these giddy bastards?" Whitaker called from the adjoining room, sounding clipped and perfunctory.

The answer came from a dozen positions, followed by the metallic sound of carbines, magazines and bolt assemblies clattering into place. "No mercy, *sir*."

They had begun as an infantry platoon of forty-seven, mostly up from New Mexico and Texas. Now, they were thirteen. Ten privates, one combat medic, and Denton the Marine, all serving under Whitaker.

Of the privates, only Grace and a trooper named Knotts were from Whitaker's original squad. The other eight and Jacobs, the medic, had come off a company that had gotten pinned down at the Air Force base and, for the most part, died there.

The base had been a short-term El Dorado, but when they arrived, their grand welcome was absent, save for a few survivors holed up in the bunkers. Some of the medical technicians had made a last-ditch effort to seal themselves in the sleep chambers. It was difficult to say whether the massacre had happened with the techs scrambling for safety or already in stasis, but one thing was certain. The flyboys had been dead for weeks.

Where Denton originated from remained somewhat of a mystery. It was theorized that he was a deserter, but in truth, Grace did not much care. Denton had the best guns.

"Smirkers," someone shouted in the front hall, immediately followed by a crash as the door splintered. Fire came in three-round bursts, rattling through the tiny house.

Grace crouched lower, sinking into her nanovest, bracing her shoulder against the radiator. She checked the cuffs of her jacket, tucked them deep into the tops of her gloves. Outside, pale hands seemed to float, palms flat against the windows. They were laughing, a storm of high-pitched giggles.

They smiled. No training in the world prepared you for that. They smiled as they slashed and bit, tearing flesh off their victims in chunks. They smiled as they ran, a merciless full-out sprint, headlong, ravenous. They smiled right before you leveled the barrel and squeezed the trigger. Sometimes, if the shot was high enough, the caliber small enough, even when they fell back—smoke rising from a neat round hole in the forehead—they were still smiling.

Jacobs said it was neurological, an involuntary tic. He talked about them a lot, his language precise, his hands sketching neural pathways. It had been his idea to come up here, strike for the research complex near Rosewood. They were close now, a couple miles off, but the slopes were crawling with smirkers and everything had started to seem wildly impossible.

A window broke somewhere and the house was suddenly awash with a new influx. They poured into the little common room. One was wearing a Christmas sweater, red, sprinkled intermittently with green trees, white reindeer.

Against the other wall, Denton was cutting swaths through the mob—systematic, businesslike. His arms were massive, the muscles displayed in sharp relief as he swung the carbine up. The smirker in the Christmas sweater was closing. It moved fast, turning on him with hands outstretched.

"Semper Fi," Denton said, but it sounded flat and ironic. He jammed the muzzle in the smirker's face.

In the front hall, Private Sutter was shouting something. He was always shouting, hooting, whooping. Sutter, with the God-awful tattoo on his neck, upwards arrow pointing to the base of his skull. Corsican script said, in an incongruously graceful hand, *Eat Me.*

Smirkers did not, in actuality, express much preference for the brain over other organs. They seemed content to take any piece they could get, but the celluloid lore of old movies was hard to shake.

In the last few weeks, some of the privates had taken to painting targets on their helmets. *Aim here in case of infection.* Whitaker didn't like it, but allowed the targets in the same indulgent way he allowed Sutter's tattoo. Harmless, letting off steam. Grace thought it was morbid.

The window above her fell in with a glittering crash, and she rose and popped the first smirker in the face. It slumped forward and she turned to meet the two that came after, dropping them on the carpet. After that, the process became automatic. Her territory extended outward for two yards and ran the distance of the wall. Every other inch of the house was someone else's problem.

Something moved behind her and she swung around, already reaching for her combat knife. It had been a boy, sixteen, maybe seventeen. The face still bore the faint interruptions of acne. He grinned and his teeth were coated in a thin veneer of blood.

The carbines were light, easy to maneuver, and the sidearm was more versatile still, but for such close quarters, Grace favored the knife. She slipped it from the sheath and brought the blade up. The throat first, and directly after that, the right eye.

Preferred it controlled, preferred it close. Some of the others couldn't stand to let the smirkers get near. Instead, they ran themselves out, not keeping count. A dull, shocked look when the handgun clicked empty. They thought about themselves before they thought about the job. That was the secret; if you thought about the job before you thought about anything else, if you just did your job, you got out. She drew her hand back, let the boy drop, and stepped over him. She wiped the blade on her fatigues and then peeled the gloves off. They were soaked.

The shooting had stopped. Grace stood, contemplating the room. Her heart beat hard and fast in her ears, and she could not precisely reckon how much time had passed. Smirkers lay everywhere, sprawled out, tangled together on the floor. After a cursory check to make sure that none were still moving, she started for the doorway.

In the front hall, she found Emery, standing with his back to her. His rifle hung at his side and he was breathing in long, whining gasps.

He was one of the ones with a target, a concentric bull's-eye painted in red on the front of his helmet. But when he turned toward her with a mystified expression, the bite on his shoulder already weeping yellow, she aimed for the eye socket. He whimpered and begged a little, but in her head, she had squeezed the trigger a thousand times, and it was no great effort to do it now, in the cramped cabin, with the daylight dropping away and the smell of bodies heavy in the air. The report was very loud in the narrow hall. At her feet, he lay still. After a moment, the blood began to pool out from under him.

Her progress through the house was slow. The floor was littered with debris, spent ammunition. Bodies lay with their limbs jutting at odd angles—smirkers and soldiers. They were mostly accounted for. She didn't recognize Denton at first, except by his size. Someone had shot him in the face. There were bite marks all over his arms. His skin oozed with the thick, pestilential yellow of infection.

In the kitchen, she found Sergeant Whitaker. He was propped in a corner, shoulders wedged in the join between two cabinets.

He looked up at her—a hard, dignified look that stopped her in the doorway. The side of his neck had been torn away, leaving shreds of muscle, exposed tendons. His voice was hoarse and liquid. "Are they dead?"

She did not know if he was referring to their makeshift squad or to the recent barrage of smirkers. "Yes, sir."

"What do you think those Washington fucks are doing right now?"

Dead, of course, all dead. Except the ones still shambling around smiling to themselves. Giggling their high-pitched giggles.

"They don't pay me to think, sir."

Whitaker laughed at that, a wet, clotted sound. "No one's paid us to do a damn thing in months. Maybe you could take up thinking as a sideline. It wouldn't have to be on the clock."

He laughed again, viscous, close to choking. The stripes on his sleeve were the brightest thing in the room. The gold looked almost white in the failing light. The blood was seeping out of him, leaving his face gray. Infection imminent.

"You should've made corporal," he said, and it sounded watery. "I'm sorry for that."

"Don't worry yourself, sir. I don't imagine I would have cared for it."

"You never know. Look at you now—you're the one who's going to walk out of here tonight."

Blood and foul yellow seepage were running down the side of his throat, soaking into his shirt.

"Do you want me to take care of it?" she said, jerking her head in the direction of his sidearm.

He smiled at her, a slow, complicated smile. "No, I got this."

She did not disbelieve Whitaker, even at the last. He was a good man, dependable. Already holding the 9mm to his temple. But she stood in the doorway to make sure. The report made her flinch. When he slumped forward and his hand let go, she turned and started back through the house.

A wooden pull-down ladder stood spindly and erect in the hall. It was fixed to the ceiling by a hinge, and led up to an open skylight. The angle of the ladder was stark, surprising. In the past weeks, the world had taken on an increasingly surreal cast and the ladder did not seem disconcerting now, but only natural and right.

"I'm coming up," Grace said, to no one in particular—to whomever might be at the top, waiting to put a bullet in the first person to stick their head through the opening.

On the roof, Jacobs the medic was sitting with his legs drawn up and his elbows resting on his knees.

"How do they always know?" he said, staring off over the hillside, the dark trees. The sky was deep purple, already speckled with stars. "We go along, covering our tracks, moving in the daytime. And still, they always know."

Grace nodded, because his assessment was true. Not a thing you argued with, but how it was. They would always find you. It was what they did.

"There aren't any bugs up here," Jacobs said.

"No," said Grace, taking a pack of cigarettes from her pocket. "No, I haven't seen any."

"It's the air. It's thin."

She wondered if he was cracking up. He didn't seem the type, but still, with these smart ones, it was hard to say. Sometimes they fell apart, just from thinking too much.

"They're not hunting people," he said.

"What do you call it then—what they're doing?"

"I mean, they're not hunting people exclusively. They're not strictly cannibals. We saw eviscerated deer when we were coming up—and rabbits—but they're not picked clean. They never eat the dead."

Grace pulled a cigarette out of the pack with her teeth, lit it. Her hands were steady, but felt light and disconnected.

When she breathed out, Jacobs coughed and fanned at the air. "How does something like this just *happen?*"

Grace observed Jacobs, his raised head, his profile, hard against the velvety sky. She assumed he must be talking in some broad, abstract sense, because the how-and-why of it was far from mysterious.

The methodology was simple. Escalating reports of a blood-borne pathogen carried by insects, high fatality rate, drug-resistant. The government had been frightened of pandemic. They had pushed immunization, pushed it hard, and in the end, they got their pandemic, all right. A vector that began at vaccination and exploded outward, extravagant. Uncontainable.

It had begun on the West Coast, vaccination facilities popping up in grocery stores and shopping centers. And everyone lined up. It had taken approximately six hours to ascertain that something was wrong, but in that time, the event had affected nearly half a million people. And it spread like fire. In a way, it was good the infection came on fast. Otherwise, they might have all had the shot, every last one of them, offering their arms to the needle without the slightest indication that anything was amiss.

"What if it's a signature," Jacobs said, turning to her.

"I don't follow."

"A carbon dioxide signature. Blood-seekers—they know to come after you. They follow a trail of chemicals, a stamp. Mosquitoes can sense living blood from almost forty meters."

Grace nodded as he spoke, not comprehending his train of thought exactly, but not needing to. The words sounded round, fat, reassuring.

"We could verify it," he said. "All we'd need is a controlled environment, some preliminary tests. We could keep going, get to Rosewood. They'll have everything we need. It would only take a few trials. I mean, then we'd *know*. And Rosewood's only four miles out. If we run—"

"If there's any still in the woods, they'll be on us in two seconds, sir. I don't see much chance."

Jacobs stood up, brushing impatiently at his fatigues. "There's a way, though. There's always a way."

He started down the ladder, his boots clattering on the wooden rungs. There was a smear of blood on the back of his shirt. Grace squashed the cigarette under her toe and wondered again if they were only prolonging something inevitable.

It didn't matter. With a purpose, a mission, the blackness of recent days did not seem so close. They would go to Rosewood and test his theory. Jacobs was not Whitaker, but he was capable. He knew things. And a short-term itinerary was better than none at all. They would go to Rosewood and find a brilliant solution. After a minute, Grace rose and followed Jacobs down.

In the bathroom, she found him standing over the body of Knotts, legs splayed to avoid the mess. He had opened the medicine cabinet and was rummaging along the shelves.

"What are you after?"

"DEET," he said, flinging bottles and tubes from cabinet haphazardly. "Why don't these rednecks have any fucking DEET?"

"You said it before, sir. There's no bugs up here."

The floor at his feet was littered with adhesive bandages, aspirin, a topical antibiotic.

"Knotts was up from Florida," she said.

Jacobs gave her a distracted look, then turned back to the cabinet.

"They got bugs in Florida like you wouldn't believe. I bet he carries it in with his personal effects. A thing like that, it just gets to be a habit."

"Check him then, check his things if you think he's got it." Another bottle hit the floor. The cap flew off and a cascade of white pills rattled across the linoleum, washed up against the motionless form of Knotts, got stuck in the congealing blood.

"And you think we could keep them off us? With mosquito repellent, sir?"

"It doesn't repel, it interferes. It corrupts receptors."

The logic was mysterious. Grace was not much in the way of parsing scientific theories, but he seemed to be missing a vital link, some key component. *A person is not a mosquito*, she thought of saying, but in the end, she knelt over Knotts's body and began to pick through his satchel. The bottle of bug spray was very small.

"Give it to me," Jacobs said, peeling his shirt over his head.

"Is this enough?"

"It'll have to be, won't it? It doesn't last more than an hour, hour and a half, anyway. We just need to get beyond them." He was already smearing the stuff down his arms. "Take off your vest."

"I'm sorry, sir?"

"Take it off. And your shirt. We need it thick, all over. Put it in your hair."

"What if it doesn't work?"

"Does it matter, then? We're dead anyway. Everyone's dead eventually."

And that was logic she couldn't argue with.

They reached the Rosewood complex shortly after midnight. The moon was pale and heavy in the sky, fat as a dogtick. Their progress went undetected, although Grace had no position as to whether it was due at all to the DEET.

They crossed the perimeter of the complex. The west entrance already stood open, a dark gaping maw. Jacobs lit his xenon lamp, holding it to the doorway. Somewhere beyond the halo of light, a shape was moving.

Grace loosened her gun in its holster. "Something's there."

"Good," Jacobs said. "We just need one. I want one alone in the lab for fifteen minutes."

Grace nodded and didn't answer. There was never just one.

From far away, a shrill giggle rose. It echoed back and forth in the corridor, trickling down the walls. Another came from somewhere in the northern sector.

At the reception station, they paused to examine the attendant signs of disuse. The control panel was coated in dust.

Jacobs indicated a bank of monitors. "See if you can bring the lights up while I find the medical bay. I need to get some supplies together."

Grace nodded again. Her skin was prickling with adrenaline, but this was not the time to go jumpy. There would be warning. There always was.

When she accessed the backup system, the lights came up sluggishly on the generator, hazy and dim, like being underwater.

She stood in the reception area and waited. The time that passed was deep and faceless and full of sound.

When an unwieldy figure came toward her down the hall, she raised her pistol, but it was only Jacobs. He wore a biohazard suit, fitted with a portable respirator and a curved Plexiglas face-mask. With one gloved hand, he gestured her to follow.

He led her through a maze of corridors to the medical wing and ushered her into a glass-fronted observation room. Grace maneuvered between counter tops and stasis chambers to peer through the long window into an adjacent exam room.

The girl was in bad shape, skin discolored, covered in welts and scratches. She was smiling the smile, gleeful, manic. Grace watched her make a circuit of the room. Eight or nine years old. Must have belonged to one of the technicians, maybe a project manager. The girl had been someone's daughter.

Jacobs turned from a cooler at the far end of the room. Cupped in his hands was a white rat.

"Is it dead?" Grace asked.

Jacobs shook his head. He had to spit out the mouthpiece before speaking. "They've got hundreds in there, in stasis. I'd say we've got five, maybe ten minutes before it revives. I need to see what she does."

Grace touched the rat's side. Its fur felt cold and matted.

Jacobs secured the face-mask again, then motioned her away from the exam room door and entered, carrying the rat.

The girl reacted with no particular venom to Jacob's presence.

When he offered his gloved hand, she took it without looking up. He lifted her and set her on the edge of a gurney. He left the rat resting beside her.

Back in the observation room, he took off the headpiece and set it on the counter.

"Now watch," he said, leaning towards the glass.

The girl sat where he'd left her, swinging her feet, smiling the deranged smile. Beside her, the rat lay peaceful and motionless.

"Right now, its body's still retaining carbon dioxide, but as it comes up, the emissions will be transiently high. It's going to be a little CO^2 bomb in a minute."

The rat twitched violently.

When the girl moved, it was with unexpected ferocity, snatching up the rat and sinking her teeth into its side. Blood ran copiously, soaking into the front of her dress.

As Grace watched through the glass, the girl's eyes turned up to meet her gaze. She was holding the animal to her mouth with both hands and then she let it fall. Blood was dripping from her chin and the rat lay motionless and red on the cement floor.

Jacobs had pillaged a battery-powered tablet from somewhere and was making rapid marks with the stylus, murmuring to himself.

There was a low, industrial whirring as the fans came on. Grace flinched as the ventilation system roared to life. Jacobs only stood with his head bent, tapping at the little screen.

On the other side of the glass, the girl began to pace frantically, scraping at the walls with her fingers.

"What's she doing?"

Jacobs glanced up. Above them, ducts ran along the ceiling, their shining planes punctuated by vents.

"She's just got a whiff of us," he said. "The air's circulating again."

In the other room, the girl was scrabbling at the floor vents and then at the edges of a broad grate in the wall. It occurred to Grace that if the DEET worked like Jacobs said it did, then the girl wasn't responding to it. That she must be smelling something else. Or maybe the DEET didn't work after all, but was only a placebo. She did not know whether Jacobs had intended the fallacy to comfort her or himself.

"Are they really mindless?" she said, with her palms against the glass.

Jacobs looked at her strangely. "You mean, did they experience brain injury? If we could mitigate the reaction to incidental levels of CO^2, we'd be certain. But no, I don't think they're stupid."

The lights failed then, and the room lapsed into blackness except for the flicker of the tablet. Without ceremony, Jacobs lit the xenon lamp and continued his notations. Grace reached for her sidearm.

Out in the corridor, footsteps echoed. Multiple people—eight, nine maybe—and coming closer, but they were unattended by the manic sounds of laughter. Grace moved so that her back was to the wall.

Jacobs still scribbled on his tablet, letters slanting down in a frantic scrawl before the CPU converted them to type. He was talking to himself under his breath, alive suddenly, animated. His intensity had become frantic, bordering on possession, and it frightened her.

The door swung open and the strangers came in slowly, with wary looks and raised guns.

"Who are you?" said a tall, craggy man at the head of the group. He stepped into the light. "What are you doing here?"

He wore no uniform. Someone had sewn stripes onto the sleeves of his jacket, but the stitches were sloppy, inexpert. A scar ran across the bridge of his nose and then jagged abruptly down one cheek. Behind him, a contingent of men held firearms. Mostly hunting rifles and shotguns.

Grace moved forward, standing at attention. "Private Maureen Grace and Sergeant Rabe Jacobs, 68W."

The man nodded. "Trask," he said.

He gave no rank and did not need to. His manner conveyed the brutal authority of a general, although the unit behind him was motley. Probably local militia. He was looking past her to the bare desk and the glassed-in examination room. "And what are you doing here, Private Maureen Grace?"

She glanced at Jacobs, who sat limply, watching the newcomers with the air of someone drugged. "We're investigating a possible course of action. The sergeant's developing a theory and has acquired a research subject."

"This research subject here?" Trask said, raising his pistol to the glass. "This raggedy little bitch right here?"

At the desk, Jacobs set the tablet down. "What are you doing? She's not a threat, you moron. She's just a little girl."

The look Trask gave him was long, calculating. "And she'd have your throat out in two seconds."

"I had her *calm*. I had her sedate, even when I was in the room. We have all the preliminary evidence necessary to pursue this. Are you listening? We could alleviate their aggression. We could *fix* them!"

"And lead them around like pets? Keep them until they've had enough one night, and kill us in our beds?"

Jacobs scrambled up from the desk. "It is our *duty* to cure them."

"There is no cure," Trask said, coming down hard on each word. "No cure but to rout them, and pick them off one at a time until it's over. There's no way to play nice and then go home."

Around him, the other men nodded, their gestures tied to his orbit like moons or planets. Grace watched them. Trask embodied all the qualities vital in a leader. His voice was low and commanding. His face was honest. It promised suffering to anyone who got in his way.

Above them, the ductwork clattered. In the eerie glow of Jacobs's lantern, the men started, raising their weapons to the ceiling.

Grace crossed to the observation window and pressed her face to the glass. "She's gone, sir."

When the ventilation duct dropped down into the observation room, the sound was very loud. The whole apparatus seemed to peel away from the ceiling—a long, shining arc that hung for an instant at its apex, then crashed to the floor with a deafening clang.

Grace watched as a dim figure scrambled out on hands and knees, slashing and clawing at everything in reach. Lank, dirty hair, tattered dress, dark splatters down the front. Then nothing but the smile. The handgun was light, not powerful, but efficient, up out of the holster and in her hand. She put the girl down from eight yards.

Beside the desk, Jacobs lay under the remains of the duct. The aluminum had torn jaggedly, like a mouthful of teeth. Her ears still rung with the sound of metal striking cement and on another plane, laid over the metallic clatter, the shot echoed again and again.

She did not recall crossing the room, but there she was beside him. His cheek had been raked open and he gasped for breath, looking up at her. A dull, shocked look, like he was offended by the treachery of the world. The wound in his side was long. Not a puncture, but a ragged gash, first through the material of the biohazard suit and then through his skin and after that, the subcutaneous fat. The blood was bright, arterial red.

Grace knelt over him and pressed her hands to the wound.

Somewhere in the ducts, a sharp, high-pitched giggle broke loose, echoing down on them like spilled nails.

"Welcome to the zoo," Trask said behind her.

"You know I'm right," Jacobs whispered. "Don't you know I'm right?"

But Grace knew nothing about chemistry or pathology. The mysteries of science were Jacobs's domain, and the brilliance of his vision eluded her.

He was coughing now, bloody saliva collecting at the corners of his mouth. On the other side of an examination table, the dead girl grinned and grinned.

Trask moved closer. He was wearing work-boots and the soles squeaked on the linoleum. "Look at his face. He's infected anyway. You know it, I know it. Just end it—for him and for us. We need to be strong if we're going to restore the nation."

All through the compound came the sounds of scrabbling, shuffling laughing. Grace had a strange, unbidden thought. *There is no nation; only people.*

Under her palms, Jacobs coughed again. The skin around his eyes had taken on a bluish hue.

Trask had nothing on his side but grim conviction and force of will. A man who was simply not afraid could persuade the masses to follow him anywhere. He might not be a war hero, but he could marshal the survivors.

Above them, the metallic clamor was much louder. Grace lifted her hands.

She raised the gun, held the muzzle to Jacobs's cheek. His eyes were pained and cloudy. She felt for the trigger and did not think, because it was easier not to.

STEVE AND FRED

By Max Brooks

Max Brooks is one of the kings of contemporary zombie fiction. He is the author of *World War Z*—which is currently in the process of being adapted into a feature film—and *The Zombie Survival Guide*, both of which were huge international bestsellers. Brooks has also published a graphic novel, *The Zombie Survival Guide: Recorded Attacks*, and he's had short stories in the anthologies *The New Dead* and *Dark Delicacies II*. Prior to becoming the world's foremost expert on zombies, he worked for two years as a writer for *Saturday Night Live*.

There comes a point in life when you must look in the mirror and ask yourself certain basic questions: *Who am I? What am I doing with my life?* And most importantly: *How will I fare when the zombies come?* As you survey the vast landscape of zombie fiction, you must appraise each character and ask: *Would that be me?*

Maybe you'll be the coward who locks himself in the basement and refuses to help fortify the house, and refuses to let any strangers into your domain, all the while ignoring obvious signs that your child will soon be among the undead. No? Then maybe you'll be the strong leader of your enclave of survivors who goes mad with power and turns into a sadistic monster more horrifying than any zombie.

Don't think so? Of course, you know *exactly* who you'll be: The hero, the one who perseveres when all others have succumbed. You'll have the weapons, the car, the steely determination, the girl. You'll ride into town like a white knight and sort the local zombie problem right out, and ride off into the sunset as the weak gather in the dusk and wave and wonder about your name. That's the way you've always imagined it, right? Well then, our next story should be right up your alley.

Think you know exactly who you'll be when the zombies come? Well, so do we. You'll be exactly like the main character in our next tale.

"There's too many of them!" Naomi shrieked, the sound perfectly matching the skidding of the motorcycle's tires.

They came to rest just short of the treeline, the Buell's engine purring between their legs. Steve's eyes narrowed as he scanned the outer wall. It wasn't the zombies that bothered him. The lab's main gate was blocked. A Humvee had collided with the burned-out hulk of what looked like a semi's tractor. The trailer must have continued forward, turning over as it slammed into the two vehicles. Bright, icelike pools shone where fire had melted parts of the aluminum walks. *Can't get in that way.* Steve glanced over his shoulder at Naomi. "Time to use the service entrance."

The neuroscientist actually cocked her head. "There *is* one?"

Steve couldn't help but chuckle. For someone so smart, Naomi sure could be dumb. Steve licked his finger and placed it dramatically in the wind. "Let's find out."

The lab was completely surrounded. He'd expected that. There had to be, what, a few hundred shuffling and groping at each side of the hexagonal perimeter.

"I can't see another gate!" Naomi shouted over the bike's roar.

"We're not looking for one!" Steve shouted back.

There! A spot where the living dead had crowded against the wall. Maybe there had been something on the other side: a living survivor, a wounded animal, who knew, who cared. Whatever it was had been tasty enough to entice enough Stinkers to crush some of their buddies against the naked cinderblocks. The pressure had created a solid mass of compressed necrotic flesh, its shallow angle allowing the still-mobile Stinkers to literally walk up it and over the wall.

The "ramping" must have happened at least a few hours ago. The original prey had long since been devoured. Only a few ghouls now stumbled or crawled over the undead ramp. Some of its parts still moved: a waving arm or a clicking jaw. Steve could have cared less about them; it was the mobile ones still slouching over them he worried about. *Just a few.* He nodded imperceptibly. *No problem.*

Naomi didn't react when Steve aimed the bike's nose at the ramp. Only when he gunned the engine, did she look straight ahead to his target.

"Are you—" she began.

"Only way in."

"That's *crazy!*" she screamed, loosening her grip on his waist as if to leap off the Buell.

Steve's left hand instinctively shot out, holding her wrist and pulling it to him. Looking back at her terrified gaze, he flashed his signature grin. "Trust me."

Wide-eyed and chalk pale, Naomi could only nod and hug him with all her might. Steve turned back to the ramp, continuing to grin. *Okay, Gunny Toombs, this one's for you!*

The Buell took off like a rifle bullet, Hansen leaning into the howling wind. Five hundred yards… four hundred… three…. Some of the zombies near the ramp began to notice them, turning and stumbling towards the oncoming crotch rocket. Two hundred yards… one hundred… and now they were massing, grouping into a small, but tight swarm blocking the ramp. Without flinching, Steve swung the M4 out of its worn leather scabbard and with eyes still fixed firmly ahead he bit down hard on the weapon's charging handle. It was a move he'd only tried once before, that night his Harrier had crashed outside Fallujah. The impact had broken one arm and both legs, but not his warrior's spirit. He'd tried using his teeth to cock the automatic carbine. It'd worked then, and damn if it worked now. The first round clicked reassuringly into the chamber.

No time to aim. He'd have to shoot from the hip. *Crack!* The closest one's left eye disappeared, a reddish brown cloud exploding out the back of its head. Steve might have commented on his marksmanship, if only there was time. *Crack! Crack!* Two more went down, falling like puppets with their strings cut. This time he smiled. *Still got it.*

The path began to open, but at the blinding speed they were traveling, would it open fast enough? "Oh my god!" Naomi screamed.

With barely half a dozen bike lengths to go before they hit the ramp, Steve squeezed the M4's trigger, spraying a fully automatic burst of copper-coated tickets to hell. *Kiss Satan for me,* Steve thought. *Or my ex-wife, whichever you see first.*

The carbine clicked on empty just as the last zombie fell, and with a soft crunch and a bang, one hundred and forty six horses thundered onto the ramp. With the Buell's wheels tearing up its putrid surface as they went, Steve and Naomi catapulted clear over the fence.

"OOOH-RAHH!" Steve shouted, and for just a split second, he was back in the cockpit, shrieking over the Iraqi desert, showering fire and death in a star spangled storm. Unlike the AV-8 jump jet, however, this machine couldn't be steered once airborne.

The Buell's front tire smashed into the parking lot asphalt and skidded on a puddle of human remains. The impact catapulted both from the custom leather saddle. Steve tucked, rolled, and slammed against the tire of a smashed Prius. The hybrid's driver, armless, faceless, stared down at him from the open driver's door. *Too bad the "save the Earth" car couldn't do the same for its owner,* he thought.

Steve sprang to his feet. He could see Naomi lying several yards away. She was face down, unmoving. *Shit.* The bike lay in the exact opposite direction. No way to tell if either of them was alive.

The moans and stench hit him like a one-two punch. He whirled just in time to see the first of the zombie horde begin to slouch towards them. Where the hell was the M4? He'd felt it slip from his grasp as they hit, heard it skitter across the hard surface. It must have gone under a car, but which one? There must have been several hundred vehicles still in the parking lot, which also meant that there must be several hundred undead former owners still on the grounds. No time to worry about that now, and no time to start looking for the weapon. The ghouls, about twenty of them now, advanced slowly towards Naomi's motionless body.

Steve's hand first went for the 9mm in his jacket. *No.* He stopped himself. If the M4 was damaged or lost, his Glock would be their only ballistic weapon. *Plus,* he thought, his finger's closing on familiar sharkskin hilt behind his back, *it just wouldn't be fair to Musashi.*

SSCHHIING! The ninjatō's twenty-three-inch blade glinted in the noonday sun, as bright and clear as the day Sensei Yamamoto had presented it to him in Okinawa. "Its name is Musashi," the old man had explained. "The Warrior Spirit.

Once drawn, its thirst must be slaked with blood." Well, he thought, let's hope that syrupy crap those Stinkers have in their veins counts.

A zombie loomed in the blade's reflection. Steve spun, catching it cleanly under the neck. Bone and muscle separated like ice under flame as the still snapping head rolled harmlessly under a torched minivan.

Ground and center.

Another zombie reached out to grab Steve's collar. He ducked under its right arm and came up behind its back. Another head went rolling.

Breathe and strike.

A third took Musashi's blade right through its left eye.

Dodge and swing.

A fourth lost the top of its head. Steve now stood only a few paces from Naomi.

Ground and center!

A fifth Stinker found its skull cleaved right down the middle.

"Steve..." Naomi looked up, voice weak, eyes unfocused. She was alive.

"I got ya, babe." Steve yanked her to her feet, simultaneously slamming Musashi's blade through the ear of a ghoul slouching between them. He thought about trying to find the M4, but there just wasn't enough time. *Plenty more where we're going.*

"C'mon!" Steve pulled her through an encroaching swarm and together they ran to the overturned Buell. When he felt the engine roar beneath him—*Made in the USA!*—he wasn't surprised. Another roar could also be heard, dull and faint and growing with each passing second. Steve tilted his head to the smoke filled sky. There it was: their ride out of here, a small black speck set against the crimson sun.

"You call a cab?" Steve said, smiling at Naomi. For just the briefest of moments, the beautiful egghead smiled back.

They were only a hundred yards from the lab's open double doors. No problem there. Four flights of stairs. Steve patted the motorcycle. Again, no problem. "We just gotta get to the heliport on the..." Steve trailed off. His eyes locked on someone—no, some*thing*. A ghoul was shuffling towards them from behind a smashed SUV. It was short and slow, and even on foot, he and Naomi could have left it in their dust. But Steve wasn't planning on leaving. Not just yet. "Keep the engine running," he said, and for once Naomi didn't question him.

Even with the rotted skin, the dried blood, the lifeless, milk-white eyes, she'd also recognized Theodor Schlozman. "Go," was all she said.

Steve dismounted the bike and walked slowly, almost casually over to the approaching ghoul.

"Hey, Doc," he said softly, his voice cold as arctic death. "Still tryin' to save Mother Earth from her spoiled children?"

Schlozman's jaw dropped slowly open. Broken, stained teeth poked through chunks of rotting human flesh. "Huuuuuuuuaaaaaaaa," rasped the former Nobel prize winner, his bloody hands reaching for Steve's throat.

The Marine let him get almost close enough to touch. "As you used to say…" he smirked, "arms are for hugging," and swinging Musashi like an honor guard rifle he sliced off Schlozman's fingers, then hands, then forearms before leaping into the air and smashing the Paleoclimatologist's head sideways with a roundhouse kick.

The brain that had once been hailed as "Evolution's Crowning Achievement" exploded from the shattered skull. Still intact, it went spinning towards the Buell, landing with a wet splat right at the base of the front tire. *Touchdown.*

The Marine sheathed his assassin's short sword and walked slowly back to Naomi.

"We all done?" she asked.

Steve looked up at the approaching Blackhawk. Five minutes till they hit the roof. *Right on time.* "Just had to take out the trash," he answered without looking at her.

He gunned the engine and felt Naomi's arms grip him tightly around the waist. "Back there," she said, tilting her head to the spot where he'd rescued her, "did you call me 'Babe'?"

Steve cocked his head in perfect innocence and spoke the only French he would ever want to learn: "Moi?"

Steve gunned the engine and the brain of Professor Theodor Emile Schlozman splattered under spinning rubber like an overripe tomato. Steve smirked as the bike thundered towards…

Fred closed the book. He should have stopped several pages back. The pain behind his eyes had now spread to his forehead and down his neck. Most of the time he could ignore the constant headache. Most of the time it was just a dull pulse. The last few days though, it was getting almost debilitating.

He lay flat on his back, his skin sticking to the smooth granite floor. He rested his head on the oily, crusty rag that had once been his T-shirt and tried to focus on the center of the ceiling. The light fixture above him almost looked like it was on. At this point in the afternoon, sunlight from the small window struck the bulb's prism glass bowl. Rainbow sparkles, dozens of them, marched beautifully across the cream-colored wallpaper. This was by far his favorite part of the day, and to think he hadn't even noticed it when he first arrived. *It's the only thing I'll miss when I get out of here.*

And then they were gone. The sun had moved.

He should have thought of that, planned better. If he'd known what time it was going to happen, he could have read up until then. He probably wouldn't have even gotten such a bad headache. He should have worn a watch. Why didn't he wear a watch? *Stupid.* His cell phone always had the time, and date, and… everything. Now his cell phone was dead. How long ago had that happened?

Way to be prepared, asshole.

Fred closed his eyes. He tried to massage his temples. Bad idea. The first upward motion tore the scabs between skin and fingernail stubs. The pain drew a quick hiss. *Fuckin' idiot!* He exhaled slowly, trying to calm himself. *Remember…*

His eyes flicked open. They swept the walls. *One hundred seventy-nine*, he counted. *One hundred seventy-eight*. It still worked. *One hundred seventy-seven.*

Counting… recounting, every bloody fist print, foot mark, panicked, frantic forehead indentation. *One hundred seventy-six.*

This is what happens when you lose it. Do NOT go there again!

It always worked, although it always seemed to take a little bit longer. The last time he'd counted down to forty-one. This time was thirty-nine.

You deserve a drink.

Getting up was painful. His lower back ached. His knees ached. His thighs and calves and ankles burned a little bit. His head swam. That's why he'd given up morning stretches. Dizziness was worse than anything. That first time he'd shot up too quickly; the bruise on his face still throbbed from the fall. This time he thought he'd gotten up slowly enough. *Thought wrong, moron.* Fred dropped back to his knees. That was safer. He kept his head turned to the right; from this angle you *always* looked to the right! One hand on the rim to steady himself. The other dipped the plastic coke bottle into the reservoir. The water was only a few degrees colder, but was enough to jolt him back to full consciousness. *I need to drink more, not just for dehydration, but when I start to drift.*

Four sips. He didn't want to overdo it. The plumbing was still on. For now. Better to conserve though. Better to be smart. His mouth was dry. He tried to swish. Another bad idea. All the pain washed over him at once; the cracks in his lips, the sores on his soft palate, the staff infection at the end of his tongue he'd gotten while unconsciously trying to suck out any last particles of food between his teeth. *Lotta fuckin' good that did.*

Fred shook his head in disgust. He wasn't thinking. He'd left his eyes open, and that's when he made the biggest mistake of the day. He looked left. His eyes locked on the floor-length mirror.

A sad little weakling stared back at him. Pale skin, matted hair and sunken, bloodshot eyes. He was naked. His janitor uniform didn't fit anymore. His body was living off its own fat.

Loser. No muscle, just fat.

Pussy. Hairy skin hung in blotched, deflated rolls.

Pathetic piece of shit!

Behind him, on the opposite wall were the other marks he'd made. Day Two, when he'd stopped trying to widen the twelve-by-twelve-inch window with fingernails and teeth. Day Four, when he'd taken his last solid crap. Day Five, when he'd stopped screaming for help. Day Eight when he'd tried to eat his leather belt because he'd seen some Pilgrims do it in a movie. It was a nice thick belt, birthday present from—

No, don't go there.

Day Thirteen, when the vomiting and diarrhea had ended. What the hell was in that leather? Day Seventeen, when he became too weak to masturbate. And every day, filled with crying and begging, silent deals with God and whimpering calls for—

Don't.

Every day that ended, fittingly, huddled in the fetal position because there wasn't any room to stretch out.

DON'T THINK ABOUT HER!

But of course he did. He thought about her every day. He thought about her every minute. He talked to her in his dreams, and in the no-man's-land between dreams and reality.

She was okay. She *had* to be. She knew how to take care of herself. She was still taking care of him, wasn't she? That's why he was still living at home. He needed her, not the other way around. She would be fine. Of course she would.

He tried not to think about her, but he always did, and of course, the other thoughts always followed.

Failure! Didn't listen to the warnings! Didn't get out when you could!

Failure! Let yourself get trapped in this little room, not even the whole bathroom, just the closet-sized toilet box, drinking out of the goddamn shitter!

Failure! Didn't even have the fuckin' balls to break the mirror and do the honorable thing you should have done! And now if they get in, you don't even have the fuckin' strength!

Failure, FAILURE!

"FAILURE!"

He'd said that out loud. *Fuck.*

The loud thumping against the door sent him crumpling against the far corner. There were more of them; he could hear their moans echoing back down the hall. They matched those coming from the street below. They'd looked like an ocean down there, the last time he'd stood on the toilet to look. Nine floors down they roiled like a solid mass, stretching almost out of sight. The hotel must be entirely infested now, every floor, every room. The first week he'd heard shuffling through the ceiling above him. The first night, he'd heard the screams.

At least they didn't understand how to open a pocket door. He'd been lucky there: If it had been the kind of door that swung instead of slid shut; if the wood had been hollow instead of solid; if they'd been smart enough to figure out how to open it; if the doorway had been in the back of the outer bathroom, instead of off to the side…

The more the ones in the bedroom pushed, the more they pinned others in the bathroom helplessly against the rear wall. If it had been a straight line, their collective weight, their sheer numbers...

He was safe. They couldn't get in, no matter how much they clawed and struggled and moaned... and *moaned.* The toilet paper in his ears wasn't working as well anymore. Too much wax, too much oil had flattened them against the sides of the canals. If only he'd saved some more, and not tried to eat it.

Maybe its not the worst thing. He reassured himself, again. *When a rescue comes, you need to hear the chopper.*

It was better this way. When the moans got too bad, Fred reached for the book, one more bit of good luck he'd found by running in here. When he got out of here, he'd have to track down the original owner, somehow, and thank him for forgetting it next to the toilet. "Dude, it totally kept me sane all that time!" he'd say. Well, maybe not quite like that. He'd rehearsed at least a hundred more eloquent speeches, all delivered over a couple of cool ones, or probably more likely a couple of MREs. That's what they'd been called on page 238: "Meals Ready to Eat." Did they really make them with chemical cookers right in the packaging? He'd have to go back and reread that part again. Tomorrow, though. Page 361 was his favorite; 361 to 379.

It was getting dark. He'd stop this time before his head hurt too much. Then maybe a few sips of water, and he'd make it an early night. Fred's thumb found the dog-eared page.

"There's too many of them!" Naomi shrieked, the sound perfectly matching the skidding of the motorcycle's tires.

THE RAPEWORM

By Charles Coleman Finlay

Charles Coleman Finlay is the author of the novels *The Prodigal Troll*, *The Patriot Witch*, *A Spell for the Revolution*, and *The Demon Redcoat*. Finlay's short fiction—most of which appears in his collection, *Wild Things*—has been published in several magazines, such as *The Magazine of Fantasy & Science Fiction*, *Strange Horizons*, and *Black Gate*, and in anthologies, such as *The Best of All Flesh* and my own *By Blood We Live*. He has twice been a finalist for the Hugo and Nebula awards, and has also been nominated for the Campbell Award for Best New Writer, the Sidewise Award, and the Theodore Sturgeon Award.

Radiation, a new and exotic phenomena for much of the twentieth century, was seized on by writers as a pretext for all manner of unlikely but exciting developments, everything from giant monsters to *Spider-Man*. Zombies too, of course: In *Night of the Living Dead*, it's suggested that the recently deceased are brought back as zombies due to strange radiation from a passing comet.

The idea of extraterrestrial influence being responsible for an exponentially expanding plague that transforms ordinary people into a sinister menace is an old one in science fiction. Perhaps the best known example is Jack Finney's 1954 novel *The Body Snatchers*, filmed in 1956 as *Invasion of the Body Snatchers* (and remade several times since), in which lurking alien seed pods grow perfect simulacra of your friends and neighbors, and the impersonators then proceed to murder and replace the originals. Another well-known example is Robert Heinlein's 1951 novel *The Puppet Masters*, about sluglike aliens that attach themselves to the backs of human hosts and take control of them. (The novel, which taps into the anti-Communist hysteria of the time, makes explicit analogies between the alien menace and the Soviet Union.)

For whatever reason, zombie stories of recent decades have tended to eschew cosmic explanations and have typically blamed zombies on man-made superviruses or else just left the question open. Our next story harkens back to this grand old tradition of zombies from outer space, and reminds us that we should never, ever forget to watch the skies.

When the rapeworms began to rain from the Ohio skies, I tossed my two boys in the truck with cases of canned food and all our camping gear, and we headed south for the Hocking Hills, far away from Columbus and the other big cities.

Too many other folks had the same idea. We found a small colony in and around Old Man's Cave, clusters of tents spilling down the gorge from the shelter of the cave all the way to the Devil's Bathtub. There were men and women both, which was just plain stupid with the rains coming this far north. Some folks were hostile, but a couple of college kids offered to help us pitch camp.

Josh hung back at my elbow, fidgeting. When the college kids weren't looking, he bumped into me and whispered, "Dad, we have to get farther away than this."

I looked down at his face, and saw the way he was trying to look mean and strong, and I hoped he wasn't imitating me. He was only thirteen, and his face still had a few soft edges to it.

"Don't be scared," I said.

"I'm not scared."

"Neither am I," I lied. "It's safe out here."

"No, it's not."

Josh was a news junkie, had been falling asleep at night with CNN, ever since the spaceship—or whatever it was—passed over Earth and the rapeworms started. At first the scientists thought it was a killer asteroid aimed at the planet. Maybe it would have been better for us all if it had been.

"Hey," one of the college kids yelled. "You can leave the kids here, go get your stuff from the car."

Nick, my nine-year-old, tugged frantically at my sleeve, his chin trembling. He talked through clenched teeth, punctuating each word with an angry pause. "Don't. Leave. Us. Here."

I put my arm around him and pulled him close, but he struggled against my grip. "I won't do that. I promise we'll stay together. We'll be okay."

So I told the college kids we'd just go up to the car together so the boys could help me carry stuff. Then when we got to the parking lot, we ran to the car and headed east on Route 56 toward Lake Hope State Park.

It was getting dark. When I first saw the man in the plaid flannel jacket on the side of the road, I figured him for another refugee. But then he saw us, and lurched out into the path of the car waving his arms for us to stop. By the way he moved, all stiff and jerky, I could tell that he was infected.

"Get down," I yelled at the boys. "Get down!"

I tried to steer around him, but he moved fast, if awkwardly. I had a brief nightmare of him flying through the windshield like a deer, because that would be it for us then. But I twisted the wheel at the last second, clipping him with the bumper, and he flew off the side of the road while I held onto the wheel and controlled the car.

"What was that? What was that?" Nick yelled.

Josh's voice was calmer. "Did you hit him? Is he gone? *Dad, did you hit him?*"

"Don't worry! Settle down!" I yelled. Fighting every natural instinct in my body to pull off to the side of the road, I put my foot down and hit the gas. "It's all right. Everything's all right."

Less than a mile up the road, I saw a car crashed into a ditch, which made me wonder: What if that man wasn't infected? What if he was just an accident victim, injured, looking for help? I pushed those questions out of my mind; I had to assume he was infected.

When I came to the Lake Hope sign, I drove past it.

Soon enough, we were on a dark, unpopulated road that led through the Wayne National Forest. If we stayed on it, we'd end up in the university town of Athens, where there were too many people. So when I saw a gate for an old logging trail into the forest, I pulled over and broke the chain on it with the tire iron. After driving the car through, I closed the gate again and poked through my toolbox for a spare lock to close the gate again. Sure, somebody else might come along and break it later, but there was no need to advertise we were here.

If I'd been thinking ahead, I would have driven all night. South toward Ironton, there were places in the woods as far away from people as we were likely to get anywhere in Ohio, and the rapeworms were unlikely to spread north into the upper peninsula of Michigan. But it was November, already after seven at night, and in the dark you can't see the rapeworms falling.

Nick was at the frazzled end of his nerves, whining and sucking his thumb, something he hadn't done since kindergarten. I just wanted to be someplace, anyplace. So we found a clearing, out of sight of the road, and we set up camp. Josh seemed glad to have some work to do. He practically put up the whole tent by himself while I talked to Nick and tried to get him to calm down.

Well after midnight, when I thought they were both asleep in their thermal sleeping bags, I tiptoed back out to the truck to listen to the radio. There were still stations broadcasting from some of the cities in the north. I sat there shivering, scanning the AM radio channels in hopes of any helpful news.

WTVN out of Columbus was dead, but I was able to pick up WJR out of Detroit. Snatches of news came in through the static.

"...scientists are still trying to understand the alien biology of the parasite infection that is sweeping the globe..."

"...officials report that the nuclear device exploded over Orlando, Florida, has sterilized the threat there, and will prevent the spread of further contamination..."

"...meanwhile in Ohio, the governor has extended martial law to the highways. All personal travel is forbidden as long as the crisis lasts. Cars on the highway may be shot without warning..."

When that signal faded, I tried a Cleveland station with no luck. I could pick up a couple Christian stations out of West Virginia, but I couldn't stomach their message. If we survived, if I saved my kids, then it wasn't the end of the world.

I was lost in these thoughts, watching the breath frost from my nose, when a tap at the window made me jump, and I jerked up my gun and aimed it at my attacker.

It was Nick. He was standing there without his coat on, bawling.

I started sobbing even before I opened the door and gathered him into my arms. I rocked him and told him how sorry I was. Snot ran from my nose while static poured out of the tinny speakers.

After a few moments, we both stopped crying. He snuggled down into my arms. "What are you doing?" he asked.

"I'm listening to music."

I reached out and hit the scan button, looking for something to distract him, but we only caught snatches of news, mostly from the Christian stations in small towns still unaffected by the plague.

"...the fifth angel sounded, and I saw a star from heaven fallen unto the earth: and there was given to him the key of the pit of the abyss..."

"...and the rest of mankind, who were not killed with these plagues, repented not of the works of their hands..."

"...hallelujah! Salva—"

I punched it off. Then I turned off the car, to save the battery and the gas. I started to sing to him, "Bye, bye, Miss American Pie, drove my Chevy to the Levee—"

"Dad, that's an old song. It's so lame."

"I'm glad you're here," I said, tousling his hair.

"Why couldn't we bring Schrody?"

"Schrody's a smart cat. He can look out for himself."

"But who's going to change his litter box?"

I hugged him close, looking through the window as the dashboard light faded. The trees formed a black wall around us, like the sides of a pit, and the darkness of the sky made the stars seem to twitch like maggots. "We get to camp out and pretend we're Indians. Won't that be fun?"

"Where's Mom? Is Mom safe?"

I checked my cellphone to see if my ex had called, but the battery was dead and I had forgotten to pack the dashboard charger. Their mother and I had gone through a bitter divorce, which we tried to keep from the boys, even though we split custody. Tomorrow was the usual day I turned them back to her. She would be frantic with worry when she didn't hear from us, but I convinced myself it was better to have no contact until the plague passed. The government had censored pictures of what happened to women infected by the rapeworm, but we heard rumors.

"Yeah, she's safe," I promised. "She wants me to tell you that she misses you."

His eyes brightened for a second, then he sank back down into my arms. "You don't really know."

I held him until he fell back to sleep. He started to wake up every time I tried to put him down or move him, so I leaned the seat back and fell asleep myself.

When I woke up in the morning, the windows were frosted over with ice, and the sun coming through them was bright and harsh. Josh was in the car too, in the passenger seat, curled up with his head against my arm.

They both looked untroubled in their sleep, the way they always had until just a few months before. I knew I would do whatever I had to do to keep them safe.

After we woke up, I checked our supplies. We had our fishing gear, and I had my grandfather's old single barrel shotgun in the trunk, with a couple boxes of shells. There was also his old .38 Special revolver, the one he bought to protect his store and then never needed. I had just the rounds inside that, and no extras. I didn't like guns, and wouldn't have owned these if I hadn't inherited them.

I checked out our supply of canned foods. If we were careful, we could get through the next few weeks until things settled down.

"Dad, you know what we forgot to pack?" Josh said while we ate canned pears for breakfast.

I picked up the can opener where he'd left it on the ground, and put it back in my kit. "No, what?"

"Twinkies. They're the perfect food. They never go stale. They survive anything."

I grinned, and he flashed a smile back. For a moment, I thought everything would be okay. "I think it's better if we have healthier food," I said.

"I thought you said we were going to have fun," he said.

The way he said it threw the lie back in my face. But I grinned anyway.

Over the next few weeks, Josh and I ate canned food until the green beans tasted like the corn like the peaches like the ham. Nick ate only peanut butter, until all the peanut butter was gone. The three of us sat inside the tent, playing Uno until the day Nick tore all the cards in half because we were out of peanut butter. We were cold all the time and we started to stink, spending day after day in the tent, until Josh started holding his nose shut every time he sat next to me. I didn't pack enough toilet paper, and I screamed at the boys when they used the last roll of it to clean up spilled peaches.

We moved camp twice. The first week, we heard cars roaring by on the nearby roads, so we moved to a clearing farther back in the woods. A week later there were days of planes flying overhead—fighter jets and helicopters—so we moved farther back under the trees. We spent our days watching the skies, staring at the roads, jumping every time a squirrel crunched through the leaves, dashing out our fire any time we heard something like a gunshot.

At night, when the boys were sleeping, I listened to the radio for news. Scientists still hadn't found a way to remove the rapeworms from brain tissue without killing the patients. We were no longer in touch with the rest of the world: the Middle East was the first to go completely silent. Americans were moving north across the border into Canada.

I thought about following with the boys, but the gas gauge in the car read empty after I fell asleep one too many times listening to the radio with the engine running.

It was the second week of December when I took the shotgun out to try for a deer, telling the boys they had to stay in the tent until I came back. I was a half mile away when I heard an explosion, and then another, something far away but powerful enough to make the ground shake. I ran all the way back to our camp, and the boys were running out to meet me, and we all waited together for something else to happen.

Snow fell that night, the first snowfall of the year that was more than just flurries, three or four inches of it before morning. There was a glow on two horizons, west toward Cincinnati and north toward Columbus, and the fresh snowfall caught the light and spread it everywhere.

Nick had the leftover peanut butter jars, which he had filled full of acorns he collected in the woods. He sat there, shaking them louder and louder, like some kind of shaman trying to ward off evil, until I snapped at him, and told him to be quiet, I just needed some quiet to think.

Before we curled up in our blankets that night, I told the boys to hold my hands. We sat there silently, but I prayed that we would make it. All we had to do was lay low and survive long enough, and my boys would have a chance.

It was in the morning, when we went outside, that we saw the footprints in the snow.

Josh spotted the tracks first when he left the tent to pee. I heard him running back, feet crunching through the snow. He yanked open the tent flap in a panic. "Dad, you gotta see this. Somebody's been watching us."

We all three went. I carried Nick, if only to keep him from hanging onto my legs and tripping me. He growled and bit my shoulder and pounded on me with his fists.

"Look, they're the same size as mine," Josh said. "It's just another kid. Maybe he's out here all by himself."

Nick squirmed out of my arms at that point, eager to take a look himself.

Together, we trudged through the snow, following the straight line of the trail through the woods. When we came to the road, I realized how stupid I'd been.

"Don't move," I whispered to the boys. And then stepping over to a pine tree, I reached inside and broke off several branches, using them to try to cover up my tracks as I retraced them.

Nick fidgeted, shifting from foot to foot, kicking up the snow, but Josh wore a look of horror. "If we can follow them, anyone who comes by here could follow us."

I nodded. "We'll go back to camp, stepping in the same footprints as we go, okay? We'll use the branches to cover our steps."

"What about the other boy?" Nick asked as I scooped him up in my arms.

"What?"

"Yeah," Josh said. "He's probably really scared out here."

"You can't leave him out here, Dad."

I damn well could, I thought, but then I saw their faces. If the boy was infected, he would have walked straight into our camp.

"Okay," I said. "But you two have to stay here. You can hide inside this pine tree, and watch me go."

I thought that would be the breaking point, that Nick would change his mind, but he scrambled through the branches, spilling snow, as soon as I put him down.

"I'll take care of him," Josh said.

I crossed the road, brushing away both sets of prints as I went. I figured to take a quick look around, then report back to the boys that I couldn't find anything. We'd move our camp again, and this time I would keep a better eye out for other people.

But I was only ten or twenty feet off the road when I saw a splash of camouflage, bright green against the snow, amid a flash of movement.

"Hey, come back!" I called.

I ran after the kid—it was definitely a kid—without bothering to cover my tracks. I came into a small clearing, and saw him standing on the other side, half-hidden by a tree.

"It's okay," I said. "I'm not going to hurt you."

"Baby?"

That was a new voice coming from off to my right. The kid said, "Dad," and ran across the clearing into the man's arms.

Another little family, surviving in the wild, just like us. I put my hands in my pockets, feeling more than a little nervous.

"Sorry, I didn't mean to scare anyone," I said, taking a step back.

This other man almost made me feel ashamed of myself. He was clean-shaven, with his hair buzzed short; his clothes were clean, and neat, not covered with stains; he had a pair of sunglasses on his face, so that he wasn't squinting at the glare of the snow, and a rifle slung over his shoulder. He had a big wad of gum in his mouth, and he was chewing with loud smacks.

He came toward me fast, hand extended in greeting. "No problem," he said. "You're that guy who's been camping up on the ridge with his two boys right?"

"Yeah—" I said.

But as soon as his hand closed on mine, I felt something snag in my coat. Looking down, I saw the tip of a hunting knife at my stomach.

He looked me straight in the eye. "Peace, okay?"

I said, "Okay."

He said, "I just want to be clear. We're not friends. If you or your boys do anything to hurt my daughter, or even attempt to hurt my daughter, I will kill you without a moment's hesitation."

I looked over at the kid. Now that he said something, I could see she was definitely a girl—the longer hair, the small chin, the thinner body—probably the same age as Josh. Her dad lowered the knife, let go of my hand, and took a step back. "Are we clear?" he asked.

I pulled my hand out of my coat pocket and showed him the .38 that I had aimed at him all along. "I feel the same way about my boys. So I think we have an understanding."

A small grin twitched at the corner of his mouth. Like he was a man who'd used a gun, and knew how to recognize one who hadn't. Holding up his knife, he said, "You should save those bullets. They may be hard to replace."

"I figure I won't use them unless I absolutely need to." I hoped that I was implying, *Don't make me need to.*

He blew a big pink bubble and let it pop. "You boys make an awful lot of noise up there."

The guy's name was Mike, Mike Leptke, and his daughter's name was Amanda. She was a year younger than Josh, but about ten years more mature in that way that girls have.

Mike would have been just as happy if we walked away and he never saw us again, but Amanda was bored with her dad's company, and used to getting her own way, so by the end of the week she was coming over to our camp every day to play with the boys. Nick came out of his shell, and would run off after Amanda and Josh, throwing snowballs at them. She got all big-sisterly around him.

One sunny morning, on a day the temperatures shot up to above freezing, we were sitting in our camp eating venison that Mike had shot and cleaned. Mike had built a good-sized fire, without much smoke, and for the first time in weeks, I didn't feel cold. The kids ran off into the woods pretending to be Indians.

"Have you ever seen the rapeworms?" I asked, voicing something that had been on my mind for a while. "What if they aren't real?"

"Oh, they're real. I was stationed at Fort Benning when they fell on Atlanta."

"No shit?"

"They look like dandelion fluff coming out of the sky. They'll hitch a ride on anything, but they only do shit to people." He shook his head. "I went AWOL—so did a lot of other guys after that—and came back to Ohio as fast as I could. Stole Amanda from my ex when she wouldn't give her up."

"Ah."

"It's us or them, us or them. I hope they nuked 'em all straight back to hell." He looked away. "What if," he asked, and then stopped.

"What if what?" I said, helping myself to another plate of stew. I had done my best to shave, and had melted enough water to wash most of the things in our camp, including myself and the boys.

"What if we're the only people left?" Mike asked, in a tone that said it was painful for him.

"That's crazy," I said around a mouthful of the best food I'd had in over a month.

He had his sunglasses on, so I couldn't see his eyes, and he always had a smile at the corner of his mouth. He lowered his head and spit between his feet. "What if it isn't?"

I didn't say anything. I wasn't ready to think about Josh and Amanda as some kind of Adam and Eve.

"You were smart enough to get out of the cities," he said, and then didn't say any more, seemingly on the principle that if you couldn't say something nice, don't say anything.

"Yeah?"

He shook his head. Then after a while, he said, "You mind if I take your older boy, Joshua, out in the woods and show him how to use a rifle?"

I was torn. I didn't let the boys touch the guns we had—my old beliefs were too ingrained. But I could see his reasoning.

Before I could answer him, Josh came running back into the camp. "Dad! Mike! Nick, he found—"

We jumped up from the log we sat on and Josh froze, his mouth moving, but no words coming out.

Mike walked toward him. "What is it? Where's Amanda?"

"Sh-sh-she was trying to help—"

"Where's Amanda?"

Josh turned and ran back the way he came, and we ran after him. I stumbled, tripped, ran into trees, trying to keep up—what had happened to Nick?

Mike trotted easily at Josh's side, his head up, eyes scanning the woods. As soon as he saw Nick's bright blue coat against the mottled brown of bark and leaves, he bolted for him.

"Where's Amanda?" he said.

I ran past Josh, who stood rooted well away from his brother, and reached Nick's side at the same moment that Mike jumped back.

There was a dog, dead at Nick's knees, a once beautiful golden retriever with a dirty white-and-green collar.

Its coat had gone gray, and it appeared to be molting right before our very eyes.

I jumped back ten feet, just as Mike had.

The dog was covered with hundreds of maggoty worms, silver-gray and slick, sprouting fluff-clouds of micro-wire-thin cilia at one end. The cilia moved, like the tentacles of tiny squids, tugging the creatures across the ground. The cilia sparked, seemingly at random, little blue explosions like static electricity.

"Nick?" I said, circling around to see his face.

His open mouth was full of the worms. Tiny tufts hung from his nose. One worm banged at the corner of his eye, pushing at his tear duct—while we watched, it shoved its way in, wiggling until it disappeared.

"Shit!"

"Dad, I'm so sorry, Dad!" Josh was crying, scared. "We were playing hide and seek—he—"

"It's okay, son," Mike said. My tongue was pinned to my throat and I couldn't speak. "Amanda ran to hide when she saw them, right?"

"She—" Josh sobbed, unable to speak.

"It's okay," Mike said, taking a step back, abrupt and unexpected, like a missed heartbeat. "Which direction did she go?"

"They got in her face!" he screamed. "Before we could stop them."

Mike walked away without a word. I stood there—staring at Josh, staring at Nick, watching the worms crawl off the dog toward my kneeling son. I was sick. I didn't know what to do, didn't know who to ask. Josh took another step away, rubbed the corners of his eyes. "It's not my fault!" he said.

I wanted to scream at him, to say, hell, yes it was his fault, it was all his fault. But I knew the words were really directed at myself.

"It's not your fault," I whispered. I wasn't sure who I was talking to.

Mike returned in moments, wearing a gas mask like some kind of steel and plastic bug. He emptied a can of gasoline all over the corpse of the dog. The smell made me think of gas stations, of normal days. I ran up and grabbed Nick by the collar, dragging his limp body back as Mike tossed a match and the dog went up in flames.

"Look," I said, pointing at Nick. "Look, he's okay! They're all off him!"

"They're not off him," Mike said as the flames danced in the reflections of his goggles. "They're in him."

"What?"

"He's too young. He'll sit catatonic like that until he dies—unless you feed him. Then he'll sit that way until he hits puberty and the rapeworm kicks in."

"What?"

"Amanda can't have gone far, not yet. We're going to catch her before she joins the bang at Athens."

Athens was the home of Ohio University, nested in the wooded hills of southern Ohio. Mike was convinced that's where the rapeworm colony had collected.

"Because it's the biggest city around?" I asked.

"No," he said, as he thumped a box of clinking wine bottles into the bed of his 4x4. "Because the dog was wearing an O.U. collar—green and white, go Bobcats."

"Ah."

We left Nick with Josh in one of Mike's deer blinds across the road. Bitter smoke filled the sky where the fire was smoldering out amid the snow-wet trees and the wet leaf cover.

"Dad, don't leave me here," he said.

"You have to be brave," I said. "We're going to go rescue Amanda, but I promise we'll come back."

After Mike and I climbed into his truck and pulled out of the woods onto the main road, he said, "Don't kid yourself—we're not going to rescue Amanda."

He had to choke out the words.

To calm himself down, he started to explain that in Georgia, they'd seen the victims of the worms follow the paths of least resistance, moving along roads to the places where they gathered, what the soldiers had called bangs.

"Why bangs?" I asked.

He looked at me like I was stupid.

"Huh?"

Mike shook his head. Then he lifted his fist in the air and made a whistling sound like a bomb falling as he lowered it toward the dash. When it touched down, he popped it open and said, "Bang."

"Ah."

"Yeah, there was that reason too. Once a bang started we used to let them gather until there were enough to make the strike count," he said. Then he had to knuckle the corner of his eye. He shook it off and kept his head up, scanning the sides of the road for Amanda as we drove toward Athens.

I had the .38 in my pocket and the shotgun on my lap. Mike had checked both of them for me. He was loaded with ordinance like some video game character. I didn't like the way this was headed.

"The people who are infected, they're still people," I said.

"Maybe not. The scientists were saying that the worms don't just rewire the brains when they lodge in them, they rewrite the DNA. The military guys thought, given enough time, they'll find a virus or something that will take it out."

"But the people, like Amanda, like Nick, we can do something for them, keep them safe, keep them comfortable, until we find a cure—"

He laughed out loud.

"Wait until we get to Athens, you'll see," he said.

But we didn't get to Athens. We came up over a hill, and Mike slammed on the brakes. "Shit," he said.

He put it in reverse and backed down below the rim of the road.

Just over the hill, there was an old white farmhouse with a wrap-around porch. Next to the house were three tall blue silos and a red barn with the name *McAufley, 1895* spelled out in colored shingles on the roof. A long, one-story animal shed stood next to an unharvested cornfield.

I had to wait until we loaded up and crouched back to the top of the road to see what Mike had seen instantly.

The farmhouse door hung open, with the ripped ends of curtains fluttering through the broken glass of the windows. On the barn, a rope hung from the hayloft pulley, spiraling around and around in the wind. A combine was tipped on its side in a ditch by the road.

There were people moving around the animal shed.

The shed was on the far side of the other buildings. We approached it carefully, creeping along the fence for cover. The stench of blood and shit and sugar was overwhelming. Anguished moans sounded and faded.

"Something's wrong here," I whispered. "The worms didn't start falling until after the harvest. There shouldn't be any corn—"

"Some folks thought it was the end of the world and stopped doing everything," Mike said, shrugging. He nodded at the combine. "Maybe there was a rapture, and this guy was the only guy who got taken."

Something rustled in the corn, the tall stalks swaying. Mike pushed me to the ground, dropped beside me, and brought up his gun.

An old man in a Tommy Hilfiger sweater walked out of the corn: his hair and beard were untrimmed and unkempt; his clothes hung from his body, tatters trailing like fringes from his arms; his smile was beatific and he mumbled nonsense words as he carried an armful of corn back toward the shed.

Mike gestured me to come along, and we followed the bearded guy around the other side of the shed, where we ducked down behind a four-hundred-gallon gas tank.

One wall of the shed had been pulled open, and the building was divided in half. On one side, a boy rested in the bed of straw. A woman crawled away from him, pulling ragged clothes back on. I was relieved to see it wasn't Amanda.

On the other side of the shed, a dozen or more women were lined up in rows. Their heads were covered with rags, and pieces of old shag carpet and odd bits of blanket were wrapped around their shoulders to keep them warm. They stood in thawing mud, bare feet shifting constantly. The sound that I had mistaken for moaning was a constant low murmur of nonsense words.

When I saw that many of them were pregnant, I wanted to puke.

Mike shifted position, crouching around the other end of the tank. He was looking for Amanda. I was too disgusted to move. Every bone and muscle in my body screamed at me to throw down my guns and run away.

One woman moaned louder than the others. Her swollen belly popped out of her sparkly tee-shirt and soiled sweatpants.

The boy rose up from his bed of straw—he was not much older than Josh, with no beard to speak of and pale as a ghost. When he leaned in to sniff the woman's mouth, she tried to bite his nose. He jerked his head away, then he bent down to sniff her crotch. Something satisfied him, because he tilted his head back and crooned in some inhuman language.

The old man in the fringe-tatter Tommy Hilfiger sweater dropped his new armload of earcorn and came, whining out his own reply. A third man, still wearing his business suit and tie, but hairy and ragdemalion like the others, came trotting around the corner.

Thing was, I could have known any of those men. I even recognized the cheerful smiles on their faces from a thousand days at the office, from the trips to the mall, from the visits to school.

While I stood there uselessly, Mike ran over to a Chevy parked near the far end of the shed and held a scope in his hand to peer inside.

Tommy Hilfiger and Three-piece repeated the sniffing at mouth and crotch while the woman moaned and panted, clearly in labor. The women around her shuffled out of her way, keeping up their continuous flow of jabberwocky.

The old man took out a knife and handed it to the pale boy. They exchanged words in their weird groaning language, and then without prelude, the boy thrust the knife into the underside of the woman's belly.

I jerked up the shotgun, banging it into the tank, startling myself. I shrank back, expecting to be seen, but the others were too focused on their task.

The ghostly boy sliced the woman open from hip to hip. At first I thought her intestines were spilling out: then I saw that it was a pile of worms, silver-gray and wet, hundreds or thousands of them, swimming like a school of squids out of the ocean of her belly.

She moaned with another contraction. Three-piece reached his hand up into her stomach and pulled.

A creature flopped out. At first I thought it was a human baby, stillborn, deformed—its head was too small to be fully developed. I thought it was just food for the worms to feed on, and I waited for the mass of tiny creatures to engulf it.

But as the bloody red thing hit the ground, it lifted its head and cried out. It pushed itself up on all fours—its limbs were as inhuman as its head—and began climbing up the woman's body. She was braced against the wall of the shed, the old man tying her to the wall to hold her upright. Three-piece and the ghost helped the monster climb, petting it and stroking it, crooning to it as it went. The baby bent its squat neck back and cried out again.

The mother cried back, word for word, weakly, fading. The sound sent chills through me, as did the sight of the baby ripping open her shirt and biting into her breast.

"Amanda!"

Mike walked into plain view, toward his daughter, who, I saw now, was hidden in the midst of a cluster of women at the farthest end of the shed.

Her head turned at his voice. She smiled as though she was happy to see him, though her eyes were blank.

Other heads also turned at the sound of his voice. The baby lifted its weirdly disfigured crown and screeched. The mass of worms on the ground wriggled and pulsed in his direction. The three men left the side of the woman and ran toward him.

Mike aimed his gun, and with short controlled bursts, dropped the old man and the ghost. Three-piece fell down, but rose again, blood pouring from his side and from the defensive wounds in his outstretched arms.

My teeth were chattering but I stepped around the tank with the shotgun raised. I was screaming curse words, the same words, over and over and over.

Still I couldn't bring myself to shoot.

Mike took a step back and shot Three-piece again, dropping him for good. The women in the shed keened and flapped their arms like a flock of frightened birds. Answering calls came from the fields and the houses.

I grabbed Mike by the arm. "We have to get out of here!"

"Amanda," he said. "I'm so sorry, Amanda."

She pressed forward, smiling at the sound of his voice: but she echoed the keening cry of the other women, and began to flail her arms.

He shot her in the head, knocking her back and leaving a hole in the wall of bodies.

There were more men coming from the fringes of the farm, out of the house and the cornfield. I had my fist in Mike's jacket, dragging him backward toward the road. He pulled away from me long enough to light one of the Molotov cocktails he had brought along. The flaming bottle arched through the air and landed in the dry straw of the shed.

The flames raced across the stalls like a golden retriever running to greet its master. The women seemed unable to flee the shed. As they jerked and struggled in the flames, their screams sounded more and more human. The men running out of the cornfields went right past Mike and me, throwing themselves into the flames to try to rescue the most pregnant of the women.

I was retreating, trying to pull Mike along. He was emptying his gun into the screaming bodies, screaming along with them, their voices merged into a single wall of sound that threatened to overwhelm and drown me.

Only the baby escaped the inferno. It had dropped from its mother's breast at the first roar of the flame, and now it ran, bloody-mouthed, on all fours with its little lizard's gait toward us.

Mike pointed his gun at the monster, but the trigger clicked on an empty chamber.

The creature stretched out its clawed hand to Mike's leg, while he tripped, staggering backward, fumbling to switch magazines.

I stepped forward with my shotgun. Raising it over my head, I slammed the butt down on the baby's head. I hit it over and over, until the stock cracked and flew off, and then I beat at it with the barrel, until the head was pulp pounded into the dirt. I couldn't even see what I was doing, my eyes were so blurry with tears, my vision red with fury.

Mike pulled me away and I threw the barrel on the monster and yelled at it. My elbow was bleeding, where the gun had gone off and grazed me with the shot. I didn't even notice when it happened.

As we drove away, the flames reflected in the window of his truck. It felt like the whole world was on fire.

When we were in the car, driving back to our camps, I kept thinking about the way Mike had shot his daughter rather than see her like that. I wanted to be like Mike. If I had to be, I wanted to be strong like he was. I didn't want to see my children suffer.

Before we went back to the deer blind, Mike made me wash up so I wouldn't scare Josh with all the blood on me. He talked a lot, more than usual for him—self-recriminations, how he should have extended his perimeter, taken out that bang earlier; talk about teaching Josh how to shoot, heading north for colder country.

We looked into the blind, and I saw that Josh had taken off his belt and tied himself to one of the corner posts.

"What's up, big man?" I said, trying to sound light-hearted.

He was shaking, sitting on his hands to keep them still. His voice was very low.

"It was only one, Dad. There was only one that got on my face, that's it, only one. I didn't know what it was. Nick was saying how they tickled—how it was dandelion seeds but they tickled."

I looked over at Nick, sitting catatonic in the corner. The Jif peanut butter jar had fallen out of his pocket; it was filled with a dozen squirming worms, setting off tiny blue sparks like little fireflies. The J had peeled off the label, leaving a glowing, brightly colored jar of if.

Josh saw me see it, and his face went sick. He gritted his teeth, put on his meanest face, and said nothing, trying not to shake.

Mike said, "Good work, Joshua. Smart. I need to talk to your dad for a second."

We stepped away from the blind. Mike put his hand on my shoulder. "I'm so sorry," he said.

I was shaking my head, rubbing my eyes.

He said, "It's all right. I'll take care of it. You had my back at the bang, I got yours here."

I swallowed deep, knowing he was right, wishing that I had known him before everything went so bad, wishing that we could have been friends, that Amanda and Josh could have grown up together. I took a deep, loud breath, and willed my chest to stillness.

Looking him in the eye, I said, "Thanks. Thanks. But I can do it. I need to do this myself."

"You sure?"

"Yeah, yeah, I'm sure."

He nodded approval, and I found myself wanting his approval as he reached into my pocket and pulled out the revolver. He flipped it open, checked the bullets, and pressed it into my hand.

"After this, we're going to go kill all those fucking alien monster bastards," he said. "All right?"

"All right."

"Dad?" Josh said uncertainly.

"I'll be right there," I said.

Mike patted me on the back. The revolver felt heavy in my hand, like an anchor keeping me in harbor during a storm.

I raised the gun and shot Mike in the face.

He toppled backward, and lay on the ground, his head a bloody wound that lay open to the sky.

"Dad!" Josh cried.

"I'm right here."

I went into the blind. Josh's teeth were chattering. He was pale and shaking, and his eyes had already started to take on the glazed look. He saw the gun in my hand.

"I don't want it to hurt," he whispered. "Don't let it hurt."

"I won't."

The thing is this: even with the alien taking over, some part of us remains in them, some essential piece of our DNA remains unchanged. I have to believe that. I thought of the way Amanda turned her head at the sound of her father's voice. Her tongue was inhuman, but her face was full of joy.

So I put down my gun. Untying Josh's bonds, I say, "Come here," and I take him in my arms. He squeezes me tight. I look at Nick, who's already somewhere else, and I pull him onto my lap. I reach down and pick up the peanut butter jar full of rapeworms.

I unscrew the lid and pull one out. Pinched between my thumb and finger, it writhes, cilia twitching and setting off tiny blue sparks.

Josh buries his face against my shoulder, torn between clinging to me and pushing away so he can follow the siren call of the worm in his brain. His voice is weak, not hardly his own voice any more. "Dad, I'm scared."

"Yeah, me too."

Holding him to me, I lift the rapeworm to my nose. It sparks as it enters, tickling, making me want to choke. I taste a spurt of hot blood. Then I take hold of Nick's hand, and Josh's, and we rise. When we go, we'll all go together.

EVERGLADES

By Mira Grant

Mira Grant is an open pseudonym for fantasy writer Seanan McGuire. Under the McGuire byline, she is the author of *Rosemary and Rue*, *A Local Habitation*, and *An Artificial Night*. Seanan is also a finalist for the John W. Campbell Award for Best New Writer. As Mira Grant, she is the author of the Newsflesh trilogy, the first of which, *Feed*, came out in May. She describes the Newsflesh books as "science fiction zombie political thrillers" that focus on blogging, medical technology, and the ethics of fear. Our next story is set in the same milieu, during a time called "the Rising," the event that changed everything.

Steve Irwin was the host of the extremely popular Australian TV show *The Crocodile Hunter*. Irwin, who had been wrestling crocodiles since early childhood, took over his parents' zoo, and married a woman who had attended one of his shows. (They didn't wear wedding rings, as these might pose a hazard to them or the animals.) He was criticized for once holding his infant son in his arms while feeding a crocodile, though Irwin maintained that the child had been in no danger. Danger was something he lived with daily. A television ad he appeared in joked about him dying of snakebite after not choosing the fastest delivery service. He eventually did die after being attacked by a stingray while snorkeling at Great Barrier Reef. Later, several stingrays were found dead on local beaches, their tails chopped off, presumably by vengeful Steve Irwin fans.

Our next tale is also about danger, death, and wild creatures. The author says, "This story is about the inevitability of natural selection. And it's about alligators. I've always had a passion for reptiles and virology, which gets you looked at sort of funny when you're a perky little blonde girl. I have been bitten by multiple kinds of venomous reptile, and one of the most chilling things I've ever done was go into the Florida Everglades to see the gators. That really makes you realize that Nature has things much more efficiently designed to survive than we are. We're just blinks of an eye to the alligator."

The smell hanging over the broken corpse of the campus is rich, ripe, and green—the heavy reptile smell of swamplands and of secrets. It teases its way past sealed windows and in through cracks, permeating everything it touches. Across the empty expanse of the quad, the green flag suspended from the top window of the Physics building flutters in the wind. It marks the location of survivors, waiting for a rescue that may never come. I wonder if they smell the swamp as clearly there, tucked inside their classrooms full of quiet air, where the search for the secrets of the universe has been replaced by the search for simple survival.

Something darts across the pathway leading toward Shattuck Avenue. I twitch the telescope in that direction quickly enough to see a large black cat disappearing under the Kissing Bridge. I haven't seen anything larger than a stray dog in the two hours of my watch. That doesn't mean it's safe to stop looking. Alligators are invisible until they strike, a perfect match for their surroundings. In this dead world, the zombies are even harder to see. From A to Z in the predator's alphabet.

This is California, a world away from Florida, but that makes no difference now; the Everglades are here. I lean back against the windowsill, scanning the campus, and breathe in the timeless, tireless smell of the swamp.

I was eight and Wes was twelve the last time we visited our grandparents in Florida. True to family form, Grandma and Wes promptly vanished to spend their time on the sunny beaches, exchanging hours for sandy shoes and broken seashells, while I dove straight for Grandpa's tobacco-scented arms. Grandpa was my secret conspirator, the man who didn't think a passion for snakes and reptiles was unusual for a tow-headed little girl from Ohio. Our visits were wonderful things, filled with trips to zoos, alligator farms, and the cluttered, somehow sinister homes of private collectors, who kept their tanks of snakes and lizards in climate-controlled rooms where the sunlight never touched them. My parents saw my affections as some sort of phase, something that would pass. Grandpa saw them for what they were: a calling.

Grandpa died five years ago, less than a month after seeing me graduate from high school. Grandma didn't last much longer. That's good. I haven't seen any reports out of Florida in days, and I haven't seen any reports from anywhere that say people who've been dead that long have started getting back up again. Only the fresh dead walk. My grandparents get to rest in peace.

That summer, though, the summer when I was eight and Wes was twelve, that was the perfect summer, the one everything else gets to be measured against, forever. Our second day there, Grandpa woke me up at four-thirty in the morning, shaking me awake with a secret agent's sly grin and whispering, "Get dressed, now, Debbie. I've got something to show you." He rolled me out of bed, waited in the hall for me to dress, and half-carried me out of their cluttered retiree condo to drop me into the front seat of his ancient pickup truck. The air smelled like flowers I couldn't name, and even hours before sunrise, the humidity was enough to twist my hair into fat ringlets. In the distance, a dog barked twice and was still. With that bark, I came fully awake, realizing at last that this wasn't a dream; that we were going on an adventure.

We drove an hour to a narrow, unpaved road, where the rocks and gravel made the truck bounce uncontrollably. Grandpa cursed at the suspension while I giggled, clinging to the open window as I tried to work out just what sort of an adventure this was. He parked next to a crumbling little dock, pilings stained green with decades of moss. A man in jeans and an orange parka stood on the dock, his face a seamed mass of wrinkles. He never spoke. I remember that, even though most of that night seems like a dream to me now. He just held out his hand, palm upward, and when Grandpa slapped a wad of bills down into it, he pointed us toward the boat anchored at the end of the dock, bobbing ceaselessly up and down amongst the waterweeds and scum.

There were lifejackets in the bottom of the boat. Grandpa pulled mine over my head before he put his own on, picked up the oars, and pushed away from the dock. I didn't say anything. With Grandpa it was best to bide your time and let him start the lesson when he was ready. It might take a while, but he always got there in the end. Trees loomed up around us as he rowed, their branches velvet-draped with hanging moss. Most seemed to stretch straight out of the water, independent of the tiny clots of solid ground around them. And Grandpa began to speak.

I couldn't have written exactly what he said to me even then, without fifteen years between the hearing and the recollection. It was never the exact words that mattered. He introduced me to the Everglades like he was bringing me to meet a treasured family friend. Maybe that's what he was doing. We moved deeper and deeper into that verdant-scented darkness, mosquitoes buzzing around us, his voice narrating all the while. Finally, he brought us to a slow halt in the middle of the largest patch of open water I'd seen since we left the dock. "Here, Debbie," he said, voice low. "What do you see?"

"It's beautiful," I said.

He bent forward, picking up a rock from the bottom of the boat. "Watch," he said, and threw the rock. It hit the water with a splash that echoed through the towering trees. All around us, logs began opening their eyes, pieces of earth began to shift toward the water. In a matter of seconds, six swamp gators—the huge kind that I'd only ever seen before in zoos—had appeared and disappeared again, sliding under the surface of the swamp like they'd never existed at all.

"Always remember that Nature can be cruel, little girl," said Grandpa. "Sometimes it's what looks most harmless that hurts you the most. You want to go back?"

"No," I said, and I meant it. We spent the next three hours in our little boat, watching the gators as they slowly returned, and being eaten alive by mosquitoes. I have never been that content with the world before or since.

I'm so glad my grandparents died when they did.

The slice of campus I can see through the window is perfectly still, deserted and at peace. The few bodies in view have been still for the entire time that I've been watching. I don't trust their stillness; alligators, all. Corpses aside, I've never seen the quad so clean. The wind has had time to whisk away the debris, and even the birds are gone. They don't seem to get sick the way that mammals do, but without the student body dropping easy-to-scavenge meals, there's nothing for them here. I miss the birds. I miss the rest of the student body more—although we could find them if we tried. It wouldn't be that hard. All we need to do is go outside, and wait for them to follow the scent of blood.

A loudspeaker crackles to life on the far side of the quad. "This is Professor Mason," it announces. "We have lost contact with the library. Repeat, we have lost contact with the library. Do not attempt to gather supplies from that area until we have reestablished communications. We have established contact with Durant Hall—" The list continues seemingly without end, giving status updates for all the groups we're in contact with, either on or off the campus. I try to make myself listen and, when that doesn't work, begin trying to make myself feel anything beyond a vague irritation over possibly losing the library. They have the best vending machines.

The broadcast ends, and the speaker crackles again, marking time, before a nervous voice says, "This is Susan Wright from the Drama Department. I'll be working the campus radio for the next hour. Please call in if you have anything to report. And, um, go Bears." This feeble attempt at normalcy concluded, her voice clicks out, replaced by a Death Cab for Cutie song. The sound confuses the dead. It isn't enough to save you if they've already caught your scent, but if the radio went offline we wouldn't be able to move around at all. I doubt we'd last long after that. A prey species that can't run is destined to become extinct.

Footsteps behind me. I turn. Andrei—big, brave Andrei, who broke the chain on the Life Science Hall door when we needed a place to run—stands in the doorway, face pale, the shaking in his hands almost imperceptible. "I think Eva's worse," he says, and I follow him away from the window, out of the well-lit classroom, and back into the darkness of the halls.

A school the size of ours never really shuts down, although there are times when it edges toward dormant. The summer semester is always sparsely attended when compared to fall or spring, cutting the population down to less than half. I'd been enjoying the quiet. The professor I was working for was nice enough and he didn't ask me to do much, leaving my time free for hikes in the local hills and live observation of the native rattlesnakes. They have a hot, dry reptile smell, nothing like the swampy green smell that rises from an alligator's skin. Such polite snakes, warning you before they strike. Rattlesnakes are a lot like people, although that's probably not a comparison that most people would appreciate.

Monday, some aspiring comedian did a mock news report on the school radio station. "This just in: Romero was right! The dead walk! Signs of life even spotted in the Math Department!"

Tuesday, half my mailing lists were going off-topic to talk about strange events, disappearances, attacks. Some people suggested that it was zombies. Everybody laughed.

Wednesday, the laughter stopped.

Thursday, the zombies came.

Some people fought, some people ran, and some people hid. On Saturday, there were twenty-six of us here in the Life Science building, half of us grad students who'd been checking on our projects when chaos broke out on the campus. By Monday, that number had been more than cut in half. We were down to nine, and if Eva was worse, we might be looking at eight before much longer. That's bad. That's very bad. Because out of all of us, Eva is the one who has a clue.

Andrei leads me down the hall, through the atrium where the reconstructed Tyrannosaurus Rex stands skeletal judgment over us all, and into the lecture hall that we've converted, temporarily, into a sickroom. Eva is inside, reclining on the couch we brought down from the indefensible teacher's lounge. She has her laptop open on her knees, typing with a ferocious intensity that frightens me. How long does it take to transcribe a lifetime? Is it longer than she has?

In the lecture hall, the smell of the Everglades hangs over everything, hot and ancient and green. The smell of sickness, burning its way through human flesh, eating as it goes. Eva hears our footsteps and lifts her head, eyes chips of burning ice against the sickroom pallor of her complexion. Acne stands out at her temples and on her chin, reminders that she's barely out of her teens, the youngest of us left here in the hall. Her hair is the color of dried corn husks, and that's what she looks like—a girl somehow woven out of corn husks that have been drenched with that hot swampy smell. She barely looks like Eva at all.

"It's viral." That's the first thing she says in her reedy little voice, the words delivered with matter-of-fact calm. "Danny's team over at the med school managed to isolate a sample and get some pictures. It looks sort of like Ebola, and sort of like the end of the fucking world. They're online now." She smiles, the heartbreaking smile of a corn husk angel. "They've been trying all the common antivirals. Nothing's making any difference in the progression of the infection."

"Hello to you, too, Eva," I say. A duct tape circle on the floor around the couch marks the edge of the "safe" area; any closer puts us at risk of infection. I walk to the circle's edge and stop, uncertain what else to say. I settle for, "Professor Mason just gave an update. We've lost contact with the library."

"That isn't a surprise," says Eva. "They had Jorge over there."

"So?" asks Andrei.

"He updated his Facebook status about three hours ago to say that he'd been bitten, but they washed the wound out with bleach. Bleach won't save you from Ebola, so it's definitely not going to save you from Ebola's bitchy big sister." She coughs into her hand before saying, almost cheerfully, "Good news for you: the structure of the virus means it's not droplet-based. So you don't need to worry about sharing my air. Bad news for me: if Jorge took three hours to turn after being bitten, I'd say I have another hour—maybe two—before I go."

"Don't say that." There's no strength in Andrei's command. He lost that when Eva got the blood in her eyes, when it became clear that she was going to get sick. She was the one who told him we needed to run. Losing her is proof that all of this is really happening.

Eva continues like she doesn't hear him: "I've been collecting everyone's data and reposting it. The campus network is still holding. That's the advantage to everything happening as fast as it has. Professor Mason has a pretty decent file sharing hub in place. If you can keep trading data, keep track of where the biters are, you can probably maintain control of the campus until help arrives." Matter-of-factly, she adds, "You'll have to shoot me soon."

Andrei is still arguing with her when I turn and leave the room. The smell of the swamp travels with me, hot decay and predators in hiding.

Minutes trickle by. Susan from the Drama Department gives way to Andy from Computer Science; Death Cab is replaced by Billy Ray Cyrus. There are no gunshots from inside. Professor Mason gives the afternoon update. Contact with the library has been reestablished. Six survivors, none of them bitten. There are no gunshots from inside. The hot smell of the swamp is everywhere, clinging to every inch of the campus, of the city, of the world. I wonder if the alligators have noticed that the world is ending, or if they have continued on as they always have...if they observe our extinction as they observed the extinction of the dinosaurs: with silence, and with infinite patience.

The risen dead have more in common with the alligators than they do with us, the living. That's why the smell of the Everglades has followed them here, hanging sweet and shroud-like over everything. The swamp is coming home, draped across the shoulders of things that once were men. Was that how it began for the dinosaurs? With the bodies of their own rising up and coming home? Did they bring it on themselves, or did the dead simply rise and wash them from the world? The alligators might remember, if there was any way to ask them. But the alligators have no place here. Here there is only the rising of the dead.

Professor Mason is on the campus radio again, this time with an update from the CDC. They're finally willing to admit that the zombie plague is real. Details are given, but the gunshots from inside drown them out. The smell of the swamp. The smell of blood and gunpowder. The smell of death.

My grandfather's hand throwing the rock. The sound of the rock hitting the water. *"Always remember that Nature can be cruel."*

"I never forgot," I whisper, and open the door.

The campus stretches out in front of me, majestic in its stillness, the smell of swamp water and the dead holding sway over everything. The door swings shut behind me, the latch engaging with a click. No going back. There is never any going back for those who walk into the swamp alone. This is cleaner. This is the end as it was meant to be—for dinosaurs, for humans, for us all.

The rock fits easily in my hand, sized precisely to the span of my fingers. I look up at the speaker that broadcasts Professor Mason's update, the masking sound that confuses the reality of my presence. Let the survivors cling to their petty hopes. I choose my window with care, making certain not to select one that shelters the living. I pull back my arm, remembering my grandfather's face, my brother's voice on the phone when his wife was bitten, the golden eyes of alligators in the Everglades. My aim is true; the sound of shattering glass is alien here. All I need to do is wait.

I close my eyes, and spread my hands, and I am eight years old. I am safe beside my grandfather, and the smell of the swamp is strong and green and sweet. The sound of water running in my memory is enough to block the sound of footsteps, the sound of distant moaning on the wind. I am eight years old in Florida, I am twenty-three in California, and I am temporary. Nature can be cruel, but the alligators, the Everglades, and the dead are eternal.

WE NOW PAUSE FOR STATION IDENTIFICATION

By Gary A. Braunbeck

Gary Braunbeck's most recent novels are *Far Dark Fields* and *Coffin County*. Other novels include *Prodigal Blues, Mr. Hands, Keepers*, and *In the Midnight Museum*. The sixth novel in his Cedar Hill Cycle, *A Cracked and Broken Path*, is forthcoming. Braunbeck is a prolific author of short fiction as well, with publications in numerous anthologies, such as *Midnight Premiere, The Earth Strikes Back, Tombs*, and *The Year's Best Fantasy and Horror*, and in magazines, such as *Cemetery Dance, Eldritch Tales*, and *Not One of Us*. The third installment of his collected "Cedar Hill" stories will be published in the first half of 2011 by Earthling Publications. Braunbeck is a five-time Bram Stoker Award-winner, including once for the story that follows.

In ancient times, bards and storytellers would speak face to face to their audiences. They could gauge the mood and reactions of the crowd and adjust their entertainments accordingly. And of course, they always knew exactly how many people were listening. Artists who perform live—stage actors, stand-up comedians, street performers—still have this (sometimes dubious) luxury, but artists directly addressing a live audience is becoming increasingly rare. Most modern entertainment consists of distributed reproductions—books, blogs, movies, TV, and, of course, radio (and its new media equivalent, podcasting). With these sorts of entertainments it can be very difficult for artists to judge exactly how large their audience actually is, especially smaller artists and outfits who don't have the benefit of Nielsen ratings and the like. The publishing industry is notoriously lacking in data about their audience, and many small-time radio hosts speak into the microphone without any real idea of how many people are tuning in. (This is one reason why it never hurts to blog about or email your favorite lesser-known artists; they probably get less positive feedback than you might imagine, and would probably appreciate the attention.)

Most entertainers today, even if they fear that nobody is listening, can be confident that anyone who *is* listening is, at the very least, *alive*. The determined radio host who stars in our next entertainment—which brings new meaning to the phrase "dead air"—doesn't have that luxury.

"...three-fourteen a.m. here at WGAB—we gab, folks, that's why it's called *talk* radio. So if there's anyone listening at this god-awful hour, tonight's topic is the same one as this morning, this afternoon, and earlier this evening...in fact, it's the same topic the whole world's had for the last thirteen days, if anyone's been counting: Our Loved Ones; Why Have They Come Back from the Dead and What the Fuck Do They Want?

"Interesting to say 'fuck' on the air without having to worry that the station manager, the FCC, and however many hundreds of outraged local citizens are going to come banging on the door, torches in hand, screaming for my balls on a platter. And to tell you the truth, after being holed-up in this booth for five straight days, it feels good, so for your listening enjoyment, I'm going to say it again. Fuck! And while we're at it, here's an earful of golden oldies for you—shit, piss, fuck, cunt, cocksucker, motherfucker, and tits. Thank you George Carlin...assuming you're still alive out there...assuming anyone's still alive out there.

"Look at that, the seven biggies and not one light on the phone is blinking. So much for my loyal listeners. Jesus, c'mon people, there's got to be somebody left out there—a goddamn *plane* flew over here not an hour ago! I know the things don't fly themselves—okay, okay, there's that whole 'automatic pilot' feature but the thing is, you've got to have a pilot to get the thing in the air, so I know there's at least one airplane pilot still alive out there and if there's an airplane pilot then maybe there's somebody else who's stuck here on the ground like I am! This is the cellular age, people! Somebody out there has got to have a fucking *cell phone!*

"...sorry, about that, folks. Lost my head a little for a moment. Look, if you're local, and if you can get to a phone, then please call the station so that I know I'm reaching somebody. I haven't left this booth in five days and that plane earlier...well, it shook me up. You would have laughed if you'd been in here to see me. I jumped up and ran to the window and stood there pounding on the glass, screaming at the top of my lungs like there was a chance they'd hear me thirty thousand feet above. Now I know how Gilligan and the Skipper and everyone else felt every time they saw a plane that didn't...Jesus. Listen to me. It's TV Trivia night here at your radio station at the end of the world.

"The thing that shocked me about all of this was that...it wasn't a thing like we've come to expect from all those horror movies. I mean, yeah, sure, the guy who did all the makeup for those George Romero films—what was his name? Savini, right? Yeah, Tom Savini—anyway, you have to give a tip of the old hat to him, because he sure as hell nailed the way they *look*. It's just all the rest of it...they don't want to eat us, they don't want to eat *anything*. All-right-y, then: show of hands—how many of you thought the first time you saw them that they were going to stagger over and chew a chunk out of your shoulder? Mine's raised, anybody else? That's what I thought.

"Oh, hell...you know, in a way, it would be easier to take if they *did* want to eat us—or rip us apart, or...*something!* At least then we'd have some kind of...I don't know...*reason* for it, I guess. Something tangible to be afraid of, an explanation for their behavior...and did you notice how quickly all the smarmy experts and talking heads on television gave up trying to offer rational explanations for how it is they're able to reanimate? Have you ever...when one's been close enough...have you ever looked at their fingers? Most of them are shredded down to the bone. People forget that it's not just the coffin down there in the ground—there's a concrete vault that the coffin goes *into*, as well. So once they manage to claw their way through the lid of the coffin, they have to get through four inches or so of concrete. At least, that's what all you good folks who've buried your loved ones have paid for.

"Think about it, folks. I don't give a Hammer-horror-film *shit* how strong the walking dead are supposed to be, *no way* could they break through concrete like that, not with the levels of decomposition I've seen on some of the bodies. So, then, how do you explain so many disturbed and empty graves in all those cemeteries all around the world? Easy—*you've been getting screwed*. Those vaults that you see setting off to the side during the grave-side service? Have any of you ever stuck around to watch the rest of it be lowered over the concrete base? Shit—it wouldn't cost anything to pour a base underneath the coffin. A lot of us have been getting scammed, people, and I think it's high time we got together and did something about it! Funeral homes and cemeteries have been charging all of us for a *single* concrete vault that never actually gets put in the ground!

"Anybody out there got a *better* explanation for how a moldy, rotting, worm-filled bag of bones can dig its way out of a grave so quickly? If you do, you know the number, give me a call and let's talk about it, let's raise hell, organize a march on all funeral homes and cemetery offices...

"But the ones who came out of the graveyards, they're only a part of it, aren't they? Remember the news footage of that Greenpeace boat that went after what they *thought* was a wounded whale, only once they got close enough to see that it was dead and had just come back to life, it was too late? One of them had already touched it by then. Christ, how many kids did we lose when they went outside to see that Fluffy or Sprat or Fido or Rover was back from doggy heaven? I smashed a silverfish under my shoe a few days ago, and what was left of it started crawling again. I've got towels rolled up and stuffed under the doors in case there're any ants or cockroaches your friendly neighborhood Orkin man might have missed the last time he was here.

"Were television stations still broadcasting when Sarah Grant came home? Wait a second...some of them had to've been or else I wouldn't remember seeing it. Okay, right. Anyway, locals will remember Sarah. She was a four-year-old girl who disappeared about five years ago, during the Land of Legend Festival. Ten thousand people and nobody saw a thing. The search for her went on for I-don't-know how long before they just had to give up. Well, about two weeks ago, the night all of this first began, what was left of Sarah Grant dug its way out of the grave in its pre-school teacher's back yard and walked home. She tried to tell them what had happened but her vocal cords were long gone...so when the police showed up and saw her, they just followed her back to her teacher's house where she showed them the grave. The police found the teacher hanging from a tree in the back yard; he'd evidently witnessed Sarah waking up from her dirt nap and knew what was coming.

"By then the police had seen more than a few dead bodies get up and start walking around, so little Sarah didn't come as much of a surprise to them. A lot of missing children started showing up at their old homes. Sometimes their families were still living there, sometimes they'd moved away and the kids didn't recognize the person who answered the door—this is when people still *did* answer their doors, in the beginning, when we thought it wasn't something that would happen here, no—it was just going on in China, or what used to be Russia, or Ireland, or…wherever. Everywhere but here. Not here, not in the good ole US of A. Downright un-American to think that. Christ, there were idiots who stood up in front of Congress and declared that all of this was just propaganda from Iraq, or Hong Kong, or Korea. Can you believe that? And *of course* it was all a plot against America, because the whole world revolves around us. *Fuck* that noise. Nations as we knew them don't exist anymore, folks—and this is assuming that the entire concept of 'nations' was *ever* real and not just some incredible, well-orchestrated illusion dreamed up by the shadows who've *really* been running the show all along. It doesn't matter. It's all just real estate now, up for grabs at rock-bottom prices.

"Remember how happy a lot of us were at first? All that news footage of people in tears running up to embrace their loved ones fresh from their graves? Mangled bodies pulling themselves from automobile accidents or industrial explosions or recently bombed buildings… all those terrified relatives standing around crash, accident, or other disaster sites, hoping to find their husbands or wives or kids or friends still alive? Reunions were going on left and right. It would have moved you to tears if it hadn't been for a lot of them missing limbs or heads or dragging their guts behind them like a bride's wedding-dress train. That didn't matter to the grieving; all they saw was their loved ones returned to them. They had been spared. They had been saved from a long dark night of the soul or whatever. They didn't have to give in to that black weight in their hearts, they didn't have to cry themselves to sleep that night, they didn't have to get up the next morning knowing that someone who was important to them, someone they loved and cared about and depended on, wasn't going to be there anymore, ever again. No. They were spared that.

"It didn't take long before we figured out that the dead were drawn back to the places or people they loved most, that meant everything to them while they were alive—at least Romero got *that* much right in his movies. At first I thought it was just a sad-ass way of reconciling everything, of forcing it into a familiar framework so we could deal with the reality of these fucking *upright corpses* shambling back into our lives—hell, maybe it was just a…I don't know…a knee-jerk reaction on the dead's part, like a sleepwalker. Maybe their bodies were just repeating something they'd done so many times over the course of their lives that it became automatic, something instinctual. I mean, how many times have you been walking home from someplace and haven't even been thinking about *how* to get from there to here? Your body knows the way so your brain doesn't even piss away any cells on that one. Home is important. The people there are important. The body knows this, even if you forget.

"But then the Coldness started. I...huh...I remember the initial reports when people started showing up in emergency rooms. At first everyone thought it was some kind of new flesh-eating virus, but that idea bit it in a hurry, because all of a sudden you had otherwise perfectly healthy, alive human beings walking into emergency rooms with completely dead limbs—some of them already starting to decompose. And in every single case, remember, it started in whichever hand they'd first touched their dead loved one. The hand went numb, then turned cold, and the coldness then spread up through the arm and into the shoulder. The limbs were completely dead. The only thing the doctors could do was amputate the things. If the person in question had *kissed* their loved one when they first saw them...God Almighty...the Coldness spread down their tongues and into their throats. But mostly it was hands and arms, and for a while it looked like the amputations were doing the trick.

"Then the doctors and nurses who'd performed the surgeries started losing the feeling in their hands and arms and shoulders. Whatever it was, the Coldness was contagious. So they closed down the emergency rooms and locked up the hospitals and posted the National Guard at the entrances because doctors were refusing to treat anyone who'd touched one of the dead...those doctors who still had arms and hands, that is.

"The one thing I have to give us credit for as a species is that the looting wasn't nearly as bad as I thought it would be. Seems it didn't take us very long to realize that material possessions and money didn't mean a whole helluva lot anymore. That surprised me. I didn't think we had any grace-notes left. Bravo for our side, huh?

"Look, I've got to...I've got to try and make it to the bathroom. I can at least cut through the production booth, but once out in the hall, I'm wide open for about five yards. The thing is, I've been in this booth for five days now, and while the food's almost held out—thank God for vending machines and baseball bats—I've been too scared to leave, so I've been using my waste basket for a toilet and...well, folks, it's getting pretty ripe in here, especially since the air-conditioning conked out two days ago. I gotta empty this thing and wash the stink off myself. If you're out there, please don't go away. I'm gonna cue up the CD and play a couple of Beatles songs, 'In My Life' and 'Let It Be.' I'm feeling heavy-handed and ironic today, so sue me. If I'm not back by the time they're over, odds are I ain't gonna be. Light a penny candle for me, folks, and stay tuned..."

"...Jesus H. Christ on a crutch, I made it! It was kind of touch and go there for a minute...or, rather, *not* touch, if you get me...but here I am, with a gladder bladder and clean hands and face, so we're not finished yet, folks. There's still some fight left, after all.

"I need to tell you a little bit about our receptionist here at We-Gab Radio. Her name's Laura McCoy. She's one of the sweetest people I've ever met, and if it weren't for her, most days at this station would be bedlam without the sharp choreography. Laura has always been a tad on the large side—she once smiled at me and said she didn't mind the word 'fat,' but I do mind it…anyway, Laura has always been on the large side but, dammit, she's *pretty*. She's tried a couple of times to go on diets and lose weight but they've never worked, and I for one am glad they didn't. I don't think she'd be half as pretty if she lost the weight.

"Laura's husband, this prince of all ass-wipes named Gerry, left her about ten months ago after fifteen years of marriage. Seems he'd been having an affair with a much younger co-worker for going on three years. Laura never suspected a thing, that's how true and trusting a soul she was. The divorce devastated her, we all knew it, but she was never less than professional and pleasant here at the station. Still, whenever there was any down-time—no calls coming in, no papers to be filed, no tour groups coming through, no DJs having nervous breakdowns—a lot of us began to notice this…this *stillness* about her; it was like if she wasn't busy, then some memory had its chance to sneak up and break her heart all over again. So we here at the station were worried. I asked her out for coffee one night after my shift. I made sure she knew it wasn't a date, it was just two friends having coffee and maybe some dessert.

"Laura was always incredibly shy when dealing with anyone outside of her job. The whole time we were having coffee she spent more time looking at her hands folded in her lap than she did at me. When she spoke, her voice was always…always so soft and sad. Even when she and Gerry were together, her voice had that sad quality to it—except at work, of course. At work, she spoke clearly and confidently. Sometimes I thought she was only alive when on the job.

"I said that to her the night we went for coffee. This was, oh…about eight months after the divorce, right? For the first time that night, she looked right at me and said, 'David, you're absolutely right. I *love* working at the station. That job and the people there are the only things I've ever been able to depend on. That's very important to me now.'

"After that, things were a lot better for a while. Laura took her two-week vacation just before everything started. In all the panic and confusion and Martial Law—which didn't exactly take very well, as you might recall—no one thought to call and check on her. She'd said she was going up to Maine to visit with her sister, so I guess most of us just figured or hoped that she'd made it to her sister's place before all hell broke loose.

"Two days ago, Laura came back to work. I can look over the console and through the window of the broadcast booth and see her sitting there at her desk. She's wearing one of her favorite dresses, and she's gotten a manicure. Maybe the manicure came before the great awakening, but it looks to me like the nail polish was freshly applied before she came in—and, I might add, she drove her car to work. I remember how excited I was to see that car driving up the road. It meant there was someone else still alive, and they'd thought to come here and check on me.

"I can see her very clearly, sitting there at her desk. About one-third of her head is missing. My guess is she used either a shotgun or a pistol with a hollow-point bullet. My guess is that this sweet, pretty woman who was always so shy around other people was a helluva lot more heartbroken than any of us suspected or wanted to imagine. My guess is she came back here because this station, this job, her place at that desk…these things were all she had left to look forward to. I wish I had been kinder to her. I wish I hadn't been so quick to think that our little chat helped, so I didn't have to give her or her pain a second thought. I wish…ohgod…I wish that I'd told her that she wouldn't be as pretty if she lost weight. I wish…shit, sorry…gimme a minute…

"Okay. Sorry about that. Forty-fucking-three years old and crying like a goddamn baby for its bottle. I'm losing ground here, folks. Losing ground. Because when I look out at Laura, there at her desk, and I remember Sarah Grant walking up to her family's home, and realize how many of the dead have been able to come back, have been able to walk or drive or in some cases take the goddamn bus back home…when I think of how they recognize us, how they *remember* us…you see, the thing is, Laura used to always bring in home-made chocolate chip cookies once a week. No one made cookies like Laura, I mean *nobody!* She'd always wrap them individually in wax paper, lay them out on a tray, cover the tray with tin-foil, and put a little Christmas-type bow on top.

"There's a tray of home-made cookies setting out there on her desk, all wrapped and covered and sporting its bow. Half her fucking brain is gone, splattered over a wall in her house…and she still *remembered.* Is this getting through to you, folks? The dead remember! Everything. It doesn't matter if they've been in the ground ten years or crawled out of drawer in the morgue before anyone could identify them—*they all remember! All of them!*

"Is this sinking in? And doesn't it scare the piss out of you? Look: if they can crawl out of a grave after ten years of being worm-food and volleyball courts for maggots and *still remember* where they lived and who they loved and…and all of it…then it means those memories, those intangible bits and pieces of consciousness and ether that we're told are part and parcel of this mythical, mystical thing called a soul…it means it never *went anywhere* after they died. It didn't return to humus or dissipate into the air or take possession of bright-eyed little girls like in the movies…it just hung around like a vagrant outside a bus station on a Friday night. Which means there's *nothing* after we die. Which means there is no God. Which means this life is *it*—and ain't that a pisser? Karma is just the punch-line to a bad stand-up routine, and every spiritual teaching ever drilled into our brain is bullshit. Ha! Mark Twain was right, after all—remember the ending of *The Mysterious Stranger*?—there is no purpose, no reason, no God, no devil, no angels or ghosts or ultimate meaning; existence is a lie; prayer is an obscene joke. There is just…nothing; life and love are only baubles and trinkets and ornaments and costumes we use to hide this fact from ourselves. The universe was a mistake, and we, dear friends…we were a fucking *accident.* That's what it means…and that makes me so…sick. Because I…I was kind of *hoping*, y'know? But I guess hope is as cruel a joke as prayer, now.

"Still, it's funny, don't you think…that in the midst of all this rot and death there's still a kind-of life. You see it taking root all around us. I suppose that's why so many of us have found ceiling beams that will take our weight, or loaded up the pump-action shotguns and killed our families before turning the gun on ourselves…or jumped from tall buildings, or driven our cars head-on into walls at ninety miles an hour…or-or-Or-*OR!*

"There's a window behind me that has this great view of the hillside. In the middle of the field behind the station there's this huge old oak tree that's probably been there for a couple of thousand years. Yesterday, a dead guy walked into the field and up to that tree and just stood there looking at it, admiring. I wondered if maybe he'd proposed to his wife under this tree, or had something else really meaningful—pardon my language—happen beneath that oak. Whatever it was, this was the place he'd come back to. He sat down under the oak and leaned back against its trunk. He's still there, as far as I can make out.

"Because we found out, didn't we, that as soon as the dead come home, as soon as they reach their destination, as soon as they stop moving…they take root. And they *sprout.* Like fucking kudzu, they sprout. The stuff grows out of them like slimy vines, whatever it is, and starts spreading. I can't see the tree any longer for all the…the vines that are covering it. Oh, there are a couple of places near the top where they haven't quite reached yet, but those branches are bleach-white now, the life sucked out of them. The vines, when they spread, they grow thicker and wider…in places they blossom patches of stuff that looks like luminescent pond-scum. But the vines, they're pink and moist, and they have these things that look like thorns, only these thorns, they wriggle. And once all of it has taken root—once the vines have engulfed everything around them and the patches of pond-scum have spread as far as they can without tearing—once all that happens, if you watch for a while, you can see that all of it is…is *breathing.* It expands and contracts like lungs pulling in, and then releasing air…and in between the breaths…if that's what they are…everything pulses steadily, as if it's all hooked into some giant, invisible heart…and the dead, they just sit there, or stand there, or lie there, and bit by bit they dissolve into the mass…becoming something even more organic than they were before…something new…something…hell, I don't know. I just calls 'em as I sees 'em, folks.

"Laura's sprouted, you see. The breathing kudzu has curled out of her and crawled up the walls, across the ceiling, over the floor…about half the broadcast booth's window is covered with it, and I can see that those wriggling thorns have mouths, because they keep sucking at the glass. I went up to the glass for a closer look right after I got back from the bathroom, and I wish I hadn't…because you know what I saw, folks? Those little mouths on the thorns…they have teeth…so maybe…I don't know…maybe in a way we *are* going to be eaten…or at least ingested…but whatever it is that's controlling all of this, I get the feeling that it's some kind of massive organism that's in the process of pulling all of its parts back together, and it won't stop until it's whole again…because maybe once it's whole…that's *its* way of coming home. Maybe it knows the secret of what lies beyond death…or maybe it *is* what lies beyond death, what's always been there waiting for us, without form...and maybe it finally decided that it was lonely for itself, and so jump-started our loved ones so it could hitch a ride to the best place to get started.

"I'm so tired. There's no unspoiled food left from the vending machines—did I mention that I took a baseball bat to those things five—almost *six* days ago now? I guess the delivery guy never got here to restock them. Candy bars, potato chips, and shrink-wrapped tuna salad sandwiches will only get you so far. I'm so...so *tired.* The kudzu is scrabbling at the base of the door...I don't think it can actually break through or it would have by now...but I'm thinking, what's the point, y'know? Outside, the field and hillside are shimmering with the stuff—from here it almost looks as if the vines are dancing—and in a little while it will have reached the top of the broadcast tower...and then I really *will* be talking to myself.

"If anyone out there has any requests...now's the time to phone them in. I'll even play the seventeen-minute version of 'In-A-Gadda-Da-Vida' if you ask me. I always dug that drum solo. I lost my virginity to that song...the *long* version, not the three-minute single, thanks for that vote of confidence in my virility. I wish I could tell you that I remembered her name...her first name was Debbie, but her last name...*pffft!* It's gone, lost to me forever. So...so many things are lost to me forever now...lost to all of us forever...still waiting on those requests...please, *please, PLEASE* will somebody out there call me? Because in a few minutes, the vines and thorns will have covered the window and those little mouths with their little teeth are all I'll be able to see and I'm...I'm hanging on by a fucking thread here, folks...so...

"...three minutes and forty seconds. I am going to play 'The Long and Winding Road,' which is three minutes and forty seconds long, and if by the end of the song you have not called me, I am going to walk over to the door of the broadcast booth, say a quick and meaningless prayer to a God that was never there to hear it in the first place, and I am going to open that door and step into those waiting, breathing, pulsing vines.

"So I'm gonna play the song here in a moment. But first, let's do our sworn FCC duty like good little drones who are stupid enough to think anyone cares anymore, and we'll just let these six pathetic words serve as my possible epitaph:

"We now pause for station identification...."

RELUCTANCE

By Cherie Priest

Cherie Priest is the author of the bestselling novel *Boneshaker*, which, as of this writing, is a finalist for the prestigious Hugo and Nebula awards. She has three other works set in the same milieu as *Boneshaker*: a novella from Subterranean Press called *Clementine*, another novel from Tor called *Dreadnought*, and the story that follows. Priest's other novels include *Four and Twenty Blackbirds*, *Wings to the Kingdom*, *Not Flesh Nor Feathers*, and *Fathom*. Forthcoming books include urban fantasies *Bloodshot* and *Hellbent*. Her short fiction has appeared in *Subterranean Magazine* and *Apex Digest* and is forthcoming in *Steampunk Reloaded*.

Priest is one of the leading writers of "steampunk," a literary subgenre of fantasy typically characterized by a Victorian aesthetic and the use of Industrial Age technology like gears and steam pipes to power wondrous contraptions such as giant robots.

Our next story, which is set in the same milieu as *Boneshaker*, is an alternate reality in which the American Civil War has stretched on for nearly two decades and which has seen the development of all manner of incredible steampunk machinery. In the novel, an inventor's ill-conceived scheme to tunnel for gold beneath Seattle ends up releasing a toxic gas that turns much of the city's population into shambling corpses called "rotters."

If just the thought of "steampunk plus zombies" has you quivering with joy, this next story should be right up your alley. The author says, "I'd been reading a lot about the Civil War, and something that nabbed my attention was how boys were occasionally sent off to fight while still horribly young. Thirteen was fairly common, and boys as young as eleven are rumored to have fought. I wanted to tell a story about one of these kids 'all grown up' and trying to move on—moving west, to make a life for himself away from the front lines. I thought such a boy might make an excellent character to dump into the creeping danger of a zombie story because he wouldn't necessarily face the steep learning curve that ordinarily whittles down a survival party; his instincts and battle experience would give him an edge."

Walter McMullin puttered through the afternoon sky east of Oneida in his tiny dirigible. According to his calculations, he was somewhere toward the north end of Texas, nearing the Mexican territory west of the Republic; and any minute now he'd be soaring over the Goodnight-Loving trail.

He looked forward to seeing that trail.

Longest cattle drive on the continent, or that's what he'd heard—and it'd make for a fine change of scenery. West, west, and farther west across the Native turf on the far side of the big river he'd come, and his eyes were bored from it. Oklahoma, Texas, North Mexico next door...it all looked pretty much the same from the air. Like a pie crust, rolled out flat and overbaked. Same color, same texture. Same unending scorch marks, the seasonal scars of dried-out gullies and the splits and cracks of a ground fractured by the heat.

So cows—rows upon rows of lowing, shuffling cows, hustling their way to slaughter in Utah—would be real entertainment.

He adjusted his goggles, moving them from one creased position on his face to another, half an inch aside and only marginally more comfortable. He looked down at his gauges, using the back of one gloved hand to wipe away the ever-accumulating grime.

"Hydrogen's low," he mumbled to himself.

There was nobody else to mumble to. His one-man flyer wouldn't have held another warm body bigger than a small dog, and dogs made Walter sneeze. So he flew it alone, like most of the other fellows who ran the Express line, moving the mail from east to west in these hopping, skipping, jumping increments.

This leg of the trip he was piloting a single-seater called the *Majestic*, one could only presume as a matter of irony. The small airship was hardly more complex or majestic than a penny farthing strapped to a balloon, but Walter didn't mind. Next stop was Reluctance, where he'd pick up something different—something full of gas and ready to fly another leg.

Reluctance was technically a set of mobile gas docks, same as Walter would find on the rest of his route. But truth be told, it was almost a town. Sometimes the stations put down roots, for whatever reason.

And Reluctance had roots.

Walter was glad for it. He'd been riding since dawn and he liked the idea of a nap, down in the basement of the Express offices where the flyers sometimes stole a few hours of rest. He'd like a bed, but he'd settle for a cot and he wouldn't complain about a hammock, because Walter wasn't the complaining kind. Not anymore.

Keeping one eye on the unending sprawl of blonde dirt below in case of cows, Walter reached under the control panel and dug out a pouch of tobacco and tissue-thin papers. He rolled himself a cigarette, fiddled with the controls, and sat back to light it and smoke even though he damn well knew he wasn't supposed to.

His knee gave an old man's pop when he stretched it, but it wasn't so loud as the clatter his foot made when he lifted it up to rest on the *Majestic*'s console. The foot was a piece of machinery, strapped to the stump starting at his knee.

More sophisticated than a peg leg and slightly more natural-looking than a vacant space where a foot ought to be, the mechanical limb had been paid for by the Union army upon his discharge. It was heavy and slow and none too pretty, but it was better than nothing. Even when it pulled on its straps until he thought his knee would pop off like a jar lid, and even when the heft of it left bruises around the buckles that held it in place.

Besides, that was one of the perks of flying for the Dirigible Express Post Service: not a lot of walking required.

Everybody knew how dangerous it was, flying over Native turf and through unincorporated stretches—with no people, no water, no help coming if a ship went cripple or, God forbid, caught a spark. A graze of lightning would send a hydrogen ship home to Jesus in the space of a gasp; or a stray bullet might do the same, should a pirate get the urge to see what the post was moving.

That's why they only hired fellows like Walter. Orphans. Boys with no family to mourn them, no wives to leave widows and no children to leave fatherless. Walter was a prize so far as the Union Post—and absolutely nobody else—was concerned. Still a teenager, just barely; no family to speak of; and a veteran to boot. The post wanted boys like him, who knew precisely how bad their lot could get—and who came with a bit of perspective. It wanted boys who could think under pressure, or at the very least, have the good grace to face death without hysterics.

Boys like Walter McMullin had faced death with serious, pants-shitting hysterics, and more than once. But after five years drumming, and marching, and shooting, and slogging through mud with a face full of blood and a handful of Stanley's hair or maybe a piece of his uniform still clutched like he could save his big brother or save himself or save anybody...he'd gotten the worst of the screaming out of his system.

With this in mind, the Express route was practically a lazy retirement. It beat the hell out of the army, that was for damn sure; or so Walter mused as he reclined inside the narrow dirigible cab, sucking on the end of his sizzling cigarette.

Nobody shot at him very often, nobody hardly ever yelled at him, and his clothes were usually dry. All he had to do was stay awake all day and stay on time. Keep the ground a fair measure below. Keep his temporary ship from being struck by lightning or wrestled to the ground by a tornado.

Not a bad job at all.

Something large down below caught his eye. He sat up, holding the cigarette lightly between his lips. He sagged, disappointed, then perked again and took hold of the levers that moved his steering flaps.

He wanted to see that one more time. Even though it wasn't much to see.

One lone cow, and it'd been off its feet for a bit. He could tell, even from his elevated vantage point, that the beast was dead and beginning to droop. Its skin hung across its bones like laundry on a line.

Of course that happened out on the trail. Every now and again.

But a quick sweep of the vista showed him three more meaty corpses blistering and popping on the pie-crust plain.

He said, "Huh." Because he could see a few more, dotting the land to the north, and to the south a little bit too. If he could get a higher view, he imagined there might be enough scattered bodies to sketch the Goodnight-Loving, pointing a ghastly arrow all the way to Salt Lake City. It looked strange and sad. It looked like the aftermath of something.

He did not think of any battlefields in east Virginia.

He did not think of Stanley, lying in a ditch behind a broken, folded fence.

He ran through a mental checklist of the usual suspects. Disease? Indians? Mexicans? But he was too far away to detect or conclude anything, and that was just as well. He didn't want to smell it anyway. He was plenty familiar with the reek, that rotting sweetness tempered with the methane stink of bowels and bloat.

Another check of the gauges told him more of what he already knew. One way or another, sooner rather than later, the *Majestic* was going down for a refill.

Walter wondered what ship he'd get next. A two-seater, maybe? Something with a little room to stretch out? He liked being able to lift his leg off the floor and let it rest where a copilot ought to go, but almost never went. That'd be nice.

Oh well. He'd find out when he got there, or in the morning.

Out the front windscreen, which screened almost no wind and kept almost no bugs out of his mouth, the sun was setting—the nebulous orb melting into an orange and pink line against the far, flat horizon.

In half an hour the sky was the color of blueberry jam, and only a lilac haze marked the western edge of the world.

The *Majestic* was riding lower in the air because Walter was conserving the thrust and letting the desert breeze move him as much as the engine. Coasting was a pleasant way to sail and the lights of Reluctance should be up ahead, any minute.

Some minute.

One of these minutes.

Where were they?

Walter checked the compass and peeked at his instruments, which told him only that he was on course and that Reluctance should be a mile or less out. But where were the lights? He could always see the lights by now; he always knew when to start smiling, when the gaslamps and lanterns meant people, and a drink, and a place to sleep.

Wait. There. Maybe? *Yes.*

Telltale pinpricks of white, laid out patternless on the dark sprawl.

Not so many as usual, though. Only a few, here and there. Haphazard and lost-looking, as if they were simply the remainder—the hardy leftovers after a storm, the ones which had not gone out quite yet. There was a feebleness to them, or so Walter thought as he gazed out and over and down. He used his elbow to wipe away the dirt on the glass screen as if it might be hiding something. But no. No more lights revealed themselves, and the existing flickers of white did not brighten.

Walter reached for his satchel and slung it over his chest, where he could feel the weight of his brother's Colt bumping up against his ribs.

He set himself a course for Reluctance. He was out of hydrogen and sinking anyway; and it was either set down in relative civilization—where nothing might be wrong, after all—or drop like a feather into the desert dust alone with the coyotes, cactus, and cougars. If he had to wait for sunrise somewhere, better to do it down in an almost-town he knew well enough to navigate.

There were only a few lights, yes.

But no flashes of firearms, and no bonfires of pillage or some hostile victory. He could see nothing and no one, nobody walking or running. Nobody dead, either, he realized when the *Majestic* swayed down close enough to give him a dim view of the dirt streets with their clapboard sidewalks.

Nobody at all.

He licked at his lower lip and gave it a bite, then he pulled out the Colt and began to load it, sure and steady, counting to six and counting out six more bullets for each of the two pockets on his vest.

Could be, he was overreacting. Could be, Reluctance had gone bust real quick, or there'd been a dust storm, or a twister, or any number of other natural and unpleasant events that could drive a thrown-together town into darkness. Could be, people were digging themselves out now, even as he wondered about it. Maybe something had made them sick. Cholera, or typhoid. He'd seen it wipe out towns and troops before.

His gut didn't buy it.

He didn't like it, how he couldn't assume the best and he didn't have any idea what the worst might be.

And still, as the *Majestic* came in for a landing. No bodies.

That was the thing. Nobody down there, including the dead.

He picked up his cane off the dirigible's floor and tested the weight of it. It was a good cane, solid enough to bring down a big man or a small wildcat, push come to shove. He set it across his knees.

The *Majestic* drooped down swiftly, but Walter was in control. He'd landed in the dark before and it was tricky, but it didn't scare him much. It made him cautious, sure. A man would be a fool to be incautious when piloting a half-ton craft into a facility with enough flammable gas to move a fleet. All things being ready and bright, and all it took was a wrongly placed spark—just a graze of metal on metal, the screech of one thing against another, or a single cigarette fallen from a lip—and the whole town would be reduced to matchsticks. Everybody knew it, and everybody lived with it. Just like everybody knew that flying post was a dangerous job, and a bunch of the boys who flew never made it home, just like going to war.

Walter sniffed, one nostril arching up high and dropping down again. He set his jaw, pulled the back drag chute, flipped the switch to give himself some light on the ship's underbelly, and spun the *Majestic* like a girl at a dance. He dropped her down onto the wooden platform with a big red X painted to mark the spot, and she shuddered to silence in the middle of the circle cast by her undercarriage light.

With one hand he popped the anchor chain lever, and with the other he reached for the door handle as he listened to that chain unspool outside.

Outside it was as dark as his overhead survey had implied. And although the light of the undercarriage was nearly the only light, Walter reached up underneath the craft and pulled the snuffing cover down over its flaring white wick. He took hold of the nearest anchor chain and dragged it over to the pipework docks. Ordinarily he'd check to make sure he was on the right pad, clipping his craft to the correct slot before checking in with the station agent.

But no one greeted him. No one rushed up with a ream of paperwork for signing and sealing.

A block away a light burned; and beyond that, another gleamed somewhere farther away. Between those barely seen orbs and the lifting height of a half-full moon, Walter could see well enough to spy another ship nearby. It was affixed to a port on the hydrogen generators, but sagging hard enough that it surely wasn't filled or ready to fly.

Except for the warm buzz of the gas machines standing by, Walter heard absolutely nothing. No bustling of suppertime seekers roaming through the narrow streets, flowing toward Bad Albert's place, or wandering to Mama Rico's. The pipe dock workers were gone, and so were the managers and agents.

No horses, either. No shuffling of saddles or stirrups, of bits or clomping iron shoes.

Inside the *Majestic* an oil lantern was affixed to the wall behind the pilot's seat. Walter grunted, leaning on his cane. He pulled out the lamp, but hesitated to light it.

He held a match up, ready to strike it on the side of the deflated ship, but he didn't. The silence held its breath and told him to wait. It spoke like a battlefield before an order is given.

That's what stopped him. Not the thought of all that hydrogen, but the singular sensation that somewhere, on some other side, enemies were crouching—waiting for a shot. It froze him, one hand and one match held aloft, his cane leaning against the dirigible and his satchel hanging from his shoulder, pressing at the spot where his neck curved to meet his collarbone.

Under the lazily rolling moon and alone in the mobile gas works that had become the less-mobile semi-settlement of Reluctance, Walter put the match away, and set the lantern on the ground beside his ship.

He could see. A little. And given the circumstances, he liked that better than being seen.

His leg ached, but then again, it always ached. Too heavy by half and not nearly as mobile as the army had promised it'd be, the steel and leather contraption tugged against his knee as if it were a drowning man; and for a tiny flickering moment the old ghost pains tickled down to his toes, even though the toes were long gone, blown away on a battlefield in Virginia.

He held still until the sensation passed, wondering bleakly if it would ever go away for good, and suspecting that it wouldn't.

"All right," he whispered, and it was cold enough to see the words. When had it gotten so cold? How did the desert always do that, cook and then freeze? "We'll move the mail."

Damn straight we will.

Walter reached into the *Majestic*'s tiny hold and pulled out the three bags he'd been carrying as cargo. Each bag was the size of his good leg, and as heavy as his bad one. When they were all three removed from the ship he peered dubiously at the other craft across the landing pad—the one attached to the gas pipes, but empty.

He considered his options.

No other ships lurked anywhere close, so he could either seize that unknown hunk of metal and canvas or stay there by himself in the dead outpost.

Hoisting one bag over his shoulder and counter-balancing with his cane, he did his best to cross the landing quietly; but his metal foot dropped each step with a hard, loud clank—even though the leather sole at the bottom of the thing was brand new.

He leaned the bag of mail up against the ship and caught his breath, lost more to fear than exertion. Then he moved the mail bag aside to reveal the first two stenciled letters of the ship's name, and reading the whole he whispered, "*Sweet Marie.*"

Two more mail bags, each moved with all the stealth he could muster. Each one more cumbersome than the last, and each one straining his bum leg harder. But he moved them. He opened the back bin of the *Sweet Marie* and stuffed them into her cargo hold. Every grunt was loud in the desert emptiness and every heaving shove would've sent ol' Stanley into conniptions, had he been there.

Too much noise. Got to keep your head down.

Walter breathed as he leaned on the bin to make it shut. It closed with a click. "This ain't the war. Not out here."

Just like me, you carry it with you.

Something.

What?

A gusting. A hoarse, lonely sound that barked and disappeared.

He leaned against the bin and listened hard, waiting for that noise to come again.

The *Sweet Marie* had been primed and she was ready to fill, but no one had switched on the generators. She sank so low she almost tipped over, now that the mail sacks had loaded down her back end.

Walter McMullin did not know how hydrogen worked exactly, but he'd seen the filling process performed enough times to copy it.

The generators took the form of two tanks, each one mounted atop a standard-issue army wagon. These tanks were made of reinforced wood and lined with copper, and atop each tank was a hinged metal plate that could be opened and closed in order to dump metal shavings into the sulfuric acid inside. At the end, opposite the filler plate, an escape pipe was attached to a long rubber hose, to which the *Sweet Marie* was ultimately affixed.

There were several sets of filters for the hydrogen to pass before it reached the ship's tank, and the process was frankly none too quick. Even little ships like these mail runners could take a couple of hours to become airworthy.

Walter did not like the idea of spending a couple of hours alone in Reluctance. He was even less charmed by the idea of spending *all night* alone in Reluctance, so he found himself a crate of big glass bottles filled with acid, and with great struggle he poured them down through the copper funnels atop the tanks. Shortly thereafter he located the metal filings; he scooped them up with the big tin cup and dumped them in.

He turned the valves to open the filters and threw the switch to start the generators stirring and bubbling, vibrating the carts to make the acid and the metal stir and separate into hydrogen more quickly.

It made a god-awful amount of noise.

The rubber hose, stamped "Goodyear's Rubber, Belting, and Packing Company of Philadelphia," did a little twitch. *Sweet Marie*'s tank gave a soft, plaintive squeal as the first hydrogen spilled through, giving her the smallest bit of lift.

But she'd need more. Lots more.

There.

Another one.

A sighing grunt, gasped and then gone as quickly as it'd burst through the night.

Walter whirled as fast as his leg would let him, using it as a pivot. He moved like a compass pinned to a map. He held his cane out, pointing at nothing.

But the sound. Again. And again. Another wheeze and gust.

At this point, Walter was gut-swimmingly certain that it was coming from more than one place. Partway between a snore and a cough, with a consumptive rattle. Coming from everywhere, and nowhere. Coming from the dark.

Up against the *Sweet Marie* he backed.

He jumped, startled by a new sound, a familiar one. Footsteps, slow and laborious. Someone was walking toward him, out of the black alleys that surrounded the landing. Nearing the ladder to the refueling platform. And whoever this visitor was, he was joined by someone else—approaching the edge near the parked *Majestic*.

And a third somebody. Walter was pretty sure of a third, moving up from the shadows.

Not one single thing about this moment, this shuddering instant alone—but not alone—felt right or good to Walter McMullin. He still couldn't see anyone, though he could hear plenty. Whoever they were, lurking in the background... they weren't being quiet. They weren't sneaking, and that was something, wasn't it?

Why would they sneak, if they know they have you?

Reaching into his belt, he pulled out the Colt and held it with both hands. His back remained braced against the slowly filling replacement ship. He thought about crying out in greeting, just in case—but he thought of the dead cows, and his desperate eyes spotted no new lights, and the sound of incoming feet and the intermittent groaning told him that no, this was no overreaction. This was good common sense, staying low with your back against something firm and your weapon out. That's what you did, right before a fight. If you could.

He drew back the gun's hammer and waited.

Lumbering up the ladder as if drunk, the first head rose into view.

Walter should've been relieved.

He knew that head—it belonged to Gibbs Higley, the afternoon station manager. But he wasn't relieved. Not at all. Because it wasn't Gibbs, not anymore. He could see that at a glance, even without the gaslamps that lit up a few blocks, far away.

Something was very, very wrong with Gibbs Higley.

The man drew nearer, shuffling in an exploratory fashion, sniffing the air like a dog. He was missing an ear. His skin looked like boiled lye. One of his eyes was ruined somehow, wet and gelatinous, and sliding down his cheek.

"Higley?" Walter croaked.

Higley didn't respond. He only moaned and shuffled faster, homing in on Walter and raising the moan to a cry that was more of a horrible keening.

To Walter's terror, the keening was answered. It came bouncing back from corner to corner, all around the open landing area and the footsteps that had been slowly incoming shifted gears, moving faster.

Maybe he should've thought about it. Maybe he should've tried again, trying to wake Higley up, shake some sense into him. There must've been something he could've done, other than lifting the Colt and putting a bullet through the man's solitary good eye.

But that's what he did.

Against a desert backdrop of dust-covered silence the footsteps and coughing grunts and the buzzing patter of the generators had seemed loud enough; but the Colt was something else entirely, fire and smoke and a kick against his elbows, and a lingering whiff of gunpowder curling and dissolving.

Gibbs Higley fell off the landing, flopping like a rag doll.

Walter rushed as fast as he could to the ladder, and kicked it away—marooning himself on the landing island, five or six feet above street level. Then he dragged himself back to *Sweet Marie* and resumed his defensive position, the only one he had. "That was easy," he muttered, almost frantic to reassure himself.

One down. More to go. You're a good shot, but you're standing next to the gas. Surrounded by it, almost.

He breathed. "I need to think."

You need to run.

"I need the *Sweet Marie*. Won't get far without her."

Hands appeared at the edge of the lifted landing pad. Gray hands, hands without enough fingers.

Left to right he swung his head, seeking some out. Knowing he didn't have enough bullets for whatever this was—knowing it as sure as he knew he'd die if any of those hands caught him. Plague, is what it was. Nothing he'd ever seen before, but goddamn Gibbs Higley had been sick, hadn't he?

"Gotta hold the landing pad," he said through gritted teeth.

No. You gotta to let 'em take it—but that don't mean you gotta to let 'em keep it.

He swung his head again, side to side, and spotted only more hands—moving like a sea of clapping, an audience of death, pulling toward the lifted landing spot. He wished he had a light, and then he remembered that he did have one—he just hadn't lit it. One wobbly dash back to the *Majestic* and he had the lantern in his hand again, thinking "to hell with it—to hell with *us*" and striking a match. What did it matter? They already knew where he was. That much was obvious from the rising wail that now rang from every quarter. Faces were leaning up now, lurching and lifting on elbows, rising and grabbing for purchase on the platform and soon they were going to find it.

Look.

"Where?" he asked the ghost of a memory, trying to avoid a full-blown panic. Panic never got anybody anywhere but dead. It got Stanley dead. On the far side of a broken, folded fence along a line that couldn't have been held, not with a thousand Stanleys.

Ah. Above the hydrogen tanks, and behind them. A ladder in the back corner of the overhang that covered them.

He glanced at the *Sweet Marie* and then his eyes swept the platform, where a woman was rising up onto the wooden deck—drawing herself up on her elbows. She'd be there soon, right there with him. When she looked up at him her mouth opened and she shouted, and blood or bile—something dark—spilled over her teeth to splash down on the boards.

Whatever it was, he didn't want it. He drew up the Colt, aimed carefully, and fired. She fell back.

The ladder behind the hydrogen tanks must lead to the roof of the overhang. Would the thin metal roof hold him?

Any port in a storm.

He scurried past the clamoring hands and scooted, still hauling that dead-weight foot, beneath the overhang and to the ladder. Scaling it required him to set the cane aside, and he wouldn't do that, so he stuck it in his mouth where it stretched his cheeks and jaw until they ached with the strain. But it was that or leave it, or leave the lantern—which he held by the hot, uncomfortable means of shoving his wrist through the carrying loop. When it swung back and forth with his motion, it burned the cuff of his shirt and seared warmly against his chest.

So he climbed, good foot up with a grunt of effort, bad foot up with a grunt of pain, both grunts issued around the cane in his mouth. When he reached the top he jogged his neck to shift the cane so it'd fit through the square opening in the corrugated roof. He slipped, his heavy foot dragging him to a stop with an ear-splitting scrape.

He'd have to step softly.

From this vantage point, holding up the quivering black lantern he could see all of it, and he understood everything and nothing simultaneously. He watched the mostly men and sometimes women of Reluctance stagger and wail, shambling hideously from corners and corridors, from alleys and basements, from broken-windowed stores and stables and saloons and the one whorehouse. They did not pour but they dripped and congealed down the uncobbled streets torn rough and rocky by horse's hooves and the wheels of coaches and carts.

It couldn't have been more than a hundred ragged bodies slinking forward, gagging on their own fluids and chasing toward the light he held over his head, over the town of Reluctance.

Walter stuffed a hand in his vest pockets and felt at the bottom of the bag he still wore over his chest. Bullets, yes. But not enough bullets for this. Not even if he was the best shot in Texas, and he wasn't. He was a competent shot from New York City, orphaned and Irish, a few thousand miles from home, without even a sibling to mourn him if the drooling, simpering, snap-jawed dead were to catch him and tear him to pieces.

Bullets were not going to save him.

All the same, he liked having them.

The lantern drew the dead; he watched their gazes, watching it. Moths. Filthy, deadly moths. He could see it in their eyes, in the places where their souls ought to be. Most of the men he'd ever shot at were fellows like himself—boys mostly, lads born so late they didn't know for certain what the fighting was about; just men, with faces full of fear and grit.

Nothing of that, not one shred of humanity showed on any of the faces below.

He could see it, and he was prepared to address it. But not until he had to.

Beneath him, the *Sweet Marie* was filling. Down below the twisted residents of Reluctance were dragging themselves up and onto the platform, swarming like ants and shrieking for Walter—who went to the ladder and kicked it down against the generators, where it clattered and rested, and likely wouldn't be climbed.

He sat on the edge of the corrugated roof and turned the lantern light down. It wouldn't fool them. It wouldn't make them wander away. They smelled him, and they wanted him, and they'd stay until they got him. Or until he left.

He was leaving, all right. Soon.

Inside the satchel he rummaged, and he pulled out his tobacco and papers. He rolled himself a cigarette, lit it off the low-burning lamp, and he sat. And he watched below as the cranium-shaped crest of the *Sweet Marie* slowly inflated; and the corpses of Reluctance gathered themselves on the landing pad beside it, ignoring it.

Finally the swelling dome was full enough that Walter figured, "I can make it. Maybe not all the way to Santa Fe, but close enough." He rose to his feet, the flesh and blood one and the one that pivoted painfully on a pin.

The lantern swung out from his fingertips, still lit but barely.

Below the lantern, beside the ship and around it, the men and women shambled.

But fire could consume anything, pretty much. It'd consume the hydrogen like it was starved for it. It'd gobble and suck and then the whole world would go up like hell, wouldn't it? All that gas, burning like the breath of God.

Well then. He'd have to move fast.

Retracting his arm as far as it'd go, and then adjusting for trajectory, he held the lantern and released it—tossing it in a great bright arc that cut across the star-speckled sky. It crashed to the far corner of the landing pad, blossoming into brilliance and heat, singeing his face. He blinked hard against the unexpected warmth, having never guessed how closely he would feel it.

The creatures below screamed and ran, clothing aflame. The air sizzled with the stench of burning hair and fire-puckered flesh. But some of them hovered near the *Sweet Marie*, lingering where the fire had stayed clear, still howling.

Only a few of them.

The Colt took them down, one-two-three.

Walter crossed his fingers and prayed that the bullets would not bounce—would not clip or ding the hydrogen tubes or tanks, or the swollen bulb of the *Sweet Marie*. His prayers were answered, or ignored. Either way, nothing ignited.

Soon the ship was clear. As clear as it was going to get.

And reaching it required a ten-foot drop.

Walter threw his cane down and watched it roll against the ship, then he dropped to his knees and swung himself off the edge to hang by his fingertips. He curled the good leg up, lifting his knee. Better a busted pin than a busted ankle.

And before he had time to reconsider, he let go.

The pain of his landing was a sun of white light. His leg buckled and scraped inside the sheath that clasped the false limb; he heard his bone piercing and rubbing through the bunched and stitched skin, and into the leather and metal.

But he was down. Down beside the *Sweet Marie*. Down inside the fire, inside the ticking clock with a deadly alarm and only moments—maybe seconds, probably only seconds—before the whole town went up in flames.

At the last moment he remembered the clasp that anchored the ship. He unhitched it. He limped bloodily to the back port and ripped the hydrogen hose out of the back, and shut it up tight because otherwise he'd just leak his fuel all over North Mexico.

He fumbled for the latch and found it.

Pulled it.

Opened the door and hauled himself inside, feeling around for the controls and seeing them awash with the yellow-gold light of the fire just outside the window. The starter was a lever on the dash. He pulled that too and the ship began to rise. He grasped for the thrusters and his shaking, searching fingers found them, and pressed them—giving the engines all the gas they'd take. Anything to get him up and away. Anything to push him past the hydrogen before the fire took it.

Anything.

Reluctance slipped away below, and behind. It shimmered and the whole world froze, and gasped, and shook like a star being born.

The desert floor melted into glass.

ARLENE SCHABOWSKI OF THE UNDEAD

By Mark McLaughlin & Kyra M. Schon

Mark McLaughlin's fiction, poetry, and articles have appeared in hundreds of magazines and anthologies, including *Cemetery Dance*, *Midnight Premiere*, and *The Year's Best Horror Stories*. His most recent story collections are *Raising Demons for Fun and Profit* and *Twisted Tales for Sick Puppies*. His first novel, *Monster Behind the Wheel* (coauthored with Michael McCarty), was a finalist for the Bram Stoker Award. His next book will be *Vampires & Sex Kittens*, a collection of essays.

Kyra M. Schon is the actress who played Karen Cooper, the trowel-wielding zombie girl in the basement in the original *Night of the Living Dead*. Since 1985, she has made her living teaching pottery and sculpture, and she also sells unique zombie memorabilia through her website, www.ghoulnextdoor.com.

In 1939, audiences at *The Wizard of Oz* were dazzled to see a black-and-white movie burst out into full Technicolor, when Dorothy departs gray Kansas and arrives in the magical land of Oz, and black-and-white has been battling it out with color ever since. In the 1998 film *Pleasantville*, twins are transported into a black-and-white 1950s-era sitcom, and as they slowly liberate the town from its oppressive staidness, residents who have broken the mold become fully colorized. In the recent video game *The Saboteur*, the hero moves through black-and-white cityscapes in World War II-era occupied France attempting to disrupt Nazi plans—if he's successful, color is restored to liberated areas.

In the world of zombies, of course, the most epic confrontation of black-and-white versus color is the showdown between George Romero's original 1968 black-and-white classic *Night of the Living Dead* and the 1990 full-color remake directed by makeup man Tom Savini. Devotees of the original will emphasize its classic status and the haunting quality of its stark black-and-white look, whereas advocates for the remake will point to its sophisticated makeup effects and stronger female characters.

Like zombies themselves, the debate just keeps on going, relentless. Our next story also features a clash between black-and-white and color. Child stars often seem to grow up to lead troubled lives, but seldom as troubled as this.

Really? Right now?

Okay.

Let me tell you about a nice lady, who lives not too far from here. She was in the movie. And still is, in a way.

Her name is Lorraine Tyler...and also Arlene Schabowski. Lorraine is in her early forties, though you couldn't tell by looking at her. She has long, wavy blonde hair. Arlene is nine years old, and she has long, wavy blonde hair, too. Most people would agree that she looks quite dead.

Lorraine played Arlene, all those years ago. Lorraine stopped, but Arlene kept right on playing.

After the zombies swarmed the building, Arlene devoured most of her parents...they were hers, so she certainly deserved the best parts...and then simply wandered off into the night. And the night was filled with shambling, ravenous corpses, feasting upon the flesh of the living. But the undead knew she was one of them, so she was safe from their hunger. Her body held no warmth, no nourishing spark of life to entice the other zombies. That was the last the viewers ever saw of her.

But she needed food, for she was... and still is... always hungry. Deliriously hungry. For there is a deep black coldness within her that constantly needs filling. Sometimes, right after she has eaten, she actually feels alive again. Perhaps even better than alive. She felt that way after she ate her parents, and she wanted to feel it again. So she wandered through the woods, through the darkness, until she came to another farmhouse.

Now at this point, one might ask, "They never showed what happened to the little girl after she wandered off. Didn't the police get her when they came and shot all the zombies' brains out?"

Obviously not.

One might also wonder: "*Fear-Farm of the Undead* was only a movie, wasn't it?"

Well, yes and no.

Lorraine Tyler's father was one of the producers and stars of the movie, which was made on a shoe-string budget. The money her family put into that movie back then wouldn't even buy a decent new car these days. Her father, mother and some of their friends wanted to make a movie, so they pooled their resources, found a few more investors and did it. And Lorraine got to play a little girl who gets bitten, turns into a zombie and eats her parents.

Lorraine went on to become a school teacher with a cool website selling *Fear-Farm* memorabilia. Teachers get time off during the summer, so she started going to conventions, meeting fans, doing a lot more to promote her memorabilia sideline. She did that for years. Made good money, too. Last year she made enough to buy a nice little vacation in Mexico.

People still watch that movie all the time. Still think about it. *Fear-Farm of the Undead* has spawned hundreds of knock-off versions, most of them released direct-to-video. And Lorraine has watched every one of them. Because she is also

Arlene Schabowski, and wants to know what other zombies are doing.

Somewhere out there, it is always night, and a little dead girl who is also a living school teacher is always hungry.

Anyway. Back to that other farmhouse.

Arlene could hear cows mooing in the distance. The sound made her hungry. She crept up to the house and looked in the window, into a quaint, tidy living room, with knickknacks on little cherrywood tables and furniture draped with lace doilies. An old woman was sitting at her desk, reading some papers. She had long white hair and wore a dark gray housecoat. Of course, everything in that world is black and white or shades of gray, just like in the movie. The old woman must not have turned on the radio or the TV that day or night... she looked so peaceful, it was clear she had no idea what was going on.

The little dead girl went to the front door and knocked. The old woman called out, as cheery as can be, "Who is it?"

Now, none of the other zombies in that movie were able to talk. All they ever did was grunt and roar and squeal. But Arlene was able to think really hard and call upon the abilities of her other self, Lorraine. And she managed to rasp out the three-word phrase from the movie for which she is best known. She also says a four-word phrase early in the movie, but most folks don't remember that. No, they only remember what she says just before she turns into a zombie: "Help me, Mommy."

"Mommy? I'm nobody's mommy!" the old woman cried. "Who's out there? Is this some kind of a joke?" So saying, she threw open the door. "My God! Little girl, are you hurt? There's blood all over you!"

Arlene held out her arms, just like she did before she killed her movie-mommy, who was played by her real-life mother. Again, she said, "Help me, Mommy."

"Of course I'll help you, you poor thing." The old woman knelt before her. She must have had something wrong with her knees, because she winced with pain. "So tell me, who did this to you? Who?"

Her next few words were lost in a thick gurgle of black blood, because by then Arlene had her little teeth embedded in the old woman's throat. And even though the dear old thing was past her prime, she was still full of warm, delicious, intoxicating life.

Arlene ate her fill and by the time she was done, that sweet old woman looked like a car-wreck victim, sans safety belt. Arlene turned and strayed into the night. She didn't wait around to watch the old woman's gnawed carcass scramble back to hungry life.

Mind you, while all that was going on, poor, confused Lorraine was hiding in some bushes in the school playground, screaming and wondering why all these bad things were going on in her head. The other kids thought she had gone nuts. Her parents and the teachers talked about it later, and based on what she'd told them, they decided she had an overactive imagination. They told her not to let the bad images scare her... they were make-believe, so they couldn't hurt her. It was all in her head, they said, and in a way it was. Hers was a sort of Reality Surplus

Disorder. It's hard to concentrate when you've got another personality playing in your mind.

My best guess is all the movie's fans created that personality, that black-and-white world of death... all those watchers in the dark, thinking about that movie, those zombies, and of course, poor little Arlene Schabowski. All that feverish brain energy. What is reality, anyway? A mental collective, that's all. The result of multiple minds, mulling over enthralling stories. I'm sure that somewhere, out there, Moby Dick is still swimming and the House of Usher is still falling. I'm sure Dorothy is still wandering down the Yellow Brick Road, having new adventures, fighting more witches and flying monkeys. And I'm sure she's still a tiny young thing, just as Arlene Schabowski is still a tiny dead thing.

But let us return to Arlene. She walked down a gravel lane until she came to the highway. Car lights were heading toward her. She held out her bloodstained, skinny arms and waited. The driver would stop. Of course they would. She was just a little girl.

So she waited. And the driver stopped—a fat, middle-aged man with a bulbous nose and horn-rimmed glasses.

"Was there an accident?" He ran up to her, crouched and thrust his fat face near hers.

"Help me, Mommy," she said.

"You poor thing," he said in a low, sad voice. "What the hell happened to you?"

Another one who thought she was simply a poor thing. She smiled, leaned forward and bit off his nose—it was too large and juicy a target to resist.

He screamed, so she bit off his lower lip, which made him scream that much louder.

She gnawed and gnawed until he was too cold for her to stomach. Then she began shambling down the road. And because that entire movie took place at night, the daylight never came. She wandered an eternal night of fields and rural back roads and farmhouses, feasting on innocent country folks who only wanted to help her.

And Lorraine... She endured Arlene's adventures in her head, and finally even got used to them. A person can get used to anything, really. Folks who live near airports soon learn to ignore the roar of planes coming and going. Lorraine grew into a tall, willowy lady. Always slender. Having a zombie in your head is enough to spoil anyone's appetite. There were plenty of times when she would sit down to dinner, and Arlene would suddenly go on a rampage in her mind. Little zombie-girl would rip apart a couple farmers, tear out their guts and gobble them down, and suddenly that plate of lasagna would seem like a hideous, visceral thing. But Lorraine wouldn't scream over it...wouldn't even bat an eyelash. She'd just push the plate away.

As I mentioned, Lorraine eventually became a school teacher. Because a part of her was still a little girl, she liked being around children. She lived in a big nice apartment building, surrounded by families—all the kids there thought she was great. Some of the people in her building had seen her movie, and they were always telling their friends that their neighbor was a movie star. Sometimes folks who had seen the movie would call her Arlene. She'd smile to be polite, but she didn't like it. "Hey, Arlene—'Help me, Mommy!'" was the favorite greeting of the fat guy who lived six doors down. She'd always try to take a different route to avoid him if she saw him coming.

Eventually she started dating the school's janitor, and all of her friends made fun of her for that, joking that the lovers were probably always sneaking off to the boiler room or some such place. The janitor, whose name was Kurt, was a good-looking man, only in his mid-thirties and in fine physical shape. And truth to tell, the two did sneak off together sometimes. To Kurt's office. His door had a fancy title—Environmental Control Specialist—but it still meant janitor.

Once while she was in his office, Lorraine saw a key hanging from a little nail on the wall behind his desk. The key had a scrap of paper taped to it. The word ATTIC was written on that scrap in blue ballpoint ink. She waited until Kurt's back was turned, and she took that key.

Even while she was reaching for it, she wasn't sure why she was taking it. She just knew she had to have it. After school, she stayed behind, waited until everyone was gone and then went up to the attic. It was all storage up there, and the things that had been packed away up there so long ago were now all but forgotten.

Remember where little Arlene ate her parents? In the attic. That's where the movie-family went to hide from the zombies. The movie-attic had a bed in it, where Arlene used to sleep. She says her four-word line while she's in that bed. The school attic had a broken cot among its various odds and ends. Obsolete school books, tennis shoes, sacks of that pinkish, pulpy stuff to sprinkle on barf to soak it up and make the smell go away. Lorraine strolled among rows of dusty boxes and stayed up there for about an hour, looking at spider webs and old papers and outdated globes. She realized then that this was the first time she'd been in an attic—any attic at all—since the filming of that movie. Her parents had always lived in apartments. Her dorm room in college had been on the ground floor. A life without attics. She now felt oddly at home—but was it a good home?

When she came down from the attic, left the building and went to her car, the world around her seemed different somehow.

A little less...colorful.

A moment later, Arlene Schabowski saw red in her night-world for the first time. Usually the blood of her victims was shiny black. But she looked down at the hitchhiker she had just torn to bits and saw red, red everywhere. Then she saw that her dress was stained not merely with various splotches of gray, but horrible gouts of rotted filth and gore—red, yellow, brown, green, a veritable rainbow of decay. It made her smile.

A few days later, Kurt was completely confused by Lorraine's birthday gift to him. "Rainy," he said, for that is what he called her, "this tie...don't get me wrong, I think it's great. And silk, it must have cost plenty. But purple? I don't know if I'm the purple type..."

"Oh," she said quite softly. "Is it purple? I thought it was some kind of dark silver. Are you sure it's purple?"

Lorraine sometimes would bring a book to school to read in the attic, after hours. In the days to come, her students became more and more confused by some of the things she said—especially during art class. Whenever one of them did a drawing, she would ask things like, "What color is that horse?" Or, "That's a very pretty mermaid—which crayon did you use for the hair?"

Arlene began to notice green leaves among the gray when car headlights hit them just right, and some of the towns she meandered through were bigger than the little country burgs she usually came across. One even had a supermarket. She would hide in the bushes bordering the parking lot and watch the front of the supermarket. Watch all the people rushing in and out. It made her hungry. Sometimes one of the shoppers would hear something rustling in the bushes and go see what it was, worrying that it might be a lost child. They were right to worry.

Lorraine found that the drive back to her house seemed a little shorter every week. And there were fewer cars on the road. Not as many buildings behind the sidewalks. Fewer kids in the school, but more birds in the light blue sky. There was still a bit of color in her world, but not much. The changes were all huge yet gradual. Kurt usually wore a nice polo shirt and jeans to work. It didn't even surprise her when he started wearing coveralls, or when his voice started to take on a rural twang. He even took to calling her "Honey."

Arlene just kept on wandering—she was so good at it. Wandering and eating, eating and wandering, always keeping to the shadows, which was getting harder, since there were so many streetlights around. But she was finding more homeless people, so at least she had been eating regularly. No more fields—she was in the suburbs now, and the skies were starting to lighten. Night was slowly giving way to a light blue morning.

You see what was happening, don't you? They were starting to meet in the middle. Why do you suppose that was happening? Maybe it was because Lorraine was spending so much time up in that attic. I suspect attics have strange powers. They come to points at the top, like pyramids. They're rather intriguing, aren't they? And bear in mind, zombie movies were becoming more modern—perhaps the imaginations that had pulled Arlene into existence were pulling her into the present day.

Lorraine was getting pulled, too, but in a different way. Into something…but what? One morning she thought she saw a tractor drive past the school. Later that day, she knew she heard cows mooing in the distance. She broke off her relationship with Kurt. He was becoming more and more rural, like some of the extras in *Fear-Farm of the Undead*. He was growing too much hair and losing too many teeth. That wasn't the kind of boyfriend she wanted and this certainly wasn't the life she wanted to lead. She didn't like it. No, not one little bit.

Especially when she found herself chewing on what was left of the Algebra teacher, late at night up in the school attic. She couldn't even remember what she had done to get him up there. Not that it mattered. There were shreds of flesh under her nails, and her belly was swollen with food.

She wasn't sure if what she had done would turn the skinny old teacher into a zombie, but better safe than sorry. She went down to Kurt's supply closet, grabbed a hammer, and used it to cave in the old man's gnawed head.

And then she waited.

Pretty soon she heard the tappity-tap, tappity-tap, tappity-tap of little-girl heels coming up the stairs to the attic. And then…

That's when you walked in, Arlene.

You walked in and said the four-word phrase that you said in the first half of that movie, in the scene when your mother was putting you to bed: "Tell me a story." Most people don't remember you said that. But you did, in that sweet, soft, cheery voice. Though that's not what your voice sounds like now. You sound like a record that's slowly melting as it plays.

So. Did you like my story, Arlene? It was all about you—and me, too. But I said "Lorraine" instead of "I" because… Well, I don't really feel like me anymore. But I'm not you.

I don't know who I am, where I am or even what I am.

Hmmm…?

No, I'm not your mommy, and I'm afraid I can't help you.

But who knows. Maybe pounding your head open with this hammer will help me.

ZOMBIE GIGOLO

By S. G. Browne

S. G. Browne's first novel *Breathers: A Zombie's Lament*, "a dark comedy about life after undeath told from the perspective of a zombie," came out in 2009 and was a finalist for this year's Bram Stoker Award for best first novel. His second novel, which comes out in November, is *Fated*, "a dark, irreverent comedy about fate, destiny, and the consequences of getting involved in the lives of humans." His short fiction can also be found in the anthology *Zombies: Encounters with the Hungry Dead*.

One of the things that's appealing about zombie fiction is that zombies used to be *us*, and we're just one bite or infected wound away from becoming one of them. That's a sentiment Browne shares, but he also believes they're experiencing their current popularity because they're no longer just the mindless, shambling ghouls we've known and loved for the past forty years. "They're faster. Funnier. Sentient," he says. "Plus there's this constant fascination with the inevitability of a zombie apocalypse. I mean, no one ever talks about the werewolf apocalypse. That would be ridiculous."

Browne's own take on zombies, in his novel and two short stories, intended to show a different side to zombies: giving them sentience, viewing the world through their eyes and what they have to deal with. "When you think about it, most zombie films and fiction are really about the people rather than the zombies," Browne says. "My fiction is about the *zombies*."

Just to warn you, our next story is a *little* gross. It was originally written for the "Gross Out Contest" at the 2008 World Horror Convention in Salt Lake City. Browne had just sold his novel *Breathers*, so, for his contest entry, he took a couple of ideas from that and ratcheted them up viscerally. The rules stated that the story had to be between three to five minutes in length when read aloud, so the authors had to be frugal with their words, maintain a decent gross-out factor, and cut out anything that didn't move the story fast enough.

Browne didn't win, but he did come in third, winning him the coveted gummy haggis prize. But if our next story wasn't gross enough to win, I'm not sure I want to know what did.

Is it necrophilia if you're both dead?

Okay, technically we're not dead. We're *un*dead. But semantics tend to take a back seat when you're banging a three-week-old corpse who's moaning that she's about to come just before one of her main body cavities bursts open.

At first I can't tell if it's the abdominal cavity or the pelvic cavity, because honestly when you're an animated corpse, everything smells like a fecal smoothie. But then I see something that looks like a partially dissolved kidney and the fluid spilling out of her has the consistency of chunky chicken noodle soup, so I'm guessing abdominal cavity.

I'm suddenly wishing I'd worn a condom.

Though I suppose it could have been worse. I could have been eating her out. But she didn't pay for the Surf and Turf.

Not that this is the first time something like this has happened to me. After all, when you're a zombie gigolo, you have to expect the smell of hydrogen sulfide and the oozing of intestinal juices and the occasional skin slip. But I should know better than to accept clients who are more than a couple of weeks past their Use By date.

If you've never had your tongue down the throat of a zombie whose liquefied brain suddenly bubbled out of her mouth, you probably wouldn't understand.

The Cavity Burster gets up from the bed, apologizing for the mess as she tries to pack her internal organs back into her Lucky Brand jeans, dripping a trail of liquefied internal organs across the concrete floor on her way out. That's why I use plastic sheets instead of Calvin Klein. They're easy to rinse off and with the set-up I have in the cellar, I just wash everything down the drain. Otherwise, I'd spend all of my time at the laundromat.

My two o'clock appointment is less than a week old. A Freshie. Still, she doesn't exactly smell like Irish Spring. More like summer compost. Her stomach is already starting to blister, she has skin the texture of a greasy banana peel, and when I slide inside her, it feels like I'm fucking a nest of mummified cats' tongues.

The thing about zombies is that, other than our internal organs turning to soup and liquid leaking from enzyme-ravaged cells, there's not a lot of natural lubrication.

However, for those of us who were fortunate enough to have been embalmed, formaldehyde is the magic elixir that allows us to maintain some sense of pride.

The Freshie wasn't one of the fortunate ones.

In addition to her cracked, bloating stomach and the aroma of rotting eggs that keeps leaking out of multiple orifices, the tips of her nipples are coming off in my mouth.

Liquid from the deteriorating cells of a corpse can get in between the layers of skin and loosen them. This is called sloughage. It usually starts with the fingers and toes. Sometimes the skin of the entire hand or foot will come off.

Not a pleasant thought when you're fucking sandpaper.

If you've never had the skin of your cock peel off like a used condom, you probably wouldn't understand.

As I slide in and out of the Freshie, I open my eyes and glance down at her face just inches from mine. Her eyes are closed in ecstasy, her mouth is open in a silent gasp, and greenish fluid from her lungs is oozing out of her nose.

Morticians call this "frothy purge," like it's some new drink at Starbucks.

Just as I'm about to blow my load, the Freshie sneezes and I've got frothy purge on my tongue and lower lip.

Some zombies are walking Petri dishes, serving host to a plethora of bacteria and fungi. These are the unlucky ones who weren't embalmed and who suffer the indignities of putrefaction as they slowly dissolve. In zombie circles, we refer to these pathetic creatures as Melters.

My last customer of the day is a Melter.

Her skin is peeling away, her body is covered with festering wounds, most of her hair has fallen out, and when she smiles, what few remaining teeth she has are coated in an oily black goo that runs down her chin because she has no lips.

Before she gets on the bed, I pull out a can of Glade Neutralizer and circle around her, covering her from head to toe. I prefer the Neutralizer fragrance because it works directly toward the source of the odor, though Tropical Mist has a nice, fruity scent.

The moment I climb on top of her, I'm wondering if I've made a big mistake.

Her breath washes over me like fresh, hot vomit. Her skin is the texture of raw chicken, sliding back and forth and tearing away in my hands. When she drags her fingers down my back, her fingernails detach. Occasionally, the pus oozing from her wounds erupts in an orgasmic geyser.

Keeping your focus when you're banging a Melter isn't easy. It's enough to deflate even a post-mortem permanent boner. So I think about human flesh and I close my eyes and I keep banging away.

But with every thrust it feels like I'm fucking mashed potatoes. Like I'm fucking overcooked rice. Like the rice is swarming around my cock.

When I pull out, my cock is covered with maggots. They're swarming around my shaft, trying to eat their way inside. At least I remembered to wear a condom this time.

I slap at my permanent erection, knocking the majority of the maggots off, but I can feel some of them scurrying across my nuts, tickling my perineum, headed for the nearest point of entry. Before I can brush the rest of them away, I have maggots squirming up my ass.

I need a bidet.

I need a Clorox douche.

I need a turkey baster and some gasoline.

On the bed, the Melter is picking larvae out of her pubic hair and asking me if I want to clean her carpet. She smiles at me, black saliva dripping from her lipless mouth. She says if I do, she'll suck the maggots out of my asshole.

I tell her to get out and to take her infested pussy with her. Then I lock the cellar door, grab a bottle of Jack, put on some Barry Manilow, and try to figure out what I'm going to do now.

You spend your entire undeath working to cultivate a reputation for affordable, high-caliber, parasite-free sex and in one moment of misguided judgment, you throw it all away.

If you've never had maggots crawling around inside your rectal cavity and feasting on your subcutaneous fat, you probably wouldn't understand.

RURAL DEAD

By Bret Hammond

Bret Hammond is the coauthor of the book *The Complete Idiot's Guide to Geocaching* and the publisher of Geocacher University (www.geocacher-u.com), a website devoted to providing education and materials to both new and experienced geocachers. This story is his first and only fiction published to date, which originally appeared on the zombie website *Tales of the Zombie War*. In addition to his interest in geocaching and zombies, he's also a pastor and has published articles and cartoons in a variety of religious publications.

The Amish are a Christian community of Swiss-German origin centered in Pennsylvania, perhaps best-known in pop culture thanks to the Harrison Ford movie *Witness*. Amish culture emphasizes hard work, humility, and family. They dress simply, largely forego modern technology (notably automobiles and electrical appliances), socialize mainly among themselves, and work in trades such as farming, construction, and crafts-making. Their main method of ensuring that members keep to Amish ways is peer pressure, known as shunning. Whether or not an individual is to be shunned is determined by the leadership, and when someone is being shunned even their spouse may refuse to speak to them. In severe cases of noncompliance a person may be expelled from the community, though they are always welcome to return if they mend their ways.

Many schisms have developed in Amish communities over the years over what rules are to be followed and how severe shunning should be. The Supreme Court case Wisconsin v. Yoder established the precedent that Amish are exempt from many American laws, including those involving compulsory education (Amish children are not educated past eighth grade), child labor, and Social Security. The Amish are also extreme pacifists, and once faced severe penalties and abuse for refusing to fight in America's wars.

Our next story, which is a *bit* more wholesome than the last one, takes a look at how this unusual and close-knit community weathers a zombie apocalypse, and what happens when extreme pacifism collides with extreme circumstances.

We've blocked off the reference room in the small community library for these interviews. Otto Miller sits across the table from me, his arms folded tightly against his chest. He is an elder in this small Amish community and looks every bit the part. I ask him to state his name and he simply stares at me and then looks down at the digital recorder I've placed on the table. He strokes his beard a couple times and then folds his arms again. I can see we're going to get nowhere with this.

I click the device off. That's not enough. I put it back down in my satchel and pull out a yellow legal tablet. As I click my pen he begins to speak.

"I have nothing against you, English, nor your devices. But you have to understand *us*. We don't cling to your machines, we don't participate in your ways, we don't ask anything of you. But you and your…things…your ways…they are constantly thrust upon us. Even your plague."

He points his finger squarely at me. I've heard of "righteous indignation," but I think this is the first time I've ever seen it. "I read your newspapers, listen to your broadcasts. You think this plague was the hand of God? Wouldn't that be convenient? If all this were simply the divine pouring out judgment and wrath upon the world? No, this was your own doing. You—you English—you played with the natural order of things and this was the result. Like breeding your livestock in one family line, sooner or later the results will haunt you. They haunt all of us."

I'm eager to get the interview on track. "Why don't we back up a bit, Mr. Miller. When was it the infection first touched your community?"

Otto Miller looks out the window for a moment and gathers his thoughts. "You are from the city, yes?"

I smile. "Yes. New York. My home is very far removed from what you have around here."

"You might think that we're completely isolated from the rest of the world, but it's not true, that's not our way. Separate but not isolated. We are not yoked to the world the way you are. So we were aware of the sickness, the "African Rabies," as they called it. We read the reports in the newspapers, listened to the radio and even watched the news on the television in the store in town. As more and more truth came out about what the disease truly was we were…cautious. But it seemed as far removed from us as…well…as New York City.

"It was in March, after that first winter. It was a hard winter, and I suppose if it hadn't been we would have seen them sooner and maybe been able to prepare ourselves better. I was up at 4:00 A.M. preparing for my morning chores. I was walking into the milking barn when I heard an odd sound in the pasture. I raised my lantern and that's when I saw my first…plague victim.

"In life he had been Jonas Yoder, a Mennonite from up the road. Jonas was a good man, I had known him all my life. There he stood in my pasture, mouth open, moaning, and what must have been a pitchfork wound through his chest."

Elder Miller looks deep into my eyes to the point of discomfort. "I suppose something you need to understand, being from the city, is that the first victims we ever saw were our friends and neighbors. People we had known our whole lives. I've read your 'survival guides' with faceless pictures of the undead. These were faces we had known and welcomed into our homes for years. You need to understand that to understand us."

I nod, and he continues. "It was still an hour or so from daylight, so I was very aware of the need to get back inside. I wasn't sure how Jonas got into my pasture, but I felt sure he couldn't get back out on the side closest to my home. I went back inside, locked the door and waited for sunup with my wife.

"Sunrise brought a horrifying sight. Jonas wasn't alone. There was Rebecca his wife. Further out in the pasture I noticed members of the King family, the Beilers and a few people from town—some of them familiar, others not. I also saw the gaping hole in my fence on the side closest to the road. That's how they had gotten in.

"Even worse they had gotten into the barn through some loose planks I had intended to fix in the spring. They were in the stalls with my work animals. The sounds were awful. I could hear my horses crying out as their flesh was torn. The sound drew the undead into the barn to feed. By the time my son arrived there must have been over thirty of them in the barn."

"So what did you and your son do?" I ask.

Otto Miller chuckles. "We simply did what needed to be done. We fixed the fence."

I laugh with him. Here was a man who faced the worst disaster in history with the simple truth he had learned all his life—if there's a hole in the fence you have to fix it. The world was going to hell but the Amish remained unchanged.

"We knew enough not to get close, we knew about the danger of the bites. But they were in the barn, so my son Amos locked them in and we went to work fixing the fence. We couldn't afford to have any more on our land so we strengthened the fence, added braces and chicken wire.

"So at this time it was just you, your wife, and your son?"

"He had brought his wife and two children with him. After we fixed the fence he went out to the neighbors and brought back everyone he could find and convince to come. We are blessed with a large home that was often used as a meeting place. By the end of the day there were sixteen of us. We were able to bring a few more of our fellowship in over the next week or so. We grew to thirty-three members in our home."

"That seems like a lot of people to house, let alone feed."

Mr. Miller straightened in his chair. If I didn't know of the humility of these people I would have thought there was a touch of pride in his response. "To be Amish is to know how to provide for your family and those you are in covenant with—even in the most difficult times. That is simply our way. Your infection simply allowed us to do for one another what we had always prepared to do.

"Canned goods were brought from other homes. There were still chickens in the coop, so we had eggs and the occasional fowl. We had to keep the birds inside the coop most of the time, though, their movement attracted too much attention from the infected and—we feared—would attract attention from survivors as well."

"You saw other survivors from outside your community?"

"Occasionally. It is very difficult to know the intentions of those outside of the fellowship. We did our best to remain out of sight—as we always had—but occasionally they would come to the house looking for help or refuge."

"Did they get any?"

"We wouldn't turn them away empty, English. That wouldn't be Christian. But we would give them some food, some water and send them on their way. 'A cup of cold water in Jesus' name' is what the Scripture commands. They received that and more.

"However, we were very aware that our supplies were limited. It was just gardening season and while we could grow plenty for ourselves it would be some time before we could harvest. And we had no idea how long the ordeal would last. We knew it was best to not attract attention to ourselves. It was then that we realized we could use the infected to our advantage. Just like with our livestock, we would release them from the barn every morning and let them into the pasture. The sight of them was enough to keep the curious away."

"So you would let them out of the barn by day? What about at night?"

Otto Miller looks at me like his next answer was the most logical and obvious. "We would herd them back into the barn. We had always done it with our livestock, it just seemed natural to do it with the undead. Also, we were uncomfortable with the idea of them roaming at night."

"I've interviewed survivors all over the world. No one else ever reported 'herding' the zombies. How did you…"

"Herding is something we've done all our lives. We were able to modify the cattle chutes that we had used to guide livestock into wagons for market. We would walk in front of them, guiding them to the barn and then use a rope ladder to get ourselves into the hayloft and back out of the barn."

It seems time to ask the question that I've been waiting for, the question that makes the survival story of this Old Order Amish community so unique. "So was that when you came upon the idea to…make use of them?"

"As spring wore on and summer was coming we became aware that we might be in for a long stay. The infected had killed my workhorses and while we wouldn't need as many crops, a few acres of corn and wheat would go a long way towards providing for us over the coming winter.

"Abraham Schrock was with us and he was an exceptionally skilled woodworker. One night as the women were putting the children to bed he showed me his plans for a new type of yoke. He estimated it would take eight of the infected to pull a plow and we would have to learn how to direct them but it seemed possible. He had brought his woodworking tools and within a few days we were ready to test the new yoke out."

Mr. Miller catches my laughter. I shake my head and comment, "You actually farmed with zombies."

His glare narrows at me. "What would you have me do? These were infected people who I had known all my life. It's not in our way to 'remove the head' as your news reporters so eloquently put it. The Word of God tells us, 'if any would not work, neither should he eat.' Well, they had already eaten my livestock. It was time for them to work."

We are silent for a moment. I use the time to collect my thoughts and clarify my notes. Finally I break the silence. "So how well did it...work?"

"Better than you might think. It took two men with ropes to hold them straight from the sides, one man to guide the plow from behind and one or two of the little ones in front to...encourage them."

"Little ones?" I ask.

"The children. We found that they made good lures for the infected—like dangling a carrot in front of an old mule. Yes, our children work, they do their share. They are strong and capable and never were in any real danger—no more danger than being trampled by a horse and we have known too many of those losses over the years.

"At any rate, the crops were in the ground. It would be a late harvest but there was still plenty of time. That winter there would be grain for flour, bread for the table, warmth in the home."

"It sounds almost ideal. You're an amazing group to have survived so well."

"We know it was the Lord's blessing. In fact, that fall we decided to hold a feast—a harvest festival. We prepared food from our crops, killed a few of the chickens and gave thanks. I remember it was the Sabbath—Sunday. We do not work on the Sabbath so the infected were kept in the barn all day.

"I suppose that's why 'they' came. They didn't see the infected and the children were playing in the yard under the trees. The adults were inside on the porch talking when my grandson brought the men to us."

He shakes his head and looks down. "They were scavengers. Vile men who were simply moving from town to town, taking what they wanted. Killing. Raping. Here they had come...on our Sabbath. On our day of thanksgiving.

"They had guns. They walked into my home and ordered us to the center of the sitting room. There were only five of them but...it's not our way to fight and with the women and children there it would have been...improper. They needed to see that our faith was strong, that our ways were steadfast.

"I spoke up and told them what I had told the other visitors over the months. We had food and would share and could provide them with water and even directions but they could not stay. They merely laughed.

"One of them spoke up. I supposed he was their leader. From his swagger and his large gun I suspect he was used to others kowtowing to him. He said, 'Well, I'm sorry, Old-Timer, but that's just not going to work for us. You see, we're going to stay for as long as we want and take what we want.'

"Those words were emphasized with a glance towards my daughter-in-law. I saw Amos bristle and step forward. I raised my palm to him and he backed down...as he should have. The outsiders just laughed.

"One of the other men must have realized that Amos was her husband, he pushed him with the butt of his rifle and Amos...poor Amos...always with the temper. He swung a fist at the man. The blow connected and he knocked him to the floor. That was when the leader stepped forward...put his gun to the side of Amos' head and pulled the trigger."

Mr. Miller stops and lowers his head. He removes his glasses and wipes his eyes, all the while in silence. I know enough to realize it's their way in prayer. I know better than to break the silence.

He sighs. "My son was gone. All those months among those undead, what some consider monsters and yet here these 'uninfected' had brought the worst plague upon my home. My wife was in tears, holding our son. His wife in tears beside her. My grandchildren simply looking on...frozen in the moment."

"I'm sorry," I offer, knowing my words mean nothing. "You have my sympathy."

"I think it was then," he continued, "that those men began to speculate on whether or not this would be as easy as they had thought. One of them said, 'We don't need this trouble, there's too many of them. It'd be a waste of ammo. Let's just take what we need and get out of here.'

"That must have sounded agreeable to their leader. He shook his head and looked back at me. 'We're going to need food. All we can carry.'

"'The women will pack it for you,' I told him, glancing over at Katie Schrock. She nodded and went to the kitchen to prepare the bags for them.

"The man tapped me on the chest with the barrel of his gun. 'You're Amish, so I don't suppose you have a car, but you must have horses around here somewhere. We're going to need transportation.'"

"I tried to tell him the horses were gone but he didn't believe me. In earnest, I didn't want to delay his leaving us so I didn't offer much more of an explanation. Finally he raised his weapon at my daughter-in-law and tapped the barrel against her head with each word: 'Where...are...the...animals?'

"I looked him in the eye—just as I'm looking at you now, English, and I told him quite simply, 'They're in the barn.'"

The words just hang there and we sit in silence as I let the full weight of them press down on me. I cannot help but think of the "scavengers" as they walked out to the barn and wonder what images of riding off into the sunset filled their minds.

Otto Miller stands and takes his hat in hand. He nods a "good-bye" my way and walks out of the room. I surmise that in his mind the interview is over. He has told his story. The rest is actually common knowledge in the area, told in hushed tones by the "outsiders." Mr. Miller led his scavengers to the barn, held the door for them as they walked in, closed it behind them and braced it. Muffled screams were heard and one or two shots were fired. The next spring he added three new members to his plowing team.

Otto Miller is a simple Amish man. His plain homemade clothes identical to those worn by his father and grandfather. His life as it always has been, revolving around his family, his fields and his faith. Whatever else he has done is between him and his God and certainly not open to the speculation of an outsider.

THE SUMMER PLACE

By Bob Fingerman

Bob Fingerman is the author of several works of zombie mayhem, including the recent novel *Pariah* and the graphic novels *Zombie World: Winter's Dregs* and *Recess Pieces* (which has been described as "*The Little Rascals* meets *Dawn of the Dead*"). Other recent works include an illustrated novella called *Connective Tissue* and the post-apocalyptic "speculative memoir" *From the Ashes*. His first novel was *Bottomfeeder* and other graphic novel work—for which Fingerman also provided the art—includes *Beg the Question*, *You Deserved It*, and *Minimum Wage*. Fingerman has also provided art for periodicals such as *Heavy Metal* and *The Village Voice* and did covers for Dark Horse and Vertigo Comics.

Fire Island, just off the southern coast of Long Island, is a bit of a mystery—no one really knows how it got its name. Historian Richard Bayles has proposed that the name resulted from a confused understanding of the Dutch term for "Five Islands," as there are a number of small islands in the vicinity. Other stories suggest that the name comes from the fires built by pirates to lure passing ships onto the sandbars, or from the island's rich autumn foliage, or even from the rashes caused by the poison ivy that grows there.

Our next story, as you might have guessed, takes place on Fire Island. "My wife and I used to rent a summerhouse on Fire Island and it struck me what a great setting for a horror story it would be during the off-season," Fingerman says. "Come October it's pretty desolate. And there are no cars. It's a weird place, like a sand-strewn version of The Village from the old series *The Prisoner*."

Fingerman never was a bike messenger like the protagonist, but as with much of his work, elements of autobiography found their way into the protagonist's personality. One way they're alike is that they both have some sympathy for zombies. "They didn't ask to be what they are and even though they want to eat humans, there's no malice," he says. "They're the average schmuck of the monster world. I can relate."

I'm looking at the red ring of fresh, shiny tooth marks on my right palm, some highlighted by small dots of blood. Not a lot of blood; in fact, quite little. But enough to have me concerned. It's times like this I get nostalgic for tetanus. Remember tetanus? When you were a kid and you'd go tearing around a vacant lot, some future construction site or some such, and you'd catch your tender young dermis on a rusty nail. Tetanus! Adults had warned you! You'd get visions of lockjaw and freak out. The grownups had cautioned you that infection with tetanus would cause severe muscle spasms and that those would lead to "locking" of the jaw so you couldn't open your mouth or swallow. It could maybe even lead to death by suffocation. Tetanus! Ah, the good old days.

Tetanus is not transmitted from person to person.

I wish I could say the same for this current unnamed affliction.

That part also sucks. I don't even know what to call this. The scientists and doctors hadn't come to a consensus by the time the broadcasts had ceased. So, what's the official classification? What's the name? I never understood the concept of naming a disease after yourself just because you discovered it. Why would you want your name associated with pain and suffering evermore? What was Parkinson thinking? If I was a doctor and I chanced upon some terrible malady I'd name it after someone awful—Hitler's Syndrome or Bush's Complex. At any rate, what would you call this latest—and likely final—pathosis? *Zombification* sounds kind of stupid. And if it's brewing, if you're infected but zombification hasn't blossomed into full-blown zombiehood, what then? What do you call its period of gestation?

I'm not man enough to go all Bruce Campbell on myself and lop off the offending extremity. Not yet. But why bother? It's in there, doing its thing, circulating. I guess. I remember hearing about this guy who was bitten on the ankle by some totally poisonous snake—in South America I think it was. Anyway, he knew he had about three minutes before the poison killed him. The guy was a lumberjack or something—maybe he was decimating the rain forest. Maybe the snake was protecting its turf. I can't remember that kind of detail. But he acted decisively and took his chainsaw to his leg and cut it off at the knee. And he lived. The guy lived. He cut it off before the poison could reach his heart. I couldn't do that. I can't. So I'm a-goner.

Why should I be any different?

Still, I feel so stupid.

I bandage the bite, more for the psychological comfort it provides. I just don't want to keep staring at it. Still, there goes my sex life, not being one for ambidexterity. I step out onto the porch and look down at the asphalt walkway. I'd call it a road, but no cars were permitted here. Sure, the occasional emergency vehicle was allowed—they didn't call it *Fire* Island for nothing—but no civilian automobiles. During the summer, just a few short, endless months ago, this road was teeming with the pasty and the tan, the fit and the flabby, all making their circuits to and from the beach, most of the guys toting coolers and cases full of cheap, low-octane suds. I never saw anyone with food. All of these beachgoers, the rare quiet ones and the common boisterous types, seemed to sustain themselves purely on beer and greasy wedges from the local pizzeria.

I'd kill for one of those mediocre slices right now.

The walkway is mostly obscured by slushy sand—just patches of buried blackness showing through here and there. I used to sit on this porch, reading—or at least pretending to read—and scoping the hotties. Right before the current, ultimate, nameless pandemic came and ruined everything, the *Girls Gone Wild* epidemic had swept the nation. Formerly normal girls, ones with a modicum of propriety, would suddenly whip off their tops and bounce up and down. All it took to loosen them up was massive quantities of alcohol, a bit of flattery, and the materialization of a video camera. How many parents cried themselves to sleep at night because of those DVDs?

Guys with oversized Dean Martin fishbowl snifters of frozen margarita would chant as these local girls made bad would frown, then giggle, then comply and let their boobs out to Neanderthal choruses of "*Whoo-whoo-whoo!*" Maybe that was a portent of the looming bestial decline of mankind. Nah. But it's amazing how fast a sexy girl can become an abject object, all desirability drained away in mere moments.

I don't know.

I thought coming back to Fire Island would be a good idea. Isolated, especially in the off-season. I liked the whole no cars thing. Back in the city, when it was really beginning to get soupy, the maniacs in their cars were more dangerous than the zombies. The roads were choked with panicky motorists attempting to flee, causing all kinds of mayhem along the way. What did they expect? Light traffic? Idiots. Of course all the roads were clogged. And every poor pedestrian schmuck one of these amateur Dale Earnhardts nailed would rise as one of the undead. Brilliant. Broken dolls peeling themselves off the pavement to wreak havoc on the ones who struck them down. Or whoever was convenient.

I used to be a bike courier, right after that movie *Quicksilver* came out—but not *because* of that movie. Never let it be said I was influenced to take a job because of a movie. Remember that thing? Kevin Bacon as a hotshot bike messenger, for the like five minutes Hollywood was convinced such a lame-ass job was cool. All those dumb movies about urban iconoclasts. Anyone for *Turk 182*?

Anyway.

Even after I moved on from that gig I remained an avid cyclist. My legs conditioned for endurance, I avoided the main arteries and biked all the way from Elmhurst to Bayshore, Long Island, which is a pretty long haul. I don't know how many miles—my odometer fell off somewhere along the way—but a lot. Especially when you consider the meandering back road nature of the trek. None of that "as the crow flies" convenience. En route I could see things worsening citywide, the zombies increasing their numbers at a dizzying pace. *Be fruitful and multiply*, I thought, ever the heretic. Even taking this shunpike route I avoided many a close call and witnessed many horrific sights. Amazing how many variations on the themes of evisceration and dismemberment there are. I splashed through more than a few puddles, and I'm not talking water. Having learned the hard way how to avoid hitting pedestrians, getting doored in traffic and other hazards of the bike courier's trade, I managed to eschew ensnarement by the hungry undead.

At least the zombies are slow.

And can't ride bikes or drive cars.

Yet.

When I got to the marina—actually, that sounds a bit grand. The wharf? The dock? Whatever—where the ferries left for the island, I realized there wasn't exactly going to be regular service. What was I thinking? Panic doesn't make for cogent planning, but you'd think on that interminable bike ride I'd have flashed on the notion that maybe ferry service to the island was terminated. Oddly, the ferries were still docked. Empty. No one was around, which was rather eerie. *Not a creature was stirring, not even a zombie.* Forgive me, but Christmas is coming. Call me sentimental.

Anyway, I boarded one and got as far as the bridge before I realized I had no idea how to pilot such a craft. I don't even know how to drive a car. And I had the brass to think those anxious drivers idiotic. Here I was, way out in Long Island, not my bailiwick, with no plan and nowhere to go. I was exhausted, too. I walked over to the vending machine to score a refreshing beverage. I'd earned that. The machine was dead, not accepting currency, paper or coin. I kicked the machine, shook it, then basically beat the hell out of it. I needed to vent. As it lay on its side, its front came undone and it spilled its innards in a cacophony of tinny—or would that be aluminumy—clanks. I chugged three cans in a row of Ocean Spray cranberry cocktail and felt better. I then stuffed a bunch in my backpack, and as I was about to check the grounds for more comestibles I spotted some interested parties dotting the periphery.

Not human.

The ruckus I'd made was the clarion, the dinner gong. I might as well have shouted, "Come and get it!" while tinkling a comical outsized triangle. If I'd entertained even fleeting hope that these callers were reg'lar folks, their herky-jerky locomotion quashed it in a trice. I gathered up a few more cans—delicious refreshment could double as solid projectile, if need be—and mounted my bike. But I wasn't sure where to go. I made a few quick figure eights around the parking lot, then made for the private boats. Many of those were missing, but a shoddy-looking motorboat was moored to the jetty. I stepped down into it, and when I didn't go straight through the bottom decided I'd be a seafaring boatnik after all. I grabbed my bike and loaded it into the dingy little dinghy, then tested the motor. A few yanks on the cord and it sputtered to life just as the lifeless approached. *Mazel tov!*

I'd never steered a boat of any size before, but for a first-timer I didn't do too badly. I managed to follow the basic course I'd remembered from all our trips on the ferry and within, oh, maybe two hours or so I made it to Ocean Bay Park, the dinky community we'd rented in.

We.

I remember the concept of "we."

"*We*" was pretty sweet. I was part of a "we." I had a wife. But guess what? She became one of those things right at the onset. On her way home from work she got bit. Well, more than bit. Consumed. I got a call from a cop who kept pausing to vomit noisily on his end of the line. He vomited, I wept. Then she came back and tore into the officer. Or at least I think that's what was going on. It sounded crunchy and wet. He kept screaming until, well, until he stopped. It was a really moist call. I'm being flippant, but sue me. It's all I have left. If I'm not flip about losing her I might just…

Anyway.

I might just what?

Kill myself?

That's a laugh.

All I know is I heard her moaning before I got disconnected—moaning and chewing. I got the picture, even without the benefit of a camera phone.

So after ramming into the side of the dock—starting it up I could work out, stopping not so much—I got out of the boat, dizzy and nauseous. I lay there for a while gasping, trying not to hurl. I must have looked like a fish out of water. It was mid-October, still not too bad temperature-wise, but drizzling. A good alternative name for Fire Island would be Rust Island. Back in the day people would ride their bikes all over, but always these ratty, rust-speckled wrecks, and here I was with my almost top-of-the-line mountain bike. Like it mattered. But at the moment I felt annoyed that my precious bicycle was going to be ruined by the elements. Priorities, young man, *priorities*.

Fog was rolling in, obscuring everything. If there were zombies afoot I wouldn't see them coming—or hear them. I hastened my pedaling and raced to our house. I say "our," but really it was just a rental. And now that I was no longer part of a "we," "our" seemed moot, too. I approached the dwelling that was little more than a shack and slowed as I heard footfalls.

Not human.

Deer.

Fire Island is rotten with these skanky, tick-encrusted deer. They're not beautiful, cute, or charming. They're the animal kingdom's answer to skid row vagrants. Dirty, infested with chiggers and lice and all manner of parasites. Their ears look like warty gourds, festooned with ticks so engorged they look fit to burst. These deer root around the trash, knock over garbage cans, mooch for scraps when you're eating outside. Where's Ted Nugent when you need him?

I got inside, locked the door, checked all the windows and then collapsed onto the naked mattress and into a nightmare-rich slumber, assuming the island to be pretty much deserted.

I was almost right.

The next morning I checked the pantry, though why I can't say. At the end of the season we cleared out all our edibles so I kind of knew it would be empty, which it was. I guess it was wishful thinking. Maybe cupboard elves had left something to gnaw on. Whatever. What else is life but hope? What would propel us forward but the inborn combination of hope and masochism? After hydrating myself with tap water I snatched up a blackened iron frying pan, cracked the front door and took a gander. Still drizzling but the coast was clear.

I tiptoed down the short flight of creaky wooden steps to the dirt path and stepped onto the sandy asphalt. Sandy Asphalt. Sounds like the name of a third-string stripper of yore. I digress. To my left was the beach followed by the ocean, a mere hundred or so feet away; to my right the ferry dock and the bay. The island's about thirty miles long, and at its most expansive only about three-quarters of a mile wide, just a long strip of sand. I mounted my bike and bay-bound made for the general store, a weathered gray clapboard number that had overcharged for everything. Ocean Bay Park—what in its heyday I'd referred to as Lunkhead Central—was silent apart from the patter of rain. Granted, even before this apocalyptic turn of events off-season would have been pretty calm, but this was different. The store's screen door hung open, not swaying on its corroded hinges. Even a rusty creak would have been reassuring. The silence was unnerving. Unnatural.

I jiggled the doorknob. Locked. A swing of the frying pan through the window later I was inside, stuffing my face like a little piggy with beef jerky, chips, and lukewarm Pepsi. I filled my pockets with snacks and potables and hit the road in search of I don't know what. Other survivors? More food? A gun? Yeah, all of the above. Inland, such as you'd call it, the roads were much clearer so biking was easy. The fog was burning off so visibility wasn't bad. I cut through Seaview and approached the larger—in relative terms—town of Ocean Beach, relishing the pleasure of riding my bike where the town ordinance had been "no bicycles allowed." The jolly scofflaw in a world where law is passé. Fun. I did a couple of laps around the center of town, checking out the spoils: general store, hardware store, a couple of shops devoted to souvenirs and beachwear, a disco, some eateries, bars, and ice cream parlors. And the old movie theater, a wooden structure I'd avoided, something churchlike in its mien that had kept me away.

I broke into the hardware store—funny how natural looting becomes—and selected a few lethal objects: a small, wieldy ax, a 12-volt battery-operated nail gun, and plenty of ammo, namely nails. I also grabbed a heavy jacket and rain slicker that were hung on a peg behind the counter. What can I say: I packed light and forgot a few things. After knocking on doors and shouting, "Is anyone there?" till my throat was raw, I rode back to the crib and charged the nail gun. It would have to do until I found a real gun. *If* I found one, that is. At least the power was still on.

As I ate a dinner of processed foodstuffs I heard a noise outside. The indicator light on the battery charger was still flashing, so I grabbed the ax and snuck up to the front door. Even with the porch light on I couldn't see anything. I heard the noise again. Something was moving out there. Had my light attracted it? Likely. I pulled on the heavy jacket and opened the door a hair, casting a focused beam from my flashlight into the hazy darkness. This fog was getting tiresome. The crunch of underbrush drew my attention and straight ahead was a ratty stag, one antler broken and dangling, the other an elaborate six-pointer. Listen to me trying to sound like the great outdoorsman. The deer on Fire Island were a protected species. They were completely unafraid of humans, so certain were they that they'd remain unharmed, like city squirrels.

It was a little early in the season for this buck to be shedding its antlers. Maybe it had gotten caught on something or been in a fight over a doe. Satisfied it wasn't a zombie I closed the door and resumed my repast, savoring each salty morsel of dry beef and chips. Amazing how salty American snack foods are. Stomach full of delicious garbage, I fell asleep easily, legs sore from all the abuse I'd heaped on them.

Over the course of the next few days my notion of retreating to Fire Island proved both a prescient blessing and shortsighted curse. It was indeed quite empty, but *too* empty. I was hoping to find *some* other refugees from the world. A young or even not so young widow. A couple with the swinger ethos. Maybe just a guy to hang with. I rode southwest through Robbins Rest, Atlantique, the aptly named Lonelyville, Dunewood, Fair Harbor, Saltaire, and Kismet. I stopped there because I didn't want to get too close to the Robert Moses Causeway, the bridge linking the island with the mainland—or at least Long Island proper. I was afraid that where there were cars there might be problems. Zombies and people in quantity.

I felt like Charlton Heston in *The Omega Man*, Vincent Price in *The Last Man on Earth*, both mediocre adaptations of Matheson's *I am Legend*. Oddly, the one that felt the least like the book was the one that used the actual title. Go figure. Anyway, tooling around like a tool on my ten-speed I was nobody's legend, that's for sure.

As a boy I'd been pretty self-sufficient, at least in terms of my ability to have fun alone. Often I'd play games like I was the last person on the planet. I'd deliberately choose routes to and fro bereft of people. I'd walk beside the tracks of the Long Island Railroad or along the traffic islands down the median of Queens Boulevard. Sure there'd be cars whipping by, but for miles I could walk without encountering another person in the flesh. My dad accused me of having a morbid fascination. I liked horror movies too much. Now, looking back, I reckon it was all a rehearsal for what was coming. Look at me, the Nostradamus Kid.

The loneliness was eroding me from within.

I tried heading in the other direction, which proved tricky. Point o' Woods was fenced off from Ocean Bay Park—no doubt to keep out the riffraff, of which in its day OBP had been densely populated. Unable to negotiate my bike over or around the fence, I climbed over and made the rest of my slog on foot. I'd never explored any of the other parts of the island back when it was alive. Sunken Forest was just that. Pretty, but creepy like everyplace else. Sailor's Haven wasn't. The super gay Cherry Grove was a bust. Hell, not that I'd have made a lifestyle change, but I craved camaraderie and so long as it was platonic I was up for anything. Anyone.

But there was nothing. No one.

I was so tired and dispirited I didn't bother schlepping to The Pines and points beyond. This was a ghost island, and I suppose as crushing as that fact was, ghosts were less harmful than zombies—at least *physically*. I'd managed to evade being literally consumed only to end up consumed by crippling melancholy. This was living?

There was no television, not even a test pattern.

Radio was fine if you enjoyed static.

I embarked on a house-to-house search for reading matter. I needed something with which to keep my mind occupied. Crossword puzzles. A Game Boy. Anything. The problem with summer rentals is that people don't leave stuff year-round. Sure I found some romance paperbacks—which I read, I hate to say—but nothing edifying. I found a cache of techno-thrillers, you know, Tom Clancy garbage. I read those, too, but stultifying doesn't begin to describe them. The bodice-rippers were better. I was in and out of almost every house between OBP and Robbins Rest before it dawned on me that I didn't have to stay in my trifling little shack. What the hell is wrong with me? Seriously. I had the run of the land and I spent my first three weeks in that drafty dive.

What a goon.

I took up residence in a sturdy and significantly more comfortable five-bedroom ranch-style number. The little pig had wised up and abandoned his straw hut for the brick palace. There was even a stash of porn in the master bedroom. I'd found my roost. With the power still on I kept my drinks cold. There was booze, and though I'd always been pretty much a teetotaler I began indulging. I'm not saying I became a drunkard, but every night after sashaying around my new demesne I took the edge off. And if that sometimes meant ending the night flat on my back, the room spinning like Dorothy's house on its way to Oz, so be it. Sobriety had lost its charm.

On a ride back from the market in Ocean Beach my front tire blew and I wiped out, spilling ass over tit into a shallow ditch opposite the ball field. Maybe I was a little hung over. It's possible. Not being a seasoned inebriate I was still defining my limits. For the first time in weeks the sky was cloudless and the sun was blinding. Even before the tumble my head ached. Now it throbbed, my palms were scraped raw and my vision was impaired. Even behind dark glasses I squinted against the glare, sprawled in the dirt angry, and even though there were no witnesses to my slapstick, embarrassed.

But there *was* a witness.

Hiding behind a water fountain near the bleachers was a zombie. How could we have missed each other this whole time? I scrabbled to my feet, groping for whatever weapon I could find, but in my pie-eyed complacency I'd left them all back at the ranch. All I could manage was my tire pump, which was pretty impotent.

The thing is, the zombie just cowered there, maintaining its position. Still wobbly from the fall and residual spirits, I stumbled backwards against a staple-riddled lamppost, gauzy remnants of weather-beaten notices for past community events clinging like scabs to the splintery surface. We stared at each other for what felt like eternity, neither of us doing anything. I began to wonder if this was a zombie or just a hallucination. Maybe the spill had given me a concussion. But it wasn't. My vision cleared, yet the zombie remained, staying put. Not attacking.

"Hello?" I asked, feeling stupid for doing so. "Can I help you?"

It recoiled at the sound of my voice. The zombie was female, and had been fairly young when she was alive—maybe a teenager or slightly older, judging by its apparel more than anything else. I'd never gotten to study one up close, most of the ones I'd seen a blur as I'd whizzed by them in transit. Her facial epidermis was taut, not slack as I'd pictured it in my mind, and the color of raw chicken skin, only the yellow wasn't quite so robust. Her deep-set eyes were filmy and lacked focus—in my present condition I could relate—yet her gaze never drifted from me. Her mouth hung slack, her breath slow and wheezy. Two things struck me: one, she was breathing, and two, her teeth were toothpaste commercial white. In the movies zombies are always snaggletoothed, their enamel grossly discolored. This undead chick had a movie star grill.

She also seemed impervious to cold, considering her bare feet and midriff, low-rider relaxed-fit jeans and thin tank top. I could see a pink bra under her low-cut white top. She had cleavage. Was I appraising this animated corpse's sexual attributes? Yes. Yes, I was. I was wondering if sex with a zombie constituted necrophilia. Who could say? The definition of necrophilia is an obsession with and usually erotic interest in or stimulation by corpses. But what of ambulatory corpses? What then? Though her body skin was a bit loose—relaxed-fit skin?—she was well preserved. Was it loneliness or madness that motivated these thoughts? Not to mention a surge of blood into my groin? Both.

"Uh, hello? Can you, uh, you know, uh, understand me?"

She cocked her head like a dog, her brow creased in concentration. It was almost adorable in a sick, macabre kind of way. Against my better judgment I took a step in her direction and she flinched, then began to back away. I took this as a sign to curtail this insanity and make tracks. I righted my bike and walked it home, looking over my shoulder at my hesitant new companion who did likewise.

I didn't drink that night, but I must have jerked off a half-dozen times.

Maybe that's too much information.

The next day I replaced the inner tube, grabbed my nail gun and hit the road. The weather had turned much colder over night and the gray misty gloom had rolled back in. As I pedaled, it began to drizzle. Soon snow would come. I considered gathering wood for the fireplace but was focused on finding the zombie girl again. I tried the ball field, of course, but she'd vacated the area. Still, I thought, slow moving as they seem to be, how far could she have gotten? Was she a local? Did she retain knowledge of her surroundings? Was she capable of anything beyond rudimentary mentation? Or even that?

As I approached Lonelyville, two does broke through the brush and blocked my path. They looked unwell, to put it mildly, even by Fire Island standards. Their fur was patchy, the bald spots scabby and oozing. Tumid ticks, as per usual, enshrouded their ears. In the rain they steamed; the smell was not good. I slowed, hoping they'd clear the way, but they just stood there looking unsure what to do next. I didn't have some fruity little bell to ring at them so I braked and shouted, "Hey, clear the road! Go on, beat it! Scram!" I made those nasty noises through my teeth that shoo cats away, but no dice. They tottered, looking drunk. I felt a flash of envy, then yelled at them a few more times, but the filthy beasts were unyielding.

I didn't feel up to a hassle with nature, so I made a U-turn and wended my way back home, zigzagging the streets up and down, looking for you-know-who to no avail. That afternoon I emptied a bottle of vodka, polished it off with a variety of mixers, then disgorged the contents of my stomach into the kitchen sink. Thank goodness for the garbage disposal. I managed to clean up before passing out on the linoleum floor.

Flashes of *Days of Wine and Roses* and *Lost Weekend* flickered behind my throbbing eyelids. When I awoke it was the middle of the night and I was disoriented as hell. At first I thought I'd shrunk—*The Incredible Shrinking Souse* or *Honey, I Shrunk the Drunk*, to keep up with the movie theme of this bender—my sightline being that of a man whose face is stuck to the floor.

I literally peeled myself from the sticky surface, rubbing my face, which had been imprinted with the texture of the linoleum. I felt like crap, but upon seeing my pattern-scarred *punim* in the mirror began to laugh until the choking curtailed my mirth. Symmetrical red striations etched the right side of my face. What a boob. I stumbled into the bathroom, urinated painfully, then gargled away the sour booze-vomit aftertaste. It hadn't been *that* long. Why was I falling apart like this? Could it be something to do with the death of humankind, especially my family, and most of all, my precious wife? Could it be because I was pining for the company of a female zombie I thought was passably attractive? Yeah, maybe that justified this rotten uncharacteristic behavior. There have been worse rationales for hitting the sauce.

I managed to get to the bed before surrendering to dormancy again.

I dreamt of a threesome with my late wife and the undead girl. Both stripped me naked and led me to a bed in the middle of the baseball diamond. The sky was black. Not nighttime dark, but black. A void. Eyes glowed from the bleachers accompanied by a chorus of chirping crickets. The two women began to run their tongues up and down my body, my wife working my upper portion, the living dead girl south of the waistline. The thing is, both of them were in that zombified state, but it was blissful—until they started devouring me. I didn't wake up. I just lay on my back watching them consume my flesh, opening my abdomen and pulling out my innards. I was paralyzed. They looked so contented.

I woke up and—goddamn if I'm not king of Mount Perverse: I had an erection.

In spite of my hangover I managed to eat and keep down a reasonably healthy breakfast, determined to find the girl. I don't like being haunted but she was doing just that. What would I do when I found her? Would she still shrink away or would the native hunger zombies seem to have—hey, I'm no expert—present itself? If so, would I flee or just let it happen? This whole survive-just-for-the-sake-of-survival thing isn't that great. It's only been weeks and already my *joie de vivre* is pretty well kaput.

I mounted up and hit the dusty—well, moist, actually—trail. The mist was icy and I had to keep my eyes squinted tight to prevent ocular abrasion, but I was resolute:

I would find this zombie girl and either court her or exterminate her, depending on her receptivity to my companionship. Maybe she just wanted a tuna sandwich. Maybe this human flesh eating was just a phase. Again, I'm no expert. Maybe she needed a hug. I know I did. I'd just like to spoon again. Be in bed and feel the small of a woman's back against my stomach, my crotch nestled against her tush.

As I pedaled I felt more and more conflicted about this loopy notion of bedding down a zombie. And it wasn't even a sex thing at the moment. I just wanted to snuggle. What man just wants a cuddle? A crazy, lonely one, that's what.

Calling out would be a no-no, she being the shy type, so I just kept my eyes peeled and pedaled slow. I skipped Point o' Woods and beyond. I just couldn't envisage the zombie girl lofting herself over the high chain-link fence. So, block-by-block I explored Seaview, pausing only to pick up a few provisions, including a visit to the liquor store. In each town I dismounted and checked the nearby beach. Nothing. Well, nothing but skanky deer. At each encounter I mused it was a good thing for them I wasn't fond of venison.

Yeah.

The first frost came in early December. Maybe my zombie heartthrob had succumbed to the elements or starvation or decomposition. I had no idea how long an undead individual lasted, with or without sustenance. How often did they eat? Could they subsist on grubs and squirrels? I hated not knowing. I hated that I couldn't log onto the Internet and Google "zombie, feeding habits, lifespan." I needed to Ask Jeeves, but couldn't. Like everything else, the 'net was down. I never realized how addicted I was to outlets of mass communication. I missed TV, radio, and the web as much as I missed human contact. Sick. Books and backdated magazines were not cutting the mustard, no sir. My nights were a debauched stag party for one, the time split between drinking to excess and masturbating when I could manage it.

It was while walking my bike through that town whose name I loved so well, Lonelyville, that I stumbled upon—literally—the undead object of my desire, but now she was just plain old dead dead, her stiff, supine body glistening with ice crystals. I knelt down beside her and stared, my grief indescribable. Her tank top had disappeared, and her bra was torn, one cup shredded revealing a pale, translucent yellow breast. Her face was angelic, at least it was to me at that moment, and I felt shame for having fostered lust for this creature. Not because it was unnatural—you can debate that all you want—but because she looked above such secular desires. Tears began streaming down my cheeks but I didn't wipe them away. I felt more loss here for this stranger than I had for my own wife, maybe because my wife's demise was in the abstract. I hadn't been there for it. I'd also been in a blind panic like everyone else.

Now, in this tranquil wintry setting, I had the luxury of time to grieve. I let it all out for this strangely captivating zombie girl, for my wife, for all of humanity. I bawled and right there in the road, lay on my side and spooned her, my body shaking not from the cold but from previously unimaginable loss.

And as we lay there a grizzled stag stepped onto the road, staring at us, its eyes black and unknowable. Steam pumped from its craterous nostrils and it grunted with bestial authority, like we were trespassing.

We. I so badly needed to be a part of "we" again. Does that make me codependent? My vision blurred by anguish, my mood black as pitch, I glared at this four-legged interloper. It grunted again and scraped a hoof against the pavement. The effrontery was too much. It was this goddamned filthy animal that was trespassing on this scene of human loss.

I disengaged from the girl's cadaver—and that's all it was now, just a plain old regular garden-variety corpse—and stood up, my fists vibrating with barely contained mayhem. I wanted to hurt this threadbare excuse for a deer, its antlers cracked and collapsing, its fur a mat of mud and grime and abrasions. I stepped toward it and it shook its head back and forth, its right antler threatening to drop off with each motion.

"I *hate* you miserable bastards," I hissed. "I've always hated the deer on this god-forsaken island, but now you, you really *put it in italics*. Can't you see this is a private moment? I know it's beyond your feeble peanut brain to show any goddamn respect, but so help me if you don't get the hell away from here I'll bash your skull in!"

It stood there, steaming away in the sleet.

So I took a swing at it. Not the brightest thing I've ever done, but I was a tad overwrought, shall we say? Open handed I made to slap it right across the muzzle and it bit me. And then it hit me why these deer looked so spectacularly putrid: *they were dead.* Undead. Whatever. They were animated corpses. Humans aren't the only ones circling the drain. It's all life. All of it.

So now I'm looking at the fresh white gauze wrapped around my right hand, a ring of small red dots seeping through. Not a lot of blood; in fact quite little. But enough to have me concerned.

And back on that road lies the undead girl of my dreams. I didn't bury her.

I guess I'm infected.

THE WRONG GRAVE

By Kelly Link

Kelly Link is a short fiction specialist whose stories have been collected in three volumes: *Stranger Things Happen*, *Magic for Beginners*, and *Pretty Monsters*. Her stories have appeared in *The Magazine of Fantasy & Science Fiction, Realms of Fantasy, Asimov's Science Fiction, Conjunctions*, and in anthologies such as *The Dark*, *The Faery Reel*, and *Best American Short Stories*. With her husband, Gavin J. Grant, Link runs Small Beer Press and edits the 'zine *Lady Churchill's Rosebud Wristlet*. Her fiction has earned her an NEA Literature Fellowship and won a variety of awards, including the Hugo, Nebula, World Fantasy, Stoker, Tiptree, and Locus awards.

This story is about a heartbroken young man who buries the only copies of some of his poems in the grave of a young woman he loves. The Pre-Raphaelite poet and painter Dante Gabriel Rossetti did exactly the same thing in real life after his wife Elizabeth Siddal, who had modeled for many of his paintings, died from an overdose of laudanum. And as in this story, Rossetti later regretted his dramatic, romantic gesture and had his wife's grave exhumed so that he could retrieve his poems, which were then published in 1870. The Pre-Raphaelites were dedicated to restoring to art the classical values of pose, color, and composition, which they felt had been denuded by the stuffy influence of art academies. (Rossetti's sister Christina is also famous for her long poem *Goblin Market,* which has influenced generations of fantasy authors.) In later years Dante Rossetti became obsessed with exotic animals, especially wombats—he finally managed to acquire one, which he would have join him for supper. His parties were also enlivened by his pet toucan, which he would dress in a cowboy hat and then have ride his llama around the dinner table. Pretty strange. Though at least when Rossetti dug up his poetry he was confident that he had the right grave.

The protagonist in our next tale is not so fortunate. And if you thought the life of Dante Gabriel Rossetti was full of strangeness, you ain't seen nothing yet.

All of this happened because a boy I once knew named Miles Sperry decided to go into the resurrectionist business and dig up the grave of his girlfriend, Bethany Baldwin, who had been dead for not quite a year. Miles planned to do this in order to recover the sheaf of poems he had, in what he'd felt was a beautiful and romantic gesture, put into her casket. Or possibly it had just been a really dumb thing to do. He hadn't made copies. Miles had always been impulsive. I think you should know that right up front.

He'd tucked the poems, handwritten, tear-stained and with cross-outs, under Bethany's hands. Her fingers had felt like candles, fat and waxy and pleasantly cool, until you remembered that they were fingers. And he couldn't help noticing that there was something wrong about her breasts, they seemed larger. If Bethany had known that she was going to die, would she have gone all the way with him? One of his poems was about that, about how now they never would, how it was too late now. Carpe diem before you run out of diem.

Bethany's eyes were closed, someone had done that, too, just like they'd arranged her hands, and even her smile looked composed, in the wrong sense of the word. Miles wasn't sure how you made someone smile after they were dead. Bethany didn't look much like she had when she'd been alive. That had been only a few days ago. Now she seemed smaller, and also, oddly, larger. It was the nearest Miles had ever been to a dead person, and he stood there, looking at Bethany, wishing two things: that he was dead, too, and also that it had seemed appropriate to bring along his notebook and a pen. He felt he should be taking notes. After all, this was the most significant thing that had ever happened to Miles. A great change was occurring within him, moment by singular moment.

Poets were supposed to be in the moment, and also stand outside the moment, looking in. For example, Miles had never noticed before, but Bethany's ears were slightly lopsided. One was smaller and slightly higher up. Not that he would have cared, or written a poem about it, or even mentioned it to her, ever, in case it made her self-conscious, but it was a fact and now that he'd noticed it he thought it might have driven him crazy, not mentioning it: he bent over and kissed Bethany's forehead, breathing in. She smelled like a new car. Miles's mind was full of poetic thoughts. Every cloud had a silver lining, except there was probably a more interesting and meaningful way to say that, and death wasn't really a cloud. He thought about what it was: more like an earthquake, maybe, or falling from a great height and smacking into the ground, really hard, which knocked the wind out of you and made it hard to sleep or wake up or eat or care about things like homework or whether there was anything good on TV. And death was foggy, too, but also prickly, so maybe instead of a cloud, a fog made of little sharp things. Needles. Every death fog has a lot of silver needles. Did that make sense? Did it scan?

Then the thought came to Miles like the tolling of a large and leaden bell that Bethany was dead. This may sound strange, but in my experience it's strange and it's also just how it works. You wake up and you remember that the person you loved is dead. And then you think: Really?

Then you think how strange it is, how you have to remind yourself that the person you loved is dead, and even while you're thinking about that, the thought comes to you again that the person you loved is dead. And it's the same stupid fog, the same needles or mallet to the intestines or whatever worse thing you want to call it, all over again. But you'll see for yourself someday.

Miles stood there, remembering, until Bethany's mother, Mrs. Baldwin, came up beside him. Her eyes were dry, but her hair was a mess. She'd only managed to put eye shadow on one eyelid. She was wearing jeans and one of Bethany's old T-shirts. Not even one of Bethany's favorite T-shirts. Miles felt embarrassed for her, and for Bethany, too.

"What's that?" Mrs. Baldwin said. Her voice sounded rusty and outlandish, as if she were translating from some other language. Something Indo-Germanic, perhaps.

"My poems. Poems I wrote for her," Miles said. He felt very solemn. This was a historic moment. One day Miles's biographers would write about this. "Three haikus, a sestina, and two villanelles. Some longer pieces. No one else will ever read them."

Mrs. Baldwin looked into Miles's face with her terrible, dry eyes. "I see," she said. "She said you were a lousy poet." She put her hand down into the casket, smoothed Bethany's favorite dress, the one with spider webs, and several holes through which you could see Bethany's itchy black tights. She patted Bethany's hands, and said, "Well, good-bye, old girl. Don't forget to send a postcard."

Don't ask me what she meant by this. Sometimes Bethany's mother said strange things. She was a lapsed Buddhist and a substitute math teacher. Once she'd caught Miles cheating on an algebra quiz. Relations between Miles and Mrs. Baldwin had not improved during the time that Bethany and Miles were dating, and Miles couldn't decide whether or not to believe her about Bethany not liking his poetry. Substitute teachers had strange senses of humor when they had them at all.

He almost reached into the casket and took his poetry back. But Mrs. Baldwin would have thought that she'd proved something; that she'd won. Not that this was a situation where anyone was going to win anything. This was a funeral, not a game show. Nobody was going to get to take Bethany home.

Mrs. Baldwin looked at Miles and Miles looked back. Bethany wasn't looking at anyone. The two people that Bethany had loved most in the world could see, through that dull hateful fog, what the other was thinking, just for a minute, and although you weren't there and even if you had been you wouldn't have known what they were thinking anyway, I'll tell you. I wish it had been me, Miles thought. And Mrs. Baldwin thought, I wish it had been you, too.

Miles put his hands into the pockets of his new suit, turned, and left Mrs. Baldwin standing there. He went and sat next to his own mother, who was trying very hard not to cry. She'd liked Bethany. Everyone had liked Bethany. A few rows in front, a girl named April Lamb was picking her nose in some kind of frenzy of grief. When they got to the cemetery, there was another funeral service going on, the burial of the girl who had been in the other car, and the two groups of mourners glared at each other as they parked their cars and tried to figure out which grave site to gather around.

Two florists had misspelled Bethany's name on the ugly wreaths, BERTHANY and also BETHONY, just like tribe members did when they were voting each other out on the television show *Survivor,* which had always been Bethany's favorite thing about *Survivor.* Bethany had been an excellent speller, although the Lutheran minister who was conducting the sermon didn't mention that.

Miles had an uncomfortable feeling: he became aware that he couldn't wait to get home and call Bethany, to tell her all about this, about everything that had happened since she'd died. He sat and waited until the feeling wore off. It was a feeling he was getting used to.

Bethany had liked Miles because he made her laugh. He makes me laugh, too. Miles figured that digging up Bethany's grave, even that would have made her laugh. Bethany had had a great laugh, which went up and up like a clarinetist on an escalator. It wasn't annoying. It had been delightful, if you liked that kind of laugh. It would have made Bethany laugh that Miles Googled grave digging in order to educate himself. He read an Edgar Allan Poe story, he watched several relevant episodes of *Buffy the Vampire Slayer*, and he bought Vicks VapoRub, which you were supposed to apply under your nose. He bought equipment at Target: a special, battery-operated, telescoping shovel, a set of wire cutters, a flashlight, extra batteries for the shovel and flashlight, and even a Velcro headband with a headlamp that came with a special red lens filter, so that you were less likely to be noticed.

Miles printed out a map of the cemetery so that he could find his way to Bethany's grave off Weeping Fish Lane, even—as an acquaintance of mine once remarked—"in the dead of night when naught can be seen, so pitch is the dark." (Not that the dark would be very pitch. Miles had picked a night when the moon would be full.) The map was also just in case, because he'd seen movies where the dead rose from their graves. You wanted to have all the exits marked in a situation like that.

He told his mother that he was spending the night at his friend John's house. He told his friend John not to tell his mother anything.

If Miles had Googled "poetry" as well as "digging up graves," he would have discovered that his situation was not without precedent. The poet and painter Dante Gabriel Rossetti also buried his poetry with his dead lover. Rossetti, too, had regretted this gesture, had eventually decided to dig up his lover to get back his poems. I'm telling you this so that you never make the same mistake.

I can't tell you whether Dante Gabriel Rossetti was a better poet than Miles, although Rossetti had a sister, Christina Rossetti, who was really something. But you're not interested in my views on poetry. I know you better than that, even if you don't know me. You're waiting for me to get to the part about grave digging.

Miles had a couple of friends and he thought about asking someone to come along on the expedition. But no one except for Bethany knew that Miles wrote poetry. And Bethany had been dead for a while. Eleven months, in fact, which was one month longer than Bethany had been Miles's girlfriend. Long enough that Miles was beginning to make his way out of the fog and the needles. Long enough that he could listen to certain songs on the radio again. Long enough that sometimes there was something dreamlike about his memories of Bethany, as if she'd been a movie that he'd seen a long time ago, late at night on television. Long enough that when he tried to reconstruct the poems he'd written her, especially the villanelle, which had been, in his opinion, really quite good, he couldn't. It was as if when he'd put those poems into the casket, he hadn't just given Bethany the only copies of some poems, but had instead given away those shining, perfect lines, given them away so thoroughly that he'd never be able to write them out again. Miles knew that Bethany was dead. There was nothing to do about that. But the poetry was different. You have to salvage what you can, even if you're the one who buried it in the first place.

You might think at certain points in this story that I'm being hard on Miles, that I'm not sympathetic to his situation. This isn't true. I'm as fond of Miles as I am of anyone else. I don't think he's any stupider or any bit less special or remarkable than—for example—you. Anyone might accidentally dig up the wrong grave. It's a mistake anyone could make.

The moon was full and the map was easy to read even without the aid of the flashlight. The cemetery was full of cats. Don't ask me why. Miles was not afraid. He was resolute. The battery-operated telescoping shovel at first refused to untelescope. He'd tested it in his own backyard, but here, in the cemetery, it seemed unbearably loud. It scared off the cats for a while, but it didn't draw any unwelcome attention. The cats came back. Miles set aside the moldering wreaths and bouquets, and then he used his wire cutters to trace a rectangle. He stuck the telescoping shovel under and pried up fat squares of sod above Bethany's grave. He stacked them up like carpet samples and got to work.

By two A.M., Miles had knotted a length of rope at short, regular intervals for footholds, and then looped it around a tree, so he'd be able to climb out of the grave again, once he'd retrieved his poetry. He was waist-deep in the hole he'd made. The night was warm and he was sweating. It was hard work, directing the shovel. Every once in a while it telescoped while he was using it. He'd borrowed his mother's gardening gloves to keep from getting blisters, but still his hands were getting tired. The gloves were too big. His arms ached.

By three thirty, Miles could no longer see out of the grave in any direction except up. A large white cat came and peered down at Miles, grew bored and left again. The moon moved over Miles's head like a spotlight. He began to wield the shovel more carefully. He didn't want to damage Bethany's casket. When the shovel struck something that was not dirt, Miles remembered that he'd left the Vicks VapoRub on his bed at home. He improvised with a cherry ChapStick he found in his pocket. Now he used his garden-gloved hands to dig and to smooth dirt away. The bloody light emanating from his Velcro headband picked out the ingenious telescoping ridges of the discarded shovel, the little rocks and worms and worm-like roots that poked out of the dirt walls of Miles's excavation, the smoother lid of Bethany's casket.

Miles realized he was standing on the lid. Perhaps he should have made the hole a bit wider. It would be difficult to get the lid open while standing on it. He needed to pee: there was that as well. When he came back, he shone his flashlight into the grave. It seemed to him that the lid of the coffin was slightly ajar. Was that possible? Had he damaged the hinges with the telescoping shovel, or kicked the lid askew somehow when he was shimmying up the rope? He essayed a slow, judicious sniff, but all he smelled was dirt and cherry ChapStick. He applied more cherry ChapStick. Then he lowered himself down into the grave.

The lid wobbled when he tested it with his feet. He decided that if he kept hold of the rope, and slid his foot down and under the lid, like so, then perhaps he could cantilever the lid up—

It was very strange. It felt as if something had hold of his foot. He tried to tug it free, but no, his foot was stuck, caught in some kind of vise or grip. He lowered the toe of his other hiking boot down into the black gap between the coffin and its lid, and tentatively poked it forward, but this produced no result. He'd have to let go of the rope and lift the lid with his hands. Balance like so, carefully, carefully, on the thin rim of the casket. Figure out how he was caught.

It was hard work, balancing and lifting at the same time, although the one foot was still firmly wedged in its accidental toehold. Miles became aware of his own breathing, the furtive scuffling noise of his other boot against the coffin lid. Even the red beam of his lamp as it pitched and swung, back and forth, up and down in the narrow space, seemed unutterably noisy. "Shit, shit, shit," Miles whispered. It was either that or else scream. He got his fingers under the lid of the coffin on either side of his feet and bent his wobbly knees so he wouldn't hurt his back, lifting. Something touched the fingers of his right hand.

No, his fingers had touched something. *Don't be ridiculous, Miles.* He yanked the lid up as fast and hard as he could, the way you would rip off a bandage if you suspected there were baby spiders hatching under it. "Shit, shit, shit, shit, shit!"

He yanked and someone else pushed. The lid shot up and fell back against the opposite embankment of dirt. The dead girl who had hold of Miles's boot let go.

This was the first of the many unexpected and unpleasant shocks that Miles was to endure for the sake of poetry. The second was the sickening—no, shocking—shock that he had dug up the wrong grave, the wrong dead girl.

The wrong dead girl was lying there, smiling up at him, and her eyes were open. She was several years older than Bethany. She was taller and had a significantly more developed rack. She even had a tattoo.

The smile of the wrong dead girl was white and orthodontically perfected. Bethany had had braces that turned kissing into a heroic feat. You had to kiss around braces, slide your tongue up or sideways or under, like navigating through barbed wire: a delicious, tricky trip through No Man's Land. Bethany pursed her mouth forward when she kissed. If Miles forgot and mashed his lips down too hard on hers, she whacked him on the back of his head. This was one of the things about his relationship with Bethany that Miles remembered vividly, looking down at the wrong dead girl.

The wrong dead girl spoke first. "Knock knock," she said.

"What?" Miles said.

"Knock knock," the wrong dead girl said again.

"Who's there?" Miles said.

"Gloria," the wrong dead girl said. "Gloria Palnick. Who are you and what are you doing in my grave?"

"This isn't your grave," Miles said, aware that he was arguing with a dead girl, and the wrong dead girl at that. "This is Bethany's grave. What are you doing in Bethany's grave?"

"Oh no," Gloria Palnick said. "This is my grave and I get to ask the questions."

A notion crept, like little dead cat feet, over Miles. Possibly he had made a dangerous and deeply embarrassing mistake. "Poetry," he managed to say. "There was some poetry that I, ah, that I accidentally left in my girlfriend's casket. And there's a deadline for a poetry contest coming up, and so I really, really needed to get it back."

The dead girl stared at him. There was something about her hair that Miles didn't like.

"Excuse me, but are you for real?" she said. "This sounds like one of those lame excuses. The dog ate my homework. I accidentally buried my poetry with my dead girlfriend."

"Look," Miles said, "I checked the tombstone and everything. This is supposed to be Bethany's grave. Bethany Baldwin. I'm really sorry I bothered you and everything, but this isn't really my fault." The dead girl just stared at him thoughtfully. He wished that she would blink. She wasn't smiling anymore. Her hair, lank and black, where Bethany's had been brownish and frizzy in summer, was writhing a little, like snakes. Miles thought of centipedes. Inky midnight tentacles.

"Maybe I should just go away," Miles said. "Leave you to, ah, rest in peace or whatever."

"I don't think sorry cuts the mustard here," Gloria Palnick said. She barely moved her mouth when she spoke, Miles noticed. And yet her enunciation was fine. "Besides, I'm sick of this place. It's boring. Maybe I'll just come along with."

"What?" Miles said. He felt behind himself, surreptitiously, for the knotted rope.

"I said, maybe I'll come with you," Gloria Palnick said. She sat up. Her hair was really coiling around, really seething now. Miles thought he could hear hissing noises.

"You can't do that!" he said. "I'm sorry, but no. Just no."

"Well then, you stay here and keep me company," Gloria Palnick said. Her hair was really something.

"I can't do that either," Miles said, trying to explain quickly, before the dead girl's hair decided to strangle him. "I'm going to be a poet. It would be a great loss to the world if I never got a chance to publish my poetry."

"I see," Gloria Palnick said, as if she did, in fact, see a great deal. Her hair settled back down on her shoulders and began to act a lot more like hair. "You don't want me to come home with you. You don't want to stay here with me. Then how about this? If you're such a great poet, then write me a poem. Write something about me so that everyone will be sad that I died."

"I could do that," Miles said. Relief bubbled up through his middle like tiny doughnuts in an industrial deep-fat fryer. "Let's do that. You lie down and make yourself comfortable and I'll rebury you. Today I've got a quiz in American History, and I was going to study for it during my free period after lunch, but I could write a poem for you instead."

"Today is Saturday," the dead girl said.

"Oh, hey," Miles said. "Then no problem. I'll go straight home and work on your poem. Should be done by Monday."

"Not so fast," Gloria Palnick said. "You need to know all about my life and about me, if you're going to write a poem about me, right? And how do I know you'll write a poem if I let you bury me again? How will I know if the poem's any good? No dice. I'm coming home with you and I'm sticking around until I get my poem. 'Kay?"

She stood up. She was several inches taller than Miles. "Do you have any ChapStick?" she said. "My lips are really dry."

"Here," Miles said. Then, "You can keep it."

"Oh, afraid of dead girl cooties," Gloria Palnick said. She smacked her lips at him in an upsetting way.

"I'll climb up first," Miles said. He had the idea that if he could just get up the rope, if he could yank the rope up after himself fast enough, he might be able to run away, get to the fence where he'd chained up his bike, before Gloria managed to get out. It wasn't like she knew where he lived. She didn't even know his name.

"Fine," Gloria said. She looked like she knew what Miles was thinking and didn't really care. By the time Miles had bolted up the rope, yanking it up out of the grave, abandoning the telescoping shovel, the wire cutters, the wronged dead girl, and had unlocked his road bike and was racing down the empty 5 A.M. road, the little red dot of light from his headlamp falling into potholes, he'd almost managed to persuade himself that it had all been a grisly hallucination. Except for the fact that the dead girl's cold dead arms were around his waist, suddenly, and her cold dead face was pressed against his back, her damp hair coiling around his head and tapping at his mouth, burrowing down his filthy shirt.

"Don't leave me like that again," she said.

"No," Miles said. "I won't. Sorry."

He couldn't take the dead girl home. He couldn't think of how to explain it to his parents. No, no, no. He didn't want to take her over to John's house either. It was far too complicated. Not just the girl, but he was covered in dirt. John wouldn't be able to keep his big mouth shut.

"Where are we going?" the dead girl said.

"I know a place," Miles said. "Could you please not put your hands under my shirt? They're really cold. And your fingernails are kind of sharp."

"Sorry," the dead girl said.

They rode along in silence until they were passing the 7-Eleven at the corner of Eighth and Walnut, and the dead girl said, "Could we stop for a minute? I'd like some beef jerky. And a Diet Coke."

Miles braked. "Beef jerky?" he said. "Is that what dead people eat?"

"It's the preservatives," the dead girl said, somewhat obscurely.

Miles gave up. He steered the bike into the parking lot. "Let go, please," he said. The dead girl let go. He got off the bike and turned around. He'd been wondering just exactly how she'd managed to sit behind him on the bike, and he saw that she was sitting above the rear tire on a cushion of her horrible, shiny hair. Her legs were stretched out on either side, toes in black combat boots floating just above the asphalt, and yet the bike didn't fall over. It just hung there under her. For the first time in almost a month, Miles found himself thinking about Bethany as if she were still alive: Bethany is never going to believe this. But then, Bethany had never believed in anything like ghosts. She'd hardly believed in the school dress code. She definitely wouldn't have believed in a dead girl who could float around on her hair like it was an anti-gravity device.

"I can also speak fluent Spanish," Gloria Palnick said.

Miles reached into his back pocket for his wallet, and discovered that the pocket was full of dirt. "I can't go in there," he said.

"For one thing, I'm a kid and it's five in the morning. Also I look like I just escaped from a gang of naked mole rats. I'm filthy."

The dead girl just looked at him. He said, coaxingly, "*You* should go in. You're older. I'll give you all the money I've got. You go in and I'll stay out here and work on the poem."

"You'll ride off and leave me here," the dead girl said. She didn't sound angry, just matter of fact. But her hair was beginning to float up. It lifted her up off Miles's bike in a kind of hairy cloud and then plaited itself down her back in a long, business-like rope.

"I won't," Miles promised. "Here. Take this. Buy whatever you want."

Gloria Palnick took the money. "How very generous of you," she said.

"No problem," Miles told her. "I'll wait here." And he did wait. He waited until Gloria Palnick went into the 7-Eleven. Then he counted to thirty, waited one second more, got back on his bike and rode away. By the time he'd made it to the meditation cabin in the woods back behind Bethany's mother's house, where he and Bethany had liked to sit and play Monopoly, Miles felt as if things were under control again, more or less. There is nothing so calming as a meditation cabin where long, boring games of Monopoly have taken place. He'd clean up in the cabin sink, and maybe take a nap. Bethany's mother never went out there. Her ex-husband's meditation clothes, his scratchy prayer mat, all his Buddhas and scrolls and incense holders and posters of Che Guevara were still out here. Miles had snuck into the cabin a few times since Bethany's death, to sit in the dark and listen to the plink-plink of the meditation fountain and think about things. He was sure Bethany's mother wouldn't have minded if she knew, although he hadn't ever asked, just in case. Which had been wise of him.

The key to the cabin was on the beam just above the door, but he didn't need it after all. The door stood open. There was a smell of incense, and of other things: cherry ChapStick and dirt and beef jerky. There was a pair of black combat boots beside the door.

Miles squared his shoulders. I have to admit that he was behaving sensibly here, finally. Finally. Because—and Miles and I are in agreement for once—if the dead girl could follow him somewhere before he even knew exactly where he was going, then there was no point in running away. Anywhere he went she'd already be there. Miles took off his shoes, because you were supposed to take off your shoes when you went into the cabin. It was a gesture of respect. He put them down beside the combat boots and went inside. The waxed pine floor felt silky under his bare feet. He looked down and saw that he was walking on Gloria Palnick's hair.

"Sorry!" Miles said. He meant several things by that. He meant sorry for walking on your hair. Sorry for riding off and leaving you in the 7-Eleven after promising that I wouldn't. Sorry for the grave wrong I've done you. But most of all he meant sorry, dead girl, that I ever dug you up in the first place.

"Don't mention it," the dead girl said. "Want some jerky?"

"Sure," he said. He felt he had no other choice.

He was beginning to feel he would have liked this dead girl under other circumstances, despite her annoying, bullying hair. She had poise. A sense of humor. She seemed to have what his mother called stick-to-itiveness; what the AP English Exam prefers to call tenacity. Miles recognized the quality. He had it in no small degree himself. The dead girl was also extremely pretty, if you ignored the hair. You might think less of Miles that he thought so well of the dead girl, that this was a betrayal of Bethany. Miles felt it was a betrayal. But he thought that Bethany might have liked the dead girl too. She would certainly have liked her tattoo.

"How is the poem coming?" the dead girl said.

"There's not a lot that rhymes with Gloria," Miles said. "Or Palnick."

"Toothpick," said the dead girl. There was a fragment of jerky caught in her teeth. "Euphoria."

"Maybe *you* should write the stupid poem," Miles said. There was an awkward pause, broken only by the almost-noiseless glide of hair retreating across a pine floor. Miles sat down, sweeping the floor with his hand, just in case.

"You were going to tell me something about your life," he said.

"Boring," Gloria Palnick said. "Short. Over."

"That's not much to work with. Unless you want a haiku."

"Tell me about this girl you were trying to dig up," Gloria said. "The one you wrote the poetry for."

"Her name was Bethany," Miles said. "She died in a car crash."

"Was she pretty?" Gloria said.

"Yeah," Miles said.

"You liked her a lot," Gloria said.

"Yeah," Miles said.

"Are you sure you're a poet?" Gloria asked.

Miles was silent. He gnawed his jerky ferociously. It tasted like dirt. Maybe he'd write a poem about it. That would show Gloria Palnick.

He swallowed and said, "Why were you in Bethany's grave?"

"How should I know?" she said. She was sitting across from him, leaning against a concrete Buddha the size of a three-year-old, but much fatter and holier. Her hair hung down over her face, just like a Japanese horror movie. "What do you think, that Bethany and I swapped coffins, just for fun?"

"Is Bethany like you?" Miles said. "Does she have weird hair and follow people around and scare them just for fun?"

"No," the dead girl said through her hair. "Not for fun. But what's wrong with having a little fun? It gets dull. And why should we stop having fun, just because we're dead? It's not all demon cocktails and Scrabble down in the old bardo, you know?"

"You know what's weird?" Miles said. "You sound like her. Bethany. You say the same kind of stuff."

"It was dumb to try to get your poems back," said the dead girl. "You can't just give something to somebody and then take it back again."

"I just miss her," Miles said. He began to cry.

After a while, the dead girl got up and came over to him. She took a big handful of her hair and wiped his face with it. It was soft and absorbent and it made Miles's skin crawl. He stopped crying, which might have been what the dead girl was hoping.

"Go home," she said.

Miles shook his head. "No," he finally managed to say. He was shivering like crazy.

"Why not?" the dead girl said.

"Because I'll go home and you'll be there, waiting for me."

"I won't," the dead girl said. "I promise."

"Really?" Miles said.

"I really promise," said the dead girl. "I'm sorry I teased you, Miles."

"That's okay," Miles said. He got up and then he just stood there, looking down at her. He seemed to be about to ask her something, and then he changed his mind. She could see this happen, and she could see why, too. He knew he ought to leave now, while she was willing to let him go. He didn't want to fuck up by asking something impossible and obvious and stupid. That was okay by her. She couldn't be sure that he wouldn't say something that would rile up her hair. Not to mention the tattoo. She didn't think he'd noticed when her tattoo had started getting annoyed.

"Good-bye," Miles said at last. It almost looked as if he wanted her to shake his hand, but when she sent out a length of her hair, he turned and ran. It was a little disappointing. And the dead girl couldn't help but notice that he'd left his shoes and his bike behind.

The dead girl walked around the cabin, picking things up and putting them down again. She kicked the Monopoly box, which was a game that she'd always hated. That was one of the okay things about being dead, that nobody ever wanted to play Monopoly.

At last she came to the statue of St. Francis, whose head had been knocked right off during an indoor game of croquet a long time ago. Bethany Baldwin had made St. Francis a lumpy substitute Ganesh head out of modeling clay. You could lift that clay elephant head off, and there was a hollow space where Miles and Bethany had left secret things for each other. The dead girl reached down her shirt and into the cavity where her more interesting and useful organs had once been (she had been an organ donor). She'd put Miles's poetry in there for safekeeping.

She folded up the poetry, wedged it inside St. Francis, and fixed the Ganesh head back on. Maybe Miles would find it someday. She would have liked to see the look on his face.

We don't often get a chance to see our dead. Still less often do we know them when we see them. Mrs. Baldwin's eyes opened. She looked up and saw the dead girl and smiled. She said, "Bethany."

Bethany sat down on her mother's bed. She took her mother's hand. If Mrs. Baldwin thought Bethany's hand was cold, she didn't say so. She held on tightly. "I was dreaming about you," she told Bethany. "You were in an Andrew Lloyd Webber musical."

"It was just a dream," Bethany said.

Mrs. Baldwin reached up and touched a piece of Bethany's hair with her other hand. "You've changed your hair," she said. "I like it."

They were both silent. Bethany's hair stayed very still. Perhaps it felt flattered.

"Thank you for coming back," Mrs. Baldwin said at last.

"I can't stay," Bethany said.

Mrs. Baldwin held her daughter's hand tighter. "I'll go with you. That's why you've come, isn't it? Because I'm dead too?"

Bethany shook her head. "No. Sorry. You're not dead. It's Miles's fault. He dug me up."

"He did what?" Mrs. Baldwin said. She forgot the small, lowering unhappiness of discovering that she was not dead after all.

"He wanted his poetry back," Bethany said. "The poems he gave me."

"That idiot," Mrs. Baldwin said. It was exactly the sort of thing she expected of Miles, but only with the advantage of hindsight, because how could you really expect such a thing. "What did you do to him?"

"I played a good joke on him," Bethany said. She'd never really tried to explain her relationship with Miles to her mother. It seemed especially pointless now. She wriggled her fingers, and her mother instantly let go of Bethany's hand.

Being a former Buddhist, Mrs. Baldwin had always understood that when you hold onto your children too tightly, you end up pushing them away instead. Except that after Bethany had died, she wished she'd held on a little tighter. She drank up Bethany with her eyes. She noted the tattoo on Bethany's arm with both disapproval and delight. Disapproval, because one day Bethany might regret getting

a tattoo of a cobra that wrapped all the way around her bicep. Delight, because something about the tattoo suggested Bethany was really here. That this wasn't just a dream. Andrew Lloyd Webber musicals were one thing. But she would never have dreamed that her daughter was alive again and tattooed and wearing long, writhing, midnight tails of hair.

"I have to go," Bethany said. She had turned her head a little, towards the window, as if she were listening for something far away.

"Oh," her mother said, trying to sound as if she didn't mind. She didn't want to ask: Will you come back? She was a lapsed Buddhist, but not so very lapsed, after all. She was still working to relinquish all desire, all hope, all self. When a person like Mrs. Baldwin suddenly finds that her life has been dismantled by a great catastrophe, she may then hold on to her belief as if to a life raft, even if the belief is this: that one should hold on to nothing. Mrs. Baldwin had taken her Buddhism very seriously, once, before substitute teaching had knocked it out of her.

Bethany stood up. "I'm sorry I wrecked the car," she said, although this wasn't completely true. If she'd still been alive, she would have been sorry. But she was dead. She didn't know how to be sorry anymore. And the longer she stayed, the more likely it seemed that her hair would do something truly terrible. Her hair was not good Buddhist hair. It did not love the living world or the things in the living world, and it *did not love them* in an utterly unenlightened way. There was nothing of light or enlightenment about Bethany's hair. It knew nothing of hope, but it had desires and ambitions. It's best not to speak of those ambitions. As for the tattoo, it wanted to be left alone. And to be allowed to eat people, just every once in a while.

When Bethany stood up, Mrs. Baldwin said suddenly, "I've been thinking I might give up substitute teaching."

Bethany waited.

"I might go to Japan to teach English," Mrs. Baldwin said. "Sell the house, just pack up and go. Is that okay with you? Do you mind?"

Bethany didn't mind. She bent over and kissed her mother on her forehead. She left a smear of cherry ChapStick. When she had gone, Mrs. Baldwin got up and put on her bathrobe, the one with white cranes and frogs. She went downstairs and made coffee and sat at the kitchen table for a long time, staring at nothing. Her coffee got cold and she never even noticed.

The dead girl left town as the sun was coming up. I won't tell you where she went. Maybe she joined the circus and took part in daring trapeze acts that put her hair to good use, kept it from getting bored and plotting the destruction of all that is good and pure and lovely. Maybe she shaved her head and went on a pilgrimage to some remote lamasery and came back as a superhero with a dark past and some kick-ass martial-arts moves. Maybe she sent her mother postcards from time to time. Maybe she wrote them as part of her circus act, using the tips of her hair, dipping them into an inkwell. These postcards, not to mention her calligraphic scrolls, are highly sought after by collectors nowadays. I have two.

Miles stopped writing poetry for several years. He never went back to get his bike. He stayed away from graveyards and also from girls with long hair. The last I heard, he had a job writing topical haikus for the Weather Channel. One of his best-known haikus is the one about tropical storm Suzy. It goes something like this:

> A young girl passes
> in a hurry. Hair uncombed.
> Full of black devils.

THE HUMAN RACE

By Scott Edelman

Scott Edelman is a five-time Bram Stoker Award finalist whose fiction has appeared in a variety of anthologies and magazines, such as *The Dead That Walk*, *The Best of All Flesh*, *Crossroads*, and *Postscripts*. When not writing, Edelman co-edits *SCI FI Wire* and in the past edited the fiction magazine *Science Fiction Age*.

In the intro to Edelman's story in the first *The Living Dead* anthology, I said that he was something of a zombie genius, but it bears repeating. In the intervening period, the smart folks at PS Publishing reached the same conclusion and gathered together all of his zombie fiction into one volume called *What Will Come After*.

Though we all live on the same planet, in a sense we each inhabit a separate reality. After all, my reality consists, to a substantial degree, of the specific building I live in, the specific location I work at, the specific stores I shop at, and the places I hang out. Yet out of the six-billion-plus people alive right now, virtually all of them have never (or barely) set foot in any of those places, let alone all of them, and by the same token I will scarcely set foot in any of the places or meet any of the people that make up, as far as they're concerned, the world. And while other people's parents are just strangers or possibly acquaintances to us, our own parents occupy a massively defining place in our own personal reality. So when a parent dies, it can seem like the end of the world.

Author Scott Westerfeld recently took his personal experience with the loss of a parent and used it as inspiration to write his novel *Leviathan*, about a fantastical alternate history of World War I, in which a parent's death—in this case, the Archduke Franz Ferdinand—actually does cause the world to come apart at the seams. Our next story is another in which the death of a parent coincides with the end of the world itself.

A zombie apocalypse seems to promise, in some sense, the end of death. For some people, that prospect might be very complicated and challenging indeed.

Paula Gaines felt herself quite ready to die.

Or perhaps it was instead that ever since the phone call that brought her to this distant place to look into her father's dead eyes and have to tell a stranger, "Yes … that's him," she was no longer ready to live.

As she sat in the bathtub, stroking her forearm with the flat of a knife she had lifted from the hostel's communal dining area, that fine a distinction no longer mattered to her. Whether she was racing toward her death, or racing away from her life, all that mattered now was the speed with which that race could be consummated.

The reflection of her face in the still water, water turned lukewarm so long had she been sitting in it, was unfamiliar to her. Her years on this earth had been full of unfortunate life lessons, and thanks to this added insult from the universe, there seemed little point in going on. Before the call that startled her in the middle of another sleepless night, before her sudden trip to London, she saw herself as a person able to at least keep up a pretense of happiness, even though happiness itself was beyond her. But this day, she no longer had the energy for false smiles, and her expression was far grimmer than she had ever known it.

Grimmer, and almost lifeless already.

As she switched the knife from her right hand to her left, her slight movement gently rippled the water, and as her reflection distorted, she could almost see her sister's face. And when the ripples were at their greatest, even her mother's. She slapped the water angrily, so that the faces went away. She just couldn't bear it. Her mother's face, her sister's face... they were both gone. The explosion that had taken the two of them had been so great that there had been no faces remaining after death, no body parts that the officials at the morgue felt it necessary for her to identify.

While the terrorist attack had left her father's body bloodied but intact, if she was ever going to see the rest of her family again, it would have to be after death.

After *her* death.

She turned the blade so that the edge pressed against her wrist. At the instant that she was about to cut deeply lengthwise—as she had learned was necessary for a successful suicide one time when she'd investigated it on the Web—there was a rap at the bathroom door. She startled, and as her hand jerked, the blade sliced shallowly into her flesh. A few drops of blood ran down her arm into the water.

"Who's there?" she asked, with a voice that sounded surprised it had the chance to speak again.

"You're not the only one who needs to use the bath, you know," called out a woman.

"Just a moment," Paula said.

She looked into the water as her red blood dissipated into pink and then was gone, almost as if the thoughts of suicide were a dream. But they weren't, and never would be again. She tried to identify exactly whose voice had called out to her, to remember which of the women with whom she had shared a bustling breakfast it could have possibly been—Lillian, who squeezed her hand briefly after passing the marmalade, Jennifer, who found it hard to meet her eyes, or perhaps one of the others—and though she could not put a face to the voice, she remembered them all as friendly, and sympathetic once they realized the purpose of her journey. And so she thought...no, not here. Don't do it here. Paula didn't want to make friends, however new, clean up the mess she'd leave behind. Whatever she was going to do, it had to be done in front of people whom she had never looked in the eye, who would not then be forced to mourn their own failures to save her. The women she'd just met here, even though just passing acquaintances, deserved better. Her mother had raised her that way.

Her mother…

Paula slipped slowly into the water until her head submerged beneath its surface and her knees popped up to cool in the chill air of the room. She held her breath, embracing the silence, and wished that she could just keep holding that breath until all breath was gone, taking with it this room, this city, *everything*. She held the air in her lungs for as long as she could, but then the air exploded from between her lips and she sat up quickly, shivering in a strange room in a strange country.

She dressed quickly and rushed back to her cramped room, which was all that she could afford, and only barely afford at that. She grabbed her backpack, stuffed it with her possessions, told no one she was checking out—almost laughing, but not quite, at the double meaning of that phrase—and fled the hostel.

If she was going to die that day, she was going to do it in front of strangers.

Paula gulped down a mouthful of coffee the moment the waitress brought it over, burning her tongue, which reminded her yet again that life meant pain. At least for her it did. She blew on what liquid remained in the cup, cursing her impatience. She had no idea how others managed to maintain pleasant lives, but hers was one filled with impatience, and blossoming with pain.

She had hoped that the despair which had settled over her, initially back home and now deepening here, would do her a favor for once and demonstrate its own patience, so that she could stave off her suicide long enough to return to die in her home country. But her latest worries made that unlikely. The intricacies of getting her family's remains released, negotiating with a local funeral home for proper caskets, dealing with the airlines to transport the bodies (or what remained of them)…it was all too much for her, and those details buzzed in her head, blotting out both sleep and reason. She found it hard to contemplate the enormity of suddenly being the responsible one in the family. No one could have ever mistaken her for the one in that role before, and now…

Identifying her father's body had been difficult enough. She just didn't have the energy to do all of the other things that remained.

And she didn't have the energy to remain alive either.

She had walked all morning through the streets of a country she had never before thought to visit, stumbled on until her aching feet insisted that she drop into a chair at a corner cafe. She'd sat in the sunshine for hours, unable to summon up the energy to move, shamed by the determination of the passersby rushing on with their lives. Picking at the remains of her plate of squidgy lemon pudding, an odd dessert with an odd name, she wondered why her father had always wanted to visit this odd country.

He had always talked about it, studying maps, poring over guidebooks, and had finally done it, and look what good chasing his dreams had done him. She never understood his dreams anyway. That had always been part of their problem, she figured; she should have been able to understand him better. But then, he never seemed to spend much energy understanding her, either. Still, he *had* reached out to both Paula and her sister Jane, neither of whom had ever married, offering to pay their ways to London to experience it with him. Perhaps she should have taken her father up on it as her sister had. If she'd done so, she would have been on that bus with the three of them, and all of her worrying and despair would now be over.

Instead, she had to sit in an unfamiliar place and contemplate how and when she would...do it. If she'd been home, she would have known exactly what to do. She had been thinking about it long enough, planning for its inevitability. It would have been easy. There was that lake, and the sunset that came with it, and those pills that since Mark had left she had been spending far too many long nights studying, even *before* every living relative of hers had been erased. She cursed her decision to remain home instead of taking her dad up on his invitation. The matter could have been taken out of her hands. She could have died with them, without thought, instead of just sitting there *thinking* about dying.

Now, sitting at the cafe, eating her pastry, drinking her coffee, pondering both her loneliness and the short time she had left in which to be lonely...she had to find another way.

Maybe she could climb up Big Ben, which her father had always talked of visiting. She could climb it and instead of admiring the intricacy of the clockwork and the view, just...jump off, giving herself over to the breeze. She wouldn't have minded that feeling of flight to be real for once, but somehow, it didn't seem right to mingle her father's goal with her own shortcomings. And besides... she knew nothing of Big Ben. She had no idea whether that tourist magnet even contained an accessible window or ledge from which she *could* jump.

Or perhaps she should fill her pockets with rocks, and swim out into the Thames until she could swim no more. A famous writer had done just that. She had even seen a movie about it. She liked the idea of floating off until consciousness faded, but the preparations—finding a river secluded enough so that no one would try to save her, finding a grouping of stones sufficient to her task—it seemed like too much work for her, regardless of how romantic it might sound. She needed a way that was almost effortless. If it could be instantaneous as well, so much the better.

As the traffic blared around her, she took another bite of her pastry and looked at the cars and trucks rushing by, and to the roadway, where she could see painted in large white letters a warning to walkers to look to their right. So many tourists visited London each year that there needed to be constant reminders that the world was not the same all over.

Reading the warning, she realized that she had finally found her answer. She could step blindly into traffic. No one would even have to know that she had done it deliberately. Americans were known for stepping off the curb while looking in the wrong direction. If anyone bothered to research her reasons for coming to London in the first place, they would simply assume that she had been distracted by grief. Unlike the case with the women back at the hostel, no one would have to feel personal responsibility, carrying the weight that it was something she could have been talked out of. There would be no guilt. They would just think it was the unfortunate, accidental passing of another sad American.

In fact, Paula could see one of those quaint double-decker busses approaching right then.

She pushed back from her table and walked away from the cafe. Her waitress stepped toward her from amid the outdoor cluster of tables, calling after her that she had forgotten to pay, which only caused her to walk more quickly. As the bright red bus neared, Paula looked the other way, feigning confusion just in case there was a witness, and began to put her right foot forward to step into the street.

Before she could set it down in the path of the bus, she heard a man scream. She hesitated, hanging there between life and death. When Paula turned, she saw that man pointing, not at her, but past her into the street. The bus went by, her opportunity gone. By then, additional people were pointing, and she followed their outstretched arms to what was revealed after the bus had moved on.

It was a dead man walking.

With his shredded clothes, bloodied body, and gray pallor, another might have thought him merely a man in make-up, costumed for a party or on his way to a movie set, but unfortunately, Paula knew what death looked like. As the creature grew nearer, she could see into its eyes. They were like those of her father; there was no there there.

Unlike her father, however, this corpse *walked*.

It shambled amidst the traffic in her direction, the cars honking for him to move and then swerving when he did not. A few drivers slowed to a crawl so they could look more closely at the impossibility. One man got out of his car and ran over to the thing, placing his hand on its shoulder. Paula could see from the driver's face, no more than ten yards away, that this was only a gesture of concern; perhaps he'd thought the bloodied walker an escapee from a hospital. As a reward for the man's good Samaritanship, the shambler slapped out with a bloodied fist and knocked him dead.

Pedestrians screamed and scattered around her, but Paula simply stood there. She wondered if she was frozen in shock, but no, she was only waiting, though she wasn't sure for what. She watched as the walking corpse punched a second man to the pavement, then lunged to bring down a third, biting deeply into a woman's neck with crooked teeth.

Then the thing saw her.

With everyone else fleeing, she was the only still target in a sea of flesh. Its lips parted, and she could hear a low, dull growl. She looked away from its bloody lips into its eyes, and thought she now saw an empty hunger there, one that was not unfamiliar to her. She began to ask what force had animated him, what had brought him back to the land of the living, but before she could utter her question, a shot rang out. A police officer had fired on the thing from behind the shelter of a car, hitting the creature in its back. It staggered slightly under the affront, but did not close its dull eyes.

"Wait," she said, holding out one hand toward the officer and the other armed men who joined him. "You can't do this. Not yet."

She took a step forward, the step toward death that she'd been interrupted from taking mere moments before, and further shots rang out. The thing's head exploded, splashing brain matter across her. It crumpled, its knees slamming into the pavement first. Then it sank forward, what remained of its head hitting the roadway at her feet, blood splattering her shoes. Only then did she sag, sitting down hard on the curb. A policeman dashed over, skirting the broken body at their feet.

"Miss?" he asked her. "Are you all right, Miss?"

She didn't know how to even begin to answer. She looked up into the policeman's face and for a moment was unable to tell whether he was alive or dead, or even remember whether she herself was alive or dead. Someone thrust a cup of water into her hands and draped a blanket over her shoulders. Someone else attempted to wipe the blood from her face.

As she sat there limp, hearing the sound of sirens and smelling the scent of death, voices reached her through her fog of shock. The police were saying that this tableaux hadn't just happened on this one street. It was playing itself out all over London. All over the world.

The dead were coming back to life.

And they didn't seem to like us.

She let herself be helped back to her feet, and then she let herself be tugged along, as she had allowed for most of her life, but when she realized that the destination she was being shepherded to was the back of an ambulance, she broke free from those who thought they were helping her. She ran as swiftly as she could, ran away, into the cafe, out a back entrance, and down an alleyway. This was no time to live meekly, to be swept along by the tide.

If the dead were coming back to life, her place wasn't in a hospital, with the living and those who hoped to rejoin the living. It was in the morgue, with the dead.

Her dead.

Paula stared down the barrel of a gun held in the shaking hands of a guard standing in the doorway to the London morgue, and was surprised to realize that all she felt was a calm disinterest.

She felt no alarm. She only thought...how ironic.

Hours before, she would have acted as provocatively as possible in the hopes of setting off the trigger finger of the jittery young man in a uniform at least one size too large for him. She would have made a lunge in his direction, walked with the staggered gait of the living corpses she had seen wandering the streets of London as she'd zigzagged her way to the building in which she'd identified her father's body...anything to provoke that bullet. But now everything had changed, for suddenly she had hope, and so she put her hands out slowly beside her, palms up, and then chose her words carefully.

"I'm not dead," she said, hoping that her calm words would distract from the bits of brain matter that had spotted the front of her blouse when that first corpse had been shot, and from the blood stain that remained on her face, impervious to washing. The guard lowered his gun slightly, but it did not appear to Paula that he had loosened his grip.

"Why did you come here?" he asked. One of his shirt sleeves was missing, and the other was dripping with blood. "This is the last place you should want to be."

"My father's here. Do you remember me? I remember you. You were standing by the elevators when I came in, I think. He died last week and I had to come here yesterday to identify him. What happened to your arm?"

He shook his head, unready to talk about it. He looked like the sort of person who might never be ready to talk about it, holding things in for a lifetime, as she had.

"I'm lucky to be alive," he said. "You should leave."

"I need to be here," she said, taking a careful step forward. "I need to see him. Please."

"No one needs to be here," he said, standing aside and letting her pass through the door to stand beside him in the entrance hall. "And I've been here long enough. They've been coming to life all day. I hope never to see this place again."

Then he was where she had been, outside looking in.

"You're not going to find what you're looking for," he said. "But you're welcome to try. The place is all yours."

He tossed her the keys.

"Just remember—some doors you're not going to want to unlock."

And then he was gone, leaving her alone in a lobby that looked even less welcoming than it had been the day before. The floor was slick with blood and littered with body parts. As she picked her way through the building, that no longer fazed her, because that's what the city had looked like as she'd made her way here. Only luck had let her get this far. She retraced her steps to the room in which she had been asked to identify her father…but it was empty. She feared that she was too late, that her father, animated by the plague that had infected the planet, had already gotten up and staggered away. It could have been his blood on the guard's sleeves. It could have been his body parts on the floor, shredded as the guard had defended himself. But as she looked around the bland room, she realized that no single body ever stayed there for long. This was just a place where people like her came face to face with death. The bodies were shuttled here from somewhere else.

Paula returned to the hallway to find that somewhere else. The floor had become so slippery that she had to steady herself against a wall to stand upright. She'd watched enough television to know what she was looking for, but it wasn't her eyes that first found her goal, that by-now clichéd room with columns and rows of refrigerated cubicles.

It was her ears. She heard her destination before she saw it.

With her hand on the doorknob and the sounds of violence raging inside, she was afraid for the first time that day. The thought that her father was inside, and that she might be stopped from reaching him, stirred up that fear. But she was more afraid of what she would learn about her father than of what would happen to her, and so forced herself into the room.

She had to lean against the door to open it, and only when she had it fully open did she see that her way had been blocked by body parts. A coroner, his internal organs chewed, was split into four pieces. She closed her eyes, took a deep breath, and stepped into the room, which still echoed with noise. Nothing moved to stop her, so she moved slowly to the center of the large room lined with small doors with handles.

She could hear muffled howling, and the dull thuds of bare feet beating against metal doors. People were trapped inside many of the refrigerated cubicles, struggling to get out.

No, not people, she reminded herself. What *used* to be people.

And behind one of those doors was her father.

She moved respectfully through the room, pausing before each column of doors. She noticed that some of the compartments emitted no sound, presumably because they contained no body. She walked by someone's mother, someone's father, someone's child, and wondered if others like her were coming to try to collect them. Slots in the doors held cards on which names had been scrawled. She had almost circled the room and returned to where she'd started before she stopped, at last, in front of a door which bore a name she shared.

She placed her hand on the cool metal handle. There was silence within, a silence that sickened her. For it could mean that he was already gone. She rested her head against the door, and was surprised to find herself praying, something she had not done since she was a small child.

She pulled the handle. Once the door opened, she tugged at the tray inside and slid it out from its compartment. It rolled out so effortlessly that she was surprised to see that her father's body was still there, unchanged since the day before.

"Oh, Daddy," she moaned.

He appeared the same as he had been when she had come to identify him. Though they had washed the blood from him as best as they could, the evidence of death was unmistakable. Whatever had brought the other dead back to this new sort of life had not yet touched him. No force had come to animate him again, to wake him so that he could say the things as yet unsaid, so that she could retract the things said that shouldn't have been said.

She dragged a chair over beside his pallet so that she could watch him, and then she sat down to await his transformation.

She jerked awake, startled to realize that she had been asleep. All she remembered was studying her father's face, just as she was doing now. There was no change. Her father still slept.

"He won't be coming back, you know."

She leapt up at the sound of the voice, tumbling her chair on its side. The guard who had earlier abandoned her knelt to pick it up.

"I'm sorry that I frightened you," he said. "But I couldn't leave you alone to face this."

Paula backed away, keeping the righted chair between them. She had not known men to act kindly to her in the past, and she doubted that it was about to start under these circumstances.

"What did you mean when you said that he wasn't coming back?" she asked warily.

"Only that it's too late for him. I've been listening to the news, what news is still broadcasting. All the others, the ones we've seen, the ones we've had to fight…they died today, and yesterday. But your father…he died last week. No one knows why, or what happened, but it's only the newly dead who return."

She sank into the chair and began to cry.

"He wouldn't have been the same anyway, Miss," he said, trying to comfort her. "He wouldn't have recognized you."

The guard didn't understand. That wasn't why she was crying this time, not because her father couldn't join her in life. She was in tears now because it was too late for her to join him in death. She was even worse off than she'd been before. Suicide had been rendered useless. There could be no end to life now. If she were to kill herself, she would just come back for another chapter. And she wanted no further chapters. She wanted her book of life to be closed.

She wanted to die, but the time for death was past. She no longer had a goal. All purpose had been stolen from her.

She dried her tears, but did not get up. She simply sat there, continuing to stare at her father.

"You should go home, Miss. If you can."

"But what about my father? What about him?"

"There is no him anymore."

"I was supposed to bring him home."

"I don't know that there's any home anymore either. From what I hear, the States are just as bad. And at a time like this, I doubt they would let you return with a dead body. I'm sorry. But it's best to just say goodbye."

The former guard backed away from her, giving her space she did not need, inviting her with his body language to leave with him.

But he didn't get it. She was dead inside. She may have looked alive, but inside, she was just like her father.

She belonged here.

By day, she wandered the wounded city, sure that her wounds were even greater, studying those who still dared to walk the streets in an attempt to get on with their lives in the midst of chaos, and being studied in return. At night, she slept by her father's side, surprised that she even *could* sleep, for the noise in that room, the moaning, the pounding of creatures that could not escape, was unceasing.

As she moved through the city, it was as if she were leading a charmed life, though she was not sure that what she still had was life. She would come upon scenes of great carnage, small battles between the living and the dead, and walk through them unscathed. It was as if the undead took her for one of their own, so dead was she inside. The fugue state in which she existed had seemed to make her invulnerable, though she didn't entirely think of herself as so, because she no longer had the level of consciousness to be self-aware. She existed without conscious choice. She just continued her walking through the city, eating when hungry, returning to sleep when tired.

Around her, some people seemed to be going about their business, but many had abandoned their routines, fleeing the city in search of sanctuary in the countryside. London had become depopulated. It was as if a great city had become a small village in a matter of days. There was no longer a problem getting a seat on the tube, though people now looked at each other with suspicion for new reasons that were just as deadly as the old.

One day after walking, she aimlessly rode the tube for hours, letting it take her where it would. It seemed as useful as anything else she could have been doing. She no longer had anywhere to go. She no longer had anywhere to be. And besides, this is how she felt closest to her family. Riding the public transportation of the city, she felt closer to her father than when she slept next to him at night, propped up in a chair waiting for a metamorphosis she now doubted would ever come. This was the sort of place in which he'd died, after all. This was the sort of place in which her entire family had died, taking her along with them.

She watched others come and go. Most were afraid, eying each other passenger and wondering whether this one or that one was a reanimated corpse. She knew no fear, for she no longer cared. No force, living or dead, had any answers for her.

But at the next station, she felt fear again, as the doors opened to reveal another who was also fearless, though for different reasons.

The man who entered the car wore a hooded sweatshirt, even though the weather had been warm that day, and on his back he carried an olive backpack. Paula tried to read his expression, but there was no expression there to read, and that told her everything she needed to know.

"Don't do it!" she shouted, no longer desiring what came after.

Then came the explosion, brighter than the sun, and then the darkness, as black as death.

Paula heard no screaming as she came to, and she thought at first that the explosion had deafened her by shattering her eardrums. But as she lifted her head, she could see that the reason there was no screaming was because she was the only one on the train left alive. She was on her back, and as she moved her hands about her to rise, her fingers swept against glass that had been blown from the windows.

She sat up in the unmoving train, and through the smoke could see the bodies of the few other occupants of the car that had been brave enough to ride the tube. She had been furthest from the bomber and had only been knocked out, but the half-dozen others had been lifted and thrown against the walls of the train.

She felt an odd sense of cognitive dissonance; it was as if she was visiting the past. This is what her father's last home had looked like, filled with smoke and dust and blood. But somehow she had escaped her family's fate. She leaned against the buckled walls as she moved along the car. She walked gingerly past the dead, the blood streaming from their ears, and threw herself against the door, which would not budge. She looked nervously at the dead, knowing what would happen next.

She had to get out.

Then she saw him, the cause of all this. Or what was left of him. A head, its hair matted with blood, was on the floor, facing away from her. The body that had supported it was nowhere to be seen. She approached the head slowly, circling it and then pushing at it with her toes so she could stare into its face. Yes, it was him. He had thought that he would be in heaven soon, but there was no heaven waiting for him in this new world.

She removed her jacket and kicked the head into the center of the cloth, hands shaking. She tied the corners together so that she could carry her burden along without having to touch it. She had to hurry, for not only would the others soon come back to life, filled with hunger, but she could hear the sounds of rescuers approaching as well, and both living and dead would only be obstacles to her now. She tucked the package under one arm, crawled through a shattered window, and ran down the tracks as quickly as she could in the opposite direction of the voices.

Back at the morgue, Paula unwrapped her parcel and put the head upright on a plate, balanced on its ragged neck. She knew that she might need to move it again, but she never wanted to have to touch it. She placed it on one of the operating tables, turning it carefully away from her, away from her father, so that all she could see was the back of its head. But then she turned it back again, so that she could watch it as she sat by her father. She needed to see the transformation when it came.

The sounds in the room had lessened since the dead first began to wake, but only by degree. The dead feet that had been pounding ceaselessly on the metal doors for hours had splintered, and the throats that roared their anger were wearing away. She imagined that if she could survive here long enough that she would see their bodies break down entirely, just like the systems that kept civilization humming seemed about to do. She wasn't sure that she could get home again even if she wanted to. And she wasn't sure that she wanted to.

She stared at what remained of a man who was willing to die for an ideology. Or, as it turned out, someone who was willing to do something even worse than that, not to die, but to choose a living, mindless death. He and others like him had hoped to bring down the workings of the modern world, but they did no such thing. The zombie plague did what they could not. Yet they still continued, not realizing that their bombs were pointless.

Night fell and morning came again, and there was no change, but then as night fell for the second day, the closed eyes of the terrorist's head snapped open. In that instant, the sounds from within the refrigerated compartments stopped, as if the dead who were locked away sensed a brother outside who might help them. But no help would be forthcoming, for all the manless head could do was rage.

She looked at her father. He had not responded to the resurrection. She guessed she didn't really expect him to. That wasn't what this was about, answers. She dragged her chair forward to sit facing her attacker, who could do nothing but look at her with mindless anger.

"Who *are* you?" she asked. "How can you keep on *doing* something like this, knowing what you had to have known?"

It growled at her, grinding its teeth loudly.

"Killing yourself so that you can go to heaven is barbaric enough. But once you knew that all you'd be getting is *this*, how could you go ahead and do it anyway? The world changed, and you paid it no attention. To choose zombiehood? To make others into zombies? You're dead forever now. I'm not sure that you were ever really alive to begin with."

The head howled, pinning her with unblinking eyes.

"Tell me," she said. "Tell me why you did this."

She stood up, and took a step closer. As she did, the thing's nostrils flared. It snapped its teeth, trying to reach her, but the gap between them was infinite.

"You're not taking a bite out of me. You won't ever be taking a bite out of anyone. Your death is as over as your life. There's nothing left for you. So you might as well tell me."

It rocked back and forth on its severed neck, but could gain no momentum.

"Tell me!" she shouted, and swatted at the head, which flew from the table and bounced several times on the floor, leaving several red splotches. The creatures behind the doors roared. She grabbed the head by its hair and lifted it up to eye level.

"I'll never know, will I?" she said. "Never."

Its answers remained the same as before. It was all senseless. She didn't know whether she could live with that. There seemed little reason to change her earlier plans. She lifted her other hand near to the thing's mouth. It snapped and snarled so ferociously that a tooth flew from between its lips and bounced off her chest. She could do it. She could do it quickly. One bite, and it would be over. She could no longer have death, but she could have something like it, and in a senseless universe, that would have to do.

But behind the head was her father, lying there quietly, speaking to her more eloquently than any member of the living dead ever could. She stepped closer to her father, holding the head out before her like a beacon.

"This is my father," she said, not really caring whether the creature even listened. "He didn't want much out of life. He just wanted to ride a double-decker bus someday, to see the Tower of London, to have a real beer in a real pub. He only wanted to see his daughters grow up to be happy..."

She grew silent. As she held the head by its hair, it rocked below her hand like a pendulum. She didn't know what else to say, but she said it anyway.

"I'm sorry, Dad. Maybe...maybe I can make it up to you."

She hadn't been able to make her father happy while he was alive. But now that he was dead…now that he was dead, maybe she had a chance.

She placed the head in one of the empty cabinets, where it once more began its howling.

"Welcome to your new home," she said. "I have to try to get back to mine."

Then she shut the door on the past and left the room of death forever.

WHO WE USED TO BE

By David Moody

David Moody's short fiction has appeared in the anthologies *The Undead* and *666: The Number of the Beast.* His zombie novel *Autumn* and its sequels were originally self-published and released for free online; the books have been downloaded more than a half-million times and are currently being rereleased in print by Thomas Dunne Books. A film based on *Autumn*, starring Dexter Fletcher and David Carradine, was released in the U.S. earlier this year. Moody's novel *Hater* is also currently being adapted for film, with Guillermo del Toro producing and *The Orphanage*'s J. A. Bayona directing. Moody's other novels include *Dog Blood* (the sequel to *Hater*), *Straight to You*, and *Trust.*

Prominent atheist Richard Dawkins was recently asked if, since he did not believe in any sort of afterlife, he was afraid of death. He replied that he was not afraid of death—after all, the universe had existed just fine without him for billions of years before he was born, so why should it trouble him to imagine that it would go on existing without him for billions of years after he's gone? Rather, he was afraid of *dying*, because current laws compel dying patients to endure a torturous gauntlet of pain and suffering rather than letting them decide for themselves when to let go.

"I think many people assume that if they really did find themselves facing-off against the living dead, they'd react like the people in the movies and books: they'd hunt out weapons and supplies and fight off wave after wave of the dead," Moody says. "I think the reality would be very different. Many people would just implode. Others would deny the impossible events unfolding around them and try to continue with their day-to-day as usual."

Our next story questions the logic of trying to survive for as long as possible when all you're doing is wasting precious time and effort prolonging the inevitable. "It's like keeping a dying patient alive by pumping them continually with drugs which make them feel worse," Moody says, "but sometimes you just have to accept that letting go might just be the kindest and most sensible option."

There was something beautifully ironic about the way mankind completely overlooked its own annihilation. Our society, for too long increasingly focused on the irrelevant, wasn't even looking in the right direction when more than six billion lives were abruptly ended. Had anyone survived, they'd no doubt have been able to come up with a thousand and one half-baked, incorrect explanations: a mutated virus, terrorism, scattered debris from a comet tail, a crashed satellite leaking radiation.... Truth was, even if by some chance they had stumbled on the right reason, it wouldn't have made any difference. And anyway, if anyone *had* been watching, then what happened next would have been even harder to comprehend than the sudden loss of billions of lives. Just minutes later, as if each person's individual death had been nothing more than an inconvenient blip as trivial and unimportant as a momentary power-cut in the middle of a reality TV program, every last one of the dead got back up again and tried to carry on.

Simon Parker had been in his home office when it happened, poring fanatically over business projections. What he'd originally envisaged as an hour's work had, as usual, wiped out his entire Saturday morning. But it didn't matter. The work needed to be done. Without the business they could kiss goodbye to this house, the cars, the holidays.... Janice and Nathan understood. He felt bad that he'd left his son on his own for so long, but he'd make it up to him when he got the chance. He knew Janice wasn't bothered. She'd just got back from shopping, arms laden with bags of clothes and other things they didn't need. Retail therapy kept her happy.

Simon mistook his death for a blackout. There were no choirs of angels or long tunnels leading towards brilliant white lights, no endless flights of heavenly steps to climb.... Instead, his death came as a sudden, crushing pressure followed by absolutely nothing. One minute he was staring at the screen searching for a particular line of figures, the next he was flat on his back, looking up at the ceiling, unable to focus his eyes. He immediately began to search for explanations. Had he suffered a heart attack? An electric shock from a faulty power outlet? A physical manifestation of the stress-related problems his doctor had repeatedly warned him about? He tried to shout for Janice but he couldn't speak.

His sudden paralysis was suffocating and terrifying but, to his immense relief, it was only temporary. With an unprecedented amount of mute effort and concentration, he finally managed to focus his eyes on the light fixture above him. Then he slowly turned his head a little. Then, with even more concentration and effort, he was able to screw his right hand into a fist and bend his arm at the elbow. He managed to draw his knees up to his chest and roll over onto his side. Then, having to will every individual muscle and sinew to move independently, he hauled himself up. No sooner had he stood upright when his center of balance shifted unexpectedly and he staggered across the room, stumbling like a new born animal taking its first unsteady steps in the wild. He tried to aim for the door but missed and hit the wall, face-first.

That didn't hurt, he thought to himself, panicking inside but unable to show it. Leaning back, he slid his hand under his shirt and pressed his palm against his chest. *Fingers must still be numb*, he decided. *Can't feel anything. Got to get help. Got to get to Janice.*

Leaning to one side until he over-balanced again, he rolled along the wall until he reached the open door and fell through. He staggered a few steps further, then landed on top of Janice who had collapsed halfway down the hallway. His son Nathan watched them both from where he lay on his back at the very top of the stairs, with his head lolling back and eyes unfocused.

Both immediately suspected as much, but common-sense prevented Simon and Janice from accepting they were dead for a considerable length of time.

They had gradually been able to move around with a little more freedom and control and, between the pair of them, had dragged Nathan down into the living room. When the TV didn't tell them anything and the phone calls they tried to make went unanswered, Simon went outside to look for help. What he saw out there confirmed their bizarre and improbable suspicions.

When he left the house, Simon had braced himself for the expected sudden drop in temperature outside. He was only wearing a thin T-shirt and jeans—putting on anything else in his current ungainly state would have been too much of an ordeal—and yet he hadn't felt a thing. He hadn't felt the rain he could see splashing in the puddles around his bare feet, or the wind which whipped through the tops of the trees he could see behind the houses at the end of the cul-de-sac.

He'd originally planned to try and get to Jack Thompson, a retired GP who lived several doors down, but he hadn't even reached the gate at the end of his own drive before he'd lost his nerve and turned around. His hearing was strangely muffled and unclear, but a sudden noise over to his far left had been loud enough to hear clearly. He turned towards the sound, struggling with knees which wouldn't bend, hips which wouldn't cooperate and feet which were heavy as lead, and saw that Dennis Pugh, the pompous, odious property developer who lived directly opposite, was trying to drive his car.

Obviously stricken by the same mysterious affliction as Simon as his family, Pugh's bloated, unresponsive right foot had become wedged down on the accelerator pedal while his left foot had slipped off the clutch. With inflexible arms he fought to control the car as it careened forward at speed, clipping the low stone wall at the end of his drive then swerving out across the road and missing Simon's gate by the narrowest of margins. Simon watched as Pugh ploughed down Kathleen Malins from number seventeen before smashing into the back of a builder's van. Pugh half-climbed, half-fell out of the wreck of his car and staggered back towards his house, crimson blood dribbling down his gray face from a deep gash across his forehead.

Simon barely even looked at him. Instead, he watched Kathleen—one of Janice's circle of friends—as she tried to get back home. She was crawling along the road, badly broken legs dragging uselessly behind.

Safely back inside his house, Simon leant against the door and tried to make sense of everything he'd just seen. He caught sight of his face in the long mirror on the wall and squinted hard to try and force his eyes to focus. He looked bad. His flesh was lifeless and pallid, his expression vacant and dull. His skin, he thought, looked tightly stretched over his bones like it belonged to someone else, as if he'd borrowed it from someone a size smaller.

Nathan sat in front of the TV while his parents had a long, difficult and surreal conversation in the kitchen about their sudden, unexpected deaths and their equally sudden and unexpected reanimation.

They had all stopped breathing but quickly discovered that by swallowing a lungful of air and forcing it back out again, they could just about speak. The Internet was still working—thank god—and they stood together over Simon's laptop, prodding the keyboard with cold, clumsy fingers. While most major news portals and corporate sites remained frozen and had not been updated, they were able to access enough personal blogs, micro-blogs and social networks to answer their most pressing questions: Yes, they were dead. Yes, it had happened to everyone, everywhere. No, there was nothing they could do about it.

The film that Nathan had been watching on TV ended and was replaced with nothing. Simon returned to the living room, his legs stiffening, to see why the sound had stopped. He picked up the remote and began flicking through the channels. Some continued with their automated, pre-programmed broadcasts as if nothing had happened. Other stations remained ominously blank. Some showed a screen of unchanging, unhelpful emergency information and one—a twenty-four-hour news channel—just showed an empty desk, the tousled hair of a collapsed news anchor visible in the foreground of the shot.

"Getting stiff," Janice said as she lurched into the room and fell down onto the sofa next to Nathan.

"*Rigor mortis*," Simon wheezed as he sat down heavily opposite them, barely able to believe what he was saying. "Won't last long. Read it online."

"Scared," Nathan said quietly, the first word he'd managed to say since he'd died.

"I know," Simon replied, trying to focus on his son's face.

"We'll all just sit here," Janice said, pausing mid-sentence to swallow more air, "and rest. I'll get us some dinner later."

Rigor mortis kept the family frozen in position for almost a whole day. For a time, they were barely able to speak, let alone move. In the all-consuming darkness of the long winter night, Simon stared into space, unblinking, and tried unsuccessfully to come to terms with what had happened.

His family was dead, and yet he felt surprisingly calm—perhaps because they were still together and they could still communicate. Maybe the loss would hit him later. He tried to imagine how any of this could be possible—how their brains could even continue to function. He wondered: Is this strange state of post-death consciousness just temporary? Would it last as long as their physical bodies held together? Or might it end at any moment?

He tried to distract himself with other thoughts but it was impossible. Everything had changed now that they were dead. Janice's earlier words rattled around his head: her instinctive offer of a dinner he knew she'd never cook. He realized they'd never eat or drink again. He'd never again get drunk. He'd never smell anything again, never sleep or dream, never make love.... For a while that really bothered him. It wasn't that he wanted sex—and even if he did, his sudden lack of circulation meant that the act was a physical impossibility now—what hurt was the fact that that aspect of his life had been abruptly ended with such dispassionate brutality.

Silent, unanswered questions about trivial practicalities and inconveniences soon gave way to other more important but equally unanswerable questions about what would happen next. What will happen to our bodies? How long will we last? For how long will we be able to move and talk, and see and hear each other?

As the long, indeterminable hours passed, still more questions plagued him. He thought about Janice's faith. (Although he believed her regular trips to church each Sunday were more about seeing people and being seen than anything else.) Was there a god? Or had the events of the last day been proof positive that all religions were based on superstition and bullshit? Was this heaven—if there was such a place—or its unthinkable opposite?

He suddenly remembered a line from a horror film he'd seen once and adapted it to fit his own bizarre circumstance. *When there's no more room in hell, the dead will walk their living rooms, hallways and kitchens.*

The next day, Janice had been the first to move. With a wheezing groan of effort she'd pushed herself up out of her seat next to Nathan—casting a disappointed glance at the large yellow stain she'd left on the cream-colored leather—then dragged herself upstairs on all fours. Simon went back to his office, leaving Nathan in front of the now lifeless TV. He needed to find answers to some of the many questions he'd asked himself last night.

Simon got lost on the still-functioning parts of the Internet. It took him a frustrating age to type and to move the mouse—he could barely hold it and click the buttons today—but he still managed to waste hours searching pointlessly as he'd regularly done before he'd died. He heard Janice crashing about in the kitchen, and her noise finally prompted him to move.

He checked in on Nathan as he passed the living room door. The boy looked bad. His legs and feet were swollen and bruised. His skin had an unnatural blue-green hue and one corner of his mouth hung open. A dribble of stringy, yellow-brown saliva trickled steadily down his chin, staining his favorite football shirt.

"Okay son?" Simon asked, having to remind himself how to talk again. Nathan slowly lifted his head and looked over in the general direction of his father.

"Bored."

"Just sit there for a bit," he said between breaths as he carried on down the hall. "Mum and I will work out what we're going to do."

Janice's appearance caught him by surprise. She'd changed her clothes and was wearing a dress she'd bought yesterday.

"Might as well get some wear out of it," she said.

"You look nice," he said automatically, even though she didn't. *Always compliment your wife*, he thought, *even in death*. Truth was, the way she looked made him feel uneasy. By squeezing herself into such a tight, once-flattering dress, she'd highlighted the extent to which her body had already changed. Her ankles were bruised and bloated like Nathan's (because the blood which was no longer being pumped around her body was pooling there—he'd learnt that online) and her belly was swollen (most probably with gas from countless chemical reactions—he'd learnt that online too). Her once-pert breasts hung heavy and unsupported like two small, sagging sacks of grain. She lurched into the light and, just for a second, Simon was thankful for the frozen, expressionless mask that death had given him and which hid his true reaction.

Janice looked grotesque. She'd covered her face in a thick layer of concealer which appeared even more unnatural than the jaundiced tinge of decay her skin had shown previously. She'd applied mascara (managing to coat her eyeballs more than her eyelashes), eyeshadow and lipstick with clumsy hands, leaving her looking more like a drunken clown than anything else. He didn't know what to say, so he said nothing.

"Just want to feel normal again," she said. "Just because I'm dead, doesn't mean I have to forget who I am."

For a moment the two of them stared at each other in silence, standing and swaying at opposite ends of the room.

"Been trying to find out what's going to happen," Simon told her.

"What do you mean?"

"What's going to happen to us. How bad things will get before..."

Janice moved unexpectedly. She didn't want to hear this. She headed for the dishwasher which she hadn't emptied since they'd died.

"Don't want to know..."

"Need to think about it. Got to be ready for it."

"I know," she wheezed. She squinted in frustration at the white china plate she held in her hand. It was dirty again now that she'd picked it up but she put it away in the cupboard anyway. "How long will we have before...?"

"Depends," he said, anticipating the end of her question. "Could be six months. Need to keep the house cool, stay dry..."

She nodded (although her head didn't move enough to notice), stopped unloading, and leant heavily against the nearest cupboard.

"We're lucky really," Simon said, pausing to take another deep breath of air. "Six months is a long time to have to say goodbye."

By mid-afternoon the street outside the house was an unexpected mass of clumsy, chaotic movement. More and more dead people had dragged themselves out into the open as the day had progressed. Simon thought he recognized some of them, although they were pale shadows of who they used to be.

What were they hoping to achieve out there? Surely they must have realized by now that the situation was beyond hope? *No one's going to help you*, he thought. You can't cure death or make it any easier—these people needed to get a grip and get back indoors. Some of them began to squabble and fight, unable to react to their impossible situation in any other way. Most, though, simply staggered around aimlessly.

Simon watched them all walking in the same clichéd, slothful way—shuffling and stumbling, legs inflexible, arms stiff and straight. That was one thing those horror film people got right, he decided. They were out by a mile with just about every other aspect of how they'd imagined the dead would reanimate, but they'd got the painfully slow and clumsy zombie walk spot-on.

Zombies, he thought to himself, smiling inwardly. *What am I thinking?* He cursed himself for using such a stupid word. He wasn't a zombie, and neither were Janice or Nathan.

Where *was* Nathan?

Janice was in the kitchen, still cleaning and fussing pointlessly, but he hadn't seen Nathan for a while. He tried shouting for him but he couldn't make his voice loud enough to be heard. The boy wasn't anywhere downstairs and Simon couldn't face the long climb up to check his room. He lurched into the kitchen.

"Where Nathan?"

Janice stopped brushing her lank, greasy hair and looked up.

"Thought you with him?"

Simon walked past his dead wife and headed for the utility room at the far end of the kitchen. Using the walls and washing machines for support, he hauled himself along the narrow passageway and looked up. The back door was wide open. The whole house would no doubt be freezing cold but, as they were no longer able to feel the temperature, humidity, air pressure, or anything else, neither of them had noticed. He squinted into the distance and thought he could see Nathan near the bottom of their long garden. There was definitely something moving around down there….

He went out to investigate, struggling to keep his balance through the long, wet grass. The shape slowly came into focus. It *was* Nathan, crawling around on his hands and knees.

"What the hell you doing?"

"Playing," Nathan answered, still trying to keep going forward, unaware he'd crawled headfirst into an overgrown bramble patch. "Lost ball."

"Inside," Simon ordered, leaning down and trying unsuccessfully to grab hold of his son's collar. Nathan reluctantly did as he was told. He reversed direction and shuffled back out, dragging spiteful, prickly bramble stems with him which refused to let go. He stood up, fell back down when one of his legs gave way, then got back up again.

"What you doing?" Simon demanded, managing to swallow just enough air to make his voice sound almost as angry as he felt.

"Fed up. Want to play…"

Simon grabbed Nathan's hand and dragged him back towards the house. He stopped and held the boy's discolored wrist up closer to his face. His paper-thin skin had been slashed to ribbons by branches and thorns. His ankles were in an even worse state. Flaps of flesh hung down over the sides of his feet like loose-fitting socks.

"Look what you done! Won't get better!"

Nathan snatched his hand away and trudged back towards the house, zigzagging awkwardly up the boggy lawn.

Simon's eyes weren't working as well as they had been earlier. It was getting dark, but when he looked outside it was still bright. The light was moving, flickering.

"Think it's… a fire," Janice gasped, inhaling mid-sentence. "House on fire."

He turned around to look at her. She was scrubbing at a dirty brown handprint on the wall, her barely coordinated efforts seeming only to increase the size of the grubby mark. He noticed that she'd changed her clothes again. Probably for the best; several large, bile-colored stains had appeared on the white dress since she'd started wearing it. Now she wore only a shapeless, baggy pullover. He noticed that lumpy brown liquid was dribbling down the insides of her bare legs and splashing on the carpet between her feet.

"What we going to do?"

Simon had been trying to think of an answer to that question all day, and he'd come to the conclusion that they only had one choice now—to barricade themselves in the house and try to maximize the time they had left together.

Earlier, when it had been lighter and he'd been able to see more clearly, he'd watched the chaos on the road outside with a mixture of fascination and unease. Their quiet cul-de-sac had become a seething cesspit of activity. There seemed to be a constant flood of people filling the street, marching incessantly towards nothing. (*Just like in the films*, he thought.) He remembered how he'd seen several of them trip and fall, only to be trampled down by countless others who were being forced forward *en masse* by the pressure of the swollen crowds behind. The street had become little more than a putrid, flesh-filled channel, ankle deep in places. But still they came, and still they fell. Stupid. Pointless. He was glad he'd had the foresight to have a gate installed across the drive. It made it easier to protect his family from the madness outside.

And what about Nathan? He'd caused irreparable damage to himself whilst on his own outside, and that had only been the beginning of his problems today. In punishment, Simon had sent him to his room, only for him to stumble back down an hour or so later, clutching his stomach. He'd fallen off his bed and had torn a deep gash in his side. Struggling to coordinate their clumsy and frustratingly slow movements, he and Janice had patched up their son as best they could. They packed his gaping wound with towels, then wrapped virtually an entire roll of gaffer tape around his misshapen gut to keep the wadding in place. He now sat on a stiff-backed chair in the corner of the room, under orders not to move.

"What we going to do?" Janice asked again. Simon had lost himself in his thoughts. That kept happening.

"Stay here," he eventually answered. "Open windows upstairs…make it cold. Block doors."

"Go out," Nathan grumbled from the corner, trying to pick a maggot out from a hole in his left leg just above his knee. The bones were sticking out of the ends of two of his fingers, making them as difficult to use as chopsticks.

"Not out," Simon snapped, conscious that their conversation was beginning to sound primitive and almost totally monosyllabic.

"Yes, out!" Nathan said again. "Bored here."

"Can't," Janice said, positioning her tottering, half-naked frame directly in front of what was left of her only child. "Listen to Dad."

"No point..."

"Go out and get hurt!" Simon yelled.

"Already dead!"

Nathan's bizarre but factually correct response completely floored his father. His response, like many parents who lose an argument with their child, was to ignore him.

"Not going out. End of talk."

The dark came again, then the light, then the dark. The family had barely moved in hours but, as dawn broke on the fourth day after death, Simon was forced to take action. When the bright sun was finally strong enough for him to be able to see out with his increasingly weak and useless eyes, he saw that the front of their house was surrounded.

He staggered towards the window and squinted out. The number of dead people crammed into their crowded cul-de-sac had continued to increase. During the night just ended, the size of the crowd must have reached critical mass. The gate had finally given way and their block-paved driveway was now filled to capacity with rotting flesh. There were hundreds of them out there, faces pressed against *his* windows and doors. Furious and frightened, he hobbled over to one side and pulled the curtains shut.

"What matter?" Janice croaked from where she lay slumped in a puddle of herself on the floor.

"Outside," was all he said as he limped past her and headed for the hall. Janice picked herself up and followed, her rapidly escaping, putrefying innards leaving a trail on the carpet behind her. Nathan watched his parents disappear into the gloom of the rest of the house.

In the hall, Simon looked at the front door. He could see them moving on the other side. Barely able to coordinate his movements, he purposefully collided with the coat stand by the mirror, knocking it sideways. It clattered down and, more through luck than judgment, became wedged across the full width of the door. Janice bent down and started to pick up the bags, coats, hats, and scarves which had fallen off and lay on the floor.

"Windows," Simon groaned, already moving towards the next room. Janice followed, desperately trying to keep him in focus as he stumbled into his office. She saw him grab at the venetian blind with bloated hands. His stiff, twisted fingers became caught in the metal slats and he fell, pulling the blind down and revealing another mass of cold, emotionless faces outside. Janice tried to help him up but she couldn't. When he crawled away from her she dropped to her knees and tried to pick up the blind.

"Out!" he mumbled, pulling himself back up, using the door frame for support. Janice, momentarily confused and disorientated, managed to work out where he was standing and shuffled towards his voice. Once she'd gone past him, Simon made a grab for the door handle, catching it with his fourth downwards swipe and managing to pull it shut.

They stood together in the hallway, leaning against each other, unsteady legs constantly threatening to buckle. Simon concentrated hard and forced himself to swallow air.

"Back door," he said. "Then safe. All blocked."

He pushed Janice away so that he could move again. She toppled back, then lurched forward, her face slapping against the wall like rotten fruit. Instinctively she took an unsteady step back and tried to wipe away the stain she'd left behind. She was still rubbing at it several minutes later when Simon limped back towards her.

"In," he wheezed, his voice barely audible now. Together they crashed back through the living room door. "Block it."

"Careful," she mumbled as he moved towards the bookcase adjacent to the door. "My things..."

She began trying to pick precious items and heirlooms off the shelves—a trophy, a crystal decanter, a framed photograph of the three of them—but Simon wasn't interested. Summoning all the effort he could muster, he pushed and pulled the bookcase until it came crashing down across the living room door, trapping them safely inside. Janice stood and looked at the mess. Simon collapsed. He aimed for the sofa but skidded in another rancid puddle and ended up on the floor. He was past caring.

They were safe. The house was secure.

After a while, he looked around the room. Something was wrong. He knew his eyes were failing, but he could still see enough to know that someone was missing.

"Where Nathan?"

Janice and Simon lasted another eighteen days together. They sat slumped on the floor at opposite ends of the living room for more than four hundred hours, longer than anyone else for several miles around, still recognizable when most others had been reduced to slurry.

It felt like forever; hour after hour, after silent, empty hour, they sat and remembered who they used to be and what they did and how they'd miss all that they'd lost. Had they been capable of feeling anything, the end would have finally come as a relief. More than a week after they'd died, first Simon and then Janice's brain activity dwindled and then stopped like batteries running flat.

Nathan only lasted a day after going outside. His dad had been right about one thing: by staying indoors, in cool, dry conditions, their rate of decay had been slowed dramatically. But Nathan hadn't wanted to sit there doing nothing. In his one long day, he played football (after a fashion), made friends with a frog, chased a cat, tried to climb a tree, and explored that part of the garden that Mum and Dad didn't like him exploring. And even when he couldn't move anymore, when everything but his brain and his eyes had stopped working, he lay on his back on the grass and looked up at the lights and the clouds and the birds and planned what he was going to do tomorrow.

THERAPEUTIC INTERVENTION

By Rory Harper

Rory Harper's short fiction has appeared in *Asimov's Science Fiction*, *Amazing Stories*, *Far Frontiers*, *Aboriginal Science Fiction*, *The Magazine of Fantasy & Science Fiction*, *Pulphouse*, and *The Year's Best Fantasy and Horror*. His first novel, *Petrogypsies*, was published in 1989 and was recently reissued by Dark Star Books.

Harper currently blogs at the zombie-themed site eatourbrains.com, where this story originally appeared. Also of interest to zombie lovers might be his two zombie songs, "Fast Zombie Blues" and "Nothing Else Better to Do," both of which are also available at eatourbrains.com.

Some of the major schools of psychotherapy are psychodynamic, psychoanalytic (e.g. Sigmund Freud), Adlerian, Cognitive-behavioral, Existential, and Rogerian or Person-Centered Therapy (PCT). In PCT, the therapist repeats key phrases that the client has said, which invites the client to elaborate and gradually reveal a wide swath of their thoughts and feelings. Author Blake Charlton, whose parents are both therapists, recently wrote a humorous piece about the first time he had a girl over for dinner, and how his parents would ask her things like, "Tell us about your relationship with your mother" and "So you're disappointed that your mother works so hard in the city?" which finally led Charlton to exclaim, "No Rogerian therapy at the dinner table!"

Our next story also deals with a counseling scenario, albeit one that's a bit more macabre. The author says, "Zombies are on my mind pretty often. I was also an addictions counselor for about seventeen years. A lot of my sessions bore some similarity to what takes place in this story—more so than you might think. There are a fair number of counselor in-jokes in this story, and one reader suggested that it be made into a short film for counselors in training, because of the way it illustrates proper responses to common issues, and illustrates how good counselors offer empathy and unconditional positive regard to their clients."

Even if your client is a zombie.

Transcript of counseling session with Michael R.—May 12, 2019

Good afternoon, Michael. I see you have a new bucket with you.

Hi, Mr. Harper. You like the Hello Kitty on the side?

Very much. [Pause.] So, what would you like to talk about today, Michael?

Nothing much happening. Same old, same old, you know.

How's your program going?

Um, work was pretty busy. I did a meeting on Thursday.

I think you told me last time that you might have found a new sponsor.

Yeah, he's a good guy. Been clean three years now. You gotta respect that.

Yes.

It's hard, you know. Sometimes I think about the old days. Back when I was all crazy. I'm a lot better now, but—

But what, Michael?

It's like... I dunno... I just don't feel... happy hardly ever any more.

That's the brain changes, Michael. Everybody struggles with it. When you give up your bad habit, and all the intensity that goes with it, it takes time for your brain to adjust. It's okay to not be happy while you're working through it. You have to honor your loss, and learn to move onward. It takes time.

Yeah, I know... I just... Is this all there is? Just making it from day to day? Is this any way to live?

You're still not sure it was worth it.

Yeah.

You'd probably be in the ground, Michael.

Sometimes I don't remember so good, but I was wild and... and free, you know? Going balls to the wall like nothing else mattered. On a terminal buzz twenty-four seven.

I understand. You're having euphoric recall. You're remembering the good parts, but not the bad ones.

It was so great!

What about your family?

That part was great, too! [Pause.] Oh, shit. That's awful, isn't it?

You killed and ate them.

[Long pause.] Yeah. I'm ashamed.

The Colonel asked me to talk with you about something. On Saturday, an elderly couple was eaten a block away from your house.

That wasn't me. No way.

I know. You were at work when it happened. I thought you might be able to help with whoever did it. You know how the Colonel is. It could get ugly.

I'm in the clear, Mr. Harper. I don't hang out with those people no more.

You don't want to go back to the bad old days, do you, Michael? That whole shoot-on-sight thing wasn't good for anybody, was it?

Oh, hell, no. That's when I lost this ear. Another inch to the left—

How about if we do a pee test? You think any DNA besides yours might show up?

[Long pause.]

I'm on your side, Michael. I want it to work as much as you do.

[Pause.] I had a bite. Just one bite. I swear.

How'd you get it?

Some guy. Over at the slaughterhouse. You know, when I took my bucket in for a refill.

The Colonel will want to talk to you after our session.

I swear, I didn't know the guy. What the fuck was I supposed to do, man? He just fuckin' walked up and gave it to me! If I wouldn't have eaten it, somebody else would have. They were already dead, right?

And that's called?

[Pause.] Shit… Rationalization….

There isn't any vague "somebody" out there that you can put this off on. You're the one that's responsible for your own behavior. Nobody else.

It smelled so damn good. You can always smell the difference between human brains and cow brains. So damn good.

This is a slip, Michael, not a relapse. The Colonel is going to have somebody keeping a close eye on you. First time you look like you're even thinking about biting somebody, it's a bullet in the head.

I gotta tell you, your brains smell great, Mr. Harper.

This isn't about me, Michael.

I mean, sometimes I wake up dreaming about eating your brains. Like they would taste better than any other brains in the whole world. I would soooo love to eat your brains.

That's called "transference." It happens in therapy sometimes. If you spend time obsessing about my brains, you don't have to face your own issues.

I bet I could just jump over the desk, and—

But you won't. [Sound of shell being jacked into twelve-gauge pump shotgun.] Michael… you're a slow zombie. I'd blow your head off before you got completely out of the chair. You know that you wouldn't be the first.

Fuck. Sometimes I wish I was a fast zombie.

They're all gone. They were an evolutionary dead end. Every human still alive has killed hundreds of zombies, fast and slow, Michael. Being slow is what saved you.

Crap. Yeah, I know. You need guys like me.

You're a great plumber, even if you are undead. Please open your bucket. Now.

[Pause.]

How does it smell?

It's cow brains. How you think it smells?

Please, Michael?

It smells... okay. All right? I could eat them. It would be okay.

Okay is what will keep you out of the ground. You stick with okay and no bullet in the head. You get too far away from okay, and you're gone, no matter how good a plumber you are. Okay?

[Pause.] Okay.... Crap.

I want you to do thirty meetings in thirty days. Here's the card. I want it signed every day by your sponsor. You need to have some long talks with him.

Aw, man! I haven't had to do that stuff since when we first started.

You ate some brains this week. If you think that was a good plan, let me know. I'll shoot you myself.

It wasn't a good plan.

Pee test every week until you get to the other side of this.

Fine. Just... fine.

I'm on your side, Michael, but you've got to be on your side, too. I believe in you. You're a good man. You can do this.

I know.

I'll see you next week, Michael.

Not if I see you first.

[Pause.]

Just kidding.

There's a meeting at Beth Israel at seven tonight. I'd like to see a signature on

your card that says you made it.

Yeah. I'll try.

Just remember: there's a bullet in the head waiting for you if you don't.

HE SAID, LAUGHING

By Simon R. Green

Simon R. Green is the bestselling author of dozens of novels, including several long-running series, such as the Deathstalker series and the Darkwood series. Most of his work over the last several years has been set in either his Secret History series or in his popular Nightside milieu. Recent novels include *The Good, the Bad, and the Uncanny* and *The Spy Who Haunted Me*. A new series, The Ghost Finders, is forthcoming. Green's short fiction has appeared in the anthologies *Mean Streets*, *Unusual Suspects*, *Wolfsbane and Mistletoe*, *Powers of Detection*, and is forthcoming in my anthology *The Way of the Wizard*.

Apocalypse Now is a strange, wild movie. In it, director Francis Ford Coppola retells Joseph Conrad's classic Colonial-era novel *Heart of Darkness* by transposing the story to the Vietnam War. In one scene, American soldiers attempt to seize a beachhead while simultaneously blasting Wagner's "Ride of the Valkyries" and surfing. Robert Duvall, playing the mad Lieutenant Colonel Bill Kilgore, stands tall as mortars land all around him, and declares, "I love the smell of napalm in the morning." From there things only get stranger and more surreal, as Martin Sheen's character Captain Willard travels farther and farther upriver, seeking a rogue colonel named Kurtz.

But the process of filming the movie was as mad and out-of-control as anything that appears on film. Drinking and drugs were rampant among the crew. A storm destroyed the sets, and the borrowed helicopters were called away to fight real-life battles. Star Marlon Brando had become grossly obese and refused to be filmed except from the neck up while standing in deep shadow. Someone on the production had obtained real cadavers to use as props, which turned out to have been stolen from local graves. And director Francis Ford Coppola, who stood to lose everything if the film failed, threatened repeatedly to kill himself.

Sounds pretty insane. But on the other hand, at least they never had to deal with zombies.

Saigon. 1969. It isn't Hell; but you can see Hell from here.

Viet Nam is another world; they do things differently here. It's like going back into the Past, into the deep Past—into a primitive, even primordial place.

Back to when we all lived in the jungle, because that was all there was. But it isn't just the jungle that turns men into beasts; it's being so far away from anything you can recognize as human, or humane. There is no law here, no morality, none of the old certainties. Or at least, not in any form we know, or can embrace.

Why cling to the rules of engagement, to honorable behavior, to civilized limits; when the enemy so clearly doesn't? Why hide behind the discipline of being a soldier, when the enemy is willing to do anything, anything at all, to win? Why struggle to stay a man, when it's so much easier to just let go, and be just another beast in the jungle?

Because if you can hang on long enough…you get to go home. Being sent to Viet Nam is like being thrown down into Hell, while knowing all the time that Heaven is just a short flight away. But even Heaven and Hell can get strangely mixed up, in a distant place like this. There are pleasures and satisfactions to be found in Hell, that are never even dreamed of in Heaven. And after a while, you have to wonder if the person you've become can ever go home. Can ever go back, to the person he was.

Monsters don't just happen. We make them, day by day, choice by choice.

I was waiting for my court-martial, and they were taking their own sweet time about it. I knew they were planning something special for me. The first clue came when they put me up in this rat-infested hotel, rather than the cell where I belonged. The door wasn't even locked. After all, where could I go? I was famous now. Everyone knew my face. Where could I go, who would have me, who would hide me, after the awful thing I'd done? I was told to wait, so I waited. The Army wasn't finished with me yet. I wasn't surprised. The Army could always find work for a monster, in Viet Nam.

They finally came for me in the early hours of the morning. It's an old trick. Catch a man off guard, while he's still half-drugged with sleep, and his physical and mental defenses are at their dimmest. Except I was up and out of bed and on my feet the moment I heard footsteps outside my door, hands reaching for weapons I wasn't allowed any more. It's the first thing you learn in country, if you want to stay alive in country. So when the two armed guards kicked my door in, I was waiting for them. I smiled at them, showing my teeth, because I knew that upset people. Apparently I don't smile like a person any more.

The guards didn't react. Just gestured for me to leave the room and walk ahead of them. I made a point of gathering up a few things I didn't need, just to show I wasn't going to be hurried; but I was more eager to get going than they were. Finally, someone had made a decision. The Army was either going to give me a mission, or put me up against a wall and shoot me. And I really wasn't sure which I wanted most.

I ended up in a cramped little room, far away from anything like official channels. My armed guard closed the door carefully behind me, and locked it from the outside. There was a chair facing a desk, and a man sitting behind the desk. I sat down in the chair without waiting to be asked, and the man smiled. He was big, bulk rather than fat, and his chair made quiet sounds of protest whenever he shifted his weight. He had a wide happy face under a shaven head, and he wasn't wearing a uniform. He could have been a civilian contractor, or any of a dozen kinds of businessman, but he wasn't. I knew who he was, what he had to be. Perhaps because one monster can always recognize another.

"You're CIA," I said, and he nodded quickly, smiling delightedly.

"And people say you're crazy. How little they know, Captain Marlowe."

I studied him thoughtfully. Despite myself, I was intrigued. It had been a long time since I met anyone who wasn't afraid of me. The CIA man had a slim gray folder set out on the desk before him. Couldn't have had more than half a dozen pages in it, but then, I'd only done one thing that mattered since they dropped me off here and bet me I couldn't survive. Well, I showed them.

"You know my name," I said. "What do I call you?"

"You call me 'Sir.'" He laughed silently, enjoying the old joke. "People like me don't have names. You should know that. Most of the time we're lucky if we have job descriptions. Names come and go, but the work goes on. And you know what kind of work I'm talking about. All the nasty, necessary things that the Government, and the People, don't need to know about. I operate without restrictions, without orders, and a lot of the time I make use of people like you, Captain Marlowe, because no one's more expendable than a man with a death sentence hanging over him. I can do anything I want with you; and no one will give a damn."

"Situation entirely normal, then," I said. "Sir."

He flashed me another of his wide, meaningless smiles, and leafed quickly through the papers in my file. There were photos too, and he took his time going through them. He didn't flinch once. He finally closed the file, tapped the blank cover with a heavy finger a few times, and then met my gaze squarely.

"You have been a bad boy, haven't you, Captain? One hundred and seventeen men, women, and children, including babes in arms, all wiped out, slaughtered, on one very busy afternoon, deep in country. You shot them until you ran out of bullets, you bayoneted them until the blade broke, and then you finished the rest off with the butt of your rifle, your bare hands, and a series of improvised blunt instruments. You broke in skulls, you tore out throats, you ripped out organs and you ate them. When your company finally caught up with you, you were sitting soaking your bare feet in the river, surrounded by the dead, soaked in their blood, calmly smoking a cigarette. Was it an enemy village, Captain?"

"No."

"Did anyone attack you, threaten you?"

"No."

"So why did you butcher an entire village of civilians, Captain Marlowe?"

I showed him my smile again. "Because it was there. Because I didn't like the way they looked at me. Does it matter?"

"Not particularly, no." The CIA man leaned forward across the desk, fixing me with his unblinking happy gaze. "You're not here to be court-martialed, Captain.

It has already been decided, at extremely high levels, that none of this ever happened. There never was any massacre; there never was any crazy captain. Far too upsetting, for the folks at home. Instead, I have been empowered to offer you a very special, very important, very…sensitive mission. Carry it out successfully, and this file will disappear. You will be given an honorable discharge, and allowed to go home."

"First thing you learn in the Army," I said, "is never volunteer. Especially not for very special, important, and sensitive missions."

"Should you decline this opportunity, I am also empowered to take you out the back of this building and put two bullets in your head," said the CIA man, still smiling.

I surprised him by actually taking a moment to think about it. If this mission was too important for the Army, and too dangerous for the CIA, and they needed a monster like me to carry it out successfully…it had to involve something even worse than wiping out a whole village of noncombatants. And, I wasn't sure I wanted to go home. After everything I'd seen, and done. I still loved the memories I had, of family and friends. I didn't like to think of their faces, when they realized what had come home to them. I didn't like to think of them with a monster in their midst, walking around, hidden behind my old face.

I didn't want to stay in Hell, but there was enough of a man left in me that I knew I had no business contaminating the streets of Heaven with my bloody presence.

So I nodded to the CIA man, and he sank back into his chair, which made piteous sounds of protest as his weight settled heavily again. He opened a drawer in his desk, put away my file, and took out another. It was much thicker than mine. The cover was still blank. Not even a file number. Just like mine. The CIA man opened it, took out a glossy 8 by 10, and skimmed it across the desk to me. I looked at the photo, not touching it. The officer looking back at me had all the right stripes and all the right medal ribbons, and a bland, impassive face with no obvious signs of character or authority.

"That is Major Kraus," said the CIA man. "Excellent record, distinguished career. Wrote a good many important papers. Had a great career ahead of him, Stateside. But he wanted to be here, where the action was…where he could be a *real* soldier. Somehow he persuaded his superiors to allow him to go deep in country, where he could try out some special new theories of his own. The first reports indicated that he was achieving some measure of success. Later reports were more…ambiguous. And then the reports stopped. We haven't heard anything from Major Kraus in over a year.

"The Army sent troops in after him. They never reported back. We sent some of our people in—good men, experienced men. We never heard from them again. And now reports have begun trickling out of that area, mostly from fleeing native villagers. They say Kraus has assembled his own private army, and turned them loose on everything that moves. They're moving inexorably through the jungle, killing everything in their path. It isn't enemy territory any more, but it isn't ours, either. Major Kraus seems intent on carving out his own little kingdom in the jungle, and we can't have that."

"Of course not," I said. "The Army's never approved of individual ambition."

"Don't push your luck, Captain. Your mission is to go up river, all the way into the jungle to the major's last reported position, evaluate the situation, and then put an end to his little experiment."

I smiled. "I get to kill a major?"

The CIA man smiled back at me. "Thought you'd like that. If the major cannot be persuaded to rein himself in, and follow orders, you are empowered to execute him. If the situation can be brought back under control, do so. If not, just present us with the exact coordinates, and we'll send the fly boys in to wipe the whole mess right off the map. Any questions?"

"Why me?"

"Because you are completely and utterly expendable, Captain. If you should fail, we'll just find another psycho and send him up the river. It's not like there's a shortage, these days. We'll just keep sending people like you, until one of you finally gets the job done. We're not in any hurry. If nothing else, Major Kraus is at least keeping the enemy occupied."

"If I do this, and come back," I said. "Do I have to go home? Or could there be more *sensitive* missions for me?"

"Why not?" said the CIA man, smiling his crocodile smile. "We're always looking for a few good psychos."

The patrol boat they gave me was a broken-down piece of shit called the *Suzy Q*. The crew of three that came with her weren't much better. I gave the pilot what maps I had, and then retired to the cabin, to be alone. I didn't ask their names. I didn't want to know. They didn't matter to me, except to get me where I was going. They didn't know it, but they were even more expendable than I was.

They didn't want to talk to me. Someone had told them who I was, and what I'd done. They maintained a safe, respectful distance at all times, and their hands never moved far from their weapons. I smiled at them, now and again, just to keep them on their toes.

I watched them die, one by one, as we headed up the winding river and deep into the dark and savage jungle. It doesn't matter how they died. The jungle just reached out and took them, in its various bloody ways. I waited for the darkness to strike me down too, but somehow its aim was always that little bit off. So when the long and twisting river finally came to its end, I was the only one left to guide the *Suzie Q* through the narrowing channels to its dark and awful source.

The jungle pressed in close around me, trees and vegetation crowding right up to the river's edge, a harsh green world impenetrable to merely human gaze. Huge gnarled trees reached out over the water, tall branches thrusting forward to meet each other, and form a thick canopy that blocked out the sky. Light had to shoulder its way in, heavy golden shafts punching through the canopy like spotlights. The air was heavy with the thick green scents of growing things, interlaced with the sickly sweet smells of death and corruption. Great clouds of insects rose up from the river to break against the boat's prow, and then reform again behind her.

The darker it got, the more at home I felt. The other three died because they were still men, while I had left that state behind long ago. In the jungle, in all the places of the world where man is never meant to live, you cannot hope to survive if you insist on remaining a man. This is a place for beasts, for nature, red in tooth and claw, for animal instincts and brutal drives. The jungle knows nothing of human limitations like honor and sentiment, compassion and sanity.

There were still some people in the jungle. I saw them, passing by. Grim gray silent ghosts, who had made their own bargain with the jungle. Black-pajama men and women, slipping along concealed trails, their supplies balanced on carts and bicycles. Peasant villagers, carrying their life's possessions, retreating in the face of something that could not be stopped, or bargained with, or survived. I let them go. Partly because my mission was too important to risk revealing myself, but mostly because I knew that if I started shooting, started killing, I might not be able to stop. I'd made a cage inside me to hold my beast, but the door was only closed, not locked.

I kept the beast quiet, traveling up the river, by considering all the awful things I was going to do to Major Kraus, before I finally let him die.

When the maps ran out, I just pointed the *Suzie Q* forward and kept going. The river narrowed steadily, closing remorselessly in from both sides, the crowded vegetation creeping right up to the edges of both banks to get a good look at me. I passed the time studying the major's CIA file. There were reports of burned out and deserted villages, and wide swathes of devastated land, radiating out from Kraus' compound at the end of the river. Whole populations slaughtered, and the bodies…just gone. Taken? Nobody knew. Kraus' private army ranged far and wide, butchering every living thing in its path, but not one dead body was ever seen afterwards, anywhere. Cannibalism, perhaps? The file had theories, ideas, guesses, but no one knew anything, where Kraus was concerned. Someone had written the words *Psychological warfare?* across the bottom of one page, but that was all.

The river finally ran out, ending in a wide natural harbor deep in the dark green heart of the jungle. The thick crumbling river banks were so close now I could reach out from the *Suzie Q* and trail my fingertips along the turgid vegetation and creepers as they drooped down into the dark waters. The thick canopy overhead blocked out the sun, plunging the river into an endless twilight, like the end of the world. I had left the world behind, to come to a place man should have left behind, long ago. We have no business here. We cannot be man, in a place like this.

The river banks came together, closing in like living gates, so close now I could barely squeeze the *Suzie Q* through, and then they opened out abruptly, revealing the wide calm waters of the natural harbor where Major Kraus had established his compound. It was very dark now, almost night, and at first all I could see were the lights up ahead. They jumped and flared, a sickly yellow, like so many will-o'-the-wisps.

The river banks rose sharply up around me, great clay and earth walls rising twenty, thirty feet above my head. Roots burst out of the wet earth here and there, curling around great open mouths, dark caves and caverns peering at me from the river banks. Huge centipedes crawled in and out of the openings, slow ripples moving up and down their unnaturally long bodies. The waters ahead of me were flat and still, disturbed only by the slow sullen waves preceding the boat's prow. The steady chugging of the boat's engine was disturbingly loud in the quiet, so I turned it off, allowing the boat to glide the rest of the way in. There were hundreds of lights now, blazing atop the tall river banks like so many watchful eyes.

There was no dock, as such. Just a natural protrusion of dull gray earth, thrusting out into the water. I eased the *Suzie Q* in beside it, and she lurched fitfully to a halt as her prow slammed against the earth dock in a series of slow, slowing bumps. I left the boat and stepped cautiously out onto dry land. It felt like stepping out onto an alien planet and leaving my spaceship behind. The tall earth banks were lined from end to end with flaring lights now. I craned my head back, and dozens of natives looked down at me, holding crude flaring torches. None of them moved, or spoke. They just looked.

A set of rough steps had been cut into the tall earth wall beside me, curving slowly upwards. They didn't look in any way safe or dependable, but I hadn't come this far to be put off by anything less than a gun in my face. I started up the steps, pressing my left shoulder hard against the yielding clay and earth of the river bank, careful not to look anywhere but straight in front of me. The steps squelched loudly beneath my boots, and my arm and shoulder were soon soaked with slime and seepage from the earth wall. I paused beside the first great opening, peering into the dark tunnel beyond. I seemed to sense as much as hear movement within, of something much larger and heavier than a centipede. I pressed on, stamping my boots heavily into the slippery steps to keep my balance. The natives were still looking down at me, saying nothing.

I was out of breath and aching in every limb when I finally reached the top. I took a moment to get my breath back, and coughed harshly on the rank air. The usual jungle stench of living and dying things pressed close together was overwhelmed here by a heavy stench of death and decay, close up and personal. It was like breathing in rotting flesh, like sticking your face into the opened belly of a corpse. It was a smell I knew all too well. For a moment I wondered whether all of this had been nothing but a dream, and I was still back in my village, cooling my bare feet in the river and smoking a cigarette, as I waited for them to come and find me, and all the awful things I'd done.... But this stench, this place, was too vile to be anything but real.

The natives stood before me, holding their torches, and every single one of them was dead. I only had to look at them to know. They stood in endless ranks, unnaturally still, their eyes not moving and their chests neither rising nor falling; flies buzzed and swarmed and crawled all over them. Some were older than others, their flesh desiccated and mummified. Others were so recent they still bore the dark sticky blood of the wounds that had killed them. Some had no eyes, or great holes in their torsos, packed with squirming maggots. Everywhere I looked there was some new horror, of missing limbs, or dropped off lower jaws, or pale gray and purple strings of intestines spilling out of opened-up bellies. They carried knives and machetes and vicious clubs, all of them thickly crusted with dried blood. They wore rags and tatters, almost as decayed as their bodies. Some wore what was left of army uniforms, north and south.

And then it got worse, as two of the dead men dropped their torches uncaringly onto the wet ground, and moved towards me. They did not move as living things move; there was nothing of grace or connection in their movements. They moved as though movement had been imposed upon them. It was horrible to look at; an alien, utterly unnatural thing, as though a tree had ripped up its roots and lurched forward. I started to back away, and then remembered there was nothing behind me but the earth steps, and a long drop. I wanted to scream and run and hide.

But I didn't. This was what I had come here for: to learn Major Kraus' awful secret.

The two dead men took me by the arms and hauled me forward. I didn't try to fight them. Their hands were horribly cold on my bare skin. They didn't look at me, or try to speak to me, for which I was grateful. I didn't think even I could have stood to learn what a dead man's voice sounded like.

They led me through the army of the dead, across an uneven ground soaked with blood and littered with discarded body parts. There were great piles of organs, torn away or fallen out, revealed suddenly as great clouds of flies sprang into the air at our approach. There were hacked off hands, and broken heads, faces rotted away to reveal wide smiles of perfect teeth. My dead guards walked right over them, and did not allow me time to be fastidious. By the time we got where I was going, my boots and trousers were soaked in blood and gore.

I should never have taken this mission. I only thought I knew what Hell was.

I'd never felt so scared, or so alive. After the village, after what I did there, I didn't feel much of anything. But now, surrounded by death, and the fear of something worse than death, I felt alive again. My heart hammered in my chest, and every breath was a glorious thing, despite the stench. I was here among things that couldn't be, shouldn't be...and I wanted to know more.

The men I killed never got up again. That would be awful, if they should rise up again and look at me with knowing, accusing eyes. The men who served beside me, who were cut down by an often unseen enemy—they never rose up again either. In Viet Nam, death was the one thing you could depend on. Except...not here. What had Major Kraus done, here, so far from civilization and sanity? Who knew what might be possible here, so far from science and logic and all the other things man depends on to make sense of his world? Perhaps...if you went back far enough, into the past, into the jungle, you could leave reality behind in favor of a whole new world where anything, anything at all, was possible.

My dead guards brought me to a great hole in the ground and stopped. They let go of me, and just stood there, looking at nothing. I rubbed my arms hard, where their cold flesh had touched mine, without menace or care or any feeling at all. I looked down into the hole. It seemed to fall away deep into the blood-soaked earth, but there was light at the bottom. A metal ladder had been roughly attached to one side of the wet earth. I started down it. I wanted, *needed* answers; if answers there were to be had.

The ladder went down and down, a descent long enough to raise fierce cramps in my arms and legs. It ended in a tunnel, dug deep into the earth of the tall river bank, lit by oil lamps set in niches in the earth walls. The red clay in the walls gave them a disturbingly organic quality, as though I was invited to go stumbling through the guts of some long-dead colossus, buried ages ago.

The tunnels were a maze, a warren of narrow inter-connecting passageways, and I soon lost all sense of place, or direction. I just lurched along, following the lit tunnels, sweating profusely in the close hot air. The lamps had to be for my benefit; dead men wouldn't need them. It was no wonder the CIA man's maps had been so vague about Major Kraus' secret compound. He'd hidden it underground, to conceal just how big it was—hidden it underground, where only the dead men go. If the CIA had even suspected how big Kraus' base was, how extensive his army, they would have sent the fly boys in long ago to burn the whole place back to bare unliving stone.

Clever Kraus.

Finally I came to the heart of the labyrinth, to the place of the monster, to the awful court of Major Kraus. There was no sign, no warning, no preparation. I just rounded a corner and found myself standing in a clean, brightly-lit earth chamber. There were rushes on the floor, shelves on the walls holding books and oil lamps and an assortment of presumably precious objects. There was a table, covered in maps and papers, and two surprisingly comfortable-looking chairs. But there was no clock anywhere, or even a calendar; nothing to tell you what time it might be, as though time had no meaning here, as though it had become irrelevant in this old, old place where the dead walked. I was in the Past now, in the deep Past, in the ancient primordial jungle, and that was all that mattered.

Kraus sat in a chair behind his table, hands clasped lightly on the tabletop before him, and he watched me with calm, amused eyes. He was alive. His chest rose and fell easily as he breathed, and his smile was real if thin. His simple vitality was like a shock of cold water in the face, breaking me out of the nightmare I'd been wandering through.

I studied the man I'd come so far to find. He was stick thin, without a spare ounce of fat on him, as though all such physical weakness has been burned away in some spiritual kiln. He had sharp, aesthetic features under close-cropped hair, and even though he was sitting perfectly still and at ease, he blazed with barely suppressed nervous energy. His spotlessly clean Army uniform hung loosely about him, as though it had once fitted a much larger man. His smile was slight but genuine, and his eyes were disturbingly sane.

I nodded slowly, to the man I'd been sent to kill. I never know what to say, on occasions like this. All my old certainties had been thrown down and trampled into the dirt, but still some small spark of stubborn pride wouldn't allow me to blurt out the obvious question. Major Kraus just smiled and nodded back at me, as though he quite understood. I had no gun or knife. Dead hands had taken all my weapons from me, before I was allowed down the ladder into the underworld. I could still kill him with my bare hands. I'd been trained. But if I should fail…I didn't want to die here. Not in this awful place, where the dead didn't stay dead.

That would be terrible: to die, and still not know peace.

Kraus gestured easily for me to sit down. A calm, casual gesture, from a man who knew he held all the power in the room. Just for a moment, the major reminded me of the CIA man, back in Saigon. I sat down. Kraus smiled again, just a brief movement of the lips, revealing stained yellow teeth.

"Yes," he said. "They're dead. They're all dead. The ones who brought you here, the ones who stand guard, and the ones I send out to kill my enemies. Dead men walking, every single one of them, torn from their rest, raised up out of their graves, and set to work by me. Everyone's dead here, *except* me. And now, you. Tell me your name, soldier."

"Captain Marlowe," I said. "Torn from my cell, raised up from my court-martial, and sent here by the CIA to kill you, Major Kraus. They're frightened of you. Of course, if they knew what you were really doing here…"

"There's nothing they can do to stop me. My army is made up of men who are beyond fear, or suffering, who cannot be stopped by bullets or bombs or napalm. Zombies, Captain Marlowe. Old voodoo magic, from the deep south of America, where the really old ways are not forgotten. You needn't worry, Captain, they won't attack you. And they certainly won't try and eat you, as they did in a cheap horror movie I saw, before I came out here. Into the real horror show, that never ends…. My men have no need to eat, any more than they need to drink, or piss, or sweat. They are beyond such human weaknesses now. They have no appetites, no desires, and the only will that moves them is mine. I give them purpose, for as long as they last. They are my warriors of the night, my weapons cast against an uncaring world, my horror to set against the horror men have made of this place.

"War…is too important to be left to the living."

"Of course," I said numbly. "The perfect soldiers. The dead don't get tired, don't get stopped by injuries, and will follow any order you give them, without question. Because nothing matters to them any more."

"Exactly," said Kraus, favoring me with another brief smile. "I just point them in the right direction, and let them roll right over whatever lies in their path. They destroy everything and everyone, like army ants on the march. Most people won't even stand against them any more; they just turn and flee, as they would in the face of any other natural disaster. And if I should lose some men, through too much damage, I can always make up the numbers again, by raising up the fallen enemy dead.

"You're not shocked, Captain Marlowe. How very refreshing."

"'Why this is Hell, nor am I out of it,'" I murmured. "I have seen worse things than this, Major. Done worse things than this, in my time."

He leaned forward across his desk, fixing me with his terribly sane, compassionate gaze. "Yes...I can see the darkness in you, Captain. Tell what you saw, and what you did."

"I have been here before," I said. "In country, in the dark and terrible place where the old rules mean nothing, and so you can do anything, anything at all. Because no matter how bad we are, the enemy is always worse. I've seen much scarier things than zombies, in country."

"I'm sure you have," said Kraus. "They have no idea what it's like here—the real people back in their real world. Where there are laws and conventions, right and wrong, and everything makes sense. They can't know what it's like here, or why would fathers and mothers allow their sons to be sent into Hell...and then act all surprised when the command structure breaks down, army discipline breaks down, and their sons have to do awful, unforgivable things just to stay alive? What did you do, Captain, to earn a mission like this?"

"I wiped out a whole village," I said. "Killed them all: men, women and children. And then refused to say sorry."

"Why, Captain? Why would you do such a thing?"

For the first time, I was being asked the question by someone who sounded like he actually wanted to hear the truth. So I considered my answer seriously. "Why? Because I *wanted* to. Because I *could*. No matter what you do here, the jungle always throws back something worse...I don't see the enemy as people any more, just so many beasts in the jungle. The things they've done...they give the jungle's dark savagery a face, that's all. And after a while, after you've done awful, terrible things in your turn, and it hasn't made a damned bit of difference...you feel the need to do more and more, just to get a response from that bland, indifferent, jungle face. You want to see it flinch, make it hurt, the way it's hurt you. That need drives you on, to greater and greater acts of savagery...until finally, you look into the face of the jungle...and see your own face looking back at you."

"I know," said Major Kraus. "I understand."

I sat slumped in my chair, exhausted by the force of my words. And Kraus smiled on me, like a father with a prodigal son.

"It's the curse of this country, this war, Captain. This isn't like any other war we ever fought. There are no real battle lines, no clear disputed territories, no obvious or lasting victories. Only a faceless enemy, an opposing army and a hateful population, prepared to do anything, anything at all, to drive us out. Any atrocity, any crime against nature or civilization, is justified to them because we are outsiders, and therefore by definition not human.

"There is only one way to win this war, Captain, and that is to be ready and willing to do even worse things to them. To embrace the darkness of the jungle in our hearts, and in our souls, and throw it in their faces. We tried to raise a light in the darkness, when we should have eaten the darkness up with spoons and made it ours—given it shape and purpose and meaning. I have done an awful and unforgivable thing here, Captain, but for the first time I am making progress. I am taking and holding territory, and I am forcing the enemy back.

"I will win this war, which my own superiors are saying cannot be won. I will win it because I am ready and willing to do the one thing the enemy is not willing to do. They are ready to fight us to the death, but I have made death a weapon I can turn against them. And after my dead warriors have subjugated this entire country, North and South, and I have won because not one living soul remains to stand against me.... Then, *then*, I will take the war home. I will cross the great waters with a dead army millions strong, and I will turn them loose on the streets of America, turn them loose on all those uncaring people who sent their children into Hell.

"I will make our country a charnel house, and then a cemetery, and then, finally, the war will be over. And I can rest."

He looked at me for a long time, and his smile and his eyes were kind. "They sent you here to kill me, Captain Marlowe, those cold and uncaring men. But you won't. Because that's not what you really want. Stay here, with me, and be my Boswell; write the record of what I am doing. And then I will send it home, ahead of the army that's coming, as a warning. It's only right they should understand their crime, before they are punished for it. Tell my story, Captain Marlowe, and when I don't need you any more...I promise I will kill you, and let you stay dead. No more bad thoughts, no more bad dreams, no more darkness in the heart. You will rest easy, sleep without dreams, and feel nothing, nothing at all. Isn't that what you really want, Captain Marlowe?"

"Yes," I said. "Oh, yes."

Major Kraus smiled happily. "I shall put an end to all wars, and death shall have dominion, when Johnny comes marching home.

"'*The horror! The horror!*'" he said, laughing.

LAST STAND

By Kelley Armstrong

Kelley Armstrong is the bestselling author of the Otherworld urban fantasy series, which began with *Bitten*, and the latest of which, *Waking the Witch*, came out in August. She is also the author of the young-adult series Darkest Powers, consisting of three books so far: *The Summoning*, *The Awakening*, and *The Reckoning*. In comics, Armstrong recently finished working on a five-issue arc for Joss Whedon's *Angel* comic book series. In addition to the previously mentioned work, which all fits into the fantasy/paranormal genre, Armstrong has also written two thrillers featuring hitwoman Nadia Stafford: *Exit Strategy* and *Made to Be Broken*.

Teachers have a rough job. Lousy pay, lots of unpaid overtime work grading papers, having to keep order alone in overcrowded classrooms full of unruly kids who would rather be anywhere than learning trigonometry. Not to mention all the abuse from crazy parents and ignorant lawmakers. In 1925, a twenty-four-year-old football coach named John Scopes was actually brought up on criminal charges in Tennessee for having taught students the scientific facts about human evolution. With all the drawbacks, it's understandable why so many teachers leave the profession after just a few years.

But bad as our educational system undoubtedly is, things could always be worse—say, the complete and total breakdown of civilization in the wake of an infection that causes the recently dead to rise again as terrifying monsters. That's the sort of event that really puts things in perspective, and makes you pine for the days of students not paying attention in class. In the 1998 movie *Saving Private Ryan*, a squad of WWII soldiers speculate endlessly about the former profession of their captain, before he finally reveals to them that he had been a simple schoolteacher.

War and upheaval can shuffle the world, thrusting us into roles we could have never imagined. In our next story we find another former teacher leading military forces under desperate circumstances, doing things she never thought she'd be capable of, and facing off against an enemy more relentless and implacable than she ever could have feared.

If you had to make a last stand for the survival of your race, Monica supposed there were worse places to do it. As she gazed out over the fort walls, she could imagine fields of green and gold, corn stalks swaying in the breeze.

How long had it been since she'd tasted corn? Monica closed her eyes and remembered August backyard barbecues, the smell of ribs and burgers on the grill, the chill of an icy beer can as Jim pressed it to her back, the sound of Lily's laughter as she darted past, chasing the other children with water balloons.

Monica opened her eyes and looked out at the scorched fields. She'd been the one who'd given the order to set the blaze, but there hadn't been corn in them, not for years. Only barren fields of grass and weeds that could hide the enemy, best put to the torch.

"Commander," a voice said behind her.

She turned and a pimply youth snapped his heels together and saluted. The newer ones did that sometimes, and she'd stopped trying to break them of the habit. They needed to believe they were in a proper army, with proper rules, even if they'd never worn a uniform before. It was what kept them going, let them believe they could actually win this war.

"Hendrix just radioed," the youth said. "He's bringing in the latest group of prisoners."

Monica nodded, and followed him off the ramparts. They passed two teenage girls in scout uniforms. They nodded, gazes down, and murmured polite greetings. Monica hid a smile, thinking that, once upon a time, she'd have killed to get that respect from girls their age, back when she'd stood at the front of a classroom.

She thought about all the kids she'd taught. Wondered where they were now, how many were Others, how many were dead… Too many in the last category, she was sure. What would they think, seeing their chemistry teacher leading the last band of resistance fighters? Could they ever imagine it? She couldn't imagine it herself some days.

As she followed the youth into the fort, Gareth swung out from the shadows. He fell into step beside her, his left foot scraping the floor—a broken leg that never healed quite right.

Before he could say a word, she lifted her hand.

"Objection noted, Lieutenant."

"I didn't say a word, Commander," he said.

"You don't need to. You heard we're bringing in a fresh lot, and you're going to tell me—again—that we can't handle more prisoners. The stockade is overcrowded. We're wasting manpower guarding them. We're wasting doctors caring for them. We should take them out into the field, kill them and leave the corpses on spikes for the Others to see."

"I don't believe I've suggested that last part. Brilliant idea, though. I'll send a troop to find the wood for the poles—"

She shot him a look. He only grinned.

"We aren't animals, Lieutenant," she said. "We don't stoop to their level."

Of course he knew she'd say that, just as well as she knew his complaint. Gareth just liked to voice his opinion. Loudly and frequently. She'd answered only for the sake of the new recruit leading them.

When they reached the main hall, she heard the cry: "Prisoners on the grounds!" For the newer ones, it was a warning and they scattered in every direction. Monica never tried to make them stand their ground. She understood too well where that fear came from, those years of hiding, watching, waiting to run again. She did, however, ask her officers to take note of those who fled and, later, they'd be taken to the stockades, so they could see that the Others weren't the all-powerful demons of their nightmares.

Once they were convinced, they'd react to that cry very differently. They'd join the other soldiers now lining Stockade Walk to watch the parade of prisoners. They wouldn't jeer, wouldn't say a word, would just stand firm and watch, the hatred so thick you could smell it, heavy, suffocating.

As they walked into the main hall, already choked with soldiers, Gareth said, "You can watch from the second floor, Commander."

"Like hell."

A wave went through the assembled men and women, grunts and nods of approval from those who'd overheard, whispers going down the line to those who hadn't. *Yet another crowd-pleasing routine*, she thought wryly. Gareth won approval for the suggestion and she for refusing.

As they entered the hall, Gareth's shoulders squared, pulling himself up to his full six-foot-five, his limp disappearing. The crowd of soldiers parted to let them through. Those who didn't move fast enough earned a glower from Gareth, and scrambled aside so fast they tripped. Him, they feared and respected. Her, they loved and respected. Yet another of their routines.

Monica took up her usual position at the first corner. When the prisoners walked into the hall, she'd be the first one they saw, waiting at the end.

She could hear them outside the doors now. This was the toughest part. Nearly every man and woman in this hall had been in this same situation, waiting in their hideouts, hearing the Others approaching, praying they passed. *Oh God, praying they passed.*

Gareth moved up behind her. Out of sight of the soldiers, he rubbed the small of her back.

When the footsteps stopped at the door, a few soldiers broke ranks and, shamefaced, bolted back to their bunks. It was still too much for them, the memories too fresh.

The door started to open. Monica's own memories flashed. In that first moment, she didn't see soldiers and prisoners. She saw the gang of Others who'd burst into her own hideaway ten years ago. She heard Jim's shout of rage as he rushed forward to protect them, yelling for Monica to take Lily and run. She heard his screams as they fell on him. She heard Lily's screams as she saw her father torn apart. She heard her own screams as she grabbed Lily and ran for the basement, as they caught her, ripping Lily from her arms. Her screams for them to show mercy—Lily was only a child, only a little girl. They hadn't.

Gareth moved closer, letting her rest against him. He leaned down to murmur reassurances in her ear, then, as she relaxed, the reassurances turned to reminders. *Stand tall, babe. You're in charge now. You own their asses. Don't let them forget that.*

Now she saw prisoners, strangers, not the monsters who'd slaughtered her family, raped and tortured her. Broken and cowed and filthy, they shuffled along the gauntlet of soldiers.

Gareth tensed. Monica looked up sharply, gaze tripping over the prisoners, trying to see which one had triggered his old cop instincts. Sure enough, there was one at the end, long greasy hair hanging in his face, but not quite hiding the furtive looks he kept shooting her way.

She stood firm, gaze on the prisoner. He looked away as he passed. Then he wheeled and lunged at her.

Gareth leapt forward so fast all Monica saw was a blur and a flash of silver. The prisoner's head sailed from his shoulders. It hit the floor with a dull thud and rolled. When it came to rest at a soldier's feet, the young woman kicked it. A cheer started to surge, choked off at a simple, "No," from Monica.

She motioned for someone to clean up the mess. The procession of prisoners continued on. None even gave any sign they'd seen what happened. They just trudged along, gazes down, until they disappeared from sight.

Word came next that the scouts had been spotted. They were moving fast, meaning they were bringing bad news. She left the hall with Gareth and headed for the meeting room to await their arrival.

As they passed the lecture hall, Monica could hear the teacher giving a history lesson for the children, all born after the Great Divide.

Three flu epidemics had threatened the world in the decade preceding the Great Divide. As they'd escaped each relatively unscathed, experts swore they'd only dodged one bullet to put themselves in the path of a bigger one.

The H5N3 virus had started in Indonesia, with sporadic outbreaks downplayed by authorities until they could announce a vaccine.

Their salvation turned into their damnation. Some said the vaccine had been deliberately tampered with. Others blamed improper testing. They knew only that it didn't work.

No, that wasn't true. If the goal was to ensure that people survived the flu, then it worked perfectly. People were vaccinated, they caught the virus, they died, and they rose again.

Even before they rose, though, they'd carried a virus of their own, unknowingly spreading it through lovers, drug use, and blood donations. By the time officials realized the problem, a quarter of the population was infected. After the vaccinations stopped, another quarter died from the influenza itself. Both viruses continued to spread.

That was the Great Divide. The human race sliced in two, one side fighting for supremacy, the other for survival.

The world will end, not with a bang, but with a sniffle.

Or, to be precise, with the risk of a sniffle.

After Monica escaped her captors, her only thought had, indeed, been survival. Her own. But as she ran from the hordes, she'd picked up others like a magnet attracts iron filings. Everyone was alone. Everyone needed help. As a mother, she wanted to protect them. As a teacher, she wanted to guide them. Within a year, she found herself leading twenty survivors. Then they found Gareth.

He'd been in the middle of what had once been a town square, fighting a half-dozen of the Others, a roaring whirlwind of blood and steel, fighting valiantly, but wounded and outnumbered.

They'd rescued him. His story was one of the simpler ones—no family slaughtered before his eyes, just one guy, living a normal life until the day he wasn't. He'd tried to stick to what he knew—being a cop, protecting the innocent, which these days meant roaming the countryside, fighting bands of Others so survivors could escape. A noble plan, if not terribly efficient. Monica had suggested that, if he really wanted people to protect, he could look after them.

And so it began. Ten years later, they were here, commanding what might well be the last of their kind, awaiting a final battle. A battle they knew they couldn't win.

The scouts' news was exactly what she'd expected. The Others were amassing just beyond a forest to the east, the only place for miles that couldn't be seen from the ramparts. When she'd ordered her troops to raze the fields, they'd started cutting down the forest, then realized the task was beyond them. Besides, she'd reasoned, that meant the Others would pick that spot for their camp, so she could concentrate their surveillance there.

Surveillance. It sounded so strategic, as if they were fully prepared to meet the enemy, simply biding their time, when the truth was that they were foxes backed into a den, waiting for the wolves to arrive.

She hadn't brought them here to die. She'd hoped by running so far, they'd send a message to the Others: "Look, you've won. We've holed up here in this wasteland and here we'll stay. Now just leave us alone. *Please* leave us alone."

One last plea for mercy. It was, she realized as the scouts gave their report, too much to hope for. Deep down, she'd always known it was.

"Prepare a reconnaissance team," Monica said as she rose from the table. "We'll leave at the first night bell."

Two of the trained scouts exchanged uneasy looks. They'd come from the true military teams, long since disbanded, where commanding officers stayed behind the enemy lines. They glanced at Gareth, as if hoping he'd advise her to stay behind.

"You heard Commander Roth," he said. "Get that team ready."

Monica was back on the ramparts, looking out over the barren fields, waiting for the team to convene below. The faint scrape of Gareth's dragging boot told her he was coming, but she didn't turn, just stood at the railing, looking out until she felt his arms around her waist.

"We knew this was coming," he said.

"I know."

"We're as prepared as we're ever going to be."

"I know."

"There's still one more option," he said.

"No."

"Just saying..."

"And I'm saying that I know it's an option. I'll remember it's an option. But..."

She inhaled and shook her head. He pulled her back against him, chin resting on her head, and she relaxed against the solid wall of his chest.

She felt his head turn, as he made sure there was no one around before he leaned down and kissed her neck, his lips cool against her skin. Those who'd been with them a long time knew they were lovers, had been for years. As discreet as they were, it was hard to hide something like that, living in close quarters. They were still careful, though, for the sake of those, like the scouts, who'd come from the troops, where such a thing would be a serious concern.

There weren't many of them left—true soldiers, trained ones. Military commander had never been Monica's role. Years ago, when they'd started meeting up with other groups of survivors, she'd made it clear that she wasn't cut out for that. She'd take charge of the civilians. Gareth had been invited to lead a military division, but he'd stayed with her, trained the civilians to protect themselves. Then, one by one, the troops had fallen, the few survivors making their way to Monica's group, until they were all that remained. Now they looked to her to protect them, and she wasn't sure she could.

By the time they left, night had fallen. That wasn't an accident. They traveled at night when they could, moving silently across the burned fields. The same open land that protected them from sneak attacks made them prisoners during the daylight.

It was an hour's walk to the forest's edge. They'd just drawn within sight of it when they heard a barely muffled gasp of pain ahead. They'd split up, Gareth and Monica proceeding, the others fanning out.

The stifled whimpers came from just past the first line of trees. It sounded like a child, but they continued ahead with caution, Gareth in the lead, machete drawn. Those were the best weapons they had—knives and spears and makeshift swords. They had guns, too, but without ammunition, they were little more than clubs. The Others were no better off. This was a primitive war of tooth and claw and steel, as it had been for years, the munitions factories among the earliest targets.

Monica's weapon of choice was a throwing knife, and she had one in each hand as she followed Gareth. At the rustle of undergrowth, he stopped, and she peered around him to see a figure rising between the trees.

"Oh, thank God," a girl's voice said. "Oh, thank *God*."

The figure wobbled, then dropped with a cry. They found her on the ground, clutching her leg as she lit a lantern. She was no more than eighteen, thin-faced and pale.

"I thought you were the Infected," she said, her voice breathy with relief. "They got the rest of my troop. I-I tried to fight—"

"Shhh," Monica said, moving closer.

The girl looked up at them. Seeing Gareth's scarred face, she gave a start, but Monica nudged him back. He slid into the shadows.

"They took the others," the girl said. "They took them all."

Monica crouched beside the girl. "We'll get you back to your camp. We just arrived ourselves. Reinforcements." She offered her most reassuring smile. "You'll have to show us the best way to go. In case more of them are out here."

The girl nodded and reached up. Monica tucked the throwing knives into her waistband halter and tried to take the girl's arm, but the girl clasped hers instead, fingers biting in as she rose slowly.

Then she yanked Monica toward her. Silver flashed as the girl's free hand pulled a knife from under her jacket. Monica's foot expertly snagged the girl's "wounded" leg and she went down, the knife flying free. Monica kicked it out of the way as the girl grabbed for it. Another kick to the girl's stomach and she fell, doubled-over and gasping.

"Did you really think I didn't know what you are?" the girl snarled between gasps. "Did you think I couldn't *smell* what you are?"

"No," Gareth said, stepping forward, machete whispering as it brushed his leg. "And did you really think we wouldn't smell an ambush?"

He swung the machete as the forest around them erupted, Others lunging out from their hiding places. The girl tried to scuttle back, but he was too fast. Her head flew from her shoulders. Blood jetted up, her body convulsing in death. The Others stopped, all frozen in mid-step, staring.

"What?" Gareth boomed, bloody machete raised. "Isn't that what you do to us? Lop off our heads? The only way to be sure we're dead? Well, it works for you, too." He smiled, his scarred face a pale death mask against the night. "Any volunteers?"

"You may want to consider it," Monica said, her quiet voice cutting through the silence. "Because, if you look over your shoulders, you'll see we aren't alone. And they won't kill you. They'll turn you." She looked around, her perfect night vision picking out each face, her gaze meeting each set of wide eyes. "They'll infect you."

Gareth roared, giving the signal for attack and the forest erupted again as their soldiers leapt from the undergrowth and swung from the trees. In that first wave of attack, some of the Others bolted. More ran after a few half-hearted swings of a blade. She had invoked the greatest weapon they possessed: fear.

Fear of becoming Infected. *Fear of becoming like us.*

Without that weapon, they'd have been massacred. Even with it, the fight was long and bloody. Finally, they were left standing among bodies, some their own, but most not and that was really all they could hope for.

They continued on. They'd come to see the Others' camp and they weren't turning back. It was a slower walk now, trudging through the forest, some of them wounded. Nothing was fatal—few things were for them—but injuries healed slowly and imperfectly, like Gareth's broken leg and scarred face. It was, as with everything about their condition, a trade-off, in some ways better than life before, in others worse.

As a teacher, Monica had been one of the first to be inoculated, along with her family. One of the first vaccinated, one of the first infected, one of the first to die. The virus had hit with lightning speed, leaving her writhing with pain and fever, listening to her daughter's screams, unable to get to her.

Then, a miracle. Or so it seemed at the time. Death and rebirth.

Before they could even decide what to do, the soldiers came, the first squads deployed with orders to annihilate the Infected. They'd gone into hiding, staying one step ahead of the death squads, squatting in abandoned homes, certain if they could just wait it out, the authorities would realize their mistake and *help* them. But the order to kill all Infected stayed. Then came the bounty. Then the gangs of blood-crazed bounty hunters. They'd escaped the death squads, but not the gangs.

Jim had blamed zombie movies. When the dead rose again, people were sure they knew what they faced—an undead scourge that would end life as they knew it.

Some of the old stories were true. The Infected could not be easily killed. They carried the pallor of death, the faint smell of rot. Their bite could infect the living. They fed on meat, preferably raw, and while they had no particular hunger for human flesh, it was true that, if driven mad with hunger, they had been known to do what they would otherwise never consider.

But, unlike the zombies of legend and lore, they were still alive in every way that counted, still cognizant, and they could be reasoned with. The same could not be said for the living—for the Others.

The Infected had been hunted to near extermination and now, when Monica finally set eyes on the Others' camp, those seemingly infinite tents, she knew their end was at hand.

"We can't fight this," she whispered to Gareth.

"But we will."

And that was what it came down to. They *would* fight, hopeless or not.

They started back for the fort. She let Gareth take the lead, her mind whirring with everything she needed to do. She didn't notice when she veered slightly off course. Didn't notice the tripwire. Didn't notice until her foot snagged it and she heard Gareth's shout and saw him diving toward her, shoving her out of the way, heard the explosion, saw the flying debris and saw him sail backward, hitting the ground hard enough to make the earth shake.

She raced over and dropped beside him.

"Shit," he said, rising on his elbows to look down at his chest, his shirt shredded, the flesh below shredded, too, a mangled, cratered mass. "That's not good."

She let out a choking sound, meant to be a laugh, but coming out as a sob. It'd been a small blast, a homemade bomb designed to do nothing more than shoot shrapnel, but all that shrapnel had slammed into Gareth's chest. If he hadn't been Infected, he'd have been dead before he hit the ground.

She waved the medic over, but one look at his face told her all she needed to know. They could recover from most injuries, but if the damage was too great, too extensive …

Oh God. Not Gareth. Please not Gareth.

She stayed beside him as the medic took a closer look. The soldiers ringed around them, solemn-faced, a few shaking, arms around each other.

When the medic looked up to give his report, Gareth waved the soldiers back out of earshot. They hesitated, but obeyed at a growl from him.

"I can make him comfortable," the medic murmured. "Get him back to the fort …"

"Waste of time," Gareth said. "Someone's bound to have heard that blast. Get them moving before—"

"No," Monica said. "You're coming if I need to carry you myself."

She expected him to argue, but he gave a slow nod. "You're right. They don't need this. Not now. Take me back, tell them I'll pull through."

That wasn't what she meant at all, but he had a point. Their best warrior—a man who'd single-handedly annihilated mobs of Others—killed by a simple tripwire bomb? That was a blow to morale they could ill afford.

The medic bound Gareth's chest while the soldiers fashioned a makeshift stretcher from branches and clothes, and they took Gareth back to the fort.

Monica stood on the guard's balcony overlooking the stockade crammed with Others. Prisoners of war. That had been her policy from the start. Leave as many of the enemy alive as possible. Bring them here. Keep them alive and comfortable. Use them as bargaining chips and as proof to the Others that they weren't monsters.

It hadn't mattered. Her missives to the government had gone unanswered, as they always had.

For years, she'd tried to reason with the Others. First to negotiate, then, as their numbers dwindled, to beg for mercy. She understood that they posed a threat. So they'd go away, far from the living.

The Others might as well have been getting letters from a colony of diseased rats. Eventually, she'd realized that was exactly how they saw the Infected—diseased rats that somehow had the power of communication, but rats nonetheless. Subhuman. Dangerous. A threat requiring swift and thorough extermination.

She looked out at the Others and thought of what Gareth had said. The final option. Back when she'd first started arguing for the taking of prisoners, the other commanders had seen the possibilities. Horrified, she'd fought until the option was off the table. Only it wasn't really. It never had been.

She left the guardroom and walked through the fort. She passed the rooms of soldiers playing card games, of civilians mending clothing and preparing meals, of children listening to stories at the feet of the old ones. Everywhere she looked, people were carrying on, hiding their fear, laughing and talking, just trying to live.

Just trying to live. That's all they'd ever asked for, and that was all she ever wanted for them. So how far was she willing to go? Not to save them—she wasn't sure that was even possible anymore—but to give them every possible chance for survival.

How far would she go? As far as she could.

Three days later, she was back on the balcony overlooking the stockade. Gareth was beside her.

"I need to be there," he'd said. "They need to see me standing there."

So the doctors had done what they could, binding him up, and she'd done what she could, washing away the worst of the stink of rot that had set in. They'd cleared the hall and carried him on a stretcher to the stockade door. He'd taken it from there, finding the strength to walk up to the guard post. He stood in front of a pillar and she knew he leaned against it, but to those below, their champion was back on his feet. And, now, with this new hope she'd given them, so were they.

Once again, she looked out over the men and women packed into the room below. Only this time, they looked back at her. More than one hundred and fifty trained soldiers on their feet, watching her.

In those faces, she saw fear and uncertainty. She saw hate, too, but less of that, surprisingly less.

Guards ringed the room. Civilians walked up and down the aisles with trays of meat. Cooked meat because, for now, that would make them comfortable. They gave the hostages as much as they wanted. That would help. So, too, would the doctors slipping along, silent as wraiths, watching for signs of trouble, others in the back room, dosing the meat with mild sedatives.

The transition had gone smoother than she'd expected. The doctors assured her it would, but she'd seen one too many hellish deaths and rebirths to truly believe them. They were right, though. After all these years, the virus had mutated, ensuring its own survival by making the process faster, less traumatic. One shot of the virus. Then a death-inducing dose of sedative. Within a day … rebirth. And now, two days later, an army to command.

She started her speech with a history lesson. How the Others had driven them to this place. How they'd fought the sporadic incursions, killing only those they could not capture. How they'd treated the prisoners of war humanely. Every man and woman there could attest to that. But now, with the wolves at their door, refusing to negotiate, they'd been forced to do the unthinkable.

"We need soldiers to fight," she said, her voice ringing through the stockade. "Right now, I'm sure you don't feel much like helping us. But you won't be fighting for us, you'll be fighting for yourselves. You are us now. You are Infected. Every one of you is now free to walk out our front gates. But you won't. Because you know they won't let you. Your brothers-in-arms, your friends, your families—every one of them would lop off your head if you walked into that camp because you are no longer human. You are Infected."

She paused to let her words sink in. Behind her, Gareth shifted, struggling to stay on his feet. She glanced at him. He smiled and whispered that she was doing fine.

She turned back to the troops. "To everyone you left behind, you are now dead. Do you feel dead?"

They shuffled, the sound crossing the stockade in a wave.

"To everyone you left behind, you are now a monster. Do you feel like a monster?"

More shuffling, sporadic grunts.

"To everyone you left behind, you have no right to live."

Another glance at Gareth. He stood straighter, chin lifting. He was dying. They all were and this was how they had to face it: stand tall and refuse to let Death win so easily. They'd cheated it before. Now they had to cheat it again.

She turned back to the crowd below. "Do you want to live?" She paused. "Are you willing to *fight* to live?"

The answer came softly at first, her own troops calling back. Gradually, more voices joined them, the new soldiers joining in, their shouts boosting the confidence of the others until the cry ran through the fort.

Gareth moved up behind her, his fingers sliding around her waist, his touch ice-cold now.

"You gave them hope," he said. "You gave them a chance."

She nodded. It wasn't much, but it was the best she could do. Maybe, just maybe, it would be enough.

THE THOUGHT WAR

By Paul McAuley

Paul McAuley is a winner of the John W. Campbell Memorial Award, the Arthur C. Clarke Award, the Philip K. Dick Award, the British Fantasy Award, and the Sidewise Award. His most recent novels are *Gardens of the Sun* and *The Quiet War*. Earlier work includes the award-winning novel *Fairyland*, *White Devils*, *Four Hundred Billion Stars*, *Mind's Eye*, and *The Secret of Life*, to name a few. His short fiction has appeared in a wide variety of magazines and anthologies, including *Asimov's Science Fiction*, *The Magazine of Fantasy & Science Fiction*, *Interzone*, *Postscripts*, and has been reprinted on numerous occasions in best-of-the-year annuals.

In Alan Moore's legendary graphic novel *Watchmen*, scientists watch in horror as one of their colleagues is accidentally obliterated by a piece of high-powered lab equipment. But as a result, the victim transcends material existence and obtains godlike powers. Later he reconstitutes his physical body, first as a walking circulatory system, then later adding bone, muscle, and finally flesh. Zombies are typically missing a lot of their skin and we can see right through to their innards. But what if, as with *Watchmen*'s Dr. Manhattan, they are in the process not of decomposing but *coalescing*? And what if, as the process continues, it becomes harder and harder to tell who's human and who isn't?

This sort of paranoia has inspired a lot of great science fiction, from *Invasion of the Body Snatchers* to the Philip K. Dick-inspired film *Blade Runner*, in which human-seeming replicants can only be identified by subtle variations in their emotional responses. In John Carpenter's *The Thing* (based on a short story by John W. Campbell), a research team at a remote arctic compound realizes that some of them have been replaced by shapeshifting aliens, and the only way to know for sure who's human is to jam a hot wire into samples of their blood and see if the blood tries to crawl away.

Our next story takes some of these notions and runs with them. But these zombies aren't just out to eat your brains. They've got something bigger in mind. Much bigger.

Listen:

Don't try to speak. Don't try to move. Listen to me. Listen to my story.

Everyone remembers their first time. The first time they saw a zombie and knew it for what it was. But my first time was one of the first times ever. It was so early in the invasion that I wasn't sure what was happening. So early we didn't yet call them zombies.

It was in the churchyard of St Pancras Old Church, in the fabulous, long lost city of London. Oh, it's still there, more or less; it's one of the few big cities that didn't get hit in the last, crazy days of global spasm. But it's lost to us now because it belongs to them.

Anyway, St Pancras Old Church was one of the oldest sites of Christian worship in Europe. There'd been a church there, in one form or another, for one and a half thousand years; and although the railway lines to St Pancras station ran hard by its north side it was an isolated and slightly spooky place, full of history and romance. Mary Wollstonecraft Godwin was buried there, and it was at her graveside that her daughter, who later wrote *Frankenstein*, first confessed her love to the poet Shelley, and he to her. In his first career as an architect's assistant, the novelist Thomas Hardy supervised the removal of bodies when the railway was run through part of the churchyard, and set some of the displaced gravestones around an ash tree that was later named after him.

I lived nearby. I was a freelance science journalist then, and when I was working at home and the weather was good I often ate my lunch in the churchyard. That's where I was when I saw my first zombie.

I can see that you don't understand much of this. It's all right. You are young. Things had already changed when you were born and much that was known then is unknowable now. But I'm trying to set a mood. An emotional tone. Because it's how you respond to the mood and emotions of my story that's important. That's why you have to listen carefully. That's why you are gagged and bound, and wired to my machines.

Listen:

It was a hot day in June in that ancient and hallowed ground. I was sitting on a bench in the sun-dappled shade of Hardy's ash tree and eating an egg-and-cress sandwich and thinking about the article I was writing on cosmic rays when I saw him. It looked like a man, anyway. A ragged man in a long black raincoat, ropy hair down around his face as he limped towards me with a slow and stiff gait. Halting and raising his head and looking all around, and then shambling on, the tail of his black coat dragging behind.

I didn't pay much attention to him at first. I thought he was a vagrant. We are all of us vagrants now, but in the long ago most of us had homes and families and only the most unfortunate, slaves to drink or drugs, lost souls brought down by misfortune or madness, lived on the streets. Vagrants were drawn to churchyards by the quietness and sense of ancient sanctuary, and there was a hospital at the west end of the churchyard of Old St Pancras where they went to fill their prescriptions and get treatment for illness or injury. So he wasn't an unusual sight, shambling beneath the trees in a slow and wavering march past Mary Godwin's grave towards Hardy's ash and the little church.

Then a dog began to bark. A woman with several dogs on leads and several more trotting freely called to the little wire-haired terrier that was dancing around the vagrant in a fury of excitement. Two more dogs ran up to him and began to bark too, their coats bristling and ears laid flat. I saw the vagrant stop and shake back the ropes from his face and look all around, and for the first time I saw his face.

It was dead white and broken. Like a vase shattered and badly mended. My first thought was that he'd been in a bad accident, something involving glass or industrial acids. Then I saw that what I had thought were ropes of matted hair were writhing with slow and awful independence like the tentacles of a sea creature; saw that the tattered raincoat wasn't a garment. It was his skin, falling stiff and black around him like the wings of a bat.

The dog woman started screaming. She'd had a clear look at the vagrant too. Her dogs pranced and howled and whined and barked. I was on my feet. So were the handful of other people who'd been spending a lazy lunch hour in the warm and shady churchyard. One of them must have had the presence of mind to call the police, because almost at once, or so it seemed, there was the wail of a siren and a prickle of blue lights beyond the churchyard fence and two policemen in yellow stab vests came running.

They stopped as soon as they saw the vagrant. One talked into the radio clipped to his vest; the other began to round everyone up and lead us to the edge of the churchyard. And all the while the vagrant stood at the centre of a seething circle of maddened dogs, looking about, clubbed hands held out in a gesture of supplication. A hole yawned redly in his broken white face and shaped hoarse and wordless sounds of distress.

More police came. The road outside the churchyard was blocked off. A helicopter clattered above the tops of the trees. The men in hazmat suits entered the park. One of them carried a rifle. By this time everyone who had been in the park was penned against a police van. The police wouldn't answer our questions and we were speculating in a fairly calm and English way about terrorism. That was the great fear, in the long ago. Ordinary men moving amongst us, armed with explosives and hateful certainty.

We all started when we heard the first shot. The chorus of barks doubled, redoubled. A dog ran pell-mell out of the churchyard gate and a marksman shot it there in the road and the woman who still held the leashes of several dogs cried out. Men in hazmat suits separated us and made us walk one by one through a shower frame they'd assembled on the pavement and made us climb one by one in our wet and stinking clothes into cages in the backs of police vans.

I was in quarantine for a hundred days. When I was released, the world had changed forever. I had watched it change on TV and now I was out in it. Soldiers everywhere on the streets. Security checks and sirens and a constant low-level dread. Lynch mobs. Public hangings and burnings. Ten or twenty on-the-spot executions in London alone, each and every day. Quarantined areas cleared and barricaded. Invaders everywhere.

By now, everyone was calling them zombies. We knew that they weren't our own dead come back to walk the Earth, of course, but that's what they most looked like. More and more of them were appearing at random everywhere in the world, and they were growing more and more like us. The first zombies had been only approximations. Barely human in appearance, with a brain and lungs and a heart but little else by way of internal organs, only slabs of muscle that stored enough electrical energy to keep them alive for a day or so. But they were changing. Evolving. Adapting. After only a hundred days, they were almost human. The first had seemed monstrous and pitiful. Now, they looked like dead men walking. Animated showroom dummies. Almost human, but not quite.

After I was released from quarantine, I went back to my trade. Interviewing scientists about the invasion, writing articles. There were dozens of theories, but no real evidence to support any of them. The most popular was that we had been targeted for invasion by aliens from some far star. That the zombies were like the robot probes we had dispatched to other planets and moons in the Solar System, growing ever more sophisticated as they sent back information to their controllers. It made a kind of sense, although it didn't explain why, although they had plainly identified us as the dominant species, their controllers didn't try to contact us. Experiments of varying degrees of cruelty showed that the zombies were intelligent and self-aware, yet they ignored us unless we tried to harm or kill them. Otherwise they simply walked amongst us, and no matter how many were detected and destroyed, there were always more of them.

The most unsettling news came from an old and distinguished physicist, a Nobel laureate, who told me that certain of the fundamental physical constants seemed to be slowly and continuously changing. He had been trying to convey the urgent importance of this to the government but as I discovered when I tried to use my contacts to bring his findings to the attention of ministers and members of parliament and civil servants, the government was too busy dealing with the invasion and the consequences of the invasion.

There was an old and hopeful lie that an alien invasion would cause the nations of Earth to set aside their differences and unite against the common enemy. It didn't happen. Instead, global paranoia and suspicion ratcheted up daily. The zombies were archetypal invaders from within. Hatreds and prejudices that once had been cloaked in diplomatic evasions were now nakedly expressed. Several countries used the invasion as an excuse to attack troublesome minorities or to accuse old enemies of complicity with the zombies. There were genocidal massacres and brush fire wars across the globe. Iran attacked Iraq and Israel with nuclear weapons and what was left of Israel wiped out the capital cities of its neighbours. India attacked Pakistan. China and Russia fought along their long border. The United States invaded Cuba and Venezuela, tried to close its borders with Canada and Mexico, and took sides with China against Russia. And so on, and so on. The zombies didn't have to do anything to destroy us. We were tearing ourselves apart. We grew weaker as we fought each other and the zombies grew stronger by default.

In Britain, everyone under thirty was called up for service in the armed forces. And then everyone under forty was called up too. Three years after my first encounter, I found myself in a troop ship at the tail end of a convoy wallowing through the Bay of Biscay towards the Mediterranean. Huge columns of zombies were straggling out of the Sahara Desert. We were supposed to stop them. Slaughter them. But as we approached the Straits of Gibraltar, someone, it was never clear who, dropped a string of nuclear bombs on zombies massing in Algeria, Tunisia, Libya, and Egypt. On our ships, we saw the flashes of the bombs light the horizon. An hour later we were attacked by the remnants of the Libyan and Egyptian air forces. Half our fleet were sunk; the rest limped home. Britain's government was still intact, more or less, but everyone was in the armed forces now. Defending ourselves from the zombies and from waves of increasingly desperate refugees from the continent. There was a year without summer. Snow in July. Crops failed and despite rationing millions died of starvation and cold. There were biblical plagues of insects and all the old sicknesses came back.

And still the zombies kept appearing.

They looked entirely human now, but it was easy to tell what they were because they weren't starving, or haunted, or mad.

We kept killing them and they kept coming.

They took our cities from us and we fled into the countryside and regrouped and they came after us and we broke into smaller groups and still they came after us.

We tore ourselves apart trying to destroy them. Yet we still didn't understand them. We didn't know where they were coming from, what they were, what they wanted. We grew weaker as they grew stronger.

Do you understand me? I think that you do. Your pulse rate and pupil dilation and skin conductivity all show peaks at the key points of my story. That's good. That means you might be human.

Listen:

Let me tell you what the distinguished old physicist told me. Let me tell you about the observer effect and Boltzmann brains.

In the nineteenth century, the Austrian physicist Ludwig Boltzmann developed the idea that the universe could have arisen from a random thermal fluctuation. Like a flame popping into existence. An explosion from nowhere. Much later, other physicists suggested that similar random fluctuations could give rise to anything imaginable, including conscious entities in any shape or form: Boltzmann brains. It was one of those contra-intuitive and mostly theoretical ideas that helped cosmologists shape their models of the universe, and how we fit into it. It helped to explain why the universe was hospitable to the inhabitants of an undistinguished planet of an average star in a not very special galaxy in a group of a million such, and that group of galaxies one of millions more. We are typical. Ordinary. And because we are ordinary, our universe is ordinary too, because there is no objective reality beyond that which we observe. Because, according to quantum entanglement, pairs of particles share information about each other's quantum states even when distance and timing means that no signal can pass between them. Because observation is not passive. Because our measurements influence the fundamental laws of the universe. They create reality.

But suppose other observers outnumbered us? What would happen then?

The probability of even one Boltzmann brain appearing in the fourteen billion years of the universe's history is vanishingly small. But perhaps something changed the local quantum field and made it more hospitable to them. Perhaps the density of our own consciousness attracted them, as the mass of a star changes the gravitational field and attracts passing comets. Or perhaps the inhabitants of another universe are interfering with our universe. Perhaps the zombies are their avatars: Boltzmann brains that pop out of the energy field and change our universe to suit their masters simply because they think differently and see things differently.

This was what the old physicist told me, in the long ago. He had evidence, too. Simple experiments that measured slow and continuous changes in the position of the absorption lines of calcium and helium and hydrogen in the sun's spectrum, in standards of mass and distance, and in the speed of light. He believed that the fundamental fabric of the universe was being altered by the presence of the zombies, and that those changes were reaching back into the past and forward into the future, just as a pebble dropped into a pond will send ripples spreading out to either side. Every time he checked the historical records of the positions of those absorption lines, they agreed with his contemporaneous measurements, even though those measurements were continuously changing. We are no longer what we once were, but we are not aware of having changed because our memories have been changed too.

Do you see why this story is important? It is not just a matter of my survival, or even the survival of the human species. It is a matter of the survival of the entire known universe. The zombies have already taken so much from us. The few spies and scouts who have successfully mingled with them and escaped to tell the tale say that they are demolishing and rebuilding our cities. Day and night they ebb and flow through the streets in tidal masses, like army ants or swarming bees, under the flickering auroras of strange energies. They are as unknowable to us as we are to them.

Listen:

This is still our world. That it is still comprehensible to us, that we can still survive in it, suggests that the zombies have not yet won an outright victory. It suggests that the tide can be turned. We have become vagrants scattered across the face of the Earth, and now we must come together and go forward together. But the zombies have become so like us that we can't trust any stranger. We can't trust someone like you, who stumbled out of the wilderness into our sanctuary. That's why you must endure this test. Like mantids or spiders, we must stage fearful courtship rituals before we can accept strangers as our own.

I want you to survive this. I really do. There are not many of us left and you are young. You can have many children. Many little observers.

Listen:

This world can be ours again. It has been many years since the war, and its old beauty is returning. Now that civilisation has been shattered, it has become like Eden again. Tell me: Is a world as wild and clean and beautiful as this not worth saving? Was the sky never so green, or grass never so blue?

DATING IN DEAD WORLD

By Joe McKinney

Joe McKinney's latest novel, *Quarantined*, was a finalist for the 2009 Bram Stoker Award. His first book, a zombie novel called *Dead City*, was recently reissued, and a sequel, *Apocalypse of the Dead*, will be published in October. A third entry in the series, *The Zombie King*, will appear in 2011. McKinney's short fiction has appeared in the zombie anthology *History Is Dead*, and a zombie anthology he co-edited, *Dead Set*, was published earlier this year. When not writing fiction, McKinney works as a Homicide Detective for the San Antonio Police Department.

Dating is hard, and that's under the best of circumstances. Throw in a few unusual complications, and going out on a date can quickly turn into the stuff of nightmares. In the movie *50 First Dates*, Adam Sandler attempts to woo Drew Barrymore, only to discover that she's afflicted by a rare condition that causes her to forget they've ever met every time she falls asleep. In *There's Something About Mary*, Ben Stiller goes to pick up Cameron Diaz for the prom, only to suffer a horrifying mishap involving a zipper. But at least those guys never had to deal with the situation presented in our next story.

The author says, "After I finish a novel, I'm usually struck by a sort of separation anxiety. So much mental effort is put into worldbuilding and getting to know the characters. So what I usually do is write a few short stories set in the world of the novel I've just finished. 'Dating in Dead World' was a part of that process." He adds, "Right before I left for my first date, my dad gave me the only bit of parental sex education I ever received. He said, 'Remember this, you will be held personally accountable for everything that happens to that girl from the moment she leaves her front door to the moment she walks back in it. Conduct yourself accordingly.' It wasn't until after I'd written this story that I realized I was channeling that advice. I guess it took."

Heather Ashcroft told me to come to the main entrance of her father's compound. She said the guards there would know my name; they'd be expecting me.

They were expecting me all right.

Four of them had their machine guns trained on me while a voice on a PA speaker barked orders.

"Turn off your motorcycle and dismount." The voice was clear, sharp, professional.

I did what I was told.

"Step forward. Stand on the red square."

I did that too.

"Stand still for the dogs."

Three big black German shepherds were led out of the guard shack and began circling me, sniffing me. Cadaver dogs, trained to sniff out necrotic tissue. No surprise there. Even the smaller compounds use them, and the one I was about to enter was no minor league operation. Dave Ashcroft controls the largest baronage in South Texas, and his security is top notch.

"I'm Andrew Hudson," I said. "I'm here to see Heather Ashcroft. We're going out on—"

Somebody called off the dogs and two of the guards came forward. One of them used the barrel of his weapon to point me towards a table next to the guard shack.

"Stand on that green square. Face the table."

"You fellas sure put a guy through a lot of trouble for a first date," I said. I gave him a winning grin. He wasn't impressed.

"Move," he said.

He asked me what weapons I was carrying and I told him.

"Put them in there," he said, and pointed to a red plastic box on the corner of the table.

"I'm gonna get those back, right?"

He ran a metal detector over my body, taking extra care to get up inside the flaps of my denim jacket, under my hair, up into my crotch.

A guard field-stripped my weapons.

"I am gonna get those back, right?"

"When you come out," he said. "Nobody's allowed to be armed around Mr. Ashcroft."

"But I'm not here to see Mr. Ashcroft," I said. "I'm taking his daughter out for a date."

He rattled a smaller box. "Ammunition, too."

I unloaded my pockets. There was no need to tell him about the extra magazines in my bike's saddle bags. They were already searching those.

He looked me over again, and I could tell by his face that he didn't see anything but a street urchin from the Zone. "Get in that Jeep over there," he said. "We'll drive you into the compound."

Several machine guns turned my way.

I shrugged and got in.

I hadn't been allowed within the inner perimeter fence on my earlier visits, so what I saw when I did finally get inside took my breath away. Outside the compound, downtown San Antonio was an endless sprawl of vacant, crumbling buildings, lath visible in the walls, no doors in the doorways, every window broken. Everywhere you turned there were ruins and fire damage and rivers of garbage spilling out into the streets. It's been sixteen years since the Fall and the streets are still full of zombies. But inside Ashcroft's compound, life looked like it was starting to make a comeback. He controlled most of the medicines, weapons and fuel that South Texas needed, and it had made him rich enough to carve his own private paradise out of fifteen square blocks of hell.

Sitting in the back of the Jeep, I rode down what had once been Alamo Street and tried not to look like a barefoot barbarian gawking at the wonders of Rome. Ashcroft had preserved a few of the main roads from the old days, and he left a few of the old buildings intact, but he had changed a lot more than he left alone.

Off to my left was what had once been Hemisphere Park. It was farmland now. Beyond that was a huge field where cattle grazed, their backs dappled with the golden copper hues of the setting sun. Men on horseback patrolled the edges of the fields, rifles resting on their shoulders.

Most of the housing was on the other side of the river, off to my right—small cottages, comfortable and clean, a few children playing in a garden under an old woman's watchful eye.

But the crown jewel in Ashcroft's compound was the Fairmount Hotel. He'd turned the ancient four-story building into his private domain. It was flanked on one side by the ruins of the Spanish village of La Villita, the crumbling adobe buildings converted into horse stables. In front of the hotel was a Spanish-style garden fed by a large, circular stone fountain. A fork of the San Antonio River curled around the rear of the hotel, supplying fresh water for the whole compound.

As we pulled to a stop in front of the hotel I said, "Looks like you guys have got room for what, about five, six hundred people here?"

"Do yourself a favor," one of the guards told me, "and don't ask no questions. You ain't gonna be here long enough to worry about it. Now get out of the Jeep."

A few minutes later I was standing in what had once been the hotel's lobby, waiting on Heather, checking the smell of my breath in my palm. I'd cleaned up as best I could, but that wasn't saying much. When you live in the Zone, in the rubble between the compounds, it shows. A lump of coal is still a lump of coal, no matter how much you polish it.

I didn't bother to make small talk with the guard off in the corner, watching me.

Eventually, Heather came down the stairs. I watched her descend, my mouth watering. She was wearing a short denim skirt that showed about a mile of bare leg and a tight black camisole that got my Adam's apple pumping in my throat. Her eyes were gray as smoke, her dark hair pulled back into a ponytail that made her jaw and throat seem delicate as spun glass.

And she was wearing makeup. You never see that anymore. Her lips were so red they actually shined. I couldn't look away, and I'm just glad I didn't start drooling.

She dismissed the guard with a wave.

"Hey," she said to me.

I tried to speak, but my throat had gone dry. "Hey," I said. I couldn't stop looking at her lips. God, how they shined. "You look great," I managed to say.

She blushed.

"They didn't give you any trouble at the gate, did they?"

"No," I said. "Well, maybe a little. No big deal."

"You sure?"

"Really," I said. "No big deal."

She smiled. "My dad wants to see you before we go. You don't mind, do you?"

Mano a Mano with Big Dave Ashcroft. Christ, I thought. "I guess I don't get to say no, do I?"

"Um, not really."

I watched golden rays of light scatter from her hair and said, "Sure, why not?"

She led me back to her father's office.

"Daddy," she said, "this is the boy I told you about."

Dave Ashcroft wasn't the giant I was expecting to meet. You hear stories about these guys, growing up in the Zone, and they're like gods, reshaping the world in their own image. You expect them to be six and a half feet tall, neck like a beer keg, arms like a gorilla's. But Dave Ashcroft, he was just a normal looking guy in a white work shirt and khaki slacks, a donut of gray hair around the back of his head.

He didn't offer to shake my hand. He pointed me to a chair opposite his desk and ordered me to sit without saying a word.

"What kind of name is Andrew Hudson?"

"It's just a name, sir."

"Yeah, but I know it from somewhere."

"My dad, probably."

"Who was your dad?"

"Eddie Hudson. He was a cop in the old days."

He perked up. "You mean the one who wrote that book about the Fall?"

"That's right." I get that bit about my dad from some of the old-timers. Dad wrote a book about the first night of the outbreak, about how he had to fight his way across the city to get to my mom and me. But his book only covered that first night. He left off at a point when it looked like we were actually going to contain the zombie outbreak. Well, he was wrong, obviously, and sometimes the old-timers who remember my dad's book look at me and I think maybe they're remembering what it was like back then, back when it seemed we might win this thing. I think, at least for some of them, the memories make them angry, resentful, like they blame people like my dad for the naiveté that allowed the Second Wave to happen. But there are others who recognize my dad and they tune out, they become distant, like they've gotten over the anger and now they're dealing with something else.

Big Dave Ashcroft—he was one of the ones who just get distant.

"What happened to your dad?" he asked.

"He and mom died in the Second Wave, sir."

"You would have been what, about six when that happened?"

"Yes, sir."

"Did they turn?"

"Mom did. Dad got swarmed trying to stop a bunch of them from breaking into our house. Mom got bit, but she managed to stash me in a hall closet before she turned."

"And you've been on your own ever since, living off the streets?"

"That's right."

"So what do you do now? How do you live?" But I could tell the question he meant to ask was, *How the hell did a Zoner like you meet my daughter?*

"Special deliveries. I take private packages all across the Zone. I've even done some work for you, sir. That's how I met your daughter."

He frowned at that.

"Where do you plan to take my daughter, Andrew?"

"Dinner, sir. And dancing. On the *Starliner*. Out on the lake."

He looked impressed, though I could tell he didn't want to be impressed.

"The *Starliner*'s not cheap," he said. "Special deliveries must pay pretty good."

"Business is fine, sir." I paused, then said, "But that's not really what you're asking, is it?"

He raised an eyebrow and waited.

"Listen," I said. "Heather's a special girl. That's not something you have to tell me. I mean I already know it. I recognize a class act when I see one, and I intend to treat her accordingly."

I'd guessed right. That was exactly what he needed to hear. He knew as well as anybody the dangers waiting for his daughter outside his compound's walls, and he knew he wouldn't be able to keep her from them forever. Sooner or later, with or without his permission, she was going to brave that world. Maybe sending her out with me, somebody who had proven their ability to survive, was his way of hedging his bets.

But whatever his thoughts, he gave his consent. He called in his senior security officer, a slender, bowlegged man named Naylor, and Naylor drove us out to the main gate in an air conditioned utility vehicle. He told the guards to give me back my gear and my motorcycle, and while they were doing that, he pulled Heather aside and gave her a little talk.

After that, to me, Naylor said, "She has a portable radio equipped with a GPS tracker. My people will be monitoring it all night. We'll be close." Then he fixed me with a meaningful glare and said, "All she has to do is call."

The message came through loud and clear.

"I'll try to be on my best behavior," I said.

Heather jumped on the back of my bike and pressed her breasts into my back. I could feel the hard pebbles of her nipples through our clothes. "You better not be on your best behavior," she whispered into my ear. "Now drive fast, Andrew. Get me out of here."

In the days after the Fall, when the necrosis virus emerged from the hurricane-ravaged Texas Gulf Coast and turned the infected into flesh-eating human train wrecks, the old world collapsed, and men like Dave Ashcroft stepped up to fill the power vacuum. They built compounds like the one Heather and I had just left to protect their interests, and everywhere else became a wasteland known as the Zone of Exclusion.

After my parents died, I became one of the fringe people, a Zoner. I was too young to be of any use to the bosses who were just then consolidating their power and building their compounds, and so there weren't any other options open to me.. These days I know the Zone better than most, and what I know I learned the hard way, fighting it out every day with the infected in the ruins of San Antonio.

I survived that way for ten years. Then, right after I turned sixteen, I stole a motorcycle. And before long, I'd worked up a reputation as someone who could get packages delivered anywhere in the Zone.

That's how I met Heather. About two months before our first date I brought her a package from a dying woman out in the Zone. How that woman got the money to pay me I don't know, because I don't come cheap, but she did pay me, in gold, and I made the delivery.

Heather opened the package in front of me and took out a badly worn pink blanket with her name stitched on it. There was a note attached, and she read it four times before she asked me about the woman who sent it.

"She's not doing so hot," I said, which was being charitable. The truth was the effort it took her to tell me what she wanted nearly killed her.

Heather nodded quietly, and then the tears came.

She told me her parents divorced when she was little, before the Fall, and when the world turned upside down, her father took her away because he could protect her better than her mom.

She didn't have many memories of the woman, but from the looks of that blanket, I figured her mom had plenty of memories of her.

Heather gave me a long letter to take back to her mother, and though she could have paid my fee ten times over with what she carried in her pocket, I didn't charge her.

I took the letter to her mother, and because she couldn't see well enough to read, I read it for her. She died a few days later, but I think she was happy during those last few days. Happier than she'd been in years.

Heather and I got close after that, though we had to steal the moments we spent together.

At least we did before tonight.

Now, sitting on the back of my bike, she squeezed my waist and put her lips to my ear. "I love the wind on my face," she said. "Go faster."

Dinner was the best thing I'd ever tasted, roasted mutton with wasabi mashed potatoes and asparagus. To this day I have no idea what the hell wasabi is, or where you get it, but I sure loved the bite it gave those mashed potatoes.

And the scenery was fantastic. The stars dappled on the surface of Canyon Lake. On the shore, the tops of the hills were silvered with moonlight. There was music, a few older couples dancing on the open air deck, glimpses of a world long gone.

The conversation, on the other hand, lagged. At least at first.

I'd never really talked to a girl. Not like you do on a date, anyway. I didn't know what I was supposed to say, how I was supposed to act. She knew little about weapons, or the Zone, and that pretty much exhausted what I knew. She was into growing vegetables and had plans for building schools.

But I told her dad I was going to treat her like a class act, and I did. The thing is, deep down inside, I am, and always will be, a Zoner. Life, as I had known it, was short and mean and cheap, and I spent a lot of time wondering if it was really worth the effort I put into it. When you think that way, it can be hard to look at a girl and think the two of you have a chance at romance.

She asked me if there was anything wrong.

"This world seems kind of pointless, don't you think?" I whispered across the table to Heather as the waiter poured each of us another glass of wine.

"There may not be a point," she said. "But even still, we're here. You and me. That's enough, isn't it?"

Her answer surprised me, the simple practicality of it. "That's true," I said. "Here we are."

After dinner we danced on the open deck of the *Starliner*. A cool, late spring breeze was in the air, carrying with it the thick, marshy smell of lake water. I held her body close to mine, the first time I'd ever held a real girl, and lost myself in the warmth of her green eyes and the smell of her skin.

That feeling, that comfort of absolute privacy, the romance of it, was why the *Starliner* cost so much. The infected were everywhere, and not even the strongest compound was completely safe from them, but when the *Starliner* was off her moorings and out on the lake, it was its own world, untouchable by the harsh realities of the Zone.

But of course there were other dangers in the Zone besides zombies. As the evening drew to a close, and the *Starliner* began her slow cruise back to the wet dock, Heather and I stood on the bow and talked about the future, about the stars, about anything and everything except the past. It was our night, and though our bonds had been forged in the heartaches of the past, we wanted our night together to be about the future. We wanted our own happy memories together.

There were no other boats on the lake. At least there hadn't been during most of our date. But as we rounded a final elbow of land and entered the cove, we saw a large cabin cruiser waiting for us, the vague shapes of men ringing the rails of the deck.

Heather broke off in the middle of a giggle and watched them.

"What is it?" I asked.

"Not good," she said. "I think that's Wayne Nessel. Daddy warned me he might try something. Daddy didn't think he'd do it out here though."

I knew of Wayne Nessel. He was Ashcroft's biggest rival, and a man with a lot of resources at his disposal. People in the Zone called him "The Bull."

"He couldn't know you're here."

"He knows," she said, and then she guided me to the far side of the *Starliner*.

"But how?"

"He's got spies everywhere, Andrew."

She crossed to the opposite side of the deck and climbed the railing.

"Wait a minute," I said. "Where are we going?"

She looked down at me. "Can you swim?"

"Yeah."

"Good." She waited till Nessel's boat lit up the *Starliner* with its spotlights, then she gave me a wink and dropped herself over the edge.

I went in after her.

I thought we'd cling to the side of the boat and wait it out, but that wasn't what Heather had in mind. She went under and kept swimming under the *Starliner*'s hull.

I followed.

Above us, through the green murky haze, I could see the glow of the spotlights and the shimmering outlines of men running on both decks. There were a lot of muffled popping sounds that I took to be gunfire, but none of that was directed down at us. It was all boat to boat.

We surfaced on the far side of Nessel's boat and swam to shore. I'd hidden my motorcycle in the brush next to the *Starliner*'s docks out of habit, and now I was thankful for my instincts. As we swam, we decided it'd be best to come ashore a little ways from the dock, just in case Nessel had men covering his back on land.

We crawled up on shore and Heather pulled her black hair back with both hands, her camisole clinging to the curve of her breasts like wet paint.

There were voices nearby, just on the other side of the bushes. Nessel's men, I thought, left here in reserve.

I spotted them a moment later. Four men, all armed with AR-15s. They were lined up on the dock, looking out at the boats, pointing and laughing.

"Amateurs," I whispered. "Look at that. They're just watching the show."

"Can you get them all?"

"No," I said. "Not all of them. Maybe one or two, but not all of them."

"What do we do?"

The switchback road we'd taken to the docks led a short distance up a steep hill behind us before curving out of sight. Low, scraggly oaks and cedars lined the sides of it. I told Heather to go up around the curve and wait for me.

"What are you going to do?"

"Try not to get shot," I said.

She frowned at that, but she made her way up to the road just the same, careful to stay in the shadows.

When she was safely out of the way, I made my move.

My bike was hidden in a clump of cedar behind an old rusted truck. I crossed behind the guards and made for the bike, praying they didn't turn around.

I got most of the way there before I heard one of them holler something. The next instant, they were firing at me. Little chunks of concrete exploded around my shoes as I made for the truck, but they didn't hit me, and if their lack of attention on the shoreline hadn't convinced me they were just hired goons, their shooting certainly did. At that range, professionals would have killed me with ease.

I got down beneath the truck, pulled my Glock, and waited. They were running up the slope of the lot, straight for me. I steadied my sights on the lead guy and dropped him with my first shot. My next three shots weren't aimed. I just sprayed the crowd to make them duck for cover.

It worked. They dived behind an old boat trailer, giving me enough time to pull my motorcycle out of the bushes, start it, and go racing up the road. They fired after me, but they never got close.

I slowed long enough for Heather to jump on the back, and then we sped off into the night.

We were still wet from the swim, and it was cold on that bike. What had been a lovely cool breeze while we were dancing was now a fierce cold snap, biting through us to the bone. Heather wrapped her arms around my waist and squeezed, and I could feel her body trembling.

I slowed the bike down enough for her to hear me. "Are you okay?"

"Uh huh."

"Why is he after you?" I asked.

"Anything to hurt Daddy," she said, her voice coming in quick, breathy stabs. "His people are always ambushing Daddy's shipments. Maybe he's upping the ante now to kidnapping. Or assassination."

"What do you want to do?" I asked.

"Warn my father," she said. "Daddy told me Nessel always attacks on two fronts at once. If he's coming after me here, he's probably trying to attack Daddy somewhere else too."

"The radio?"

She nodded. "I tried back at the lake. Nobody answered. We'll have to get closer into town and try for my father's safe houses."

"You got it," I said, and laid into the throttle.

When we got closer into town, I pulled off the highway and parked in a lot on the top of a small hill and Heather called Naylor on the radio.

"Are you sure it's Nessel's people?" he asked.

"I'm sure," she said.

He told us not to use the radio any more than we had to. Besides a good share of the gasoline market, Nessel controlled the sale of most of the electronic equipment in the area. The radio Heather was using was probably stolen from one of his shipments, and there wasn't much doubt he'd be able to overhear her transmission.

"Can you get to the pickup point?" he asked.

Heather gave me a sidelong glance and a smile. "I'm pretty sure we can," she said.

We moved out, and as we rode, I thought about this old-timer I used to know who told me what life was like before the outbreak. He said people were pretty much the same then as they are now, and that turning into zombies hadn't changed them much. What was different, he said, was the noise. It was noisy back then. There were cars and planes and trains everywhere, not to mention all the crowds. He said you couldn't escape it.

But these days, there are so few cars left you can drive around all day and never see another driver. Heather and I hadn't seen any all night. I couldn't remember the last time I'd heard a plane fly overhead. I'd never seen a moving train. Life in the Zone was quiet, even though it was rarely peaceful.

That's how I knew something was wrong. Heather and I got up on the highway again and started driving, but we hadn't made it very far before I heard the high-pitched whine of a pack of sport racing bikes.

We glanced around, looking for them. They were behind us, coming down from an overpass and getting onto the freeway at top speed. I didn't need to ask if they were Nessel's men. All of them had machine guns slung over their backs, and the way they were riding, they clearly knew who we were.

I got my bike up to top speed, but they were faster. My bike was just a beat up Harley Sportster, but they were riding Honda CXRs—top of the line racing bikes. I didn't have a snowball's chance of outrunning them in a dead sprint, so when they got close enough to take their shots, I did the only thing I could think of and veered over to the far left lane, let them come up on us, then downshifted and banked the bike hard to the right, taking the connector ramp to the Connelly Loop at almost a hundred miles an hour.

Heather yelled out in surprise. Nessel's men overshot us. I saw them lock up their brakes and slide, but none of them reacted fast enough to take the ramp with us.

Their mistake bought us a few valuable seconds. The Connelly Loop led right into the heart of the Zone. There was nothing in there but crumbling buildings and legions of the infected. As a result, it was a low priority for the bosses who made it their business to keep the roads clear, and so it was still choked with long lines of abandoned cars.

My old-timer friend told me that rush hour traffic used to be so bad the freeways would turn into parking lots, and when it was really bad, you could sit in your car for half an hour or more and never make it more than a couple of miles. Looking out over the abandoned cars ahead of us I felt like I knew what he meant. It was a three-lane bumper-to-bumper junkyard as far as I could see.

As I slowed down to thread the gap between the cars Heather yelled in my ear, "What are you doing? You're going the wrong way."

I looked behind us and saw Nessel's men coming for us. They looked like a squadron of mad hornets buzzing down the ramp, shooting the gaps between wrecks at fantastic speeds.

"Hold on," I said.

A zombie was stumbling along between two rows of cars about a hundred and fifty yards ahead of us. I dug into the throttle and went straight for him, darting

through the narrow gap, feeling a *thump thump thump* echoing in my ears as we passed all the cars.

Zombies are predictable. When they see you, they stumble after you. They don't care if you're on foot or driving a truck, they stumble after you just the same, which is exactly what the zombie ahead of us was doing.

And about ten yards ahead of the zombie was a gap in traffic. It looked like a driver in the middle lane had tried to turn into the lane to his right, and had hit another car in the process. The car was stuck at a forty-five-degree angle, with just enough room for me to slip alongside it and cross over to the gap between the middle and right lanes. But I had to time it just right. I had to get there just a fraction of a second before the zombie if I was going to make it work.

It was close.

When I got to the gap I hit the brakes, rocked the bike hard to the right, then hard to the left, feeling Heather gasping as she squeezed me. We threaded into the opening and took off at full speed.

I looked back just as one of Nessel's goons hit that zombie. He must have been doing at least ninety miles per hour when he realized what was happening and hit his brakes. But at that speed, not even the Honda's oversized racing brakes could help him. He hit the zombie, and both bodies went tumbling over the wrecked cars. The bike went sideways, hit the trunk of a car, and shot twenty feet up in the air, spinning end over end the whole way back to the ground.

That slowed the other three down, but not by much, and I knew I couldn't play those games forever. I took us up another hundred yards or so until we came to a small box van. There I slowed, turned the bike around, and headed back the way we'd come.

"What are you doing?" Heather said.

But I didn't have time to answer. I ducked my head and charged.

One of the remaining three riders was in our gap, and even though he was wearing a full helmet and face shield that kept his face hidden, I could tell by the way his body stiffened that his eyes were going wide.

I pulled my Glock and fired. I'm not sure if I hit him or not, but the bike shimmied beneath him, he lost his balance, glanced off a car, and crashed out.

I saw his head smack a bumper as he fell.

I stopped the bike and told Heather to get off. She looked panicked, but she did like I asked.

"What are you going to do?"

I pulled out my other Glock. "Just stay down, okay? I got this."

Those huge green eyes of hers melted me.

"We're going to be okay," I said.

She nodded, and I moved out on foot. The other two riders were going slow now, practically walking their bikes through the cars, looking for us. I crouched down below the top of the cars and jogged into position. When the rider I was targeting got close enough, I stood up and fired both Glocks into his chest, knocking him backwards off the bike.

The other rider tried to react, but he was stuck between two pickups. I threw a lot of ammunition at him with both guns and managed to catch a lucky shot. He spun around, hit in the shoulder, and went down.

I ran over to where he fell and saw him rolling on the pavement, wounded. He pushed off his helmet and let it tumble away. He looked up at me, his eyes pleading with me. Most of the time my moral compass swings closer to the good than the bad, but some people just aren't worth the effort.

I shot him in the head.

When I got back to Heather, she was holding that portable radio in her hands and crying.

"What's wrong?" I asked her.

"Daddy was right about Nessel," she said. "The bastard used me as a decoy."

"What do you mean?"

"Daddy sent a squad of his best men to the safe house where we were supposed to go." She looked up at me and choked back tears. "Nessel was waiting for them. They're all dead. Now he's attacking the compound."

"Oh Jesus."

"He said for us to stay away." She looked deep into my eyes. "But my God, Andrew. It sounded so bad. I heard explosions. And Daddy was screaming at people while he was talking with me."

I had no idea what to say. She told me while we were dancing that she had begged her father for a week to let her go out on a date with me, and now his empire was in serious risk of crumbling and it was all because of our date.

I was feeling lousy, because I knew the role I played in wrecking her family, but then she surprised me.

"Andrew," she said. "You were telling me the truth about my mom, weren't you? You really did read her my letter?"

I nodded.

"You worked a miracle bringing her back into my life."

I shook my head.

"You did," she said. "I believe that. And I believe you can do it again. I believe you can give me my father back."

I felt confused. "What are you asking me to do?"

"Help me save my father, Andrew. Please."

She turned those big green eyes up at me, a tear welling up and running down her face, and in that moment, I knew I was powerless to refuse. I'd have handed her my soul for the asking.

"Let's go get your dad," I said.

I started toward the main gate because that was the only way into Ashcroft's compound that I knew of, but when Heather saw where I was going she pointed me in a different direction.

She had me go to the west side of the compound and drive into a crumbling building that looked like it had been a bakery before the outbreak. It was the corner shop in a block-long strip mall. She told me to stop, got off the bike, opened a door that had been made to look like it was rusted shut, and ushered me into a freshly painted white corridor.

"This leads right into the compound," she said.

I nodded, impressed. Concealed doors and hidden tunnels were the kind of thing you'd expect from a powerful boss like Ashcroft, but it was still weird to actually see it in real life. That kind of engineering was way beyond what most bosses were capable of.

We took the motorcycle all the way to the end of the corridor, where we were met by guards who took us to see Ashcroft.

Ashcroft and Naylor were watching the battle from the third floor of the Fairmount. Nessel had focused his troops around the main gate, but they were hitting the wall of flattened cars in a couple of different places, forcing Ashcroft's troops to divide up their strength.

Heather and I stood back a little, listening, as Naylor relayed updates of the battle he was receiving over the radio to Ashcroft.

The outer perimeter of Ashcroft's compound was made up of smashed and stacked cars. Nessel's men had used rocket-propelled grenades against that wall and it had partially collapsed in two places. A large group of Ashcroft's men were boxed in near the gate, fighting a close-quarters battle in the rubble left from the explosions, and Nessel's superior numbers were starting to wear them down.

Ashcroft surveyed the scene with night-vision goggles. "Pull them back, Naylor," he said. "Tell them to regroup around the courtyard."

Ashcroft's troops began falling back. Heather reached over and touched my hand as the soldiers ran back toward the hotel. I looked over at her and saw she was holding her breath.

Just then another blast from a rocket grenade lit up the night, and when the smoke settled, we saw there was a huge hole in the wall.

Naylor was watching the space beyond the wall. "Something's happening," he said. "They're bringing up buses."

"Buses?" Ashcroft said. He focused his binoculars on the hole. "My God," he gasped.

Two yellow school buses broke through the burning debris that had once been the wall of flattened cars and rolled to a stop not far from Ashcroft's retreating troops. Some of the men stopped to fire at the bodies getting off the buses, but took off running again when they realized they were the infected.

"That is fucking brilliant," Ashcroft said, impressed despite himself. "Using the infected like that. I didn't think Nessel had it in him."

"Problem, sir," Naylor said.

Ashcroft smirked. "What now?"

"There, sir. To the right of the main gate. See him?"

I followed Naylor's finger to a high point on the wall. There was a man crawling to the top of it, but he was too far away for me to see what he was doing.

"Sniper," Ashcroft said. And then, one at a time, Ashcroft's retreating troops started to fall, the only clue as to why were the bright muzzle flashes of the sniper's rifle.

In the confusion, Ashcroft's men didn't know which way to run.

"They're getting slaughtered out there," Ashcroft said. "Get some of your men back up to the front and take that sniper out."

Naylor said, "I don't have anybody, sir. Prescott is the only officer I have left, and he's coordinating the retreat."

Ashcroft said nothing. He gripped the railing and stared down at the battlefield.

"Mr. Ashcroft," I said.

"What?" he growled.

"I can get him, sir."

"Just stand still and shut up," he said.

For the second time that night I met his gaze and didn't look away.

It looked like his first instinct was to throw me over the railing, but then he stopped himself. "Okay," he said. "You want to do it, go ahead."

I turned to go.

Heather followed me.

"Andrew, wait." She said, "You're not serious? You can't go."

I nodded in her father's direction. "Heather, do you really think he'd ever let us be together if I don't do this? He'll always have it in the back of his mind that this happened because of me. But I can change that if I do this."

"Don't be stupid, Andrew. He's got people to deal with this."

"I'll be all right," I said. "I promise."

"God, I hope you're right," she said.

"Yeah, me too."

The battle had reached the courtyard right in front of the hotel. Ashcroft's men had taken up defensive positions behind the fountain and the rows of small garden walls leading up to the front doors. Nessel's men were still moving into position, using the infected as a moving barrier.

That sniper was the key to the battle. From his position he was picking off Ashcroft's men no matter how well-hidden they were, and it was only a matter of time before he got so many of them that there wouldn't be enough of them left to put up a fight.

I moved out across the right flank of the battle and headed for a ditch that ran through the cow pasture. I figured as long as I stayed inside it I'd be able to make it all the way to the wall of cars. I had no idea what I was going to do from there, though.

I got most of the way across the yard before I saw a small group of the infected wandering on the fringes of the battle. I was so intent on reaching the wall that I didn't even notice them until I was right on top of them, and by then it was too late. I jumped out of the ditch and ran for it.

The infected followed me.

I veered right and ran along the inside of the wall until I got to a section where rocket grenades had blown it apart. I jumped over the debris and landed outside the wall—right in front of a military-style Humvee where Nessel and two of his lieutenants were watching the battle unfold.

I wasn't wearing one of Ashcroft's uniforms, so they didn't know what to make of me for a second. I might have been a civilian, or even one of their own hired goons. That hesitation saved me. With the infected hot on my heels, I drew both Glocks and ran straight for Nessel, firing the whole way.

I wasn't aiming, just spraying and praying, but I got one lucky shot and hit Nessel's driver in the head. He went down onto the hood of the Humvee. The other lieutenant tried to break and run, but he got caught by the infected and went down screaming.

That left Nessel.

He fell over the back of the Humvee and landed face first in the grass. Before he had a chance to get up I shot him three times, once in the neck and twice in the chest. With Nessel dead, I turned to face the infected. There were eight of them, and using the Humvee for cover, I used up the last of my ammunition on them. That left me with nothing but my machete to fight the sniper.

I started to climb up the wall of flattened cars as quietly as I could. I heard him up there, popping off shots every few seconds with a bolt-action rifle. Maybe, if I'm lucky, I thought, he'd be so into his shooting rhythm that he wouldn't hear me coming.

But that was just wishful thinking. I made it most of the way to the top when I heard something moving below me. It was one of the infected, and he was coming up after me. He made a gurgling, moaning sound as he bumped and clanged his way up the side, and I knew he was making enough noise that the sniper would be able to hear him even over the sound of his rifle.

I was stuck.

I couldn't go up, because I would lose the element of surprise and probably get killed, and I couldn't go down, either. But there was a little gap between two of the cars on the top row, and I ducked into that, facing outwards. I waited to see who would get to me first, the sniper or the zombie.

It was the sniper. He poked his head over the side, his face barely a foot above my waiting hands. I reached up, grabbed him by the back of the head, and yanked down as hard as I could. He came down the side of the wall like a snowball going downhill, picking up lose car parts as he hit the sides, trying to hold on, only to keep tumbling downward, right into the waiting arms of the zombie below us. The two of them hit hard, and both ended up on the ground.

I didn't waste any time. I jumped over the top and picked up the sniper's rifle. The sniper was fighting the zombie barehanded, and doing pretty well, until I shot them both.

Then I took up the sniper's post. I looked through the scope and watched the battle taking place around the fountain. Ashcroft's men, who had a reputation as the best private army in the Zone, were earning their stripes. I saw at least fifty of Nessel's soldiers dead in the courtyard, and it looked like their advance was starting to break apart. Despite their numerical superiority, they just weren't as well-disciplined, or as well-trained, as Ashcroft's troops.

Ashcroft himself was leading the fight now. I saw him waving a machine gun over his head, yelling at his men to hold their positions.

I went to work on Nessel's men, and as I started putting them down, one by one, I swept the scope across Ashcroft's position. He stopped yelling long enough to look my way. All at once he realized it was me doing the firing now, and he gave me an exaggerated overhand salute.

The tide of the battle turned, and soon Nessel's men broke ranks and ran. Ashcroft followed up their retreat, and his men carved the retreating enemy up into pockets, showing no mercy.

Gradually, the steady, thunderous roll of the battle faded, and all that was left was the occasional sporadic popping of small arms fire. Ashcroft's men were still dealing with the infected, but those too were getting mopped up.

I could see the mood among Ashcroft's men changing. They had won big, and now they knew it.

With nothing left to shoot at, I got down from the wall and went over to where I'd left Nessel to die. I tossed his body onto the hood of the Humvee and drove straight through the gates to the hotel.

I parked in front of the fountain.

Ashcroft's men stopped their celebrations to watch me, and Ashcroft himself came over to see what was going on. He took one look at Nessel's body and whistled. Then he looked at me and smiled.

Behind him, coming out of the hotel at a run, was Heather. She ran right past her father and straight into my arms.

Ashcroft came over to us. "You did real good," he said, and offered me his hand.

"Thank you, sir."

"I owe you big, Andrew."

I shrugged.

In the background I heard Naylor giving orders to the men to start damage control. After he got the men moving, he came back to Ashcroft and gave a report. Ashcroft listened in silence, nodding his head, and when Naylor was finished, he gave him some more orders to relay to the troops.

Then he turned to me and said, "Andrew, it looks like we've got a lot of rebuilding to do." He glanced down at Nessel. "And I seem to have inherited several new businesses. I'm going to need some good men to help me run them. You interested in a job?"

Heather was smiling.

"Uh, a job would be great," I said.

"I heard a 'but' in there."

"Well," I said, "what I really want is a second date with your daughter."

FLOTSAM & JETSAM

By Carrie Ryan

Carrie Ryan's first novel *The Forest of Hands and Teeth* debuted to great acclaim when it was released in 2009. The sequel, *The Dead-Tossed Waves*, came out earlier this year, and the third volume, *The Dark and Hollow Places*, is due out in Spring 2011. Our next story shares the same milieu as her novels, but takes place several hundred years earlier. Another piece of Ryan's zombie fiction appears in the anthology *Zombies vs. Unicorns*. Her love of zombies is all her fiancé JP's fault. Since becoming infected with the zombie bug, she has begun converting her friends and family to her cause, much like a zombie would.

In *Poetics*, Aristotle recommends that storytellers observe a unity of time (no large jumps forward in time), place (one location), and action (few or no subplots). Well, things don't get much more unified than a couple of characters on a lifeboat. Hitchcock used this scenario to great effect in his World War II-era film *Lifeboat*, in which the survivors begin to suspect that one of them is a German agent. Gary Larson, author of the beloved newspaper comic *The Far Side*, repeatedly used gags involving lifeboats. (In one such strip, three men and a dog draw lots to see which of them will be eaten—the dog comes up a winner, and looks suitably smug.)

Our next tale also utilizes the grim immediacy and forced intimacy of a lifeboat scenario. "My original idea for this story was to have infection break out on an airplane, which caused airports to constantly divert it," Ryan says. "As I thought more about the idea, I wanted to simplify it and boil it down. I was out to dinner with friends and talking about my idea, and my fiancé suggested using a boat instead. I'd been doing a lot of research into *The Rime of the Ancient Mariner* for another project so the first line was obvious, and the entire story unfolded from there. I love using zombies in my fiction because it allows me to ask what differentiates the living from the dead. How do we determine our own lives and futures beyond mindlessly doing what someone tells us?"

"Water, water everywhere, and—"

"Damn it, Jeremy! If you say that one more time..." It's when I see his face fall that I swallow the rest of what I'm going to say. But the unspoken words circle my head, the rage stinging just under my skin. Honestly, I'd love nothing more than to reach across the tiny little raft and rip his throat out with my bare fingers.

I close my eyes, try to inhale slow and deep. I feel him shift, feel the ripple and dip of the rubber underneath us that pushes me just a little off balance. To avoid the urge to kick him, I pull my legs up to my chest, resting my forehead on my knees.

"Sorry, man," he says, his voice a tiny defeated squeak.

I press my face harder against my kneecaps, digging the prickle of my unshaven chin into my skin. Trying to focus all my pain into a single point. Trying to burn out my frustration. Waves dip and tumble underneath us, tilting us toward the sun and then away, water whispering around our tiny octagonal rubber island.

The cruise ship still hulks on the horizon and no matter how hard I try, I can't resist staring at it. Bright orange specks hover around it like chiggers—other lifeboats stuffed with other potential survivors. I start to unroll the nylon canopy, attaching it to the raft walls and pulling it over the inflated cross bar arcing across the center of the raft when Jeremy glances at me, looking startled.

"We could go back," he says, hesitant. "We could try to get closer. Just to see."

I stop struggling with the canopy and close my eyes tight again, curling back over my knees. "No," I tell him, my voice echoing between my legs.

He sighs and dips his hand over the edge of the raft. I can hear the drip of the salt water as it plinks from his fingers. I should tell him to stop, tell him that the salt's not good for him.

But we both know it won't matter. Not in a few days if the reports have been right.

Jeremy has nightmares. Not that I don't, but Jeremy's are bad—worse than bad: horrific. The first two days on the life raft neither of us sleep. Instead, we sit here, eyes riveted on the gigantic cruise ship as we drift farther and farther away.

It's during the second night when he finally falls asleep. I'm still staring at the ship, struck by how bright and dazzling it is—how it looks exactly like all the commercials as it lights up the night. I even start to think that perhaps we'd been stupid to evacuate so hastily and that maybe we should circle in closer, see if they've somehow been able to contain the infection.

That's when Jeremy starts screaming and thrashing around. It makes the little raft buck and dip, one of the sides catching a wave and letting water slosh in. I jump on him, pinning him down and he swings at me before I'm able to get to his hands.

He wakes up with me straddling him and panting hard, my heart loud like gunshots in my ears. He doesn't know he'd been having nightmares and he frowns, his face draining.

"Get off me," he says, twisting to the side, and I let go his hands and scuttle back to the other side of the raft. He looks at me like I'm a monster and it makes me feel awkward and weird.

"You were screaming," I tell him but he just grunts and won't look at me. He keeps staring at the ship, watching the lights glitter like nothing's changed. I pull my legs up to my chest and tuck into one of the corners, making sure no part of me touches any part of him for the rest of the night.

Smoke billows from the ship on the fourth day. It's been dry, the sun burning and keeping us sweltering under the sagging canopy. I think about licking the sweat from my arms but it's full of salt—just as useless as the water surrounding us.

"You think Nancy and them are still on there?" Jeremy asks. He's pressed against the only opening, blocking the fresh air. I nudge him with my foot and he moves over slightly. I wonder how the hell eight people are supposed to survive on this tiny thing, how they could ever stand each other.

Eight supply pouches ring the inside of the octagonal raft, one per potential survivor, and I give each a name. A friend who was on the ship with me that I've left behind: Francis, Omar, Leroy, Margaret, Nancy, Micah, and Tamara. I know that leaves Jeremy out, but I don't care. I wasn't supposed to end up on this stupid life raft with him in the first place. He wasn't even supposed to be going on the damn cruise and wouldn't be here if it weren't for Nancy and her soft heart and inability to say no to losers.

Jeremy cranes his neck around and looks at me. "Should we look for them? Maybe pull a little closer to see if they're on other rafts?"

I shake my head, dig my fingers into my arms until I'm pinching the muscle. I should tell Jeremy I saw them already. The night we jumped ship I saw them running. Saw the blood and bites. Saw the expression on Francis's face.

Fucking Francis, I think to myself. Of course he'd have been the first one bitten.

Jeremy wears glasses and the lenses are crusted with salt. Everything's so layered with it that he can't even find a way to clean them anymore and so he doesn't bother. Just stares at everything through the white haze.

I hate looking at him like that. It makes him look like he's already gone. Like he's already one of them.

He doesn't think I know about his bite. His hand keeps slipping to it, pressing against it, tracing the outline of it under his shirt. I pretend not to notice but it's not like he's being subtle about it. If I hadn't seen the raw red ring of bite marks along his ribs that first night I'd struggled with him during his nightmares, I'd have figured it out eventually.

I mean, Christ, it's running towards one hundred degrees every day and even though we huddle under the canopy of the life raft, it's not like it's cool in the shade. I ditched my shirt the first day but Jeremy still keeps his on and I don't care how self-conscious and scrawny he might be: when the temperature hits triple digits and you're stranded with a guy in the middle of the damn ocean while the world falls apart, you lose things like modesty.

If I can watch him slip into the water to take a dump, I can deal with his pale thin muscles and a chest like a plucked turkey. I may not be the smartest, but I'd have figured out he was hiding something under that shirt.

"How long you think it takes them to turn after they're bitten?" I ask him. I know I'm an asshole but I'm bored and I wonder how much I can prod and poke at him before he admits the truth. Plus, he's smarter than I am. Jeremy's the one who first figured out that we needed to get off the ship, even though they hadn't called an official evacuation. He was the one keeping up with the news when the rest of us were testing out our fake IDs in the bar and pretending everything was going to be okay.

He swallows, sharp dagger of an Adam's apple dragging along his throat. "Depends how bad the bite was," he says, pinching the web of skin between his thumb and forefinger.

I stare at him, willing him to have the balls to tell me himself but he just shifts and stares back at the boat. "Maybe we should pull in closer," he says. "Just in case someone needs our help."

I shake my head. "No," I tell him. "Too risky."

The thing Jeremy doesn't understand is that the first time he fell asleep, I couldn't resist the pull of all those lights. That promise of safety and warmth—the idea that everything was under control. So I'd paddled us closer.

There were people everywhere, all over the decks. Running. Screaming. Jumping. They were panicked and desperate. I saw other lifeboats rocking as they fought against them, the living and the dead.

Something had flashed in one of the windows and I stared at it, trying to see what was going on inside. That's when I saw a hand, fingers scratching at the glass. That's when I saw the teeth and mouth, banging against the window again and again, desperate to get out.

Even though I'd smothered our emergency beacon light, I felt like the thing was staring straight at me. That more than anything else she wanted to rip every bit of flesh from my bones and pull apart every muscle. Open me up like a frog on the dissection tray.

I'd let us drift back away then. Just before Jeremy started screaming. Just before I saw the bite marks along his ribs.

"You ever had sex?" I ask him.

His back stiffens, his shirt sticking to his body. Even though we've been rationing water he's been sweating a lot—too much. His skin's hot and flushed and he wants me to think it's from the sun and heat but I can smell the way his wound's festering, the sweet putrid stink of it. He pulls his head under the canopy and slumps against the wall. "Why?" he asks.

"Why sex? It's supposed to be pretty damn good," I tell him, trying to lighten his mood.

"Supposed to be?" he repeats, raising an eyebrow.

I scowl, cross my arms over my chest. "Don't you think about those things, being out here?" He starts to look at me funny and I think about the night I pinned him in his sleep. I roll my eyes. "I just mean, it's not like we have anything else to do but think. It's just sex is one of those things I'd planned on doing before I died. I'm kinda pissed it might not happen."

He shrugs. "Who says you're going to die?"

I notice he doesn't say "we" and I swallow, my tongue suddenly feeling a little thick. Scrunching down until I can prop my feet against the raft wall, I stare up at the peak of the canopy, watching it stretch and ripple over the inflated support bar. "What do you think's happening back home?" I say. It's a question I've been trying desperately not to ask but it's all I can think about recently. Well, that and sex.

Jeremy's silent and I let my head flop over until I'm looking at him. He's staring out at the horizon but from here all I can see is gray water, gray sky, gray life. Slowly I push myself to my hands and knees and crawl until I'm sitting next to him.

The ship's farther away now. We'd lost sight of it the day before and for a while we'd been panicked, not realizing until then how much we needed to have it out there even if we kept our distance. How empty everything seemed without it.

But then we'd seen the smoke rising out of nowhere and we'd paddled toward it until we saw it billowing from the decks of the ship. For most of the day it's been listing to the side, slowly and inevitably capsizing.

"I think they might all be gone," Jeremy finally says softly, before dancing his fingers along his side as if I don't know what he's hiding.

Every time he falls asleep, Jeremy screams. He never remembers it, or at least never acknowledges it. It's driving me insane and a part of me hopes the infection goes ahead and takes him soon so I can be done with it.

The thing is, it's not like Jeremy or I were being stupid. It's not like we didn't know how the whole thing works: someone gets bitten, gets infected, dies and comes back from the dead hungering for flesh. We'd seen the movies and played the video games. We *knew*.

It's just...when it came down to it, it wasn't that easy. It was never supposed to be real, never supposed to actually happen. Everything got confused and strange. We lost our friends trying to run through the cruise ship and we fought over taking a life raft and ditching or staying for official evacuation orders.

Really, this isn't what was supposed to happen at all—this isn't how it was supposed to end up. We'd treated it like a joke because we'd have panicked otherwise. "Ha-ha, the zombie apocalypse's hit, let's take a life raft and run."

Ha-ha, joke's on us. Or them. I can't remember anymore.

Sometimes I wonder if it wouldn't just make more sense to confront Jeremy and force him overboard. After all, it's not like he has a chance of surviving this, and in the meantime he's taking up resources that I might need.

Neither one of us says anything but we both know: if there was going to be a rescue, it'd have happened by now. There've been no planes, no coast guard or bright orange helicopters. Our little raft beacon chirps and blinks away merrily, sending little distress "rescue me" signals out into the world that either no one's there to hear or they're too busy ignoring us.

We *know* this. Just like we know that land can't really be that far away—we'd been on a cruise after all. The whole point is to visit all the islands—they have to be out here somewhere.

But we can't bring ourselves to lose sight of the ship to find out. Just in case.

I don't realize what it is at first, the huge groaning noise like a whale's swallowed us whole. There's this massive, deep popping sound, a high-pitched whine and then the sound of the world sucking itself up with a straw.

The wave hits not too long after, tossing us around the boat. I grab the canopy trying to hold on and end up tearing part of it away from the sides.

"What the hell?" I ask, running my fingers over the raft to make sure nothing's damaged.

Water knocks us around, up and down and up and down, and Jeremy's at the flap, staring out in the night.

"No!" he shouts into the darkness and I suddenly realize just how dark it is. It's nothing; pure absolute emptiness. The cruise ship's gone, devoured by the ocean.

Jeremy jumps into the water and starts swimming as if he could somehow bring it back from the depths. I can't even see him, he's been swallowed up already, but I hear his splashing.

"It can't go yet!" he screams. "I'm not ready. I'm not ready!"

I kneel in the boat, my arms over the side trying to feel for him as I listen to him beat at the waves and curse everything for taking away the ship once and for all.

When I finally get him back on board he shivers in my lap, his arms crossed tight over his chest. "I'm not ready," he mutters, turning his face to my chest as tears burn hot against my skin.

I hold on to him, letting the raft rock us both, the silence of the sea settling around the sunken ship our only lullaby.

"Jenny Lyons," I tell him and he cracks a small smile.

"Her?" he asks. "Really?"

I shrug. "It was eighth grade and computer class."

"Didn't she have braces then?"

"Oh yeah."

He shakes his head.

"How about you?" I ask.

If possible, his cheeks pinken even more.

"Oh don't tell me, sweet sixteen and never been kissed?" I mean it like a tease.

"More like eighteen," he says staring at his lap.

I feel my smile tighten as I think about the bite on his ribs and suddenly it doesn't seem so funny anymore.

It's pitch-black dark when he finally comes clean. "Listen, I gotta tell you something," he says. He must have known I was pretending to sleep because he doesn't bother trying to wake me up first.

I shift a little, feeling the boat rock slowly under my movement. We haven't seen anything else for days: no ship, land, rafts. Only so much nothing that it feels like we have to be the last people left.

As he explains I bite my teeth together as hard as possible, wondering if I can break them—break everything and be done with it.

"I'll go overboard, if you want," he says. In the darkness his voice has no body, no infection. It just is.

"But then you'll turn into one of those things," I tell him.

His breath shakes. "I'm going to turn into one of those things no matter what," he says.

I push my fingers into my eyes, trying to poke them hard enough to bring tears because it's the only way I can think of to unleash the searing pain inside. "Is that what you want?" I ask him.

"If I stay on this raft and turn, I'll go after you," he finally says. He pauses and in the emptiness our hearts keep beating. "I don't want that," he adds softly.

"So you think you can take me?" I ask him.

He doesn't laugh, not really. It was a lame joke anyway, but I do hear him exhale a little harder as if he'd thought about laughing. "You have to promise me you'll throw me over when it happens," he finally says. "Promise me you'll make me sink."

I press my fingers harder against my eyes.

"Promise me." His voice is urgent.

I shake my head. "I promise," I mutter.

"I think Nancy had a little crush on you," I tell him. It's a thick soupy day, taunting us with rain and I'm organizing our water bottles to catch what I can. My mouth tries to salivate at the thought of it, cool and wet, sliding down my throat, filling every dry space inside me.

"I hope so, since she's the one who bit me." He's leaning back in the shade of the canopy, shirt off now that I know his secret. I can't look at him without glancing at the bite festering along his ribs. It's like he's proud of it, forcing us both to deal with it.

And then I realize what his words mean. "So you knew." I don't ask it as a question. I turn to face him. "If she's the one who bit you, you knew about everyone else. Francis, Nancy and the others."

"Why do you think I told you we shouldn't wait for them?" he asks. Red streaks along his skin, marking every vein through his body with an infection whose heat sometimes radiates along the rubber of the raft.

"Then why did you keep asking to go back if you knew?"

He shrugs, stares at his hands. "I wanted to be wrong. Doesn't matter now, I guess."

And he's right. We lost sight of the last raft two days ago.

His hands are hot as he grabs for me. He's gasping for breath and at first I think he's turned, gurgling on moans, but then I realize he's trying to say my name. "Get up," he says, shaking me, but his muscles are weak from so many days of disuse and I'm still much larger and stronger than he is.

"Get up," he prods again.

He shoves something into my hand, the lanyards that lashed the flap of the canopy shut. "Tie me up," he says. "It's time. Tie me up, sink me."

It's been harder and harder for me to surface from sleep and I struggle to understand what Jeremy's saying. He's wheezing now as he takes my hands, wraps my fingers around the ropes, pulls them tight along his wrists and elbows.

His skin's dry and cracked and I try to blink the salt from my eyes so I can focus on what's going on. It's dark in the little raft, pitch-black swallowing us everywhere with just the tiny hiccups of the alert beacon flashing.

-flash-

Jeremy knotting the ropes. Using his teeth to tighten them.

-flash-

Me winding them around his torso, tucking up his knees.

-flash-

Jeremy's eyes glassy and bright. His chest barely moving.

-flash-

I don't know what to say. What to do. What to tell him.

-flash-

I slip my fingers into his. "I'm sorry, Jeremy."

-flash-

He's nothing.

-flash-

Dead eyes. Still heart.

-flash-

Waves tilt and whirl as his body becomes a shell.

-flash-

I breathe in. Hold it.

-flash-

-flash-

-flash-

I exhale.

And before the light can flash again he explodes, straining and struggling.

I see the perfectly straight teeth, the gleaming white as he tries to lunge for me.

As he snaps at the air.

Screaming, I throw myself across the raft. Pushing and forcing myself back. Wishing the walls could absorb me. Keep me safe. His moans are like growls, guttural and wet. He's insane with what looks like agony and rage and a desire so intense I can smell it.

Beneath me the entire raft bucks and swirls, his movements teetering us around, his feet ripping at the canopy overhead as he tries to gain his balance, tries to push himself closer to me.

I can't get near him, can only watch as he pulls and pops against the ropes. Can only hear the strain on his joints, the snap of his wrist breaking apart under the twisting jolts. It's too much. I can't stand it, can't be near him anymore. Can't see him like this.

I dive through the opening in the canopy into the night, letting the waves close over my head until I can't hear, can't see, can't forget as the raft twists and shudders above me.

"Do you believe in God?" I ask Jeremy. Water pools around the divot in the raft where I'm crouching and I've pulled open the canopy, hoping the sun will burn it away so that my poor chaffed skin can find relief.

Jeremy bucks against the soggy ropes holding him tight. I've lashed him to the other side of the raft and used strips of my shirt to tie his mouth shut. He still manages to moan, deep nasal sounds that reverberate through the raft so that I'm always feeling them even when I shove my hands to my ears.

I tried to push him overboard, I swear. But I just couldn't do it. I couldn't let go of him.

He's all I have left. I couldn't drift away from him on the empty horizon.

"Blink once for yes, twice for no," I tell him, staring into his face. He doesn't blink, just tries to lunge for me, his shoulder buckling back at a sickening angle.

"Jeremy?" I whisper. It's night, pitch black, and I swore I woke up to screaming. I swore I woke up to Jeremy and his nightmares.

The raft shudders. Jeremy still desperate to escape. Still desperate for me. I shake my head, feeling like my ears are full of water, every sound distant and dull.

"Jeremy?" I ask again.

Carefully, I crawl across the raft, my muscles having a hard time keeping me from falling over. The bottom sags every place I set my hand and knee, feeling as if it too is giving up. I pull myself face to face with Jeremy, too close to be safe.

"Is there anything left?" I ask him.

And I can't tell if he's shaking his head or if he's just twisting against his ropes to get closer to me.

I'm pretty sure Jeremy's been talking to me. When I wake up I'm positive I hear his voice in my head. And when I'm staring at the horizon, trying to find shapes in the wavering distance, I swear he's saying something.

"You promised." He's starting to sag against his ropes. His body's pretty torn up, joints dislocated and his left arm fractured where he pulled too hard. His skin's tight over his face, cheekbones sharp and accusing.

"I'm not ready," I tell him.

"Neither was I," he says.

I turn away again. Nothing inside me is willing to cooperate anymore. Everything shudders and falls apart, muscles failing to fire, bones shifting under my skin so that I always hurt.

"You promised," he says over and over and over again until I almost do want to throw him over just to shut him up.

It's raining, so our water bottles are full again. One of the survival pouches has a fishing kit and I've been sitting here for a while staring at the gleaming little hook. Part of me wants to draw it along the raft, wondering if it's sharp enough to gash the boat and sink us both.

We ran out of food three days ago, so I don't have anything to use as bait. I've tried using just the hook but nothing bites. I stare at Jeremy, at the flesh flayed off his broken thumb. His moans are more like whimpers now and my stomach heaves as I pinch at his skin, tearing the little flap off.

I shove it on the hook and toss it in the water and wait, thinking of the fish circling underneath us, wondering if eating Jeremy's undead flesh will cause them to turn as well. Thinking of the feel of their meat on my tongue, the thick oily taste of it, makes me weak with desperation so intense I tremble.

Hours pass, the storm dwindles and nothing. Wincing, I close my eyes, cut a sliver of my own skin away. As soon as the scent of my blood hits the air, Jeremy explodes, thrashing harder than he has in days. Startled, the hook slips through my fingers and falls away into the depths.

I sit staring at the bloody flesh in my fingers, red and bright and wet. Inside I'm empty, nothing but water sloshing through my veins, nothing but the taste of salt coating my tongue. Slowly I raise the bit of skin to my lips and close my eyes.

Jeremy moans and writhes as I force myself to swallow.

It's dark again, so dark that nothing makes sense. There's a storm whipping around outside, dragging the raft and tossing it around. I brace my hands against the walls and try to hold on tight but still I'm thrown into Jeremy, thrust against him again and again.

Everything's soaking wet, water seeping through tears in the canopy even though I've done my best to lash it shut. It's slippery and I can't keep my balance. I reach for Jeremy's hands.

"*I don't want to be alone*," I scream at him, my throat raw and cracked. "I'm scared."

It's too hard to keep doing this, to keep surviving. I'm exhausted and my body's beyond pain: salt leaches into my cuts, my skin's tight and shrunken with sunburn and my stomach is so empty I'm frightened it no longer exists.

"I'm afraid to die," I tell Jeremy. His fingers grab for me, clutch on to me as if he understands what I'm saying. He seems so much stronger than I am.

I kneel in front of him and pull the scrap of shirt from his head, unleashing his jaw. He snaps and moans, louder than the roar of the storm. My breath is shaking as I reach my arm up to him, push it toward his mouth.

A wave crashes down on us, flooding the tiny raft and in the murk of it I feel the sharp sting of his teeth closing around me.

I rest my head in Jeremy's lap and stare up at the calm blue sky. There's something comforting about him, about the feel of him underneath me like I'm a kid curled up on my parents' bed on a Saturday morning.

Already I feel the sear of the infection, my body offering up little resistance. I've been shutting down, muscles twitching, throat closing, stomach ceasing to rattle and growl and my heart a bare whisper. I haven't felt my toes for a day and what bothers me is that I no longer care.

"My dad made the best waffles," I tell Jeremy, staring at the clouds. "He'd leave the butter out overnight so it was soft and melty. I'd drown them with syrup." I run the tip of my tongue against the roof of my barren mouth, trying to remember the feel of it.

I'm so wrapped up in the memory that seeing the bird doesn't make sense, doesn't penetrate the fantasy I have in my head of a table heaped with food. But then the bird screams and I jolt up, my head colliding with Jeremy's chin, snapping him back.

"Oh my God!" I shout. "Oh my God!" There's a tiny spit of land cresting over the horizon. Exerting every force I can muster from my muscles, I hold my hand up, trace the curve of a tree with my finger. We draw closer and closer, the island growing larger and larger, the infection inside me roaring hotter and hotter.

I'm weeping, barely able to move.

Jeremy sags against the wall next to me, red gashes covering his body where the rope's rubbed him raw. I put my hand on his foot and he twitches, leans toward me. "We made it, Jeremy," I say with cracked lips.

He leans toward me, his mouth finding my knuckles. He's so weak now, so torn apart from struggling that he can barely bite, and what hurts more than his teeth grazing my flesh is the sting of salt from his lips penetrating the raw skin.

My eyes blur with tears. "We made it," I whisper. Overwhelmed with a crush of emotions so intense I can't even untangle them, I hug him tight, press my face into the curve of his neck and pretend his struggles are joy at being saved.

THIN THEM OUT

By Kim Paffenroth, R. J. Sevin, & Julia Sevin

Kim Paffenroth is the author of the zombie novels *Dying to Live* and *Dying to Live: Life Sentence.* A third volume in the series is due out later this year. Paffenroth is also the editor of the anthologies *History Is Dead* and *The World Is Dead.* A new novel, *Valley of the Dead* is due to come out around the same time as this anthology.

Julia and R. J. Sevin are the proprietors of Creeping Hemlock Press, which launched its own line of zombie novels this summer with Kealan Patrick Burke's *The Living.* Together, they are the editors of the Stoker-nominated anthology *Corpse Blossoms*, and individually they have each published fiction in *Fishnet, Postcards from Hell, War of the Worlds: Frontlines, Cemetery Dance*, and the anthology *Bits of the Dead.*

All of George Romero's zombie films—*Night of the Living Dead, Dawn of the Dead, Day of the Dead*, etc.—feature at least one character who spends the entire movie being shrill and obnoxious and totally impervious to reason. In *Night* it's Harry Cooper, who is crassly possessive of the presumed safety of the cellar. In *Day* it's Captain Rhodes, the unreasoningly aggressive military commander.

When author Carrie Ryan—whose story you just read if you're reading the book in order—saw *Night of the Living Dead* for the first time, she thought it was stupid: The characters are in so much danger, but rather than working together they spend the whole movie bickering with each other in a pointless way. But then someone explained to her that that was the whole point: Romero was saying that this is what humanity is—that we're doomed by our inability to just get along with each other even in the face of life-or-death challenges. After that, she completely changed her mind about the movie. "This made the film absolutely brilliant to me," she said.

In the face of current calamities—global warming, economic collapse, AIDS, overpopulation—to which humanity's response has been mostly just a lot of pointless political sniping, Romero's warning seems more pressing than ever, and our next story is another that plays with the idea that interpersonal drama can be an even bigger problem than zombies.

He was on his back, looking up at the sky.

He felt a little cold, but overall not too bad. Hearing sounds to his left, he turned his head. Another person stood nearby, eyeing him. Her face, hands, and arms glistened red, and she held something pink in her hands, which she raised to her mouth. Slurping sounds followed, then she wiped her hands on her dress.

He sat up and examined himself. He too was covered with red. He tried to say something, but all that came out was something between a roar and a moan. The red lady returned the greeting, so he thought she might be friendly after all.

He pulled aside the tatters of his shirt, and found a large hole in the middle of him. That must be where the cold was coming from. He reached into the hole and felt around. Mostly it was squishy, but nearer the back, there were hard parts, too. He thought the hole looked nice, all colorful and mysterious, and he thought it might be useful, as a place to put things. But he couldn't think of anything he had to put there.

He stood up and took a step toward the red lady. The stuff on her neck wasn't shiny and wet, like the stuff on her mouth and hands, but all caked and dark. Even so, she looked very pretty. The sun made her blond hair shine, where it wasn't matted with the red stuff. He tried to touch her hair, but she growled and pulled away.

After a while, they both sat down on the pavement. She still wouldn't let him touch her hair, but she did let him hold her hand. There was a big, shiny metal band around her wrist. That looked nice, too.

He looked around. A large blue sign nearby read WELCOME TO LOUISIANA. Another sign, not far from that one read, simply, I-55. He didn't know what either sign meant, but somehow he did.

There was a roar, and a metal thing on wheels stopped near them. The people who got out of the wheeled thing didn't have red stains on them. They weren't missing any parts. They were whole, but he didn't like the way they looked. They looked ugly and plain. They also had ugly, dull metal things in their hands. The ugly people smiled and laughed and pointed, then the dull metal things roared louder than the wheeled thing had. He fell on top of the red lady, laying there till he heard the wheeled thing roar off.

Sitting up, he found she no longer pushed his hand away, but she also didn't move. This made him sad. He took the metal band off her wrist. Now he had something to keep in the hole in him.

The other people had seemed much happier and more satisfied by what they did, and he wondered if he could ever be whole like they were. He doubted it. But sitting there in the fading light, running his dead fingers through such luminous blond hair, he didn't feel completely empty, either.

"Okay." Zach brought the Jeep to a halt. "We're on foot from here."

To his right, Ted grunted something and the two men hopped out. In the back seat, Wayne looked at his gun and wondered if he should have shot them both as soon as Zach threw the vehicle into park.

The opportunity passed, Wayne stepped from the Jeep and into the early morning light. Not even nine o'clock, and already the Louisiana air was cloying. The interstate sliced through a dense pine forest. They'd stick to the shade for as long as they could.

At the rear of the Jeep, they suited up: backpacks stuffed with supplies (in case they got separated and were unable to return to the Jeep), gloves, hinged face-shields, filtered dust masks, and wooden baseball bats. There was also a furniture dolly, for boxes. Wayne grabbed it.

"Cars are tight here," Zach said, real low. "Keep quiet and watch your asses. If you get bit, I'm calling the Doctor." He patted the .357 Magnum on his right hip. The bastard had actually painted it white. There was a small red cross on the grip. A .40 Taurus rested beneath each arm.

"What if *you* get bit?" Wayne asked, grabbing a bat.

"Then *I'll* see the Doctor."

"That one is mine," Ted said, pulling the bat from Wayne's hand. His dark eyes, darting leftrightleftright, resembled empty zoetropes. There was more than a little crazy there.

"Oh-kay."

"It's the marks right here." Ted pointed at some deep gouges in the business end of the bat. "That's how I can tell. This is the one I always use, it has the marks." He turned and trotted off.

Wayne looked at Zach, who nodded once and walked away. Wayne grabbed another bat, slipped it through a loop on his belt and, pushing the dolly, followed them onto the interstate. Since their little community of survivors had come together four months ago outside of Baton Rouge, they'd searched over forty miles of I-12. They now moved along the choked northbound lanes of I-55, and were less than fifty miles away from the Mississippi border.

Zach and Ted walked shoulder-to-shoulder two paces ahead of him, chuckling over stories they'd told each other several times before. They'd been buddies before the outbreaks, and it didn't seem fair.

Wayne didn't have any real friends among the three-dozen men in the warehouse. Ian was trustworthy enough but pretty unpleasant to be around, always talking about needing pussy, always picking at his ears and nose and fingernails and scalp. You'd think with a perpetual hygiene jones like that, he'd smell a little better than he did. Then there was Sue, who he hardly knew, really. It was hard to talk about things now in any normal way, but he guessed he wasn't really interested in her religion or her favorite music, anyway.

But goddamn Ted and Zach went on chatting about the Saints and the niggers and the fucking Waffle House like any of it still mattered. Scanning the area for dead folks, Wayne wondered again if he should just pull his piece and pop each of them in the back of the head. He wondered if he could.

"That one there," Zach said, indicating an 18-wheeler a few hundred feet away.

"What about those?" Ted was talking about the four smaller delivery trucks between them and the semi. "Could be some good shit in there."

"Could be. Probably is," Zach said. "But we try the big truck first. Find what we need and get the hell out of here."

Wayne looked around. No movement anywhere, only cars and trucks bumper to bumper for all-time, some of them unscathed, some blackened and twisted, others glass and steel tombs whose misshapen and sun-baked occupants watched soundlessly as the three men strode between them.

It would be so damn easy now. A little later, and he'd lose his chance to get the drop on them. The whole thing could fall apart. And if his suspicions were true—if the last five guys to die on supply runs with Zach and Ted had been popped to keep rations fat back at the warehouse, couldn't they already have the drop on him? Could he be walking toward his execution?

"Slow day," Wayne said. Ted grunted again.

"The fuck you talking about?" Zach asked. Wayne could hear the disdain in his voice.

"None of them around yet."

"Yeah," Zach said. "So far so good, I guess."

About twenty feet from the semi, Zach cursed. The loading door was partially open, and the ground around the truck was littered with rusted and broken kitchen appliances—toasters, blenders, indoor grills—sitting among the faded and disintegrating remains of cardboard boxes. They lifted the door and peered into the trailer. The boxes near the door were weathered and rippled. Toward the back, they were intact, their contents as useless as the trailer in which they sat.

"Okay," Zach said. None of them were surprised. "We'll go back and check the smaller trucks, and then we'll—damn."

"What?"

"Here we go." Zach nodded in the direction from which they'd come. A few hundred feet away, a lone form shuffled toward them.

"Ah, jeeze," Ted said. He scampered onto the cab of the semi, shielding his eyes and scanning the area. "Three more. Half a mile or so north."

"No problem," Zach said.

"Just stumbling around—they don't know we're here yet."

"Good. Now get down before you fall and break your fucking leg. I'll leave your ass, I swear."

"I got this one," Wayne said, leaving the dolly and walking toward the slowly moving corpse. Fifteen feet away from the thing, he stopped. He smelled it through the dust mask. In a van to his right, what had once been a small boy of no more than three years watched him from its car seat. Desiccated hands pawed at the restraints. There was no one else in the van.

The other thing was closer, but not by much. It was a slow one. Its flesh was purplish-black and swollen, and its massive, rigid stomach was split down the middle like a tomato rotting on the vine. Its gaze rarely rose from the ground, and it seemed unable to lift its head. Its eyes lifted in its sockets and found Wayne. It tried to grunt, hands twitching at its sides and trembling upward. Wayne pushed down his face-shield and lifted the bat.

Three blows, and the corpse went down, its head a lumpish black sack. Wayne walked to the van and opened the door. A dry yelp escaped the dead kid's drawn lips. He placed the blunt end of the bat to the side of the child's head and pushed. It didn't take long.

There was a Batman action figure on the floor of the vehicle. He picked it up and placed it in the child's lap. Saying nothing felt wrong, but nothing he could think of sounded appropriate. As he shut the door, he noticed two cases of water in the back of the van along with several unmarked boxes. He went around back and checked them. Each contained various canned goods, as well as several packs of pasta and ramen. Whoever had left the kid had been in a hurry.

He looked around. No walking corpses, no sign of Zach or Ted. They'd moved on, taking the dolly with them.

Wayne removed the face-shield and wiped sweat from his brow. He plucked a bottle of water from the van and, pulling the dust mask beneath his chin, downed it. His heart raced, and just like that, the silence and the heat were almost too much. He felt alone and small, and he wanted to be with Zach and Ted, even if they were maybe going to try and kill him today.

Wayne tucked three bottles of water under his arm and walked until he saw Zach and Ted. They were standing at the rear of an unmarked truck that had stalled in the wildly overgrown grass beside the freeway.

Ted looked back and smiled. "You're not going to believe this," he said.

Wayne handed them each a bottle of water and let what he was seeing sink in: pallet upon pallet of military rations, the kind he and his family had lived off of in the weeks following Katrina.

Wayne said, "Damn."

"Yeah," Zach said. "Damn."

There were hundreds of boxes, each containing sixteen complete meals. From what he could see, several pallets toward the back were piled with cases of bottled water. The same stuff as in the van.

"See that," Ted said. "FEMA is good for something after all."

"Okay," Zach said, all business. He hopped into the truck, ripped away the thick plastic wrap securing the boxes to the pallets, and began tossing boxes down to Ted and Wayne.

The dolly held five boxes. Wayne pushed it back to the Jeep, walking behind Ted and Zach, who each carried one box.

The first trip was without incident.

On their second run, Ted got a chance to use his bat. The thing that clambered like a lizard out of the forest was naked, creeping around on the ragged stumps of its arms and legs. No ears, lidless eyes, lipless mouth. Ted enjoyed putting it down.

"Damn," Ted said on their third trip to the truck. He knocked back a water bottle and belched. "Can we start the truck? Maybe move it or something?"

Zach stared at him for a moment, blinking, his face glistening with sweat. Dark stains seemed to emanate from the guns beneath his armpits. "Yeah, Ted," he said, half-grinning and nodding. "Sure. But first we have to clear out all these pine trees, maybe cut a path all the way to 190."

"I don't know," Ted said, shrugging. "I was just saying."

"Yeah, yeah. Okay. Moving on. We need to load up what we can for now and come back tomorrow with the truck. We'll get Seth to—"

Somewhere nearby, a dead thing howled, long and mournful.

"Aw, crap." Ted said. "Where the hell is that coming from?"

"There," Wayne said. Not far from where he'd encountered the first corpse of the day, another form stood. It howled again, louder and longer. There was urgency in the thing's voice.

"Oh, shit," Zach said. Here and there, the creature's call was answered. "Not good. Run."

They ran, their bats raised and ready. On either side of the interstate, the walking dead emerged from within the cool confines of the forest. Soon there was a chorus.

They overtook the howler. Not slowing, Ted took a swing at it. He missed, staggered, and almost fell, dropping the bat, and then the Jeep was in sight. Zach leaned against a tree, winded. Ted bent over, his hands on his knees, panting.

"You not going back for your bat?" Wayne asked, his back to the Jeep.

"Why the fuck would I do that? There's like six more in the back of the Jeep," Ted said, and Wayne shot him in the face, blowing away most of his jaw. Ted dropped, mewling and clutching at where his chin used to be. Blood poured between his fingers.

He should have shot Zach first—Zach was always more on the ball and now he was just gone, dropped from sight. "Shit," Wayne said, and Zach appeared from behind a tree and started firing the Tauruses.

Wayne got the Jeep between himself and Zach. From all sides, the dead closed in.

You knew it was a real shit day when killing the class cat was the high point.

That was the first thing Sue did in the morning, and her mood had not improved. Mr. Stripestuff had been pretty sickly for a while, was probably fifteen years old and going blind, and there was no way anybody in the warehouse would take adequate care of him after she left. She hoped they'd have a little more compassion for the kids she'd be leaving behind, but deep down she doubted it.

She let him lick the scraps from a can of tuna mixed with a packet of old government-issue powdered creamer and a couple of crushed Tylenol PMs. Then she laid him in her lap and petted his head for a while, then she put a towel over his face, and a plastic bag over that. She thought not about how she should just set him free, but how slim his odds were out there. She was doing him a favor, but it wasn't easy for either of them. She was gentle, gentle as she could be while getting the job done, and she laid him in his bed for the class to find.

They were on lockdown and Sue couldn't get downstairs to the trash in the night. She had no place to stash Stripestuff in the couple of upstairs offices where the orphans lived every minute. In the daytime, the kids—the non-orphans at least—got into everything, even downstairs where they were supposedly not allowed. Might as well make the discovery foreseeable and respectful. Educational, too, she thought, wondering if maybe she was getting a little teacher in her after all. Then again, each and every one of these kids had already seen death firsthand in unimaginable manners and quantities. What could they learn from a cat? Her smile evaporated.

The class—such as it was, twenty kids spread over ages three to ten, being overseen by a clerk and a dental assistant, whose only qualifications were that they *looked* like teachers, both being middle-aged females—found him in his bed, having passed peacefully in the night when they assembled at eight. After a little death-lesson-cum-ceremony by Sue, they interred him by wrapping him in plastic sheeting and throwing him out one of the second-story windows into the piles of red earth of the unfinished construction site next door. The plastic came partly unraveled and the cat fell a little short of the dirt, landing on the warehouse's own blacktop. What could you do but pull the shades? The kids mostly cried or moped, but not Jayson, which just confirmed everything Sue felt about him.

He was just lucky he wasn't an orphan.

"I'm hungry!" the little animal yelled, and Sue nearly lost it right there. Everyone in the warehouse had eaten carefully meted crackers and peanuts for lunch, for Christ, and this little fatty was the only one bitching about it. One of the oldest kids in the group but stupider than the youngest by half.

Sue took a breath and, clutching it inside her, strode past the other children to grab Jayson by his filthy collar and hiss in his face, "You. Are. Not. A good. Child." That made her smile a little bit, and she set him down.

"I hate you!" he shrieked, with his horrible little nubby teeth and his filthy face. "I'm telling my dad!"

That made her smile even more. She reached down and pinched his cheek hard, harder, keeping in the thing that she wanted to growl, that Jayson's father was part of the reason Jayson was hungry. Every time that asshole went out on runs, the truck came back half-stuffed with liquor, and all the guys cheered, not considering that a few cases of saltines and applesauce only went so far.

Another child said it. "I'm hungry."

Sue turned, feeling revived. "I told you, Leticia, there's no food yet. We're waiting for the supply run to come back."

"When are they gonna be here?"

Sue looked to Patty, the dental assistant, the other woman who passed for an elementary-grade teacher in the upper-level conference room of this welding and steam-fitting warehouse. In truth they were babysitters at best. Patty was at least slightly more experienced, having had a daughter until the outbreak. She had a dozen new lines on her face this week and seemed a little stoned, with her eyelids not quite reaching the tops of her broad pupils.

"Well," Sue said, leaving Patty staring at the wall, "they were supposed to have been back a little while ago. For lunch." It was quarter past one. "My guess is, they found a really nice grocery store or something, and they took their time, and they're almost back now with a truck full of cookies and spaghetti and tuna. How does that sound?"

Some of the younger kids gave out a little "yay" chorus. Then they were all back to doodling on their math sheets or punching at their board games.

Sue hated them. Most of them. Wayne said there was only room for eight people on the Jeep, a couple more if the kids were little.

Sue had eight orphans in her class and eleven children of other adults holed up in the warehouse. She didn't have to worry about the eleven, but with her and Patty not minding them during the day or sleeping on pissy mattresses with them in the classroom at night, the orphans were as good as dead.

Pushing it, *pushing it*, she and Patty could maybe bring five kids. That meant she had to eliminate three.

Obviously, she should have done this before noon but her hangover was still wearing off then.

She scanned the pitiful crowd. It was easy enough to gravitate toward the younger students, the kindergarteners whom life hadn't yet broken, but that just made them a liability. It meant Sue would have to be the one to watch or assist the breaking.

Devon, a four-year-old black kid, gave out a horrible snorking cough, the apparent culmination of some symptoms that had been dribbling out of him all day and a validation ticket for some thoughts Sue had been having on the subject. She sighed thanks. *Goodbye, Devon.*

Sue sidled over to Patty and whispered. "I'm thinking we take Leticia, Morgan, Shawn, and Greg. They're all over six...for the last one, it's between Sophia, Sarah, and Avery. What do you think? Sarah's youngest but she's got it together, listens well."

Patty grunted.

"That's all we can take. Five is a lot even for two of us to wrangle, out...on the road. Christ, Patty, say something, we have to—"

"Wha?"

"You have to pick: Do you want Sophia, Sarah, or Avery? Devon's got that horrible cough. It seems serious. All we need is for the kids to all get sick."

"I can't do it."

"Yes, you can, Wayne and Ian have it all planned out. We can't stay here forever."

"I can't pick them, I'm not going."

"You're not making sense. We've been talking about it for a week. Christ, we've all been thinking about it for a month, ever since Ian said Seth wanted to quit doing rescue runs and stick to supplies. You can do this. We have to do it. The warehouse is a dead-end situation. Picking the kids—that's all hypothetical anyway, if Wayne can come back with hard proof that Zach and Ted are murderers, then maybe Seth will see that we all have to go."

"Of course I'll go if we all go. But if he doesn't, if Seth wants to stay, I'm not just...I'm not just going to leave, it's too dangerous. I'll stay here with the kids. There's food—"

"No there isn't!"

"Usually, usually there is. There's protection..." Patty said. "Seth keeps things running here pretty well."

Sue rubbed her face. "Ohhh, my god. You really believe that, you'd really rather stay."

"It doesn't matter, I can't leave any kids. None of them... none of them deserve that."

"Shhh!" So that was it. It was a goddamned mother thing. Sue stole a look out the window; no Jeep yet. "Sweetie, Brandy's gone, you can't help her. Let me put it to you this way: What would Brandy want you to do? She'd want you to do the thing that was best for everyone, right? Well, staying isn't good for anyone. This is a place for dying. Think about Plaquemines Parish. Did you ever take Brandy down to Port Sulphur? Did she like it? Well, it's great, that area, you can grow just about anything, fish, shrimp, it's breezy.... Think about the kids that are here."

"I *am*."

"Think about them growing up here, in this building. They're not even going to last long enough to grow up. They're going to starve here."

"No...they're exploring I-55, there'll be something up there."

"Bullshit. There's fewer men practically every week to do that, and you know why. You want to do something good for these kids, pick which ones we can take and let's get the fuck out of here."

Now Patty was weeping. Jesus, what a drama queen. "You don't have to take any, if you want. I know you don't really—"

"All right, all right." She squeezed Patty's shoulder and peeked out the window again. "I'm taking the four I said I'd take, and then Sarah, with or without your sorry ass." She smiled as she said this, realizing that some kids' eyes were on her.

That woke Patty up. "You can't. You can't possibly manage five kids..."

"I can and I will." Her face was getting warm but she anchored the smile. "Watch me. I'm making this shit happen. I'll be goddamned if I'm gonna stay here and rot—"

"Sarah's too little, leave her—" and then Sue stopped hearing. She must have been hyperventilating, because her head felt hot but her mouth felt cold. She ran her fingers through her hair and left the room, went for the stairs. She looked down into the main warehouse area, fully lit now by the afternoon sun through the skylights.

Wayne was downstairs. How did he get here so quietly? She didn't see a Jeep. He was already talking with Seth, who had on his stained pink shirt and striped tie, like he was still middle management.

Sue ran down the rattling iron stairs.

"...both of them," Wayne was saying.

Seth nodded gravely and looked up at Sue. She had her mouth open but something in Wayne's eyes told her to shut it.

"Bad news, Sue: Zach and Ted are dead. Call everyone around."

The manager's office bathroom was the only real private room in the warehouse. That's where Sue waited for Wayne after the meeting, drinking a long-hoarded Abita beer, playing with the candles on the rust-stained toilet that could no longer be used, fixing herself up as best she could in the mirror. Finally, he came in.

"What happened out there? Where's the Jeep?"

"Shh," he said.

"They tried to kill you, didn't they? Why didn't you tell Seth?"

"I...not really. Maybe they were going to."

"Maybe? What did Seth say? Will they come?"

"I didn't put it to them, I don't think that's wise." Wayne put his hand on the wall behind Sue.

"What, we're just going? Just us, no caravan?"

He dropped his arm. "Seth can't be trusted."

She stamped her foot. "How are we going to make it anywhere without that kind of backup, Wayne?"

"Do you hear me? I don't trust Seth anymore. I don't think Zach and Ted were acting alone. I think it came from higher up."

Sue leaned back against the wall. "They *did* try to kill you."

"Well, they didn't get a chance."

"The dead got them first."

"*I* got...you know, I went ahead and shot them."

"Oh, Christ."

"I was scared, I kept thinking about the plan, I don't even know if we were right anymore. I panicked."

"Shh, it's okay." She put a hand on his chest. "You were right, you were right, just like we planned, just a little different. And it's good you told Seth and all that they were killed by the dead, that's fine cover, you did good."

"I don't know...I worry that they, that Ted or Zach, might..."

"What?"

"Might wander back here, I don't know. I can't stop thinking about it."

"You didn't finish them?"

"I don't know!"

"Christ, Wayne. You're unbelievable, that could really be—"

"Shut...just, be quiet. Listen." He held her wrists to her chest but she didn't like the maneuver and pushed back away from him. "Go talk to Patty, get the kids' stuff ready so we can go. I'll talk to Ian."

"Ugh. Where's the Jeep, anyway? How are we leaving?"

"It's four blocks from here, loaded up with MREs and water." Her eyes went wide. "Don't freak out, just get the shit ready, tell Patty so we can go."

"We'll have to *walk?*"

"A little ways, yes. It's no real problem."

She swallowed then, leaned against his chest and whispered, "Can we just go now, forget the kids?"

"No. The kids." Now he pushed her away. "The kids are half the damn point, Sue."

"What do you care. You don't even know their names," she said. "Patty's not coming."

He sighed. "Whatever. Just get everything together, keep it quiet, don't spook anyone. Give me that beer. We're leaving at daybreak. Get some sleep."

She left the bathroom and headed upstairs, shaking and wondering if she could sleep: tomorrow would start no better than today had. In the classroom/orphan bedroom, she stepped over the mattresses in the dark and just grabbed clothes from unwashed piles as she passed, stuffing them into a backpack, trying to get things for the ones she'd decided on but just not entirely sure, in the dark, with this pitiful flashlight. Children slept like the dead. Patty was asleep on the floor. Devon breathed and it sounded like a greasy drain gurgling. The shoes: she had to be sure of the shoes. She put the correct pair next to each child's head. Morgan, Leticia, Greg, Shawn, Sarah. These were the ones; she could help these ones.

Sue had just fallen asleep when Wayne woke her up to say the dead had found the warehouse.

The sun vanished, and others like him emerged from the forest. They shambled by, paying him little mind, some marred and broken and beautiful beyond expression, others as plain and dull and ugly as the laughing ones with the roaring metal things and the wheels.

The night was cool and damp. When he tried to breathe, the air felt empty and used up. It had nothing to give him. Fortunately, he needed nothing right then—nothing physical, at least. He could just sit there, oblivious and unknowing.

Unknowing, but not unthinking. His mind was a blur of images and feelings—people and places and things, and all the emotions they evoked in him. Several times in the long night, he clutched at his head and rocked back and forth, moaning, because the thoughts hurt him.

It wasn't that they were all images of violence or terror—very few of them were, in fact. The pain was from the cacophony of his mind, for all the images and feelings came at him without order, logic, or connection. He could not choose what he would think, or even pick from among a certain set: he could not call forth thoughts—he was only assailed and bombarded by them, and the assault seemed as painful as any kind of physical torture.

He lacked words for most everything that passed through his mind, and that contributed more to his mental anguish. Without labels or categories, even pleasant feelings seemed disorienting and disappointing, for he could not understand or explain his pleasure. And this pain was increased by his inability to hold on to anything, or to anticipate what thought or feeling might come next. Instead, he was constantly subject to the whim of some unknown force inside or outside himself.

When he could calm himself enough to observe and not be tormented by his mind, he noted that one person appeared repeatedly in his thoughts: a young girl with blond hair and fair skin. Her age and looks varied in his different thoughts of her, but he recognized her as the same girl. She was surrounded by different people, in various clothes, often outside among trees and flowers; in many thoughts she was making a happy sound with her mouth that he tried to duplicate, but could not, but the memory of it still gave him joy and contentment. But his contentment was disturbed, because he could not understand her connection to him or why he should think so much of her. He did not know her name. His inability to articulate or specify who she was increasingly oppressed and confounded him, till he let out his second loudest and longest moan of what seemed an endless night.

The longest and loudest wail came from him a couple hours later, when an even more fundamental deficiency tore at what was left of his mind and soul. He realized shortly before dawn that he could not name or understand his feelings for her. Seeing her with his mind's eye was a pleasant experience: it was not fear or pain or anger, for example—feelings of which he seemed to have retained a better, fuller conception. It was not a need or hunger, exactly, even though he intensely wanted to see and hear the girl again. But his wanting her was not the same as the physical thirst and hunger that wrenched his insides from his throat to his abdomen and twisted them into a knot of burning pain and grasping desire. If anything, thinking of her made him forget about his broken, torn body. It made him forget himself entirely and think only of her, and what she might need or feel or want.

It seemed all the more imperative to know what such a self-annihilating feeling might be called, and what might be expected of one who felt such a thing so intensely. As any understanding of this feeling seemed completely beyond the grasp of his damaged mind, he loosed a cry to the uncaring stars as long and piercing as any sent forth from a living man as he died, forsaken and alone. The fact that he was already dead only seemed to increase his loneliness and separation from anyone or anything that might ease his pain.

As the orange orb of the sun pushed up above the tops of the cool forest around him, the light soothed him somewhat, and he could let the feelings and thoughts of the girl occupy him, rather than hurt him. He would simply have to go on with them as his mental landscape. Looking at the stiffened female body across his lap, the smears of his blood and hers on the pavement around him, he realized these did not frighten or hurt him; and if they did not, then he would ignore the pain of his thoughts, perhaps even let their beauty distract him from the ugliness and destruction all around.

He laid the woman gently on the ground and folded her hands across her chest. Smoothing her beautiful hair one last time, he pulled himself up to his full height and shuffled away from the body. He had no plan, but something in the words on the sign—WELCOME TO LOUISIANA—made him think of her, the girl in his mind.

His shoes crunched on broken glass. He didn't like the sound.

Wayne watched from the darkness at the foot of the stairs. His flashlight hung from his belt. His right hand rested on his holstered gun.

The skylights were just useless blue rectangles now. All the lower-level windows were long-since boarded up. You couldn't see the dead amassing outside, but you could hear them, shuffling and grunting in the primeval twilight. Occasionally they banged on the aluminum walls and it echoed through the building to sound like a stage storm, making it hard to hear the living as they scuttled in between points of artificial light. Wayne held his watch to his face and pressed the light button. The sun would be down in half an hour. Five minutes and they were out of here, ready or not. Where the hell was Ian?

"Keep your voices down," Seth said, hissing, trying to rally the troops and failing miserably. Several men clustered around him, voices raised in the darkness, their wan faces washed in the cold light cast by various battery-powered fluorescent lanterns. Outside, the dead moaned.

"Listen, listen," Seth said, and someone shouted him down. They needed to get out of here, and now.

"No," someone else said. It may have been Hank, but Wayne wasn't really sure.

"How did they find us? How did so many…"

"…gotta get to the trucks and…"

"…to shut up. They can hear…"

"…already know we're in here…"

"…how many are there…"

Gunshots from above brought silence, then the hollow thump of the aluminum roof sheets shifting beneath the weight of the gunmen.

"If you'd just listen for a minute," Seth said, no longer bothering to keep his voice down. "I was trying to—" Another shot interrupted him. He raised his voice: "Steve and Brian are on the roof. We're safe here. That's why we—"

Static, and then a voice: "Seth. It's Brian. Over."

Motioning for those around him to stay silent, Seth plucked the walkie-talkie from his hip and held it to his face. "Talk to me. Over."

"There's gotta be fifty or sixty out here right now. Over."

"We can handle that."

A few seconds of silence. Wayne looked at his watch again. He could hear one of the kids upstairs, crying. Somewhere, a walking corpse pounded on the side of the warehouse with what sounded like a pipe. More gunshots.

"Brian? Over."

"Yeah, we can, but we're making a hell of a lot of noise. They might just keep coming. You know how—"

The shouts from those around Seth drowned out the rest. The large group splintered into smaller groups, the familiar cliques coming together at last.

"...it's Wayne's fault..."

"...finish the job!"

"...followed his trail..."

"...that's not how it works. They're not that smart..."

"...led them right to us..."

"...where is he..."

Crouching in the darkness, Wayne pulled his gun, killed the safety. Almost. Almost.

Seth's small group pulled together, shouted for everyone to listen, said that they had to work together, that they'd survive if they could just—

"The trucks," one of Zach's pals said, his own group advancing on Seth's. Everywhere, people scurried, vanishing into the offices that served as their living quarters. Above, the gunfire continued. Outside, the dead howled and pressed in. "Give us the keys. We're getting the fuck out of here."

"I'm not giving you the keys, Tevin. Just take a minute and think about what you're—"

Someone shot Seth, and then the air was buzzing with lead.

Wayne dropped low and let the whole thing play itself out. A second of silence, followed by the cries of the wounded. On the roof, the men continued to fire their guns. The dead hammered the building. Someone ran by, their flashlight beam bobbing.

Wayne leapt to his feet and took the stairs two at a time.

"Here they are," someone said. Wayne heard keys jingling, and then he was in the classroom. He closed the door behind him.

Sue held the small black boy to her chest. He pressed his face to her neck, weeping. Some of the kids were standing, tears in their eyes. Others still sat amid their sheets and pillows, stuffed animals held to their chests. Patty sat at the back of the class, just out of the glow cast by Sue's lantern. She held two children close to her.

"What's happening?" Barely holding it together. "Who's shooting?"

"Some guys are on the roof picking them—"

"No. Someone in the warehouse fired a gun."

"Seth. Someone—"

"Seth shot somebody?"

"No. Somebody shot Seth. We have to—"

"Oh, God. Is he—"

"Are you ready? Wayne said.

"Now?" Sue asked, looking around, jittery. "Wait, where's Morgan?"

"Bathroom," Patty said.

"Jesus." Sue bit her lip and stood. "Kids, get up, we're going."

"Not you, hearts," Patty said to the kids in the back, and closed her eyes.

Leticia, Greg, and Shawn gathered by Wayne's side. Sue looked around. "Where's Sarah? Sarah?"

"She's staying with me," Patty said, pulling one of the shadows closer, her voice slurred.

Wayne said, "We can come back. You can fit. We all can fit. We can—"

"Goddamn it." Sue made fists at Patty and screamed, "You idiot!"

"You're going on foot?" Patty said.

"The Jeep is just four blocks away," Wayne answered. "We can—"

"You told Seth that you left it behind," Patty said. "You're going to get them killed."

"Do you have your gun?" Wayne asked, staring at Patty's shadowed form.

"I have three."

"Okay. Let's move." More gunshots. Shouting from downstairs. The drone of the gathering dead. The kids wailed. They closed Patty in the back room and stopped in the hall to the stairs.

Wayne looked at Sue and whispered, "I didn't know you wanted that one."

"He won't let go of me," she sighed. "I don't know where…he couldn't tell me where his shoes were, I just have to fucking carry him."

"We can make it." Wayne said, fighting back the urge to yell and curse. "We just need to be fast. Just—wait…"

"What is it?" Sue asked.

"I think I heard the motor pool loading door rolling up."

"Damn it. They're gonna get in."

An eruption of gunfire. Sue switched the small boy—*Devon*, Wayne remembered—to her left arm and pulled her gun. She nodded.

Wayne pulled Leticia, the smallest of the three standing around them, onto his right hip. She wrapped her arms around his neck. "Now hold on tight, okay?"

"Don't let them get me."

"Okay," Wayne said, sucking in a deep breath. "Sue, behind me. You cover our right. I have the left. Get them between us."

Sue nudged the two crying boys between them. Wayne winced. There were seven or eight in all, but damn it, they were so small.

"Hold onto my belt," he told Shawn. "Now." He looked at Sue. "Just like we planned. Okay?"

"Okay."

He opened the door and led them out. The vast expanse of the warehouse was lost to darkness. Their flashlight beams seemed to die on black air.

A row of offices separated one warehouse from the other. The dead may have been packed shoulder to shoulder in the motor pool, but there were none to be seen on this side of the facility.

They took the stairs slowly. Somewhere, voices raised in anger. More popping gunshots from outside. Heavy footsteps on the roof.

At the bottom of the stairs, Wayne stopped. The kid's head bumped into his back. Feet shuffled somewhere nearby. Ian stepped from the darkness and sank his teeth into the soft flesh of Leticia's shoulder. She screamed.

Wayne's gun thundered. Ian dropped. Sue and the kids screamed, retreating, falling over one another. She opened fire, shooting at nothing. Leticia's hot blood doused Wayne's hand. Her grip on his neck tightened. She screamed and screamed, and then there were more of them shambling through the darkness toward them.

Wayne screamed, "Go back!" and trailed Sue and the kids to the top of the stairs. "I'll take care of these. I'll get the Jeep. Wait in here." He pried the screaming and wounded child from his neck and passed her to Sue.

"Take care of her," he said, and with the click of the door shutting, was gone. At the bottom of the stairs, two more dead things bumped into one another. Trace and Mark, killed in the shootout over the keys. He took them down and moved toward the loading door, his flashlight beam passing over Seth's body. In the direction of the motor pool, someone yelled. An engine revved.

There would only be a few of them milling around outside—most of them would have flocked toward the motor pool loading door, some forty feet to his right. He could get through with ease. Probably.

Holstering his gun and still gripping the flashlight, he grabbed the chain with both hands, hoisted the massive door some five feet from the ground, and dashed into the night. Cold hands groped for him, and he stumbled over a fallen corpse—they were everywhere, thanks to the snipers, now long since gone. The walking ones closed in, grunting and eager. He rolled, kicking and thrashing and fumbling for his gun.

"Fuck." His holster was empty. One of them threw itself onto him. His chin hit the concrete. Blood flowed.

Rolling from beneath its thrashing dead weight, he scrambled to his feet and ran into Zach. The dead man gasped, its breath rank.

Wayne jerked back, pulled the Doctor from the holster on Zach's right hip, and blew the thing's head into pulp.

A pickup truck burst from within the motor pool, tires screeching and bouncing over the parking lot dividers. Screaming and flailing, several people flew from the truck-bed and slammed against the concrete.

Wayne ran. The further he got from the warehouse, the less activity he found. Within five minutes he found himself sliding behind the wheel of the Jeep, panting. Two minutes later, the headlights passed across the nightmare taking place outside of the warehouse.

Sue walked toward him, clutching Devon to her chest, her gun held high. There was no sign of Shawn or Greg, save the glistening red tangle over which the things fought just inside the loading door. Its ragged jaw twitching and useless, Ted's corpse dragged its baseball bat through the blood pooled around the feast. On the roof, someone waved and yelled for help.

Wayne brought the Jeep to a halt.

"Are either of you bit?"

Sue shook her head.

"Good. Get in."

She did.

They drove away.

He walked for days, thinking of the girl and of her hair, though not entirely sure which hair or which girl. Sometimes he wondered where she was, what had happened to her or if the signs around him had anything to do with her. NEW ORLEANS 65, one of them said, but that wasn't quite right. Almost right, maybe, but not quite. It was and it wasn't.

His wandering carried him from the highway and into a town. HAMMOND, the sign said, and that meant something to him, or had. The town was shattered and wrecked and broken, like the stumbling forms who were so like him and not at all like him.

One storefront was more thoroughly destroyed than the others he had seen. The front doors were lying on the ground, ripped from their frames. He looked past them and saw a small machine, about the size of a man, lying further from the store, as though it had somehow been yanked through the doors, tearing them out along with it. The small machine had three letters across the top—"ATM." He didn't recall what it was used for, but it looked sad lying there.

He looked back to the devastated store. To the left of the entrance, a dead woman stood raking her head back and forth across the wall. Little pieces of her face clung to the bricks. As he stepped into the store, she pulled her forehead away from the smeared rainbow of filth to watch with listless eyes as he passed. Because so much damage had been done to the front of the store, it wasn't as dark inside as the others. Boxes and trash were everywhere. The floor was slick with dirty water. The broken doors let the rain in, and this reminded him of something else, something that came to him only in images: the interior of the place he shared with the girl sodden and ruined, black stuff growing on the walls. He moaned once, and a dead boy sitting in the middle of the candy aisle moaned in return. He peeled the crinkly and shiny paper away from something colorful. Dropping the paper, he placed the colorful thing into his mouth, retched, and spat.

He made his way slowly to the back, where there were hundreds of little plastic bottles all over the floor; a few were also on metal shelves. He picked one up. It rattled.

Unlike his random thoughts in the night, one now came to him with some logical connection, though it was as unbidden and unpredictable as any of the others. He remembered the girl needed what was inside these little bottles. He remembered opening them for her and very carefully counting out two of the little white disks into her palm. He fumbled with one bottle now, but there was no chance of him opening it. He raised it up to look at the label, but the print was too small for him to read. When he noticed this problem, he instinctively reached for his shirt pocket: he remembered there was always something in that pocket that would help him read things that were too small, though he couldn't remember what the device was called or what it looked like. But his pocket was now empty.

He began going through all the bottles, arranging many of them on a counter there in the back of the store. He couldn't read any of the labels, but he tried different ways of arranging the bottles—from biggest to smallest, or in an undulating "wave" of descending and then ascending sizes, or separating the round bottles from those with squared corners. Then came combinations of the various organizational methods he'd tried. He was very careful and spent most of the day on this project.

He didn't know why he did this, or what exactly guided his hand, but he knew when he had the bottles arranged in the "right" way, the way that formed the perfect pattern on the counter. He stepped back to admire it. Then he stepped forward and counted the seventh bottle and removed it. Stepping back, the pattern still looked "right." Counting another seven, he removed a bottle, and still the pattern looked to him unmarred by this removal. He repeated this process five more times, and, when he was satisfied the remaining pattern was still the correct one, he looked at the seven bottles he had chosen. He nodded. These too were correct, he thought, and put them in the hole in his stomach, next to the metal band he had taken from the woman. He walked from the store and continued down the street, feeling somewhat more full and satisfied than before.

Eventually he worked his way back to another highway. I-10, the signs said. NEW ORLEANS 50. His mind buzzed and he walked and walked. The sun sank and rose, and he walked and sometimes he sat down and closed his eyes or pulled the round thing out of his stomach and held it. When the sun got too hot on his skin, he sought peace in the shade of the forest or beneath one of the large wheeled things or sometimes even inside one of the smaller ones.

He walked and walked, and sometimes those like him walked with him, side by side, as if he had someplace to go and they wanted to be there with him. Other times they ignored him, busy with their own broken journeys.

Once he came across a dead man being pursued by four others. The man crawled and gasped and tried to stand, but the four grunted and pushed and would not let him rise, battering him with loose fists and rocks, bashing away his nose and shattering his teeth. He moved toward them, wondering in some way if he could help the man, but the others pushed him away and lashed at him with sticks. One of them tried to take the things in his stomach. He slapped them back and, as they turned their attention to the pitiful shape writhing on the ground, crept away.

He walked and walked. NEW ORLEANS 35 and 20 and 10, and though he didn't know what that meant, he nonetheless knew it when he saw it, silent and dark and still.

The sun was again going down as he ambled across a large bridge. All over the roadway were large machines of metal and glass, all of them smashed, many of them burned. There were motionless bodies inside most of them, with many more on the pavement. Many were not whole, but were just limbs or torsos in dried-up pools of blood. There were swarms of loud, ugly flies all over. He shook his head and kept walking, looking up at the beautiful angles of the bridge's proud steel frame. There was another bridge next to the one on which he walked, and this meant something to him, too, though it made little sense: CCC. And: GNO.

Halfway across the bridge, he saw a yellow metal box attached to it at eye level. The box was open and a plastic thing hung from it by a cord. The plastic thing was grasped by a right hand, severed sloppily just below the elbow. He looked above the metal box and read the sign there: "Call Now. Life is Worth Living. There Is Hope."

He stared at the words for some time. He tried mouthing them, but his lips and tongue felt like cloth flaps attached to his body without really being a part of it. The words were simple, but he couldn't quite grasp them, or why those ones in particular would be written on a bridge. More and more, he concentrated on the first word of the second sentence. He tried to breathe out as he mouthed it, but he couldn't control the vowel sound properly, or how to press his lower teeth against his upper lip to make the "f" sound, so it kept coming out differently as "Laf… lav… laf… lof… lov…."

The effort taxed him mentally, but he nodded. He had made the right sound.

He continued to the middle of the bridge. Here the wind whipped across him, driving off the flies. One vehicle in the center of the bridge was undamaged. He ran his hand along the smooth, warm metal. It remained a beautiful thing—a most pleasing combination of curved and straight, glass and metal, all of it governed by symmetry and grace. He balanced the little plastic bottles on the roof of the vehicle, stacking them in two little pyramids of three each. He put the circular, metal band between the two pyramids, and placed the last bottle inside the circle. As he knew they would be, the pyramids were precisely the same height, and they were spaced perfectly. The band and bottle in the middle were also formed and spaced to complete the whole. It was good how they combined, with each other and with the lines of the vehicle. If there were any people left, perhaps they would see it and admire or enjoy it.

He turned from this creation to the guardrail. Behind him, the city was motionless, dead, and silent in the day's dying light. Beneath the bridge, the water seemed to sit bloated and unmoving, a thing dead and stagnant, but if he concentrated, he knew he could hear its whispering rush, full of power, mystery, and promise—qualities he heard more and more distinctly as he spun toward the water's black surface and his uncertain rebirth.

Wayne had been counting on the path still being there, and it was. One of the very last efforts in the city during the outbreaks had been the National Guard attempting to organize things, forbidding unauthorized vehicle use. For their own travel, they had to clear two lanes of the Crescent City Connection. It was the only job they finished. Wayne drove them over the city.

"I always found that amazing," Sue said, "that you could pass through the center of New Orleans, right over the St. Charles cable car line, French Quarter to the north, Garden District to the south, and never even touch down, never even have to get your tires dirty."

"Mm."

"Just float thirty feet above it like a bird on a wire." She sighed. "You can't even see it now." Wayne slowed as they went up the CCC ramp. The Guard had cleared it, yeah, but there were still bits of junk everywhere. Devon coughed. He looked like he was trying to sleep, or cry. Sue was holding him in the front seat, starting to cry herself, and Wayne was turned to look at them, like an idiot, when the Jeep went ba-KUNK. There was a huffing sound and Wayne knew they'd busted a tire. Devon was awake now, and definitely crying. He sounded worse than he had even an hour ago.

Wayne pulled over, then got out and paced around the Jeep. He'd wedged the right front tire over a rusted bumper. It had sliced clean through the rubber. The tire was already empty. There was a spare on the back, but Christ was it dark. Sue said, "What is it?"

"Just the tire, I'm fixing it."

"*What?*"

"Stay there, Sue." He heard her door open. Shit. "Get back in the car, I'll be done in five minutes."

He had the spare and the jack already. This was ridiculous. "Where are you going?" He heard her blubbering further up the bridge. She'd grabbed Devon and was carrying him on her chest with his arms wrapped around her neck.

"Christ, Christ," she panted, as Devon's green snot wet her shoulder. There were bodies all over. She jogged up the lane as fast as she could, thinking, *There might be a car up there. Something with the keys in it, and some juice.* She was hyperventilating again. She had no plan. Her face was hot with tears.

Mosquitoes and flies fluttered in the headlight's beams. She could only hear her sneakers thumping the asphalt and her own sticky breathing. She held Devon tighter.

She reached the crest of the bridge to look down into Gretna on the other side. It was dark over there. She turned. Wayne crouched next to the car. There were no dead in sight, not walking, anyway. Maybe she should go back.

She spun around again, and saw the pill bottle pyramids. Cefdinir. Citalopram. Prazepam. Tramadol. Amoxicillin, more. They were pasty-flaky with dark blood, but Sue could read the labels, and she recognized some of the names. Peggy had once told her the names of some medicines she gave to Brandy after she was attacked, the ones that should've helped but didn't. Which were they?

Devon whimpered into her neck, "I don't like the dark."

"I know, baby." Sue grabbed all of the bottles, stuffed them between her body and Devon's and turned back toward the Jeep.

ZOMBIE SEASON

By Catherine MacLeod

Catherine MacLeod has tried to watch *Night of the Living Dead*, but every time she does, she spends so much time with her hands over her face she can't actually claim to have seen it. When not cowering behind her hands, she writes fiction, which has appeared dozens of times in the Canadian science fiction magazine *On Spec*, and in other magazines such as *Talebones*, *TransVersions*, and the French-language magazine *Solaris*. Her work has also appeared in anthologies *Tesseracts 6*, *Bits of the Dead*, and *Open Space*. Forthcoming work includes her story "Stone," which will appear in *Horror Library #4*.

Death is a horrible and terrifying thing, but it's a reality that has to be faced. When a loved one dies, most people don't feel like doing anything but grieve. Sadly, there are a whole host of practical issues that have to be attended to—phone calls to make, financial affairs to be put in order, and funeral arrangements to be made. A coffin must be picked out, the body must be prepared, and a service planned. And, of course, before a person can be buried in the ground, someone's got to dig the hole, and that's when society turns to our gravediggers.

We all know this is a vital occupation, but perhaps because of our discomfort with the idea of death, we tend to form some pretty strange ideas about those who dig graves. Ask your average person to picture a gravedigger and what do they imagine? Some weirdo, right? Some lurking creep with frenzied hair and haunted eyes, a guy with a strange voice who spends too much time by himself. It's an ugly stereotype, and it's high time that something was done to set the record straight. Gravedigging is an honorable profession, and our gravediggers deserve better treatment at the hands of authors and moviemakers.

We hope that our next story, which portrays a gravedigger as a brave, zombie-battling hero, will eliminate those negative preconceptions and give everyone a more positive, wholesome image of gravediggers everywhere.

The secret's all in the salt. People just expect the town zombie hunter to carry it, along with a shotgun and squirt-bottle of gasoline. I don't believe it'll protect me, but if carrying it makes folks feel safer, that's fine.

Of course, I've always carried salt, but not for reasons that would make anyone feel safe, and that's fine, too.

The first shriek shreds the air at 7 A.M., and I'm ready. I was a gravedigger, back before Judgment Day put me out of a job—no use digging holes if the deceased aren't going to stay in them—and these days people say I just have a natural way with the dead. Privately, I don't think much of their appetite for living flesh, but I don't judge.

Some people fear the dead, no matter what, and back then I didn't understand. Now I do. The dead know too many secrets, and some folks have reason to worry.

Like Adam Wade saying his crazy wife ran off to New York, only to have her shamble on home with her head stove in. Or the preacher's pure-as-new-snow daughter dying of pneumonia, then wandering into church yesterday with the remains of a dead baby caged in her ribs.

But everyone has secrets. I suppose how bad they are is just a matter of opinion.

Then again, concern for opinion has always kept me closemouthed about my own.

My seven o'clock job is a zombie on Main Street, who probably wouldn't even have noticed Miretta Jackson if she hadn't started screaming at it. Then again, it's Henry Jackson, Miretta's late husband. She screamed at him non-stop when he was alive, and old habits die hard.

I shoot him down, spare the gasoline, and drop a match on the chance that—yup, you can always tell who's been embalmed; they go up like marshmallows.

I watch the fire from the coffeehouse as I eat pancakes and ketchup. The waitress, Gina, says, "Billy Martin, I swear you have no taste," just like always. Then, like always, she glances at my shotgun and moves off.

It's coming on fall now, and the dead slow down in cool weather. They're no good at all in winter. I'll have to start curing meat to put by while the hunting's still good. Gina has no idea, saying I have no taste. After all, isn't my salt mixed with parsley and thyme?

Life is easier these days. I don't have to dig the dead up anymore, or worry about getting caught; and no one wants to watch me roast zombies, especially when one might be their own dearly departed. Still, I'm discreet. Only the dead know my secret, and I doubt they'll judge.

People say I just have a natural way with the dead, and I think that might be true.

That, and the secret really is all in the salt.

TAMESHIGIRI

By Steven Gould

A Hugo and Nebula Award finalist, Steven Gould is the author of the novel *Jumper*, the basis for the recent film of the same name. Other novels include *Reflex*, *Blind Waves*, *Helm*, *Greenwar*, and *Wildside*. A new novel, *7th Sigma*, is scheduled for May 2011. Gould is currently working on another entry in the Jumper series. His short fiction has appeared in *Analog*, *Asimov's Science Fiction*, *Amazing Stories*, *The Year's Best Science Fiction*, and *Tor.com*. When not writing, Gould spends entirely too much time killing zombies on his Xbox 360.

Ninjas were spies, saboteurs, and assassins in ancient Japan. In Japan the equivalent term "shinobi" is more common, but Westerners prefer the sound of "ninja." Ninja was an officially recognized job, and only those of a certain income were allowed to keep ninjas on the payroll. Ninjas commonly wielded swords (katanas), throwing stars (shuriken), and chain and sickle weapons called a kusarigama. While popular imagination pictures ninjas clad in black, in real life ninjas probably tried to blend into the local population by dressing as priests, entertainers, and merchants. Much of Japanese architecture was originally developed as a defense against ninjas, including the use of gravel courtyards and nightingale floors that made it difficult for intruders to move about silently.

Gould says that this story is all my fault: "I made the mistake of saying on Twitter something like 'Ninjas awesome. Zombies awesome. Ninjas and Zombies? Double awesome!' John Joseph Adams saw it and asked if I was writing such a thing. I wasn't, but I said that I could."

A student of Iaido—the Japanese sword as a martial art—for over twelve years, Gould didn't need to do much research for the story, but he says he did stand out in the middle of his backyard with a bokken (wooden sword) for a while, working on some of the moves depicted in the story.

Why zombies? "The scary thing about zombies, slow or fast, is that there will always be more," Gould says. "It doesn't matter how many you kill, eventually more will arrive. Zombies are a palpable, biting representation of our own mortality. And mortality stinks. And it has rotting flesh."

In medieval Japan there was a swordsmith who volunteered to execute a felon so he could perform *tameshigiri*—test cutting—on his latest blade. When the convicted man saw the sword maker he said, "If I had known it would be you, I would have swallowed stones to ruin your blade!"

Some days you're the sword maker, slicing cleanly through flesh and bone, and some days you're the poor bastard forcing rocks down your throat right before they put the steel to you. Sure you're going to die, but you don't have to go *easy*.

We walked twenty minutes through the kitchen gardens before we got to the southern wall. The gate wasn't manned but we only had to wait a few minutes before the guard walking the parapet got there, slung his rifle, and came down the ladder, huffing and puffing.

He checked Sensei's pass and then Richard pushed forward, like he does, to be next. The guard glanced at Richard's pass and then up at his face. "Richard Torres? You look like your brother. Didn't he go missing a few weeks back?"

"You think?" snapped Richard. "Why do you think—"

Sensei touched Richard on the arm. "No sign of Diego, I take it?" Sensei said to the guard.

"Not on my watch, no." He gave Richard back his pass, took Lou's, looked at her, and blinked. They all do when they see her. I mean she's gorgeous most days but for some reason, today she glowed.

"Louise Patterson? I think I knew your sister in high school. How is she?"

"Dead," said Lou.

Nine out of every ten died in the infestation. You'd think he'd know better.

He swallowed, gave her back the pass, and took mine. "Hello. I don't think I've met you before. New to town?"

I laughed sourly. "You sat behind me in Algebra, Danny. You kept copying my work."

He took a step back and stared down at my pass. His free hand touched the opposite elbow. "Wow, Rosa. You've, uh, filled out."

"Yes," I said. I was skinny back then but now I had curves. He was stocky before, and still was. Surprising, that, considering the rationing. I didn't comment, though, about his weight or what had happened back in high school. We wanted to get through the gate after all.

He turned back to Sensei, as if I wasn't there. "Weapons? Just the pig stickers, right?"

We held open our packs so he could see. Guns and ammo were reserved for the defense of the community. You could travel outside but ammo and guns stayed in unless it was the guards going out to watch the fields during planting, weeding, or harvest. There are other reasons, too.

"Just the swords," said Sensei.

Danny undid the massive padlock holding down the hinged bar, then said, "Don't open it until I've checked from above, right?"

Sensei nodded, his face impassive. "Understood."

Of course Sensei understood. He'd been outside more than anyone else in town.

Danny went back up the ladder and unslung the rifle. "There's some in the cornfield over there." He pointed to the left of the gate. "Maybe six or so standing up, but there could be more lying down. The corn is getting pretty high." He pointed to the right. "The soybeans are only knee-high and there's one wandering around in there. The road—" He lifted his rifle and fired one shot. "There, the road is clear until it dips down toward the river."

Sensei glared at Danny.

Lou frowned. "What'd he do that for? He's going to draw them to the gate."

Sensei sighed. "It's not as if we're trying to avoid them, Lou." He gestured, and I went to the bar and lifted it. Richard drew his sword and held it *hasso*, pointed straight up near his right shoulder. I heard Sensei sigh slightly but he didn't say anything. Sensei gestured again and I pushed. The left-hand door opened outward on well-oiled hinges until it was ninety degrees open. Richard sprang out, looking around wildly. Lou rolled her eyes, and I nodded.

The asphalt was cracked and weed-lined, but the field crews had cleared any sizable brush away twenty feet on either side. A hundred feet in front of the gate, a body sprawled across the faded median stripes—Danny's target. Richard took several steps forward and stopped in the middle of the road, sword still raised on high.

I looked behind the door, before moving forward, but it was clear.

Sensei said, "Richard, put away your sword."

Richard looked back at Sensei, his eyes wide.

Sensei said, "What do we study?"

"*Batto-ho*, Sensei. The art of drawing and cutting."

"Yes. So, save your strength. Trust your training. We are out in the open. You will have lots of time to draw."

"Yes, Sensei." Richard did *noto*, the sheathing of the sword, in the *Shindo Munen Ryu* style, first lowering the tip forward, reversing the grip, and swinging the blade up so the *mune*, the back of the blade, rested on his shoulder, then bringing the *saya*, the wooden scabbard, forward until it touched the *mune*. He brought the *tskua*, the handle, forward until the sword's tip crossed the opening of the *saya*, and then reversed, sliding it home. Done smoothly and quickly it is beautiful to see.

I winced. This was not beautiful. Richard nearly stabbed himself in the hand.

Sensei stepped forward, close to Richard, and said something quietly. Richard blushed, but he stepped back and said, "Yes, Sensei."

From the wall, Danny said loudly, "Be back before dark, right?"

Lou held her finger to her lips and Danny laughed, making no effort to keep his voice down. Once an asshole, always an asshole.

We turned away and a minute later I heard the gate shut and the bar drop. Sensei led us on, sticking to the road first, going toward the zombie that Danny had shot from the wall. Ten feet short, Sensei stamped his foot hard on the ground.

The body twitched.

Sensei shook his head and stepped back.

Danny had made all that noise for nothing. The shot had grazed the side of the zombie's head, tearing away an ear, but the central nervous system disconnect hadn't happened. It pushed itself up on all fours and looked at us. It was bald and scabby but it had been a woman once. A pearl earring, still shiny in the sun, hung from the remaining ear. Once I saw that I couldn't help looking for the other earring. Yep, there it was on the asphalt, six feet up the road, still attached to the other earlobe.

"Lou," said Sensei.

"*Hai.*" Lou slid forward, feet brushing across the asphalt.

Richard gave her an angry glance but Lou's attention was focused on the zombie. As she moved closer it shoved up with its arms, coming upright on its knees. Lou drew and cut with one motion, horizontal, her left arm pulling sharply back on the scabbard as the tip cleared.

The sword cut cleanly through the neck. The body dropped down and the head bounced off the payment and rolled to the side.

Sensei nodded.

Lou cleaned her blade with alcohol, put the sword back in its *saya*, and threw up in the ditch.

Richard opened his mouth to say something but I turned sharply so my *saya* struck his hip. When he turned, frowning, to look at me I said, "Oh. Sorry."

Sensei glanced back at us, then pointed out across the soybeans to a figure shambling in our direction. "Yours, Rosa. Richard, you go along and observe." He lifted two fingers up and pushed them toward his eyes.

"Yes, Sensei," I said. "Eyes open."

Richard walked directly toward the zombie but I said, "Walk in the rows. Come winter, we'll be eating these beans if you leave any alive." I didn't look to see how he took that but set off briskly between two rows of plants at right angles to the road. My zombie swung its head toward me and changed course. It was one of the stupider ones, unable to predict an intercept point, so it walked in a constantly changing curve, always turning toward me.

When I was halfway there I saw a dark spot, two rows over. I held up my hand and looked back at Richard but he wasn't watching me or the rows; his eyes were on the moving zombie. "Richard!" I hissed.

He jerked to a stop. Ten feet in front of him, the dark spot sat up. It was missing one arm from the elbow down, possibly shot off by one of the wall guards, but it got to its feet surprisingly quick. It had been a man, tall and thin, and it was closer to Richard than I was. When it lurched toward him, Richard, his face white as a sheet, took a step forward, drew, and cut.

Richard's arm was clenched so tight that the cutting arc was abbreviated, slicing the air in front of the zombie.

I reached it, then, from the side, and hamstrung it, cutting the tendons behind the knees. It flopped down but kept crawling forward, toward Richard.

"Finish it!" I said quietly, and headed back toward my original target.

This one had been a soldier, combat fatigues still recognizable, but too stained to read the insignia. I took a stance ten feet before it, *hasso*, sword above my right shoulder. As it took one last step I went forward and cut, *kesa*, upper right to lower left. When I'd finished the stroke, its head and right arm lay to my left and the rest of it lay at my feet.

I turned back, to see how Richard was doing.

He'd managed to cut off the other arm and into the zombie's spine, mid-back, which had at least stopped it shoving forward with its legs. At that point, finally, Richard had managed the head, though it had been high. He'd cut through even with the ears so the top of the head was on the ground but the lower jaw, tongue extending oddly upward, still hung on the neck.

"Lovely. Clean your sword," I said, getting out my own baggie of alcohol-soaked rags.

We'd all had the vaccination but it was only seventy-five percent effective. Better to take all precautions.

Sensei and Lou joined us then. Sensei examined both kills quietly. When we'd sheathed our swords he said, "Right. This way."

There were a lot more of them down in the river bottom. There were vacation homes on the high banks and a series of fishing camps, but mostly it was the water that drew them. They drink a lot if they can. The scientists aren't sure if they need the water but the speculation is that they feel a burning and they try to quench it. It's the same burning that drives them at the uninfected, drives them to consume something that they don't have anymore, as if eating it will give it back.

Sensei took the next group, three zombies, giving a lecture first.

"When there are more than one, you can't afford to wound. You must disable or kill. Wounded they just keep coming. So, sever the spine or split the brain or take a leg. Once they are down you can finish those that need to be finished."

Then he showed us.

He took the first one with a *shomen* cut. *Shomen* means head, after all, but it refers to the vertical cut which, in this case, came down from the top of the skull right between the eyes, all the way into the throat before it stopped. Sensei stepped aside as the next one rushed through and he cut into the neck from behind, cleaving the spine but not the entire neck, for the head flopped forward and hung there as it made one more stumbling step before sprawling forward. He took the last zombie's leg from the side, cutting through the femur right above the knee. While it was trying to struggle upright again, he decapitated it, like an executioner.

The next zombies came as a pair, moderately spaced. Sensei gestured. "Okay, Richard. Just relax. Remember that you're cutting with the last four inches of the blade. Extend. Be aware of your environment."

Richard moved forward with Sensei following a bit behind. Lou and I stood back to back, our eyes checking all around.

"You okay?" I asked. Since she'd thrown up, I hadn't had a chance to talk to her.

"Yeah. Something I ate, I guess."

"Well, it would've bothered me, too. I just couldn't help thinking that she was a person once. Someone raised her, tucked her into bed, gave her those pearl earrings."

"Yeah, someone did and *it* probably ate them."

"Cynic," I said.

"What was that with Danny boy back on the wall? When he remembered who you were, he backed away quick enough."

"He tried to grope me once. I'd been with Sensei for a year already. I dislocated his elbow."

Richard and Sensei were closing on the two zombies, Richard in the lead.

"I don't think I can look," Lou said.

"Well," I said. "He hasn't stabbed himself yet." I held up my left hand. There were three triangular scars on the webbing between my thumb and forefinger. "I got myself enough times at the dojo."

"It would be better if he had. He'd have the respect he needs for the blade."

There was truth in that. You shouldn't be afraid of the blade but you should certainly be respectful of it.

Richard drew his sword ahead of time and held it behind him, low, in *waki gamae* the hidden stance. When the first zombie approached, he cut up from the side, trying to do a reverse *kesa*, but the blade stuck in the ribs, short of the spine. Richard threw himself to the side, wrenching hard, and the blade came free but he stumbled backwards and fell.

Sensei tensed but didn't move.

Richard got up on his knees and stayed there. When the zombie with the slashed ribs approached, he cut horizontal, right below the zombie's knee. The zombie, went down, forward, trying to step on a foot that was no longer there. Richard twisted to the side and decapitated it cleanly.

I heard Lou's sigh of relief.

Richard kept it simple for the next one, a straight *shomen* cut to the forehead. He must've tensed for it was more of a chop, but the blade got deep enough into the brain to drop it.

We joined them. Sensei was saying, "...can't throw everything you learned out the window now that it counts." He held up his left hand and extended the pinky and ring fingers. "Squeeze. Relax. The blade is sharp enough to do the work *if you let it.* Speed and the correct angle matter far more than muscle."

Richard nodded.

Sensei had Lou go next, a group of four clustered close together.

Lou ran toward them, then moved quickly to the side and away, so that when they turned to track her, they strung out in a line. She didn't draw her blade until the first cut but took a leg with it, then danced past the falling zombie to kill one of the rear ones with a *kesa* cut to the neck. She sidestepped again, causing the last two to tangle with the fallen zombie, now struggling up on one knee. She stepped forward and killed one of the standing with a *shomen* cut, stepped back, and repeated the cut on the last standing zombie. The one missing a leg crawled forward and she pivoted and took the head.

Sensei nodded in satisfaction. "See how she separated them? Took them one at a time? Isolate them. Don't let them surround you. Work around the edges. Turn and keep turning."

We heard running feet then and Sensei said, "Rosa. Watch out, it's recent."

We all looked, fearful, but when it came out of the trees near the river, we saw it was a woman, almost normal looking, clothes still intact, not as pallid, but there was blood down its front and the eyes were insane. The recent ones, infected within a month, are much faster. Not supernaturally fast—just human fast and not as stupid. They retain more of their physical skills.

"Jesus," said Richard. "It's Mrs. Steckles."

The Steckles had left three weeks before, traveling to the city, looking for family.

I walked out, putting myself well ahead of the others and it tracked on me. Excuse me if I still use "it"—all of these things were human once but no more.

I knelt, *seiza*, sitting back on my heels. It came on and its arms came up as it neared. I took both feet off slicing through the ankles, sliding off to the right to avoid the flailing, clawing hands. It thrashed as it fell but was up on knees and hands remarkably fast, coming back toward me. Standing, I cut down, aiming for the neck but it lurched forward and I ended up cutting through its spine lower down, below the shoulder blades. It lost control of it's abdominal muscles and legs but it flopped down and pulled itself forward with its arms. It's teeth snapped together within inches of my knee.

I jumped completely over it, turned, and cut its head off as it dragged itself back around. The rictus of the face relaxed and the eyes lost their focus. She looked like Mrs. Steckles again.

Now I felt like throwing up.

The others came up and Sensei was saying, "Imagine facing a large group *and* one of these faster ones charging into the mix." He searched my face for a moment.

"I'm okay, Sensei," I said, wiping the blade.

He gestured back toward the river. "Let's see what we can find closer to the river."

We dispatched over a hundred by mid-afternoon and still they marched out of the woods. We'd engage the larger groups in a line and, as we cut them down, we'd slowly move back to keep them from flanking us. The sheer monotony of it finally overcame Richard's tenseness and he started looking more like he did in the dojo, relaxed and focused, spending his energy at the right instance to accelerate his blade instead of slowing it with excess tension.

We ran into two more from the Steckles' party, or more specifically, they ran into us. One of them carried a baseball bat, his hands hadn't lost their cunning. It came in and swung at Sensei, like a slugger going for a fast ball, and Sensei took one step back and cut the wrists, then finished it, *kesa*. Richard finished the other after Lou took off its leg mid-thigh.

It was so much worse, recognizing them. Fortunately the older ones are so changed—their hair falls out and their skin is scabbed, flaked, and swollen—that even if you knew them before, your chances of recognizing them are small.

That helps. Well, it helps a *little*.

Sensei led us back up the hill, to where an old soccer field gave a good view in all directions. "Rest," he said. "Eat."

I didn't think I'd be able to eat but I washed carefully with my alcohol rags and waved my hands through the air to dry them. I served Sensei first, of course. It was tortillas with onions, eggs, and beans and my first bite showed me I *could* eat. That I was really hungry. Lou barely touched hers.

"Okay," Sensei said. Let's get back to the gate."

Richard protested. "Sensei, we haven't begun to look. Diego could be holed up somewhere, starving!"

Sensei shook his head. "Perhaps. But we need the light. It gets dark early down in the bottoms. We can try again, tomorrow."

Lou looked miserable but she didn't say anything. I was unhappy, too.

Diego had studied with Sensei longer than any of us, since before, when our sword study was just an adjunct to the aikido. Diego had brought his little brother, Richard, to learn the sword when it had become a practical matter, after ammo became scarcer and it became clear that noise would just bring more of them.

As far as I was concerned, Diego was like a brother to me and Lou, as if we'd shared parents. In a way, we did, in Sensei.

Danny wasn't at the gate.

Sensei shrugged. "Walking the wall, perhaps."

Lou asked, "Is he still on duty?"

"Oh, yes," said Sensei. "Shifts change at eight, four, and midnight. He should be on for another hour easily."

Richard went over and pounded on the gate, three times, hard.

"Stop it!" said Sensei, but it was too late.

There was a heavy rustling in the cornfield.

I wish I'd never read that book.

Lou was mad. "Are you insane? Why don't you just put a cowbell on and run back to the river!"

Sensei shook his head. "Spilled milk. Keep your mind focused."

The rustling got louder. I mean really loud. They must've been lying among the stocks like cordwood before the pounding roused them.

"Why didn't they come out when Daniel fired that shot this morning?" I wondered aloud.

"Maybe they weren't here yet," Lou said. "Maybe it was the shot that drew them here."

Twelve walked out of the corn at once, then five more. And then I lost count.

"Sensei," said Lou. "Maybe we could throw Rosa up onto the top of the wall, so she could open the gate."

Sensei drew his sword. "It'll be padlocked, remember? And I don't think she'd make it over the razor wire."

Another wave walked out of the corn.

Sensei pointed back along the wall, in the other direction, through the soybeans. "At a jog, Lou, lead. Look ahead. Keep your eyes open. We'll watch behind."

"Now, Sensei?"

"Five minutes ago."

I left my sword undrawn and hung back with Sensei, letting Richard keep pace behind Lou. There was a recently infected, vigorous zombie further back in the cornfield and it got up a serious head of steam before it burst out of the stalks. It was across the road in seconds and ten more seconds saw it out in front of the others.

I breathed out. It wasn't Diego.

"Sensei?" I said.

"I see it. I'll make the first cut, you finish it." He kept jogging but slowed slightly, drifting further back.

The zombie sped up and, just when I thought it would leap on Sensei's back, he sidestepped and turned, so fast, the sword coming across waist high, cutting deep across the zombies abdomen. It folded over, but didn't fall, staggering.

I pivoted and took the head.

The zombie dropped. We kept moving.

It's three miles to the town's west gate but there's a deep culvert where the outflow from the city's water treatment plant flows through a grate under the wall on its way to the river. If we went far enough away from the wall it became more shallow, but that was in the woods.

"Sensei?" Lou asked.

Sensei and I caught up to Richard and Lou, and looked down. It was steep, fifteen feet down, then back up the same on the other side. Also, there was a trio of zombies crouched in the shallow stream.

"Follow," Sensei said, and dropped over the edge with his sword drawn.

The zombie Sensei landed on didn't stand a chance. Neither did the one he cut as he dropped, but Sensei fell backwards into the stream, after landing, and the other zombie leaped at him.

Richard jumped. He missed with his feet but he fell over and knocked the zombie sideways, away from Sensei. He swore sharply. Sensei got up and cut the zombie down.

I looked behind. The crowd was fifty yards behind and coming steadily, some of them almost jogging if you could call a quick, step-drag, a jog.

"Go," I told Lou. "Carefully, though. I think Richard's broken his foot."

She slid down the steep side in a shower of rocks and dirt, pulled Richard to his feet, and began climbing up the other side, supporting Richard. I waited until Sensei had joined them, supporting Richard from the other side, then slid down myself.

I wanted to reach the far side before them. If anything came out of the woods, they'd be handicapped as they came over the edge. I ran ten feet down the gully and scrambled up to where I could grab a root sticking out of the bank. With it,

I reached the top in time to see two zombies come out of the woods. Very old zombies, probably early infected. They hardly looked human. All their clothes had rotted off and with it lots of skin. I couldn't even tell what sex they'd been, but thank goodness they were slow ones. I had time to pull Richard over the lip before they were even close.

The one in front reached out its left arm and I just cut it off above the elbow. It staggered in the other direction, suddenly heavier on its right side. It would probably have recovered its balance in another step but the gully was right there and it went over the edge. I split the other one down through the sinuses and turned back before it fell. On the other side of the gully the first of our pursuers had jumped down into the gully and was starting to claw its way up our side.

Sensei tilted his neck side to side, stretching. His voice was calm and low. "Lou, check his leg. If it's a sprain, bind it. Rosa, you're with me, on the edge."

It was a good place to make a stand. They were clumsy and, even unopposed, it took them several tries to get up the bank to the rim. Mostly we just split their heads open, letting them dislodge others as they fell.

The problem was they were still coming. I didn't really see an end to them, and some of them were being driven down the gully into the woods where I knew they'd be able to climb out easily.

We'd put twenty or so down for good when Lou said, "Bad sprain, I think. I duct taped it."

"Then we should go," said Sensei. "Start off. We'll follow."

We killed fifteen more.

Richard was moving okay, limping heavily, but he and Lou were working well as a team with Lou taking the legs and Richard finishing them. We went through a field of sugar beets, moving down the rows parallel to the wall.

"Go for the gate," someone said, loudly.

I looked up. One of the guards—not Danny—was watching us from the wall but he kept his gun slung, thankfully.

"I'll be waiting!" He headed down the parapet at a slow jog, light-footed. He'd still get there well ahead of us.

The next field was hay, cut short and harvested recently, for it felt like a stubbly lawn. Without Richard's sprain, we could've sprinted across it, but at least we could see everything come at us.

I was expecting to see more ahead of us, for the wall and the gates draw them, but instead I started seeing bodies. Bodies in pieces.

"Sensei, Diego's been here."

There were sharp cuts, heads, arms, legs. Not a few were cleaved entirely through the chest from the shoulder down through the ribs.

He nodded and frowned. One of the bodies had not been infected for it had also been eaten. The infected don't eat other infected, not after the first day or two. Something about the taste. But this body had been sliced first, several times. Including the neck.

"Sensei?"

He frowned. "I don't know. Maybe the zombies had already killed or mortally wounded him, er, her, and Diego put her out of her misery."

I was looking at the blood spray. "Definitely alive during the first cut."

We pushed through to the apple orchard beyond the hay. The field hands had done a good job of keeping the underbrush down, but the trees were unpruned and many of the branches dipped down close to the ground, heavy with unripe fruit, obscuring the sight lines.

The crowd of zombies on our tail hadn't entered the hayfield and it was clear that they were beginning to tail off as the ones in the rear got distracted and wandered away.

We moved carefully into the orchard, looking in all directions. The orchard predated the wall and the rows ran at an angle, making it hard to see too far ahead. We rounded one low-branched tree and saw him, two rows over.

Diego was sitting on a pile of bodies, his arms resting on his thighs, his head hanging. The sun was behind him, casting his figure in silhouette, but he was instantly recognizable by his size, posture, and especially his hair, which he wore in a top knot, like the samurai *chonmage* style.

Lou's hand went to her mouth and froze but Richard saw him and cried out, "Diego!"

He turned then, and the light fell across his front.

In one hand he held his sword, in the other he held an arm. Someone else's arm. His chin was covered with blood as was his shirt front.

"Oh, no." Lou fell to her knees. One hand went to her stomach and the other covered her mouth.

"Rosa, take them around." Sensei gestured at the side of the orchard closest to the wall. "Keep them moving to the gate." He didn't look at us as he said this. Instead, he walked forward, his hands resting on the scabbard and handle of his sword.

"Sensei, shouldn't we take him together? *He's still holding his sword!*"

As I said, the recently infected retained their physical skills and Diego had been studying with Sensei for twenty-five years. His physical skills were considerable.

"Could you cut him, Rosa? I'm not sure I can, but I must. Get Lou and Richard to the gate. My will is in the *Kamiza* at the dojo. I haven't changed it but you are listed as my preferred successor, after Diego." He finally looked around at me. The corners of his mouth were drawn down hard, but they twitched up briefly in an almost smile, and then he winked at me.

He stepped out briskly toward Diego.

Damn him!

I grabbed Lou by the arm and said, "Help me with Richard. We've got to run for it."

She was sobbing, but she staggered to her feet and grabbed Richard's other arm. We began running toward the wall.

Diego ignored Sensei and ran toward the wall, too, blocking our path. He raised his arms to hold the sword *jodan*, over his head, but realized he still held the arm in his hand. He shoved it down into his shirt where it hung, the fingers just sticking above his collar, then took the sword up high.

"*MA-TE!*" screamed Sensei, and Diego jerked back slightly and looked confused. Sensei had used that command thousands of times during Diego's training. It meant stop or wait. Diego turned back toward Sensei who still hadn't drawn his sword.

"See," said Richard, reaching out. "He's still in there! Diego, it's okay!"

Diego turned and slashed at Richard's extended arm. I pulled Richard back. The sword cut through Richard's shirt sleeve.

Sensei drew then, and Diego turned and slashed, *kesa*, at Sensei's neck.

Sensei blocked, absorbing the strike and drawing his elbows into his body, then slid his sword down Diego's blade, going for the thumb. Diego drew back to cut *kesa* on the other side.

Sensei drove forward, letting Diego's strike pass behind him and then turning away from Diego while very close, and bringing his blade around to cut Diego's exposed side.

The arm, Diego's snack, stuck down his shirtfront took the brunt of the cut, and, though Sensei sliced all the way through it, his sword only cut an inch or so into Diego's abdomen.

Diego turned like a snake and cut at Sensei's back but Sensei had kept going, putting him just out of range. Sensei pivoted and sliced up vertically, the move from the *Suburi Happo*, designed to cut from groin to chin, and Diego jerked backwards to avoid it.

I tried to get Richard and Lou moving again, and Diego saw or sensed the movement. He leaped back into our path, blocking the way.

"No, Diego!" Richard yelled.

Again, Diego hesitated, looked confused.

Sensei closed in again, and Diego faced him, moving away from us without unblocking our path. Diego struck, lightning fast, *shomen*, and Sensei slid off the line, guiding the sword away, to cut back *shomen*. Diego moved sideways, without blocking, and struck again, so fast, that Sensei barely had time to get his head out of the way. The sword bit hard into Sensei's shoulder but Sensei's rising block kept it from cutting all the way through the bone.

Sensei fell and Diego raised his sword again, to finish Sensei, but I drew and thrust quickly into Diego's back.

It didn't kill or disable but it got his attention.

He turned and cut viciously, *kesa*, but I'd stepped back. As his sword went by I tried to cut his wrist, but I hesitated and nicked his forearm instead. He came back horizontal and Lou's sword blocked it. At the same time, tears streaming down his face, Richard thrust into Diego's stomach.

Diego stepped back and put his hand to the wound, then held it, looking at the blood. He sniffed it and his nose wrinkled. He gripped the sword again, both hands, and I dropped to my knees and said loudly, "*Da-TO!*" When we bow out of class, the first thing we do is take our sword out of our *obi* and put it down on the floor before us. I set my bare sword down, not in its scabbard, like we'd normally do, but in the same position, edge toward me, handle to the right.

Diego almost did it, starting to lower the sword and bend his knees in reflex, but then he stopped and raised it again.

Lou lowered her sword and said, "Diego, love, come to me."

Diego froze, his mouth opening and his face softening, and I snatched up my sword and, left hand flat on the *mune*, thrust it up through Diego's jaw and all the way into his brain.

Diego fell to the side, his sword still gripped solidly in his hands.

Lou dropped back to her knees and threw up. Again.

We made Richard limp by himself as we carried Sensei to the gate. We kept him from bleeding to death but it was a close thing. Richard brought back his brother's sword, and we're saving it. Boy or girl, his child deserves something of her father's.

All that throwing up wasn't just something Lou had eaten.

"Sensei would never have allowed you to come along if he'd known you were pregnant."

Lou nodded and kept crying.

Danny, the southern guard, was discharged from his post and set to garbage detail. He wasn't at the gate because he was pilfering in the kitchen gardens. Had a nice business in black market tomatoes.

Sensei's shoulder was never the same. He still lives at the dojo and he makes comments from the side of the mat, but mostly he leaves it to me, and he never went out of the gates again.

But I did.

THE DAYS OF FLAMING MOTORCYCLES

Catherynne M. Valente

Catherynne M. Valente is the critically acclaimed author of *The Orphan's Tales* series, which has won the Tiptree Award, the Mythopoeic Award, and was a finalist for the World Fantasy Award. Her novel, *Palimpsest*—which she describes as "a baroque meeting of science fiction and fantasy"—is a finalist for the 2010 Hugo Awards. Her young adult novel, *The Girl Who Circumnavigated Fairyland in a Ship of Her Own Making,* which was originally self-published online and is forthcoming in print from Feiwel and Friends, recently won the Andre Norton Award. A new series, beginning in November with *The Habitation of the Blessed*, retells the legend of Prester John. Her short fiction has appeared in the magazines *Clarkesworld*, *Electric Velocipede*, and *Lightspeed*, and in the anthology *Dark Faith*, where this story first appeared.

The inspiration for this story came when Valente visited Augusta, Maine, for the first time. "Augusta, despite being the state capitol, is an extremely economically depressed region, and the dilapidation of the downtown area and the general atmosphere of silence and a city long past its prime truly struck me," she says. "It looked like the zombies had taken over in 1974 and people just said: 'Well, we have to go to work tomorrow.' The idea of that quiet apocalypse took hold of my heart; an apocalypse you just have to live through and find a way to co-exist with was fascinating. I finally felt like I had something new to say about zombies."

Zombies may be caused by any number of factors—a supernatural event, a man-made virus, or radiation from a passing comet—but one thing is nearly universal: you have to kill them to survive, and killing them is completely justified because it's self-defense and you have no choice. But what if zombies didn't have to be killed? What if they *shouldn't* be? What if you could live side-by-side with them and make a new kind of life for yourself among them, even as the world around you has fallen to pieces?

To tell you the truth, my father wasn't really that much different after he became a zombie.

My mother just wandered off. I think she always wanted to do that, anyway. Just set off walking down the road and never look back. Just like my father always wanted to stop washing his hair and hunker down in the basement and snarl at everyone he met. He chased me and hollered and hit me before. Once, when I stayed out with some boy whose name I can't even remember, he even bit me. He slapped me and for once I slapped him back, and we did this standing-wrestling thing, trying to hold each other back. Finally, in frustration, he bit me, hard, on the side of my hand. I didn't know what to do—we just stared at each other, breathing heavily, knowing something really absurd or horrible had just happened, and if we laughed it could be absurd and if we didn't we'd never get over it. I laughed. But I knew the look in his eye that meant he was coming for me, that glowering, black look, and now it's the only look he's got.

It's been a year now, and that's about all I can tell you about the apocalypse. There was no flash of gold in the sky, no chasms opened up in the earth, no pale riders with silver scythes. People just started acting the way they'd always wanted to but hadn't because they were more afraid of the police or their boss or losing out on the prime mating opportunities offered by the greater Augusta area. Everyone stopped being afraid. Of anything. And sometimes that means eating each other.

But sometimes it doesn't. They don't always do that, you know. Sometimes they just stand there and watch you, shoulders slumped, blood dripping off their noses, their eyes all unfocused. And then they howl. But not like a wolf. Like something broken and small. Like they're sad.

Now, zombies aren't supposed to get sad. Everyone knows that. I've had a lot of time to think since working down at the Java Shack on Front Street became seriously pointless. I still go to the shop in the morning, though. If you don't have habits, you don't have anything. I turn over the sign, I boot up the register—I even made the muffins for a while, until the flour ran out. Carrot-macadamia on Mondays, mascarpone-mango on Tuesdays, blueberry with a dusting of marzipan on Wednesdays. So on. So forth. Used to be I'd have a line of senators out the door by 8:00 a.m. I brought the last of the muffins home to my dad. He turned one over and over in his bloody, swollen hands until it came apart, then he made that awful howling-crying sound and licked the crumbs off his fingers. And he starting saying my name over and over, only muddled, because his tongue had gone all puffy and purple in his mouth. Caitlin, Caitlin, Caitlin.

So now I drink the pot of coffee by myself and I write down everything I can think of in a kid's notebook with a flaming motorcycle on the cover. I have a bunch like it. I cleaned out all the stores. In a few months I'll move on to the punky princess covers, and then the Looney Tunes ones. I mark time that way. I don't even think of seasons. These are the days of Flaming Motorcycles. Those were the days of Football Ogres. So on. So forth.

They don't bother me, mostly. And okay, the pot of coffee is just hot water now. No arabica for months. But at least the power's still on. But what I was saying is that I've had a lot of time to think, about them, about me, about the virus—because of course it must have been a virus, right? Which isn't really any better than saying fairies or angels did it. Didn't monks used to argue about how many angels could fit on the head of a pin? I seem to think I remember that, in some book, somewhere. So angels are tiny, like viruses. Invisible, too, or you wouldn't have to argue about it, you'd just count the bastards up. So they said virus, I said it doesn't matter, my dad just bit his own finger off. And he howls like he's so sad he wants to die, but being sad means you have a soul and they don't; they're worse than animals. It's a kindness to put them down. That's what the manuals say. Back when there were new manuals every week. Sometimes I think the only way you can tell if something has a soul is if they can still be sad. Sometimes it's the only way I know I have one.

Sometimes I don't think I do.

I'm not the last person on Earth. Not by a long way. I get radio reports on the regular news from Portland, Boston—just a month ago New York was broadcasting loud and clear, loading zombies into the same hangars they kept protesters in back in '04. They gas them and dump them at sea. Brooklyn is still a problem, but Manhattan is coming around. Channel 3 is still going strong, but it's all emergency directives. I don't watch it. I mean, how many times can you sit through The Warning Signs or What We Know? Plus, I have reason to believe they don't know shit.

I might be the last person in Augusta, though. That wouldn't be hard. Did you ever see Augusta before the angel-virus? It was a burnt-out hole. It is a burnt-out hole. Just about every year, the Kennebec floods downtown, so at any given time there's only about three businesses on the main street, and one of them will have a cheerful We'll Be Back! sign up with the clock hands broken off. There's literally nothing going on in this town. Not now, and not then. Down by the river the buildings are pockmarked and broken, the houses are boarded up, windows shattered, only one or two people wandering dazed down the streets. All gas supplied by the Dead River Company, all your dead interred at Burnt Hill Burying Ground. And that was before. Even our Wal-Mart had to close up because nobody ever shopped there.

And you know, way back in the pilgrim days, or Maine's version of them, which starts in the 1700s sometime, there was a guy named James Purington who freaked out one winter and murdered his whole family with an axe. Eight children and his wife. They hanged him and buried him at the crossroads so he wouldn't come back as a vampire. Which would seem silly, except, well, look around. The point is life in Augusta has been both shitty and deeply warped for quite some time. So we greeted this particular horrific circumstance much as Mainers have greeted economic collapse and the total disregard of the rest of the country for the better part of forever: with no surprise whatsoever. Anyway, I haven't seen anyone else on the pink and healthy side in a long time. A big group took off for Portland on foot a few months ago (the days of Kermit and Company), but I stayed behind. I have to think of my father. I know that sounds bizarre, but there's nothing like a parent who bites you to make you incapable of leaving them. Incapable of not wanting their love. I'll probably turn thirty and still be stuck here, trying to be a good daughter while his blood dries on the kitchen tiles.

Channel 3 says a zombie is a reanimated corpse with no observable sell-by date and seriously poor id-control. But I have come to realize that my situation is not like Manhattan or Boston or even Portland. See, I live with zombies. My dad isn't chained up in the basement. He lives with me like he always lived with me. My neighbors, those of them who didn't wander off, are all among the pustulous and dripping. I watched those movies before it happened and I think we all, for a little while, just reacted like the movies told us to: get a bat and start swinging. But I've never killed one, and I've never even come close to being bitten. It's not a fucking movie.

And if Channel 3 slaps their bullet points all over everywhere, I guess I should write my own What We Know here. Just in case anyone wonders why zombies can cry.

What Is a Zombie?
by Caitlin Zielinski

Grade... well, if the college were still going I guess I'd be Grade 14.

A zombie is not a reanimated corpse. This was never a Night of the Living Dead scenario. The word zombie isn't even right—a zombie is something a voudoun priest makes, to obey his will. That has nothing to do with the price of coffee in Augusta. My dad didn't die. His skin ruptured and he got boils and he started snorting instead of talking and bleeding out of his eyes and lunging at Mr. Almeida next door with his fingernails out, but he didn't die. If he didn't die, he's not a corpse. QED, Channel 3.

A zombie is not a cannibal. This is kind of complicated: Channel 3 says they're not human, which is why you can't get arrested for killing one. So if they eat us, it wouldn't be cannibalism anyway, just, you know, lunch. Like if I ate a dog. Not what you expect from a nice American girl, but not cannibalism. But also, zombies don't just eat humans. If that were true, I'd have been dinner and they'd have been dead long before now, because, as I said, Augusta is pretty empty of anything resembling bright eyed and bushy tailed. They eat animals, they eat old meat in any freezer they can get open, they eat energy bars if that's what they find. Anything. Once I saw a woman—I didn't know her—on her hands and knees down by the river bank, clawing up the mud and eating it, smearing it on her bleeding breasts, staring up at the sky, her jaw wagging uselessly.

A zombie is not mindless. Channel 3 would have a fit if they heard me say that. It's dogma—zombies are slow and stupid. Well, I saw plenty of people slower and stupider than a zombie in the old days. I worked next to the state capitol, after all. Sometimes I think the only difference is that they're ugly. The world was always full of drooling morons who only wanted me for my body. Anyway, some are fast and some are slow. If the girl was a jogger before, she's probably pretty spry now. If the guy never moved but to change the channel, he's not gonna catch you any time soon. And my father still knows my name. I can't be sure but I think it's only that they can't talk. Their tongues swell up and their throats expand—all of them. One of the early warning signs is slurred speech. They might be as smart as they ever were—see jogging—but they can't communicate except by screaming. I'd scream, too, if I were bleeding from my ears and my skin were melting off.

Zombies will not kill anything that moves. My dad hasn't bitten me. He could have, plenty of times. They're not harmless. I've had to get good at running and I have six locks on every door of the house. Even my bedroom, because my father can't be trusted. He hits me, still. His fist leaves a smear of blood and pus and something darker, purpler, on my face. But he doesn't bite me. At first, he barked and went for my neck at least once a day. But I'm faster. I'm always faster. He doesn't even try anymore. Sometimes he just stands in the living room, drool pooling in the side of his mouth till it falls out, and he looks at me like he remembers that strange night when he bit me before, and he's still ashamed. I laugh, and he almost smiles. He shambles back down the hall and starts peeling off the wallpaper, shoving it into his mouth in long pink strips like skin.

There's something else I know. It's hard to talk about, because I don't understand it. I don't understand it because I'm not a zombie. It's like a secret society, and I'm on the outside. I can watch what they do, but I don't know the code. I couldn't tell Channel 3 about this, even if they came to town with all their cameras and sat me in a plush chair like one of their endless Rockette-line of doctors. What makes you think they have intelligence, Miss Zielinski? And I would tell them about my father saying my name, but not about the river. No one would believe me. After all, it's never happened anywhere else. And I have an idea about that, too. Because people in Manhattan are pretty up on their zombie-killing tactics, and god help a zombie in Texas if he should ever be so unfortunate as to encounter a human. But here there's nothing left. No one to kill them. They own this town, and they're learning how to live in it, just like anyone does. Maybe Augusta always belonged to them and James Purington and the Dead River Company. All hail the oozing, pestilent kings and queens of the apocalypse.

This is what I know: One night, my father picked up our toaster and left the house. I'm not overly attached to the toaster, but he didn't often leave. I feed him good hamburger, nice and raw, and I don't knock him in his brainpan with a bat. Zombies know a good thing.

The next night he took the hallway mirror. Then the microwave, then the coffeepot, then a sack full of pots and pans. All the zombie movies in the world do not prepare you to see your father, his hair matted with blood, his bathrobe torn and seeping, packing your cooking materiel into a flowered king-size pillowcase. And then one night he took a picture off of the bookshelf. My mother, himself, and me, smiling in one of those terrible posed portraits. I was eight or nine in the picture, wearing a green corduroy jumper and big, long brown pigtails. I was smiling so wide, and so were they. You have to, in those kinds of portraits. The photographer makes you, and if you don't, he practically starts turning cartwheels to get you to smile like an angel just appeared over his left shoulder clutching a handful of pins. My mother, her glasses way too big for her face. My father, in plaid flannel, his big hand holding me protectively.

I followed him. It wasn't difficult; his hearing went about the same time as his tongue. In a way, I guess it's a lot like getting old. Your body starts failing in all sorts of weird ways, and you can't talk right or hear well or see clearly, and you just rage at things because everything is slipping away and you're never going to get any better. If one person goes that way, it's tragic. If everyone does, it's the end of the world.

It gets really dark in Augusta, and the streetlights have all been shot out or burned out. There is no darker night than a Maine night before the first snow, all starless and cold. No friendly pools of orange chemical light to break the long, black street. Just my father, shuffling along with his portrait clutched to his suppurating chest. He turned toward downtown, crossing Front Street after looking both ways out of sheer muscle memory. I crept behind him, down past the riverside shops, past the Java Shack, down to the riverbank and the empty parking lots along the waterfront.

Hundreds of zombies gathered down there by the slowly lapping water. Maybe the whole of dead Augusta, everyone left. My father joined the crowd. I tried not to breathe; I'd never seen so many in one place. They weren't fighting or hunting, either. They moaned, a little. Most of them had brought something—more toasters, dresser drawers, light bulbs, broken kitchen chairs, coat racks, televisions, car doors. All junk, gouged out of houses, out of their old lives. They arranged it, almost lovingly, around a massive tower of garbage, teetering, swaying in the wet night wind. A light bulb fell from the top, shattering with a bright pop. They didn't notice. The tower was sloppy, but even I could see that it was meant to be a tower, more than a tower—bed-slats formed flying buttresses between the main column and a smaller one, still being built. Masses of electric devices, dead and inert, piled up between them, showing their screens and gray, lifeless displays to the water. And below the screens rested dozens of family portraits just like ours, leaning against the dark plasma screens and speakers. A few zombies added to the pile—and some of them lay photos down that clearly belonged to some other family. I thought I saw Mrs. Halloway, my first grade teacher, among them, and she treated her portrait of a Chinese family as tenderly as a child. I don't think they knew who exactly the pictures showed. They just understood the general sense they conveyed, of happiness and family. My father added his picture to the crowd and rocked back and forth, howling, crying, holding his head in his hands.

I wriggled down between a dark streetlamp and a park bench, trying to turn invisible as quickly as possible. But they paid no attention to me. And then the moon crowned the spikes of junk, cresting between the two towers.

The zombies all fell to their knees, their arms outstretched to the white, full moon, horrible black tears streaming down their ruined faces, keening and ululating, throwing their faces down into the river-mud, bits of them falling off in their rapture, their eagerness to abase themselves before their cathedral. I think it was a cathedral, when I think about it now. I think it had to be. They sent up their awful crooning moan, and I clapped my hands over my ears to escape it. Finally, Mrs. Halloway stood up and turned to the rest of them. She dragged her nails across her cheeks and shrieked wordlessly into the night. My father went to her and I thought he was going to bite her, the way he bit me, the way zombies bite anyone when they want to.

Instead, he kissed her.

He kissed her on the cheek, heavily, smackingly, and his face came away with her blood on it. One by one the others kissed her too, surrounding her with groping hands and hungry mouths, and the moon shone down on her face, blanching her so she was nothing but black and white, blood and skin, an old movie monster, only she wept. She wept from a place so deep I can't imagine it; she wept, and she smiled, even as they finished kissing her and began pulling her apart, each keeping a piece of her for themselves, just a scrap of flesh, which they ate solemnly, reverently. They didn't squabble over it, her leg or her arm or her eyes, and Mrs. Halloway didn't try to fight them. She had offered herself, I think, and they took her. I know what worship looks like.

I was crying by that time. You would, too, if you saw that. I had to cry or I had to throw up, and crying was quieter. Your body can make calculations like that, if it has to. But crying isn't that quiet, really. One of them sniffed the air and turned toward me—the rest turned as one. They're a herd, if they are anything. They know much more together than they know separately. I wonder if, in a few decades, they will have figured out how to run Channel 3, and will broadcast How to Recognize a Human in Three Easy Steps, or What We Know.

They fell on me, which is pretty much how zombies do anything. They groped and pulled, but there were too many of them for any one to get a good grip, and I may not have killed one before but I wasn't opposed to the idea. I swung my fists and oh, they were so soft, like jam. I clamped my mouth shut—I knew my infection vectors as well as any kid in my generation. But they didn't bite me, and finally my father threw back his head and bellowed. I know that bellow. I've always known it, and it hasn't changed. They pulled away, panting, exhausted. That was the first time I realized how fragile they are. They're like lions. In short bursts, they'll eviscerate you and your zebra without a second thought. But they have to save up the strength for it, day in and day out. I stood there, back against the streetlamp, fingernails out, asthma kicking in because of course, it would. And my father limped over to me, dragging his broken left foot—they don't die but they don't heal. I tried to set it once and that was the closest I ever came to getting bitten before that night on the river.

He stood over me, his eyebrows crusted with old fluid, his eyes streaming tears like ink, his jaw dislocated and hanging, his cheeks puffed out with infection. He reached out and hooted gently like an ape. To anyone else it would have been just another animal noise from a rotting zombie, but I heard it as clear as anything: Caitlin, Caitlin, Caitlin. I had nowhere to go, and he reached for me, brushing my hair out of my face. With one bloody thumb he traced a circle onto my forehead, like a priest on Ash Wednesday. Caitlin, Caitlin, Caitlin.

His blood was cold.

After that, none of them ever came after me again. That's why I can have my nice little habit of opening the Java Shack and writing in my notebooks. These are the days of Punky Princesses, and I am safe. The mark on my forehead never went away. It's faint, like a birthmark, but it's there. Sometimes I meet one of them on the road, wandering dazed and unhappy in the daylight, squinting as if it doesn't understand where the light is coming from. When they see me, their eyes go dark with hunger—but then, their gaze flicks up to my forehead, and they fall down on their knees, keening and sobbing. It's not me, I know that. It's the cathedral, still growing, on the banks of the Kennebec. The mark means I'm of the faith, somehow. Saint Caitlin of the Java Shack, Patroness of the Living.

Sometimes I think about leaving. I hear Portsmouth is mostly clean. I could make that on my bicycle. Maybe I could even hotwire a car. I've seen them do it on television. The first time I stayed, I stayed for my father. But he doesn't come home much anymore. There's little enough left for him to scavenge for the church. He keeps up his kneeling and praying down there, except when the moon is dark, and then they mourn like lost children. Now, I think I stay because I want to see the finished cathedral, I want to understand what they are doing when they eat one of their own. If it's like communion, the way I understand it, or something else entirely. I want to see the world they're building out here in the abandoned capital. If maybe they're not sick, but just new, like babies, incomprehensible and violent and frustrated that nothing is as they expected it to be.

It's afternoon in the Java Shack. The sun is thin and wintry. I pour myself hot water and it occurs to me that apocalypse originally meant to uncover something. To reveal a hidden thing. I get that now. It was never about fire and lightning shearing off the palaces of the world. And if I wait, here on the black shores of the Kennebec, here in the city that has been ruined for as long as it has lived, maybe, someday soon, the face of their god will come up out of the depths, uncovered, revealed.

So on. So forth.

ZERO TOLERANCE

By Jonathan Maberry

Jonathan Maberry is the bestselling author of several novels, including *Ghost Road Blues* (winner of the Bram Stoker Award), *Dead Man's Song*, *Bad Moon Rising*, and *The Wolfman*. *Rot & Ruin*, the first book in a new young-adult zombie series, was just published; a second volume, *Dust & Decay*, will appear in 2011. Maberry's other recent novels *Patient Zero* and *The Dragon Factory*, along with the forthcoming *The King of Plagues*, are set in the same milieu as our next story and are in development for television. Other work includes the non-fiction books *THEY BITE!*, Stoker Award-finalist *Zombie CSU*, *Wanted Undead or Alive*, *Vampire Universe*, and *The Cryptopedia*.

September 11, 2001 changed the world, and also changed science fiction, fantasy, and horror. Civilization collapsing had always been a topic of perennial interest in the field, of course, but after 9/11 magazines were positively deluged with this sort of material. And of course zombies, the ultimate symbol of societal breakdown, went from being a niche interest to one of the dominant images in the popular imagination, familiar to everyone. Before 9/11, characters in a zombie story might speculate about the cause of the epidemic without ever mentioning the word "terrorism." Afterward, of course, that's tended to be the first word on every character's lips.

America's War on Terror has had many casualties, chief among them the nation's view of itself. Images of U.S. soldiers torturing naked, helpless (and in many cases innocent) prisoners at Abu Ghraib prison in Iraq haunt the American psyche, and are all the more disturbing given the lingering sense that those truly responsible have never been punished. (In her memoir *One Woman's Army*, Janis Karpinski maintains that she was scapegoated due to sexism and that the soldiers sent to prison for the crimes were acting according to policies issued by the White House.)

Nietzsche famously warned: "He who fights with monsters might take care lest he thereby become a monster." Our next story is a military thriller about zombies, terrorism, war, and some very grim and unsavory interrogation techniques. It's a powerful story and, much as we might wish otherwise, a tale of our time.

-1-
Battalion Aide Station
Near Helmand River Valley, Afghanistan
One Hour Ago

"I never thought that anyone that beautiful could scare the shit out of me." The Marine sergeant sounded like he had a throatful of broken glass.

"Tell me about her, Sergeant," I said.

He looked away so quickly that I knew he'd been waiting for that question. He tried to keep a poker face, but he was a couple tics off his game. Sleep deprivation, pain and the certain knowledge that his ass was in a sling can do that to you. Even to a tough son of a bitch like Sergeant Harper. As he turned I saw the way guilt and shame twisted his mouth; but his eyes had a different expression. One I couldn't quite nail down.

"Tell you what? That I can't bear to close my eyes 'cause when I do I see her? That I've had the shivering shits ever since we found her out there in the sand? I don't mind admitting it," said the sergeant. He started to say more, then closed his mouth and shook his head.

Harper's uninjured hand was freckled with powder burns and skin was missing from two knuckles. He ran his trembling fingers through his sandy hair as he spoke. He did it two or three times each minute. His other hand lay in his lap, the hand cocooned inside gauze wrappings.

I waited. I had more time than he did.

After a full minute, though, I said, "Where did she come from?"

Harper sighed. "She was a refugee. We found her staggering in the foothills."

"A refugee from what?"

"From the big meltdown out in the desert."

"In the Helmand River Valley?"

"Yes."

He didn't tack on "sir." He was fucking with me, and I was okay with that for now. He didn't know me, didn't really know how much shit he was in, or how deep a hole he'd dug for himself. All he knew was that his career in the Marines had hit a guard rail at seventy miles an hour, and now he was sitting across a small table from a guy wearing captain's bars and no other military insignia. No medals or unit patch. No name tag. Harper had to be measuring that against the deferential way the colonel treated me. Like I outranked him, which I don't. I'm not even in the military anymore. But in this particular matter I was able to throw more weight than the base commander. More weight than anyone else in or out of uniform on the continent. As far as Harper was concerned, when it came to throwing him a lifeline it was me and then God, and God was off the clock.

Harper couldn't really know any of that, but he was smart enough and sly enough to know that I had some juice. On one hand, he rightly figured that I could drop him into a hole deeper than the one he'd dug for himself. On the other hand, he had information that I wanted, and he was stalling to see how best to play his only good card.

"How long are they going to keep me here?"

"To be determined, Sergeant. Do you feel you're being inconvenienced?"

He didn't rise to the bait.

"It's been three days."

"Not quite. Forty-seven hours and change."

"Seems longer." He didn't even know that we'd already met. Not sure when I was going to spring that on him. It wouldn't do anything to calm him down.

I opened my briefcase and took out a file folder.

"I'd like you to look at some photos," I said and took two color eight-by-tens from my briefcase and laid them on the table. If I'd tossed a scorpion on the table he couldn't have jerked back faster.

"Jesus Christ!"

I nodded at the print. "That's her?"

"Fuck me," muttered the sergeant. "Oh fuck me fuck me fuck me."

Take that as a yes.

I sat back and waited him out. Sweat popped all along his forehead and leaked out from his hairline. He smelled like urine, cigarette smoke and testosterone, but I could smell fear, too. A whole lot of it. I used to think that was a myth, or something only dogs and horses could smell, but lately I've learned different. The kind of shit I deal with? I smell it a lot, and on myself, too. Like now, but I wasn't going to let this asshole know it.

"Could…could you turn the pictures over? I don't mean to be a pussy, but I don't want her staring at me the whole time, y'know?"

"Sure," I said, and did so. But I left them on the table. "Try to relax. Smoke one if you got any."

He shook his head. "Never took it up. Jesus H. Christ. Wish I did."

I opened my briefcase and took out two bottles of spring water, unscrewed one and handed it to him. He drank half of it down. Then I took some airline bottles of Jack Daniel's and lined them up in front of him. One, two, three.

"If it helps," I said.

He snatched one off the edge of the table, twisted off the cap and chugged it, then coughed. More bravado than brains.

"Tell me about the woman," I said. "And what happened in the cave."

He gave that some thought, drank half of the second bottle of Jack.

"Do you know my outfit? Second Marine Expeditionary Brigade, Light Armored Reconnaissance Battalion. We were part of Operation Khanjar, working that corner of Helmand Province, doing some recon stuff up in the hills," he began. "Counter-insurgency work, and some fox hunts to flush the Taliban teams running opium through the area. That whole part of the province is nothing but dead rock riddled with a million caves. You could hide a hundred thousand people in there, camels and all, and it would take us fifty years to find half of them. That's why this war was fucked from the snap. The Russians couldn't do it twenty years ago, and we can't do it now. Besides, nine out of ten people you meet are friendlies who look and dress just like the hostiles, so how you going to know?"

"Skip the politics, Sergeant. Talk about the woman."

He shrugged. "It was weird out there because last week the whole place was lit up by some kind of underground explosion. We got word that some Taliban lab blew up, but the blast wasn't nuclear. Something to do with geo-thermal chambers or shifting plates or some bullshit like that. A whole section of desert just fell into itself and there was this spike of fire that shot a couple hundred feet in the air."

"No radiation?"

"No. Most of us still had TLD badges and the badges stayed neutral. The area was hot, though…not with radiation, but actually hot. Like a furnace. When we reached the outer perimeter of the event zone we could see a weird shimmer and I realized that big sections of the desert had been melted to glass. It looked like a lava flow, rippled and dark."

"And is that where you found the woman?" I asked.

He drank the rest of the second bottle of Jack Daniel's, and chased it with a long pull on the water bottle. He was pale, his eyes sunken and dark, his lips dry. He looked like shit and probably felt worse. Just mentioning the "woman" made his eyes jump.

"Yeah," he said. "Locals started calling in sightings of burned people, and then word came down to scramble a couple of recon teams. We went in…and after that everything went to shit." He turned away to hide wet eyes.

-2-

The Warehouse
DMS Tactical Field Office / Baltimore
Ninety-two Hours Ago

I was on the mats with Echo Team's newest members—replacements for the guys we lost in Philadelphia. There were four of them, two Rangers, a jarhead and a former SWAT guy from L.A. For the last couple of hours Bunny and I had taken turns beating on them, chasing them with paintball guns, trying to carve our initials in them with live blades, swinging at them with baseball bats. Everything we could think of. Actually, let me rephrase that. There were ten of them this morning. The four who were left were the ones who hadn't been taken to the infirmary or told to go the fuck back to where they came from.

We were just about to enter a practical discussion on pain tolerance when my boss, Mr. Church, came into the gym at a fast walk. He only ever hurries when the real shit is coming down the pike. I crossed to meet him.

Church nodded toward the recruits. "Are these four in or out?"

"Is something up?"

"Yes, and it's on a high boil."

"They're in."

Church turned to Bunny. "Sergeant Rabbit, get these men kitted out. Afghanistan. No ID, no patches. You're wheels up in fifteen." Bunny flicked a glance at me, but he didn't question the order. Instead he turned and hustled them all toward the locker room. Bunny was a nice kid most of the time, but he was still a sergeant. And we'd been through some shit together, so he knew my views on hesitation: Don't.

"What's the op?" I asked.

Church handed me the file. "This came in as an email attachment. Two photos, two separate sources."

I flipped open the folder and looked at two photos of an incredibly beautiful woman. Iraqi, probably. Black hair, full lips, and the most arresting eyes I'd ever seen. Eyes so powerful that despite the low res of the photos and graininess of the printout, they radiated heat. Her face was streaked with dirt and there was some blood crusted around her nose and the corner of her mouth.

I looked at him.

"These were relayed to us by the people we have seeded into a Swiss seismology team studying an underground explosion in the Helmand River Valley. We ran facial recognition on them and MindReader kicked out a ninety-seven percent confidence that this is Amirah."

My mouth went dry as dust.

Holy shit.

When I was brought into the DMS a month ago my first gig was to stop a team of terrorists who had a bioweapon that still gives me nightmares. I'm not kidding. Couple times a week I wake up with the shivers, cold sweat running down my skin, and clenched teeth that are the only things between a silent room and a gut-buster of a scream.

There were three people behind that scheme. A British pharmaceutical mogul named Gault, a religious fanatic from Yemen called El Mujahid, and his wife, Amirah. She was the molecular biologist who conceived and created the *Seif al Din* pathogen. The Sword of the Faithful. They test-drove the pathogen with limited release in remote Afghani villages, trying out different strains until they had one that couldn't be stopped. *Seif al Din.* An actual doomsday plague. El Mujahid brought it here, and Echo Team stopped him. But only just. If you factor in the dead Afghani villagers and the people killed here, the body count was north of twelve hundred. Even so, Mr. Church and his science geeks figured we caught a break. It could have been more. Could have been millions, even billions. It came down to that kind of a photo finish.

Most of the victims turned into mindless killers whose metabolism had been so drastically altered by the plague that they could not think, had no personalities, didn't react to pain, and were hard as balls to kill. The pathogen reduced most organ functions to such a minimal level that they appeared to be dead. Or...maybe they *were* dead. The scientists are still sorting it out. We called them "walkers." A bad pun, short for "dead men walking." The DMS science chief is a pop culture geek. My guys in Echo Team called the infected by another name. Yeah. The "Z" word.

And you wonder why I get night terrors. Six weeks ago I was a Baltimore cop doing scut work for Homeland. Sitting wiretaps, that sort of thing. Now I was top dog for a crew of first-team shooters. Do not ask me how one thing led to another, but here I am.

I looked at the photos.

Amirah.

"The rumors of her demise have been greatly exaggerated," I said.

Church managed not to smile.

"If you're sending us, then she hasn't been apprehended."

"No," he said. "Spotted only. I arranged for two Marine Recon squads to locate and detain."

"What if Amirah's infected?"

"I shared a limited amount of information with the appropriate officers in the chain of command. If anyone reports certain kinds of activity—from Amirah or anyone—then the whole area gets lit up."

"Lit up as in—?"

"A nuclear option falls within the parameters of 'acceptable losses.'"

"Can you at least wait until me and my guys reach minimum safe distance?"

He didn't smile. Neither did I.

"You'll be operating with an Executive Order, so you'll have complete freedom of movement."

"You got the president to sign an order that fast?"

He just looked at me.

"What are my orders?"

"Our primary concern is to determine if anyone infected with the *Seif al Din* pathogen is loose in Afghanistan."

"Yeah, that'll be about as easy to establish as bin Laden's zip code."

"Do your best. We'll be monitoring all news coming out of the area, military, civilian and other. If there is even a peep, that intel will be routed to you and the clock will start."

"If I don't come back, make sure somebody feeds my cat."

"Noted."

"What about Amirah? You want her brought back here?"

"Amirah would be a prize catch. There's a laundry list of people who want her. The vice president thinks she would be a great asset to our own bio-weapons programs."

"And is that what you want?" I asked, and then he told me.

-3-

The Helmand River Valley
Sixty-one Hours Ago

We hit the ground running. When Church wants to clear a path, he steamrolls it flat. Our cover was that of a Marine SKT—Small Kill Team—operating on special orders. Need to know. Everybody figured we were probably Delta, and you don't ask them for papers unless you want to get a ration of shit from everyone higher up the food chain. And when we did have to show papers, we had real ones. As real as the situation required.

Just as the helo was about to set us down near the blast site, Church radioed: "Be advised, I ordered the two Marine squads to pull out of the area. One has confirmed and is heading to a pick-up point now. The other has not responded. Make no assumptions in those hills."

He signed off without explanation, but I didn't need any.

The six of us went out into the desert, split into two teams and headed into Indian country. We ran with combat names only. I was Cowboy.

Twilight draped the desert with purple shadows. As soon as the sun dropped behind the mountains the furnace heat shut off and the wind turned cool. Not pleasantly cool: This breeze was clammy and it smelled wrong. There was a scent on the wind—sweet and sour. An ugly smell that triggered an atavistic repulsion. Bunny sniffed it and turned to me.

"Yeah," I said, "I smell it, too."

Bob Faraday—a big moose of a guy whose call-sign was Slim—ran point. It was getting dark fast and the moon wouldn't be up for nearly an hour. In ten minutes we'd have to switch to night-vision. Slim vanished into the distance. Bunny and I followed behind, slower, watching as darkness seemed to melt out from under rocks and rise up from sand dunes as the sparse islands of daytime shadows spread out to join the ocean of shadows that was night.

Slim broke squelch twice, the signal to close on him quick and quiet.

As we ran up behind him I saw that he'd stopped by a series of gray finger rocks that rose from the troubled sands at the edge of the blast area. But as I drew closer I saw that the rocks weren't rocks at all.

I followed my gun barrel all the way to Slim's side.

The dark objects were people.

Eleven of them, sticking out of the sand like statues from some ancient ruins. Dead. Charred beyond recognition. Fourth-, fifth- and sixth-degree burns. You couldn't tell race or even sex with most of them. They were like mummies, and they were still too hot to touch.

"There was supposed to be some kind of underground lab," murmured Slim. "Looks like the blast charbroiled these poor bastards and the force drove them up through the sand."

"Hope it was quick," said Bunny.

Slim glanced at him. "If they were in that lab then they were the bad guys."

"Even so," said Bunny.

We went into the foothills, onto some rocks that were cooler than the sands.

The other team called in. The Marine was on point. "Jukebox to Cowboy, be advised we have more bodies up here. Five DOA. Three men and two women. Third-degree burns, cuts and blunt force injuries. Looks like they might have walked out of the hot zone and died up here in the rocks." He paused. "They're a mess. Vultures and wild dogs been at them."

"Verify that what you are seeing are animal bites," I said.

There was a long pause.

And it got longer.

I keyed the radio. "Cowboy to Jukebox, copy?"

Two long damn seconds.

"Cowboy to Jukebox, do you copy?"

That's when we heard the distant rattle of automatic gunfire. And the screams.

We ran.

"Night-vision!" I snapped, and we flipped the units into place as the black landscape suddenly transformed into a thousand shades of luminescent green. We were all carrying ALICE packs with about fifty pounds of gear—most of it stuff that'll blow up, M4 combat rifles, AMT .22 caliber auto mags on our hips, and combat S.I. assault boots. It's all heavy and it can slow you down...except when your own brothers in arms are under fire. Then it feels like wings that carry you over the ground at the speed of a racing tiger. That's the illusion, and that's how it felt as we tore up the slopes toward the path Second Squad had taken.

The gunfire was continuous.

As we hit the ridge, I signaled the others to get low and slow. Bunny came up beside me. "Those are M5s, boss."

He was right. Our guns have their own distinctive sound, and it doesn't sound much like the Kalashnikovs the Taliban favored.

The gunfire stopped abruptly.

We froze, letting the night tell us its story.

The last of the gunfire echoes bounced back to us from the distant peaks. I could hear loose rocks clattering down the slope, probably debris knocked loose by stray bullets. In the distance the wind was beginning to howl through some of the mountain passes.

I keyed the radio.

"Cowboy to Jukebox. Respond."

Nothing.

We moved forward, moving as silently as trained men can do when any misstep could draw fire. The tone of the wind changed as we edged toward the rock wall that would spill us into the pass where Second Squad had gone. A heavier breeze, perhaps? Moving through one of the deeper canyons?

A month ago I'd have believed that. Too much has happened since.

I tapped Bunny and then used the hand signal to listen.

He heard the sound, then, and I could feel him stiffen beside me. He pulled Slim close and used two fingers to mime walking.

Slim had been fully briefed on the trip. He understood. The low sigh wasn't the wind. It was the unendingly hungry moan of a walker.

I finger-counted down from three and we rounded the bend.

Jukebox had said that they'd found five bodies. Second Squad made eight.

As we rounded the wall we saw that the count was wrong. There weren't eight people in the pass. There were fifteen. All of them were dead. Most of them moving.

Second Squad lay sprawled in the dust. The night-vision made it look like they were covered in black oil. Jukebox still held his M4, finger curled through the trigger guard, barrel smoking. A man dressed in a white lab coat knelt over him, head bowed as if weeping for the fallen soldier, but as we stepped into the pass the kneeling man raised his head and turned toward us. His mouth and cheeks glistened with black wetness and his eyes were lightless windows that looked into a world in which there was no thought, no emotion, no anything except hunger.

Spider and Zorro—the L.A. SWAT kid and the other Ranger—were almost invisible beneath the seething mass of bodies that crouched over them, tearing at clothing with wax-white fingers and at skin with gray teeth.

"Holy Mother of God," whispered Slim.

"God's not here," I said as I put the pinpoint of the laser sight on the kneeling zombie. It was a stupid thing to say. Glib and macho. But I think it was also the truth.

The creature bared its teeth and hissed like a jungle cat. Then he lunged, pale fingers reaching for me.

I put the first round in his breastbone and that froze him in place for a fragment of a second, and then put the next round through his forehead. The impact snapped his neck, the round blew out the back of his skull, and the force flung him against the rock wall.

The other walkers surged up off the ground with awful cries that I will never be able to forget. Bunny, Slim and I stood our ground in a shooting line, and we chopped them back and down and dead. Dead for good and all. Painting the walls with the same dripping black. The narrow confines of the pass roared with thunder, the waves of echoes striking us in the chest, the ejected brass tinkling with improbable delicacy.

Then silence.

I looked down at the three men. They'd been part of Echo Team for a day. Less. They'd been briefed on the nature of the enemy. They were highly trained men, the best of the best. But really, what kind of training prepares you for this? The first time the DMS encountered the walkers they'd lost two whole teams. Twenty-four seasoned agents.

Even so, the deaths of these good, brave men was like a spear in my heart. It was hard to take a breath. I forced myself to be in the moment, and I slung my M4 and drew my .22 and shot each of the corpses in the head. To be sure. We carried the .22s because the low mass of the bullet will penetrate the skull but lacks the power to exit, and so the bullet bounces around inside the skull and tears the brain apart. Assassins use it, and so does anyone who has to deal with things like walkers.

"Bunny, drop a beacon and let's haul ass."

Bunny dug a small device from a thigh pocket, thumbed the switch and tucked it under the leg of one of the dead walkers, making sure not to touch blood or exposed skin. The beacon's signal would be picked up by satellite. Once we were clear of the area, an MQ-Reaper would be guided into the pass to deliver an air-to-surface Hellfire missile. Fuel-air bombs are handy for cleanup jobs like this. When you don't want a single fucking trace left.

We didn't take dog tags because the DMS doesn't wear them. We try to have a "leave no one behind policy," but that doesn't always play out.

We moved on.

The night was vast. Knowing that helicopters and armed drones and troops were a phone call away didn't make the shadows less threatening. It didn't make the nature of what we were doing easier to accept: hunting monsters in a region of the Afghan mountains dominated by the Taliban. Yeah, find a comfortable space in your head for that thought to curl up in.

This was pretty much the opium highway. The friendlies who lived in the nearby villages were little or no help, because even though they idealistically supported us and hated the Taliban, they also feared the terrorists more than us; and without the trickle-down of drug money, they'd starve to death. It was a devil's bargain at best, but it was the reason that no one can win this war. The best we could hope for was to slow the opium shipments and keep the Taliban splinter cells underfunded and ill-prepared for a major, coordinated terror offensive of the kind they've always promised and we live in fear of.

Something flared ahead and I held up my fist. The others froze.

The pass we were following curled around the mountain like the grooves on a screw, turning and rising toward the peak on the far side. Sixty yards ahead, half-hidden by an outcropping of rock, light spilled from the mouth of a small cave. The overhang would have made the light invisible from aircraft, but not for us on the ground. A shadow seemed to detach itself from the wall and as I watched through narrowed eyes it resolved into the shape of a man. A Marine.

He walked to a spot outside the spill of light, looked up and down the pass, and then retreated to his nook. He didn't see the three big men crouched behind boulders in the dark. The sentry went to the mouth of the cave and peered inside. The glow let me see his face. He was grinning.

Then we heard the scream.

A man's voice, pleading. A string of words in Pashto, ending in a screech of pain that was cut off by the sharp crack of a palm on flesh.

And then the sound of a woman laughing.

It was not a pleasant laugh. It held no cheer, no good will. No warmth. It was deep and throaty, strangely wet, and it rose into a mocking screech that turned my guts to gutter water.

We did not hail the guard. The situation felt wrong in too many ways. I signaled Bunny to keep his eyes and gun barrel on the sentry as I circled on cat feet behind a tall slab of rock. That put me on the man's six, ten feet from his back. Even if this all proved to be a zero-threat situation I was going to fry this guy for his criminal lack of attention to duty. A sentry holds everyone's life in their hands; this guy was handing me everyone in that cave.

I screwed the .22's barrel into the soft spot under his left ear, grabbed him by the collar and slow-walked him back. Slim was there and he spun the guard and put him down. I didn't see the blow, but it sounded like a tree being felled. The guard went out without having said a word. Slim watched our backs as Bunny and I crept to the cave entrance…

…and looked into a scene from Hell.

The cave was clearly one that saw regular use. There were chairs, a card table, ammunition cases, cots, and a stove with sterno burners. A Taliban soldier was tied to a folding chair, ankles and wrists bound with plastic cuffs. His clothes had been slashed and torn away to reveal his pale chest and shoulders. His turban hung askew, one end trailing down behind him where it puddled on the rocky ground between his heels. Several Kalashnikovs stood against the wall, magazines removed.

The other three men of the Marine squad stood in a loose semicircle around the man, laughing as he screamed and begged and prayed. All of them were sweating; a couple had red and puffy knuckles that spoke to the way this session had started. If this was just a group of frustrated Marines knocking the piss out of a Taliban grunt, partly to blow off steam and partly to try and get a handle on something that might result in some real good being done, then I might have just stepped in and calmed it down. Yelled a bit, given them the appropriate ration of shit, but basically dialed it all down with no charges being filed.

But that's not what we were seeing. These guys had taken it to a different level and in doing so had crossed the line between an attempt to gather useful intelligence and something else. Something darker that was not part of soldiering. Something that wasn't even part of torturing or "enhanced interrogation." Something that went beyond Abu Ghraib and into the darkest territory imaginable.

They had Amirah—scientist, designer of the *Seif al Din*, wife of one of the world's most hated terrorists. There were two ropes looped around her neck, each end pulled to an opposite side by a Marine so that she could not approach either of them. All she could do was lunge forward toward the prisoner. Her wrists were bound behind her. Her ankles were hobbled by a length of rope. She couldn't flee, couldn't run. The men had stripped her to the waist, revealing a body that was beautifully made but which now inspired only revulsion. Her once olive skin had faded to a dusty gray-green and there were four black bullet holes—one in her stomach, three in her back—that were crusted with dried blood and wriggling with maggots.

Amirah lunged forward to bite the man, but the Marines jerked on the ropes and stopped her when her gray teeth were an inch from the Afghani's face. Amirah snarled and then laughed. It was impossible to say whether she was enjoying this game, or if she was completely mad.

As the men struggled to keep her in check they danced and shifted around and I could see that there were two other Afghanis in the room. They lay sprawled like broken dolls. It looked like their faces had been eaten, and their throats were tangles of red junk.

"It's getting tough to hold this bitch," growled one of the men, though he was smiling when he said it.

"Please, in the name of God, keep her away!" begged the bound man. He was already bleeding from half a dozen bites. Thin lines of dark red spiderwebbed out from each bite. The infection was slow for some, faster for others. Snot and spit ran from his nose and mouth as he pleaded in three different languages.

A big man with sergeant's stripes—the only one not holding a leash—bent down behind the man and spoke with sharp impatience. "We'll fucking stop when you fucking tell us what we want to know."

"But I don't...I don't..." He was filled with too much panic to complete a sentence.

The sergeant straightened and nodded, and the men slackened their holds on the rope leashes. Amirah instantly lunged forward and sank her teeth into the flesh of the man's shoulder. Blood spurted hot and red beside her cheeks, and even from where I crouched I could see her eyes roll high and white with an erotic pleasure. The man's piercing shrieks filled the whole cave.

"Okay, pull the bitch off him," snapped the sergeant, and she fought them, her teeth sunk deep into muscle. It took all three men to haul her back, two pulling and the sergeant pushing. He punched Amirah in the face and that finally broke the contact, but as they dragged her away a piece of sinew was clamped between her jaws and it snapped with a wet pop.

She licked her lips. "Delicious..." she said in English, drawing the word out, tasting the soft wetness of it, savoring the way the syllables rolled between teeth and tongue and lips.

Bunny made a soft gagging sound beside me.

This was what I was afraid of. What Church had been afraid of. During that fight against El Mujahid, we'd encountered several generations of the *Seif al Din* pathogen. Most of the early generations transformed the infected into mindless eating machines. The walkers. But at the end, when I'd squared off against El Mujahid himself, he'd been among the dead but he still retained his intelligence. It was the result of Generation 12 of the disease. He bragged about how his princess—the name Amirah meant "princess"—had saved him, had elevated him to immortality.

That had to be what we were seeing here. Amirah had become one of her own monsters. Was it an accident or part of some twisted plan? From the way El Mujahid bragged about it—right before I gave him a ticket to paradise—I had to believe that Amirah had chosen this path.

Chosen. God almighty.

"Fuck this," I murmured and stepped into the cave. Bunny was right beside me. I held my .22 in a two-hand shooters grip; he had his M4. Our night-vision was off but we wore black balaclava's that showed only our eyes.

"United States Army," I bellowed. "Stand down, stand down!"

The sergeant whirled toward me, his right hand going for his sidearm. I put the laser sight on him.

"Stand down or I will kill you!"

He believed me, and he froze.

The other Marines froze.

The man in the chair froze.

Amirah, however, did not.

With a snarl of hunger, the mad witch twisted so suddenly and violently that she tore the ropes from the hands of the startled Marines. She tore her hands free from the plastic cuffs. She screamed like some desert demon from legend, leapt into the air and slammed into the sergeant, driving him against the torture victim. They crashed to the ground amid shrieks and blood and biting teeth.

The two Marines began to move toward the sergeant, but Bunny shifted to cover them with his M4. That left me.

I stepped in and kicked Amirah in the side of the head. The blow knocked her off of the sergeant, but she had his hand clamped between her jaws. And the bound man was screaming and beating his forehead against the side of the sergeant's head, mashing his ear.

"Holy shit, boss—on your six!"

It was Bunny. I pivoted in place in time to catch the rush as something came out of the shadows and tackled me. It was one of the other Afghanis. One of the dead Afghanis.

His teeth were bared and spit flew from cracked lips as he lunged for my throat.

I braced my forearm under his chin as I fell backward, and then clenched my abs so that my flat back fall turned into a curled back roll. The Afghani went into the tumble with me and instead of him pinning me down we ended the roll with me straddling his chest. I jammed the barrel of the .22 into his left eye-socket and fired. The bullet tore all his wiring loose and he transformed from murderously vicious to sagging dead weight in a microsecond.

There were shouts all around and I had to shove at the body to get free. As I came up, I saw that the second Afghani had clamped his teeth around the windpipe of one of the Marines. Bunny put six rounds into the Afghani: the first one knocked him loose from his victim, the second punched him in the chest to stall him, and the last four grouped like knuckles in a lead fist to strike him above the eyebrows. The man's head exploded and his body spun backward in a sloppy pirouette. The Marine dropped to his knees, trying to staunch an arterial spray with fingers that shook with the palsy of sudden understanding. His companion crouched over him, pressing the wound with his hands, but the Marine drowned in his own blood in seconds.

Slim was in the cave mouth, his weapon sweeping quickly back and forth from target to target, not knowing whether to take a shot or not.

I dove at Amirah, who had crawled back atop the sergeant. For his part, the Marine was putting up a good fight, but it was clear that terror of the woman he had been using as a tool of interrogation was off the scale, too much for him to handle. He shot me a single, despairing glance, and I saw the moment when he gave up. It must have been one of those instantaneous moments of clarity that can either save you or kill you. His interrogation had failed. His method of interrogation was indefensible, a fact that would never have mattered if we hadn't shown up. But we were here, and he was caught. His world had just crashed, and he knew it.

I locked my arm around Amirah's throat and squeezed, bulging my bicep on one side to cut off her left carotid and my forearm to cut off her right. In jujutsu that puts someone out.

It didn't do a fucking thing to her.

She bucked and writhed with more force than I would have thought possible for a woman of her size, alive or dead.

I shoved the hot barrel of the .22 against the back of her head, bent close, and whispered in her ear, speaking in Farsi.

"There is no shame to die in the service of Allah."

Her muscles locked into sudden rigidity. The cave was instantly still. Even the Afghani and the sergeant had stopped screaming. I held her tight against my chest and my back was to the cold stone wall. She smelled of rotting meat and death, but in her dark hair there was the faintest scent of perfume. Jasmine.

"Amirah," I said. "Listen to me."

I whispered six more words.

"Your choice, Princess," I said. "*This*...or paradise?"

I leaned on the word "this." From the absolute stillness, I knew that she understood what I meant. The cave, these men, all this destruction. She knew. And even though she had meant to sweep the world with her pathogen, the end goal—the transformation via Generation 12 of a select portion of Islam and the total annihilation of the enemies of her people—that was impossible. All that was left to her now was to be a monster. Alone and reviled.

The moment stretched. No one moved. Then Amirah leaned her head toward me. An oddly intimate movement.

She said, "Not...this."

I whispered, "*Yarhamu-ka-llâh.*"

May God have mercy on you.

And pulled the trigger.

-4-
Battalion Aide Station
Now

I sat back and studied Harper for a long time.

He said, "What? You going to sit there and tell me that you wouldn't have done the same thing?"

I said nothing.

"Look," he said, "I know that was you in the cave. What are you? Delta? SEALs?"

I said nothing.

"You *know* what we're up against out there. They want us to stop the Taliban, stop the flow of opium, but our own government supports the brother of the Afghan president, and he runs half the opium in the frigging country! How the hell are we supposed to win that kind of war? This is Vietnam all over again. We're losing a war we shouldn't be fighting."

I said nothing.

Harper leaned forward, anger darkening his face. He pointed at me with the index finger of his uninjured hand. "You think Abu Ghraib's the only place where we had to do whatever it took to get some answers? It goes on all over, and it's *always* gone on."

"And look where it's gotten us," I said.

"Fuck you and fuck that zero tolerance bullshit. We were trying to *save* lives. We would have gotten something out of that man."

"You didn't get shit from the first two."

Now it was his turn to say nothing. After a minute he narrowed his eyes. "When you spoke to that…that…*thing*. That woman. At the end, you gave her a blessing. You a Muslim?"

"No."

"Then why?"

"Honestly, Sergeant, I don't think I could explain it to you. I mean…I could explain it, but I don't think you'd understand."

"You think I'm a monster, don't you?"

"Are you?"

"No, man," he said. "I'm just trying to…." And his voice broke. At first it was just a hitch, but when he tried to catch it and hide it, his resolve broke and he put his face in his unbandaged hand and sobbed. I sat back in my chair and watched.

I looked at him. The bandages on his other hand were stained with blood that was almost black. Red lines ran in a crooked tracery from beneath the bandage and up his arms. I could see the same dark lines beginning to creep up from his collar. It was forty-eight hours since he'd been brought to the aid station. Fifty-nine since Amirah had bitten him. Strong son of a bitch. Most people would have turned by now.

"What's going to happen to me?" he asked, raising a tear-streaked face.

"Nothing. It's already happened."

He licked his dry lips. "We…we didn't know."

"Yes you did. Your squad was briefed. Maybe it was all a little unreal to you, Sergeant. Horror movie stuff. But you *knew*. Just as you know how this ends."

I stood and drew my sidearm, and racked the slide. The sound was enormous in that little room.

"They're going to want to study you," I said. "They can do that with you on a slab, or in a cage."

"They can't!" he said, anger flaring inside his pain. "I'm an American god damn it!"

"No," I said. "Sergeant Andy Harper died while on a mission in Afghanistan. The report will reflect that he died while serving his country and maintaining the best traditions of the U.S. Marine Corps."

Harper looked at me, the truth registering in his eyes.

"So I ask you," I said, raising the pistol. "This…or paradise?"

"I…I'm sorry," he said. Maybe at that moment he really was. Deathbed epiphanies aren't worth the breath that carries them. Not to me. Not anymore.

"I know," I lied.

"I did it for *us*, man. I did it to help!"

"Yeah," I said. "Me too."

And raised the gun.

AND THE NEXT, AND THE NEXT

By Genevieve Valentine

Genevieve Valentine's first novel, *Mechanique: a Tale of the Circus Tresaulti*, is forthcoming from Prime Books in 2011. Her short fiction has appeared in the anthology *Running with the Pack* and in the magazines *Strange Horizons*, *Futurismic*, *Clarkesworld*, *Journal of Mythic Arts*, *Fantasy Magazine*, *Escape Pod*, and more. Her work can also be found in my anthology *Federations* and in my online magazine *Lightspeed*. In addition to writing fiction, Valentine is a columnist for *Tor.com* and *Fantasy Magazine*.

In *Dawn of the Dead*, George Romero's follow-up to his classic, genre-defining *Night of the Living Dead*, we see hordes of zombies converge upon a shopping mall, bust through the doors, and proceed to shamble aimlessly up and down its halls. We are told that they remember what was important to them in life and are moved to re-enact their routines in death, and so we are moved to reflect that these mindless dead are not so very different from our own consumerist neighbors who also seem to converge on the mall and wander its tacky displays for no better reason than a kind of grim atavistic inertia and lack of conscious thought.

As terrifying as it is to imagine being bitten by a zombie and transformed into a mindless shell of your former self, even more terrifying is the idea of having to pretend to be one of them, to enact a meaningless ritualized existence while fully conscious and never giving away that you are actually wide awake. Many stories have played with this theme, from its humorous treatment in *Shaun of the Dead* to its more serious treatment in the 2007 film *Invasion* to its positively grueling treatment in Adam-Troy Castro's "Dead Like Me," which appeared in the first *The Living Dead* anthology.

Maybe you feel like you're surrounded by mindless drones and that you have to pretend to be something you're not just to fit in. If so, the scenario presented in our next tale may feel eerily familiar.

You know them by their milky eyes, but they're easy to fool. If you survive the first crush of them, and can master the art of walking slowly and staring straight ahead, none of them in the packed train car will even look at you.

(Once you get their interest, it's over. Someone in the car behind you tries to run for it near Prospect Avenue and gets swarmed. If you glance over, it will look like a glass box stuffed with maggots. Do not glance over; you must look straight ahead.)

You will do better to ignore the smell of rotting apples that's seeping into the train car from all their open mouths hanging limp.

You need to get to open water—you're trying to get to Coney Island, to get someplace where they haven't devoured everything.

(You're already too late.)

As you hit New Utrecht, two men run into the train car. They're holding baseball bats, looking over their shoulders, smug and relieved to have escaped.

Every head turns, every milky eye in the train car fixes suddenly on them, and the slack mouths pull up into a hundred rictus grins.

The men turn and bolt. One of them gets caught in the closing doors, and as the train pulls away from the station his arm drops out of sight, and something tears.

That man is lucky.

The other man is trapped in the train car with them (with you). He gets two or three good swings in before they swarm him, and after a few seconds his screaming gets eaten up by a single, sucking, wet sound that you don't want to think about.

(You must look straight ahead.)

All along the open-air platforms they gather, headed south, pressing themselves into the cars whenever the doors ding open. They step on in twos and threes, pulling children or parts of children, patiently grasping the little hands carrying the little arms that lead to empty shoulders.

They line the tracks all the way south, five deep, then eight, then ten, waiting for the train to stop so they can get on.

(They're not fast, it turns out, but they're patient, and there are more of them every minute.)

The boardwalk is packed shoulder-to-shoulder, all of them moving slowly and without direction, shambling onto the beach and back again. Some of them, the ones with dents in their skulls, walk in small circles with their heads cocked like birds.

(You are too late; any hope of finding others is gone. You walk slowly alongside all the others, out of the train and down the concrete path and up the ramp to the wooden walk. There is nothing else, now, that you can do.)

At first it's hard to see much through the boardwalk crowd, but there is enough movement for you to slip forward by degrees. Your goal is Brighton Beach (anything where you can duck into a side street, get out of the sun), but when you reach the fencing you stop alongside the others and stare into Astroland.

The grown ones have all brought their children, hundreds of them waiting patiently in lines that snake back and forth beside the little rollercoaster shaped like a dragon, the little flying boats shaped like whales, the carousel.

The adults trudge up to the ride in pairs and deposit a child into an empty seat, one child at a time until the ride is full. Then the switch is thrown. (The park employees must not have been fast enough to get out; they pull their levers with the same clockwork motions you've always seen.) The little children with their milky eyes turn slowly with the engine-wheel, rising up and down. Every once in a while, one of them utters a sound through its slack mouth, bleating and wordless as a calf.

From time to time the ride stops, and they march up and lift a child—any child—out of the seat and wander to the next event. The carousel is crowded; the adults forget to leave, and they sway unsteadily as the horses lurch into motion.

Over at the rollercoaster, a child has come back without a head. A pair of parents picks the body up by the shoulders, carries it away.

(You must not run.)

When the crowd moves forward, it dissolves into the park, little wandering circuits. Now you can break away, you think. If you can get past the Wonder Wheel and back onto the street there has to be some apartment left empty where you can take refuge.

You walk carefully past the whales and the roller coaster, down the maw of the Wonder Wheel. The metal corrals are full, but the crowd is so quiet that you can hear the creaking carriages as the wheel stops and the doors open, and the line moves forward all at once, like a worm surging over the grass.

The girl operating the wheel has green eyes, bright and clear, and you're so surprised that you stop in your tracks. You startle her (bad sign, the last thing you need is to draw their notice), and when she looks at you she sucks in a breath like she's about to call out to you, but remembers herself and flips the switch instead. As the wheel lurches into motion, a chorus of half-hearted groans floats down from the cars.

You wait in line, snaking closer, and when you're at the center of the line and the car swings into place you step aside and let the ones behind you haul themselves into the carriage, their slack jaws swinging back and forth as the wheel carries them away.

"How many of us are left?" she asks under her breath. Her legs are trembling; you wonder how long she's been trapped here, pulling the lever back and forth. It's taken you since yesterday to get this far; has she been trapped here all that time?

"I don't know how many," you say.

(It's a mercy not to tell her the truth about what the city looks like now; what good would it do her to know that it's too late?)

"Help me," she says. Her eyes are bright and fixed on you, and the panic is starting to set in. You know what she's feeling; you had this same desperate hope, just for a moment, when the two men ran into the train car. You almost stood up.

(Once you get their attention it's all over).

You can't help her; they would notice if the wheel didn't stop.

"I'm sorry," you say, and walk slowly between the cars, threading your way into the departing riders and out the wheel on the other side.

"No," she says softly, and then louder, more shrilly, "Help me! You have to help me! Fuck you, come back!" but by then they've noticed her.

You sit in the nearest photo booth, safe behind the flimsy curtain, until all the sounds have stopped.

You sit there for a long time, looking down at the edge of the curtain, watching them pass slowly back and forth.

You don't know where you can go. You can't swim very far. You'll need a boat, you think.

(You can't drive a boat. You can barely swim. You sit in the booth a long time. You do not admit you are stranded. How can you?)

Outside the booth, through the little spaces between the bumper cars, you can see that the streets are crawling with them. There's no escape there. You have to keep going the way that you came.

In the arcade, three children are playing basketball. The balls fly away from the tips of their fingers in a waltz beat, one-two-three, and they scoop up the next without looking; their blind white eyes never move from the basket.

Amid the sound of the bumper cars, you walk out up the ramp, under a banner printed in bright block letters: *Deno's Wonder Wheel: Open This Year, and the Next, and the Next, and the Next, and the Next...*

At the top of the ramp you risk a look behind you; the girl is still standing at the Wonder Wheel. Now she's milky-eyed, one hand on the lever, the other hanging slack at her side. The top of her head has been opened like a soft-boiled egg.

You turn away too fast; you have to steady yourself before you keep walking out and up to the boardwalk.

(Don't glance over. You must look straight ahead.)

On the boardwalk, the adults are absently feeding the children, their little mouths mechanically chewing. It looks like funnel cake, but you know better by now what they eat, and you don't investigate.

The sun is blazing. The whole place is starting to smell like a fish market.

Out on the beach it's easier to walk the way you should; the sand sucks at your feet, forces you to be slow and careful.

Some of them are walking out into the water. They walk straight out until the water's too deep to stand in, and when the current takes them they give in, float with arms and legs loose.

(You remember, suddenly, the summer you were ten years old and the kid a few doors down from you drowned in the pool in his backyard. For the rest of the summer none of the neighborhood kids were allowed to go out of sight of their parents, which ruined everything your friends had planned all year.

They moaned all summer about how boring it was to have to stay so close to the house. You agreed.

You were tired all that summer, because whenever you closed your eyes at night you imagined that kid in the moment before he fell into the water, when he had just begun to lean forward, when it wasn't too late for someone to pull him back and save him.)

You walk towards the surf, picking your way over the ones on the beach. Where they have laid out flat in the sand, white eyes turned to the sun, there's the rancid smell of eggs gone bad.

You wonder how long you can last this way, sneaking amongst them. Will you have to go back on the train, make it through the city, head south on the highway walking one mile an hour? How far will you have to go before you reach someplace where this hasn't happened?

(You will never find that place. There are more of them every minute.)

By now there's a web of them across the water, floating akimbo. In some places they're locked together tight as puzzle pieces. If you were brave enough, you could walk across them.

Behind you, someone has figured out how to start the Cyclone. There's the crank of cars on the way up the rails, a collective off-key moan as they plummet. On the stretch of boardwalk behind you, some of them turn to look at the sound, lose interest when they recognize what it is.

They seem sad to see that it's nothing exciting. It's strange to watch them looking disappointed; you don't know what will happen to them when there are no real people left.

(You have already given up hope. They will win. They are patient.)

When you step into the ocean, the water is already cool on your ankles. By nightfall it will be cold. You don't know how far you can swim in cold water.

(Not far enough.)

You take another step. The water soaks into your shoes, your pants. The next step is more difficult than the last one.

Behind you, they are coming, sloshing dutifully into the water the way they remember doing. They will not make way for you to turn around. You cannot go back now.

You think about the moment before the child falls into the pool.

(You must look straight ahead.)

THE PRICE OF A SLICE

By John Skipp & Cody Goodfellow

If George Romero is the father of zombie cinema, then surely John Skipp is the father of zombie literature. He, along with Craig Spector, edited the first all-original zombie fiction anthologies in the '80s: *Book of the Dead* and *Still Dead*, then, more recently (and on his own), *Mondo Zombie* and *Zombies: Encounters with the Hungry Dead*. He is also the author of several novels, such as the splatterpunk ecocidal classic *The Bridge* (co-written by Craig Spector) and *The Emerald Burrito of Oz* (with Marc Levinthal).

Cody Goodfellow's novel, *Perfect Union*, was published earlier this year, and his short fiction has appeared in *Bare Bone*, *Black Static*, *Shivers V*, and *Dark Passions*. Skipp and Goodfellow's collaborative novel *Fruiting Body*, publishes in December.

If you've read the first *The Living Dead* anthology, you may remember a searing science fiction tale called "Meathouse Man," one in a series of stories by George R. R. Martin that concern remote-controlled zombies being used as slave labor. Our next tale brings the same concept to a decaying near-future San Francisco, and concerns not only zombie laborers but also soldiers.

In our own present, war by remote control is becoming increasingly commonplace, as detailed in P. W. Singer's recent nonfiction book *Wired for War*, which delves into some of the issues surrounding soldiers who pilot Predator drones into combat in Iraq or Afghanistan from the safety of a cubicle in Colorado or Nevada. The book describes the unease felt by many elite pilots, whose training has cost upward of a million dollars, as they watch missions similar to their own being flown by teenagers sitting at computer monitors. One drone pilot describes the physical qualifications needed for his job as not being able to do a hundred pushups, but rather having "a big butt and a strong bladder"—literally being able to sit at the controls for an extended period of time.

War is changing before our eyes, though as this next story reminds us, the more things change the more they stay the same. Workers and soldiers may be replaced by remote-controlled zombie slaves, but somebody's still got to deliver the pizza.

I.

(Excerpted from WHY WE STOOD: THE NEW UTOPIA *by Jerrod Unger III):*

"A city is to a planet what a person is to a city. One out of many. A star shining in a firmament filled with constellations. With some shining a little bit brighter, more beautiful or otherwise luckier than the rest.

"By any standard, San Francisco was one of the luckiest, and the most beloved. To those who called her home, San Francisco was *The City*—the quintessential, the only *real* city.

"She was a survivor. Of booms and busts, earthquakes and plagues. In the face of every disaster, she always found a new way to thrive, and came back smarter, grander and richer than ever before.

"Few others could claim the same.

"When the dead rose up, most of the world's cities died just like their people. Winking out, then blindly rising to attack their neighbors.

"Like very few others—and Tokyo came closest—San Francisco kept the lights on throughout the crisis, and shone a beacon to the world. The New San Francisco would not just be the last city on Earth, she would be the greatest.

"We never set out to merely rebuild the old order; we used the breakdown to sweep away old mistakes, and make the kind of world we always knew we should have.

"And while the rest of the world sank deeper into chaos, we toiled and dreamed and dared to grow our City for three hard, uncertain years, until—as viewed from space—she was clearly the brightest light yet emanating from our godforsaken planet, and the only real, living city left on Earth.

"History is full of tough, rotten choices and unfair judgments. And few will be more unfair than the condemnation of what we made, by those who failed even to keep the lights on in their own homes."

II.

4:47 a.m. Down at Candlestick Park, twenty miles outside the Green Zone, the predawn gloom gave way to icy castles of toxic fog. "The Bargain of Kali Yuga," his Master had called it, once again proving his divine prescience.

Everywhere upon the earth, darkness had won. But here, there was still hope.

This house is surrounded by light…

Ajay Watley was on guard duty on top of the east pedestrian ramp of the long-dead athletic stadium, holding down the sacred perimeter. Below him, the parking lot was a ten-acre graveyard of gutted cars and scattered bones he scanned with amped thermal imaging goggles. He had a sixty-caliber Squad Automatic Weapon, a walkie-talkie, and an old iPod blasting his alertness mantra.

This house is surrounded by light…

Ajay had been a devotee of Bhagwan Ganguly for four years before the Master's prophecies came true, and he had never had reason to doubt. All of the Master's visions had come to pass, even the date and hour of his death.

But since then, his commands had become erratic, and tended to change, depending on who transcribed them. When he said to move the ashram to the city, Ajay almost risked his karma by raising doubt.

The dead had indeed been swept out of San Francisco.

But their worst enemies here were not the dead…

No birds called, and no fish swam, as the Higgins boat sailed out of the fog and into the lagoon behind the stadium. In this place where hopeless Giants fans in kayaks used to paddle around waiting for Barry Bonds' home runs, the vintage military ship-to-shore vessel ran aground like a sea lion, unnoticed.

The ramp dropped and slammed the mud.

And the Oakland Raiders came stomping out onto land.

A flurry of movement in the parking lot depths caught Ajay's sleep-deprived eye. Nobody'd spotted a deadhead in weeks, and the ones still walking around were nothing to waste ammo on.

Cranking up the volume on the Master's chanting voice, Ajay cracked his knuckles and waited for whatever it was to come into range.

"I am surrounded by light…" he murmured, drawing a bead with the big sixty caliber…

…just as the hot wind brushed him back…

A drone helicopter no bigger than a toy hovered before him. Its miniature fuselage pointed a camera lens, a parabolic mic, and a shotgun barrel at his face.

He blinked, tried to hoist the heavy gun off its bipod.

The shotgun blew off the left half of his scalp.

Ajay yelped and squirted, dropping his machinegun over the railing. "*Wake up!*" he screamed into his walkie-talkie, belly-crawling down the ramp to the guardhouse, wiping blood out of his eyes.

A hollow, unfamiliar robotic voice hissed back from the handset, "*All your base are belong to us.*"

The Raiders double-timed it to the gatehouse under scattered wild fire from above. They wore SFPD tactical body armor draped with silver duct tape, Raiders jerseys, and dented football helmets.

The first one through the turnstile set off a homemade claymore filled with bathtub napalm. It set him alight, but did not stop him. Sheathed in flames, he stalked through the atrium yard, raking the guardhouse with a belt-fed automatic shotgun as flares, bricks, and small arms fire rained down.

One crazy devotee jumped from cover and charged, but his M16 jammed. The burning Raider cornered and hugged him as its ammo cooked off.

Aerial recon had the ashram's sixty-four devotees holed up in the press boxes. Moving as a hedgehog, the Raiders crossed the courtyard and tossed grenades into the spiral pedestrian ramp. They never spoke or cried out when they got shot. They spent their bodies as cheaply as their bullets.

A gang of wild-eyed devotees dressed in dhotis or long underwear charged down the ramp, brandishing machine pistols and howling the Master's name. Another drone chopper swooped into the open well around which the spiral ramp wound, a toy with twin fléchette cannons in its nose. They sounded like tambourines shaking, but they reduced the defenders to a blizzard of red confetti before they could get off a single shot.

The only effective resistance the Raiders faced was the sluice of gore they slipped in as they climbed the ramp.

On the press level, Ajay ran past a barricaded snack bar with two machine guns.

"*Get down!*" Sister Sharon bellowed from inside. "Move your skinny ass, Ajay!" And opened fire.

She cut the first Raider in half, blew his torso clean off his hips, but still couldn't stop him. He dragged himself up to the snack counter while his teammates laid down withering cover fire.

Ajay prayed for a weapon. He prayed for the courage to do something.

The mangled upper half of the Raider crawled right past him. He saw a gray human face behind the facemask, but telescoping goggles covered its eyes. It had no lower jaw. Earbuds in its helmet screamed loud enough for Ajay to hear the Raider's tinny mantra: *"Get some, 49, get some, get some… take that nest, you little bitch."*

The Raider tossed two grenades in through the gun slits. They bounced off the menu board and detonated in Sharon's lap.

Ajay ran without looking back until he'd hopped the barricades and found them unmanned. He picked up an MP5 off the sandbags, but before he could find the safety, the corridor was engulfed in flames.

The Raiders swept into the luxury skyboxes, where the Master's favorites were kept. Their guards resisted with pistols that didn't dent the Raiders' body armor. Room to room they stalked, giving out headshots or grenades.

Ajay shot one of them in the back without even getting its attention. He almost threw himself upon them with his fists, but he knew it would be suicide, and the Master forbade martyrdom. It would be easier to die than see the end of everything they had built, of everyone he loved.

Ajay went to the window in the owner's box and looked out on the field. Together, they'd bulldozed the wreckage of a relief center into the cheap seats to make room for a massive tented victory garden, and a parking lot to mirror the one outside.

Hundreds of Jaguars, Rolls Royces, and Bentleys filled the infield.

Before the eye of Kali Yuga opened on the world, the media had mocked Master Ganguly's weakness for British luxury cars, but the fleet had brought them all here from the ashram in Big Sur quickly and in fine style.

He could get the keys to one of the Range Rovers they kept in the underground VIP parking. He could get away, and live with a coward's karma. But he heard his brothers and sisters chanting in the big room. If this was truly their karma, they would gather at the Master's feet to meet it.

Ajay ran into the banquet hall with his hands on his bleeding head. There were at least three dozen of them, and even the women and kids were armed and shooting at the double doorway entrance.

The Master sat at the wheel of his favorite Silver Ghost Rolls on a dais in the center of the room. He gunned the engine and honked the Rolls' regal horn. The inner circle of devotees locked arms around the car.

A hulking Raider linebacker stepped into the room and got its face shot off. Inside its hollowed-out torso was a veritable Whitman's Sampler of grenades, RPGs, and a TOW missile.

Even as the hail of lead chewed its helmet and head off, the linebacker fell to its knees and unleashed a holocaust.

The windows and walls blew out of the banquet hall. The secondary explosions brought the upper tier bleachers down on the banquet hall.

But when the smoke cleared, four Raiders were still standing.

"*Game over, bitches,*" said Ajay's walkie-talkie. He threw it away and ran for the VIP staircase.

The corridor was choked with burning bodies, but nobody stopped him as he barged through the door and ran down the stairwell.

He got four steps before he crashed into a Raider's back and hit the stairs on his tailbone. His legs went numb.

DEATH MACHINE, said the name above the number 24 on its shredded jersey. It turned and looked down at him, cocking its head and popping its goggles. Ajay's skin crawled as he felt someone intelligent looking at him. Someone who was probably miles away.

"I am surrounded by light," Ajay prayed. "This house is surrounded by light. I am—"

The zombie in the Raiders helmet stopped over him and put a gloved hand on his shoulder, gave his arm a gentle little squeeze. "*I'm sorry, dude, but my pizza's here,*" it said.

The gentle hand shoved the nozzle of a flamethrower in his mouth, and pumped a jet of high-octane gasoline down his throat.

"*Vaya con huevos, Gandhi,*" said Death Machine #24. The jet of gas ignited, and Ajay was surrounded by light.

III.

The Dungeon Master peeled off his VR goggles, and shucked his data gloves. Checked his pulse rate. *Breathe, barbarian, breathe.*

"Holy shit, that was brutal!" He shivered with a bowel-clenching adrenaline chill, despite the suffocating kiln atmosphere of his server bunker. His muscles tensed and twitched like the dregs of an amyl nitrate rush, still juiced from something that happened to somebody else's body. He'd sweated right through his silk Dethklok pajamas. It felt like someone had dumped a cooler of Gatorade on him, from somewhere up above.

Sherman Laliotitis blinked out of his mystic warrior trance and buzzed in the delivery boy, put his hands behind his head and stretched in his ergonomic office chair. His catheter jabbed his semi-tumescent wang as he emptied his bladder. The tube snaked out of his PJ bottoms to join the spaghetti of cables on the floor to the reclamation tub in the closet. *Christ*, he thought: *Life during wartime.*

The door thudded shut behind him. "So, uh… Seagull, how much for the pie?" His headset burped in his ear. "Wait. Hold that thought."

His eyes unfocused as he gritted his teeth and listened to Charlie Brown's teacher natter in his ear. "*Front office is pissed. You're breaking too many eggs.*"

"Excuse me, but you weren't there, and neither were they! No strategy survives first contact with the enemy—"

"*We're watching the streaming feed now. They wanted to fire you. I told them you knew what you were doing. They're starting to think you're doing it on purpose.*"

"Wait a goddamned minute! Those eggheads built these teams to take deadheads, but we haven't seen free-range street-meat in weeks—"

"*Calm down, Sherman.*"

"No, you calm down! You have no idea what it's like, running a squad in a hot combat zone! You wouldn't last two minutes in my fucking chair! Dungeon Master out."

God damn it. Sherman pushed aside the pill bottles and Hot Wheels cars piled up around his keyboard. He forgot what he was looking for, then remembered he wasn't alone.

"So who were those guys?" The pizza guy pointed at the screens.

"Those hobgoblins were a doomsday cult from Big Sur. Moved in after we cleansed the city, and started poaching our supply lines, snatching our immigrants. We warned them, but they fed our messenger to their dear leader. That's him right there."

With a loaded slice precariously balanced in one hand, Sherman zoomed in on a pasty mummy with a beard down to his knees, licking the windows of the Rolls with a black, cracking tongue. "Watch this, dude."

Sherman made one of his Raiders punch in the window and feed the mummy a phosphorus grenade. *Poom.*

"Wow," said Falcon, or whatever his name was. "I read that dude's book. So you're using dead guys against live guys now?"

Sherman killed his Coke and tossed the empty in the trash, found his vasopressin, and shot a blast of synapse-sharpening mist up his nose. Jesus, he was discussing strategy with the pizza boy. Only difference between this bottom-feeder and the meatbags he controlled was that zombies couldn't ask irritating questions.

His headset bawled like a baby with a dirty diaper. "Hold on. Julio? Sharp air support, dude. Love the way you ghosted my whole op by winging that sentry."

"*Suck it, Halitosis. I didn't hear you bitching when I saved your team on that ramp.*" Julio noisily high-fived somebody, and Sherman almost hung up. God, he hated speakerphone. "*Kid, you are making fucking up into an Olympic event.*"

Sherman was a sponsored pro gamer on the Xbox Live circuit before he turned fourteen. The Pentagon's strategic solutions teams all played *Necropolis Online*, and he pwned their asses daily. Air Force and Army were in a bidding war for his services before he finished high school. If the dead had come a year later, these Navy reserve dipshits would be calling him *Sir*. "Julio, anytime you want to get promoted out of air support, I always got openings on my team. You'd look good in a Raiders uniform, bro."

Behind him, Pizza Boy cleared his throat. "Look, man, my other pies are getting cold…"

"Fuck. Hold on, losers." With a wave of his laser pen over the subcutaneous chip in the hippie's wrist, he paid for the food.

"*Hey, Halitosis*," Julio shouted. "*Are you gonna stop jacking off and move your team, so we can clean up this mess*?"

The Dungeon Master slapped on his goggles. "Please get out of here now, Pizza Boy." But he was already gone.

IV.

Jeez, thought Eagle. *What a douche*. Nice tip, though. Thirty-eight creds. That was the thing about rich motherfuckers. They thought they could pay off their contempt with pocket change. And they were right.

They also all liked pizza.

Eagle's bike was parked outside the penthouse door. It was a chrome green Moots Gristle—a $6,000 mountain bike—the one he chose out of thousands when they gave him a hero's parade, and his old job back. Talk about perks.

He took a moment to savor the view from the uppermost inner balcony of the Hyatt Regency: gorgeous tiered ultra-modern architecture, sloping down to reveal 802 luxury rooms, all occupied, thanks to him and his friends. His own was #615, and he could see it from here.

Hey, Ma! he thought and waved. But she was dead. And that wasn't funny.

Eagle rode to the elevator bank, hopped the glass diving bell down to the lobby. Sheets of illuminated crystal dangled overhead, an indoor aurora borealis that looked awesome when stoned, which he was, waving bye to his friends and neighbors as he hit the domed streets of New San Francisco.

Everybody knew Eagle. That was the great thing. Beneath the sheer poison-and-shatterproof plastic that encased the twenty-block bubble of the Green Zone, roughly 8,000 still moved and breathed, and he saw them all each and every night as he made his rounds through the former financial district, spreading joy with whole-wheat crust, fresh tomatoes and veggies, prewar sausage and pepperoni.

Half the open spaces in the Green Zone were vertical farms now, hydroponically providing for the needs of the city; and thank God they understood that quality weed was every bit as fundamental as rice and beans, in this new economy.

Eagle wheeled around the Embarcadero, past tribal art galleries and acid jazz bars where third-shifters decompressed, downed shots of sketchy bathtub liquor and hoped for the best.

Outside the bubble, the world was still dead. And you could still see it, if you wanted to look. The black ash fields that used to be parks. The ferry terminal mausoleum. The south side of Market Street, where the lights were still off. All just a window away.

But just a stone's throw from the edge—one block from the Transamerica Pyramid, on the corner of Front and Clay—was Pizza Orgasmica: the only surviving 24-hour gourmet pizza emporium.

"Couple of outcalls, if you want 'em," said Bud, as he entered for refills. "One code red, and one from somewhere out in the Black. I told him fuck no, but the guy said he knows you."

"Really?" Eagle said, grinning.

Sometimes it was fun to go outside.

V.

Death Machine #24 stood at attention in the outer courtyard of the defeated enemy objective. He had orders not to move.

#24 followed orders.

Sweep and clear, hold and defend, seek and destroy. #24 had survived eighteen engagements because he hardly needed the voices in his ear to do what he had to do.

He could follow orders almost before they were given.

His armorers and handlers were sure he was a professional athlete or a vet, probably a Marine. Tully Forbes, the machinist who rigged the steel beartrap replacement for his missing mandible, swore that once, when he shouted, "Gimme ten!" #24 assumed the position and did pushups until Tully made him stop with a sleep spike.

But that wasn't true. #24 could count to ten, and sometimes even higher, when his medpak was working overtime.

Over and over, he tried to count the bodies laid out in front of him. After ten, things got foggy, but he didn't have to use his fingers. If he used his fingers, he'd only be able to count up to seven.

The bodies were covered in sheets. The cleanup crew dropped color-coded tags on them. Green, red, or black. Hardly any green ones; the sheets over them were only spotted with blood. Lots of red and black. The red ones were a mess, but the black ones were yard sales of loose and charred body parts.

A couple of men and a woman walked down the line. They wore white pressurized biohazard suits, but #24 smelled the bracing stink of their breath and sweat venting out of their gas masks. Even as his medpak kicked down a bolus of tryptophan to make him drowsy, he ached to have them.

The woman was different. She smelled dead, but she walked and talked and the others listened to her angry orders.

The dead-smelling lady came over to review the surviving Raiders offensive line. Her skin was a dull gray-green behind her mask, shot through with black capillaries. He could ignore the itching hunger aroused by her assistants, but her rank aroma screamed at #24 to shoot, burn and behead her, sweep and clear.

But the order never came.

As she inspected them, she snapped over her shoulder, "Who runs these fucking rodeo clowns?"

A flunky checked his PDA. "A civilian contractor, Sherman Laliotitis. He was a professional gamer prewar, the best in the world at squad-based combat simulations."

"Reliable?"

"He's a sociopathic little prick, ma'am, but he'd do the work for free. Loves his toys."

"Get him on the phone. If he still can't deliver viable candidates, then he's either incompetent or he's a saboteur."

She stopped and looked into the eyes of #24. Her eyes were the color of bile. She never blinked. "Check the headset on this one."

"We did, ma'am. It sustained no cranial damage during the engagement."

"Check it again, and double its downers. They're supposed to be in a coma, and this one's looking at me."

A flunky unscrewed the bolts on #24's helmet with a drill, while the other tugged it off. Several shots had cracked the high-impact plastic helmet, but the Kevlar liner had stopped them from damaging the electrical wiring and neurotransmitter pumps screwed into the dome of his skull.

He wanted to stop them and gut her, but he had orders not to move.

#24 followed orders.

VI.

On the dead side of Market, the Berkeley social science geniuses were building museum dioramas in the old storefronts, re-creating the bustling life of the old City. Celebrating its heroes—both the surviving and the fallen—in frozen pantomimes of earnestly rosy history.

You couldn't see it at night, but they'd actually sculpted a plaster statue of Eagle and put him on a bike—next to Lester the Professor in his wheelchair and crazy-eyed Emperor Norton II, his courageous freak comrades in that first desperate year of rescues and food runs, before Big Brother came back to take over the job. A plaque at their feet said: *They Kept the Embarcadero Lights Burning, And Kept The City Alive.*

They'd posed for it together, three unlikely loners who had just tried to stay alive and protect their neighbors, when nobody else could. It was hella fucking surreal, hilarious, and also an incredible honor.

But under the self-deprecation and pride was a creeping sense of *having already died.* Their purpose fulfilled. Their glory days noted, memorialized, and gone.

Like the boy in the hundred-year-old statue behind him, on the domed-in corner of Montgomery and Market at which Eagle paused, finishing his joint before rolling out into the toxins.

It was a monument erected in 1850, or at least that was the date of the quote on the base. It showed a handsome young fellow in miner's togs with a pickaxe in one hand, a flag in the other, standing tall against all comers.

The inscription read:

"The unity of our empire hangs on the decision of this day." W. H. Seward, on the admission of California vs. Senate.

And now, San Francisco was a sovereign nation.

"Pffffft...Thanks, America!" Eagle said. "It's been fun!" And then coughed up a plume of Master Kush and Kilimanjaro.

The Market Street South airlock was four lanes wide and a city block long, which included the sealed-off BART station just past Montgomery.

He snuffed the roach and swallowed it on his way through the door. No waste in this city. No littering, either.

Eagle's locker was near the back and the showers, with the rest of the regulars. He suited up, put on his goggles and gas mask, checked the hazmat seals on the pizza cozy one more time.

Then he rode out through the gate and into the Red Zone.

The New City reclaimed the corpse of the old a block at a time. Clearing the wreckage off the streets, purging the buildings of any lingering human wreckage—dead or alive—was only the first step.

They were also repairing infrastructure, and cleaning up the chemical residue from the bombs that had leveled the playing field—or at least cleared it.

Eagle had watched from his bolthole in the Hyatt when the Navy choppers flew over the City that day. He watched the chemical bombs descend, on what they all unofficially called Black Flag Day.

He couldn't tell what kind of bug spray they dropped this time, but the thousands of loitering dead that filled the streets didn't respond to the powdery gray clouds like all the other times: getting all tweaked and fidgety, or eating themselves, but still standing.

This time, they just melted. *Like the Wicked Witch of the West, an army reduced to runny, rancid meat that pooled in their shoes and overflowed the gutters around their fizzing, blackened bones. Then all was still, and death was dead.*

Nearly a million zombies, dispatched in an hour and a half.

Along with every plant, animal, insect or human being that wasn't safely under glass.

Black stains like Hiroshima victims, silhouettes etched deep into the pavement wherever they dropped. Static shadows of what once was, ghosts of an explosion still lethal two years later...

Eagle rolled over them, coasting the cleared stretch of Market, where the work crews were now opening up the frontier.

A few other cyclists passed Eagle as he hopped the curb and crossed the plaza with its defunct fountain and dead ginkgo groves. They wore elaborate Hopi sacred clown gas masks, and shouted his name as they passed.

The big red City truck was parked at the edge of Civic Center Plaza, with a string of worker trailers behind it. The crews worked in a long line, scrubbing the buckled marble flagstones and shoveling concrete debris into a sinkhole that had gobbled up half of Grove Street.

The workers wore orange convict jumpsuits and skid-lid motorcycle helmets. They played sandblasters over the marble to scour away the black scabs where the dead had melted. A cancerous seagull from somewhere far away wheeled down and perched on the head of one of the workers, pecked at its runny gray eyes.

Eagle saw a few other encouraging signs—sickly yellow weeds pushed through the cracks in the sidewalk, cockroaches ran in the gutter—but the domed palace of the Civic Center still looked like an ancient ruin. He remembered the day he'd delivered twelve pizzas to a wedding feast on the steps, the last weekend gay marriages were legal in the City. All of them now, as dead as the Romans.

The airlock on the back of the truck hissed and irised open as Eagle parked his bike and hefted the thermal pouch with their order in it.

Eagle stepped in and closed his eyes to the spray and blowoff. He kept his mask on until the inner airlock popped. The lucky pizza pies were way better protected than Eagle. A piping-hot message of love in a hermetic polystyrene metaphorical bottle, they would stay warm, yet crispy for at least twenty-four hours. Or until someone opened their boxes.

(Some Navy jerk on Treasure Island had bitched about the soggy cardboard when Eagle shipped a batch of deep dish pies out there; but the next day, he shipped a batch of these space age containers the submariners designed for keeping food hot without noisy microwaves. Another breakthrough for the evolving world.)

"Hey, Eagle," Ernie cheered. "You remember that pizza place, Escape From New York, over on Van Ness? Ada says they gave you free pie if you could order in Italian. Is she full of shit or what?"

Eagle peeled off his mask, but he was in no hurry to jump into the argument, or breathe the air in there. Ernie Nardello and Ada Glaublich worked Red Zone cleanup 24/7, so they practically lived in the truck. Somebody must've pissed in their air recirculator. Hazmat suits, masks, dirty longjohns, and more than a few of Eagle's special pizza boxes lay ankle-deep on the floor.

"I dunno, Ernie. I never delivered for them." Popping the seal on the pouch made the truck warmer by five degrees. Garlic and oregano overpowered the truck's manifold stinks. Even Ada made a noise, and Eagle had never heard her say a word. At least not to the living.

Born Adam Glaublich, the shy civil engineer was on top of the list for sex change surgery when the dead fucked up everything. Ada was a stone bummer, but Ernie loved her, and talked more than enough for both of them.

Ernie cracked the top box and nearly fainted. "Aw shit, I thought you said there was no more pineapple!"

"We got a couple more cans out of the Holiday Inn, so I saved 'em for you."

"Dude, I could blow you right now."

Eagle held out his wrist. "I love you, too. But how's about you just pay me instead?"

Laughing, Ernie scanned him with a light pen. "They don't pay you enough to come out here, man."

"No, that's your job." He looked at the screens, the fly's compound eye view of the Civic Center, the sinkhole, his bicycle. "Working hard?"

Ada munched a slice while she monitored their crews. "17, you're cold," she purred. "Warm up and work. Shovel faster." She jogged Ernie's elbow and pointed at a blinking indicator, but Ernie ignored her.

"This is bullshit busy work, man," Ernie said. "The Navy says the shit got washed out and neutralized eighteen months ago. That's why the fuckin' Bay is dead, right? There's never gonna be enough live people in this city for them to open the Green Zone this far."

"I beg to differ, dude," Eagle said, wiping the steam out of his goggles. "There're still *people* out there. It's our town. You're cleaning it up, so the people will come back."

"We're just polishing rocks for a life-sized museum, but thanks. They'll have meat puppets good enough to do our jobs by then. Hey, if anybody shows up at the gates who can turn my partner's hot dog into a taco, let me know, okay? Then I'll be at peace with the world."

Ada punched his shoulder. "17's acting up. Seagull ate his eyes."

"So shut him down," Ernie growled. "I'm not suiting up now. I'm eating lunch. You going back to the Bubble?"

"Not right away." Eagle picked the old boxes out of the mess on the floor. "Got another delivery."

"Out here? Where?"

"Haight and Stanyan." Eagle strapped on his mask in the airlock.

Ernie's eyeballs bounced off his HUD goggles as he dropped the first seal. "Say what?"

"It's a long story. I gotta go, guys. Take care."

Eagle popped the outer airlock and jumped down.

The zombie was waiting for him.

#17 stenciled on its helmet. Seagull shit and a sparking wire in its empty eye-sockets. It dropped its shovel and lurched at Eagle, who threw the empty pizza boxes in its face and instinctively backed into the gate of the truck, groping in vain for a weapon worth having.

He hated guns, but he always carried one. A cop-issue Glock 9mm with soft hollowpoint rounds hung in its holster on his bike, next to his canteen, about ten unreachable feet away.

"Ernie! Call off your fucking dog!"

Ernie's voice popped his headset. "*What? Oh, holy shit… Ada!*"

"MAKE IT STOP!" Eagle shrieked as #17 pawed his gas mask with one work-gloved hand.

Up close, the employed dead—the slave dead—glistened. Hi-tech Glad Wrap vacuum-sealed their skin, locked the sickness in and the freshness out. It was the only way to slow their inevitable decay, and make them humanly tolerable.

Under the industrial worklights, #17 glowed like a leftover angel. But underneath the shrink-wrap was the same old hunger. Its humanity was just a mask.

Up close, Eagle recognized that mask.

#17 had a Kirk Douglas chin. A Bruce Campbell chin. A chin among chins, with a nose to match.

That red-headed guy who used to barback at the Albion… Short-tempered, the regulars called him Fireplug…

I used to deliver pizzas to this guy, he thought.

Ernie and Ada were both hollering in his headset, but Eagle couldn't hear it. He was lost in the moment. Pushing at #17, both hands on its chest, boxed in tight with no exit room. Watching it stagger back, lurch in, moaning.

"*Ada, pop 17! Just do it! We got you, Eagle! Duck and cover, brother!*"

Eagle dropped to his knees. The charges in the rogue worker's head went off like firecrackers in a watermelon, wetware jumping out the top of its skull and spraying all over the fucking place.

"*Eagle, you okay? Jesus, man, I'm so sorry!*"

#17 wobbled and dropped. Eagle checked himself, wiped a few black specks off his parka. Willed his heart to slow down.

"Yeah, I'm good. Fucking freaked, but good."

"*Okay. We're okay?*"

"We're okay."

"*Just…*"

"Yeah. Just… yeah. Don't worry about it."

"*You sure…?*"

"Not gonna say a fucking thing, all right? We're good."

"*Thank you, man.*" Ernie exhaled, and chugged antacid. "*Stay safe, buddy. We got your back.*"

Eagle scooped up and stowed the pizza boxes, pocketed his gun and hopped on his bike as two more remote-controlled workers swept in to scrape up the mess.

Working together, making the world a better place.

VII.

The Dungeon Master had just burnt his tongue on the microwaved ricotta in his calzone—at least a three-hit-point wound—when the Love Line rang.

He washed the glutinous lava down with a splash of root beer, checked his hair, and let the phone ring.

For allegedly living humans, the science division sure seemed to enjoy chewing on human asses. When they couldn't bitch about his kill ratio, they whined that his tactics were overkill; when his meat puppets weren't lagging and bugging out like an NT server, they were dangerous rabid dogs.

The Love Line blinked faster. His pager trembled and jittered off the edge of the desk into an empty pizza box.

He wondered which of the Brain Trust would be dining on his haunches today. Of the three-headed nerd colossus that ran New San Francisco, he got the least friction from the Livermore geeks. Nasty little crypto-fascist elves, but they made the best toys, and bitched the least about his tactics.

His tongue throbbed and told him everything tasted like sandpaper. Perfect. He might as well throw the rest of the calzone back in the fridge.

Well, he thought, killing his root beer and reaching for another, *somebody in the world probably has even worse problems.*

He hit the Accept button.

Fuck my eyes, he thought.

Poison Lady.

Sherman sat up in his chair and brushed his oily hair back out of his eyes. "Dr. Childers, you're looking lovely today."

Meredith Childers' gray-green face tightened on the monitor. She wasn't just the chief researcher on the City's medical research Brain Trust. She was also their star guinea pig. It was easy to see why the other scientists called her The Hippie. *"Sherman… Laliotitis, is it?"*

"Round these parts, they call me the Dun—"

"This is not a game, Sherman. You were briefed by your superior about today's primary objective?"

"To secure the borders of Fortress Frisco against hostile invaders, ma'am. And phase one was a big win."

"Don't fuck around with me. You know what we're doing here. What needs doing."

Sherman looked around the control room. The Raiders' POV monitors showed the cleanup crews carting off the last of the bodies. "I, uh… I am sorry if you're unhappy with my performance, but… you know, capping enemies in the heat of battle isn't like cutting the heads off guinea pigs in the lab—"

"When you're fighting for your life, the person next to you who can't stomach the fight is just another enemy. This war turned our dead against us, because it was the only way the Earth could purge itself of the living. They still rule the rest of the world, and we only have a home here so long as we have the manpower to reclaim this city."

I'll bet the cultists would've done it, he thought. You could've paid them in lentils and Bentleys.

The order had come down last night to target all the squatters on the peninsula in a one-day blitz, using all meat-puppet crews. Every squad operator was on duty today or tonight. The machinists pulled double-shifts refitting assault teams and converting run-down workers into walking bombs.

All the targets were armed; most were subhuman freaks, but none of them was an imminent threat to the city. Most of the Green Zone was still half-empty, but they were expanding it again, and the whitecoats always needed more cold bodies to play with.

"I'm just," he finally said, "trying to do my job, ma'am."

"If you're as good as advertised, you should be able to control your team. Do you verbally monitor all of them at once?"

"That'd be impossible. I'm all over them in real-time for the real precise wetwork, but they're all running a bunch of apps, most of which I wrote myself."

"You've changed their programming for today, though, correct?"

"Well, sure…"

"No more headshots. You will be docked for each non-viable body—"

"Docked?" Sherman sputtered. "How much?"

"How much is a human life worth on the current market? Harden the fuck up and do your job, Sherman."

"Yes, ma'am."

"You'll have no excuses for me next time?"

"No, ma'am."

"You're not the only warm body in San Francisco who's good at videogames, Mr. Laliotitis. But if you're not the best in town from here on out—or if I hear of any more leaks in your operation—the machinists will help us discover a whole new world of uses for you. Am I clear?"

"Um, yes, ma'am." Voice choked. His catheter popped out. Cold piss streamed down his leg.

The line went dead. *Motherfucker!*

Sherman got an aluminum baseball bat and strode out into the hall, away from the mainframe made from 900 chained PS3s and the banks of refrigerated processors running every zombie in the city.

His eyes alit on the vending machine in the hall, but it was the only one in the whole building that worked.

A janitor pushed a floor waxer in loopy circles in front of the elevators.

He didn't flinch or look up as Sherman ran up on him and smashed his face in.

The janitor wore a cheap motorcycle helmet with an enormous smiley face sticker on the visor. It took four whacks to crack the helmet, but another twenty to kill the fucking thing.

It never raised a hand to block the blows with its nylon idiot mittens. Just kept stumbling back and back as he pummeled it again and again, driving it into the wall and making doorknobs rattle halfway down the hall.

By the time the shrink-wrap snapped and the septic contents exploded outward, he could barely swing the bat. His lungs vapor-locked, knees went wobbly, but he couldn't stop until the medpak in its skull cracked open, sprayed a little drugstore everywhere, and it finally spasmed and keeled over.

Sherman fell down hard on his hands and knees next to the bloodless corpse, blowing goat cheese in the beyond-septic waft, streaming snot and tears.

The door behind him clicked and hissed open. Wiping his eyes, Sherman saw a very old, very drunk man in a plush bathrobe hanging on the doorknob as he scowled at the mess. "*Was ist passiert? Ist alles in Ordnung*?"

Why was everything in the real world so fucking hard?

VIII.

The Black Zone party was down by Golden Gate Park, at the end of Haight. Less than ten minutes out of the Red Zone, as the Eagle flies.

A universe of difference, by any other standard.

But every so often, Pizza Orgasmica would get an urgent call from one of the outlaws who had managed not to melt in the post-human hinterlands, or had snuck back into town after Black Flag Day. There were enclaves dug in all over the City, more than anyone knew. And they loved pizza, too.

These streets were not clear, so Eagle ducked and dodged between the cars: glad the Moots was good on rugged terrain, and thinking about how sweet it was to be seeing some long-lost friends.

If you were a bunch of college dropouts living in an empty metropolis, you would probably think it was the best idea in the world to hole up in the Haight-Ashbury Amoeba Records.

The front windows were boarded up, but a guy waiting on the roof with an M16 shouted, "Pizza man!" and buzzed the front door for him.

Eagle rode into the open floor of the record store. It was an impressive setup. Anywhere else, it might have even had a chance. The front counters were fortified with thick plexiglass from a bank. A portcullis made of wrought-iron spikes was hoisted up to let Eagle in, then dropped behind him.

The ground floor of the record store was still a mess, but someone had been restocking the CDs. Along the far wall, a bunch of young guys and a couple girls sat on stationary bikes wired to car batteries, pedaling and watching cartoons as they kept the lights on and powered the big club soundsystem on a dais in the center of the store, where a pale guy with black dreads and a droopy mustache spun a deepdish dubstep mix. He saluted Eagle as the pizza guy parked and popped the hotbox on the back of his bike. "Hey, Tweak, you got any real music?"

Tweak flipped him off and tapped the sign on the decks: NO GRATEFUL DEAD—PLEASE DON'T ASK.

The second floor was a loft where the DVDs were stored. The new occupants had replaced the old staircase with a cantilevered drawbridge.

A couple semi-feral kids came hopping down the stairs to meet him, chanting, "Pizza! Pizza!" Black circles under their eyes. Bleeding gums. The adults looked worse.

Eagle dropped the stack of pies on the table and immediately wished he'd brought more. Fourteen hungry people converged on the boxes, making noises like Ernie's broken worker.

"Dude, thanks for coming out," Lester Wiley rolled over and pumped his hand. "You're a lifesaver. I don't have one of those pen things…"

Eagle sat on a milk crate next to Lester's wheelchair and passed him a fat joint. "No sweat. You got the Sly Stone and Hendrix catalogs on vinyl?"

"If the kids haven't burned 'em. Little Philistines melted most of the classic rock to make into swords and throwing stars and shit…" Lester's eyes glistened as he watched his people eat. "Really, thanks for coming out, man…"

"It's just a couple pizzas, Les. How're you guys living out here?"

Lester lit up and took a stupendous hit. "It's not easy, but when was it ever? At least the traffic's gone."

"Haven't seen you in ages. When did you come back?"

Lester sketched out the last year and change since he and his gang left the City to try a commune in the San Joaquin Valley. "Everywhere else was worse, so we came home. But we're not going back in the Green Zone, man. Don't know why you stay."

"Because it's safe."

"Nowhere's safe. At least out here—"

"You're not safe out here." *You're not safe from them.*

"We've been here a couple months, and it was working out pretty good... There's a cistern in the park, behind Kezar Stadium, and we had gardens on the roof under pressurized tents—"

"What do you mean, you *had* gardens?"

"Last night, somebody burned us out."

Gracie took Eagle up to the roof. Rows of burst bubbles and black crops. Gracie spat in the ashes. "Whole thing went up before we got up here. Chimi was on guard duty, but he was huffing something last night. He said he saw—"

Eagle said, "Toy helicopters." He ran back downstairs.

Lester followed him, passed him the joint. Eagle stubbed it out. "You guys gotta get out of here today. Now."

Lester coughed. "No way. We've got everything we need here. If they'd just leave us alone—"

"They can't leave you alone. They need you—" He stopped. "Did you hear that? Turn down the music!"

It sounded like thunder.

It was dark in the back of the garbage truck. Soothing miasma of rot inside, pushing out bad thoughts. In the dark, in the stench, #24 couldn't see the new recruits, couldn't smell their freshly welded metal and plastic new-corpse stink.

The Commander's voice recited a litany in his ear, over and over. The pre-engagement medpak spikes made him restless. When that happened, #24 got bored, and he started to picture something else happening, and remembering it, or imagining it. Wishing...

"*Hold and contain. Wait for the gas to clear. Target center-of-mass. No headshots. Don't screw your Dungeon Master, kids...*"

On and on. Over and over, like teaching a parrot to talk. If something else happened, anything, it would be better.

One of the Raiders moaned, a low, hungry sound in the dark. The others took it up. They did it every time. The drugs and the voice in their ears wound them up, so they must be getting close.

A flat, deafening boom lifted the truck and stood it up on its back wheels, then dropped it on its side. The Raiders were thrown into a pile. #24 was on top, but he couldn't move. Static chewed his ears.

The rear hatch hissed. Jerry the handler pried it open with a crowbar.

"Motherfuckers," he kept saying, like a parrot. Blood streamed from his ears and hundreds of cuts all over his face and chest that shone like rubies—half-melted glass embedded in his skin. "Used our own fuckin' mines on us, Tooz..." Woozily, he punched #24 in the shoulder. "*Fuck 'em up, O-Town!*"

"*What is the fucking situation out there, over?*" The Dungeon Master screamed in their ears. "*Gordo, Jerry… where are my dogs, goddamit?*"

Jerry sat down in the street and lit a cigarette, started coughing. Blood squirted out of the holes in his neck. The Raiders spilled out of the trash truck. Three of them rushed Jerry and tore him apart. They looked funny to #24, trying to stuff gobbets of steaming meat into their toothless mouths and into their rubber food-tubes.

"*Raiders! Sound off, you cocksuckers!*"

#24 growled at the PDA duct-taped to his forearm and tapped the touchscreen. Green dots on the map were friends. The red spot on the edge of the map was hot. Move closer, get warmer. Feels good. When you were hot, you got to fight.

"*#24, you're my quarterback, baby! Are you the only one left? Fuck… The transmitter in the truck is toast, I'm rerouting through here. I can't see shit on the satellites, and my air support is a fuckin' noob. And I'm pretty much talking to myself right now, huh?*"

#24 counted his comrades, tapping the touchscreen six times… Two Raiders still lay in the back of the truck. One flopped from the waist down. The other one's head was twisted around backwards, and could only bite his own back.

"*OK, helmet-cams are live… Fall in, bitches, it's medication time!*"

As one, the Raiders jerked to attention. Their medpaks whined under their helmets, pumping drugs and barrages of electroshock to jump-start sluggish, decaying synapses. Shreds of Jerry's septic gut dangled from the facemasks of the three backsliders, but they shambled into the huddle.

The new guys were stripped. Slim green metal tanks jutting out of their chests, stuffed with C4 bricks.

They marched in staggered formation along both sidewalks, hugging the scorched brownstone townhouses and concrete lofts that lined Haight Street.

On their screens, the meaningless map glowed red in the direction of west. #24 took point with a sixty-caliber SAW in his hands.

The Dungeon Master spoke in his ear, coaxing them around piles of wrecked cars and booby traps. "*Okay, you're coming up on the park, go left, you're getting warmer…*"

#24 didn't need directions. His brain glowed, pulsing in time with the Red Zone on the map. The light from the intense shocks sparked behind his dull gray eyes and through the bulletholes in his black and silver helmet, making him look like a wrathful, dick-swinging god of the underworld.

The mix downstairs rudely cut out, and Bob Marley's "Iron Lion Zion" shook rat turds out of the record store's rafters. It was their burglar alarm.

The pizza feast disbanded with fire drill discipline. Even the kids grabbed guns. Tweak pulled a metal chain to drop the steel curtains in front of the store, but something roared out in the street and burst through the plywood and plastic windows. It burst in midair before crashing at their feet. A canister flooded the loft with yellow smoke.

Eagle pulled on his mask and pushed Lester's chair away from the gas. Gracie herded the kids and the pedal-pushers towards the rooftop stairs, but she dropped dead before she could say the words.

Eagle shouted, "Masks! Get your masks—" Most of them had masks or filters around their necks, but the gas rolled over them before they could spit out their pizza. Half a dozen of them died in a sprawling pile at the foot of the stairs. A kid rolled on the floor clawing at her mask, drowning in her own vomit.

Lester slid out of his chair and tumbled to the floor.

Eagle took his gun out and looked for something to shoot. His goggles were fogged up. All he could see was smoke. The white stuff that killed everyone thinned out into cotton candy streamers oozing down the stairs. Black smoke came from the roof. Shooting from outside, but almost all of it was hitting the building.

Eagle charged down the drawbridge stairs just as a car crashed through the portcullis and plowed into the electronica section. Nobody was driving the burned-out Subaru wagon, but four Oakland Raiders were pushing it.

The second the Subaru crashed through the wrought-iron gate, a ring of claymore mines on the cashier's counters popped up like sprinklers to shoulder height before exploding. Thousands of steel ball bearings flew out like a multiball monsoon in a tight, utterly devastating radius.

Two Raiders stumbled into each other as their perforated heads drained like dribble glasses. Tweak capped a third with a shotgun, but the headless Raider self-destructed and doused the DJ with flaming jelly.

The fourth Raider had dozens of steel pinballs embedded in its armor, but it gamely came over and climbed the stairs. Dragging a huge machinegun on one arm like John fucking Wayne, #24 clomped up the steps as Eagle tried in vain to figure out how to raise the drawbridge.

He looked at the pile of people behind him. Dead kids with guns and pizza in their hands. The roof stairs were on fire. He put away his gun and picked up the last pizza box. Olives, artichoke hearts, and anchovies, less than half-eaten. Why did nobody appreciate anchovies?

"Hey, Sherman, hold up, man! It's me, Eagle. The pizza guy." He waved his chipped wrist at the approaching zombie Raider. Like he deserved to live, while these chipless nobodies deserved to get gassed in their own home.

As if the Dungeon Master, looking at him from behind his game console, would see a human being at all.

#24 lifted the gun to Eagle's head, then froze, looking down. Eagle felt shit pushing at his sphincter. Sweat popped out of his forehead.

"I'm not fighting you," he told #24. "Nobody here wanted to fight you. They just wanted something to eat."

#24 scanned the loft, from the neat pile of bodies by the stairs to the harmless, hopeless pizza guy standing in its way. Looking back at the dead bodies for a long moment, it finally turned to Eagle and raised its gun.

"Hey, big guy, you want a slice?" Eagle held out and opened the box.

And he wanted to say, *Please, in the head, if you have to*. Which was to say, *Please,*

I don't wanna come back.

Looking past the camera goggles, stared straight into #24's runny gray eyes. Just pouring his soul out. Being human. The only thing he'd ever been.

#24 gurgled, and a rope of spittle dripped down from its steel-plated jaws.

"*Huck… anchowies…*" it said.

And Eagle was running even before the barrel dropped, running and laughing with tears in his eyes, thanking God in whatever form it chose for this awful moment of mercy and grace…

…as the Dungeon Master went *click click click*, stomped his feet. Went *click click click* again. Repeating it over and over.

Staring furiously at the game that utterly failed to obey him.

Betrayed, with every click.

Fifteen minutes later—as he *click click clicked*—a text window popped up on his primary screen. MUCH IMPROVED.

Good news. *Was* good news. It was good to be useful. He got recognition, bonuses and perks all the time. He deserved them. Because he was the best.

And yet, with his free hand, he grabbed at his straggly goatee and tugged until the pain cleared his mind, then reached out and grabbed the joystick again, squeezing and squeezing the trigger.

On the screen, #24 suddenly locked on a worker and shot him in the back, cutting him in half. His crew went on bagging and tagging the bodies, all green tags. Definitely not an equipment failure.

"I shot you," he said to the screen. "I told you to shoot. I gave you a fucking order…"

The replay of Eagle staring down his favorite Death Machine ran on a corner screen until Sherman kicked it in.

It made his foot hurt like a bastard.

War was just so unfair.

ARE YOU TRYING TO TELL ME THIS IS HEAVEN?

by Sarah Langan

Sarah Langan is a three-time winner of the Bram Stoker Award. She is the author of the novels *The Keeper* and *The Missing*, and her most recent novel, *Audrey's Door*, won the 2009 Stoker for best novel. Her short fiction has appeared in the magazines *Cemetery Dance*, *Phantom*, and *Chiaroscuro*, and in the anthologies *Darkness on the Edge* and *Unspeakable Horror*. She is currently working on a post-apocalyptic young adult series called *Kids* and two adult novels: *Empty Houses*, which was inspired by *The Twilight Zone*, and *My Father's Ghost*, which was inspired by *Hamlet*.

Benjamin Franklin said, "Fish and houseguests start to stink after three days." It can really be a strain, sharing your living space with another person, and so the decision to have a child is one of the biggest gambles a person can take—you're essentially inviting a complete stranger to come live with you for a few decades and to be a major part of your life until you die. Most of the time it works out pretty well, at least we like to think so, but there are exceptions—children who are desperately unhappy no matter what you try to do for them, who run away, or get mixed up in crime. Parents torment themselves over how they should handle situations like this—Do you draw the line somewhere? Try to enforce strict discipline or maybe ship your child off to a prison-like reform school? Or do you provide unconditional love and support and hope that somehow they find their way in the world? Sometimes nothing you do seems to work.

Our final story tells of a parent who was in just such a predicament, and who is trying to reach his wayward daughter in the wake of a zombie apocalypse. He knows that his daughter is not the child he might have wished for, but he loves her nevertheless and is willing to do anything to protect her. Or at least...*almost* anything. After all, the world can be a terrifying place, a place full of monsters.

I.
He Gets Bit

The midday sun slaps Conrad Wilcox's shoulders and softens the blacktop highway so that his shoes sink just slightly. It's a wide road with a middle island upon which Magnolias bloom. Along the sides of the street are parked or crashed cars, most of them rusted. He's got three more miles to go, and then, if his map is correct, a left on Emancipation Place. Two more miles after that, and he'll reach whatever's left of the Louisiana State Correctional Facility for women. He'll reach Delia.

Along the highway-side grass embankment lies a green traffic sign that has broken free from its metal post. It reads:

Welcome to Baton Rouge—Authentic Louisiana at Every Turn!

And under that, in scripted spray-paint:

Plague Zone— Keep Out!

Conrad wipes his brow with the back of an age-spot-dappled hand and keeps walking. He's come nearly two thousand miles, and he buried his fear back in Tom's River, along with the bodies. In fear's place came hysteria, followed by paralysis, depression, the urge to do self-harm, and, finally, the enduring numbness with which he has sustained his survival. But so close to the end, his numbness cracks like an external skeleton. His chest and groin feel exposed, as if they've loosened from their bony cradles, and are about to fall out.

"I'm almost there, Gladdy," he says. "You'd better be watching. You'd better help me figure out what to do when the time comes, you old cow."

"I am." He answers himself in a fussy, high-pitched voice, then adds, "Don't call me a cow."

Another quarter-mile past the city limits brings him to a kudzu-covered 7-Eleven. It's the first shop since the Hess Station in Howell that doesn't look bombed out or looted. "Water. Here we go, Connie," he mumbles in that same, wrong-sounding voice. "See? It's all going to turn out great!"

He shuffles toward the storefront on a bent back and spry, skinny limbs, so that the overhead view of him appears crablike. He is sixty-two years old, but could pass for eighty.

His reflection, a grizzled wretch with a concave chest and hollowed eyes, moves slowly in the jagged storefront glass, but everything else is still. No crickets chirp. No children scream. It's too quiet. He grabs his holster—empty—and remembers that he lost his gun to the bottom of the Mississippi River two days ago, and has been without water and food ever since.

"This looks like Capital T trouble. Right here in River City," he says in the high-pitched voice. It belongs to his wife Gladys. He's so lonely out here that he's invented her ghost. "Keep walking, Connie."

He knows she's right, but he's so thirsty that his tongue has swollen inside his mouth, and if he doesn't find water soon, he'll collapse. So he sighs, angles himself between the shards of broken doorway glass, and enters the 7-Eleven.

It's small—two narrow aisles flanked by an enclosed counter up front. Dust blankets the stock like pristine brown snow. A morbidly obese woman with a balding black widow's peak and chipped purple nail polish stands behind the counter, holding a bloodied issue of *The Enquirer*. "Zombies rise up from Baton Rouge Ghetto!" the lead article screams.

"Hi," Connie says.

The woman drops the magazine and bobbles in his direction. Something has eaten most of her abdomen and in the weeks or months since her death, the wet climate has not dried her out, but instead made a moldy home of her. He pictures lizards, crickets, even unborn children flying out from her gaping hole. Her apron, which presumably once read, "Thank Heaven for 7-Eleven!" now reads: "Heaven-Eleven!"

"Are you trying to tell me this is heaven?" Conrad asks.

She lunges at him and the force of her weight against the three-foot-high counter opens her stomach, spraying the shrunken Big Bite Hot Dogs' spit glass and *Enquirer* with gangrenous green fluid.

"Sorry. I didn't mean to tease you," he grunts as he wipes his face and pitches toward the darkened glass refrigerators in the back.

Behind him, Heaven figures it out and climbs the counter, then falls to the floor and crawls after him on a leaking stomach.

Conrad tries to pick up his pace, but he's so dehydrated that his heart is a trapped bird in his chest, fluttering and in pain.

Do zombies eat cold meat? Do they dream of electric sheep?

"Shut up about the poor, innocent zombies and find the water, Con!" he hisses, only he's too tired to use Gladys' voice, so now it's just him, talking to himself, which strikes him as sort of sad.

Behind, Heaven pushes herself to her feet. Her lips spread into a grin, and then keep spreading until they split open. The heat has turned her blood to thick soup that doesn't run.

He hurries, but his heart's not in it. Literally. It's pumping spastically, as if to Muzak—his wedding song forty years ago:

With all of your faults, I love you still. It had to be you!

Lovely young Heaven lunges and swipes at him. He reaches the refrigerator, whose shelves are lined with new world gold, and lifts a gallon-sized container of Poland Spring Water. Though Heaven's gaining, he chugs for one second... two... three... as he rounds the second aisle and doubles back toward the exit.

Just then, something cracks. "What the—?" he asks.

Glass skids like sand under Heaven's feet. To his shock, she isn't shambling anymore; she's running. Bad luck. Runners are rare.

"Hurry up, Con," he pants, but he's rooted there for a second, water in hand, as her voluminous flesh bounces and thuds. He's wondering if maybe this is the second coming and he got left behind, because Heaven's lips have split length-wise like a hag's clit, and inside, all her teeth are gold.

She dives, fast this time. He doesn't know she's got hold of his denim jacket until she reels him into a festering embrace. She's strong and tall—his toes don't even touch the floor, so he uses her body as a hinge and kicks up as hard as he can. His knees slop against her chest, hooking gristle as something cracks (her ribs? her hardened kidneys?), and she drops him.

Back muscles screaming like cop sirens, he dives over the counter. His hands find the twelve-gauge on the shelf beneath the cash register, and he reaches over and presses it against Heaven's ugly face before his physical mind ever recognizes that it's a gun.

"I'm sorry, Heaven" he intends to say as he squeezes the trigger. But instead, Freudian slip: "I'm sorry, Delia."

The mention of his daughter's name trips him up. He hesitates as he shoots, and by luck or intention, she knocks the gun out of the way. He hears the sound of shattering glass, but doesn't see what the slug hit. All he can see is Heaven as she sinks her gold teeth into his shoulder, down to the bone.

There's no time to think. He reaches inside her open belly with both hands and pulls her spine until it cracks. She hugs him tighter and then lets go, falling backward and in half.

"I loved you where the ocean met the sky," he tells the thing named Heaven, though he does not hear himself say those strange words. She blinks, only her eyelids aren't long enough to cover her rot-bloated eyes. So she watches him, perhaps seeing nothing, perhaps seeing everything, as he pulls the trigger and her head explodes.

When he's finished, he stands over her remains while his shoulder bleeds and infection worms its way through his heart and into his frontal lobe. "I'm sorry, Delia," he tells her, "for that bloodlust. For Adam, and not testifying. For not believing you that time you called. Especially for that. I'm sorry for everything," he says. Then he staggers out, a damned man down a long, lonely road that is almost over, toward Delia.

II.

How Rosie Perez Foretold the End

Some blamed cockroach feces. Others, the hand of God. Whatever it was, nobody who got the virus survived. It attacked the immune system first, then it devoured the entire frontal lobe. The sick forgot who they were or how to walk, and eventually, how to breathe. After they died, the virus worked its way into the hindbrain's instinct center, and kept eating. Then something funny happened. They woke up, only this time, the virus was in charge, and it was hungry.

Fox News broke the story on April 1, 2020. At first, everybody thought it was a joke: the dead rising from embalming and autopsy tables, sick beds, basement bedrooms. They spread the blood-borne disease with their bites. It started in Baton Rouge, but quickly spread to all of Louisiana. Overnight, hospitals throughout the south were full. A week later, national radio signals and satellites were offline. Two weeks after that, the army disbanded and went rogue. By Easter, America had dissolved.

Conrad had only been walking for three months since the world ended, but it felt like years. He didn't like to think about the old days. They were bittersweet.

When his wife got pregnant with Delia more than twenty years ago, Gladys had called the child a gift from God. After three miscarriages, two years of fertility treatments, and, finally, experimental blood transfusions, they'd almost given up hope. "She's the best thing we could have hoped for," Gladys said the day she arrived at the hospital, and for once, cynical Conrad had agreed: Delia Christen Wilcox was perfect.

Smart, pretty, full of giggles. They'd doted, indulged, hugged, and kissed until their hearts had overfilled, broken, and grown back larger and more accommodating. And she'd taken. And kept taking. It had started at her mother's tit, which she'd suckled too hard and drawn blood. Then the bigger things: backyard swing-set, horseback riding lessons, her own room, a lock on her door, hand-sewn boutique clothes, ski vacations, all-night curfews, and finally, the silver and crystal, and even their flat screen television.

Drugs, they'd guessed, though they'd never known for sure. After their dog Barkley went missing, Conrad had imagined it was something much worse. Bloodier. Probably, one of them should have asked.

She moved out at sixteen and began couch surfing at boyfriends' houses. "Back surfing," he'd once called it, for which the kid had slapped him. He'd slapped her right back. Then she'd bit his arm hard enough to draw blood.

There were more shenanigans. The house got broken into. The Dodge stolen. Some fool named Butter had called them at all hours, asking for his "Sweet Momma." They instituted a curfew when the high school kids at Tom's River started turning up dead, but she'd climbed out the window and come waltzing back at dawn. Then she went missing entirely, and though both of them had imagined this absence in their darkest moments and assumed it would bring relief, it only ushered more misery. Was she cold, frightened, alone? Did she need them, only she was ashamed to ask?

Two years later, they got the call from a special victims unit detective in Louisiana—Delia had been arrested for the human trafficking of her own child.

He'd learned but had promptly forgotten the particulars: A son named Adam born a year after she left home, a kiddie-porn ring, a trannie boyfriend who'd kept her high and happy, a $1000 payoff for her infant son. It amounted to less than the going rate for any of the boy's individual organs on the black market, as if the living child as a whole was worth less than the sum of his parts.

Though he considered it, in the end Conrad decided not to testify in his daughter's defense. She was sentenced to eight years at the Louisiana Women's Correctional Facility. He never visited. She never wrote. He and Gladys legally adopted Adam. They gave away Delia's pretty things and painted her old room blue. Adam never learned to attach significance to the word mother, and for this they considered themselves lucky.

"It's like she's dead," Gladys once said. Behind her, the section of wall where Delia's picture once hung had appeared especially white.

"It's not like she's dead," Conrad replied. "It's like she was never born."

After some time, they got used to the boy. They cherished his coos, and the way he cried out with glee when he woke from naps, so happy, once again, to find them waiting. This second time around the scale tilted in the opposite direction, and they did not spare the rod. For this they were rewarded with an obedient, if less spirited child.

Trouble came when the boy turned five. It started with the fevers. When the welts appeared, the specialists diagnosed him with viral meningitis. He'd gotten it, the best anyone could figure, from an act of sodomy while under his mother's care. This was also how he'd gotten the syphilis.

Conrad and Gladys sold everything Delia had not stolen, from the diamond ring to the Belgian lace linens. When insurance wouldn't cover the experimental spinal filtration, they mortgaged their house. Little Adam lived in the Columbia-Presbyterian Intensive Care Unit, and as much as they could, they lived there, too.

Two months later, they saw firsthand in the hospital what the virus did to its victims. They survived somehow, in the way that people meant to live through every kind of misery always do. To his own surprise, Conrad got cold blooded. He bashed two infecteds' heads with an IV pole while Gladys pulled the tubing from Adam's wrists, and together they ran. Most others, from the administrators to the doctors, surrendered with open hands and horrified expressions. Fighting meant believing, and they hadn't been ready for that. But by then Conrad's daughter was a jailbird junkie, his grandson's skin too tender to touch, and his wife a new-age Jesus freak, praying for the health of her lost family, so what the fuck did a few zombies matter?

He and Gladys took the boy back home to Tom's River, where he wheezed his final breaths in their arms. Throughout, Adam wore this betrayed expression on his face, like he'd died under the misapprehension that Conrad was God and could have cured him, but had chosen otherwise, to teach him a lesson.

Outside their manicured split-level ranch, sirens blasted. Carnage littered the streets. Inexplicably, his walking buddy Dale Crowther, slick with soap, ran naked down Princeton Road. But the animated dead stuck to old routines, and in the suburbs nobody visits their neighbors, so Conrad dug the shallow grave in the backyard next to the family dog's bones unperturbed.

On the television the next night, they learned that the research institutes were close to a cure. With Martial Law declared and Civil Rights rescinded, the CDC had turned the southern prisons into laboratories, and begun experimenting on convicts. In thick Brooklyn-ese, Rosie Perez, the fill-in WPIX news anchor, announced that the government had discovered a twenty-three-year-old convict who was immune.

"Isn't that the lady from the lottery movie?" Gladys asked. Conrad shushed her by putting his hand over her mouth, and they'd sat erect and tense as metal tuning forks while a still photo of their daughter had illuminated the television. She'd looked younger and more pissed off than he'd expected.

"They shot her full of the virus and she's not sick?" Gladys whispered. "Thank the Great Buddha. My baby, I love you so much. Momma loves you," she told the angry woman on the glowing screen while Conrad inspected his hands, because the sight of his wife's tears, when he was helpless to console her, was intolerable.

Then Rosie returned, and spoke off teleprompter. "So, basically, we're killing a buncha prisoners even though there's like, a million zombies out there we could capture and test instead. So if this Delia Wilcox winds up curing everybody, then I guess it was worth it. But if she doesn't…" Rosie had looked directly into the camera, through the screen, at Conrad, and he'd felt like someone who's done wrong, and been caught.

"Think about it, people! They can't see and they can't hear but they'll still chase you twenty miles, 'cause it's not your skin these fuckin' things want. This virus eats souls. That's not gonna be me. Is it gonna be you?"

Rosie glared. Connie thought about Delia, and the dog Barkley, and that day the ocean met the sky. Then Rosie produced a gun, pressed it to the side of her head while the cameraman shouted, thought better of her strategy, placed the gun in her mouth, and fired. The program went offline.

Conrad and Gladys got close enough to press their faces to the snowy screen, just in case Delia came back. She didn't. After a half-hour, a rerun of *America's Funniest Home Videos* played. Somebody's cheeky monkey stole a bunch of bananas from a grocery store. Then the signal went out, the television was gone, and America died, just like that.

That night, Gladys shook him awake. The bed was just a mattress on the floor—he'd broken apart the cedar frame, along with the rest of the wood furniture, and nailed it against the windows and doors. They were living on saltines and defrosted vegetables. Some days it felt like camp, but mostly it didn't.

"I'm dying, Connie," Gladys said.

His belly filled with cold and his heart slowed as it pumped. "You're healthy as a cow, Gladys," he told her, though in fact she was sweating now, her breath shallow, and he understood with increasing alarm that there was something he'd forgotten.

"It's my heart. We're out of the digitalis."

"I'll get it right now," he answered. The digitalis—why hadn't she reminded him?

"It's no good, Connie," she said, and he realized then that she hadn't been too *upset* to help dig Adam's plot: she'd been too *sick*. "I didn't tell you because I didn't want you to risk it."

"Stop this talk," he answered, standing now, in the dark. Orange light played through the cracks in the windows, because something out there was on fire. "I know a little high school chemistry. We'll cook it on the kitchen stove. What's digitalis made of?"

"No, Con. I'm on my way, and you've got to promise me something."

He ran his hands along the sheets, and found that they were wet with her sweat. "I won't promise you anything. You tricked me, you coward."

Gladys shook her head. "Stop that, Connie. Now promise. I won't rest peacefully knowing she's alone. Locked up, even, with no one to remember to feed her. Remember the time with the blood? She drank it all straight out of the freezer bag.

Maybe there's a reason she ran off and it wasn't just the drugs. We were wrong to give up on her like that. You've got to promise to see what's become of her."

He looked at his wife, whose complexion had turned orange with the fire. Over these last thirty-nine years, she'd grown wrinkled and fat and timid. He hated her whiny voice, and her old lady stink, and her sagging tits. Mostly, he hated her worthless ticker. "I'm empty, Gladys. I don't love anything anymore. Not even you."

She shook her head in what he would later remember as amusement. You're married to somebody that long, you know better than to pretend like love is a fish. "Oh shut up and find her, you big baby!"

In the morning he dressed her in her comfy bathrobe and plastic-soled slippers, then cut off her head just in case, and buried her next to the boy and the dog. By noon he was gone. Walking south, toward Delia.

III.
He Finds the Dog

It's only been two hours since he left the 7-Eleven, but his water is gone and he's thirsty again. Dusk has settled like a tall man's shadow, and though the prison is still two miles of dark, broken road to go, he doesn't have time to set up camp for the night, so will instead persevere.

His back went out during that last fight, so his crab-walk is exaggerated, but at least his shoulder has stopped hurting and become numb. Veins along his neck shine bright blue and green with infection, and he wonders what those little virions are eating. His defenses probably, then his memories.

That's when he hears the howl carrying across the broken blacktop. It sounds human—a soulful lament. He thinks it must be the thrumping bass of old world music since he can't imagine there are any survivors left who'd be so incautious as to wail.

Then again, maybe it's his imagination. Since he got bit, he's been hearing voices. They don't belong to Gladys.

—*Sorry I bit you, mister.*

—*Could you help an old altar boy, Father?*

—*I saw the multitudes to every side of me, and their howls were loud.*

He thinks it might be a disorder of the brain. He hopes so, at least.

"Maybe you didn't even get bit, Con," he says in the wrong voice. Gladys' voice. "Maybe you just imagined it, and you're totally fine."

"No, Gladdy. I'm losing it," he says as a second howl interrupts him. He spots the thing in the middle of the magnolia-strewn street. A black Lab retriever. A dog! It cowers with its head between its paws.

He can't help it. He smiles and comes to life a little. A dog! He thought they all were dead—eaten up first by the infected, and then by the survivors. He shambles faster. Grinning like an idiot. Remembers games he taught his old mutt Barkley—*fetch my beer* and *lift Gladys' skirt.*

As he crab-walks, he passes a crawling zombie without legs, that is chewing its own flesh—

I like it because it is bitter, and because it is my heart.

—but is too decomposed to chase him.

When he gets to the pup he offers it his closed fist. Out of habit, he pulls back when he sees the thing's chewed-up snout and bloated, white eyes. It doesn't try to bite him, and he's confused until he realizes that it smells his infection and knows they are kindred. So he does the dog a favor. With one hand, he takes it by the chin, and with the other he draws the butt of his shotgun and smashes it over the mutt's skull. It whines, just like a real dog.

I loved you where the ocean met the sky, he thinks, *even though your mouth was bloody*. Then he keeps walking, toward Delia. By his map, he's almost there.

IV.

Bestial Creatures

He's seen a lot of things, none of them good. In Tupelo he met a band of lunatics who sacrificed their healthiest to the infected in the hopes of pleasing God. Still, they'd been company. In Delaware he met a couple who traveled with him until they got botulism from canned Spam. How can you taste the difference? In Asheville he took pity on an old shut-in and stole a kitchen's worth of food for her before leaving. On his way out she said, "Stay. Take care of me. You can't really think your daughter's still alive." She wept as he shut the door to her small, airless basement, and it occurred to him that in the old days, he might have wasted more time trying to comfort her.

When Delia was small, he'd carried her on his shoulders from place to place, and pitied his bosses at the accounting firm, who'd considered their children's rearing the domain of women. Now that seemed smug. Who had he been, to judge? Shit happens. You can blame yourself and God and everybody around you, but sometimes shit just happens.

Like when they went fishing, and the trout flopped in the plastic bucket filled with water. The stillness of the ocean had mesmerized him, and for a moment, he mistook nine-year-old Delia's bloody mouth for a fever dream. But then he heard the slurping. The sun began to rise, and its color married the water to the sky. Maybe it was the blood treatments, or bad genes, or bad rearing. Maybe some people are just born wrong, and there is nothing you can do. "I love you," he told her as he'd dumped the dead bluefish back into the water.

A few years later, Barkley turned up drained and hanging from the roof like a Christmas suckling pig. He buried the dog before Gladys ever saw how badly it was mangled.

Once, a long time ago, he got a phone call. Gladys slept through, even while he spoke in hushed tones next to her. The voice on the other line came reluctantly. "...Dad?"

"Yeah?" It had been months by then. She'd left on a Sunday afternoon while they were at church, and had taken her mother's heirloom pearls with her.

"...I need help," she said. "Money. I'm in trouble."

He looked at the phone a long while, thinking. "Did you hurt somebody?"

"It's not about that. It's a debt. About five thousand."

"We're out, D. You robbed us blind and I'm not working full-time like I used to."

"They'll make me pay for it with my body," she said. "And I'm pregnant, Dad." She'd been crying, but that hadn't meant it was true. He'd been so angry, or maybe so shocked, that he'd hung up.

Next time they heard from her was two years later, in Baton Rouge. His heart swelled like a leaking sponge when he found out she'd been telling the truth.

"Did you ever imagine she had a baby?" Gladys asked as they sat on the plane headed south, their IRAs cashed in for bail. "It's a blessing, maybe," she said with tearful eyes. "Little feet running around. Burping and pooping. God, I've missed that."

Connie looked out the window at the clouds as they'd kissed the ocean. He thought about how, in purgatory, you relive your life over and over without ever finding resolution or redemption. The colors outside the plane had been blue ocean on blue sky, and, in between, the red of a sunset. "I had no idea," he'd said.

V.
Delia and the Start of It All

The prison is an ordinary building. The cast-iron gate surrounding it is open and rusted. It's dark out, but with the infection threading his veins, Connie can see. He can hear, too. Already, he knows that the prison is lousy with the dead. They're looking for things they've lost. Children. Love. Ambitions. Their souls.

"Maybe she wasn't immune, and they only told people that to keep hope alive," he says in Gladys' voice as he comes to the end of Emancipation Place. "It's a lie, just like everything else. Maybe she wasn't the cure; she was the cause."

"You're the optimist, Glady. Not me."

"You should shoot yourself now while you still can. I hate the idea of you turning into one of *them*. What if there's a heaven, and you're not allowed, because your soul is gone?"

He stops and looks up at the vast, brick prison whose windows are all barred. "I've come this far, Glady. We both know she was never right, but I can't chicken out now," he says, then climbs the steps to the entrance.

The lobby inside is small and long, with reception stations down the entire length of the building. He wanders first the east wing, then the west, where he passes a slender child who sways to the rhythm of the vents that pump hot, wet air. Her eyes are bloody, and out of habit, he kicks her so that she lands against the tiled hall wall. Something cracks (her femur?) but she doesn't come after him. Only lies against the cafeteria wall like a fractured doll.

"Sorry," he mumbles, then keeps walking.

It's okay, she answers in his mind. *Have you seen my daddy? He abandoned me.*

"That's a low blow," he mumbles back, only maybe he doesn't say the words. Maybe now, he and the dead understand each other.

She grins.

The holding cells are in the back of the building. About thirty in all, they border the periphery of a large, two-story room. Connie walks from cell to cell. Half are empty, the other half singly occupied by emaciated, uninfected women lying mostly in their beds. None bear Delia's face. It seems a waste to Conrad that no one thought to set them free or feed them. In cell nine, a woman clings to the bars with locked fingers. Her front teeth are worn down to the gums from where she tried to bite her way out.

There are zombies, too, of course. They walk in aimless circles, and have spread nearly equidistant—about one per every ten square feet—like air molecules in stasis, mindless and inanimate. For the most part, they don't notice him, though he can hear their thoughts:

I'm hungry.

I'm thirsty.

I'm lonely.

It's so dark in here, and my love is so dry.

In the basement of the west wing, he finds the makeshift laboratory where it looks like surgeries happened in the hallways. He sees the IV trees, monitors, and needles that remind him of Adam. It occurs to him that he and Gladys never asked Delia if she wanted the child. Instead they took him, then abandoned her as if she were junk. In admitting his own fault, it's easier to admit the greater truth: she murdered the fish, and Barkley, and those high school kids, too. She was born with a bloodlust.

In the basement, he finds the rest of the prisoners chained to gurneys. They must have been injected with the virus, because their heads are cleanly sawed away.

A doctor and nurse, both infected, wander the aisles, forever trapped in their roles of sick and, well, prisoner and captive. They seem to believe they are ministering comfort as they check lifeless wrists for pulses.

"Delia!" he shouts. They look at him for a moment, then return to their work. *If she is alive, and I find her, I will be happy*, he thinks. *Even if she has not changed, I will take comfort from finishing this journey, and be fulfilled.*

"Delia!" he cries. Like his joints, his throat is beginning to lock.

Just then, a tiny, faraway voice shouts back: "Here!"

It's been years since he's seen her, but her voice transcends time. It is imprinted upon him and dwells in the reptile part of his brain that even the virus cannot devour. His body moves, almost of its own volition. Not even his back hurts anymore. He is entirely numb.

"Delia!"

In reply is that same hesitation from years ago, when she called late at night while Gladys slept. He's run that moment over in his mind every day since, and recognizes now that her hesitation was shame. It was always shame.

"...Dad?"

He's racing on stiff, rigor mortis legs, while his favorite memories, long forgotten, surface: the night she stayed home from a party to play chess with him; the poster of dogs playing poker in her bedroom that he never took down, even after Adam moved in; the color red, that he has forever associated with Delia, his perfect child, who was born with a taste for blood. These memories surface like exploding stars, and then just as quickly, disappear. He tries to catch them, but they are mist. By the time he reaches the lower level of the basement, he is aware only of their loss, and not what they contained.

"Delia!" He cries, and now he can't remember—is he chasing her ghost, or the actual girl?

"Dad, I'm here. In the bomb shelter!" she answers.

He shambles, standing tall now, past the walking dead National Guard and orderlies and reporters, through the second examination room, where the rest of the headless prisoners lay, and toward the back stairs that lead farther down. His muscles tear and creak as he descends. He unlocks another door to another wide room, where there are no zombies. Just a single cell in the center of the room. Several bodies lay half inside the bars, their legs and chests chewed down to the bones. He looks up, and there is Delia, red-cheeked and glowing, peering out from her cage.

"Dad," she says.

He doesn't remember her name, and her young, vigorous face doesn't look familiar, but he knows her, and he loves her like red dawn. He walks stiff-legged to the bars. She's crying. The sound is both terrible and beauteous.

There are voices, many voices, whispering words of nonsense.

I'm hungry.

I'm lonely.

It's so dark.

Nine hundred ninety-nine times out of a thousand, my master will lie.

And then, through all that, so softly he can barely hear it: *Connie, promise me. She's all we've got.*

The woman is small and sharp-featured with a round belly. Though he has no evidence or memory, he knows she is his daughter. "You're immune?" he asks.

"Sort of," she says. She can't look him in the eyes.

"Why didn't they make a vaccine?"

She shakes her head. He waits for more. She doesn't ask about the boy, Adam. He doesn't remember the name or what the word represents. He only knows he's disappointed, like always. And she's ashamed, like always. And the chasm between their two distinct natures is red.

"I got bit," he tells her. "Where are the keys? I better get you out so you can run away."

She nods her head at the key ring about twenty feet away and he retrieves it. There is only one key, and it occurs to him that to put her here, they must have thought she was very dangerous.

"Don't worry about me," she says. "I can't get what you have."

Something clicks inside him. The part that knew this all along. The part that came all this way because it knew, and needed to finish what it had started.

He comes closer. In one hand, he's got the shotgun. In the other, the key. He feels himself nodding off. He thinks about the ocean and the sky, and the time they went fishing at dawn, and how she told him she loved him, too.

And then there is Gladys, looking down on them both with the baby in her arms like the Virgin Mary.

"Why are you immune?" he asks.

She points to the back of her cell. He notices that the structures he'd first imagined as furniture are bones. She has fashioned a chair, a bed. The rest are piled and polished like shiny rocks. He realizes why this room is free of zombies. Little is left, save their bones. "I feed on their blood. Any blood. It keeps me young. But you knew that."

He nods, but doesn't answer, because he has lost the words. He is losing himself, one brain cell at a time.

She licks her lips, and he sees that she's less happy to see him than hungry. But this is the nature of parents and children. The former give, the latter take. "The key, Dad?" she asks.

It feels sharp in his hand. He remembers those missing high school kids, and after that, the junkies' bodies he read about in the paper that had been drained of blood. No wonder she developed a taste for heroin.

"The virus came from me," she says. "I bit someone and they lived. It mutated inside them and spread."

"I'm dying," he says.

Her orange jumpsuit is slack in the hips and waist. It's probably been a while since she fed. If he opens the door for her, she'll make a meal of him. But what are fathers for, if not sustenance? "Fuck you, Dad. You never understood it was a gift. You made me ashamed."

He shakes his head. Feels his heart slowing in his chest. It doesn't remember how to pump, so he hits it, hard. "I love you," he says.

Her eyes water. He thinks that means she's sad, but he can't really tell. Monsters don't act like normal people. "I love you, too," she answers. "Now give me the key."

Are you lonesome, just like me?

Connie, did you know? Gladys asks. Maybe it's coming from him. Maybe it's her ghost.

"Yes, I knew," he whispers. "So did you."

Behind the bars, Delia licks her lips. "The key."

He doesn't remember his name anymore, or this woman before him. All that is left is the emotion underneath it, and instinct.

"Now, Dad."

He fires the shotgun. His aim is true.

Then he turns the shotgun on himself, but it is too long and his fingers won't obey him, so he drops it.

The young woman lies motionless while blood pools around her. He thinks about the color blue as he reaches through the bars that will now separate them for an eternity, and squeezes her fingers. She squeezes back as if she is relieved, and then lets go.

In sadness he can no longer comprehend, his heart tears itself into wings and flaps blood. It is a caged bird in there, that has shred itself inside-out but still can't get free.

ACKNOWLEDGMENTS

Many thanks to the following:

Jeremy Lassen and Jason Williams at Night Shade Books, for letting me edit all these anthologies and for doing such a kick-ass job publishing them. Also, to Ross Lockhart and Michael Lee at Night Shade for all they do behind-the-scenes, and to Marty Halpern for his copyediting prowess.

David Palumbo, for yet another fantastic cover.

Gordon Van Gelder, who first infected me with the editorial bug, and made me into the zombie editor I am today.

My former agent Jenny Rappaport, for helping me launch my anthology career. Enjoy retirement!

David Barr Kirtley for his assistance wrangling the header notes. All the clever things in the header notes are all his work. Anything lame you came across is mine.

Rebecca McNulty, for her various and valuable interning assistance—reading, scanning, transcribing, proofing, doing most of the work but getting none of the credit as all good interns do.

Christie Yant, my self-described "minion," for her friendship and her tireless devotion to making my life easier.

My mom, for the usual reasons.

All of the other kindly folks who assisted me in some way during the editorial process: Charlie Campbell, Ellen Datlow, Pablo Defendini, Diana Fox, Regina Glei, Susan Marie Groppi, Wake Lankard, Seanan McGuire, Tom Piccirilli, Julia & R. J. Sevin, Patrick Swenson, Jeremiah Tolbert, Ryan West, Renee Zuckerbrot, and to everyone else who helped out in some way that I neglected to mention (and to you folks, I apologize!).

The NYC Geek Posse—consisting of Robert Bland, Desirina Boskovich, Christopher M. Cevasco, Douglas E. Cohen, Jordan Hamessley, Andrea Kail, and Matt London, (plus Dave Kirtley, who I mentioned above, and the NYCGP Auxiliary)—for giving me an excuse to come out of my editorial cave once in a while.

The readers and reviewers who loved my other anthologies, making it possible for me to do more.

And last, but certainly not least: a big thanks to all of the authors who appear in this anthology.

ACKNOWLEDGMENT IS MADE FOR PERMISSION TO PRINT THE FOLLOWING MATERIAL:

"Last Stand" by Kelley Armstrong. © 2010 Kelley Armstrong.

"Danger Word" by Steven Barnes and Tananarive Due. © 2004 Steven Barnes and Tananarive Due. Originally published in *Dark Dreams*. Reprinted by permission of the authors.

"Pirates vs. Zombies" by Amelia Beamer. © 2010 Amelia Beamer.

"We Now Pause for Station Identification" by Gary A. Braunbeck. © 2005 Gary Braunbeck. Originally published as a limited edition chapbook by Endeavor Press. Reprinted by permission of the author.

"Steve and Fred" by Max Brooks. © 2010 Max Brooks.

"Living with the Dead" by Molly Brown. © 2007 Molly Brown. Originally published in *Celebration: 50 Years of the British Science Fiction Association*. Reprinted by permission of the author.

"Zombie Gigolo" by S. G. Browne. © 2010 S. G. Browne.

"The Anteroom" by Adam-Troy Castro. © 2010 Adam-Troy Castro.

"The Human Race" by Scott Edelman. © 2009 Scott Edelman. Originally published in *Space and Time*. Reprinted by permission of the author.

"The Summer Place" by Bob Fingerman. © 2010 Bob Fingerman.

"The Rapeworm" by Charles Coleman Finlay. © 2008 Charles Coleman Finlay. Originally published in *Noctem Aeternus*. Reprinted by permission of the author.

"Tameshigiri" by Steven Gould. © 2010 Steven Gould.

"Everglades" by Mira Grant. © 2010 Seanan McGuire.

"The Mexican Bus" by Walter Greatshell. © 2010 Walter Greatshell.

"He Said, Laughing" by Simon R. Green. © 2010 Simon R. Green.

"Rural Dead" by Bret Hammond. © 2008 Bret Hammond. Originally published in *Tales of the Zombie War*. Reprinted by permission of the author.

"Therapeutic Intervention" by Rory Harper. © 2008 Rory Harper. Originally published on eatourbrains.com. Reprinted by permission of the author.

"Lost Canyon of the Dead" by Brian Keene. © 2010 Brian Keene.

"Alone, Together" by Robert Kirkman. © 2010 Robert Kirkman.

"The Skull-Faced City" by David Barr Kirtley. © 2010 David Barr Kirtley.

"The Other Side" by Jamie Lackey. © 2010 Jamie Lackey.

"Are You Trying to Tell Me This Is Heaven?" by Sarah Langan. © 2010 Sarah Langan.

"Twenty-Three Snapshots of San Francisco" by Seth Lindberg. © 2001 Seth Lindberg. Originally published in *Twilight Showcase*. Reprinted by permission of the author.

"The Wrong Grave" by Kelly Link. © 2007 Kelly Link. Originally published in *The Restless Dead*. Reprinted by permission of the author.

"Mouja" by Matt London. © 2010 Matt London.

"Zero Tolerance" by Jonathan Maberry. © 2010 Jonathan Maberry.

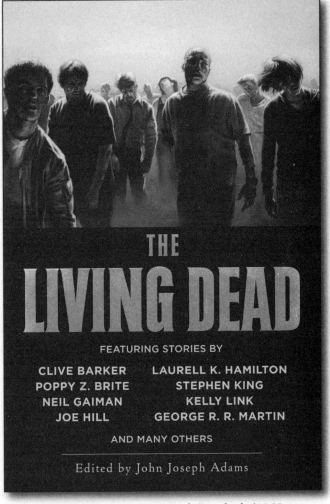

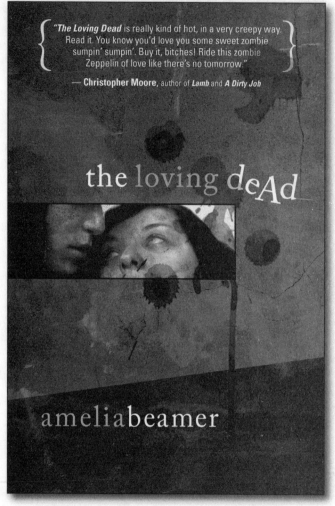

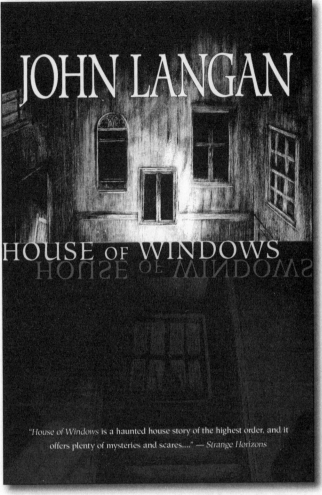